Leigh's face felt hot

She tried fanning herself with a napkin, which did absolutely no good. The corners of the festive room looked cool and shadowy, and she drifted toward one. She noticed that this Christmas tree was decorated differently from the one around which her family was congregating. The ornaments seemed to be tiny, wood folk carvings. She gravitated toward the tree for a closer look, and then, as if in a dream, she heard his voice.

"Leigh?"

She whirled around. The man was silhouetted against the fire, but because he stood so close, she saw his face distinctly. She would have known him anywhere.

Her breath caught in her throat. "Russ?" she whispered.

In that moment there was no one else around. No family, no holiday travelers—just the two of them, their faces illumined by the twinkling white lights on the huge Christmas tree. . . .

CW00719846

Dear Reader,

Season's Greetings!

The magic of Christmas has been captured in this special Silhouette collection. Read in *Second Chances* how the kidnapping of her young daughter forced Leah to seek out her embittered ex-lover. And how Bret in *Under the Mistletoe* was compelled to return home after receiving a long-lost mystery letter from his close friend, Dani. Our third seasonal novel, *For Auld Lang Syne*, celebrates a wedding at Christmas and we share in the warmth and hope which comes with the beginning of a New Year.

Join with us and celebrate Christmas – the season when wishes really *can* come true.

The Editors,
Silhouette Books,
Eton House,
18-24 Paradise Road,
Richmond,
Surrey.
TW9 1SR

PAMELA BROWNING
For Auld Lang Syne

SILHOUETTE BOOKS

*First published in Great Britain in 1992
by Silhouette Books, Eton House, 18-24 Paradise Road,
Richmond, Surrey TW9 1SR*

© Pamela Browning 1991

Silhouette Books and Colophon are
Trade Marks of Harlequin Enterprises B.V.

ISBN 0 373 58628 0

95-9211

Made and printed in Great Britain

Chapter One

It was already late afternoon, the pale, wintry sunlight filtering through the almost-bare hickory branches outside the studio window. Leigh Cathcart stood back from the easel and studied the pansies she was painting on the canvas in front of her. Perhaps it was only the waning of the sun that made the brush strokes on her canvas seem lifeless, she thought, but by the time she decided to add the slightest touch of cadmium yellow to the mixture of oils on her palette, she heard the slam of the mailbox lid outside. *A good excuse to take a break,* she thought, glancing at her watch.

With one last doubtful glance at the painting, she wiped her hands on a turpentine-soaked rag and ran lightly down the stairs. When she pressed her face against the cool glass of the sidelight beside the front door she saw that the mailbox was stuffed with envelopes.

A crisp breeze blew a skitter of dry leaves across the sidewalk as Leigh stepped onto the front stoop. The mail carrier was retreating down the brick walkway, and he turned and waved. Leigh waved back. He wasn't her regular carrier, he must be one of those temporaries hired for the holidays. Funny, but with his long white beard and roly-poly figure, the man could have been a stand-in for Santa Claus. The idea made her smile.

The mail yielded a couple of bills and the first Christmas cards of the season, easily identifiable by their pristine white or festive red envelopes. One yellowed envelope, frayed around the edges, stood out from the rest, and Leigh pulled it from the pile out of curiosity.

She was surprised to see that the envelope was addressed to Miss Leigh Richardson, which had been her maiden name. No one had called her by that name for more than twenty years.

As she puzzled over the sprawling handwriting a sudden freeze-frame of a memory tugged at her heart. In her mind's eye she saw the image of a tall, dark-haired boy whose broad shoulders swung distinctively when he walked.

Russ, she thought with a shock of recognition. *Russ Thornton.*

The envelope bore his return address—or at least it had been his return address when she knew him twenty-two years ago.

She walked numbly into the living room and sat on the edge of the wing chair in front of the window. The postmark on the envelope was dated August 18, 1969.

A not-so-good year, Leigh thought. It was the year that Russ left for Canada in order to avoid the draft, the year that he had skipped out on her without a word. On the other hand, it was also the year that her daughter, Wendy, had been conceived, which more than made up for the rest.

But where had this letter been all this time? And why had it been delivered now? With trembling fingers she slit the envelope, unfolded the paper within and began to read.

Dearest Leigh,

You took a piece of my heart with you when you drove away from our special place yesterday. Please forgive the things I said in anger; you know I love you.

I must leave for Canada, and I believe that in time you will come to understand why I'm going. But Leigh, I cannot live my whole life without you. There can never be anyone else for either of us.

Marry me, Leigh. Don't let me leave the country with this unsettled between us! Whatever the difficulties, we can work them out. Say yes, wonderful Leigh, and we'll be together always. Knowing that you are my fiancée will make our separation so much easier.

I don't think I could bear to part from you if your answer is no. If it's yes, meet me on Sunday as usual at our special place. If it's no, you need not come and I will know.

Please say yes. We belong together.

I love you with all my heart, now and for always.

Yours,
Russ

Russ. Russ Thornton. If she closed her eyes she could picture him—the crisp, wavy hair, almost black, that curved over the back of his collar; snapping dark eyes; a wide smile slightly off-center. *Russ*.

Leigh slumped back in the chair and stared out at the tree branches whipping in the wind. Russ had wanted her to marry him. She hadn't known.

All the pain of his desertion came back to her in a flash. Stricken, she buried her face in her hands; tears streamed between her fingers and rained into her lap. At first she wept softly, but before long she was wrenched by great, gulping sobs.

Russ would have married her.

She had believed for all these years that Russ hadn't really loved her. But she had been wrong. He had written this letter and proposed to her. He had loved her even after their quarrel and in spite of all the cruel things she had said to him. *He had wanted to marry her!*

When her sobs finally died, she brushed the tears away and willed her stomach to stop churning. Slowly she bent to retrieve the letter, and in the fading light she read it once more to reconfirm its contents. She had not mistaken the words.

If only she had known back in August of 1969 that he wanted to marry her! Instead she had thought that Russ wanted her out of his life, and she'd been too proud to contact him first. After all, he was the one who wanted to leave, and she hadn't approved of his evading the draft by running away to Canada. In her heart of hearts, she had been terrified that she'd never see him again if he went either to Canada or to Vietnam, but to her way of thinking in those long-ago days, it would have been better to fight than to be branded forever a coward. And so he had gone, and she had never heard from him again.

Until now.

Leigh roused herself. How long had she been sitting there? Outside she heard the neighborhood children dispersing to their homes, and lighted windows sprang to life up and down the winding street. In a daze, she moved through the half darkness like a sleepwalker and turned on a lamp so that it spilled a shaft of golden light into the hall.

Slowly she walked into the kitchen and removed her paint-spattered smock. She set the letter on the counter, ran water from the tap into a kettle and put it on the stove to boil for a cup of tea. She stopped and stared at the letter for a moment in disbelief. Yes, it was real. It hadn't gone away.

The phone rang, but the sound didn't register at first. She didn't pick it up until the sixth ring.

"Mom?" It was her twenty-one-year-old daughter, Wendy, calling from college. Wendy was a junior at Duke University in Durham, North Carolina, and she was going to be married on December 26. "Mom, I've got the latest bulletin from Wedding Central."

Leigh sank down on the wide window seat in the breakfast area, her eyes resting on the letter. "What's going on?" she asked. Wendy's late-afternoon phone calls had become standard since she'd set the date for her wedding, but this time Leigh had to force herself to pay attention.

"Today at the bridal shop I saw the most beautiful satin roses. They hold rice or confetti or birdseed for the guests to toss. I want them for my wedding, Mom, but they can't order the exact shade of red I want. Can you make them?"

Leigh stifled a sigh. "I don't know. I can't promise anything until I've seen one."

"I'll send you a sample. I'm sure you can figure it out. I want them to be made out of the same satin as my maid-of-honor's dress. Oh, Mom, these roses would be just the right touch. In the shop, they were arranged in a gilt basket with small sprays of baby's breath, and the guests pull the roses out just before they throw the rice or confetti or whatever, but I want to use birdseed in my roses for the birds that stay around for the winter."

Leigh pinched the bridge of her nose between her thumb and forefinger. She felt a headache coming on.

"Mom?"

"I've never made satin roses before," Leigh said.

"You're the artist in the family—you're the only one I know who could get them exactly the way I want them."

It's amazing what we do for our children, Leigh thought, distractedly twisting a strand of auburn hair around her fingers.

"Do you need one satin rose for each guest? Is that the idea?"

"Oh, maybe we'll need a few extra so the basket will look really full. We're only having fifty guests, after all. I want a *big* basket of satin roses right by the door of the Timberlake Room when Andrew and I leave on our honeymoon."

"I wonder if I'll have time to do all this," Leigh said.

"I'm not getting married until the day after Christmas! Today's only December 1, you know. Do you realize I'll be Mrs. Andrew Martin Craig in only twenty-six days?" Wendy sounded enthralled.

Leigh managed a smile. "Wendy, darling, I certainly do. You and Andrew did a wonderful job of convincing me that you couldn't wait until after graduation to be married. If only—"

"Now, Mom, don't start again. Anyway, if we'd waited we wouldn't be able to have a winter wedding at The Briarcliff, and you have to admit that the setting is perfect."

"Oh, I'll grant you that, although I must say that dealing with the staff of an inn on the top of a mountain in western North Carolina is rather difficult when working from my home base of Spartanburg, South Carolina."

"How do you think I feel, stuck way over here in Durham? Thank goodness for the telephone. Maybe we should set up a conference call between you in Spartanburg, me in Durham and the inn staff on top of Briarcliff Mountain.''

"Maybe someone at The Briarcliff knows how to make satin roses," Leigh said, snatching at this ray of hope.

"They wouldn't do half as good a job as you will, I'm sure of it. Oh, I almost forgot. Do you think Andrew and I could have that little bookcase in my room? The one with the glass doors on the bottom? It will look great in our apartment."

"Sure, I'd be glad for you to have it. In fact, Dad and I bought that bookcase when we first got married."

"Did I mention yesterday that Andrew has a job lined up for this summer? He's going to work in the local library. With my waitress job at Murgatroyd's we should just be able to make ends meet. In fact, I'm thinking of working there through my whole senior year."

"And Andrew?"

"We don't know if his library job will extend past August. Don't worry, Mom. We'll manage."

"So you say. Things happen," Leigh said before she could stop herself. She wished suddenly and poignantly that David were here. He had always been able to make Wendy see his point of view, and she was sure that he'd have wanted Wendy and Andrew to postpone their marriage for another year and a half. But David was dead, killed over two years ago by a drunk driver. She missed him; to this day she often expected to round the corner into the den and see her husband sitting in his favorite chair reading the paper.

"Must I remind you that you and Dad were married early in your senior year? I was born right before school was out. And you graduated with a baby in tow. Andrew and I don't plan to have children for a long time, so I'm sure we'll both finish college. Don't worry, Mom. Trust me.'' Wendy's tone was light and cajoling, and she couldn't possibly know that for Leigh, her careless words packed an emotional wallop.

Trust me. The expression, tossed so matter-of-factly into the conversation, echoed inside Leigh's head. They had been two of Russ Thornton's favorite words. *Trust me, I'm going to Canada. Trust me, you won't get pregnant.*

"Oh, I've got to run," Wendy said in a burst of energy. "I just realized that I'm meeting Andrew for dinner in ten minutes. 'Bye, Mom. Thanks for everything. Love you.''

"Love you, too," Leigh said faintly. She hung up, reached automatically for the ever-present Things to Do list in the pocket of her jeans and wrote down "satin roses." She glanced at Russ's letter on the counter to make sure it was still there. Nope, it hadn't gone anyplace. She'd better stop thinking it wasn't real.

It was time to eat dinner, but she didn't feel like eating. All she wanted to do was read Russ's letter over and over again. She retrieved the letter, settled herself amid the bright cushions of the window seat with her cup of tea, and studied every word. She ran her fingers across the lines of script, touched the letters of his name.

Russ Thornton. Oh, how she had loved him.

The world had been so different in 1969. The Vietnam war had been raging full-force. Apollo 11 landed on the moon. A crowd of four-hundred-thousand people gathered at a farm in the Catskills for the Woodstock Music and Art Fair.

And Leigh Richardson and Russ Thornton had fallen in love.

She'd actually met him the summer after high-school graduation when she'd vacationed as usual at The Briarcliff with her family. Russ had been the skinniest busboy working in the dining room, and he'd always smiled at her if he happened to pass by their table. She'd felt none of his attraction then; Leigh had been enamored of one of the lifeguards, and she and her friend Katrina, who had accompanied the Richardsons to The Briarcliff that year, had ignored the restaurant help completely.

Then in January of their junior year at Duke, Leigh and Russ happened to be sitting next to each other at one of the campus hangouts, and he'd remembered her. They struck up a lively conversation which they couldn't conclude on the spot, so he escorted her back to the dorm. She was taken by his engaging personality as well as his angular good looks. By that time, though he was still a bit gangly, his spare frame had filled out. For Leigh, the awkward look only added to his charm.

He'd worn his fraternity sweatshirt under a warm wool jacket, and she'd worn a black-watch-plaid pleated skirt and a demure white blouse beneath her winter coat. He'd tried to kiss her good-night at the door of the dorm, and she had surprised him by letting him, but that was only because she'd known before they'd walked half a block that this was the man she wanted to marry.

Russ had been her first lover, just as she had been his. His room at the dorm, his car parked on a deserted lane, the apartment of married friends who often went out of town on weekends—all were pressed into service for their rendezvous. They had been so young and so much in love, and their passion had seemed boundless. In April of their junior year, when Russ had dropped out of school to return to his hometown of Charlotte after his father's heart attack, Leigh had ached with loneliness.

After he left college that spring, Russ pitched in with his mother to run the family furniture business. On weekends he'd make the three-hour drive from Charlotte to Durham, and he and Leigh would have two precious nights together. Every time he left, she had felt the pain of his leaving anew; it never became any easier, especially since she needed all the moral support she could get.

Most of Leigh's friends at Duke were doves, and with unrest on college campuses increasing that year due to the government's failure to bring the war to a close, she had taken a lot of flak for her hawk stance.

"My brother is in Vietnam," she would say quietly when pressed, and then her antagonists would usually back off. If Russ were present, he'd fervently defend her, which made her quietly proud. She'd never guessed in those days that Russ would make a complete about-face and begin to speak out against the war.

In June, Leigh went home to Spartanburg to stay with her family. Her sister, Bett, who was only eight that summer, was away at camp. Since her brother, Warren, had recently left for Vietnam, Leigh thought her parents needed her.

At the beginning of the summer she sensed a change in Russ, but she'd ignored it at first. It was easier that way; after all, her parents were often visibly upset by the constant television coverage of antiwar demonstrations, and they made no secret of their prowar sentiments.

Her father often said, "I'd like to know what kind of mess this country would be in if we'd all decided not to fight Hitler." He had enlisted in the army with pride at the beginning of World War II.

And once when a small group of antiwar protesters appeared on the local TV news to explain their views, Leigh's mother burst into tears.

"I can't bear it when they make it sound as if Warren is fighting for nothing," she said, her voice muffled by her handkerchief. Leigh tried to comfort her, but her soothing words had little effect. After that, her mother always left the room when the network news was on.

Leigh's father, fervently outspoken, declared several times that the government should round up all the protesters, give them guns, and send them over on the first ship bound for Vietnam. "That'd show those jokers what's what," he said grimly.

Aside from Warren's participation in it, the war meant little to Leigh. She spent more time thinking about Russ than about the war, which was half a world away. Their own primary problem was getting together, and she spent most of her time and energy trying to figure out ways to bring it about.

After suffering through the long spring at Duke without Russ, Leigh had looked forward to weekends during the summer when Russ could visit her in Spartanburg. She'd also thought that he could drive over from Charlotte, less than a hundred miles away, a couple of times during the week, as well. Before the month of June was half over, however, she began to see that these plans were hopelessly unrealistic.

On the second night that Russ visited her in Spartanburg, she walked him out to his car to say goodbye at the end of the evening. She was delighted to have him to herself after sitting in the same room with her parents for two hours. The night was peaceful; there was no moon, but the stars were out in force and she was crazy with wanting him. It had been torture to be able to look at him but not touch.

"I can't stand it when your father talks that way about the war," Russ said unexpectedly through clenched teeth.

Her father had been particularly vocal about his belief that the President should bomb Vietnam out of existence.

Leigh drew closer and hugged his arm. "My brother, Warren—" she began. It was her stock answer.

"Don't tell me about your brother again," Russ said wearily. "Why can't any of you see that it's precisely because of Warren that you should be against the war?"

"Mother says that to speak out against the war is to demean what our men are doing there," Leigh replied self-righteously.

"'Mother says, Dad says'—Leigh, what do *you* think about it?" He pulled away from her embrace and swiveled so that he was looking her square in the face.

"Why, I think we should fight to win," she answered slowly, wondering how anyone could think otherwise. In any case she was bored with the topic and considered it irrelevant now that they were alone for the first time since Russ had arrived.

Russ's eyes searched hers. "We should bring the troops back home," he said abruptly. "It's a dirty, rotten war, Leigh. We never should have become involved."

Russ could be so exasperating. "Why are we talking about the war?" she asked playfully, slipping her arms around his neck and stretching to kiss the corner of his mouth. "Let's talk about you and me instead."

He had surrendered to her urgency, pulling her into the front seat of his car and kissing her so passionately that after he drove away she had to wait on the front porch until her flushed cheeks cooled and her racing heart slowed to its regular pace before she could rejoin her parents.

It had all happened such a long time ago.

Unbidden tears sprang to her eyes when she thought about how innocent they had both been. Innocent and in love. It was a bad combination.

When the front doorbell chimed, the sudden noise startled Leigh back into the present. She had a headache; she didn't want to talk to anyone, and she didn't want to see anyone. But her visitor was persistent, and so finally, limping slightly because her right foot was asleep from sitting so long with it curled beneath her on the window seat, she went to the door and recognized her friend Katrina through the sidelight.

She threw the door open without hesitation and was instantly enveloped in Katrina's hug.

"I thought I'd missed you," Katrina said. "I hope I didn't interrupt anything." She studied Leigh in the glow of the overhead light in the foyer.

"No, I was just—drinking tea," Leigh said.

"I'd have called, but I got stuck in a huge warehouse with this funny little guy who insisted on pulling out bolts of fabric, and since I wanted to find exactly the right print for the DeRuiters' bedroom draperies, I—but, Leigh, is anything wrong?"

Leigh sighed, blowing the air out of her mouth so that it ruffled her bangs. "That depends, I guess. I'm glad you're here, Katrina. I missed seeing you last month."

Katrina grinned. "Me, too, you. I couldn't get away because my assistant quit, and I didn't want to leave my studio without someone to oversee current projects. Speaking of which, how are you doing on that pansy painting for the Caldwells' cottage? And have you eaten? You look ghastly."

"I'm doing fine on the painting, but I think the pansies need to be more yellow, and I haven't eaten, and thanks for the compliment. I needed to be told I look ghastly, I really did."

"Well, I suppose you merely look tired. You never did say if anything is wrong, by the way."

"You didn't give me a chance, and why don't we go in the kitchen?"

"Great idea. Again, have you eaten?" Katrina slung her shoulder bag onto an antique rocking horse that was stationed at the foot of the stairs and trooped after Leigh, the heels of her boots echoing loudly as she walked.

"I haven't had dinner, but I'm not especially hungry. We could heat up some lentil soup. You like it, and one pot seems to last forever with only me in the house."

"You heat the soup, I'll set the table. Nice place mats. Are they new?"

"New since you visited in October," Leigh said. She was glad for this activity; spooning the soup into a casserole dish and sliding it into the microwave oven gave her something to do. While the soup heated, she automatically felt in the pocket of her jeans for Russ's letter, and it crackled against her fingers. She shot a surreptitious look at Katrina to see if she'd noticed, but Katrina seemed oblivious.

"And then Mother said, 'Let's go out to lunch,' and I agreed, and after we ate I hurried to the warehouse, and there's never a phone handy in those places, so that's why I didn't call," Katrina explained as she set out bowls and spoons. She spared Leigh a keen look. "Have you been paying attention to anything I've said?" she asked in exasperation.

The microwave oven beeped, signaling that the soup was hot. Leigh avoided answering Katrina's question by tossing a plastic-wrapped loaf of pumpernickel bread on the counter and asking her friend to stack slices on a plate, which Katrina did while talking nonstop.

Katrina Stimson had been Leigh's best friend since they'd found themselves sitting next to each other in a ninth-grade art class. They'd roomed together in college, and Katrina had served as maid-of-honor at Leigh's wedding. Katrina, who had never married, was now a successful interior designer with her own studio in Florida, where she catered to a rich and exclusive clientele. She returned to her hometown of Spartanburg once a month both to visit her elderly mother and to make rounds of the local textile factories in search of unique fabrics for her customers.

This evening Katrina was full of plans to design the interior of a mansion in Palm Beach. After they ate, she pulled out preliminary sketches of bedrooms and guest houses galore, and although Leigh had always enjoyed acting as Katrina's sounding board, this time she knew that she was merely sounding bored.

Just when Leigh began to wish that she could pull out Russ's letter and read it one more time, Katrina impatiently swept her materials into a portfolio and hitched her chair closer to Leigh's.

"All right," Katrina said. "Something's up. What's going on, Leigh? You're not acting right."

"Well," Leigh said, taking a deep breath. She studied the fringed edge of her place mat and avoided looking at Katrina.

"Why, Leigh, you have tears in your eyes! Leigh, for heaven's sake, what's wrong? It's not Wendy, is it? Is the wedding off?"

Leigh lifted stricken eyes to Katrina's. She shook her head mutely, unable to trust herself to talk. And yet she wanted Katrina to know.

She reached into the pocket of her jeans and withdrew the yellowed envelope, staring at it for a long moment before passing it to her friend, who looked totally perplexed.

"Read this. It arrived today," Leigh whispered. Katrina, after all, knew the whole story involving Russ and David; she might as well be party to this, too.

The room was quiet except for the rustle of the paper as Katrina withdrew the letter. Leigh sat unmoving, her hands clenched tightly in her lap.

Katrina read quickly. "He wanted to marry you?" she asked incredulously.

Leigh nodded and bit her lip, her eyes anguished.

Slowly Katrina held the letter out to Leigh, who accepted it and stared at the all-too-familiar handwriting with blurred vision.

"Why—why wasn't the letter delivered back in 1969 when it was written?" Katrina asked.

Leigh shook her head. "Your guess is as good as mine."

"But this is downright criminal!"

"There's certainly nothing we can do to change things now."

"You and Russ, though. Oh, Leigh, you were so perfect together."

"I thought so at the time. But I married David, and we had a good life. A happy life. And everything that happened with Russ was just—just—" She had started to say that it was inconsequential, but she couldn't possibly deny the importance of their relationship. It had been wonderful and warm and real, and she and Russ had shared a love such as few people are lucky enough to experience during the course of a lifetime. No, there had been nothing inconsequential about it.

"What are you going to do?"

"Do?"

"About this letter. Russ must have thought your answer to his proposal was no when you didn't show up at the park that Sunday."

"I'm still reeling from the shock of this. I don't think a plan of action is necessary," she said.

"The draft evaders who went to Canada rather than serve in the war were granted amnesty in 1977," Katrina said gently. "Many of them came back to the United States."

"I haven't heard anything about Russ Thornton in years, Katrina," Leigh said.

"Neither have I. But you could ask around. You could—"

"I couldn't," Leigh said firmly.

"Leigh, for heaven's sake. The man asked you to marry him back in 1969, and you never got his letter. He has a right to know."

"That's ridiculous. He got over me a long time ago, just as I got over him. He's made a good life for himself since then, I'm sure."

"Maybe not," Katrina said thoughtfully.

"I wouldn't have been exactly overjoyed if Russ had shown up a few years back when David and I were content and carrying on with our lives. I have no desire to stir up this particular stew, Katrina, believe me."

"What if Russ has never been happy without you? What if he's still in love with you?"

"It's been twenty-two years, and few torches burn that long. Grow up, Katrina. You're too old to have stars in your eyes."

"And you're too young to sit around here brooding. Your husband has been dead for over two years, and you need to get out and see more people. You've gone out with some duds since you started dating, I'll grant you that, but maybe Russ Thornton is what you need to make you smile again."

"Ah, Katrina. You're nice to be concerned, but no thanks. Anyway, let's go up to my studio and take a look at that painting. I have an idea that you can tell me exactly what it is that I need to do to make those pansies look more lifelike."

"Aren't we going to clean up the kitchen first?"

"Nah. Pansies first, pans later." Leigh stood up and led the way upstairs.

"You could at least send him a Christmas card," Katrina said as they walked through the door of the studio, but Leigh pretended not to hear as she turned her easel toward the light.

Katrina suggested a paler shade of yellow on the outer edges of the pansies' petals, admired another of Leigh's works-in-progress, and departed early in order to catch up on her sleep.

"I'll call you before I head back to Florida," she promised as she waved goodbye.

Leigh stood shivering on the porch until Katrina was gone, missing the easy companionship of their hours together. She always thought that she was adjusting beautifully to the empty house until Katrina came and showed her how much fun it was to have someone who understood your thoughts before you even voiced them, who shared private jokes of long standing, and who liked to laugh. For Leigh, the hardest part about living alone was not being able to share laughter with a kindred spirit.

On the way back to the kitchen, she passed the boxes of Christmas cards she had bought earlier in the week. They were sitting on the hall table; Katrina must have seen them. That must be why she suggested sending one to Russ.

A crazy idea, for sure. Anyway, Leigh had no inkling where to send it. And what would he think?

Send Russ a Christmas card? No. Absolutely not. But still, she found herself imagining how surprised he'd be to get it, and she knew for certain that he wouldn't be half as stunned as she'd been when she'd opened his long-lost proposal of marriage.

Chapter Two

The next day when Leigh sat down at her desk to address Christmas cards, she couldn't stop thinking about sending one to Russ. The cards were simple—large and white with an embossed message. *Peace and joy,* the cards said. They seemed particularly apt, since peace was what Russ had worked to achieve in Canada.

If—and only *if*—she sent the card, she could send it to the Charlotte furniture store. Russ Thornton was the only child of doting parents, and she had no doubt that they would forward it to wherever he was living now.

But should she? Would Russ want to hear from her?

She figured he was probably married with a lot of kids. Russ had always wanted children. No "lonely onlies" for him—that's what he'd always said.

Did his marital status matter? Couldn't she wish him peace and joy in this special season even if he was a married man who had begotten a whole army of children? She hesitated, her pen poised over the card.

Of course she *could* mention that she'd never received his marriage proposal back in 1969. But how do you throw something like that at a person you haven't seen for twenty-two years? Maybe he couldn't care less. Maybe he'd forgotten all about her.

Maybe he hadn't.

Finally, still feeling ambivalent, she scribbled both her maiden and married names and stuck the card in its envelope. By this time, she wasn't doing it for him—she was doing it for herself.

Later she walked through the cool dusk to the mailbox a few blocks away. For some reason she hesitated to toss the card addressed to Russ into the box along with the others. She stared at the envelope before closing her mind to her objections. This was the season for peace and joy, and she needed to make her own peace with the past.

She tilted the door to the mailbox, sailed the Christmas card into the opening and let the door clang shut behind it.

RUSS THORNTON DIDN'T open his own mail anymore. His secretary had some kind of fancy machine that neatly slit the tops of the envelopes. This meant that he didn't spend much time on his mail, which was a good thing during the Christmas season. Here it was December 5, and already his desk at the Charlotte main office of the Thornton Furniture chain was piled high with Christmas greetings.

Thornton Furniture always received lots of Christmas cards. Cards from pleased customers, cards from creditors, cards from debtors. If you asked Russ, and no one had, Christmas was becoming entirely too commercial. It seemed as though he sent cards to a lot of people he didn't care about one way or the other; in business, it was prudent to send season's greetings.

Not that he was a Scrooge or anything, and he certainly hadn't reached the *bah humbug* stage. What he longed for was a return to the simple meaning of the Christmas season, which he believed boiled down to—

well, to the message expressed by the card he now held in his hands.

Peace and joy. That was it. Peace, both in the world and within each person. And joy, because Christmas was the celebration of the Christ child's birth.

He inspected the card more closely, trying to figure out if he actually knew the person who had signed it. Leigh Richardson—Leigh Richardson? Leigh Richardson *Cathcart?*

He felt as if all the air had suddenly exited from his lungs. He leaned slowly back in his chair, staring at the signature. The handwriting was familiar. He could never have forgotten the distinctive wide lower loop of her *L*s, nor did anyone else he knew form *G*s in precisely that way. It had to be Leigh. *His* Leigh.

No, he corrected himself, not *his* Leigh. David Cathcart's Leigh. Why in the world was Leigh sending him a Christmas card after all these years?

He turned it over, searching for a clue. Nothing on the back. No handwritten message, no explanation, no nothing. And no mention of Dave.

"Want another cup of coffee?" asked his secretary, momentarily popping her head in the door.

"No, thanks," he said, and she tripped away down the hall.

He stood up, still clutching the card in his hand, and paced from one end of his office to the other. Something like twenty years without a word from Leigh, and now this card. It didn't make any sense.

Not that he'd expected her to forget him entirely any more than he could forget her. Leigh Richardson was a name engraved on his heart. He'd loved her, and even though he'd married Dominique, he couldn't help thinking about Leigh from time to time and hoping that she had found happiness.

It had almost destroyed him when he'd heard that she'd married David only a couple of months after he went to Canada. At first he couldn't figure out what she saw in David, who was the kind of nice, all-around guy that all the girls liked but seldom dated. Dave Cathcart hadn't even been particularly handsome, at least not by Russ's standards, and he was pretty sure that Leigh hadn't thought so either.

Why she had married him Russ couldn't imagine, and at first it had made him angry. After that, the despair had set in, and in a few years he had learned to accept the fact that Leigh belonged to someone else. He threw himself into building a meaningful life for himself in Canada, and the people he had known back home, even Leigh, began to fade in importance.

He glanced at the return address on the envelope. It sounded like Leigh's parents' address in Spartanburg, and he was curious. Did Leigh and her family live with her parents? Hadn't he heard that David had become a successful businessman? What was it—real estate? No, it had been insurance, that was it. He couldn't recall where or when he'd heard it.

Russ didn't know whether to put this card in the stack to keep or the one to throw away. Maybe he should send a card to Leigh at the address on the envelope and wait to see what happened.

No, there was a quicker way. He turned to his desk and picked up the phone. Then he just as quickly replaced the receiver in its cradle. He couldn't call her. He wouldn't know what to say.

But even after twenty years there must be things they could talk about. His mind tested an imaginary conversation.

"Hello, is this Leigh Richardson Cathcart? You may not remember me, but—"

No. If she hadn't remembered him, she wouldn't have sent the card. Maybe he should aim for a chattier tone.

"Hi, Leigh, I got your Christmas card. How's things? How's the husband and kiddies?"

That definitely wouldn't do—much too casual.

"Leigh? You won't believe who this is. No, you'll have to guess. Ted Quincy? Well, uh, no. Actually, it's Russ Thornton."

No way. Ted Quincy was the fellow from Chapel Hill that Leigh used to go out with before they met. Russ wondered if she'd sent Ted a Christmas card, too.

"Hello, Leigh, Russ Thornton here. I was wondering if you have a happy life. Me? Well, it's been an experience, I'll say that for it. Yeah, I worked to bring the war to an end, and after a while I married this girl in Canada who is beautiful and brainy, but, no, she doesn't look a bit like you. We're divorced now. What do you say we get together sometime? Can you bring David along? Why, uh, sure. We'll have a great time, the three of us, talking over old times. Your husband would probably like to know all about how I used to sneak you into my room at the dorm, and not only that—"

His mind was veering away into dangerous territory, and he'd better nip this train of thought in the bud. Thinking about Leigh lying in the narrow bed in his room at the dorm, her auburn hair glowing in the light of a forbidden candle, was enough to make him catch his breath. She had been so beautiful.

"If you don't have anything else for me to do before I go, I'll drop this deposit off at the bank," his secretary said from the doorway.

Russ wheeled around, embarrassed to have her catch him with such complex emotions visible on his face. She homed in on him with a penetrating look.

"Sure, Gail, go right ahead. Take your time," he said.

"It'll be about twenty minutes, the same as always," she said.

"Fine," he said abstractedly, sitting down and shoving Leigh's Christmas card under a pile of invoices.

"Is everything all right?" she asked.

"Yes, of course. When you come back, will you bring me the Henry file?"

"You want it before I go?"

"No, later will be fine." He tried to look as though he was busy with the papers on his desk.

With one last meaningful lift of her eyebrows to express doubt, Gail hurried away, and when Russ was sure that she was gone, he pulled Leigh's card out again. Peace and joy, peace and joy. She was wishing him peace and joy.

On impulse he dialed Information and asked for the telephone number of a David Cathcart in Spartanburg, South Carolina. The number stated by the mechanical voice on the telephone line sounded familiar, yet Russ found it hard to believe that Leigh would have the same phone number that her parents had had after all these years.

His heart said to go ahead, but his hand hesitated. Then, feeling slightly unnerved by the rapidity of his decision, he was punching out the South Carolina area code followed by the phone number in rapid succession. His

mouth grew dry when he heard the phone ringing, and he
almost hung up. He had no idea what he would say to her.

"Hello?"

It was Leigh's voice, and her hello ended on the same
cheerful lilting note as always, although perhaps she
sounded a bit huskier. He thought he would have recognized her voice anywhere.

"Leigh, this is Russ Thornton," he said.

She made a sound that could have been a gasp, and he
thought she muffled the receiver. Perhaps there was
someone with her; he'd better make this quick.

"Russell," she said, recovering quickly. "What a
pleasant surprise." She was the only person in the world
who had ever called him Russell.

"I received your card in the mail today," he said, hoping he sounded casual. "It was good to hear from you."

"Well, I—I—" She seemed unable to go on.

He decided to act as though he hadn't noticed her confusion. "Your card reached me at my office. My father
died back in 1980, and Mother died a couple of years ago.
It's been a challenge to take on the responsibility of a
chain of furniture stores, but I enjoy it. How about you?
What are you doing now?"

She spoke rapidly, and he sensed that she was as nervous as he was. "I taught art in the public schools for ten
years, but now I'm painting full-time. My friend Katrina—remember her? Well, she's an interior designer,
and she commissions paintings from me for her clients. It
gives us a chance to work together," she said.

"That's nice, Leigh. You've always been so talented.
I'm glad you're working in your field." He hesitated before taking the plunge. "And David—how is he?"

A long pause. "He died, Russ, a little over two years
ago."

"I'm sorry. I didn't know. Do you have children?"

"Yes, a daughter. Wendy. She's a student at Duke. And you, Russ? Do you have a family?"

"I wish I did," he said. "Unfortunately, my wife and I were divorced several years ago, and we didn't have any kids."

Leigh sounded surprised at this. "You always loved children," she said softly.

"And still do. Like I said, I wish—but wishing won't make it so."

An awkward silence. Perhaps they had said everything there was to say. He had the inordinate desire to ask her if she looked the same, but of course, none of them did. He had put on some pounds, and a few gray hairs had sprouted at his temples. He couldn't imagine Leigh Richardson's rich auburn hair turning gray.

"Isn't this the same phone number your parents had?" he asked.

"Yes, I live in their house. After Dad died, we moved in with Mother so she wouldn't be lonely. She died about five years ago, which left me and David and Wendy. I live here alone now, but I love this house."

"It was a pretty Williamsburg-style house, wasn't it? Yellow, with white trim?"

"It's blue now instead of yellow."

"You always did like blue. I'll bet you painted the shutters green."

Leigh laughed. She had gone through a blue-and-green phase in the days when she knew Russ; her trademark had been blue oxford shirts worn with dark green skirts, and she had painted a green stripe on her blue Volkswagen Beetle.

"Actually, the shutters are white. I got over the blue-and-green thing a long time ago."

"That's too bad," he said, because the combination had brought out the myriad blue-green shades in her eyes.

Suddenly there seemed to be nothing else to say. "Well," he said reluctantly, and "Well," she said simultaneously, so that they both laughed in embarrassment.

"It's been good to talk with you," he told her.

"Thanks for calling," she said. He wondered if she felt the way he did. He would have liked to talk with her longer, but he'd be embarrassed to say the things he was really thinking. He felt as though they knew each other so well, and yet they had been strangers for the past twenty-two years.

"Have a merry Christmas," he added, knowing that his would be less than merry but trying to sound upbeat. He didn't want the conversation to be a downer.

"Merry Christmas to you, too, Russ."

"Goodbye," he said.

"'Bye," she replied softly, and then he heard the click of the broken connection in his ear.

Gail stopped at his office door. "Heidi wants to know if you've checked on those oriental rugs," she said.

He stared at her, drawing a blank.

"Oriental rugs?"

"From that dealer who stopped by last week. The one from New York."

"Oh, *those* oriental rugs," he said.

"Heidi said you were going to place the order. The woman she was working with—the one who bought a whole houseful of furniture from us—wanted to know how long it would take to order one."

"It only takes a few minutes to order it, but it could take weeks to get it. I suppose she wants it by Christmas," he said wryly.

"You guessed it," Gail said.

"Tell Heidi I'm checking," he said as he picked up the phone.

Gail went away again, and Russ called the oriental-rug dealer, concluded the conversation and decided to go out for lunch instead of ordering in.

"I'll be back in an hour," he said on his way past Gail's desk.

He walked out into the sunshine and got in his car. It was a warm day for the season, with the temperature in the seventies, which didn't help to put him in the mood for Christmas. He slid open the sunroof of his BMW and turned onto the four-lane highway fronting the store. The whole world seemed brighter than it had been earlier today, but then his life had taken an unexpected turn since then. He had never in his wildest imaginings dreamed that he would ever speak with Leigh Richardson again.

Leigh *Cathcart,* he reminded himself. He had liked David Cathcart, and he certainly hadn't known that David was dead. Leigh was so young to be a widow, and he felt a pang of sadness on her behalf.

He was no stranger to sorrow himself. His divorce had almost devastated him. He realized now that he had married Dominique with such unrealistic hopes that he would have had to come down to earth sooner or later, but he had never imagined that she would become totally dedicated to her career to the exclusion of almost everything else, including him.

A line of orange caution cones appeared on his left, warning him of a road-construction job ahead, and as he slowed his speed, a convertible with the top down passed him on the right. The driver was a woman with reddish hair whipping in bright tendrils around her face. It was almost the exact auburn shade of Leigh's hair.

Stop it, he told himself. Leigh's hair was probably not the same burnished copper that it had been when she was twenty. She probably had wrinkles. But her eyes, those incredible wide-set eyes, the irises the palest blue-green, they couldn't have changed much. He had never known anyone with eyes as beautiful as Leigh's.

And what was Leigh like after twenty-two years? Was she as much fun as she had always been? Had marriage lived up to her expectations? He wanted to see her again. But to what purpose? After that last day together before he left for Canada, the tenderness of their lovemaking, the terrible quarrel that tore him apart, his desolation when she hadn't shown up at their special place in the park on the following Sunday—why would he want to recall those memories?

Ah, well, they were both older now, and it had all happened such a long time ago. Maybe they could reminisce about the good times. He hadn't maintained a relationship with many people who had known and understood him when he was young. There was something special about old friends, and although he and Leigh had been lovers, they had also been the best of buddies.

His other friends from that time period were scattered. Sam lived in Chicago with his wife and children, Phil had moved to Arizona, and Terry, poor Terry, had been seriously wounded in Vietnam and never left the veteran's hospital in California. Leigh was the only one who lived in this area of the country.

He braked at a stoplight and squinted at the woman in the convertible. If you blocked out the details, she could have been Leigh. Then she turned her head, and disappointment washed over him. Her nose was long and hooked; Leigh's nose was short, straight and dainty.

He turned at the corner, but his mind was made up. He wouldn't go see Leigh. But he would call her again. He'd wait a few days so he wouldn't appear too eager. And he'd think of an excuse for calling; he wouldn't pick up the telephone and then find himself with nothing to say like he had this morning.

Interesting that she still had the same phone number. He wouldn't even have to look it up. It was engraved on his heart, just like her name.

USUALLY LEIGH DIDN'T retire for the evening at nine o'clock, but tonight she was so tired. Another marathon phone call with the supervisor of catering at The Briarcliff had taxed her patience, and then there had been the call from Russ this morning, which had knocked her for a loop. Now she switched off the light to go to sleep, but when the ring of the bedside telephone jolted her to attention, she sat up straight and reached out to pluck the receiver from its cradle.

"Leigh, this is Russ Thornton," said the familiar voice.

She was so surprised to hear from him again so soon that she couldn't make her tongue separate from the roof of her mouth. She groped for the switch on the lamp beside the bed, and when the light came on, she blinked. It was several seconds before she could speak.

"Why, Russ," she said, struggling to get her bearings.

"Have I reached you at a bad time?"

"No, not at all," she said, but she couldn't keep the amazement out of her voice. She hadn't expected him to call again.

"Something you said earlier today when we talked interested me," Russ said. "You mentioned that Katrina incorporated your pictures into the houses she designs. It occurred to me that we could do the same thing at Thornton's."

"Why, perhaps you could," she said, grasping at this bit of reality.

"We have two decorating consultants who advise our customers on what furniture will go in which room, things like that. They're always looking for accessories. If you'd like to bring some of your work over to the store, we'd like to see it."

Her mind raced. Was he serious? Did he really want to use her paintings or was this an excuse to see her?

"Well, I've never thought about increasing my output. Katrina keeps me busy," she said. She didn't want to see him again.

"Oh, if you're not interested, that's fine," he said, his disappointment evident.

Leigh tried to sound brisk and businesslike. "It's just that with the holiday season and everything, there isn't much time. Perhaps after the first of the year...." She let her voice trail off.

"Oh. I see."

He sounded so curt. She fought to regain her equilibrium. She hadn't meant to hurt his feelings.

"You know, there's always so much to do for Christmas," she added. She couldn't tell him about the wedding because then she'd talk about Wendy.

"I always leave my shopping until I can't possibly put it off any longer," he said.

"Not me. I like to be organized. I can enjoy the holiday so much more if I don't have a lot of things to do at the last minute."

"You always were good about that. For instance, the way you kept your class notebooks with neat sections where everything was labeled."

"I could never understand why you used to throw all your notes from every class onto the back seat of your car. You'd have to dig through all those papers before you could study for a test." Too late, she realized that she had been drawn into conversation.

He laughed. "I'm better now. I have a secretary who takes me to task if I don't keep things in the proper folders. It's done wonders for me. Anyway, that wasn't so much a car as it was a filing cabinet."

His car had been a two-door white Corvair Monza. Leigh could even remember the way it smelled—like Old Spice after-shave mixed with lemon drops. Russ had always carried a pocketful of lemon drops in those days. Whenever he thought she needed cheering up, he'd give her one.

"Whatever happened to that car?" she asked. She couldn't help her curiosity; she had felt a certain affection for that Corvair.

"A guy hit it broadside when he ran a red light, and that was the end of it."

"Oh," Leigh said, disappointed. "That's too bad. Were you hurt?"

"No, but Dominique—my wife—was in the hospital for a week or so."

Leigh wanted to ask what year that had been. How long had it taken Russ to marry? Instead she said, "Dominique—was she French-Canadian?"

"Yes, from Montreal." He wasn't sure how much else to say about Dominique, so he said nothing.

"Did you live there?"

"No, we lived in Toronto. She owned a boutique and— but this can't possibly be interesting to you."

Leigh sank back into her pillows. She was trying to imagine Russ with this woman, this Dominique. She tried to picture her. Oh, Leigh was interested all right, curious to know what kind of woman Russ would have married.

"Leigh?"

"I am interested, it's just hard to imagine your living in Canada for so long. Did you mind the cold?" He had always been so sensitive to cold weather; he'd claimed it made his teeth hurt, although she had never been sure that she believed him.

"I came back to Charlotte as soon as I could. I was sick of snow tires and snowshoes and snow shovels. Especially snow shovels. The winter is very long in Toronto."

"But at least you had white Christmases," she said. Spartanburg, South Carolina, with its mild climate, was not conducive to snow.

"Oh, lots of white Christmases," he agreed with a chuckle.

"Every year I've dragged boxes of ornaments out of the attic to decorate the house, and every year one of us would say, 'It's sure to snow this Christmas,' and almost every year we were disappointed. And after the holidays we'd carry the boxes of decorations back upstairs again, and we'd say, 'Maybe next year,' and next year we'd go through the same thing all over again. There's something so special about snow at Christmas."

"Those sleigh bells jing-jing-jingling," Russ agreed.

"Snowflakes that stay on your nose and eyelashes," she said.

"Walking in a winter wonderland," he added, and they both laughed, borne along momentarily on the same wavelength.

Leigh reflected with stunning clarity that she felt so comfortable with him. Had *always* felt comfortable with him, dating from that first night that they'd met in the little off-campus coffeehouse.

"Well," he was saying, "I've enjoyed talking to you, Leigh, but it's getting late. I wish you could bring some of your work into the store soon, but I understand. Why don't you call and set up an appointment when you're ready?"

"I will," she said. "Actually, I have some things that are almost finished. They just need a bit more work."

He sounded encouraged. "Good. That's great. And, Leigh," he said, hesitating, "would you mind if I phoned you again? Just to chat? I've enjoyed talking about old times with you."

Now she was wide-awake. "If you want to," she said, wondering if she dared to encourage him.

"I do want to," he said firmly. "I'll call you soon."

"Thanks," she replied, but that sounded silly. "I mean, I'll look forward to it." She wasn't sure he actually would call; perhaps he was only being polite.

"Goodbye, then," he said.

"Goodbye, Russ," she answered, and then hung up.

She switched off the lamp and lay staring up at the soft pattern of light reflected on the ceiling from the bathroom night-light. He sounded exactly the same. A voice that wound itself softly around the syllables of the words; a voice still sweet enough to make her tremble when she heard it. She pictured him in her mind as he had been then, but then she canceled the image. He wouldn't look the same after twenty-two years. She certainly didn't.

This morning when he called, she'd been so tongue-tied at the thought of him on the other end of the phone line that she hadn't said any of the things she would have liked to say. Nothing, for instance, about Vietnam or about Warren's not returning from the war. Nothing about their love affair, nothing about the letter she had just received, and certainly nothing but the most basic information about Wendy. They'd covered none of these topics to-night, either, but it was probably just as well.

She wondered lots of things about Russ, like if he still wore Old Spice, and if he still liked lemon drops, and if he was one of those guys who had more hair in their ears than on their head after the age of forty.

But she couldn't make an appointment to see him now, not before the wedding. Because no matter how much she wanted to see him, it wasn't worth the risk. The wedding had to be perfect for Wendy's sake, and the last thing Leigh needed was for Russ to show up and realize that he was her real father.

Chapter Three

It was December 24, two days before Wendy's wedding, and she and Leigh were on their way to The Briarcliff. Afternoon traffic was heavy on I-26 because of the holiday, and Leigh, suffering a case of wedding burnout, had declined to drive, so Wendy was driving Leigh's Cadillac. In the trunk reposed Wendy's wedding dress in all its white satin splendor, and in the back seat was stacked a precarious pile of Christmas presents.

Wendy glanced across the front seat of the car at Leigh. "You were up awfully late last night, Mom. Who were you talking to, anyway? Katrina?" she asked.

Leigh faced front so Wendy couldn't see her face. "For a while," she said, which was true. She had been chatting on the phone with Katrina when her call-waiting beeped, and after Katrina hung up, she'd talked with Russ for over an hour.

"I'm sorry Katrina can't come to the wedding. It won't be as festive without her," Wendy said. She checked the rearview mirror and pulled into the passing lane to overtake the next few cars.

Leigh held her breath. Wendy was a competent driver, but Leigh would have felt more comfortable if she didn't drive so fast.

"Katrina's mother won't be able to put her full weight on her broken foot for six or eight weeks, and Katrina can't leave her alone," Leigh said.

"Katrina is such a good nurse. Remember when she came and stayed with you after your hysterectomy?"

"I'll be eternally grateful for Katrina's kindness in those days. I was still grieving for Grandma, and having a hysterectomy on top of it was almost too much. And Dad was so busy at work—wasn't he in the process of moving his office?"

"Yes, and I was a bratty fifteen-year-old and no help at all. How did you ever put up with me?"

"Katrina and I managed to grin and bear it. We remembered how we were when *we* were fifteen. I was awfully glad when you grew out of that stage, though. You have no idea how pleased I am that you've become a kind, caring human being."

Wendy laughed. "That's exactly why I'm worried about Katrina. I know she was looking forward to my wedding, and Christmas certainly won't be the same without her. Are you sure she'll be all right in Spartanburg alone?"

"She's with her mother and the rest of their family, so that's hardly alone. Anyway, last night Katrina mentioned the possibility of taking her mother to Florida for the holidays."

"Florida for the holidays? No white Christmas? Oh, that's too bad. I hope it snows at The Briarcliff on Christmas Day. That would make my wedding perfect, just perfect."

"There's certainly much more chance of snow in the mountains, but snow or no snow, your wedding will be perfect," Leigh said firmly. It ought to be; she had worked hard enough making those tedious satin roses and firming up plans for the wedding and reception with The

Briarcliff's catering staff and running from bridal shop to bridal shop at the last minute trying to find a blue garter for Wendy, who had misplaced the one she'd borrowed from a friend.

"A perfect wedding," Wendy said dreamily.

"Watch the pickup truck behind you on the right," Leigh said sharply. "He's speeding."

Wendy let the pickup pass her before easing back into the right-hand lane. "Was your wedding wonderful, Mom?" she asked.

Leigh focused her eyes straight ahead on the undulating blue mountain range in the distance. Wonderful? She wouldn't exactly put it that way. Her wedding had been a relief more than anything else, but at least David had been happy. And sweet. And gentle.

"Well, was it?"

"Oh, yes," she said, and thought of Russ. Last night he had tried to convince her that they should see each other over the holidays and she'd continued to put him off, telling him once more that she was too busy, that she had a lot to do to get ready for Christmas. She'd been telling herself that where Russ was concerned, it was best to let bygones be bygones, to let sleeping dogs lie, to leave well enough alone.

When it seemed as if he wasn't going to take no for an answer, she had sought to end the conversation with an exasperated, "I'm not even going to be home for Christmas," followed by his incredulous question, "Well, why not? Where would you go at Christmas, anyway?"

"To The Briarcliff," she'd said, none too gently, and then she'd regretted it. They'd met there, after all, and the name would bring back more memories than she wanted him to have at the moment.

"The Briarcliff?" he'd repeated in mystification.

"For a family gathering, a whole bunch of us. I'd better hang up and get some sleep."

"You're going to The Briarcliff in winter? I thought you only went there in the summer."

"We've always wanted to celebrate our family Christmas at The Briarcliff. There's more chance of snow in the mountains," she replied.

"Oh. Snow. Well, merry Christmas," Russ said lamely.

"Merry Christmas to you, too, Russ."

"I'll give you a call afterward," he'd said, sounding miffed, and then they'd hung up.

Not that she hadn't enjoyed his frequent phone calls over the past couple of weeks, but after Wendy arrived home from college Leigh had been frantic with trying to answer the phone at times when she thought Russ might call. Wendy, enthralled with being a bride, knew nothing about Russ or his phone calls, and Leigh didn't want her to hear Russ's voice. She didn't want Russ to hear Wendy's voice, either. All she wanted to do was to keep them away from each other.

"Let's stop and grab a hamburger, okay?" Wendy said, steering onto an off ramp that led to a pair of golden arches, and Leigh nodded in assent.

Maybe Russ would stop calling her, she thought. She had been so prickly and cross during the past few days that she wouldn't blame him if he did. Especially since she had refused to see him over and over again.

LEIGH AND WENDY arrived at The Briarcliff ahead of a winter storm front, and the wind was already blowing mightily when they drove between the two stone pillars that marked the entrance to the inn's grounds. Ahead of them they could see golden light spilling from the windows, and Wendy leaned forward in excitement.

"The inn looks beautiful. I knew it would," she said in satisfaction.

"It looks like a fairy-tale castle," Leigh said, and Wendy laughed.

"There's something elegant about The Briarcliff, all right, but it's homier than a castle; it reminds me of one of those châteaus in the wine country of France," Wendy said. They drove around the sweeping driveway circle at the front entrance, where a uniformed attendant whisked away their luggage and promised to park the car.

After a few check-in formalities, Leigh looked around the lobby for their family group. She didn't have to look for long, because her sister Bett called to them immediately.

"Leigh! Wendy! Oh, I'm so glad to see you!"

Bett and her three children swarmed across the crowded great hall of the inn to greet them. In the background the fires in The Briarcliff's massive four-sided fireplace leaped and danced. Carson, Bett's burly good-natured husband, ambled over and embraced Leigh first and then Wendy.

"How's our bride doing?" he asked, holding Wendy at arm's length.

"Great," Wendy answered, her eyes sparkling up at her uncle.

"Are you sure you still want me to give you away? I'm worried about this wedding-march business. You know I've got two left feet. Bett says I'm the worst dancer she's ever experienced."

"Follow me, I'll lead," Wendy assured him, and everyone laughed.

Bett's children were stair steps: Darren, Billy and Claire-Anne, ages eight, six and five respectively. All of them had inherited their mother's pale red hair and freckles, and all of them were built like their father. They flocked after Carson and Wendy, who went to bask in the glow of the fire.

A sharp and biting wind was tossing the tops of the trees outside the mullioned windows. Early winter darkness had already closed in upon the picturesque inn on the top of Briarcliff Mountain, but the inn was cozy and warm and echoed with the pleasant sounds of conversation and laughter.

"We're in luck—the weatherman is forecasting snow tonight," Bett said, linking her arm through Leigh's as they moved toward the fire.

"Thank goodness. Wendy will be disappointed if it's not a white wedding in every way," Leigh said. She noticed a group approaching from the other end of the hall. "Oh, there's Andrew and his family," she said happily.

The Craigs—Andrew, his parents, Nancy and Jim, and his grandmother, Vera—met them in front of the Christmas tree. Andrew was tall, much taller than Wendy, with a thick thatch of brown hair and warm brown eyes. He and Wendy threw their arms around each other, much to the delight of Bett's brood.

"The inn is so beautiful when it's decorated for Christmas," Nancy Craig said, as she looked approvingly at the garlands of greenery looped from the ceiling.

The huge stone chimney, erected by Italian masons in the late 1800s when The Briarcliff was built as a mountain retreat for a wealthy philanthropist, was situated in the middle of the great hall of the inn and divided it into four distinct areas, each with its own hearth flanked by huge pots of poinsettias. Every area was dominated by its own enormous Christmas tree, and each tree was decorated in a different style. In their section, small unblinking topaz yellow lights twinkled from the branches of the tree; gilt balls of various sizes swung amid ribbons of silvery tinsel. Frothy golden garlands swooped from branch to branch, clasped with tiny angels made of papier-mâché.

Andrew brought Leigh and Bett cups of eggnog from one of the bustling waiters who crisscrossed the hall periodically bearing laden trays. He and Wendy stood close together, gazing raptly into each other's eyes. As the mellow tones of Christmas carols played on hand bells wafted in from the adjoining music room, Leigh felt an emotion that seemed ridiculously close to envy. Wendy looked so very much in love. *Oh, to feel that way again,* she thought with a stab of longing. Then Wendy turned and smiled at her, and envy melted into pride. Andrew was a fine person, and though Leigh had originally wished they had waited until after graduation to be married, she approved wholeheartedly of her daughter's choice of him as a husband. Impulsively she leaned over and kissed Andrew's cheek.

"I'm so glad you're the one Wendy is going to marry," she whispered, and he beamed with pleasure.

"Everyone gather in front of the Christmas tree for a picture," Carson called, fiddling with the adjustment of his Minolta as though he meant business.

They crowded close together, and Carson enlisted a hotel employee to do the honors.

"Say 'cheese,'" called one of the children.

As she faced front and arranged her expression for the camera, Leigh caught a startling glimpse of a tall man on the other side of the chimney. He was wearing a blue sweater with a wide red stripe across the chest and standing with his hands in his pockets, watching them intently. Her jaw fell; there was something about his utter immobility, something about the way he was studying their group.

"Don't say 'cheese,' say 'wedding,'" insisted Wendy, inspiring a burst of laughter, and the flash went off.

Leigh could have sworn—but it was impossible. She had been thinking about Russ Thornton so much that she was beginning to see him everywhere. She blinked rapidly until the man was gone.

"One more picture," Carson insisted, while they were all still seeing floating blue spots as a result of the last one.

"Let me straighten Billy's collar," Bett said.

"Oh, Mom," groaned Billy.

"He's chewing gum," Darren was only too happy to point out.

"I'm not. It's candy."

"Well, get rid of it," Carson ordered.

Billy spat into a napkin while Bett rolled her eyes in exasperation and stepped back into place. Leigh, distracted by the byplay, noticed with a start that the man who had been watching them was edging around the corner of the fireplace again.

She squinted her eyes, trying to refine his image, and decided that he wasn't as thin as Russ. Of course, she hadn't seen Russ in twenty-two years. It *could* be Russ. Or could it? If only she could observe him walking, she'd know. The way Russ's shoulders swung would have given him away.

"Leigh, stop scrunching up your forehead," Carson ordered. "All right, everybody, say 'wedding.'"

"No, say 'happy,'" Wendy said, and she was smiling up at Andrew when the shutter clicked. Leigh had barely managed to rearrange her face in time, and she was relieved when Carson called a halt to the photography session.

"Okay, that's enough pictures for the present," he said, tucking the camera back into its case. "But be warned—

I'll be taking plenty of candid shots by order of the bride and groom.''

They began to drift away in clumps of two or three people, and Leigh was about to ask Andrew's grandmother if she would like another cup of eggnog when she saw him again, the man in the blue-and-red sweater. Leigh refused to blink this time. She forgot about Andrew's grandmother and summoned all her concentration to study his face, paying special attention to the shape and line of it. It could be Russ. It *could* be.

But why? *Why?* She felt a sudden chill when she realized that he knew she would be at The Briarcliff because she had told him so herself. The recollection of this oversight on her part sent cold ripples of anxiety up her spine.

"Oh, here's Jeanne," Wendy cried, running to meet her college roommate, who was to serve as her only attendant. Jeanne was breathless from the cold, and introductions had to be made all around, which kept Leigh from watching the man who was so intently eyeing their group. A waiter appeared with trays of cake and cookies. In the general confusion, Darren chased a squealing Billy around the room, and Carson took off in pursuit. When Leigh managed a quick glance toward the corner of the fireplace, the man was no longer there.

Leigh decided that she definitely needed a few minutes to pull herself together. During a quiet moment, she separated herself from the group as if to inspect the fragrant cascades of greenery adorning the mantel and stood for a long moment inhaling the sharp, pungent scent of fresh-cut blue spruce.

It's natural to feel keyed up, she told herself. *My daughter is going to be married the day after tomorrow.* She stared into the fire's golden depths, thinking that she should get back to the group. She felt suddenly thankful for social obligations; they would keep her securely anchored to reality for the next few days.

As she moved away from the hearth, she glanced over her shoulder. In front of the neighboring fire, a young couple on the couch were totally absorbed in each other. There was no sign of anyone else, and her knees felt rubbery with relief.

She briefly considered asking the couple if they'd seen a man in a blue sweater with a red stripe across the chest, but she thought better of it. Of course, there were the other two hearths, but there seemed to be noisy family groups on those sides. No, there was no sign of a man alone.

I was only seeing things before, she told herself. *I must be more tired than I thought.*

Her face felt so hot. She tried fanning herself with a paper napkin, which did absolutely no good. The corners of the room looked cool and shadowy, and she drifted toward one. She noticed that the Christmas tree in this section of the hall was decorated differently from the one where her family was congregating. The ornaments on this one seemed to be tiny wood folk carvings, and they looked handcrafted. She gravitated toward the tree for a closer look, and then, as if in a dream, she heard his voice.

"Leigh?"

She whirled around, suddenly wary. The wide skirt of her simple red dress flared against her knees. The man in the blue-and-red sweater was silhouetted against the fire, but because he stood so close, she saw his face distinctly. She would have known him anywhere.

Her breath caught in her throat. "Russ?" she whispered.

He strode forward, and in that moment there was no one else around. No family, no couple on the couch, no waiters bearing trays—just the two of them, their uncertain faces illumined by the twinkling white lights on the huge Christmas tree.

She drank in his face; it was so much the same, yet different. His eyes, dark and lustrous, with a web of fine lines at their corners that hadn't been there before; the straight planes below the cheekbones squaring off at the jawline; the broad shoulders so much the same; and he was tall, but not as thin as she remembered him. She had forgotten the tangle of his curly eyelashes. Her heart swooped down to her toes, then up again. She couldn't speak.

For a moment she dreaded that he was going to throw his arms around her in enthusiastic greeting. But somehow she had extended her hands involuntarily toward him, and he reached for them as if for a lifeline and clasped them between his. Her fingers fluttered and were still. She was locked in his gaze as she tried to comprehend his presence. Behind her the noise of the group diminished; they could have been strangers, not members of her family and Andrew's.

"Leigh," Russ said, his voice grating under the force of suppressed emotion. "I had to see you."

"No," she whispered. She spared a wild-eyed glance at the family party, looking for Wendy. He mustn't see her; he mustn't guess.

"I knew you were going to be here, you see, and I didn't want to spend Christmas alone. I flew up here this afternoon—"

"Flew?" she repeated distractedly. She would have flown if she could, but she was incapable of movement. Besides, he was still holding her hands.

"In my plane. A four-passenger Beechcraft—I use it for business. Another Christmas spent with my aged uncle and aunt and all their children and grandchildren would have given me the willies. I'll try not to interfere with your plans, but I *had* to see you."

In desperation, Leigh squeezed her eyes shut and opened them again. He was gazing down at her with an expression of such bright expectancy that she wanted to cry. Why couldn't he have waited until later, until after the wedding when Wendy would be safely away on her honeymoon?

"You shouldn't have come," she managed to say.

"I hoped you'd understand. I know I'm putting our relationship in jeopardy by doing such a crazy thing, and I understand your obligations to your family. If you only have ten minutes, I'll take that. Or five. Anything at all, Leigh."

Russ had never begged her for anything before, but it sounded suspiciously as though that was what he was doing now. She tried to summon her anger from the ample reservoir that had fed her past hurts, but at this moment she could find none. Instead she only felt bewilderment. She had no idea what she was going to do about him.

She swallowed and inhaled deeply. "I can't think. I don't know what to say. I didn't expect this," she said.

"Can we meet later tonight?"

This is awful, she thought. *I can't let Wendy see him. Or Bett. She might guess—well, something.* Which was probably a ridiculous thought. She didn't think that Bett had ever met Russ, and even if she had, she'd only been eight years old in 1969.

"We could meet in the library," Russ said urgently. "Just to talk. You're still so lovely, Leigh. I can't believe it's been twenty-two years."

Leigh shot a worried look toward Wendy. She and Andrew stood with their arms linked around each other, holding court for the admiring group of children. Claire-Anne, the five-year-old, was yawning. Everyone would go to bed before long; the kids had been reassured that Santa Claus could find them here at The Briarcliff, and they would be up at the crack of dawn to make sure that he really had.

"I—I—" She saw that Bett was looking around, and probably she was trying to figure out where Leigh was.

"Meet me for a few minutes," Russ urged. She pulled her gaze away from the group; Russ's determined face filled her vision.

She mustered the strength to yank her hands away. "In the library, then. Around eleven o'clock," she said quickly. She turned on her heel and fled—no, floated—toward the other side of the fireplace, leaving him staring after her. She felt his eyes on her back; her cheeks suffused with rising warmth. Embarrassed, she pressed ice-cold hands into the hollows beneath her cheekbones.

Russ was here. How in the world was she going to handle it?

Bett's voice broke through the fog surrounding her. "Leigh? We're going to gather around the piano at the end of the hall and sing a few Christmas carols," she said. Despite Leigh's flaming face, she seemed to notice nothing amiss.

A limp Leigh let herself be carried along with the group. They had begun to sing "The First Noel" when Russ quietly approached the other side of the piano and began to sing, his eyes never leaving Leigh's face. The words to the carol died in her throat.

Russ had always been a terrible singer, she remembered, and the thought brought a smile to her lips. In midsong he smiled back, that wonderful lopsided smile that had always endeared him to her.

Leigh felt as though everyone around the piano must see that Russ was looking at her. He sang gustily, his voice ringing out over the others, and she lowered her face to hide her expression. From the sound of it, he didn't sing any better than he ever had. When she lifted her head he was grinning at her and his eyes were dancing, and she knew that he knew what she was thinking.

Leigh bit her lip and looked away. Russ had always been able to read her; why should it surprise her that he was doing it now?

Because it's been twenty-two years, she told herself vehemently. *Everything is different.*

She stole a look at Wendy. Her daughter was singing softly, her eyes alight, her hand nestled trustingly in Andrew's. Wendy had dark, wavy hair, its texture remarkably like Russ's. And she had broad shoulders and a pointed nose, a square jawline and small, even teeth—in short, she looked so much like Russ that anyone who saw them together would have to know that they were father and daughter. Except for her eyes; she had Leigh's sea-blue eyes.

A faint queasiness made it difficult for Leigh to go on singing. For all these years she had kept the secret, and now Katrina was the only living person besides herself who knew the truth about Wendy's paternity. No matter how much Leigh wanted to renew her relationship with Russ Thornton, her daughter's well-being was paramount. Leigh could not let Wendy find out here and now about her real father. A possessive ferocity arose in Leigh's chest, and she moved slightly forward so that her body blocked Wendy and Russ's view of each other.

This is insane, she thought as the pianist played the introduction to "Silent Night." *Silent in the night,* Leigh thought, *how apt.* Never telling anyone but David and

Katrina about Wendy; keeping the secret so that Wendy wouldn't be hurt. And now here was the one person who could destroy the world she'd made for her daughter, *their* daughter, and she was actually planning to meet him in the library later. Worst of all, she was still attracted to him.

When the last strains of the carol faded, Leigh turned away so that she wouldn't have to look at Russ, although she felt his probing eyes on her back. She covered her confusion by bending down to kiss little Claire-Anne good-night. When she straightened, Russ was gone.

Relief made her garrulous, and she found that she was overdoing her good-nights. Finally, after bidding the Craigs an effusive farewell, she helped Bett shepherd the children toward the elevators. Wendy, Andrew and Jeanne followed.

"I guess it'll be an early morning," Jeanne said, once the elevator doors had closed and they were headed upward.

"We're all going to meet in Bett and Carson's suite to open presents at eight o'clock, and then it's down to brunch with the other guests in the dining room. Everyone will be free to pursue various activities throughout the day before the wedding rehearsal at seven sharp, followed by the rehearsal dinner in the Balsam Room," Leigh said. She felt as if she were speaking by rote; no one seemed to notice.

"I don't know about everyone else, but I'm ready to pack it in," Andrew said.

"Me, too," Wendy replied as they stepped out of the elevator. "I hope you're not up for any late-night chats, Jeanne."

Jeanne laughed. "Today I helped my brother put together a bicycle for my nephew, a chore which had to be accomplished at five in the morning so my nephew wouldn't see it. No, I think I'll sleep early and well.''

Andrew kissed Wendy good-night in front of the room she was sharing with Jeanne, and he escorted Leigh to the single room that she was occupying alone.

''Good night, Andrew,'' she told him.

''Is there anything you need? Anything I can get for you before I leave?'' he asked.

Leigh smiled and patted his arm. She couldn't believe how normal she managed to look and sound. ''Thanks, but I'll be fine. In fact, I'm going to read a bit before I go to sleep.''

''See you in the morning, then,'' he said.

Leigh went into her room and pressed her back against the closed door. She felt a wild, nervous impulse to laugh hysterically. Or cry. Or something.

What if Russ had looked into Wendy's beautiful face and had seen the resemblance? What if, during those moments when they were all gathered around the piano, he had guessed?

Wendy didn't have a clue, she was sure of that. Wendy was so wrapped up in Andrew that she had no thought of anything else. But Russ—he could have put two and two together easily. For that matter, anyone could have. Wendy was so clearly her father's daughter.

The red digits of the clock on the round table beside the bed indicated that it was now ten-thirty, which meant that she had time to call Russ's room to tell him that she wouldn't meet him in the library as planned. To tell him that he'd better leave The Briarcliff now, because she didn't intend to talk to him at all. The telephone stared up at her from the table beside the bed.

She had no idea whether Russ would honor such a request even if she summoned the strength to make it. Certainly Russ was every bit a gentleman; he would probably depart quietly and without a fuss. Although hadn't he said he'd flown his plane here? A snowstorm would keep him from leaving.

She brushed aside the folds of the long blue velvet drapery at the window. There was no moon and no stars, and the wind had died. It wasn't snowing, though. If she met with Russ for a few minutes—he had asked for five or ten—perhaps she could convince him to go back to Charlotte where he belonged.

She went to the mirror over the big double dresser and stared at her reflection. Her face was thinner than it had been when she was twenty; her laugh lines showed, and her freckles did not. Her hair was worn in the same flowing style, reaching almost to her shoulders with wispy bangs across the forehead. And it was still the same copper color, thanks to the skills of an excellent hairdresser.

No, she didn't look the same. Russ was only being kind when he said so. And he didn't look the same, either. He had changed. But she liked the changes. Even though he posed a threat to her peace of mind, she couldn't help admitting that Russ Thornton looked better than ever.

LEIGH'S FEET MOVED soundlessly and reluctantly along the thick carpet in the hallway. A pause at Wendy's door assured her that her daughter and her roommate were serious about getting a good night's sleep, and she was sure that no one else in her family or Andrew's would be up and about. She rode the deserted elevator to the first floor where she halted outside the paneled library door and fought to surround herself with an air of detachment. She was determined that he would leave. Tonight, if possible.

Russ stood when she entered the library. On the way downstairs in the elevator, Leigh had prepared a fine speech. Now, however, facing his serious, unblinking scrutiny, all the words deserted her. His eyes searched her face, looking for something he had hoped to find; whether he found it or not, she couldn't tell. He smiled, a warm smile of welcome.

"We're lucky," he said, moving forward to take her hand. "There's no one else here. Come sit beside me on the couch. There are still coals in the grate."

In the face of his obvious pleasure, she caved in. She let herself be led to the leather couch and sank down beside him, halfheartedly planning her escape. She could say the words now. The words refused to come, however, and she gazed helplessly at Russ Thornton, understanding completely in that moment of looking deep into his dark eyes how she had fallen in love with him in the first place.

The only light in the room was a small lamp on the table beside the chair where Russ had been sitting. The walls were lined with the books that inn guests were encouraged to take to their rooms and read; the fireplace was small, and the embers within it lit their faces with a golden glow.

He held one of her hands. "I was afraid you wouldn't come," he said. His hopeful expression brought back so many feelings of loss and longing that she turned her head away.

"I almost didn't," she said faintly, keeping her face carefully averted.

"I'm glad you did," he said.

She forced herself to lift her head and look him in the eye. "You have to leave," she said as sternly as she could manage, but she realized too late that her forcefulness had only piqued his curiosity. "I mean, I wish you'd leave," she amended, pulling her hand away from him.

He looked suddenly deflated. "That's not what I wanted to hear," he said.

"This situation isn't easy for me," she said. "Here I am celebrating Christmas with my family, and you show up unannounced."

"You seem to enjoy our phone conversations," Russ pointed out.

"Phone calls, yes. But this—" and she shook her head in despair.

He let out a deep, lingering sigh and slid down on the couch so that his long legs extended toward the fire. He folded his arms across his chest and stared moodily into the fireplace.

"I wouldn't have thought you'd come here at Christmas," she said after a moment. "Doesn't your family expect you?"

"Now that my parents are gone, I often spend the holidays alone. When I was watching you in the great hall with your family, I realized how much I'd been missing. Was that your sister in the gray dress? Are those her children?"

"Yes, that's Bett," she said, and when he looked interested, she haltingly told him about Bett's whirlwind of a family.

"Does she live near you?" he asked.

"Less than an hour's drive away," she told him.

"And Warren?" he asked.

"Warren was killed in Vietnam, Russ," she said.

She swiveled her head in time to see the color drain from his face, but he recovered rapidly and shook his head. "I'm sorry, I hadn't heard," he said.

"Anyway, we're not a big family now, but we are close," she said.

"I figured out that the girl with the dark hair was your daughter," he said. "But I was mostly looking at you."

He doesn't know, Leigh thought in a moment of amazed revelation. *He hasn't guessed!* Wendy's resemblance to him, so obvious to Leigh, seemed to have escaped Russ completely. Her relief was instantly diluted by her sense of responsibility toward Wendy. Russ couldn't stay here. He *couldn't.*

She faced him squarely. "Russ, I meant it when I asked you to go. My daughter is getting married here the day after tomorrow. I'm very busy. I don't need this."

He seemed taken aback. "She's getting married? To whom?"

"To Andrew Craig, a boy she met at college. The point is, this isn't a good time for this—this reunion of ours."

"You seem glad to see me," he said after a moment.

"Do I?"

"Well, aren't you?"

"No. Not now."

"When? Next week? Next year?"

Leigh averted her eyes. He was so earnest. So genuine. If only—but she couldn't live the "if onlies." She'd learned that long ago.

"You've upset me so by showing up like this," she said in a rush.

"I figured we had a lot to say to each other," he said.

"We do, but not now. It's—it's—" She felt hysteria rising within her, but she pushed it away.

"If I'd known your daughter was getting married," he said with the utmost sincerity, "I probably wouldn't have come. But I didn't know, and I did come, so I want to make the most of it. I told you I won't interfere with your family plans, but any time that you have left over—"

"I won't," she said firmly.

His eyes were rueful. "Perhaps you could make time?" he suggested.

Leigh shook her head. "It's doubtful," she replied, feeling sad.

Russ stared at her for a moment before standing abruptly and walking to the shuttered window. He pushed back the shutters with one hand. "I can't fly in this weather," he pointed out. "It's a snowstorm." With his free hand he drew her close, so close that her hair brushed his shoulder, and she didn't have the heart to resist.

Then she looked out the window and saw that Wendy would have her white Christmas. Snow swirled in eddies around a post light near the path outside; it drifted into billowy mounds in the sheltered angle of the low wall defining the courtyard beyond. Dancing, whirling, sparkling magical snow—and somewhere a clock chimed the hour.

Leigh counted twelve silvery chimes. When she looked up at Russ, he was smiling down at her, and the rapt expression on his face was her utter undoing.

"Merry Christmas, Leigh," he whispered, and then he inclined his head slowly, so slowly that her heart stopped beating, and kissed her.

Chapter Four

The next morning Leigh awoke abruptly, and the first thing she thought was, *Russ is here*.

She had no idea what she was going to do about him. Last night he'd made it clear that he had no intention of leaving. She'd repeated her point that he couldn't count on her for company; he'd insisted that he didn't care. He just wanted to be near her, he said.

With her lips still warm from his kisses, she had asked him—no, begged him—to leave her alone today. Not that she thought he would. She was all too well acquainted with the stubborn spark she'd seen in his eyes last night. She only hoped that he'd have the good sense to time his approaches so that no one else in her party noticed him among the throng of people who had chosen to celebrate the holidays at the well-known Briarcliff.

At least he hasn't guessed about Wendy, Leigh thought thankfully. She slid out of bed and padded as soft-footed as a cat to the window to see the new-fallen snow. How he could have seen Wendy and not suspected, Leigh couldn't imagine. The features that they shared were so familiar to her that she thought they should be obvious to anyone. She had to admit that Russ's sharp nose was softened a bit in Wendy's face and that the similar texture of their hair might be a characteristic that only she would notice. But the squared jawline—wasn't that unmistakable? And the broad shoulders—weren't they a sure giveaway? Maybe not. Maybe it was her guilt that made her catalog resemblances that were not really as striking as she thought.

When she raised the shade, she saw that the grounds of The Briarcliff seemed silvered in misty light; the fresh snowfall blurred the shadows of the mountain ridges and unfurled around the inn like a glistening white bridal train. The scene was so quiet and peaceful, a direct contrast to Leigh's complicated emotions.

As she dressed, she wondered if she really wanted Russ to leave. On her mothering level, where she instinctively wanted to protect her young, she believed that he must go. If he stayed, he might guess about Wendy. On another level, the one where she operated like any other woman who hoped for an all-encompassing relationship with a man, she wished that things could be the same between them as they had been twenty-two years ago. Or was she merely overwhelmed by Russ's sudden presence in her life at a time when she was bound to be sentimental, anyway? Leigh was smart enough to recognize her own vulnerability.

After the wedding, if Russ stayed around that long, and Leigh had no doubt that he would, she would figure out what to do about him. Before she could think this through, Wendy and Jeanne burst laughing through the connecting door to their room, shouted "Merry Christmas!" and swept her up on a wave of enthusiasm and hilarity that effectively ended Leigh's reflections.

The three of them gathered up their presents and arrived breathlessly with the others at Carson and Bett's suite where they were greeted by the excited squeals of the children, who had been awake since the first tentative rays of sunlight crept over Briarcliff Mountain. There were repeated jovial exclamations about the appropriateness of last night's snowfall, and Wendy and Andrew seemed wrapped in their own particular bliss, which was exactly, Leigh thought, as it should be.

After much oohing and aahing over presents, they all trooped downstairs to brunch. The dining room had been draped with red velvet ribbons for the occasion, and a sculptured-ice Santa presided from his spot in the middle of the buffet table. All the while Leigh was tending little Claire-Anne and watching Wendy, who was glowing with happiness, her eyes were darting into the corners of the room and past the garlanded entrance searching for Russ. She saw no sign of him. Well, what had she expected? She had asked him to leave her alone, hadn't she?

By the time brunch was over, the great hall of the inn was abuzz with children trying out their new toys; a quartet of carolers moved from one section of the hall to another singing Christmas songs.

"This is the kind of Christmas I've always hoped for," Wendy said, swooping up behind Leigh during a lull.

"Isn't it lovely," Leigh murmured in agreement.

"Mom, is anything wrong? You look—well, so *removed*. It isn't like you." Wendy regarded her with mild concern.

"I'm just being a bit reflective," Leigh replied.

"I was thinking earlier how much Dad would have loved all of this," Wendy said softly, her gesture taking in the decorations, the smiling faces of their family and the glittering snowscape beyond the wide windows.

"Yes," Leigh agreed wistfully.

"If only he could have lived long enough to meet the man I'm going to marry. Dad would have loved Andrew, wouldn't he?"

"I'm sure he would have," Leigh said. Suddenly her heart ached with a pang of disloyalty to David. All this thinking about Russ meant that she'd given David no more than a passing thought, and this at a time when she should have been thinking about David more than ever. David had, after all, embraced Wendy as his own. No man could have done more than that.

"Don't cry, Mom. This is the happiest time of my life. Dad wouldn't want you to be sad," Wendy said. She drew a lacy handkerchief out of her pocket and passed it to Leigh.

Leigh dabbed at the tears threatening to overflow her bottom eyelids, and as she returned the handkerchief to Wendy, she saw Russ standing unobtrusively at the other end of the hall. His smile was tentative, and, her heart laden with sadness, she let her eyes meet his for one long moment.

He was struck by the pain he saw and stunned by the rawness of her need. The droop of her head, which she tried to disguise when her daughter approached; the strained expression around her eyes; she touched him to the very core of his being in some indefinable way. In her, Russ saw all the uncertainty and disillusionment that he felt about his own life. In that moment he felt more than an attraction to her, he felt a kinship. In the twenty-two years that they had been apart, they had both suffered. Now they had the opportunity to come together again, if that was what they both wanted, and to comfort each other, if that was in their power.

Leave her alone—hell, he thought fiercely. Today was Christmas Day. No one should be as much alone as he sensed Leigh was, even in the rush of activity surrounding her family. He knew all about keeping busy so you wouldn't have time to let the feelings surface. He knew what it was like to pretend to be happy and cheerful so that other people wouldn't feel concerned about your own sadness. And that was what Leigh was doing—she was pretending. The Leigh he saw this morning wasn't the spontaneous, happy-go-lucky girl he had known. And yet that girl was somewhere inside her, and perhaps he would be the one to set her free.

He wheeled abruptly and went back to his room. He had a card up his sleeve, and he sensed that this was the time to play it.

LEIGH REALIZED, when she looked up and saw that Russ was gone, that he had pulled another disappearing act. At least he was respecting her wishes so far. He wasn't embarrassing her in front of the family. She would embarrass herself, however, if she didn't keep up a cheerful front.

"Anybody want to build a snowman?" Carson wanted to know, and Leigh, feigning a gaiety that she didn't feel, quickly took up the cause. They all bundled up in their warm coats and woolly mittens, flocking outside to join several other families in the construction of an immense snowman in the circle created by the grand loop of the inn's driveway.

Once Leigh looked up to see Russ watching her intently through a window of the great hall. She made a wry face at him without thinking as she helped the boys roll a large snowball for the snowman's head. The next time she sneaked a covert glance at the window, Russ waved. She shook her head slightly in disapproval, but she couldn't help smiling at him. He grinned back.

After the snowman had been built and Carson had taken pictures of all of them gathered around it, Nancy, Andrew's mother, said that she felt like spending the afternoon napping. Vera said that sounded like a good idea, and Bett soon followed them into the inn, insisting that a protesting Claire-Anne lie down on her bed for a while so that she wouldn't fall asleep in the middle of the rehearsal dinner that night. Carson, Jim and the boys wandered toward the creek, where a snowball fight was in lively progress.

Andrew threw one arm around Wendy and one around Leigh. "It's a fine snowman," he said expansively. "Look at everyone inside the inn admiring him."

Leigh glanced at the window where Russ had stood. She didn't see him, but a couple of children standing there with their parents were applauding. Andrew swept a comic bow in their direction, and one of the children mimicked him.

"I'm so cold that my feet feel like blocks of ice," Wendy said, stomping her boots in the snow.

"Come up to my room," Leigh said. "I brought a hot-water bottle."

Wendy darted a hasty glance in Andrew's direction. "Andrew and I thought we'd warm ourselves in front of the fire in the library," she said apologetically.

"Of course," Andrew hastened to add more out of sense of duty than a desire for Leigh's company, "we'd love for you to come with us."

Leigh, stung by her own insensitivity, realized immediately what she should have understood before she spoke—that Wendy and Andrew would naturally want to spend time alone together.

"No," she said briskly, "I'll be perfectly okay on my own. *My* feet are cold, too, and a hot cup of tea in my room sounds more than inviting. You two run along."

Wendy looked indecisive, torn between wanting to be alone with her husband-to-be and her obligation to her mother.

"No, I really mean it," Leigh insisted. She started to walk toward the inn.

"Mom," Wendy said, still unsure.

"You worry too much," she said, going back to where Wendy stood and slipping her arm through her daughter's. Leigh turned to Andrew for support. "Andrew, how about helping me out?"

"Come along," he said, appropriating Wendy's other arm. "We'll have those feet of yours warm in no time."

Wendy followed, knowing when she was outnumbered, and in the lobby Leigh bade them a cheery goodbye. Once in the elevator, however, she let her determined smile fade and rubbed her eyelids with a cold thumb and forefinger. Of course Wendy would disdain a hot-water bottle in favor of Andrew; Leigh should have known better than to offer it. Somehow she must learn to let go of Wendy, little by little, bit by bit, even though she knew it would be one of the hardest things she had ever done. She and Wendy were closer than most mothers and daughters, perhaps because they had depended so heavily on each other for comfort ever since David's death. It would be a real challenge to back off in the months ahead, because she was already feeling shut out.

Leigh's room was an oasis of quiet after the hubbub everywhere else at the inn; it was a good place to nurse her rejection. The bright sunlight penetrated into all the corners of the room, bringing out the glow of the cherry furniture and casting rainbow reflections from the prisms of the light fixture onto the cream-colored walls of the room, and Leigh immediately felt better.

She hung her coat in the closet, draped her muffler over a doorknob, and only when she was about to pick up the receiver to order a cup of tea from room service did she notice that the red message light on her telephone was blinking.

She knew that there was only one person who could have left her a message. Everyone in her party had been outside with her for the past couple of hours.

Common sense advised her that to ignore the winking red light would be the utmost folly. Leigh had absolutely no doubt that Russ Thornton would appear knocking at her door if she didn't respond to his message. And that simply wouldn't do.

She picked up the phone and telephoned the desk. As she waited for the clerk to answer, she felt a hundred misgivings.

"Yes, Mrs. Cathcart, we do have a message for you," observed the desk clerk. "I'll send a bellman to deliver it."

"Please read it to me on the phone," Leigh said.

"I'm sorry, but we can't do that. The sender asked specifically that it be delivered."

"But—"

"The bellman will be there shortly" was the firm answer, and Leigh suspected that the wheels of this particular Russ Thornton gambit had been greased with a liberal tip. Impatiently she hung up and awaited the inevitable knock. When she opened the door, a uniformed inn employee handed her not only a white envelope but a small green-and-gilt-wrapped box. After he disappeared down the hall, she stared at the tiny package and let her apprehension give way to dismay. Why was Russ giving her a gift?

The wrapping paper fell away to reveal a white box. *Jewelry,* she thought with foreboding. *But why?*

She lifted the box's lid and removed a layer of cotton. A golden glimmer... a familiar shape. Her eyes blurred for a moment when she saw the heart-shaped locket against the black velvet lining. As she lifted the locket on its chain, it winked seductively in the gossamer rays of sunshine filtering through the snow-laden branches of the oak trees outside her window.

On the back were engraved their initials, L. R. and R. T. *Just the way we'll engrave our wedding bands someday,* Russ had whispered on that spring night so long ago when he'd given her the locket to reassure her that their separation because of his father's illness was only a temporary interruption of their relationship; that night neither of them had thought that anything could come between them.

Leigh remembered that the locket's chain had broken sometime during that last summer when they lay together in their secret green glade in the park, and Russ had scooped the locket up from where it had fallen amid the pine needles and he said, "I'll take it to the jeweler's and have it repaired for you." Later, in the heat of their disagreements, they had both forgotten the locket, although Leigh had thought about it many times since, wondering if it was still waiting unclaimed in some Charlotte jewelry store after so many years.

Russ had kept the locket all this time. How incredible, and how crafty of him to present her with it now. He knew that it was the one gift that she wouldn't send back to him, the one gift that would touch her more deeply than any other.

Clutching the locket in her hand, she picked up the phone, hesitated, and then dialed Russ's room.

"Russ," she said when he picked up the phone. "I don't know what to say."

"How about Merry Christmas for starters?" he said.

"Merry Christmas, then, but—oh, Russ, thank you for the locket. I—I often wondered what became of it." She held it at eye level and watched the gold heart twisting on its chain so that their two sets of engraved initials blurred into each other. *I am you and you are me,* she thought, the words surfacing from somewhere in her subconscious. It was what they used to say to each other all the times that they felt inseparably close. She folded her fingers around the heart until she felt her own pulse.

"I meant to give it back to you, but the opportunity never arose. Now I think you should have it," he said. "Anyway, Christmas is a most appropriate time for gifts, if you consider something that was always yours a gift. Look, I don't know what's on your agenda this afternoon, but would you like to join me for a walk? Now?"

"I'm supposed to be drinking a cup of tea," Leigh told him. She set the locket carefully on the table beside the bed; having it back was one thing, but wearing it was another.

"You don't sound the least bit thirsty," he pointed out, and she smiled.

"Actually, I wasn't," she admitted.

"How about it? Doesn't a walk seem like the perfect way to spend such a beautiful afternoon?"

Leigh glanced out the window. The sky was a bright crystal blue, and sunlight fairly bounced off the blanket of snow covering the mountain. She really didn't want to coop herself up inside the inn. She did, after all, have a life of her own.

"I'll put on my coat and meet you somewhere away from the inn," she said, feeling her heart lighten with joy at the very thought of seeing him.

"I'll be waiting beside the stone pillars at the main entrance to the grounds. Can you be there in ten minutes?"

"Seven," she said, and he laughed.

"That's even better. Bye," he said.

Leigh caught a glimpse of her reflection in the mirror as she hung up the phone. She was smiling, and who could blame her? After all this time, she and Russ were planning to go somewhere together again, and it was just as it had been in those long-ago days when they took each other's presence in their lives so much for granted. Twenty-two years seemed to melt away in the force of their attraction to each other; in some ways, it was as though they had never been apart.

She threw on her coat and literally ran from her room, feeling furtive and yet exhilarated as she traversed the great hall as unobtrusively as possible, and finally she breathed a sigh of relief as she escaped the confines of the inn without seeing anyone she knew. She drew long drafts of air into her lungs, heady with her freedom.

Russ was waiting, and he waved and bounded toward her across the snow when he caught sight of her approaching from the direction of the inn. When they met in the middle of the driveway, he caught both her mittened hands in his; she could feel his warmth through the thick wool.

"I'm so glad you decided to join me," he said, his eyes sparkling as they took in the sight of her. He looked boyish and carefree and unabashedly happy to see her. She smiled up at him, a dazzling smile, and clung to his hands for a few seconds longer than necessary before releasing them.

"Race you to the road," she said, flinging the words back over her shoulder, and he laughed and said, "Be careful! There may be ice in the drive!" but there wasn't, and Leigh skimmed past two startled parents who were pulling their bundled-up baby on a small sled in the snow alongside the driveway. The incongruity of it amused her: a few years ago, she would have been one of those totally responsible parents who was looking askance at any crazy adult who wasn't acting her age. And now she didn't even care how she appeared to these people or to anyone else as long as she was having a good time. She laughed with the sheer delight of it.

When she breathlessly skidded to a stop on the narrow path bordering the highway, Russ was beside her. "As someone who runs every day, I'm ashamed to admit that you almost beat me," he said.

"Almost? I *did* win. I was a whole nose ahead of you on the straightaway."

"I won't quibble. Want to run with me tomorrow morning? I usually go before breakfast."

"Tomorrow I'll be busy," she said, reminding him.

"Ah, that's right. Well, for now you're mine," he said lightly, taking her hand as they started their downhill walk.

The gesture surprised her in a way, although it seemed perfectly natural. He grinned at her and reached in his pocket with his other hand. "Want a lemon drop?" he said, offering her the package.

"You still have lemon drops," she said softly, feeling a tiny pang at the sight and scent of them.

"Of course," he said. She held out her mittened hand and he slid one out of the bag and into her palm. She put it into her mouth before it could stick to the wool of her mitten. The sour-sweet taste brought back so many memories, all mixed up with the way Russ's car had always smelled, the way *he* smelled, even the way he tasted. Last night when he had kissed her, she had marveled that he tasted exactly the same and had been amazed that she actually remembered.

Leigh shivered slightly as a cold wind blew through the stand of trees on the slope, and Russ squeezed her hand. She might remember the taste of him, but this was something she had forgotten—they had communicated so much to each other through touch in the old days; Russ had liked to punctuate conversations with meaningful little squeezes of her hand, and she had often squeezed back in agreement. She had never done that with anyone else; how could that have escaped her memory?

Maybe too many things had slipped her memory, after all. Oh, she remembered the big things, like the seriousness of the moment when he had first slipped the chain of the heart-shaped gold locket around her neck and the pain on his face when she left him that last day in the park. She'd *thought* she remembered the little things, too, such as the lemon drops. But in fact she only recalled the obvious—for instance, the way the lemon drops smelled and tasted. She wasn't ready for the emotional response she was experiencing. She wasn't ready at all.

"The craft village is down the hill. The stores won't be open because it's Christmas Day, but we can window-shop. Heidi, one of my decorators, told me to be on the lookout for colorful quilts, and she also said that if I can find any authentic antiques, I should buy them. I don't know how to tell if they're authentic, that's the problem."

"My mother owned an antique store for a few years after Bett left home," Leigh said. "Maybe I can advise you."

"You'll be busy with the wedding tomorrow," Russ reminded her.

"Oh. Yes, that's true," she said, pulling herself up short. For a moment she had been thinking that she would be at The Briarcliff longer than she actually was. Time had a way of warping when she was around Russ.

"As for quilts, Heidi says they're great for the country style of decorating that's so popular now," Russ said.

"Katrina knows this little old lady who lives deep in the mountains and who makes the most marvelous quilts. I'll see if I can get an address for you."

"That would please Heidi no end," Russ replied.

They heard a shout from the top of the hill and stopped short as a boy riding an upside-down garbage-can lid swooped in front of them, barely avoiding their toes. He tumbled sideways and rolled in the snow, then sat up with a jaunty grin, picked up the lid, and ran downhill to meet his friends.

"That looks like fun," Russ said, glancing up the hill. "I wonder if we could do it."

"If we had a couple of garbage can lids, maybe we could. I remember when Wendy was little and it would snow, the kids would use anything to slide down the hill on the next street over. Pizza pans, cafeteria trays, all sorts of things became toboggans for them."

"It must have been fun raising a child," Russ said wistfully.

"Oh, it was," Leigh began before remembering that she didn't want to talk about Wendy. And yet Wendy had been such an important part of her life that it was almost impossible not to inject her into the conversation.

The boy with the garbage-can lid and his friends ran noisily past them up the hill. One boy hollered an invitation to the others to come over to his house to play a new video game. Their voices fairly crackled in the crisp cold air.

"At Christmas, I really start feeling down sometimes," Russ said. "That's when it's painfully clear to me that I've missed out on so much by not having a child. Or children. I'd always thought I would have a family."

She shot him a curious look. "I was surprised when you told me you hadn't," she said, knowing full well that she was treading on dangerous ground.

"It never seemed to be the right time to have a child. At least for Dominique." He tried to keep the bitterness out of his voice, only partially succeeding.

"She didn't want children?"

"I thought she wanted them when we got married, and maybe she did at the time, I don't know. Later, when she told me that kids didn't fit in with the kind of life she wanted to lead, I tried to accept that. I thought I had come to terms with our childlessness until we divorced; afterward I had to realize that probably I'd never be a father."

Leigh held her breath; what if she were to tell him flat out, right this very moment, that he *was* a father? That his daughter was smart and beautiful and that she was everything anyone could hope for in a daughter? What would he do? What would he say?

They walked on in silence, which she hoped he would interpret as sympathetic. He could have no idea of the pain she was feeling at this moment, and yes, of the terror. She had kept the secret so well; even thinking of telling it made her mouth go dry and her knees feel weak.

"So, now I'm resigned to not having kids," Russ said. He kicked a pinecone out of the path and it rolled downhill, giving Leigh time to think. What she thought was that she didn't want to think about it, and with the craft village looming in the distance, she was able to manage a quick change of subject.

"Look," she said. "The craft village looks so beautiful under its blanket of snow."

It *was* lovely. Bare snow-frosted tree branches arched through the wintry blue sky to shelter the little rustic stone cottages arranged neatly along the sides of the highway, and snow glittered from the windowsills and in the niches between the stones. It could have been a Christmas-card scene depicting a small New England village, but in fact the Briarcliff craft village was something quite different.

A hundred years ago, the wife of the philanthropist whose retreat this was had sought to extend her good works to the impoverished mountain people who lived nearby. She had been entranced by the folksy crafts of the mountain people; the wood carvings, the weaving and the sturdy furniture would, she was sure, find a ready market in the North. And so she had built a village where the mountain artisans could work, and the craftspeople had formed the Briarcliff Crafts Cooperative, which had sold handmade items to some of the most exclusive shops in New York, Chicago and Philadelphia.

Now that The Briarcliff was an all-season resort, the cooperative sold most of their crafts on the premises, functioning as a series of gift shops for the inn. Today other guests enjoying the bracing mountain air browsed among the shops as they admired the window displays, and as she and Russ joined the crowd, Leigh recalled how during past summers spent here with her family, the craft village had always been a treat.

In the window of the first house, an old loom built of woods native to the mountains dominated the setting. Soft homespun cloth spilled over the weaver's bench, and several bedspreads and tablecloths in different patterns were knotted loosely and draped artistically around a basket.

In the next shop, Russ found the antiques he had been looking for. "What do you think about that handcrafted pine shaving stand?" he asked, shading the glass from the reflection of the sun and peering inside.

"Very nice," Leigh said approvingly.

"I don't know. I have no imagination about decor. I should send Heidi up here to look at some of these things," Russ said as they moved on.

"Heidi—you've mentioned her a number of times," Leigh observed.

Russ slowed his steps. "I suspect I know what you're thinking, and no, she isn't. She is twenty-four years old, has worked for me for six months and lives with her boyfriend in a house decorated with old Coca-Cola signs and curtains made of mosquito netting dyed army green. I have absolutely no interest in her at all. Anyway, she's practically young enough to be my daughter."

Leigh felt her face flush. "I wasn't implying that you had an unusual interest in her," she said, wishing the subject had never come up. It struck too close to what she didn't want to think about, to what she didn't want Russ to know.

"You were wondering about Heidi. You might as well admit it," Russ said good-naturedly.

"I couldn't help but be curious about someone you mention often," she said in a small voice.

"For your information, there isn't anyone else in my life at the moment. How about you?"

"No," she said slowly, "there's no one."

"Then let's have a lemon drop. To celebrate," he said solemnly. He handed her one and ate one himself. "Now, we might as well check out the wood-carving place. And I promise I won't mention Heidi again."

Feeling chastened and on edge, Leigh kept a considerable distance between her and Russ as they walked across the street. She was annoyed to feel tears sting the inside of her eyelids. She blinked, willing them to go away.

They stood in front of the wood-carver's house, and Russ said something, the words sounding to her ears like a blur. She fought to recover her composure.

"Leigh, what's wrong?" he said, all concern.

"Nothing," she said, rolling the lemon drop from one side of her mouth to the other. "Nothing."

"I looked down at you and all of a sudden you weren't there," he said, half to himself.

"I'm here," she said, forcing brightness.

"Just for a moment—"

"Just for a moment perhaps my attention wandered," she said as briskly as she could manage. She focused her attention on the objects in the window, which consisted of carved chipmunks and elves that seemed to have cornered the market in cute. They were definitely not her type of thing nor did they fit her mood, and she turned and began to walk back up the hill.

Russ followed her, catching up with her in a few steps.

"I know you've got a lot on your mind with your daughter getting married," he said.

"Yes," she admitted.

"If you want to talk about it, I'll be glad to listen."

"There's not much to say," she said tersely.

"Where's Wendy going to live after she's married?" Russ asked.

Leigh's mind raced. If she didn't talk about it, she would be upset. If she did, she might say too much. Leigh decided to take the latter course and to keep her remarks brief.

"She and Andrew are both still juniors at Duke, and they found a lovely apartment not far from campus."

"Does it worry you that they haven't graduated from college yet?" he asked.

"I'd hoped they would finish college before they got married, but they didn't want to wait."

"Well, they're young and in love. That can make up for whatever material things they're lacking."

"Yes. I suppose it can," Leigh said, and she was thinking, *Young and in love. The way she and Russ had been twenty-two years ago.* She sped up her step, unwilling to pursue the topic. She hoped Russ wouldn't either.

"Leigh, wait. You're walking so fast," he said.

She reluctantly slowed her step, and he caught up. He slid an arm around her shoulders, sensing her mood. "I guess some things are still too difficult to talk about. Right?"

She didn't know what irritated her more, his chatty tone of voice or the fact that he always had been able to read her. Now, as much as she wanted to renew their relationship, she felt on very shaky ground with him. She couldn't figure out the guidelines, hadn't managed to establish any boundaries. She was used to dealing with him as though they were both still twenty, and yet they had each lived a lifetime, a *separate* lifetime, in the intervening years. She still felt the same magic when she was near him, but it wasn't enough to carry her safely through the mine field of her emotions. And right now the mines were exploding all around her.

She turned to face him, her hands stuck deep in the pockets of her coat. They were clenched into fists.

"Look, Russ, I'm completely at a loss right now. One minute I'm glad you showed up at The Briarcliff, and the next minute I think it was the biggest mistake in the world.

And I've got this wedding on my mind and—oh, I don't know. It's a really emotional time for me, as you can surely imagine. This on top of it—well, it's crazy, that's all." She lifted her shoulders and let them drop, then resumed walking.

Russ, his mouth clamped in a tight line, was right beside her. "Crazy? Yeah, I guess you're right. I'm crazy, you're crazy, the whole world is crazy. So let's make a little time in our lives for something real and warm and happy—like getting to know each other again. Like spending part of Christmas Day together and enjoying it."

Leigh forged ahead, walking faster now. "I don't think I'm enjoying it," she said.

His face fell. "You *were*. *I* was. Until you started thinking about things that don't have anything to do with us."

"Oh, don't they?" she muttered under her breath. She didn't think he heard her.

"All right, I'll butt out of this picture. I'll get away from The Briarcliff as soon as I can, leaving you to get on with the wedding. That's what I did twenty-two years ago, and I can do it again," he said.

Stricken, Leigh lifted her head and gazed at him. He was staring straight ahead with an anguished expression.

She stopped, saw a stone bench that had been brushed free of snow. "Wait," she said, reaching out blindly.

"Wait? Oh, that's funny. *You* didn't wait, did you, Leigh? You married David Cathcart as soon as I left for Canada. Now you expect me to wait? I told you, I'm out of here."

She hadn't expected this. He had always been calm in the face of chaos. Now she knew that his mental state was as agitated as hers was; the difference was that he held his feelings inside. Suddenly his pain was real to her, and she knew in that moment how much she had hurt him.

It was then that he noticed the tears welling up in her eyes, saw that she was struggling to maintain her composure. He swept aside his own anger long enough to caution himself that he didn't want her to become as frustrated as she had been on that last day they had met in the park before he fled to Canada, and from the looks of things, she was well on the way. He exhaled in one long breath, and all the fight went out of him.

"All right," he said heavily. "All right. I didn't mean it. Or at least I don't mean it anymore."

She took his hand and led him over to the bench, stumbling once and righting herself by clinging to his arm. He sat down, barely conscious of the high laughter of the children playing nearby.

She clasped her mittened hands together in an effort to keep them from trembling, and she struggled to find the words. They didn't come easily. Finally she lifted her head.

"Russell, I have something to tell you. Your letter—the one in which you asked me to marry you, the one you sent to me right after our last argument that day in the park—I never received it, Russ. I never knew you wanted to marry me. I didn't find out that you had proposed to me until the letter was delivered early this month." The tears spilled over now, sliding down her pale cheeks.

This information sent him reeling; he was thunderstruck.

"I thought you had refused me when you didn't show up at the park," he managed to say.

"I didn't *know,*" she said, the words extracting themselves with the utmost pain. "I didn't know."

He stared at her helplessly, hardly able to believe it but knowing, from the tormented expression on her face, that he would *have* to believe it because it was, God help him, the truth. He was numb, and she looked more wretched than he had ever seen her. He could only imagine how heart-wrenching it had been for her to find out now that he had wanted her to marry him.

"Leigh," was all he could say. "Oh, Leigh." Nothing he could do or say about the past would make things right after all this time, so he did what he could about the present. He pulled her gently into his arms and kissed away her teardrops one by one.

Chapter Five

That evening Leigh moved woodenly through the wedding rehearsal. She entered the chapel at the appropriate time, sat alone in the first pew and watched Wendy and Andrew practice the ceremony. She felt as if she were only going through the motions, because telling Russ about the letter had left her feeling drained and devoid of energy.

He had taken it hard. She had expected bewilderment and perhaps even anger, but she had not been prepared for the raw expression of grief that sprang to Russ's face before he pulled her into his arms. Sitting on that bench, lost in their private sorrow, they had clung together for a long time, oblivious to passersby.

During those moments, splintered images eddied through her mind; the heat of her anger on that day so long ago when he told her that he planned to leave for Canada, his face contorted by grief when she told him to get out of her life. She'd meant it.

She'd never meant it. All she'd really wanted was to be with Russ forever.

Finally the memories had receded and the cold had seeped through to their consciousness, and shivering, they had reluctantly forced themselves apart. Still shaken, Russ had walked her back to the inn, where they had separated before they came within sight of the windows and where Leigh had proceeded zombielike to her room and gone through the motions of bathing and dressing for the rehearsal and the dinner that would follow.

The proceedings at the altar forced Leigh to pay attention. This wasn't the time to be thinking about Russ's reaction to her revelation; she was a key player in Wendy's wedding, and she'd better shape up. She riveted her gaze on the scene being played out in front of her.

The minister, a relative of Andrew's who would officiate at tomorrow's ceremony, said, "I'll ask, 'Do you take this man to be your lawful wedded husband, to have and to hold from this day forward, for better, for worse, for richer, for poorer, in sickness and in health for as long as you both shall live?' Then, Wendy, you will reply 'I do.'"

"I do," Wendy said softly as though trying the words on for size.

Leigh thought of how proud Russ would be of Wendy and how he also deserved to share this day. Suddenly it didn't matter that he hadn't been able to be part of Wendy's life; he had been part of her begetting, and as her real father, he should be present for her wedding. Their love for each other in those long-ago days was the reason that Wendy existed. Yet Leigh knew that if he showed up at this small wedding, his presence would surely be noticed.

No, Leigh could not invite him. It was impossible. She made herself stop thinking about it and forced herself to listen to the minister's instructions about the recessional.

When the practice ceremony was over, Wendy and Andrew stopped to consult with the leader of the string quartet that was to play at the wedding in lieu of an organist.

"Shall we go in to dinner?" asked Jim Craig, offering one arm to his wife and the other to Leigh.

Leigh pulled herself together, and with the Craigs, led the procession into the small private dining room that the Craigs had reserved for the occasion. Dinner seemed interminable. Leigh caught herself barely responding to questions that were put to her and feeling as if she were operating on the fringe of reality.

Other scenes flashed through her head; she was thinking of Wendy as a teenager, with braces on her teeth; she was thinking of Wendy as a young, gap-toothed girl in a Girl Scout uniform and as a toddler trying to learn to ride a tricycle.

"Coffee?" asked a waiter at her elbow, and she shook her head. Try as she might, she could not clear her mind of scenes of Wendy growing up, parts of Wendy's life that Russ had missed and from which Leigh had, by her marriage to David, effectively shut Russ out.

Even so, now Leigh was at a loss to know what else she could have done under the circumstances. Alone and pregnant, she hadn't known Russ's address in Canada, and she had been too dazed by her plight to think clearly. The only thought that had penetrated her consciousness at the time was that she and Russ had parted in anger and that she had never heard from him afterward. Her pregnancy had capped off a summer that had been miserable from the beginning. She remembered; she remembered it all.

During the summer of 1969, Russ, who was caught up in the anti-Vietnam-war movement full-force by that time, refused to accept her family's hospitality after the first few uncomfortable visits to her parents' home. Leigh had been secretly relieved when he stopped coming over. She was unhappy with her position between opposing camps, and she was sure that she'd soon coax Russ back to her way— and her family's way—of thinking.

Her persuasion hadn't worked, of course. Soon Russ joined a group to send out flyers protesting the government's actions in Vietnam, and subsequently he organized a protest march on Raleigh, the North Carolina state capital, on the Fourth of July.

Because of Russ's awkward antiwar stance, Leigh had let her parents assume that the romance was winding down, and when, flabbergasted, they recognized Russ on television burning his draft card in front of the North Carolina capitol building, her father had erupted from his recliner chair with an oath.

"What the hell is this country coming to?" he had asked angrily. "Who do those people think they are? Who does Russ think *he* is?"

"He has a right to speak out, if that's the way he feels," Leigh said.

Her father's keen look pierced through her. "If you ask me, you need to give that boy the old heave-ho. I'd better not see him around here again."

Leigh thought about defending Russ, but she realized that it wouldn't do any good, especially when her father stomped out of the room. She knew her father well enough to know that once he had taken a stand, he would not back off. That afternoon she crept away to her room and cried, knowing that as long as Russ held his radical views, he would not be welcome in her parents' home.

She loved Russ as much as ever, of course, but in view of the growing tension between Russ and her family, they had begun meeting secretly on weekends in a state park halfway between their two cities. When they met on the weekend after the Fourth of July, Leigh attacked Russ viciously.

"How was I supposed to explain to my parents when they saw you burning your draft card? Why did you do it, anyway? What good did it do? When I saw you on television, I didn't even know who you *were* anymore!" she said, tears streaming down her face.

"Leigh, calm down," Russ said, attempting to take her in his arms. They were standing on a small arched bridge in the woods in a secluded area of the park, and the only sound other than their own voices was of the creek below singing against the stones.

"I can hardly wait until this fall when we're back at school and things are normal again," she said, because it seemed to her that all their troubles had started once they left the college milieu, but Russ grabbed her wrist and twisted her around so she'd have to look at him.

"I'm not going back to Duke," he said softly. His eyes were dark and liquid, flecked with green glimmers of light from the sun filtering through the trees overhead.

"Not going back?" she replied incredulously. "I thought your father would be well enough to return to work in September."

"He will, but this doesn't have anything to do with him. Leigh, I can't conscientiously continue to accept a student draft deferment. I want to work against the war, to do something positive, something that will make a difference. I met this guy when I was in Raleigh, he knows about an organization in Canada—"

Russ was serious. He wasn't joking. Leigh knew all about draft resisters and how they were leaving in droves for Canada; she knew a friend of Warren's who had skipped the country instead of waiting for his army induction. Her parents had called him a coward and worse.

"Don't you see, Leigh? This is something I *have* to do." Russ cupped her face gently between his hands, and as always when he looked at her with that expression of love and openness, her knees went weak and the palms of her hands grew damp.

"I thought you loved me," she said, her voice quavering with uncertainty.

"I do. Oh, you know I do," he said softly.

"Then how can you go? How can you possibly leave me?"

"Because I *do* love you. What's happening in the world scares me, Leigh. I can't think about planning a future the way things are now. Look at the mood of the people in this country—it's ugly. I want to work to make it better for us."

"The war will be over soon, you won't have to go anywhere, there's no need, don't you see, Russ? Don't you?" She was babbling now, and crying, and her damp cheek was pressed so hard against his shirt that the buttons bit into her flesh.

"I have to go," he said, and that was all he said, but she knew he meant it and that there was no point in arguing.

She needed his reassurance, needed to know that he cared. In their secret green glade she drew him down on top of her, and they made desperate love. Afterward, spent and shaking, they clung to each other, each terrified of the future.

"What will happen to us?" she had asked fearfully. She couldn't imagine life without Russ.

"We'll be together," he told her, but she was not so sure.

As he slowly walked Leigh back through the leaf-filtered light to her little blue Volkswagen, Russ said uncertainly, "Next week?"

"Next week," she'd answered dully, and he'd bent down to kiss her through the open window, his lips warm and tender.

No matter how much she had thought about it, no matter from what angle she considered it, she couldn't figure out how to change Russ's mind about going to Canada. He was sure that he was doing the right thing, and nothing would persuade him otherwise. He had always been stubborn.

"Going to Canada to evade the draft is illegal," she had said forcefully in continuation of their argument when they met in the park the next weekend. "If you leave, you'll never be welcome in this country again."

"Someday I'll come back," he said with a faraway look in his eyes.

"And what about me in the meantime?"

"You could go to college in Canada."

"It's so far away, Russ! Why, I've never been north of Durham, North Carolina! It gets too cold in Canada. Besides, we don't know anyone there!"

"Ontario is right across the border from Detroit. There's a university in Windsor, I checked it out. I'm going to get my degree there, and you could, too. As for the cold—we could keep each other warm. If we have each other, we won't need anyone else." He'd smiled at her so engagingly and with so much charm that she'd almost capitulated before she realized it, and the fact that Russ would use his charm to get around her made her even more angry.

She'd beaten her fists against his chest, and she'd ranted and she'd raved, but nothing she said seemed to make the slightest difference.

They kept meeting at the park that summer; her parents thought she was out with friends on those lazy summer weekend afternoons, and she had no idea what Russ's parents thought. If she'd had the strength to do it, she might have broken up with him. She couldn't stand the agony he was heaping on her, but the overriding factor was that she knew it would be worse, far worse, not to have him at all. He was leaving soon enough, and she wanted to hold him and kiss him and make love with him as much as she could now. She lived in the Now, she wished that Now could last forever, and she tried to memorize every look, every touch, every gesture, every word to take out and examine later. Later, when she would be alone.

Their last day in the park together had been a nightmare.

It had started out pleasantly enough; Leigh had brought a picnic lunch, which included Russ's favorite brownies. They had walked in the woods, dabbled their bare feet in the creek, and in their glade after lunch they had made love slowly and languorously in the somnolent mid-August heat.

It was after they dressed that Russ pulled her on top of him in what she had thought was a playful mood. When he captured her face between his hands so that her long hair curtained both their faces, hers above and his below, something had changed in him and she had known with growing fear that what he was about to say was momentous.

"I'm leaving for Canada over Labor Day weekend," he said quietly before lifting his head from the blanket to kiss her, and at first she had been so stunned that her lips remained motionless against his. Then she had been overwhelmed with rage.

She rolled away from him, off the blanket and onto the cushion of pine needles, and she had scrambled to her knees.

"You coward," she said, venom dripping from her every syllable.

He sat up. "Leigh," he began, but she was determined that he would not talk her out of her anger.

"Men are dying in Vietnam, Russ. They're fighting for what they believe."

He looked as though she'd punched him in the stomach. "I'm doing what *I* believe is right," he said, his eyes beseeching her.

"You believe it's right to run away? To let someone else fight your battles for you?"

"Vietnam is not my battle," he said unhappily and with an aloofness that only angered her more.

"It isn't my brother's battle, either, but he's doing his duty. *He* didn't head north; he saw a job that needed to be done and he's doing it, and he's fighting for people like you who look down on him and his fellow soldiers."

"The way I see it is that there's a job that needs to be done, but it's certainly not the job of killing people. My duty to my country is to make people see what an immoral war we're conducting, so that eventually we can put an end to it." Russ seemed imperturbable, which only intensified Leigh's fury.

"There'll be an end to it, all right, no thanks to people like you. The war will be over because of Warren and others like him, not because of guys who tucked their tails between their legs and ran out of the country."

"Leigh, sweetheart, listen to me. You're entitled to feel any way you like, but this isn't as easy for me as you seem to think. I'm leaving everything I know and love to carry on this work, and I'd like your support."

She stared at him. How could he be so calm and level-headed? How could he think that anything he could do in such a faraway place as Canada would help at all? He was stupid, stupid!

"Russ, you're making a terrible mistake! Classes at Duke start the day after Labor Day. Please come back to school. We were so happy before you left," she pleaded. It was all she could do to keep from throwing her arms around his neck and begging him.

He eased himself up onto his knees so that he was facing her. His face was solemn, and he slowly raised one finger to caress her cheek. "I can't," he whispered. "Don't you see?"

All her pain and anger beat against the inside of her head until she couldn't think or reason; she only knew that Russ was determined to proceed on this foolhardy course and that nothing she did or said made any difference. She threw herself at him, sobbing and screaming in frustration.

"I hate you! I hate you! How can you do this to me, to us? Oh, God, go! Get out of my life! I never want to see you again as long as I live!"

He had grabbed her wrists to hold them immobile against his chest, and she had the satisfaction of watching his face turn chalk-white beneath his summer tan. In his shock he relaxed his grip so that she was able to pull away, and she held his gaze triumphantly for one long moment, grimly satisfied that she had finally hurt him. For far too long she had been the only one suffering.

She left the picnic basket and the blanket behind, running like a fury to her car and starting it with keys left earlier in the ignition. She jammed the gearshift into reverse, hardly looking where she was backing and barely missing a tree. Russ stood at the edge of the woods staring, but she was gone like a bat out of hell before he could run after her.

She thought she heard a muffled shout as she rounded the curve onto the main road, but she couldn't be cer-

tain. The only thing that she was sure about was that there
had been tears gleaming in his eyes after she told him to
get out of her life, and she told herself that she should be
happy that the awful things she'd said had found their
mark.

But she hadn't been happy; she'd only been sad. And
although she'd hardly strayed from the telephone all
week, Russ hadn't called, not even to say goodbye before
he left the country.

The only good that had come out of that day was that
it was, by Leigh's obstetrician's calculation, the day that
Wendy had been conceived.

Of course, Leigh knew now that Russ had written her
that long-lost letter. But little good that did either of them
now; they had lost so many years. Wendy had never
known her real father. And tonight, instead of rejoicing
along with everyone else, all Leigh wanted to do was go
back to her room and cry.

"Join us in the lounge for a drink?" Andrew's father
suggested after the rehearsal dinner.

Leigh managed a smile. "I'm really very tired," she
said. "I think I'll go upstairs."

"We'll see you tomorrow," Nancy told her. Wendy and
Andrew said that they were going out to the great hall to
sit in front of the fire and listen to a folk group singing
Christmas carols with the rest of the party except for Bett
and Claire-Anne.

"Honestly, I've lugged Claire-Anne around so much
today my arms are aching," Bett complained as the three
of them crowded into the elevator.

And my heart is aching, Leigh thought involuntarily.

Bett and Claire-Anne left the elevator on the second
floor, leaving Leigh to ride to the third floor alone. Gala
New Year's Eve Celebration—Make Your Reservations

Now, urged a bright red-and-green poster on the wall of the elevator. Leigh turned her face the other way. New Year's Eve? She would be doing well to get through Christmas.

She left the elevator and hurried to her room, closing the door behind her with a relieved sigh. She really did want to go to bed, though she felt so keyed up that she had scant hope of sleeping. She ran hot water into the tub for a bath and doffed her clothes, leaving them lying where they fell. Once in the tub she lay back, succumbing to the soothing steam rising against her face and smoothing out the tired lines between her nose and mouth with her fingers. She had smiled so many false smiles tonight that her face hurt.

Russ didn't know and hadn't guessed that Wendy was his child. She was thankful for that. If he hadn't guessed by now, she didn't think he would. Time was growing short, and Wendy would soon be married and gone, leaving her and Russ to—well, what? Say their goodbyes and return to their respective cities?

Leigh didn't know how Russ was feeling, but she couldn't easily forget the moments of tenderness they had shared earlier. Later she'd call Katrina and tell her all about it. She needed to talk to someone, she needed a shoulder to cry on and—

The unexpected trill of the phone startled her. The caller wouldn't be Wendy, and it probably wasn't Jeanne or Bett. Russ. It had to be Russ.

She stood up, flipped a towel around her, jumped out of the tub and raced for the phone.

"H-hello?' she said.

"I hope I didn't wake you," Russ said.

"No, I just got back from the rehearsal dinner."

"How did it go?"

"It was lovely." She would have liked to tell him the truth, that she had been overcome by her memories, but this didn't seem like the time.

"Will you meet me somewhere? In the library? The lounge?"

She thought for a moment. She wanted to be with him. "Not the lounge. Andrew's parents are there having a nightcap. And not the library—anyone could walk by the door and see us there."

"Must we be a secret? Can't you tell your family that we ran into each other and are old friends?" He sounded hopeful.

"I'm too exhausted to do any explaining tonight," Leigh said in a strained voice.

"I hope I'm not disturbing you, Leigh, but I've been pacing the floor ever since we came back from our walk. I couldn't eat dinner and I know I won't be able to sleep. I'm so—oh, I suppose you'd call me distraught. What you told me today has my mind jumping around on several different tracks. I—I just want to talk about it."

"Me, too, but right now I'm dripping water on the floor. I got out of the tub to answer the phone," Leigh said. "I'll call you back as soon as I get my robe on."

Russ squeezed his eyes closed, and a picture of Leigh wearing nothing but a towel appeared on the inside of his eyelids.

"I was hoping you'd come to my room for a while. Will you, Leigh? For, say, an hour?"

"I'll have to get dressed," she said doubtfully. She hadn't bothered to pin her hair up before getting in the tub, and the back of it was wet and clung damply to her neck.

"Throw something on—anything," he urged. "It doesn't matter how you look."

"Okay," she said. "I'll come for an hour. Maybe less."

"Good, I'll be waiting. My room's on the third floor in the old wing. Walk right in—I'll leave my door unlocked."

After they hung up, Leigh slowly unwrapped the towel and studied her reflection in the cheval mirror in one corner of the room. Now there was no makeup hiding her tiny facial flaws; no eye shadow brought out the complex blues and greens of her eyes. No clothes covered her figure faults, and she conceded that there were a few. Her hips had spread a bit too wide, and her abdomen bore faded stretch marks left over from her pregnancy with Wendy. Her breasts, which had once been firm and had needed little support, now sagged slightly. Russ remembered the way she had looked when she was twenty. If their relationship became sexual, and she knew that this was an option if they continued to see each other, how could she bear the look of disappointment in his eyes if he saw her the way she was now?

With one last despairing look into the mirror, she threw open her closet door and pulled out a sweater and a pair of jeans, which she pulled on as quickly as she could. She fluffed her hair with a warm stream of air from the blow dryer and tucked the still-damp strands behind her ears. Then she remembered that she'd better do something about makeup, so she dabbed on a bit of foundation, some blusher and lipstick.

She navigated the familiar hallways of The Briarcliff as quickly as she could, and when she arrived in front of Russ's room, she paused with her hand on the doorknob. Did she really want to do this? Was it *wise* to do this? No matter; she needed to be with him. To talk it over. To set her mind at ease.

When she pushed open the door to his room, he was lying on the bed leafing through a magazine. As the door opened, he tossed the magazine aside and leaped to his feet, hurrying to greet her.

She closed the door gently behind her. He stopped in front of her and hesitated, then held her firmly by the shoulders as he leaned down and kissed her cheek. She swayed for a moment, staring up at his handsome features. She thought quickly and irrelevantly that he no longer used Old Spice, and she thought he would smile if she told him she'd noticed. But he was gazing at her so soberly, his dark eyes illuminated by such a serious expression, that she said nothing. Without a word, he led her to a small love seat in one of the window alcoves and pulled her down beside him.

"I didn't want to be alone after you told me about the letter. I thought I would go out of my mind blaming the postal service, the government, anybody. Then I began to understand that I was to blame. Not anybody else. *Me.* I didn't try to contact you before I left. I was so shaken when you didn't show up that all I wanted to do was get out of town and get on with my life," he said.

"Don't blame yourself," she said gently. "I was wrong, too. I told you to get out of my life, and then I foolishly waited to hear from you because I was young and silly and thought you owed it to me to apologize for all the pain you had caused me by what I considered your stupid antiwar stance. Please forgive me for the things I said, the things I did—"

"There's nothing to forgive, Leigh. I could have handled it better. Maybe if I hadn't been in such a hurry to leave for Canada, we could have figured out a plan to be together. And as for writing you a letter to propose, that has to go down as the all-time dumbest idea ever. I should have come to your house and asked you properly."

"You weren't exactly welcome," Leigh reminded him.

"So what? I should have broken down the barriers, carried you off on my white charger—"

"White Chevrolet Corvair," she reminded him. "With red upholstery, and scented with lemon drops and Old Spice after-shave."

He smiled for the first time since she'd arrived. They were both quiet for a moment, and then he slid an arm around her and pulled her close. She rested her head against his shoulder and felt his breath against her hair. It seemed so fitting and right to be together like this, and she closed her eyes, savoring the moment.

He rested his cheek against her hair. Pensively he thought of the pain and emptiness of his life. During his marriage, he had needed something he didn't get from Dominique, and the strange thing was that he hadn't even known it was missing until they split up for good. Then he had realized how barren their relationship had been right from the first, not only as far as having children was concerned, but in all the intimate ways, too. For a long time he had doggedly tried to repair the relationship over and over, and it had never worked. Now, here was Leigh. And remembering what the two of them had together in those days so long ago made him hope that somehow they could recapture it.

She stirred, and her hair, still damp from her bath, brushed against his cheek. He raised his hand to stroke her head, and she lifted her face to his. He gazed soul-deep into her eyes, those beautiful eyes he remembered so well. Her eyelids fluttered downward like butterfly wings, and he saw her pulse beating at her temples. He was overwhelmed with tenderness for her.

He lowered his face to hers, their cheeks grazing momentarily, and he felt her catch her breath. She shifted so that she was able to slide her arms around him, and he held her close, feeling the rise and fall of her ribs as she breathed, getting used to the rhythms of her again. Without a warning, he felt a lump rise in his throat. She meant so much to him, even now. She was an important part of his past, a memory that he had held dear for so long, and now that she was part of his present he was electrified by the possibilities.

His lips found the hollow of her cheek and rested there before seeking her mouth. He resisted the impulse to touch her breasts, to trace the curve of her hips with his fingertips. Instead he concentrated on the sweet sensation of her kisses, losing himself in the nearness of her even as currents of impatience threatened to displace all his rational thoughts.

When his mouth found hers, she was amazed at how hungrily she returned his kisses. Despite her growing physical excitement, she felt comfortable and easy with him, much like the way she had felt with David.

David. Even though Russ's kisses were nothing like her husband's, the thought of David and all he had meant to her sent a chill rippling through her. She pulled away, interrupting the silken flow of kisses and closing her eyes against the expression on Russ's face.

Russ kissed her eyelids one by one. "What's wrong?" he asked.

She opened her eyes and sat up straight. "I'm not feeling comfortable with this," she said. "It doesn't have anything to do with you."

Russ smoothed her hair back behind her ears, his eyes twinkling with amusement. "I'm glad to hear that," he said. "For a moment, I thought I was somehow lacking."

She caught his mood and couldn't help smiling back. "No, um, I'd say you were pretty much up to your old standards," she said. "As I remember them, that is."

"Maybe sometime you'll let me refresh your memory," he said.

She didn't know what to say. It wasn't as though her memory needed refreshing. She remembered everything all too well.

"Look," he said, "I know you have a busy day scheduled tomorrow. Are you planning to go back to Spartanburg after the wedding?"

"I'd planned to drive back tomorrow night."

"Stay, Leigh. Let everyone else go home, and after they've gone the two of us can spend the following week alone together. The Briarcliff is famous for its New Year's Eve party. I'll make reservations for two. You'd like that, wouldn't you?" His eyes searched her face eagerly.

She answered slowly. "Oh, I'd like it, all right. But—"

He laid a finger across her lips. "No arguments. Let's just do it and figure everything else out afterward."

Leigh's thoughts raced. She wasn't looking forward to returning to her big, empty house alone. If her memories of David made her uncomfortable here, they'd be even worse there.

Of course, staying on at The Briarcliff might raise some questions, but then again, who would have to know about it? Only Wendy, because Leigh would want her daughter to know where she could be reached in case of emergency. Everyone else would leave for their respective homes as soon as Wendy and Andrew departed on their honeymoon.

Russ seemed to be holding his breath as he waited for her answer. His uncertainty was written all over his face; clearly, he thought she might refuse. She lifted her hand and touched his cheek, then swiftly bent forward to kiss him.

"I'll stay until New Year's Day, Russ. I want to."

He stood when she did and took her into his arms. "It'll be terrific," he whispered close to her ear. "You'll see."

She still felt shaky about giving her assent, but maybe if they took things slowly she would feel reassured, not only about David but about all the rest of it.

He walked her to the door. When she turned to face him, every detail about him seemed clearer than ever. The dark eyes shadowed by tangled eyelashes, the clean, spare line of his jaw, the long curve of his neck. Everything about him seemed precious to her in that moment. She swallowed, her mouth suddenly dry. There was one other thing she wanted to say now that she was sure that he didn't suspect anything about Wendy. She knew of no other way to go about it but to ask him straight out. She drew a deep breath and plunged ahead.

"I'd like—I'd like you to come to Wendy's wedding, Russ. She's being married at two o'clock tomorrow afternoon in the inn chapel." As soon as she spoke the words, she stopped breathing.

She had taken him by surprise, she knew, when his brow wrinkled in mild concern.

"You're sure my presence wouldn't cause any problems for you?" he asked.

She managed to meet his eyes but kept her expression casual. "I'll explain somehow if it becomes necessary. But I really want you to attend. It would make me very happy." She tried to read his expression, but if he sensed anything amiss, he gave no sign.

"If it means so much to you, Leigh, I'll be there," he said, bending to kiss her cheek before she left.

She returned the kiss, mostly to hide the rush of relief that she knew would show on her face. And then she fled to her room, hoping she hadn't done something unbelievably stupid.

Chapter Six

The next day, Leigh's daughter's wedding day, Russ arrived at the chapel where the wedding was to be held as the last of the guests were being seated. Even so, he managed to get an aisle seat on the groom's side. He estimated that there were only about fifty guests, none of whom he knew. He recognized Bett, Leigh's sister, but she didn't show even a flicker of acknowledgment when she passed him. That wasn't surprising. To his recollection, they had never met when he was dating Leigh.

The small chapel glowed with candlelight; candles were everywhere—at the altar, flanking the entrances to the pews, even in the window alcoves. Decorations consisted of red and white poinsettias in keeping with the season, and the pungent green scent of spruce and balsam hung in the air.

He sat back and listened to the string quartet, which was a nice touch, he thought. He wondered if that had been Leigh's idea or Wendy's. He didn't think it was something Leigh would have thought of, yet he didn't know Wendy and so had no clue as to her tastes.

It was hard to think of Leigh as a mother. Not that he had any doubt that she was a good one, but it was a whole segment of her life about which he knew very little. They used to talk about the family they planned to have—two boys and two girls. A big family, they both had decided. But the way things turned out, he had no children and Leigh only had one. He wondered why Wendy was an only child. Perhaps Leigh and Dave had decided to limit their family. There was nothing so unusual about that, and yet Leigh had been so fervent in her wishes to have "a whole houseful of kids," as she had put it.

Dave might not have shared Leigh's wish for a big family, and maybe he had been the one to say that one child was enough. The early years of their marriage could have been financially difficult, with Dave building up that insurance business of his, or—well, maybe either Dave or Leigh had been physically unable to have any more kids after Wendy for some reason.

Now Leigh, as mother of the bride, glided past on the arm of one of the groomsmen, her face slightly flushed, her long hair folded into an intricate smooth twist at the back. He caught his breath when he saw the gleam of the gold locket in the sleek hollow of her throat. He was surprised that she had chosen to wear it for the wedding of her daughter.

He didn't stop to ponder the meaning of the locket. Leigh, wearing emerald-green wool crepe with a wide satin cape collar, looked beautiful, more like a bride than the mother of one. He noticed a strand of hair fluttering at the nape of her neck and resisted the urge to go to her and tuck it into the twist.

Leigh reached the front pew where she sat down and composed herself, looking as though she couldn't be happier. Russ wondered, though. From some of the things Leigh had told him, he thought she might have mixed feelings about her daughter's marrying so young.

But is twenty-one really so young? he asked himself. When he and Leigh were twenty, they had known with the conviction of the very innocent that their love was enough to last a lifetime. Maybe they had been wrong. It hadn't sustained them even through the bitter battle over his leaving the country.

He still thought their love would have weathered any circumstance if it hadn't been for the lost letter. Leigh wouldn't have refused his marriage proposal, he was sure of that. Thus they would have been engaged when he went to Canada, and she could have followed him there at the earliest opportunity. If her parents, because of his anti-war stand, hadn't gone along with their plans, Leigh could have dropped out of school for a semester to earn money for her plane fare to Ontario. Or she could have joined him the following summer, and they could have been married in June and both worked for a while before finishing college. So many plans he had worked out in his mind, and it had all come to nothing in the end! If only Leigh had received the letter before he left.

If only, if only...

The door swung open behind him, and at this cue that the bride was about to enter, Leigh stood. The rest of the guests followed her lead, and he stumbled to his feet. First the little flower girl, who magnanimously scattered red rose petals by the handful, her brow furrowed in concentration. She was dressed in long-skirted red velvet with a wide velvet hair bow trailing past her waist. Then the maid-of-honor, Wendy's only attendant, wearing red satin. She carried a lighted candle wreathed with holly leaves instead of the traditional bouquet.

Finally, with all eyes upon her, Wendy began her walk down the aisle on the arm of a male relative—probably Bett's husband, Russ figured. As Wendy passed, he studied her, searching for resemblances to Leigh, and he was immediately struck by her sea-blue eyes, Leigh's eyes. He was stunned, because they were *exactly* like Leigh's, and he hadn't been prepared to see those eyes in another woman's face, even her daughter's.

Wendy was a beautiful girl. *Woman,* Russ reminded himself. She had long, dark hair, and that was nothing like Leigh's, although she wore it long and loosely curled the way Leigh usually did. Instead of a veil Wendy wore a white fur circlet clasped in the back by a spray of pearls; her gown was a sleek sweep of white satin with a deep V-back edged in beaded flowers. She swayed slowly down the aisle, holding her head like a princess, her hand resting lightly on her uncle's arm.

Russ would have liked to have a daughter like that; a lovely child who, when she was little, liked to sit in his lap and listen to him read stories about poky puppies and marching ducklings and little engines that could. A daughter to ferry back and forth to school dances as she giggled over boys with her girlfriends in the back seat of the car. A young woman who would seek his advice about her choice of career and whether she should marry the man of her dreams before they both finished college.

In answer to that question, Russ would have said yes, he thought, without any qualms about it. He would have advised Wendy to hold on to her love, hold on tight and never let it go. To fight for it unto the death, because although he was a pacifist, he knew from bitter experience that the only thing in the world worth fighting for was love and love alone.

IF SHE TURNED her head ever so slightly, Leigh could barely glimpse Russ out of the corner of her eyes. He was standing in the last pew of the tiny inn chapel, his face angled toward the door as they waited for the bride to appear on the arm of her uncle.

The string quartet was playing a classical piece that Wendy especially liked; she had decided to forgo the traditional here-comes-the-bride wedding march in favor of something softer. Andrew stood at the altar with his best man, smiling broadly.

And then, an auspicious pause in the music, and Wendy appeared on Carson's arm, wearing the gown that, by a laborious and often stressful process, she had selected for what she called "the most important day of my life."

She looks so beautiful, Leigh thought in a burst of well-justified maternal pride. The gown, with its delicate embroidery and fur cuffs to match the circlet on Wendy's head, her satin shoes with the high, high heels chosen because Andrew was so much taller, the dewy smile that might have been only for Andrew. As Wendy passed, she blew a kiss toward Leigh. And then there she was standing before the minister, Leigh's little girl, all grown up and about to be married.

Leigh was so absorbed in her own thoughts that she almost forgot to sit down. Bett leaned forward and touched her shoulder, and then she remembered. Following her lead, the guests resumed their seats in a rustle of movement.

"Dearly beloved," the minister began, and as Leigh listened to the words, she thought of the many other weddings she had attended, including her own. She could think of no other couple who evidenced so much love for each other as Wendy and Andrew. Andrew couldn't take his eyes off Wendy, and she was smiling up at him so sweetly that Leigh felt suddenly confident that this marriage was absolutely right for both of them. And to think that she had tried to talk them out of marrying right away;

well, it was what most parents would have done under the circumstances.

Leigh shifted slightly in the pew so that if she cast a sidelong glance, Russ would be in her line of vision. When she allowed herself a peek, she saw that he was staring squarely at her. Her eyes shot front again, and she felt the color rising on her neck. She prayed that Bett, who was sitting behind her, wouldn't notice.

Leigh wanted to telegraph to Russ, *Don't keep looking at me! Look at Wendy.* But there wasn't any way for her to get the message across to him; she could only hope that he would realize that he was embarrassing her by his avid and obvious stare.

"I wish Wendy's father could be here," Bett leaned forward to whisper suddenly as Wendy and Andrew embraced and kissed at the conclusion of the ceremony, and Leigh's heart skipped a beat.

She wanted to cry out, *He is here,* but she only whispered, "Yes." As if to reassure herself, her hand rose quickly to touch the locket at her neck.

FROM WHERE RUSS SAT on the aisle, he had a good view of the ceremony. Wendy Cathcart was a looker, all right, but his critical eye told him that she would be even more beautiful in five or ten years. She looked so young. So unformed. Like a blank slate. And the groom—he seemed, well, nice enough, but *callow.* Had he, Russ, ever been like that? He had no sense of himself when he was younger.

Wendy and Andrew stood in front of the minister now. Russ couldn't help seeing Leigh, because she was within his field of vision when he looked at the young couple standing at the front of the chapel. He willed Leigh to turn her head and look at him. Briefly he thought he saw her eyes slide sideways before facing front again. He supposed it was the most he could hope for at present.

"Do you, Wendy," began the clergyman, and Russ forced his attention to the couple standing before the altar. When the minister had finished, Wendy spoke a clear "I do." The minister addressed Andrew, who gazed lovingly at his bride and said his "I do" so forcefully that the married couple in front of Russ exchanged amused but understanding smiles.

Russ had to admire Andrew. If he, Russ, had been speaking those same vows to Leigh at the height of their love for each other, he might have shouted them.

For a moment he allowed himself to imagine that Wendy was Leigh and that he was Andrew, that they had somehow found themselves in front of the altar in this little chapel and were being married. In his imagination, twenty-two years had disappeared without a trace, they had never been separated by Russ's antiwar activities, and they were marrying with the blessing of both sets of parents. If he were standing before the altar at this very minute, he would hardly be able to take his eyes off Leigh's face as she spoke the words that would make her his.

He yanked himself back to reality. Why was he thinking this way? The truth was that Leigh had married David Cathcart only a couple of months after he, Russ, left for Canada. It had been David into whose eyes she had adoringly gazed when she repeated those all-important vows, David who had left on his honeymoon with Leigh in a flurry of rice, David who had signed the hotel register on their honeymoon as husband and wife, and it was Leigh *Cathcart,* not Leigh Richardson, who was sitting so primly in the first pew.

He sat back and tried to study Leigh dispassionately. Why was he so hung up on her? Why had he never been able to get over her? If she had loved him, *really* loved him, she would have waited for him. Never mind that his letter proposing marriage hadn't been delivered. The truth was that she had married another man almost immediately after he, Russ, left the country.

And despite his hardheaded pursuit of her, he was beginning to realize that he was going to have a hard time forgiving her for doing it.

THE CEREMONY seemed so short, Leigh thought as Wendy retrieved her bridal bouquet from Jeanne and the string quartet struck up the recessional. Wendy and Andrew started their triumphant walk up the aisle, but here Wendy defied tradition and flew directly to Leigh, enveloping her in a big hug.

"Thanks, Mom," she whispered, her eyes bright with joyous tears, and after Andrew hugged Leigh, the happy couple were on their way out of the chapel.

With the eyes of the other guests on Wendy and Andrew, Leigh allowed herself to look Russ full in the face, hoping in that moment to share with him a silent communion. She was expecting a look of recognition, a meaningful glance or maybe even a smile, but when she saw the expression on his face, it was enough to make her heart clench in her chest. His eyebrows were drawn to the middle of his forehead and he was staring at her as if she were a fly under a magnifying glass. She hadn't expected this from him—not here and not now, anyway.

She felt as if someone had stuck a pin into her and let all the air out. As she waited for Andrew's cousin, who was supposed to retrieve her after the ceremony, she steadied herself against the back of the pew. Russ's look had rocked her to her foundations; there was something dark and foreboding about it, and it was a side of him that she didn't recognize.

She could have looked away immediately, but she was so stricken that she found it impossible to pull her gaze away. She was barely conscious of the reflexive upward tilt of her chin as a proud defiance surfaced from her subconscious.

I raised my daughter entirely without your help, she found herself thinking. *And I—no, David and I—did a wonderful job. You missed the chicken pox and the broken front tooth when she fell off her bike, and that awful boy she said she was in love with when she was in the tenth grade. You can't even imagine the sacrifice involved in being a parent; how dare you look at me like that!*

At that moment Andrew's cousin arrived and offered his arm, and Leigh swept out of the pew and past the guests. When she passed Russ, Leigh's smile froze on her face, and she refused to look at him. She wished she hadn't invited him. He didn't belong here—didn't deserve to be part of Wendy's life.

As for staying on at The Briarcliff, it was not too late to change her mind.

THE RECEPTION TURNED out to be a sit-down dinner in the Timberlake Room for about fifty people, and Russ found himself sitting beside a garrulous grand-uncle of the groom on his right and a little girl on his left who kept hiccuping. The conversation on both sides left a lot to be desired, and he tried in vain to catch Leigh's eye. She was definitely avoiding looking in his direction, so he resigned himself to listening to his dinner partner's tiresome monologue about municipal bonds.

The little girl finally stopped hiccuping, and Russ turned his attentions to inquiring politely about her

Brownie troop activities. Across the table, two college friends of Wendy and Andrew's were flirting outrageously. He doubted that he and Leigh had ever gone about getting to know each other in such a silly fashion.

He felt so out of place that he was enormously relieved when the tiered wedding cake, adorned with swags of spun-sugar filigree, was wheeled in.

Wendy and Andrew cut the cake, drank a toast, and the cake was served.

"'S bad for the digestion," said Russ's male dinner partner, who proceeded to consume three slices, anyway.

"Excuse me," Russ said, getting up as his companion was quaffing his third glass of champagne. Russ had every intention of bolting for the men's room and thence to the peace and quiet of his own room. He had been unsuccessful in catching Leigh's eye and now she had disappeared altogether. Furthermore, no one seemed interested in cultivating his acquaintance, and he wished he had turned down Leigh's invitation. He was even beginning to question whether this wild-eyed flight to The Briarcliff in search of Leigh had been a good idea in the first place.

The rest rooms were in a short corridor just outside the door to the Timberlake Room, and as he was going in the men's, he met Leigh coming out of the ladies'. He automatically stepped to the right to let her pass, and she dodged in the same direction. He moved to the left; so did she.

"Shall we dance?" he said, and he was unexpectedly rewarded by the reluctant upturn of the corners of her mouth.

Clearly neither of them had expected to encounter the other in this narrow passageway, but Russ knew immediately that something was wrong from her point of view.

Her ruffled feathers surprised him. He'd thought he owned the rights to all the misgivings.

"I shouldn't have come to this wedding," he blurted.

"I invited you," she said uncomfortably. He wished she would smile again.

Too long a pause, and then, "It was a beautiful wedding," Russ said.

"I think so, too," Leigh answered. Two women unconnected with their party pushed past them into the ladies' room, one of them stepping on Russ's toe. He winced.

"We shouldn't stand here," Leigh said.

Russ remembered a pantry that opened off this corridor; when he used to work here during summer vacations from high school, he and his buddies had used it when they wanted a break from the headwaiter's strident demands. Since then the door had been wallpapered so that it was barely discernible, but he nudged it with his foot and much to his surprise it swung open. "In here," he said, pulling Leigh in after him.

The space was a broom closet now; they found themselves standing amid a bristly forest of mops, brooms and assorted brushes hanging from hooks.

Leigh struggled to prevent it, but she couldn't help laughing.

"You always did take me to the nicest places," she said. "How did you know about this closet, anyway?"

"During the summer when I met you and was lusting after you as you ate in the dining room with your family, I used to dream of being alone with you. Some of the other guys used to bring girls in here."

"In *here?*"

"It was a pantry then, and slightly cleaner. As I understand it, there were these large sacks of flour and cornmeal that could be pressed into use as an instant couch."

"Pressed?"

"Messed?"

"Undressed in a little love nest?"

"And after that they'd need a rest," he said, and whatever had been wrong between them evaporated and drifted away on the low notes of her laughter.

He grasped both her hands in his. "How long until this wedding is over?" he asked her.

They smiled at each other, old friends, their pleasure in each other's company illuminated by the harsh electric light bulb overhead.

"Not long," she replied. She wished that she could stay angry with him, but how could she when he made silly jokes and smiled that comical crooked grin that had always been her undoing?

"Your daughter is quite lovely," he said in all seriousness. "In fact, she looks a lot like you."

"Do you think so?" she said, but she was thinking, *Take another look. Haven't you guessed? Can't you see?*

Any resemblance must have gone right over Russ's head, because he said, "I've only known two people with eyes that exact shade of sea blue. And that's you and Wendy," he said.

"We've got all the genes for that shade locked up," Leigh said lightly.

"Can we get together after everyone leaves?"

"I don't know. I'll think about it."

"Why couldn't you tell everyone you need a rest?" he said. "You could go to your room, and I'll call you."

"I said I'll think about it," she said firmly. She pulled her hands away from him as two female voices receded in the hallway. Leigh looked distracted. "I wish I knew of some way to get out of this closet without anyone seeing us," she said.

He opened the door a crack. "The coast is clear. You go first, I'll wait a respectable minute or two and follow you."

"Okay," she agreed.

He held the door for her, and she slipped past him. Someone outside spoke to her, and he smiled at the effusiveness of Leigh's greeting. Whoever it was would never guess that she had spent the last few minutes in a broom closet.

After a decent interval had passed, he stepped outside and closed the closet door firmly behind him. It seemed to him that he had no choice but to return to the wedding reception and try to press his case with Leigh.

When he reentered the Timberlake Room, Wendy was circling the room, bidding goodbye to her guests. Russ edged toward Leigh, determined not to let her get too far away from him.

"You wouldn't have to follow me around the room," she pointed out in an undertone.

"I'm not," he said. "I'm only waiting for you to tell me when and where we can meet."

At that inopportune moment, Leigh's sister, Bett, hurried past with one of the boys in tow.

"I'm taking Billy upstairs," she said to Leigh. "Can you believe he spilled a glass of water all over his new suit? It was a full glass, too. Oh, I'm sorry, I didn't mean to interrupt." Bett's eyes flashed from Leigh's face to Russ's in clear mystification.

Leigh drew a deep breath. "Bett, this is Russ Thornton. We're old friends, and when I ran into him here at the inn I invited him to the wedding."

Bett stared at her for a moment, taking in the red spots high on Leigh's cheeks, but Leigh had to give her sister credit for recovering quickly. Bett offered her hand and said cordially, "How do you do, Russ. I'm glad you could come. Now if you'll excuse me, I really must get Billy into some dry clothes. I'll see you later, Leigh. And it was nice meeting you, Russ." With one last quizzical lift of her eyebrows in Leigh's direction, Bett hurried off in pursuit of her offspring.

"Your sister hardly batted an eyelash. I suppose she wouldn't really remember me, would she?" Russ asked.

"I doubt it. She was only eight that summer, and she was away at camp when—when—"

"When we were in love," Russ supplied.

"Exactly," Leigh said in a small voice.

They stopped talking when they noticed the photographer heading their way, and they unfurled pleasant smiles across their faces when he paused to take their picture. Afterward, knowing that Leigh could be called upon to pose with the bride at any moment, Russ said, "I'm making things awkward for you, and I'm not so comfortable myself. I really do think I should leave, but not before you tell me where we can meet."

"I haven't said I would," Leigh said distractedly. "I can't even think about it now because Wendy and Andrew will be going soon."

As if to underline her statement, Jeanne hurried past. "Wendy is going to throw her bouquet," she told Leigh. "She wants all eligible females to gather at the end of the hall. You included."

"Not *me*," Leigh said with a vigorous shake of her head.

"Yes, you," Jeanne said, urging her forward. Leigh sent a helpless backward look at Russ, who was smiling a bemused smile.

"You're supposed to stand with your back to the crowd," someone called out from the knot of people surrounding Wendy as she prepared to throw her bouquet.

"Don't be silly," was all Wendy said, and then, with a mischievous wink and no preamble, she lofted her bridal bouquet into the air. Leigh, speechless, knew in that moment that Wendy had deliberately tossed her bouquet in her direction, and she instinctively put out a hand to catch it.

Everyone laughed and clapped at Leigh's obvious astonishment when she looked down in confusion at the bouquet of white roses in her hands.

"That's not fair!" Leigh exclaimed, as she looked at the disappointed faces of several young women, friends of Wendy's, who might have caught the bouquet.

Wendy smiled broadly and hurried to put her arm around Leigh. "I'm the bride, and this is my special day. If I want to throw my bouquet to my mother, I will! Anyway, who was that handsome man who was talking to you?"

"Why—why—"

"Mom, you're blushing! For goodness' sake, I must meet him," Wendy said, craning her neck to look over the heads of her wedding guests as she tried to spot Russ in the crowd.

"I don't think that's such a good idea," Leigh said tightly, but Wendy had already spied Russ, who was edging toward the door at the other end of the room. Wendy took Leigh's hand and tugged her, protesting all the way, in Russ's direction.

"Now," Wendy said peremptorily as they intercepted him at the door, "introduce us." She smiled up at Russ, completely unaware that her smile was almost his smile.

Seeing the two of them side-by-side unnerved Leigh so much that she could hardly speak. Suddenly she felt totally irresponsible; what an impetuous idea it had been to invite Russ; how foolish she was!

Russ, seeing how flustered she was, stepped in. "I'm Russ Thornton," he said smoothly. "I'm an old friend of your mother's. We ran into each other in the inn library, and she was kind enough to invite me to the wedding. You are a beautiful bride, Wendy, and your mother is justifiably proud of you. I wish you and Andrew every happiness."

Wendy smiled. "Thank you. And I'm glad you could come to the wedding. Are you here alone?"

"Yes," Russ said, but he leaned almost imperceptibly closer to Leigh, who thought that this conversation had gone on quite long enough.

"Oh," she said, touching Wendy's arm. "There's Andrew, and I believe he's looking for you."

"I'm sure he is. He's eager to get on the road. Goodbye, Mr. Thornton, I'm glad I got to meet you," Wendy said.

"Call me Russ. And I hope we'll meet again." He smiled.

"Excuse me, Russ," Leigh said. She was still holding the bridal bouquet; she felt ridiculous. Whoever heard of the bride's mother catching the bouquet? She felt irritated at the idea, but there seemed to be nothing she could do but hang onto it and follow in Wendy's wake as Wendy hurried to Andrew's side.

"Come upstairs with me," Wendy urged, turning to Leigh after a whispered consultation with her new husband. "Andrew wants to leave right away, and I'm going to need some help getting out of this dress."

Leigh felt absurdly grateful to Wendy for providing her with a chance to leave, but in the spirit of letting go of Wendy, she felt that she should protest. "Perhaps Jeanne should go with you," she said.

"Jeanne is deep in conversation with Andrew's cousin, and since he's hinted that he'd like to see her again, I have no intention of breaking up their little tête-à-tête. Come to think of it, I wish I hadn't interrupted your conversation with Russ Thornton."

"Wendy, you're stepping on your train," Leigh said.

Wendy paused to give the train an impatient twitch. "Andrew will be livid if I prolong this any longer than necessary," she said. "He wants to get to—well, our honeymoon hideout is a secret, but it's a long drive from here."

"Not too long, I hope," Leigh said, following Wendy's train out the side door through which they could reach the service elevator.

"Too long to suit Andrew," Wendy said with a laugh. "Sometimes I think the bridegroom feels left out of things. Oops," she said once they were in the elevator, "the door's going to close on my skirt!" But it didn't, and they were both quiet on the ride to the third floor.

In Wendy's room, Leigh set the bridal bouquet in a vase of water and unbuttoned the slippery satin-covered buttons at the back of Wendy's dress. When Wendy had slipped the gown over her head and stood in front of Leigh in her lacy underwear, Leigh thought, *That's how I used to look. Slim. No stretch marks. No cellulite. And that's how Russ remembers me.*

Wendy hurried around the room, unself-conscious as she kicked off her white satin pumps, shimmied into her going-away suit and pulled on matching hose.

Leigh heaved a shaky sigh, mourning her own lost youth.

Wendy mistook her expression. She slipped her foot into one leather shoe and stood uncertainly on her left foot, frowning slightly. "Aw, Mumsie, don't take it so hard," she said. "I'll call you tonight to make sure that you've reached home safely. Andrew and I will be back in Asheville with his parents by January 3. And you haven't lost me, you've gained a son. I know it's trite, but it's also true." Wendy hobbled across the room and hugged her.

Leigh returned Wendy's hug. There was no point in telling Wendy how far off the mark she was. How could she tell her daughter that the thing that was really worrying her was the possibility of going to bed with a man?

Much to Leigh's embarrassment, it was almost as though Wendy could read her thoughts. "That man I met—Russ," Wendy said, retrieving her other shoe and perching on the edge of the bed to put it on. "How long have you known him?"

"Oh, quite a while," Leigh said as she turned away to arrange a helter-skelter pile of what must be Jeanne's cosmetics on the dresser top.

"How long? He looks kind of familiar."

Leigh's head shot up. She used the mirror to eye Wendy's reflection; behind her, Wendy seemed calm and matter-of-fact. No, Wendy didn't suspect anything, didn't realize that the reason Russ looked familiar was that every time Wendy looked in the mirror, she was confronted with the selfsame features.

"Dad and I knew him at Duke," Leigh said carefully.

"How nice that you happened to run into him here. He said he was alone—does that mean he's not married?"

"He's not married."

Wendy shut her purse with a snap. "He seems to like you. I think you should try to see him again," she said. She looked around the room. "Where have I put the car keys? You'll need them for the drive back home."

Leigh found them on the dresser. "Here they are. And actually, Wendy, I'm not going home yet." She slid the keys into the pocket of her suit.

Wendy's eyebrows flew up. "Not going home? You mean you're staying here at The Briarcliff? Whatever for?"

Leigh drew a deep breath and tried to look nonchalant. "Well, Russ asked me to stay on. I said I would. Until New Year's Day."

Wendy stared at her, speechless. "Why—"

"Don't look so surprised. You *said* I ought to see him again," Leigh said, unexpectedly amused at Wendy's amazement.

"I didn't expect it to happen so suddenly," Wendy said, but she was grinning.

"At any rate, when Russ suggested that I stay, I thought it might be a good idea. I wasn't relishing the idea of going home to that big empty house," Leigh said, tracing the marquetry pattern on the dresser top with one manicured fingernail.

"Of course you weren't. And I'm delighted. Honestly, Mother, I would feel so much better if you weren't all by yourself. You *need* someone."

"Hey, who's the mother here? I'm the one who is supposed to be worrying about you. You're the one who just got married."

"Which is why I recommend it. If you could just find someone nice, someone as much like Andrew as possible—"

"Speaking of Andrew, he's probably pacing up and down the corridor wondering what happened to you. Don't you think we'd better go downstairs?"

"I certainly do. I think I've got everything. My bags were stowed in the trunk of Andrew's car this morning, and I don't need anything but my purse, and—"

Jeanne burst into the room. "Andrew is having fits wondering where you are, Wendy. My, don't you look fantastic! Come on, I've been deputized to make sure that you arrive in the Timberlake Room posthaste," and Jeanne made an exaggerated bow toward the door.

"I *was* going to hang up my dress. . . ." Wendy said.

"That's what maids-of-honor are for, and I'll do it later. Shall we?"

Wendy hurried out of the room, turning to Leigh for one last hug before she appeared before their guests for the run to the car.

"Bye, Mom," she murmured to Leigh. "I'll call you. Promise."

"I love you, dear. And don't worry about me."

"I love you, too, and I promise not to worry about a thing," Wendy said. She looked radiant as Leigh followed her into the elevator.

Guests lined up on the sidewalk under the portico outside the reception room and Wendy and Andrew, hand in hand, ran the gauntlet as people called "Goodbye!" and pelted them with birdseed from the satin roses that Leigh had so painstakingly made.

"Birdseed," sniffed Vera, Andrew's grandmother. "In my day we threw rice."

"It's because of the birds," Darren said importantly. "Wendy explained all about it. If you throw rice, the birds eat it and it makes the birds swell up and pop open. Then they spill their guts all over the—"

"Darren!" said Bett in horror, as she clapped a hand over her son's mouth.

"The birds in winter appreciate the birdseed so much," Leigh said, tactfully drawing Vera away from Bett's family. Bett was rolling her eyes, and Billy said plaintively, "I didn't think birds *had* guts," before Carson popped a candy cane in his mouth.

Wendy, happily oblivious to this discussion, blew a kiss to her guests out the window of Andrew's small car, and then the newlyweds were off, rolling down the driveway in front of a plume of exhaust.

"Brrr! It's cold out here," Claire-Anne said, despite the furry white cape and muff she wore over her velvet dress.

"Let's hurry back inside, then, before we all catch cold," Bett said, as she shepherded her brood. "Leigh, the wedding was perfect."

Leigh, who had been borne along on a crest of emotion all day, felt a sudden letdown. The wedding that she had planned carefully for so many months was over; Wendy was married.

"I was happy with the way it turned out," she admitted, her eyes searching for the familiar shape of Russ's head over the heads of the other guests. She didn't see him; she wondered where he was.

"Carson and I are all packed to leave, and we're going to head home right away," she said. Bett lived in Shelby, a little over an hour's drive from The Briarcliff.

"Thanks for everything. It was a wonderful Christmas," Leigh said, stooping to kiss Claire-Anne goodbye.

"I'll call you one of these days after I've rested up," Bett promised.

After Bett, Carson and family had gone, Leigh lingered in the lobby of the inn to bid farewell to some of the other wedding guests. When the last one had driven away, she walked slowly through the great hall, wondering where to find Russ. To tell the truth, she was exhausted. Her feet hurt. She could use a nap or a hot bath or— "How about joining me for a drink?" asked Russ as he stepped out from behind a pillar, and when she saw the certain pleasure that leaped into his eyes at the sight of her, she thought involuntarily and with a shiver of happiness, *At last we're alone.* She thought no more of weariness, and then the room darkened and receded so that the two of them with their bright faces might have been the only people in it.

Chapter Seven

"Well, it's over. Wendy is married," Leigh said with relief and more than a little regret. Somehow it didn't seem possible; in many ways, Leigh still thought of Wendy as her little girl. It would be hard to think of her as a grownup, mature and sensible married woman, although Leigh had no doubt that Wendy was indeed all of those things.

"Wendy was a beautiful bride, and Andrew seems like a fine young man, but they seem so young," Russ said, meeting her eyes over the little table in the lounge where he had steered her after their meeting in the lobby.

"That's what I thought when Wendy and Andrew first came to me and said they wanted to get married. I have to admit that I tried to change their minds; I told them how hard it would be to deal with the pressures of the first year of marriage while worrying about college grade-point averages and final exams—but no matter what the Craigs or I said, they wouldn't listen."

"At that age, I suppose they aren't so much deaf as they're blinded by the stars in their eyes," Russ observed.

"Spoken as one who knows," she said.

"Yeah, I suppose so," he said ruefully, and they were quiet for a moment, each lost in thought.

Leigh used this lag in the conversation to study him; Russ looked so suave and urbane in his dark suit—like a man of the world from head to toe. She supposed he was. He seemed so *finished*. When she had known him before, he'd had many rough edges. Katrina used to refer to Russ as "Mr. Knees and Elbows" until Leigh persuaded her to stop. Now Leigh smiled at the memory.

"What's so funny?" he asked.

She shook her head. "I can't tell you."

"Why not?" he asked in a bemused tone.

"Secret," she said, and smiled again. She wished Katrina could see Russ now. She decided she could tell him that, so she did.

"I expected Katrina to be at the wedding," he said. "I looked for her among the guests."

Leigh quickly told him how Katrina would have come to the wedding if her mother hadn't fallen and broken her foot during the week before Christmas.

He leaned across the table. "I always liked Katrina a great deal. Not as much as I liked you, of course, but a lot. And as much as I'd like to see her again, I'm not as desperate to see her as I was to see you."

"You didn't tell me you were desperate," she said.

"I wanted to see you. Nothing less would do," he told her.

"And now that you have?" She wondered if her voice sounded as small to him as it sounded to her.

"I'm bowled over. Knocked out. You're as lovely as ever, Leigh. I was prepared for—well, something different."

"Different?" She felt a certain tightness in her chest, as though she were beginning to have trouble breathing.

"So many people our age are tired, bored, jaded. You're not. You're energetic and vibrant, and very refreshing."

"When I see my sister Bett I feel—oh, somehow passé. Bett's so involved in her children's lives, and I feel old when I'm around her. Now, with Wendy gone..." She shrugged, and a shadow fell over her features.

She's feeling Wendy's flight from the nest more than she's admitting, Russ thought to himself when he saw that momentary sadness flit across her face. He decided to steer the conversation down another path.

"I like your sister, Bett," he said. To his relief, Leigh smiled.

"Bett and I are very close," she told him. "There's such an age difference between us that we didn't really know each other until we both grew up."

"I envy you," Russ said. "I always wished I'd had a brother or a sister."

Leigh became reflective. "I missed my brother, Warren, today, Russ," she said. "He always enjoyed family gatherings so much."

"I suppose it's at times like this that you can't help thinking about him," Russ said.

"Warren and I were pals when we were kids, mostly because we were only a few years apart. After he died, it was hard for me to believe that he'd never walk through the front door of our house and toss his jacket over that rocking horse at the foot of the stairs, never sneak up behind my mother and distract her while he reached around and stuck his finger in the bowl of frosting for a forbidden taste, never chase Bett around the house threatening to skin her alive for disturbing things in his room."

"I wish I'd met him."

"He was a likable guy. There will always be a terrible emptiness inside me where Warren is supposed to be, but I came to terms with his death long ago, Russ." She paused, choosing her words very carefully. She had wanted to say them for so long, and now that she had the opportunity she didn't want to botch the job.

"In the course of accepting it," she said slowly, her eyes boring into his, "I realized that you were right and I was wrong. About Vietnam, I mean. Our troops had no business being there."

At first he froze, his features an unreadable mask, and then his eyes clouded over with sadness. "You know," he said, his eyes never leaving hers, "there's no satisfaction anymore in knowing I was right. I wish that none of us had ever had to concern ourselves with that war."

Russ paused to sign for their drinks. "This is supposed to be a happy day for you," he said ruefully as the waiter retreated. "I didn't mean to make you sad."

"Sad? I'm not sad. And Wendy's wedding has made me see that life goes on. No matter what." She was thinking about David now, something that Russ intuited immediately. His heart ached for Leigh; she seemed, in that moment, very forlorn.

"You've had a hard life, haven't you, Leigh? It hasn't been easy," Russ said. He touched her hand, which was resting on the edge of the table.

"Is anyone's?" she asked him, turning her hand over so that their palms touched. "Was yours?"

"Not very," he admitted.

"Things haven't turned out as either of us expected, yet neither of us has wasted time wallowing in self-pity," she pointed out, her tone upbeat now.

"We're survivors," he said.

"Survivors," she agreed, seeming to take heart. "We accept reality and go on."

"Today's reality may not be tomorrow's," he said.

"But today's reality is the only important one," she said softly, searching his eyes to see if he understood.

"Yes," he said, squeezing her hand. "And tonight's."

He held fast to her hand as they walked out of the lounge, and she was aware of heads turning as they passed. She caught a glimpse of them in the mirror on the wall; they *were* a handsome couple. They always had been.

In the great hall, the sounds of people having a good time swept over them in waves. A large awestruck group was clustered around a storyteller in front of one of the hearths. From the dining room sounded the clatter of cutlery, and behind them in the lounge they heard a shrill peal of feminine laughter.

So many sights, so many sounds. Leigh hesitated, thinking that she didn't want to be around so many people after being on display all day. She was reluctant to put on her public face again. Yet where could she go? She didn't feel as though she could invite Russ to her room; Jeanne might still be in Wendy's room straightening up before she left to spend the night with relatives.

Lights from the nearest Christmas tree played across Leigh's features, illuminating the uncertainty she was feeling. Russ felt helpless to banish that hint of shadow from Leigh's eyes. He could understand her sadness, but he didn't want to accept it. Perhaps he could change it— but he immediately admitted to himself that that was an arrogant assumption on his part, because what he was really thinking was that if only she'd go to bed with him, she'd be all right.

Don't think that making love will be as wonderful as it was before, he cautioned himself. It was as close as he had come to admitting to himself that he had a few reservations about resuming a sexual relationship with her. He wasn't twenty years old anymore, and he knew now that sex wasn't the all-important cure-all for relationships that he used to think it was in his younger years. This time around he was more interested in Leigh's head and heart than he was in other parts of her anatomy.

Yet there was no dodging the issue; they would have to confront it eventually if they continued to see each other. *If* they continued to see each other! Maybe they wouldn't. But how could they *not*?

If *he* decided that sleeping with each other wasn't in their best interests.

If *she* said she didn't feel like going to bed with him.

However: If they didn't feel like going to bed together, *he* would never know if that part of their relationship would have worked. And he had to know.

Therefore: He would make love to her tonight.

Damn. Maybe they didn't know each other well enough for him to initiate lovemaking yet.

This is Leigh, he reminded himself. Of course they knew each other. She was probably as curious as he was to know if the sexual part of their relationship could still work.

"Maybe—maybe you'd like to come up to my room?" he said, his voice low.

She nodded silently, her lower lip caught between her teeth. She wasn't at all sure that she was ready for what Russ probably had in mind, but she'd deal with that later. She knew him so well that all she'd have to do was tell him she wasn't ready and he'd back off quickly, perhaps too quickly. What she probably needed was a little persuasion.

A little persuasion? No, a lot of persuasion. Tonight she was still keyed up from the wedding; she was exhausted. This shouldn't be the first time they made love after so long. It would be better to wait.

They were the only ones in the elevator as they rode it to the third floor, and as they disembarked he slid his arm around her shoulders. Leigh held her breath as they passed her own door; she half expected Jeanne to pop out like a jack-in-the-box. But in a few moments they stood in front of the door to Russ's room and he was swinging it open and indicating that she should precede him inside.

The bed was neatly made; the love seat where they had sat when she paid her last visit looked inviting.

"I could order something from room service if you'd like," Russ suggested. "Maybe a light supper? Drinks?"

"I'm not hungry," she said, but she hastened to add, "If you want something, please go ahead." She went to the long recessed window and brushed the filmy casement curtains away from the glass with one hand; below, a mound of snow glistened in a spotlight and a group of children were sliding on it. A draft of cold air whistled through the sides of the window, and Leigh shivered.

Russ bent to light the fire in the fireplace. Then, as the flames caught, mingling the scent of burning logs with the fragrance of the evergreen boughs heaped on the mantel, he joined her, lifting the heavy velvet drapery so that they could both see out. As they watched the children, Leigh's shoulder brushed his chest, the emerald satin of her wide cape collar whispering against the fabric of his suit. He caught a whiff of her perfume; it was Arpège, the same as she used to wear. Once shortly after they started dating, he had spent his lunch money to buy her a small flacon of it, and he had gone hungry for a week. He had considered the sacrifice well worth it.

"Leigh," he said, and her name was a sigh on his lips. She turned to him, her eyes searching his face for one long moment. He felt a catch in his throat, almost as if he wanted to clear it, but this was entirely emotional. Her expression had taken on a softness, a pliability. He bent to kiss her parted lips.

Leigh lost herself in his kiss. With the touch of his lips, without warning, all doubt fled, and along with it, her fatigue. She didn't want to wait; she had waited long enough. It had been twenty-two long years since they had made love; twenty-two very long years. She slid her arms around him, and burgundy velvet draperies swung around them as he crushed her in his embrace.

They had touched many times since they'd found each other again, but not like this, not with this heat and urgency. They sought each other's mouths hungrily as though they could not get enough of each other, his fingertips exploring the lines of her face and the curve of her neck as if to reassure himself that it was really Leigh.

She felt as if none of this could be happening to her. Since David died, she'd gone out on a few dates, but she hadn't let the men kiss her the way this man was kissing her, with sheer male greediness, nor did she tremble within the circles of their arms or cling to them for support.

This isn't just any man, she reminded herself, *this is Russ.* And her knees turned to jelly at the thought.

She had only loved two men in her life, and Russ Thornton was one of them. Her heart filled with wonder at the odd circumstances that had brought them together again after such a long parting. That mail carrier, his long beard whipping in the wind as he walked away from her house; the Christmas card she had sent to Russ and his subsequent phone call. It seemed so unreal, like a story she had read about somebody else.

But this was no story, nor was it a dream. His lips and tongue and teeth were real, and his hands were real as they moved reverently, then more urgently over her body. She felt herself melting into him, felt clothes falling away, felt skin soft against skin, felt her hair tumbling from its twist. She had no time to worry about how she looked. She only knew how he looked: flat belly, firm thighs, broad shoulders. And he wanted her; that was apparent.

As if through a haze she saw him smiling at her, and then he was swinging her into his arms and she was protesting that someone might see through the curtains, and he laughed low in his throat and said how could they when the room was on the third floor facing the side of the mountain, and she said that was exactly the point, and he said that no one would be up on the mountain on this cold night and if they were, they could go ahead and look, and she didn't care if the whole world watched them by that time, but he turned out the lamp, anyway.

When she lay against the pillows on the bed and gazed up at him in a moment of pure, crystalline happiness, he paused to cup her cheek in the palm of one hand. The flickering firelight softened the square line of his chin and gilded the wide pupils of his eyes. His eyelashes cast feathery shadows on his cheeks.

I will remember this moment forever, Leigh thought as he studied her intently, and she lifted her arms to embrace him.

"I think I never stopped loving you," he said unsteadily.

At first she thought that such love could not be possible, but then, overcome by the tenderness she felt for him in that moment, she admitted that perhaps it was. Maybe the first love was the seed from which all other loves grew; maybe that seed could sprout again. After all, the things she had originally loved about Russ then were the things she loved about him now.

His hand lay on her breast over her heart and she covered his fingers, so familiar, with her own. And then, barely breathing, she closed her eyes so that he could tenderly kiss her eyelids one by one; she traced the tips of his curly eyelashes with one finger, and he trailed a chain of kisses to the hollow of her throat where the gold locket gleamed. She arched up to meet him as he settled himself over her, and she opened her mouth to his kisses as she opened her body to the rest of him. All of her open, letting in the warmth and the joy and the life, everything that she had been missing for such a long, long time. And it was Russ, her wonderful Russ, and it was so much the same that tears sprang to her eyes when she thought of being without him for all those years. She pulled him closer, wanting to feel all of him, the weight of him, everything. She twined her legs around his and wound her fingertips in his hair. As much as two people could be connected; that was the way she wanted to be enmeshed with him. Bodies and hearts and even souls flowing one into the other, so that she could once again say, "I am you and you are me," and it would be the truth.

The truth. The truth. The truth.

The words thudded against her brain in time with her heartbeat. Above her, Russ shuddered, and she realized too late that it was over.

His body, sheened with moisture, lay heavily upon her, crushing her against rumpled sheets. She lay wide-eyed beneath him, and she could hardly breathe.

As he rolled to one side he buried his face in her hair. His left hand rested on her thigh, and she sensed that he was reluctant to break contact with her. She felt that she needed more space but not because of anything that he had done: he'd been everything she'd expected and more. It was her own deceit that disgusted her and had curdled the act of love in its final moments.

She sat up. He reached out to her, but slick with his sweat, she eluded his grasp.

"Leigh?" he murmured, wanting her in his arms.

"I'd better get back to my room," she said clearly and distinctly, turning her head away so she wouldn't see the wounded look in his eyes.

"It's still early," he protested. A slightly panicky feeling settled over him; what was wrong?

"I've been on my feet most of the day," she answered, slipping off the bed. She walked unsteadily to the pile of clothes on the carpet and wordlessly began to sort them out. The fire had died and an icy chill had settled over the room.

Russ watched her in disbelief as she fumbled with soft tangles of lace and a pair of panty hose that seemed tied in knots.

Well. That's it, then, he thought, trying to keep his cool. *So much for retracing our footsteps. Now we can both get on with the rest of our lives.* He should have felt relieved, but he only felt numb at the way things had turned out.

Without saying a word, he got out of bed. She put on her skirt, fumbling with the clasp on the waistband, and she shrugged into the jacket and fastened it with clumsy fingers.

"If only—" he said heavily, but seeing the look on her face, he stopped. He shook his head. "How could it go so wrong when everything was so right?" he asked.

"I wish I could tell you," she said, and before he could figure out what she meant, she had slipped out the door.

LEIGH WOKE UP THE NEXT morning in her own room, her head hurting and her mouth dry. She felt as though she'd had too much to drink last night, only she hadn't. When her eyes opened, she recognized her surroundings immediately as The Briarcliff, and the memory of last night's debacle flooded into her consciousness. She sat up in bed, silently contemplating what she should do next.

Nothing, she thought, and then she proceeded to the bathroom where she filled a glass with water from the faucet. She swallowed two aspirin and headed back to bed with every intention of going back to sleep, but before she had pulled the covers up around her shoulders, the telephone rang.

"Leigh?" said Katrina in response to her groggy "hello."

"Yes," Leigh said, abandoning in that moment any hope of going back to sleep. "Where are you, Katrina? Are you in Florida?"

"No, Mother and I decided to stay in Spartanburg. I called your house a few minutes ago to see if you wanted to come over and meet my cousin, and I was worried when you weren't home yet. Is anything wrong? Why didn't you drive home after the wedding?"

"I—" Leigh said, but then she stopped. She had no idea how to tell Katrina what was going on in her life.

"You sound sick," Katrina said. "What is it—the flu?"

"Worse," Leigh said with conviction.

"*Nothing* is worse than the flu. Last year Mother made the foolhardy mistake of saying rather dramatically that she'd rather have a broken foot than the flu, and look what happened to her. Don't tell me you have a broken foot, Leigh. It couldn't happen to two people I know at the same time. Or could it?''

"Something's broken, but it's certainly not my foot," Leigh answered, propping herself up on two pillows.

"Well, what is it? Stop acting so mysterious," Katrina said.

"A broken life? A broken heart? I don't know," Leigh said miserably.

"I'm more in the dark than ever now," Katrina replied in sheer bafflement.

"Russ Thornton followed me to The Briarcliff, and I invited him to Wendy's wedding," Leigh said.

"You *what?*" Katrina yelled, nearly shattering Leigh's eardrum.

"I ran into Russ Thornton and asked him to come to the wedding. He sat in the last pew and stared at me throughout the ceremony."

Dead silence. Then a giggle of disbelief. "Back up just a minute, please. How did he know you'd be there for Christmas?''

"I made the mistake of telling him," Leigh said.

"Well, that's what I call foolishness on your part and pure nerve on his. Or bravado. Or something."

"Try insanity."

"That's more like it," Katrina said. "Whatever possessed you to invite him to the wedding?"

Leigh massaged her eyelids. "I wanted him to see Wendy being married. He's her father, and I figured he had a right."

"He has no idea that Wendy is his, does he?" Katrina asked in alarm.

Leigh sighed. "No, I don't think so, although she looks so much like him that I don't see how he can miss it."

"She resembles you, too, Leigh. Those eyes. The way she moves. I can understand why the thought might not occur to him. After all, he doesn't know when Wendy was born. As far as Russ is concerned, she could very well be David's."

"In all the ways that matter, she *is* David's, Katrina," Leigh said. "He made her his own daughter by accepting her wholeheartedly from the very beginning. I hope she never finds out differently. You know how it was with Wendy and David. They were so close."

"True," Katrina said. "So what are you going to do now? I suppose Russ has left."

"No, he's still here. We—we decided to stay over and—and spend some time together," Leigh said.

"Spend time together? As *what?*" Katrina asked incredulously.

"As friends," Leigh said, although she considered the whole plan off after last night.

"Remember I told you that you two were perfect together? Are you still?"

Leigh wasn't sure now to answer this. She had no intention of telling Katrina about the fiasco of their lovemaking, at least not now while it was so fresh in her mind.

"I told him about his marriage proposal arriving twenty-two years too late, and he was terribly shaken," she said, ignoring Katrina's question. She thought about that day—was it only the day before yesterday?—and felt her heart soften toward him. Russ had been so kind and so sweet when she told him about the long-lost letter. So accepting.

"What did he say?"

"Oh, not much. But in its way, the moment after I told him was beautiful. We reached out to each other, and then we had to part because of the wedding rehearsal, and we talked afterward, and—"

"Leigh, wait a minute! You're moving too fast! You've hashed over your whole romance except the fact that Wendy is his daughter? When do you plan to drop that little tidbit of information?" Katrina asked.

"Never," Leigh said as positively as she could. "That's a secret that no other living person knows except you and me. And no one needs to know, either."

"It's not fair, Leigh," Katrina said pointedly.

Leigh sat up and swung her feet over the edge of the bed. "Fair to whom? I have to protect Wendy, you know."

"Wendy is an adult now, my friend. She's quite mature—you've said so yourself—and stronger than you think. If you *really* want a chance with Russ, you've got to tell him about Wendy. Or else he may find out later in some way that you won't like, and the news could drive you apart. Think about that."

"I think you're borrowing trouble, Katrina," she said. She didn't want to admit that the longer she was awake, the clearer it was that she'd better pack and leave The Briarcliff before Russ came looking for her.

"Okay, okay," Katrina said, "I'll back off. But I'm always available if you need me."

"Thanks. I'll tell you all about it when I get home," she said, adding to herself, *It'll be sooner than you think.*

"Leigh," Katrina said and then hesitated. She drew a deep breath. "Be careful, won't you?"

"Trust me, Katrina," Leigh said, picking the expression out of the air, not thinking about it at all, and it wasn't until after she hung up that she realized in horror that she had just spoken the two words she had never said before, two words that had wreaked utter havoc in her life.

Chapter Eight

"Trust me."

That was what Russ used to say about so many things. It was a catchphrase for everything, from whether he would be able to pick her up at the dorm in time to hurry to a concert to letting her know that he had taken responsibility for birth control. As far as birth control had been concerned, she had trusted him and it had failed. And as always she, the woman, was the one who had paid the price.

It was in September of 1969, shortly after Russ left for Canada, that she missed her period, and she had always been so regular that she began to worry immediately. In those days, there had been no drugstore kits for determining pregnancy, and she had waited on tenterhooks for some sign that she wasn't pregnant. Instead her breasts began to swell, something that had never happened before. And on the morning when she had awakened feeling queasy, she had known immediately that it meant the worst. She was pregnant. And she was alone.

Not entirely alone, however. David Cathcart had been following her like a shadow ever since she'd arrived on campus for the start of the semester. Leigh and David had been friends ever since they were freshmen, and she had always liked him. With Russ gone, it seemed entirely natural to sit together in the library as they studied and to walk somewhere afterward for a late snack, to attend fraternity parties as his date and to call him when she felt low, which was often.

David noticed, as the days wore on, how downcast Leigh was. He had tried everything to snap her out of the depression that was so obvious from the beginning of the school year, but nothing had worked. Finally he had subsided into the perfect companion for that time in her life—one who unfailingly bolstered her spirits by merely being there and asking no questions.

One windy Saturday when everyone else had gone to the big football game of the season and the two of them were strolling rather aimlessly across the almost deserted campus, David said earnestly, "I care, you know. I know something is bothering you, and I wish I could help."

David's kind remark was more than Leigh in her wretchedness could take, and she had burst into tears. For the past couple of days she had been frantic. Katrina knew, of course, that Leigh thought she was pregnant, but outside of her best friend, Leigh had told no one. Informing her parents was out of the question, because she had no idea how they would react. Furthermore, abortion in those days was illegal, and even if it hadn't been, Leigh couldn't have aborted this baby. *Russ's* baby. And yet what was she to do? Russ didn't love her, he wasn't around to help her, and the problem was more than she could handle alone.

David found a quiet corner where a brick wall formed a shelter from the wind, and there beneath a bright pyracantha vine he had spread his jacket so Leigh wouldn't have to sit on the ground. Once she stopped sobbing, Leigh told him the reason for her misery. She didn't look at him the whole time she was explaining how it must have been the last time that she and Russ had been together in the park that she got pregnant, and when she looked up David was gazing at her with both love and tenderness.

"Leigh, I can help. I love you, Leigh, and I always have, even when you and Russ were so wrapped up in each other. I've been crazy about you since the day I met you in freshman year, but I never thought until recently that you could accept me as more than a friend."

Thoroughly confused, Leigh had stammered, "Of—of course I consider you my friend, David. But you can't love me," and she blotted at her tears with a tissue she pulled from the pocket of her skirt.

David, sweet David, had taken her chin in his hands and lifted her tearstained face so that she would have to look at him. His round face was solemn, and his eyes behind the horn-rimmed glasses were kind.

"You'd better believe I love you, because we're going to be married," he said, and then he kissed her for the first time.

It had never occurred to her before that she could marry David, and she was astonished. After he kissed her a few more times, she pulled away and clasped her hands protectively over her abdomen. "I can't marry you, David," she whispered. "It wouldn't be right. I don't love you."

"I have enough love for both of us," David said stubbornly. "In time maybe you'll learn to love me."

She had told him she would think about it, and she had walked back to her dorm in a daze. *Marry David?* How could she when she loved Russ?

But Russ didn't love her. If he did, he wouldn't have left without a word.

The more she thought about marrying David, the more possible it seemed. He was, above all, a nice person and a decent human being. Her parents had met him and liked him. His thoughtfulness and kindness in the days following his unexpected marriage proposal convinced her that he would be a wonderful husband. *Marry David?* Well, maybe.

Katrina said in disbelief, "How can you, Leigh? You don't love him."

"He loves me," Leigh replied as she thumbed through books she had checked out of the library. They illustrated the development of the embryo day-by-day; by this time, her baby was no longer a little pin dot floating in a uterine sea; it had sprouted tiny buds that would soon grow into arms and legs. The idea of the baby was becoming more real to her every day.

David had a part-time job and an ample allowance from his parents. Leigh had been offered a student assistantship in the art department, and if she took it they could just get by if they rented a cheap apartment near the campus. She had counted the days and knew that the baby would be born in May; her due date was during the week after exams and before graduation. If the baby cooperated, she wouldn't even have to miss a day of classes.

David hovered over her protectively whenever they were together, and he called her at least three times a day to ask how she was feeling. He brought her crackers for her morning sickness, and he held her in his arms for hours at a time to comfort her. He was patient in waiting for her answer to his proposal, and finally when Leigh missed her second period, she knew she'd have to do something.

She called David at four o'clock one afternoon in early October and asked him to meet her outside the dorm. As they walked in the waning afternoon sunshine, she shivered. She knew that once she had taken this enormous step there would be no turning back.

Leigh was honest. "I've always liked you, and you're one of the best friends I've ever had. But I don't love you. I think it's important for you to know that," she told him.

David sighed and looked away, but then his eyes unflinchingly met hers. "And?"

"And if you still want to marry me, I will. I—I do think we could be happy living together, you and me." She watched him uncertainly, unsure of his reaction.

He had broken into a wide smile, enveloped her in his arms and covered her face with kisses. And then they had laughed, and he had whirled her around in excitement and they had gone straight to the student-housing office to check the bulletin board for a likely apartment.

That night they called both sets of bewildered parents, and without telling them why haste was necessary, they informed them that they planned to elope. Their parents convinced them to wait until the following weekend so that they could be married properly in the campus chaplain's study with both immediate families hastily assembled for the occasion. And that was what they had done.

Truly, marriage to David was pleasant from the very beginning. Going to bed with him for the first time had seemed strange, and there had been a certain amount of inexperienced fumbling on his part, but Leigh was patient and David was a fast learner. He had delighted in her pregnancy, and by the time they had been married four months, both of them forgot for long stretches of time that the baby Leigh was carrying was not David's child.

And whenever any thought of Russ surfaced, Leigh put him firmly out of her mind. It was as though his child growing within her edged him ever so slowly and surely out of her mind and her heart, leaving only David and her memories. In time even the memories receded so that her whole world became David and Wendy, and when she thought of Russ at all, it was with a sweet nostalgia and only a passing regret for what might have been.

Yes, she had learned to love David, and she had been enthralled by her daughter, and after all was said and done, theirs had been a marriage more successful than most of her friends'. They had hoped for more children after Wendy, but unfortunately Leigh hadn't become pregnant again. David had often said how thankful he was that they had Wendy, and Leigh had echoed his thoughts. When David died, she was devastated because she couldn't imagine life without him. But she had adjusted. And now here she was, with Russ creating problems in her life again.

She headed for the shower, turning the spray to its most forceful setting. The stinging jets of water jarred her into action, and she dried herself quickly and with a sense of purpose. She'd toss everything into her suitcase, gather Wendy's belongings from the room she had shared with Jeanne and be on her way before Russ Thornton was even out of bed.

She slammed out of the bathroom, rummaged in the closet and straightened abruptly when she heard the unmistakable clearing of a throat. She looked up to see Russ, wearing a gray sweat suit, sitting on the edge of the bed.

She did a quick double take. He was the last thing she would have expected to see.

"How did you get in here?" she demanded.

"Last night you dropped the key to Wendy's room next door," he said, dangling it in front of her before slamming it down on the table beside the bed. Leigh winced, hoping he hadn't damaged the finish of the lovely cherry wood. Her eyes darted to the connecting door. It hung slightly ajar.

"You shouldn't have come in uninvited," she said. Her hair was dripping on the carpet.

"I knocked, but you didn't answer," he told her.

"Still," she said pointedly.

"All right, all right," he said. "I wanted to see you, and I was afraid you had other ideas."

"I think it would be best if I went home this morning," Leigh said with dignity.

"I don't," Russ replied, studying her from head to toe. She was thankful that it was a very large bath towel; nothing showed that he wouldn't have seen if she were wearing a dress.

"A matter of opinion," she said.

He ran a hand through his hair. Wendy had the same habit when she was upset. Leigh turned away, unable to look at him.

"I went for a run this morning and gave this matter quite a bit of thought," he said.

"Russ, I wish you would go so I can get dressed."

"Since you were in my bed and entirely naked last night, I don't see what difference it makes if I see you in the altogether now," he pointed out.

"Technically I suppose it makes no difference. But I do want you to leave," she said. She turned her back on him and walked to the closet, striving for a nonchalance that she didn't feel. Her heart pounded against her rib cage so loudly that she was sure he could hear it, too.

She found underwear in her suitcase and ripped a pair of slacks and a shirt from their hangers. She would go into the bathroom to get dressed since he refused to leave. Not that she was above calling the management and complaining if she had to, but at the moment she had everything under control.

She acted as though he wasn't even there; Russ couldn't believe it. Or maybe he could, come to think of it. She'd always had a way of distancing herself from any unpleasantness between them. That's how they'd gotten into the mess they were in when he left for Canada.

He propelled himself off the edge of the bed and grabbed her arm as she was about to retreat into the bathroom. He startled her so that she dropped the armload of clothes and almost let the towel fall, too.

"You can't do this," he said tightly.

"Have you been drinking, Russ?" she said through gritted teeth.

"I told you, I went for a run and I've been thinking. About you and me, and I can't let it end like this."

"End? It never began," she said bitterly, her eyes flashing. She twisted out of his grasp.

"Don't be a fool," he said.

"Last night was a mistake," she retorted angrily.

"It may have been a lot of things, but it was no mistake," he replied. He wrapped his arms around her so she couldn't move. Trapped in his embrace, she reminded him of a frightened rabbit tangled in a snare, ready to bolt at the first opportunity. He wasn't trying to frighten her, he only wanted her to admit what they both already knew.

"Russell," she said on the edge of a sob. "Please."

He realized how frightened she was and relaxed his arms. "It's okay, Leigh," he said with a hint of tenderness. "Whatever was running through your mind last night doesn't matter. We're a lot of other things besides lovers. Friends, for instance. That's important to me— maybe more important than the other. I don't want to lose you again."

Leigh closed her eyes and drew a deep breath. How could they be friends? There were some things she could never tell him.

But then she and Katrina were friends, and she didn't tell Katrina everything, either. About how last night had ended, for instance. Of course she would, in her own good time, speak to Katrina about what had gone wrong, but not until she, Leigh, was ready to talk about it.

When she opened her eyes again, Russ was gazing down at her with eyes full of love. *Love,* she thought in a daze. *He is still in love with me. He really cares about me,* and the thought was overwhelming. After all, who else cared about her in such an intimate, loving way? Wendy, whose husband would require most of her attention now? Bett, whose life was filled with her active family? Katrina, who lived so far away that they saw each other only once a month?

She was silent for a long time, so long that he began to chastise himself for barging in here like this. Just when he was on the verge of stammering an apology and beating a hasty retreat, she spoke.

"I just don't know how to act around you," she whispered. "I—I'm lost."

"No, my Leigh, at last you are found." Hiding his relief, he kissed her on the forehead and deliberately stepped away. "And now, to prove to you that I really am a gentleman, I'm going to leave you to your privacy. But let's meet for breakfast in the dining room in, say, one hour?"

Fifteen minutes ago, she couldn't have imagined that anything would change her mind, but then she hadn't reckoned with Russ's charm and earnestness, which she couldn't discount because he was so obviously sincere.

"I'll be there," she said, her heart lightening at the thought of looking at him over the breakfast table. Suddenly she was ravenous.

"I knew you would be," he said and smiled before he left her room, closing the door quietly behind him.

IN THE HALL, Russ released the doorknob and sagged against the wall. He wasn't nearly as self-assured as he looked or acted. When she'd told him to leave, he'd almost done it, and when she acted so distant, for a moment or two he'd thought there was no point in continuing; it was clearly a problem that could not be solved by handing her a lemon drop.

But she hadn't been able to hide her need for somebody, and that somebody might as well be him. Her loneliness was so real that he'd have to be blind not to see it.

And he wanted her in his life. He was lonely, too, and at no time was he aware of being alone as much as he was during the holiday season. This year, she had made him feel alive and hopeful again, the way he *should* feel at Christmas. She had given him joy. He'd like to continue their sexual relationship, but if she didn't want that, then it was enough to be friends. *No*, he thought, *that isn't quite right. I want her as much as I ever did, maybe even more, now that I've been around a bit and know how important it is to find the right woman.*

He actually ached to be near her. To be *with* her. No, more than that. Putting it more poetically, he longed to immerse himself in the experience of her; in doing so, perhaps he could recapture the magic of their love.

He recognized how foolhardy it was to pin his hopes on that, but he felt that he had to try. Their love had been so special. They had been good for each other, he and Leigh.

He had always regretted their being separated by circumstance; how unfair the circumstance, he had never realized until she told him about the lost letter.

A second chance seemed almost too good to be true, but here it was and he wasn't about to let it slip by. He was ready to concede that he might have to make a few adjustments in his expectations.

At first, when their relationship had begun in this, its second incarnation, he'd thought that they could pick up exactly where they left off twenty-two years ago. She looked so much the same, still the most beautiful woman in the world to him, and she smelled the same and laughed the same and smiled the same brilliant smiles.

Now the more reasonable side of him knew that nothing was really the same at all. Everything had changed. But his idealistic side told him that somewhere inside Leigh Cathcart was the Leigh Richardson he had once known. The shining core of her might have been tarnished by layers of living, of watching the world swallow up her hopes and dreams, of trying to come to terms with reality. In this she was no different from anyone else, and he of all people was well-equipped to understand. It just made what he needed to do more difficult, that's all.

He had so little time. Soon they'd each go back to their ordinary lives, living out their ordinary days, and he wanted so desperately to change that. To find the extraordinary thing that the two of them had had together and, this time, to make it work.

He shrugged out of his sweatshirt before the door of his room had closed behind him. He had fifteen minutes to meet her in the dining room for breakfast.

He usually sang in the shower, but this time he didn't. He would save the singing for later when it was time to rejoice.

BREAKFAST COMMENCED in uneasy silence and progressed in nervous fits and starts to cautious observations about their fellow diners and eventually about each other. Leigh was surprised that Russ ate so little.

"I ate earlier," he said, offering no more explanation, and she doubted that he had really eaten. He looked confident and sure of himself, but she wondered if that was only a façade to hide his real feelings. She hadn't mistaken the love in his eyes earlier; it had changed her mind about leaving. Now he seemed very quiet, withdrawn into himself. As if he were thinking things over, and she wouldn't blame him. After last night and her histrionics this morning, he was probably reconsidering. But, oh, she hoped that he'd reach the same conclusion that he'd reached before—that she was worth pursuing.

She made an extra effort to be pleasant, then wondered if she was overdoing it. She forced herself not to speak in order to give him a chance, but the long silence made her so uncomfortable that she finally stammered a request for the maple syrup, which he passed to her without comment. She desperately racked her brain for something intelligent to say, but nothing occurred to her. She began to wish that she had left the inn after all.

She could still leave. She could get up from this table and go to her room, resume packing, and be on the road in fifteen minutes. The only trouble was that it was a long road, and there was nothing at the other end.

All of her life she had been something to someone, and now she was nothing to anyone. She had been child of her parents, wife to her husband, mother of her child. Now her parents were dead and so was her husband, and her child no longer needed her. What was left?

Her work. Of course she had her work, and it was important to her. Long years of teaching art to kids who really had no passion for it and were only taking the course because they thought it would be an easy credit toward graduation had sharpened her appreciation for the freedom she had now as a free-lance artist. Her work was absorbing, but it was not as demanding as a family. Her paintings didn't *need* her.

Did Russ *need* her? She stole a glance at him from beneath lowered eyelids. He didn't look as though he needed anyone. Divorced, successful, competent—that was Russ. He had managed to get along without her or anyone else for a very long time, and although he had admitted that he was lonely at Christmas, so were a lot of other people, even some who were married.

If he needed her, he could give her life the direction it had been lacking. If he loved her—but it was too soon to be thinking about lasting love. The emotion that she had seen in his eyes was real enough, she was sure of that. But there was still last night's fiasco to be overcome, and a whole lot of other things, too.

Russ signed for their meal, and they walked into the lobby. Today it seemed that many people were checking out, and small children were running up and down the polished floor of the foyer.

"Too noisy in here," Russ said, raising his voice over the din. "How about a walk outside?" He looked unnaturally serious, and she wished he would smile. She needed some indication that he was glad she hadn't left.

She'd brought her coat with her because she had thought she might suggest a walk herself. He helped her put it on, and they walked past the crying babies in the lobby out into the frosty air, where it seemed unnaturally quiet.

"There's new snow," she pointed out unnecessarily as they set off on one of the paths.

"It fell early this morning," he said, his words a white plume in the chill air.

"Where did you run? Not outside, I gather."

"They've built a gym above the ballroom. There's a weight room, a place for aerobics classes, and a track. That's where I ran."

"Why do you do it? Run, I mean?" she asked.

He shrugged. "Trying to stave off the aging process," he said.

She looked slightly startled. "Most people say it's for the exercise," she said.

"It's the same thing. Exercise is for the purpose of feeling young. How do *you* feel about getting older?"

The question surprised her; she hadn't expected it. "Kind of sad," she admitted. "There are compensations, I suppose. Wendy, for instance." She slanted him a look out of the corners of her eyes. She had forgotten and let down her guard. She shouldn't have mentioned Wendy.

"I don't see anything remotely good about being middle-aged," he said. "In fact, last time a woman made eyes at me, I found out she was just trying to get used to her bifocals."

She looked up sharply, trying to figure out if he was joking and decided that it was at least an attempt. *We're making progress,* she thought. She stuffed her hands down into her pockets and walked slightly ahead of him down the path, which was cleanly shoveled. It wound around a stand of spruce trees and skirted a flat, snowy area which, in warmer months, was the golf course.

"Let's walk to the overlook," Russ suggested as they approached the turnoff that led up the mountain.

"Good idea," she agreed, falling into step beside him. The overlook was reached via a steep path faced with a sheer rock cliff on one side and snow-laden spruce trees on the other. Beneath the drooping spruce branches a purling stream ran headlong over a rocky bed, its edges glittering with crystals of ice. Their boots crunched through the thin layer of snow on the path, leaving dark footsteps in their wake. It seemed to Leigh that there was nothing to say, or at least nothing right. She couldn't crack jokes the way he could; maybe it would be best to center the conversation on him.

"Tell me how you ended up taking over the family business," she said. "After you became an antiwar activist, I figured that would never happen."

"It was what I originally intended to do after college, although I got sidetracked a bit," Russ told her. "Then when my parents died, I was faced with the choice of selling the business and living happily ever after on the proceeds or making a go of it myself. A life of leisure never appealed to me. I saw a chance to improve the stores and was excited by the prospect. I sold off some of the less-profitable stores, improved the main store, and added new lines of furniture. The business is in good shape now, and I'm proud of that. I'm financially secure, and now I've got a little spare time to spend doing things I like, such as flying."

"I remember that you used to think that people who were well-to-do owed something to society," she said.

"I still do. I support several worthy causes, such as Big Brothers and Big Sisters and a school for migrant children. The money I've made makes it possible for me to do these things. Oh, when I was in Canada and involved in the antiwar effort, I suppose I thought that living my life only to accumulate a lot of money would be a sellout. Now I see that having money allows me to help the less fortunate more than I could if I were poor. The realization didn't come upon me all at once. It dawned on me gradually."

"David arranged our finances so well that I'll never have to worry about money again," Leigh said, glad that they were finally managing to make something besides small talk. She glanced at him to see if he was really interested in any of this.

He didn't look bored, so she took a deep breath and went on talking. "It's a lot different now from the early years when David was struggling to establish his insurance business and I worked right alongside him," she said. "I was his secretary and his bookkeeper, his answering service and even his janitor. At this point in my life I like having enough money, but there are more important things. I often think—" and she stopped, unsure that she wanted to steer the conversation in the direction it was going.

"You think what?" he probed gently, looking interested.

"Well, that I'd be better off if I'd had to work—really work—for a living after David died." This was something she'd never revealed to anyone else.

"You work. In fact, I envy your career."

She shrugged. "It's not a big deal. I mean, I'm not a wonderful artist, only adequate. I'm certainly not under the illusion that the pictures I paint for Katrina are great art."

"They fill a need, and that's important. I still hope you'll bring some of your paintings into the store sometime, so my designers can look at them. I'd like to see them, too. To this day I treasure that little portrait you painted me for my birthday when we were at Duke together."

"You still have it?" she asked in surprise. The painting had been a self-portrait in oils. She'd always considered it one of her best.

"Of course I do," he said. "It hangs at the end of the hallway in my house."

She was unnerved by this information; the picture had been painted at the height of their love affair, and she had portrayed herself as she thought she looked after lovemaking—eyes drowsy, hair slightly disheveled, lips swollen with kisses. It seemed to her to be too intimate a painting to hang in a hallway.

"You hung the painting in the house you shared with Dominique?" she blurted.

He smiled faintly. "She never saw it. I found it at my parents' house after Dominique and I were divorced. I couldn't bear to hang it in my bedroom, so I put it in the hall. It's a lovely painting, and I'm fond of it. Always have been."

"I see," she murmured, but she was staggered by the idea that Russ Thornton had been looking at her picture every day for many years. She would have thought that he'd tossed it out in the garbage long ago.

"We're almost to the overlook," he pointed out as they rounded a curve in the path. He clasped her hand to help her cross an icy patch where water had trickled out of a crack in the rock face of the cliff, and he held on to it as they mounted the steps to the overlook.

I'm reading too much into the fact that he still has the painting, Leigh told herself. *Maybe he's just one of those people who can't stand to throw anything away. Maybe he's a born pack rat. It doesn't mean anything.*

The importance—or unimportance—of the painting flew from her mind at the sight of the panorama spread out below, when she stopped and caught her breath at the overlook. The valley stretched vast and white, the sweep of snow interrupted only by a small cabin from whose chimney a spiral of smoke wafted upward. Beyond the valley rose the Great Smoky Mountain range, cloaked in a gentle smoky blue mantle. Overhead, the sky was a blue so brilliant that it was not found on any painter's palette.

"How lovely," she breathed, instinctively moving closer to Russ. He squeezed her hand in reply, and even though he did not speak, she understood that he was as awed by the scene as she was. Gone was any discomfort they felt in each other's presence; they were drawn together by their appreciation of the scene before them.

Up here where the air was so light and cold, they seemed far above trouble and care. Last night seemed to have been a long time ago, and the world below so tiny and insignificant. Leigh felt centered in herself, her mind expanded, and suddenly she saw everything more plainly.

With luminous clarity, she finally understood. She could not merely wait for a good relationship to develop with Russ, and she couldn't expect him to do all the work. If she wanted more than they had now, she would have to take positive steps in that direction.

She saw now that nostalgia might have been enough to bring them back together again, but it was not enough to keep them together. The truth was that they could not have the kind of relationship she wanted if she continued to keep the secret that weighed so heavily on her mind— the secret that Wendy was Russ's daughter.

But how could she tell him? Did she *want* to tell him?

His arm, quite naturally and almost of its own accord, encircled her shoulders and pulled her against him. She liked being there, but she knew that if she told him about Wendy, things would never be the same. Maybe she'd lose him.

How can you lose what you don't have? asked the small voice inside her head.

We have something, she answered. *I'm not sure what it is, but there's love. And respect.*

But she didn't need that small voice to remind her that without honesty, love and respect were of little use.

Telling Russ about Wendy wasn't the only problem, and it certainly wasn't the most immediate. Leigh knew that soon she would have to face the task of sorting through her feelings about Russ, keeping some and discarding others. It seemed like a monumental task to face those feelings, and she was well aware that if she said goodbye to Russ forever after these next few days, she would never have to face her feelings at all.

But to say goodbye forever seemed unthinkable, as unthinkable as it had been when he told her that he was going to go to Canada.

The sunshine felt warm on her face, and it felt right to be standing beside Russ, looking out over the valley. She knew she didn't have to do anything right away, right this very moment. For now, there was only this—a beautiful, shining moment when the world seemed far away, a moment to treasure, perhaps as long as she lived.

But was it enough? Enough to last her for the rest of her life?

Chapter Nine

That night they dressed and went to dinner in the inn dining room, and afterward they wandered into the Grand Ballroom where a band played for dancing.

They sat at a small table, and Leigh felt completely and utterly relaxed. Maybe it was the champagne that Russ ordered, or maybe it was that she felt good about their day together.

"Wendy called while I was dressing for dinner," she told Russ. "She asked about you and me."

"What did you tell her?" Russ asked with more than a little interest.

"That we're spending a lot of time together," she said.

"And her reaction was—?"

"Interested, to say the least. She's always wanted to pair me off with someone since I've been alone."

Russ laughed. "I hope I'm the right someone," he said. "And how are the newlyweds?"

"Blissfully happy," Leigh said.

"Where are they honeymooning?" Russ wanted to know.

"She wouldn't say. All she said was that it was beautiful and cold and that she is very happy," Leigh replied.

"And may she live happily ever after," Russ said, raising his glass.

Leigh took a small sip of champagne and set her glass down. "Do you suppose it's possible?" she asked wistfully, wanting to believe.

"What?"

"Do you suppose anyone can live happily ever after?"

"Maybe 'contented ever after' is a better way to say it," Russ amended. "It'd be hard to be happy all the time. Besides, if you were, you'd probably be crazy. *Nobody* can have it that good."

"I worry about Wendy and Andrew," Leigh said slowly, tracing a damp ring on the tablecloth with one fingernail. "They think they know all the answers."

"So did we, remember? And we didn't even know all the questions. Speaking of questions, here's one that only you can answer. Would you like to dance?"

Leigh broke out of her contemplative mood and rested her hand in his. "Yes, I most certainly would," she said, smiling at him.

He led her out onto the floor, proud to see how all eyes turned their way. Leigh looked exquisite in a flame-colored chiffon dress that molded to her figure and broke into a cascade of ruffles at the hip. The back scooped low, revealing creamy skin; the sleeves were long and flowing.

He held Leigh in his arms, marveling at the lightness of her, at the grace with which she moved. They had always danced well together, but he was a bit rusty; nevertheless, he remembered all the moves and she followed him perfectly.

"I've always liked dancing with you," he told her, leaning away so that he could take in her face. She wore simple diamond studs in her earlobes; they glittered in the lights from the bandstand when she laughed. He loved the sound of her laughter.

"Remember the dances we used to do? The Frug? The Watusi?"

"Don't remind me," he said with a groan.

"They were kind of outdated by the time we were in college, but I distinctly remember one fraternity party where—"

"If you're going to talk about the time we had a toga party and invited two girls for every guy—"

"Was it only two? It seemed like three. What was the purpose of that, anyway?"

"My frat brothers and I wanted to meet girls," he said.

"Well, you certainly did. Not that *you* needed to. You knew far too many girls as it was."

"After I met you, I thought so, too. Remember that Betty Whatsername, the one who was slightly obtrusive of tooth?"

"Obtrusive of tooth!" Leigh said, stifling a laugh.

"She had *huge* teeth," he said.

Leigh snickered but managed to recover.

"She wouldn't stop calling me, even after I told her I was in love with you."

"I thought her name was Bonnie, and you *didn't* tell her you were in love with me. That was the problem," Leigh said.

"Oh, *Bonnie,* the one whose calves bulged like wine bottles. I was never into wine, I'm strictly a beer man," he said. He remembered that he hadn't liked Bonnie much. After he started going out with Leigh, he hadn't been interested in anyone else.

"Bonnie, Betty! I certainly had a lot of competition."

"No, Leigh," he said, suddenly serious. "You never had any."

Her smile faded into a nostalgic, faraway look. "Neither did you," she said.

He drew her closer so that her temple rested against his cheek, reflecting that he had never looked at another woman after he started dating Leigh.

When the song ended she smiled up at him, a bright spontaneous smile that melted his heart. They danced again and again, whirling around the floor, causing people to look up from their drinks and their conversations and remark about how well-matched they were.

And they were. She followed him instinctively, anticipating every movement, adjusting to him gracefully.

Like good sex, Russ thought. *Like last night.* It had been good until something had happened and she had run away. He pulled her close, feeling the way she adjusted to him, and he wondered what was going to happen tonight. Should they make love again? Should he wait for her to make the first move?

They drank another glass of champagne when they sat down, and her smile became softer and more reflective. She had so many faces, and all of them beguiled him with their countless expressions and the feelings that flitted so quickly across her features. His gaze followed the curve of her neck downward to where her breasts swelled beneath the bright fabric of her dress. She was womanly, desirable, and his throat tightened with the memory of how she had looked last night.

But Leigh coaxed him onto the dance floor again, and when she was in his arms, she tilted her head back and gazed up at him dreamily.

"I haven't danced like this in years," she said.

"Neither have I," he said.

"Why not?"

"I never had a partner as good as you," he told her truthfully, and was happy that the compliment pleased her.

"You taught me to dance," she said, surprising him.

"Not true," he said. "Definitely not true. You learned to dance in your cradle."

"Oh, I had the usual ballet and tap lessons at Mrs. Hand's School for Feet, but—"

"Mrs. Hand's School for Feet? You're pulling my leg!" His eyes glinted with humor.

"The neighborhood dancing teacher was named Mrs. Hand. I'm afraid her students added the part about feet. Anyway, I wasn't good at dancing until I met you. I remember how you taught me to waltz at the big fraternity dance that spring."

"I don't recall that at all. I remember what you wore, though. A dress with gold threads that shimmered when you walked."

"I loved that dress. But most of all I remember the corsage you bought me to wear that night. White orchids. My *first* orchids. They were beautiful."

"You were beautiful. And you still are."

"Oh, Russell. You always say the nicest things." She was gazing up at him mistily, and he would have kissed her then and there if he'd thought it wouldn't raise eyebrows among the others on the dance floor.

"You *are* beautiful," he said, his voice low. "I had thought you would have changed, but you haven't. You look the same to me, those same blue-green eyes, the same scent, the way you feel in my arms, the way you—" and he stopped, suddenly abashed. He had been on the verge of mentioning the way she murmured his name over and over during lovemaking, something she had done from the very beginning and which always had made him feel as though his name on her lips was some powerful kind of aphrodisiac that only he could supply.

"The way I whisper your name when we're in bed. I know what you were going to say," she finished softly, resting her cheek against his. He was stunned that she would speak the words out loud, but then he wondered why he was so surprised; she had never been shy about sex.

The song ended, and the band began to leave the bandstand. The other dancers drifted toward the door, and they realized abruptly that the dancing was over.

Reluctantly they broke apart, suddenly self-conscious with each other. She slid a slow glance toward him, wondering if he felt the same rising heat that she did. She wished it could be easy. If she could design lovemaking the way she wanted it, they would not have to worry about logistics—where it would happen, when it would happen, who would initiate it. It would occur spontaneously according to appetite, and people would have some sort of sixth sense that would tell them when and how and where. The thought made her giggle, and he said, "Too much champagne?" and she said, "You can't have too much champagne," and he laughed and pulled her close.

She felt so attuned to him that she knew he wanted to make love to her in spite of what happened last night. And she also understood that he was reluctant to be the one to suggest it in case she still had misgivings. She felt slightly tipsy; *had* she drunk too much champagne? No. She'd only taken a couple of glasses, and they were small ones at that. It seemed to her that the champagne had made things easier. Simpler.

She could think of no earthly reason why they should not make love. Her inhibitions had been carried away on champagne bubbles. Had floated away on the strains of music as they danced. Today they had grown closer; she was clearer in her own mind about what she wanted to happen. She had not resolved the problem of telling him about Wendy, and she knew it would have to be done sooner or later. But now she was operating under the heady influence of champagne and the physical attraction of a man who thought she was beautiful. She had never thought she would hear those words from a man again.

Silently she walked beside him to the elevator, and as it climbed past the second floor and came to a jarring stop on the third, she considered her options. She could ignore the enormous physical attraction between them and go to bed alone. She could wait for him to ask her to his room. Or she could invite him into hers.

He walked her to her door, and once there, he turned her around to kiss her good-night. Her desire for him flooded her senses; when she looked at him, he filled her mind and her heart. She lifted her arms around his neck and let her head drop until her forehead rested against his shoulder.

"Oh, Russ," she said on the breath of a sigh. "I had forgotten it could be like this."

"I hadn't," he said, his voice unsteady.

She felt warm and aroused and very, very lucky. If she had left this morning, this wouldn't be happening. She would be alone in the big, old house in Spartanburg, walking barefoot on cold floors because there was no one to remind her to put on her slippers when she went downstairs to check the doors. She would be drinking a solitary glass of milk and watching late-night television, worrying in her head about whether she should go to the store to buy another tube of naphthol crimson paint tomorrow, and the truth of it was that she didn't care one way or the other and neither did anyone else.

Instead here she was with a most attractive man, perhaps *the* most attractive man to her, and she knew that she did not want to sleep alone tonight, that if she did she would feel the utmost privation, and that waking up by herself tomorrow morning in the big queen-size bed would be depressing in the extreme.

She moved away slightly and rummaged in the small purse she carried, trying to find the key to her room, and he said, "Here, let me," and he reached into her purse, his big hand dwarfing it, and pulled out the key. She tried to take it from him, fumbling in her nervousness, and it slipped from her hand. He caught it in mid-fall, which elicited a gasp from her, and then he inserted it into the lock and swung the door open. When his eyes met hers, they spoke a question.

After one long, mute look she pulled him inside after her, and she stood before him, searching his face as the door clicked closed behind them.

She felt unsteady on her feet, but not from the champagne. She felt overwhelmed by the sheer import of this moment. Last night was nothing; it was a bridge they had to cross and that was all. The experience had served a purpose. Now whether they would make love was not an issue, and she was thankful for that. The issue here was something more; it was deciding if their lovemaking could represent anything more than good, quick sex, could transcend the physical.

She held out her hands and pressed them against the front of his suit, reaching for his heartbeat. She felt it, slow and steady, beneath her palms. Somehow it made her feel less tentative and more sure of herself. He reached up and circled her wrists with his thumb and forefinger, spanning them easily.

"So delicate," he said, rubbing his thumb against the bones.

She bent to him like a willow wand, and he slid his hands up her arms. He dipped his head and kissed her, a soft, swooping, brief kiss, and he inhaled the scent of her hair, sent feathery breaths along her jawbone, touched his lips to the warm shadowy hollow of her throat. Her hands fumbled with his tie, lost the knot, found it and untangled the silk until it fell away; the buttons on his shirt slid easily through the buttonholes. He shrugged out of his suit jacket, letting it fall, and it seemed to float away in slow motion. Everything seemed heavy, weighted with meaning, with time. Away fell his belt, his pants, his underwear, and somehow he found the tricky zipper of her dress and she was shivering out of it, so cold standing there in her underwear, and while she was pulling his head down for a long, searching kiss he dispensed with the gossamer wisps of lace and she was standing before him wearing nothing at all, champagne singing softly in her blood.

His hands began a slow exploration of her body. They were cool and smooth against her skin, and she knew she was shivering, but how could she feel so cold and so hot at the same time?

"Sweet, so sweet," he said, devouring her in a long kiss, and she clung to him, her limbs winding around him like tendrils. Once she had seen a slow-motion nature documentary depicting the way plants responded to light. Their stems and leaves had rotated to follow the sun in its course through the heavens; light was something they'd had to have in order to survive. She felt like that plant, a plant that had lived too long in the darkness and had discovered the warmth of the sun. If Russ turned, she would turn. If he moved, she would follow. He was the sun, and she needed his warmth.

His body, fit and lean, felt hard and smooth beneath her fingertips. She cupped her palms around his shoulders, slid them to the shoulder wings below, followed the curve of his waist and continued to the tight buttocks beneath. She pressed him against her, aware of his own hands curved around her breasts and amazed at how alive she felt. Compared to the way she felt now, she had been sleepwalking through life. Going through the motions. Doing what was expected of her. It all seemed flat and dull, from this perspective. Flat and dull and tiresome. But this—*this* was real.

He was lifting her up, and her legs twined around his waist, and their mouths were joined so that she could hardly tell where she left off and he began. He lowered her to the bed, his eyes dark behind tangled lashes, the pupils wide with pleasure. She felt him pressing against her, grinding down upon her, pushing her wide; she rose to meet him as if on wings, curving upward in flight, wild flight, opening to him as his lips bore down upon hers, and she couldn't breathe, only felt his breath hot upon her face, or was it hers? An exquisite tension built inside her, a singing electricity humming through her body, concentrated here and here and here, and mostly here, and mostly, mostly, mostly... ah! She gasped and pressed her wet mouth to his shoulder, tasting salt, tasting sweat and tears and whispering his name over and over, trembling beneath him, barely conscious of his own shuddering and release, and the tears were on her lips, her tears, and he tasted them on her kiss.

She sobbed in his arms, she couldn't help it. It had been so long, and it was still so good, so perfect with him. As though they had been doing it for years, with all the right moves committed irrevocably to memory, understanding things about each other that no one else could know.

"Leigh, Leigh, what's wrong?" he asked urgently.

She sobbed harder, wetting his chest and his neck, her fingernails digging sharp half-moons into his back.

"Nothing is wrong. It's *right*," she said through her tears, and surprised herself by laughing.

"Crying, laughing, what is it with you?" he asked, rocking against her.

"Oh, I don't know. Whatever it is, I like it," she said.

"Since you like it, let's do it again," he said, sliding down until his lips found her breast.

"Mmm," she murmured, guiding his hands downward.

"There?"

"No, more—yes. *Yes,*" she said as his fingers found the right place.

"Ah," he said, and she lay back, letting his mouth and his fingers draw out delicious sensations more slowly this time.

"Enough?" he said later, when it wasn't nearly enough.

"Not yet," she said, sliding over him and teasing him with her tongue.

"It's like champagne—you can never have enough," he said, and in that moment she agreed.

Later, when their passion was spent, she lay in his arms in the quiet, darkened room and wondered why she had ever thought this would be complicated.

Because of Wendy, her conscience murmured, but she ignored it. Right now it was just her and Russ, and soon would be the beginning of the new year. It was a hopeful season, and she knew everything would be all right. It had to be. This was perfect. Wasn't it?

Russ dreamed that night, but it was not the kind of dream he usually had. Most of the time he dreamed action scenes where he was the principal player, reminding himself of Arnold Schwarzenegger. Afterward, when he remembered them, he was amazed at his feats of derring-do. This time, his dream resembled an impressionist painting—soft and blurry and emotional.

In the dream, he held Leigh's hand and they were strolling through a field of frothy wildflowers—Queen Anne's Lace, he thought they were called. The edge of the field was dotted with trees, and Leigh was wearing something filmy and yellow that billowed around her bare legs. As if he were looking through a zoom lens, Leigh's smiling face filled his vision. And then, surprisingly, the laughter of children, as liquid and warm as sunshine, swirled around them.

The children were his and Leigh's. There were four of them, the exact number they had decided they would have back in the old days when they planned to marry. Two boys and two girls, and one of the girls reached up trustingly and nestled her pudgy little hand in his. Her touch was so real that he could feel it.

He felt a sudden draft and opened his eyes. His legs were constricted, and as he began to understand where he was, he realized that his legs were tangled in the sheet. There was no field of flowers and his hand wasn't holding that of a small girl with blue-green eyes. Instead he was gripping Leigh's shoulder, and she murmured something and rolled over with her back to him.

Drowsily he pulled the sheet up and billowed it over both of them; he adjusted his position until he and Leigh lay as close as spoons. His hand rested in the hollow of her waist, his face was burrowed in her sweet-smelling hair, and he felt so content that he should have been able to go back to sleep but couldn't.

The children had seemed disturbingly real. He thought the boys had looked like him, and the girls had definitely resembled Leigh. Their faces had seemed so familiar that he thought he might have dreamed them before.

He couldn't remember such a dream. Perhaps he had pictured such children in his mind, however, during the years that he had been married to Dominique and she had kept refusing to start a family. They had argued about it frequently, and Dominique had stated obstinately that she wasn't about to give up her hard-earned gains in the business and that she had no intention of losing her figure. He had countered with a question about what good did it do to have all the proper female equipment if she wasn't going to use it, and she had commented heatedly that this was a particularly sexist remark and unworthy of him, and he had apologized, but he had still hoped that she'd see his side of it eventually. She never had.

Russ had thought often in those days about Leigh and the four children she'd probably had with David, and he'd envied her. He'd always known that Leigh would be a good mother, and now that he'd seen her with her daughter, he knew she was. Too bad that she hadn't had any more children; someone who is good at parenting should have a large family. *He* would have been a thoughtful, wise parent. He wished he'd had a chance to prove it.

Maybe he'd be a father someday, though he had come to doubt it as the years passed. He had a couple of buddies who had become parents after passing the age of forty, and fatherhood seemed to agree with them. They had married very young women, though, which wasn't an option for Russ. He liked women who could carry on a decent conversation about a variety of topics, women who had weathered a few storms in their lives, much as he had. Women like Leigh.

Leigh. If he married her—

But no. It wasn't time to be thinking of that. Maybe she didn't want to marry again. Maybe *he* didn't.

But children. If they married, would Leigh object to starting a new family? Probably their old dream of having four children was an impossibility, but perhaps she would like to have one more. A son, maybe. With his dark hair and her eyes. With curly eyelashes and a jaunty grin. He could picture such a boy if he let his mind drift... dreaming and drifting with Leigh's soft body pressed close to his.

Her daughter was grown. Why should he think that Leigh would want to start over again with diapers and sour milk and two o'clock feedings? She was forty-two years old and so was he.

He would help with a baby. He wouldn't mind. He was financially able to hire someone to run the stores; he'd be a better father than some of the younger guys who were never home because they were building a career. He had the energy to cope with kids. But what about Leigh?

She stirred and moved against him, and his mind focused on the present. She was warm and welcoming, and her skin was soft. Soon all thought of children fell away, and his whole awareness centered on the joining of their bodies, the joy and pleasure of it, again and again and again.

Chapter Ten

It was amazing, Leigh reflected as she waited for Russ to get out of the shower the next morning, how in certain circumstances making love obscured all the real issues in a relationship.

Not that she cared *why* they made love. At the moment, it seemed right. Oh, it was right to wake up in Russ's arms and to mold her body to his for warmth, and it was right to pick up the phone and call room service while one of his hands inscribed lazy circles around her breast. And it was right for him to head for the shower in her room, not his, and for him to sit with her at the small table by the window as they ate pancakes and sausage.

They could not stay inside; indoors seemed stifling and confining in light of this newfound freedom of their bodies. Instead Russ asked the restaurant staff to prepare a picnic lunch, and though the staff found it odd that two people would want to eat lunch outside in the snow, they obliged.

Leigh and Russ stopped to visit an antique toy train displayed in one of the rooms off the great hall, holding hands as they watched children approach with eyes that grew even rounder when the train chugged out of the tunnel and they saw that a small replica of Santa Claus sat in the locomotive. One little boy clapped his hands with delight when women dressed as Santa's helpers passed out lollipops all around, and Leigh and Russ took them, too, grinning at each other as they unwrapped them and popped them in their mouths.

Being around children and acting like children made them feel like children, and so they romped and chased each other around the small lake behind the inn until they reached the picnic area where they suddenly became grown-ups again and embraced and kissed and smiled at each other, scarcely believing their good fortune at being together again. Then, struggling to catch their breath in the thin mountain air, they cleared the snow off one of the stone picnic tables and a bench before sitting down to eat their lunch.

Leigh felt replete with happiness, so much so that she ate very little. Russ took up the slack, downing two chicken drumsticks, two ham sandwiches and a huge piece of chocolate cake. When he had finished, he swept the wrappings off the table and turned around so that he could use the table as a backrest, holding one of her hands in his.

Above them, snow blazed in the ridges of Briarcliff Mountain, and in front of them, the lake glittered with reflected sunlight. A bird landed in a spruce tree nearby, shaking clumps of snow to the ground. It took flight and wheeled in the air, a black speck silhouetted against the sky. Leigh sighed with pleasure and leaned back against Russ, surrendering herself to the moment.

The sun was warm, melting little rivulets that sparkled like jewels as they ran off the warm gray stones forming the bases of the picnic tables. The air was pure and fresh, and Leigh drew a deep breath into her lungs, energized by its crispness.

"Katrina and I used to come to this spot often during that summer when I first met you," she said dreamily. "It was where we met our boyfriends after dark."

"Boyfriends? And where was I?"

"In the kitchen. The boys we liked worked at the lake; they were lifeguards."

"They must have seemed glamorous compared to us kitchen rats," Russ said with a wry flicker of amusement.

"I'm not so sure of that. I can't even remember the name of the boy I liked."

"His name was Cal, and I was jealous," Russ told her.

She sat upright and turned to look at him. "Imagine your remembering that!" she said.

"Of course I remember," he said with an aggrieved air. "I spent the whole summer trying to get you to notice me, but I didn't have a chance with that guy walking around in a pair of skimpy swim trunks and flexing his biceps every chance he got."

"He did not. Besides, by this time he probably weighs three hundred pounds and has lost most of his hair."

"I'll bet that's what you thought about me before you saw me," he teased.

She laughed. "I didn't think you'd be fat. But I wondered if you were bald," she admitted.

He kissed the corner of her eye. "I was sure you'd be wrinkled," he said.

"I *am,*" she told him.

"Not very. And not where it matters," he said, kissing her mouth.

"What does *that* mean?"

"It means that I like the little crinkly places at the corners of your eyes. It means you've laughed a lot, and I'm glad. And I love the way your breasts have become more round, more full—"

She twisted away from him. "More fat?" she asked skeptically.

"Not fat. Round. I like it. I only wish I'd been around all these years to watch you develop and change." He seemed suddenly serious as he picked up her hand and traced her fingernails with one of his own.

She leaned back against him, uncertain about his change of mood. The sun flitted behind a cloud, then peeked out again.

"I dreamed last night about our children," he said at length.

She turned and regarded him with a puzzled frown. "I don't understand," she said.

"Have you forgotten? We were going to have four. Two boys and two girls."

"So we were," she said lightly, bending over to pick up a piece of plastic wrap from one of the sandwiches. She crumpled it in her hand, distracted by the sound of it, and dropped it in the basket that they were supposed to return to the inn.

"Anyway, there they were in my dream. One of the little girls held my hand so trustingly, looking up at me with enormous blue-green eyes. She had dark hair like Wendy's."

Something in his tone of voice made her catch her breath. Had he guessed?

"But," he continued, looking out over the valley, "the dream ended abruptly. Dreams often do."

He hadn't guessed. He didn't know Wendy was his daughter. If he knew, he wouldn't be so casual. In that moment, she realized that she wished he *did* know, because then all she would have to do was confirm his suspicions. If only she could tell him and be done with it!

I'm a coward, she thought with sickening clarity. It occurred to her that she could tell him right now, but in doing so, she knew full well that she would risk her happiness.

Leigh jumped down off the wall. "I think we should go back to the inn," she said abruptly. "It looks to me as if the sun is going to hide behind that bank of clouds, and it will be too cool up here if it does."

"The weather report distinctly predicted sunny weather today," Russ objected, but after studying her face for a few moments, he helped her pack up the basket.

She pretended to concentrate on the task, feeling that his eyes were on her whenever she turned her back. When they had finished, Russ hoisted the basket in one hand and followed her along the path beside the lake. She barged ahead, not waiting for him.

He caught up with her quickly. "Leigh, you're acting differently," he said.

She seemed to take stock of what he'd said. She shook her head. "I don't think so," she said, but he noticed that she avoided looking at him.

"It started when I was talking about the dream I had. You act as if I've struck a nerve."

"Nonsense," she said briskly.

"Do you have something against children?"

"Of course not."

"This isn't the first time you've shut me out," he pointed out. "Don't you think I get tired of this everlasting tango—forward and back, then forward and back again?"

"What I think is that this silly conversation is going nowhere," she said.

A boisterous group of cross-country skiers crossed the path where it forked toward the inn, and while he and Leigh waited for them to pass, Russ brushed the snow off a nearby bench.

From the set of Leigh's shoulders he knew that something was wrong. What it was, he couldn't say, but he was sure it had something to with his mentioning children. Why didn't she tell him what was on her mind? Why couldn't she be as open with him as he was with her?

The problem was that he didn't like unpleasantness any more than she did, which was why a lot of things never got said. He was struggling just as she was with trying to get their relationship back on track with too little time to do it; he was painfully aware that they had only a few days left. After that, he didn't know what would happen.

If she wouldn't discuss, however, then she wouldn't discuss. He would have to wait until she wanted to confide in him about whatever was bothering her, and there was no way he could force her to trust him with her innermost feelings. Either it would happen or it wouldn't. In the meantime, they might as well enjoy themselves; that was the way he looked at it.

"Have you ever tried that?" he asked, gesturing toward the skiers. "It's fun."

She sat down beside him and leaned forward, gripping the edge of the bench with her hands. "Cross-country skiing? David and I took it up one year in Utah," she said.

"I missed my morning run today. If you'd like, we could rent skis at the inn this afternoon. Are you game?"

"I was thinking of taking a nap. You could go while I sleep," she replied.

"I don't want to ski unless you do," he said, watching the skiers' retreating backs. His shoulder brushed against one of the laurel branches behind him, and it dumped a wad of snow down his neck.

"Ugh," he said, swatting at it, and Leigh said, "Let me." She whisked the snow away with one of her mittens. The wool felt harsh against his neck.

"Mountain laurel," he mused, looking over his shoulder at the big green, glossy leaves. "I've always liked it, especially when it blooms. Those huge pink clusters of flowers are one of the prettiest sights in the world. That reminds me—weren't we going to name one of our children Laurel?"

"The second girl," Leigh said faintly.

"The boys were Dirk and Matthew. The first girl was Elizabeth."

"Elizabeth is Wendy's middle name," Leigh said recklessly. *Let him make of it what he will,* she thought.

Russ focused a long, hard, incredulous look upon her.

Flustered, Leigh stood up. He was still staring at her when she turned her back and headed toward the inn.

He caught up with her near the gardeners' hut.

"I would have thought that the name was already taken," he said, his voice unnaturally quiet.

"Elizabeth is my sister's name. It's always been special to me," she said. The truth was that she had sentimentally bestowed the name upon Wendy in remembrance of the love affair in which she'd been conceived, but no one knew that, not even Katrina.

"If I'd been lucky enough to be a father, I would never have named my children any of those names. Never," he said, sounding slightly bewildered.

Leigh slowed her pace as they approached the inn entrance. She felt shaken; guilt stabbed through her. She wanted to say, *Wendy is our daughter. Can't you guess? Don't you see?* but the words stuck in her throat.

"I really think I'd like to take a nap," she said tonelessly once they were inside the inn. She looked pale, and Russ told himself that he could understand her fatigue. They hadn't fallen asleep until the early morning hours, and then they'd kept waking up, surprised and unaccustomed to finding themselves together. But they'd been happy. *She'd* been happy, but she wasn't now.

"All right," he said easily. "I'll go upstairs and jog around the track a few times." He made himself sound as natural as possible, but inside he was still reeling with the information that she had named her daughter Elizabeth; how could she have done that?

"Yes, do," she said, sounding immeasurably relieved, and when he walked her to the door of her room, she presented him with a cheek to kiss before slipping quietly inside. She didn't invite him to join her for her nap.

Russ went to his room, changed clothes, and ran around the track until he was so exhausted he almost dropped. Then he went to his lonely room and lay on the bed, trying to sleep. He never did, however; his mind kept trying to untangle some unknown puzzle and wondering what in the world it was.

THAT NIGHT THEY WERE lying in bed when Russ thought, in a burst of courage, that it was as good a time as any to broach the subject that he was sure she'd been thinking about as much as he had.

Leigh had never been one of those women who hurried away to wash after lovemaking; she was the kind who liked to kiss and cuddle and fall asleep wrapped in his arms. For that he was thankful. He was also glad that she liked the lights low so that she couldn't see his face when he first said the words.

"I've been thinking," he said slowly, "about what would happen if we got married."

He felt her shoulder muscles tense against his arm, and he stroked her cheek with his free hand. She remained completely motionless.

"Well?" he said, when there was no reply.

"Is this a proposal or what?" she asked finally.

"It's more like an 'or what,'" he said. "I'm merely throwing the idea of marriage up for discussion. You can do whatever you want with it—ridicule, argue, say you'll think about it tomorrow. I thought you should know that it's on my mind."

"On your mind," she repeated.

"You sound like a parrot," he told her, and he commenced sucking on her little finger, which happened to be handy.

She pulled her finger away. "It's a bit sudden," she said in a quavering voice.

"Hey, we've known each other for more than twenty-two years," he said, shifting his weight so that he could peer at her in the half darkness.

"Not all the time. It's not the same as *really* knowing each other," she objected.

"Nevertheless," he said. He paused. "You don't think we should be considering it?"

"I don't know," she said, sounding troubled.

"We wouldn't have to get married right away. We could be engaged."

"For how long?" she asked.

"A couple of days? Weeks? A few months? Whatever seems practical."

"Where would we live?"

He honestly hadn't considered this. He'd pictured them in his house in Charlotte, however; her self-portrait had decorated his hall for years; and it seemed only right that she should be there in person.

"My house," he said firmly. Then, seeing the dismayed expression on her face, he realized that it probably would not be so easy for her to leave the big, comfortable home where she had grown up, raised her child and lived so happily with her husband. "Maybe your house," he said in a spurt of generosity.

"What about your business?" she asked.

"I have employees who can take care of things with only an occasional visit from me," he said.

She rolled away from him and lay on her stomach with her chin propped on her folded arms. She stared broodily at the headboard of the bed.

He caressed her back, marveling at the silkiness of her skin. She seemed not to notice him, to be lost in some thought of her own. He wished she'd say something.

"Like I said, you don't have to make a decision right now," he reminded her.

Suddenly he was startled to see the silvery tracks of tears glistening on her cheeks. He reached out a forefinger and touched one; his finger came away wet.

"What in the world are you crying about?" he asked in mystification.

"About what we had. And about what I don't deserve," she said, turning her head sideways and away from him so he wouldn't have to look at her ravaged expression.

"Leigh, for God's sake," he said. He slid one arm beneath her and the other arm around her. Her tears fell on his clasped hands and he felt at a loss. What should he do? How could he comfort her? *What* was he comforting, anyway?

While he pondered this, she seemed to shrink within herself. Maybe he had been insensitive, although he couldn't figure out how. What was this rubbish about not deserving? *What* didn't she deserve? A marriage proposal? He thought he'd made it clear that he was only beginning a discussion; didn't she understand?

Twenty-two years ago he'd written her that fool letter, and she'd never received it; that was his first attempt at proposing marriage to anyone, and he had botched it. Now, as two adults without illusions about life or love, he thought that he and Leigh should be able to reason things out together; wasn't that what other people did? Or did Leigh expect surprise and hoopla and romance?

Not that he didn't feel romantic about her. He thought that this was a very romantic situation, lying in bed, engrossed in each other, the rest of the world busy someplace else. What could be more romantic than that? All the rest of it—the flowers and love letters and diamond engagement rings—weren't real. *This* was real, two people naked in each other's arms. But maybe Leigh didn't think so.

"I didn't mean to make you cry," he said.

"It's not your fault," she replied.

"If you're thinking about the past—"

"How can I help thinking about it?" she said.

"You could think about the future, instead. That's what I'm doing."

"Somehow I can't picture it."

"That's because you're not trying. You're clinging to old memories, and it's time to let go."

She sighed deeply and turned within the circle of his arms so that she was facing him. In the dim firelight, the shadows beneath her eyes looked deep and dark. She looked tormented and miserable, and his heart went out to her.

He stroked her hair as he would that of a child. She let her head drop against his shoulder, and he wondered what he could do or say to make her feel better. Since he didn't know the origin of her pain, he didn't know where to begin.

"I'd let go of the past if I could, but it's not that easy," she said finally, her voice barely audible.

"If I can, you can," he said firmly.

"I don't know what you mean."

He leaned back on the pillow and shoved one hand behind his head. In the fireplace, the logs glowed with an eerie light; one split and fell, shooting a shower of sparks up the chimney.

"I've had to live with the knowledge that you married David only weeks after I left for Canada," he said, deciding to lay it on the line. "It hurt. Oh, how it hurt."

She brushed away the dampness on her cheek with a sharp movement of her hand.

"Anyway," he continued, "it's past. Over. *Finis.* And what we have left is you and me. Now. Not then." The words were emphatic.

She brushed her hair back from her face with a weary hand. "It's not as finished as you think," she said.

He thought he understood. "I know you cared for David very deeply," he said gently. "I'm so sorry about what happened to him."

"It's not David," she said, her voice choking on the words. "It's Wendy." She looked so devastated that he drew her into his arms.

He was surprised to find that her skin was gooseflesh and that she was trembling.

"You're cold," he said. "I should put another log on the fire."

"No," she said. "No." She huddled against him, uncommunicative. He wrapped himself around her and eased her back under the blankets until their heads were side-by-side on the pillow.

"I would be good to Wendy," he said.

"It's not that," she said, her teeth chattering.

"She's gone, Leigh. Married. You have to let go of her."

He felt the infinitesimal shake of her head, a denial. He might have guessed that it would be hard for her to let her only child go so soon after her husband's death.

"Don't worry," he said soothingly. "It'll be all right. You have me now, you know."

Her eyes drifted closed, and he kissed her forehead, dismayed at the teardrops seeping out from under her lids. But he didn't speak of them and neither did she, and eventually they both slept.

Chapter Eleven

In the morning, neither one of them referred to the night before. Leigh marveled at how they could both get up, shower, dress and go on as though no unusual conversation had taken place. Russ was as even-tempered and smiling as always, and Leigh found herself thinking that this might be his greatest strength—his ability to remain on an even keel no matter what happened. It was one reason that she should feel comfortable telling him about Wendy, and yet she couldn't bring herself to do it. At least not yet.

But, she decided as she brushed her teeth, she wouldn't feel comfortable discussing marriage with Russ until he knew about Wendy. If she let him go on talking about getting married, she wouldn't be playing fair. *How* to tell him was the problem. All in all, she'd much rather he guessed.

Luckily the problem of how to tell Russ about their daughter did not overshadow the joy and pleasure of being with him. She was able to compartmentalize her feelings in such a way that their happiness in being together again was not overshadowed by her fear and uncertainty. She still looked forward to every minute they spent together, she enjoyed their companionability, and she soaked up his compliments and his admiration. Each magical day they had spent together was embellished with smiles full of memories, and the chemistry between them sparked the same old rapport.

"How would you like to get out of the inn today? We could go antique shopping on behalf of my staff," Russ suggested at brunch, leaning forward and smiling at her over the white tablecloth on their table in the dining room. Around them chimed the gentle clink of glassware and silver, and at the buffet table busy waiters were clearing away the last of the scrambled eggs and sausage, the French toast and cantaloupe.

"I'd like that. I think I can help you," she answered happily, and soon they were walking with light footsteps down the hill to the craft village, sucking on lemon drops and with Leigh's hand tucked inside Russ's big pocket for warmth.

She'd brought her camera; she hadn't taken any pictures at The Briarcliff yet, an omission that she intended to correct while everything was still covered with snow.

"The weatherman is predicting a thaw," Russ said. "It's supposed to rain tonight and become warmer by tomorrow morning."

"I thought I smelled a thaw in the air," Leigh said. "I'll hate to see the snow melt. This Christmas has been so beautiful. I've been so happy."

He squeezed her hand and smiled at her. "This has been the best Christmas ever, and it's because of you. By the way, I've bought our tickets to the New Year's Eve party."

She gave a little skip of delight. "I've always wanted to go to New Year's Eve at The Briarcliff. People come from all over to attend. They're having a jazz band, and a comedian in the lounge, and—and I don't have anything to wear!" she said at the sudden realization.

He laughed at her astonished expression; she looked as though the thought that she needed a dress to wear on New Year's Eve had never occurred to her.

"Wear what you wore to Wendy's wedding," he suggested.

"That suit is not the kind of thing I'd wear to a New Year's Eve celebration," she said.

"How about that bright dress with the ruffles? The one you wore dancing?"

"Oh, no, not that one. I'll buy something in the inn's boutique. Something special," and she smiled up at him, thinking that he would love the way she looked in the black sequined dress that she had spied in the boutique window on their way to breakfast this morning.

They turned into the antique shop, the little brass bells on the door tinkling merrily to announce their arrival.

Inside, Leigh steered Russ away from a rough-hewn cradle that she suspected was a copy, but cheered when he discovered an antique maple drop-leaf table that was suited to many uses. He also liked a small but authentic pie safe that had been painted Wedgwood blue and a lovely rocking chair with a handwoven rush seat, and he bought them all and asked that they be sent to the Charlotte store.

While Russ was standing at the counter arranging for the shipping, a man carrying a small child walked up and began to look at the cradle. The child was a boy, his chubby cheeks as round and red as apples as he peered out from under a bright green peaked cap, and Leigh thought that he looked like a little elf. He made a wild grab at her scarf as his father carried him past, and she was captivated by his wide grin.

"How old is he?" she asked as the man waited at the counter to be helped.

"Eighteen months," the man said. "And I have a newborn daughter, too."

"Bababa," said the boy.

"He can talk," the man said proudly. "Kenny, can you say 'doggie'?"

"Doggie," Kenny said obediently.

"That's very good," Leigh said. Russ turned and looked at them, and he smiled at the sight of Leigh and the baby together.

"Kenny, say 'cookie,'" the man said.

"Cookie? Cookie? COOKIE?" Kenny said, his voice rising on a shrill note of hope. He wriggled in his father's arms.

"Bad choice of words," the father said ruefully.

Leigh laughed. "Here, maybe this will help," she said, handing over a packet of melba toast that she had stashed in her coat pocket a few days earlier.

Russ folded the receipts for the furniture and stuffed them into his back pocket.

"It's all set," he said. He paused for a moment to chuck Kenny under the chin before they walked outside into the bright sunshine.

The snow had already begun to melt and was dripping steadily off the steep shingled roofs of the craft houses. Leigh felt a sudden pang, mourning the loss of the snow.

"I should take a picture of this," she said, snapping the lens caps off her camera. She set the shutter and the aperture in a businesslike way and experimented with several angles until she found one she liked. She clicked the shutter and advanced the film, and Russ thought how capable her hands were, how they belied the soft, gentle woman that she was. She saw him looking at her and sent him a questioning look, but he only smiled and slid his arm around her shoulders as they headed back toward the inn.

It felt right to be walking beside her, measuring his long footsteps to her shorter ones so that they stayed together. It was, he thought, a metaphor for marriage. If they were married, he would adjust his footsteps to hers; that's the way it should be both for husband and wife, but it hadn't been that way with Dominique.

He wondered about Leigh and David—how they had negotiated the inevitable compromises that go with being married. He gathered that they had adjusted very well, which should have made him jealous, but he only felt glad for them, both of them.

"I should take a picture of those bare tree branches— see how the branches make triangles out of the sky?" Leigh said suddenly as they began their walk up the hill. Ahead the forest loomed before them, the trees starkly beautiful against the snow-covered mountain.

Russ had never considered trees as geometric shapes, but now he did. The rays of the afternoon sun limned the branches in light; the effect was startling in its simplicity. Leigh fiddled with the camera, experimented with different angles, and snapped several pictures. He watched her, liking the way she concentrated so completely on what she was doing, entranced by the sparkle of her coppery hair in the sunshine.

"Why are you looking at me like that?" she said suddenly, as if she'd just noticed.

"I like the way you look," he answered. "You never gave me a Christmas present, you know."

"The two things," she said, "don't have anything to do with each other. And I apologize about the Christmas present, only I didn't know you'd be here."

"I'd like a picture of you," he said. "It would be the perfect present."

She laughed and looked embarrassed. "It wouldn't," she said.

"It would. Let me take one of you now. You could stand on that log over there," he said, pointing to a fallen tree trunk in front of a boulder shaded with interesting shadows.

"I don't want my picture taken," she said, but he pushed and prodded her until she was standing exactly as he wanted her, with her face slightly in profile and one leg on the log, and he snapped her picture just as she turned her head and taunted him with an appealing but saucy grin that made her look about ten years old.

"Now you," she insisted, making him sit on the fallen log and lean his elbows on his knees so that he was exceedingly uncomfortable, and then she ordered him to relax, which was impossible.

"You clicked the shutter before I smiled," he complained afterward, so over his good-natured protests she sat him down again and took another picture.

"Anyway, I wouldn't take a picture of you if you weren't smiling," she insisted as she put the lens cap back on the lens.

"Why's that?" he asked.

"I wouldn't want to miss capturing that off-center smile of yours for posterity," she said.

He had forgotten until now that she always referred to his smile as "off-center"; she was the only one who had called this particular peculiarity to his attention. He supposed his smile appealed to the artist in her, or at least the part of the artist that appreciated shapes.

"I'll ask the concierge at the inn about getting these photos developed," she promised as they hurried back to the inn. "You'll be pleased when you see how yours turns out."

"I can't wait," he said, and she laughed.

"If you don't like it, I can always take another one later," she told him.

This statement implied that they would have a future together, and this unexpected bonus made Russ's hopes turn optimistic. He was suddenly overwhelmingly glad that he'd taken a chance, that he'd tracked Leigh down at The Briarcliff. He'd had so many doubts about it at first. Back in Charlotte, when he was thinking it over, he hadn't been sure that it was the right thing to do. And then when he'd found her and she'd asked him to leave, his spirits had reached a new low. But now, things looked promising. He wasn't sorry; he'd never be sorry that he'd spent this special time with Leigh, no matter what happened in the end.

Leigh glanced at her watch when they reached the inn lobby. "Let's meet in the music room for tea in half an hour," she suggested.

"Good idea. I'd like to check on our dinner reservations for tonight," he said.

"And I'd like to change out of these wet boots," she told him, and when she left Russ watched her walking across the lobby, saw how other men turned to look at her, and felt wildly possessive in a way he had not felt about anyone in years.

In her room, Leigh changed into a pair of comfortable shoes and was preparing to go downstairs for tea when her phone rang.

"Mom, hi!" Wendy said, her voice brimming with happiness. "I'm so glad I caught you in. Where have you *been* all the times I've called, anyway?"

Leigh laughed. Wendy's curiosity about Russ was about to get the best of her, she could tell.

"Oh, I might have been at the craft village, or dancing in the Grand Ballroom, or walking to the overlook with Russ, or—"

"He really likes you, doesn't he?"

"Mmm-hmm, it's safe to say so," Leigh admitted. She was enjoying the suspense; Wendy seemed so surprised that she was actually keeping steady company with a man. *Keeping steady company,* she thought. My, those words would date her. What was the proper way to say it? Oh, *seeing.* She was *seeing* a man.

"Am I going to get to see him again? I mean, where does he live?"

"In Charlotte," Leigh said.

"Oh. So far away. Well, will the two of you get together after this week?"

Leigh thought about it. How much should she tell Wendy? That Russ had mentioned marriage? That the man was her real father? She felt slightly sickened at the idea.

"I suppose that Russ and I will see each other again," she said carefully.

"I'd like to get to know him better. He has kind eyes," Wendy said.

"Is that all you noticed?" Leigh asked, wondering if Wendy had picked up on any resemblance to her; probably not. Wendy was not one to beat around the bush. She would have come right out and mentioned it if she had.

"I noticed that Russ seems quite taken with you," Wendy said.

"I'm fond of him, too," Leigh said.

"Fond? Is that all? Merely fond? Or something more?"

"Wendy, ease up. We've only been together for a few days."

"I'm so glad you've found someone. I really am. Oh, here's Andrew. He wants to say hello," and Wendy put Andrew on the line.

They said a few obligatory words to each other, exchanging their usual friendly greetings, before Wendy returned.

"I'll call you again to wish you a Happy New Year," Wendy promised. "That is, *if* I can find you."

"I'll be in my room getting ready for the big party from about four o'clock until seven or so on New Year's Eve. You can call me then if you'd like."

"Will do. I envy your going to the New Year's Eve celebration," Wendy said.

"Will you and Andrew be going out to celebrate New Year's Eve?" Leigh asked.

Wendy laughed. "It's not likely. Andrew says I can tell you where we are—we're in a sweet little cottage on an island off the coast. The view of the ocean is wonderful and we're having a good time, but I'd love to go to a party." Andrew said something in the background, and Wendy laughed again. "Andrew says that the island's beautiful but cold. We think the heater is on the blink."

"Have you called a repairman?"

"There's only one man on the island who fixes things. He's at his sister's on the mainland. But don't worry, Mom. We're keeping warm."

"I know you can always go to Andrew's parents' house a day or so early if you'd like," Leigh said.

"They're not expecting us, but I'm sure it would be no problem. We're hoping the heater will be okay. Anyway, I'll call you on New Year's Eve, Mom, and in the meantime, say hello to Russ for me."

"Yes. Yes, dear, I will."

Leigh felt pensive as she hung up, and she remained so as she slowly descended the stairs to the music room. It seemed that there was no easy way to end the lie that she had been living for so long. She was painfully aware that when she divulged the information that Russ was Wendy's birth father, she would irrevocably change two lives.

You changed those lives before, you should be able to change them again, she told herself, but she was older now and much wiser. Things had turned out well enough for her and David and Wendy; in retrospect, she felt sad and increasingly guilty over her decision to keep the secret, because she knew now that it hadn't been good for Russ. He had never really found happiness, and perhaps it was her fault.

Also she cringed from letting Wendy know what she, Leigh, had done all those years ago. Once Wendy knew that Leigh had deliberately hidden her existence from her real father, her view of her mother would be forever changed. Leigh couldn't bear the thought that anything could disturb her happy relationship with her daughter; on the other hand, it was already changing because of Wendy's marriage. Perhaps Wendy was mature enough to take everything in stride. Katrina thought she was, but then Leigh was having a hard time accepting the fact that Wendy was an adult, a married adult who had shown every indication that she was capable of taking charge of her own life and in fact already had done so.

With these thoughts heavy on her mind, Leigh arrived in the music room before Russ. She sat down at a small card table in a corner and ordered tea for both of them, wishing there was some way to dispel her doubts and fears. She could think of no way out of the trap she had backed herself into; bleakly she acknowledged to herself that she was the one who was responsible for the current state of affairs, and ironically she had thought she was taking charge of *her* own life at the time she had made those far-reaching decisions.

Russ came in smiling, and in spite of her troubling thoughts, a tremor of recognition danced up her spine. *My love,* she thought involuntarily, and knew that it was true. She *did* love him, perhaps now more than ever before.

"Dinner is set for seven o'clock in the dining room," Russ said, sliding into his chair across from her. He smiled at her, and she relaxed. Nothing had to be done now, nothing but enjoying the present.

"I had a good time today," she said, picking up on his mood. "Going into the antique shop, taking the pictures—"

"Eating lemon drops, walking in the snow," he said, grinning at her. "And wasn't the kid in the antique shop cute?"

"He was adorable," she agreed without much enthusiasm; there were other things she'd rather have talked about.

What she lacked in enthusiasm was more than compensated for by Russ. "Eighteen months old—can all kids that age say a lot of words?" he asked.

"I suppose most of them can talk a little," she said, thinking back. Although her memories of Wendy at that age were vivid, she found more and more that she couldn't recall the specific ages at which Wendy learned the skills that all babies must learn. What was more, she didn't care. Every little accomplishment had seemed earth-shattering; now each one had diminished in importance. What was paramount in her memories now were her own feelings at the time—the sense of relief when Wendy first slept through the night, the delight when Wendy spoke her first word, the pride when Wendy took her first steps.

"That man—I think he said he had a newborn daughter, too," Russ said.

"Mmm-hmm," Leigh said, not really paying attention. A pianist walked through a door not far away and sat down at the grand piano in the middle of the room. He played a scale, a series of soft, tinkling notes, and the conversation in the room hushed and receded.

"His children would only be fifteen months apart. That seems a bit too close in age," Russ went on. He was oblivious to her lack of interest.

"Perhaps," she said.

"If we had children, we wouldn't have to have more than one," Russ said, and she turned astonished eyes upon him.

"We've talked about getting married," he said evenly, and she thought, *You've talked about it—I haven't,* but she held her silence.

"Oh, Leigh, don't look at me like that," he said seriously. "With marriage goes children. You're still young enough and so am I, and—" He stopped when he saw how pale she was.

She was speechless. She'd had no idea that he'd been thinking about this, no idea that he actually expected that if they got married, they would undertake raising a family together. It was so removed from the kind of things that she'd been thinking about that she was truly and utterly aghast.

"Leigh, don't look so—well, I'm not sure how you look. What's the matter?"

When she could make her mouth work again, she closed it, and for want of a better place to look, inspected the inside of her teacup, trying to gather her thoughts. She had the outlandish urge to giggle, but this wasn't funny. He was serious.

Russ leaned forward, his tea forgotten. He waved away the uniformed waitress who was approaching with a tray of dainty sandwiches.

"I know some people who have had children when they were in their forties," he said coaxingly. "It worked out well."

Piano notes filled the air, bridging the dead silence between them.

Leigh drew a deep, shaky breath. "I can't have any more children, Russ. I had a hysterectomy when I was thirty-five," she said. She was thinking that this was as good a time as any to tell him about Wendy. Or was it? He looked pained; no, it was more than that. He looked stabbed to the core.

"I see" was all he said.

"It wasn't elective surgery," she said, her words tumbling over each other. "I had a lot of physical problems and more than one indication that surgery was necessary. I'd always hoped to have more children and never became pregnant, but then I had the hysterectomy, and on top of the operation I had to realize that all hope for David and me to have any more kids was gone. It was tough, I'll admit that."

"That's why you never had the houseful of kids you planned on," he said. He felt sorry for her, but he felt sorrier for himself. He had woven a nest of dreams, and it was already unraveling.

"I've come to terms with it," she said.

He heaved a great sigh. "It makes no difference to me," he said heavily. "I want you more than I want kids. I hope you'll marry me. That way I'll gain not only a wife but a lovely daughter."

Leigh's knee jerked involuntarily and hit the side of the table, sending her tea sloshing into the saucer. When he saw the panicky look in her eyes he realized that he had upset her terribly, but he was confused. What had he said to set her off like this? What was going on in her head, anyway?

A waiter hurried forward with extra napkins and offered to bring a fresh cup of tea, but Leigh stood up abruptly. "That won't be necessary," she said to the waiter, and before Russ could speak, she ran blindly from the room.

He hurried after her, aware of the startled glances of the other people in the music room. When he came to the great hall, she had reached the row of elevators behind the bank of poinsettias, but when she punched the call buttons a few times, she must have realized that all the elevators were busy elsewhere and she headed up the large, sweeping staircase.

"Leigh! Wait!" Russ called, taking the stairs two at a time. A woman with a small child in tow stopped and stared after them openmouthed, but Russ didn't care. He only wanted to reach Leigh, to find out what the hell was going on.

She didn't stop until she reached the door of her room, where she fumbled in her pocket for the key.

He pinned her against the wall before she could unlock the door. His face was inches from hers and she closed her eyes to shut him out. Unfortunately he knew exactly what she was doing.

"Look at me, Leigh," he ordered, and slowly she opened her eyes. His expression was fierce and loving, and she tried to look away but he wouldn't let her.

"You have to face the fact that I love you and want to marry you. Why is it so hard to accept?"

"I'm not ready," she said miserably.

"I don't believe you," he said.

She swallowed, but the lump in her throat wouldn't go away. She heard the sound of children's laughter at the far end of the hall.

"We can't stay here," she said, twisting in his embrace. "People are coming."

Slowly he released her, and she shakily slid the key into the lock. "Come in," she said, when he hesitated.

He walked through the door and closed it firmly behind him. He looked around, not sure what to do with himself. Leigh was taking off her coat, and wordlessly he did the same. He felt exhausted after their exchange, almost too exhausted to go on.

It shouldn't be so hard, he thought wearily. When they were young, nothing had been easier than falling in love. All he'd had to do then was pick up on a certain look of Leigh's, act on an indefinable attraction to her, and after that everything—sex, intimacy, happiness—had happened naturally. Now love was so much more complicated—past issues to resolve, old hurts to be healed. And it was harder to love once you were experienced, because you knew that it could never be easy.

Leigh had wrapped her arms around herself as though she felt cold. He looped his coat over a doorknob and put his arms around her.

"I'm sorry," he said. "Sorry about Laurel, Elizabeth, Dirk and Matthew. And about everything that came between us. If it'll help you to know it, I'm sorry about the whole past twenty-two years. I wish things could have been different."

She looked up at him, her eyes haunted by ghosts of the past. "I had a happy marriage," she said.

"I'm glad," he said, meaning it. "You may not believe it, but I'm happy for you."

She drew away from him and sat down on the edge of the bed. When he didn't speak, she said, "David always liked and respected you, you know. He often said he admired you for the stand you took against the war."

He sat down beside her. She slid one of her hands into his, and he thought that she wouldn't have to tell him these things, that it wasn't necessary. She seemed to need to talk about it, though, and he'd always been curious about her life with her husband.

"David never was drafted?" he asked.

He could think of no explanation for the way her lips tightened into a grim smile. "He had a student deferment, and then we married and had a baby. Some men were drafted even though they were married, but fathers weren't subject to the draft. Wendy saved David from having to go to Vietnam," she said.

He sensed that she wanted something from him. She looked at him half-expectantly, but over and above her expectancy there was a tension and a fearfulness that he couldn't explain.

"Lucky David" was all he said, and he lay back on the bed and pulled her down beside him. She made no move toward him, only lay there with a look of despair and desperation on her face. He turned to her, slid his hand up the side of her neck, and turned her face toward his.

Slowly he lowered his lips to hers, seeking something in her response to him. Her passion and excitement and even her love for him had been amply expressed in their past lovemaking, but what he wanted and needed from her now was the certain knowledge that he brought her as much happiness as she brought him. He wanted to see his own pleasure reflected in her eyes; he wanted her to know the exhilaration that he felt when they were together.

But that was not what he found in her. Instead of joy, there was only melancholy.

She turned to him swiftly, pressing closer. "Oh, Russ," she said brokenly, burying her face in his collar. "I do love you, you know. I can't help loving you, even though—" Here she stopped, and he realized that she was trembling.

"Even though what, my darling?" he asked gently.

"Even though it may not be best," she answered in a tone so low that he could barely hear her.

"How can it not be best?" he asked. "Why shouldn't we love each other? I'll tell you this, Leigh—I never stopped loving you, and I never will. This time it's forever."

Her face was wet with tears when he kissed her, and before he knew it she had unbuttoned his shirt. He shrugged out of it and helped pull her turtleneck sweater over her head. Soon they lay together on top of the pile of clothes in the dim purple half-light of dusk, and when she reached for him tentatively, he yanked the phone cord out of the wall, gathered her into his arms and decided to forget about their dinner reservation. Outside a warm rain beat softly against the windowpanes.

He stroked her hair, and his mouth brushed her cheek, his breath gentle against her ear. *Just make love to me so I can forget everything else,* she said silently, feeling tired. Her emotions were tearing her apart, and she'd found no way to tell him why she was hesitant about marrying him. No way to tell him about Wendy. He hadn't picked up on her mention of Wendy's keeping David from being drafted, but then, why should he? All along she had tried so hard not to give Russ any clues, not to let any important details slip. Apparently it had never occurred to Russ to ask when Wendy had been born or to count up the months; he must have thought that his method of birth control in those days was foolproof. He had absolutely no idea that Wendy was his daughter.

His hand wandered lower, tracing her spine, and when she opened her eyes he was looking at her. He took in the long, slender curves of her legs, touched the indentation at her waist, slid his hand upward until it cupped her breast.

"You are so lovely," he said. "You always were."

He slid his leg over hers and pulled her so close that no space was left between their bodies. His mouth covered hers, and she felt herself opening to him, pleasure chasing care, eagerness overcoming doubt. This part was good; this had always been good.

She let her fingertips move of their own will, exploring the territory she knew so well; the wide shoulders, the firm pectoral muscles, the long, flat abdomen. His skin was hot against hers, and she melted beneath him the way the snow melts in the sun. Went all watery and weak because she loved him, and because she loved, she wanted to give him the most exquisite pleasure. And for an instant, only an instant, she could believe that this was twenty-two years ago and that they were in their secret glade in the park, loving each other as though they would never stop, no matter what.

"Russ, oh, Russ," she murmured, and he said, "Now I am you and you are me," and she answered, "Yes, yes," and felt him filling her at last.

When the world returned to normal, he said, "I love you so much, Leigh."

"I love you," she said, her voice a mere whisper.

He twined his fingers through hers and listened as her breathing became slow and regular. In this season of hope, she had brought him more hope than he could have imagined; he fell asleep beside her, his face nestled in her hair.

It was very late when a sharp knock on the door disturbed them.

Leigh sat up, her breasts shining white in the moonlight pouring through the window. She was disoriented until she felt Russ stirring beside her.

"Don't answer it," he said. "Whoever it is can go away."

She started to lie down when she heard a voice. "Mrs. Cathcart? Are you there? I'm afraid it's an emergency."

"I'll go," Russ said, pushing her back into the rumpled sheets with a cautionary hand, and he pulled on his pants and shirt and hurried to the door.

The word "emergency" woke her completely. Leigh sat in the dark with the bed covers pressed to her chest, trying to hear the subdued conversation, but she could make out none of the words. She struggled to stand up, wrapping the bed sheet around her.

Russ flipped the light switch as soon as he closed the door. Harsh incandescent light flooded the room, and she saw that his face was ashen and his look was pitying.

"What is it?" she asked sharply. "It's not Wendy, is it?"

"An accident," Russ said. "Andrew called and left a message at the desk when no one answered your phone. He and Wendy were driving back to the inn to surprise you and to spend New Year's Eve with us. Leigh, I'm sorry, but their car slid off the road. Wendy's hurt. Oh, Leigh, I am so sorry."

Chapter Twelve

The world began to spin and Leigh heard a roaring in her ears. She was only marginally aware that Russ was easing her onto the edge of the bed, was holding her head down between her knees, and she thought, *Am I fainting?* She had never fainted in her life.

When she lifted her head, Russ drew her into his arms. "It's all right, Leigh, it's going to be all right," he said. His voice sounded faraway.

"Where is she?" she managed to ask.

"The desk clerk wrote the telephone number of the hospital on this piece of paper," Russ said. "It's a hospital in Kettiston, North Carolina, not far from Fayetteville."

"*Kettiston!* What were they doing there? Andrew—is he all right?"

"Minor cuts and bruises, that's all."

"Thank God. Oh, Russ, I'd better call the hospital," she said. Her voice was shaking.

"Here, let me," Russ said, taking the phone receiver from her hand. Russ dialed the number and handed her the telephone.

The person Leigh talked to was an emergency-room nurse, who told her little more than what she already knew. Wendy had been brought in over an hour ago with a head injury. Period. For more information, Leigh would have to talk to Dr. Miller, the doctor in charge.

"May I speak with him, please?" Leigh asked.

"I'm sorry, he's with a patient," the nurse told her.

"With Wendy?"

"I don't know, Mrs. Cathcart."

Leigh's voice rose. "May I speak with my son-in-law? Andrew Craig. He was in the same accident, but I understand that he wasn't seriously injured."

A whispered consultation on the other end of the line, after which the nurse said, "He sustained a minor injury, a cut on his hand. He's being looked after by the doctor on duty now."

"I need to speak to him," Leigh said firmly, balancing on a thin edge between control and hysteria.

"I'm sorry, it's impossible."

"Page my daughter's doctor, then," she said, willing herself not to get angry.

Having the doctor paged yielded no results. The nurse, as impersonal as ever, noted the telephone number of The Briarcliff and promised to give it to Dr. Miller, Wendy's physician.

Leigh slowly lowered the receiver of the phone. She knew nothing. She could find nothing out.

"I have to go to Wendy. They won't even tell me how she is," she said. She lifted troubled eyes to Russ, who was standing beside her and looking concerned.

"Of course," he said immediately. "I'll take you."

"My car—it's probably low on gas," she said, beginning to function more normally. She let the sheet fall to the floor, gathered up her clothes and began to put them on.

"I'll check with flight service and see what the weather is like between her and Kettiston. I'll fly you, if it's okay. We could be there in an hour and a half."

With a sense of unreality that this was really happening, Leigh picked up a rubber band off the floor where it had fallen earlier and bundled her hair back into a ponytail. Her face looked so pinched and white, reminding Russ of another day when she had been upset, the day that he'd told her he was going to Canada. His heart went out to her; he could see her pain written all over her face.

"I'd better get ready," she said distractedly. "I'll have to pack something, anything..."

"Wait until I call flight service," he urged. He dialed the number and the phone rang on the other end, but no one answered. He glanced at his watch. It was after midnight; flight service was supposed to be available twenty-four hours a day to give weather reports to pilots. *Answer, damn it!* he thought, and at last someone picked up the phone.

He listened, then hung up and turned to Leigh.

"The airport's fogged in, but they expect the fog to lift in another hour or so. If we fly, it will take us a little over an hour to get to Kettiston; if we drive, it would take five."

"We'd better fly," she said tersely.

"It could take a while for the fog to clear," Russ warned.

"How long?"

"You never know what the weather will do," he admitted. "Still, flying would be faster, even if we have to wait a couple of hours."

"A couple of hours!" Leigh exclaimed. In her mind's eye she saw Wendy, bleeding and broken, lying in a hospital bed.

"It's possible," Russ said.

She wondered for one brief moment if he was trying to get out of this. "You don't have to go with me, you know," she reminded him.

"I want to," he told her firmly, allaying any doubts that she might have had. He gathered her hands in his. "You can't go alone, Leigh. You shouldn't drive when you're this upset."

At the look of concern on his face, concern for her, she broke. She began to sob quietly. For a minute or more he held her tight against his chest until she managed, with great effort, to pull herself together.

"I'll pack," she said, easing away from him.

"I'd better throw a few things in my duffel bag," Russ told her.

"You can still back out of this," she told him.

"Leigh," he said in a tone of reproof, and when she saw the reproachful look on his face she said nothing more.

When the door had closed behind him, Leigh moved like a robot to the closet. She threw the first things she saw into her smallest suitcase. Pants, sweaters, a skirt. Blouse, shoes, boots. In the bathroom, she yanked the curling-iron cord out of the wall plug. Shampoo. Brush. Mascara? No, she tossed it back onto the counter. She wouldn't need it.

In five minutes, she had finished. She zipped the suitcase closed and slipped on her parka, grabbed her warmest gloves off the closet shelf and opened her door as Russ was arriving, his muffler flying behind him.

"All set?" he asked in a low tone.

Mutely she nodded. She hadn't even brushed her teeth; she belatedly recalled that she wore no makeup. Neither seemed important.

He picked up her suitcase and set off at a trot. She had to run to keep up with his long legs.

Like Wendy's, she thought with a jolt, and then she thought, *She's Russ's daughter, too.* It seemed appropriate for him to be there, and strange. It was hard to reconcile herself to the idea that Russ was actually around when he was needed. It had always been David who had been there during other crises in Wendy's life.

People were still up and about in the great hall of the inn, walking in twos past the huge fireplaces where the fires were being banked for the night. Bright chatter wafted from the direction of the lounge. Russ turned to Leigh in the foyer.

"I'll get the car. It'll take just a minute."

She watched Russ as he loped down the curving driveway toward the parking lot. He was a good runner; after all, he ran every morning. She was immensely thankful for that. For *him*.

She saw a pair of headlights swinging toward her, recognized Russ behind the wheel of the car and picked up her suitcase. By the time she had reached the door, the car had screeched to a stop in front of her.

The trunk lid popped up, released from inside, and Russ erupted from the driver's seat to help her stow the suitcase in the trunk beside his duffel bag. He opened the door on the passenger side and made sure she was secure in her seat before he closed it after her. In a few moments they were on the highway to the airport.

Damp patches of fog swam past the car's headlights; wet tree trunks loomed on each side. Ragged remnants of snow remained here and there in places that the sun couldn't reach, and the pavement was slick from the thaw.

Leigh leaned forward in her seat, peering ahead. Russ masterfully guided the car around several curves where it was impossible to see what was coming from the other direction. They were descending the mountain; the airport was located at one end of the valley. The fog grew denser as they reached the lower altitude. Leigh's ears popped, adjusting to the change. All she really wanted was to get to Kettiston. The fog looked thick, too thick. They couldn't take off in this.

Russ sensed her agitation. "Don't worry," he told her. "I think the fog will lift before we reach the airport."

Leigh tried to relax, but it was impossible. The moment she let down her guard, her hands clenched and her fingernails bit into her palms. She prayed that Wendy would be all right and that the fog would lift so that Russ's plane could take off. She thought that she had never prayed so hard in her life.

When she stopped praying, she thought about Wendy and how she was beginning a new life with Andrew. She was so young, only twenty-one; surely Wendy deserved a chance to live the happiness that she had so recently found? And Andrew—he must be beside himself. He loved Wendy so much; together the two of them had planned their careers and had talked about having a family when the time was right. They had so much ambition and drive, so much love!

Great clouds of fog engulfed them within a mile of the airport, and Russ was forced to slow down. Visibility was so limited that it was impossible to see the curves in the road until they were upon them; the fog was a wall of white.

"We won't be able to get out if it's like this, will we?" Leigh asked nervously. She bit on a fingernail, a habit she'd thought she'd broken over a year ago.

"No," Russ said, clipping the word off short, and she sank back into the soft leather seat.

"Could we—could we still drive to Kettiston?"

"If you'd rather," Russ said.

"I don't know," she said fretfully, staring out at the mist. Russ had turned on the windshield wipers, and they seemed to taunt her. *Will you, won't you, will you, won't you,* they mocked, and she remembered that the refrain was a line from *Alice's Adventures in Wonderland,* one of Wendy's favorite books when she was a child.

She swallowed the lump in her throat and tried to think. She didn't doubt Russ's ability as a pilot; she only worried about the weather. She wanted to get to Wendy as soon as possible. What should they do?

Blindly she turned to Russ. "Tell me what you think," she said.

He braked the car to a stop outside a small white building—the airport. Somewhere out there in the fog were the hangar and planes, but they couldn't see the outlines of the building. Leigh had the crazy idea that maybe the hangars and planes weren't there after all, that this was some kind of nightmare from which she would soon awaken.

"I'll call flight service again," he said, going around to the trunk and getting their suitcases.

"I'll carry mine," she said, but he replied, "No, I've got it," his voice echoing eerily in the fog, and she followed him silently into the building where a stout man sat in an orange pool of light behind a messy counter and looked up in surprise as they entered.

Russ immediately picked up the phone and Leigh paced the small waiting area, barely conscious of the dog-eared magazines and the old leatherette furniture with its stuffing falling out.

"They say the weather should clear up soon," Russ told her, but when he saw her bleak expression, he hurried across the floor to where she stood. "We can drive if you want to," he told her gently. "My car has plenty of gas in the tank."

"It would take five hours," she said.

"Yes, I'm afraid so."

She whirled and looked out the window. If anything, there was more fog than before. Still, one hour was better than five.

"I'll hold out for the fog to lift," she decided.

"Okay," Russ said. "I'll get you some coffee, all right?"

She nodded, and the man behind the counter said, "Wouldn't you like to sit down, ma'am, and be comfortable?" but she shook her head, attempted a smile, and remained at the window, searching for a hole in the sky.

Russ brought her a paper cup filled with black coffee, and she tried to drink it. The first sip burned her tongue and she winced, but after that she didn't feel the pain of it. She was growing numb, both physically and mentally. She had slept earlier, but it was hardly enough rest. She knew she should probably sit down, perhaps lie down, on one of the couches, but she felt too jittery for that.

"Maybe it won't be too much longer," Russ said. "I'm going over to the hangar to do my preflight check on the plane. I'll be back in a little while."

Russ completed the preflight check; he came back and filled a cup of coffee from the pot. Once she glanced at him and he was staring out at the fog, a worried crease bisecting his eyebrows.

One hour passed and they were still waiting; flight service could offer no explanation for the continuing fog.

"I should have gone ahead and obtained my IFR rating last spring when I was thinking about it," Russ said.

"IFR?" Leigh repeated.

"Instrument rating. It means Instrument Flight Rules," Russ told her. "I could fly in this soup if I were instrument-rated."

"Oh," Leigh said, uninterested.

"Maybe we could find a pilot with an IFR rating who could be hired to fly us there," Russ suggested in a spurt of unexpected energy. He and the man behind the desk held a hurried consultation, and the man immediately began dialing numbers on the telephone. One after another, all the pilots he called said that they were unavailable.

"Another half hour gone by," Leigh murmured with one more despairing look at her watch.

"We could still—" Russ began, but the man behind the desk interrupted. "Look," he said. "I think the fog is lifting!"

The three of them went outside, slamming the door behind them. The hangar, which was about fifty feet away, was beginning to emerge; wispy tendrils of mist still curled around the roof.

"I'll get the plane out," Russ said, and he and the man took off at a run.

Slowly the plane rolled out of its shelter and headed toward the runway. Leigh went inside and tossed her coffee cup in a trash bin. The clock on the wall indicated that it was almost two-thirty; it had been hours since she'd learned of Wendy's accident, and she was still no closer to Kettiston than she had been at the beginning.

Russ slammed back inside and made a hurried telephone call. After he hung up, he grabbed Leigh's hand.

"Come on," he said. "The weather's clear all the way there. We'll be on our way in minutes!"

She ran beside him, her shoulder bag bumping against her hip, her heels barking against the asphalt runway.

When they reached the plane, Russ boosted her up on the wing. She angled into her seat, buckled her seat belt. The propellers began to whirl, slowly at first, then faster. The engine caught. And then they were lurching along the runway, the sky miraculously clear. Above them, Leigh could see a few faint glimmering stars.

Russ talked into the microphone, getting his guidance from the man back at the airport, who was now talking on the radio. The plane hurtled through the darkness, the familiar buildings receding into the night. Then the plane left the earth behind and below, leveling out above the trees. They were on their way.

Russ had to shout to make himself heard over the drone of the engine.

"Hang on to your seat, Leigh! We'll be there before you know it!" he said, and she ventured a halfhearted smile because he looked so jubilant.

Engine noise made it impossible to talk, so Leigh's thoughts turned inward. Her thoughts flew to Wendy. She had been such a beautiful bride. Such a happy bride. Had Andrew been driving when the accident happened? Or was it Wendy?

She glanced at Russ. He was concentrating on the remote and crackly sound of the radio, which Leigh found extremely hard to understand. Russ was much too busy flying the plane to talk to her, so she slid down in the seat and closed her eyes, but no sooner had she started to relax than they hit a pocket of turbulence. Her eyes flew open, and Russ touched her knee reassuringly.

Leigh settled back into her seat. Below a series of small towns skimmed by, their shapes discernible by the pattern of lights. She closed her eyes again, but she soon discovered that relaxation was impossible. She felt slightly sick to her stomach, which was probably a result of the turbulence. Russ did something to direct a small stream of cool air into the cabin, and after that she felt better. She did breathing exercises to relax, and she tried to remember the names of all the original Mickey Mouse Club Mouseketeers, and she counted backward from five hundred. Anything, anything she could think of to dispel the image of Wendy in her hospital bed.

At last she felt the plane descending, and she bent forward, watching for the runway. Finally lights rushed up out of the blackness and the plane touched down, a rough landing that bounced her against Russ. She didn't mind being jostled, as long as they were here.

When Russ helped her out of the plane, she felt stiff and sore, but her muscles limbered up again as they took off at a trot for the Quonset hut where a single vapor light showed a cab waiting.

In answer to her questioning look, Russ told her, "I called ahead and asked them to have a taxi ready," and he hustled her into the back seat and climbed in after her.

They rushed past darkened houses and stores, and Leigh gripped the armrest as the taxi careened into a long driveway that puzzled her until she realized that it was the entrance to the hospital; it was such a small, forlorn-looking hospital with a too-bright light in front of a door labeled EMERGENCY ENTRANCE. She clambered out of the taxi with a feeling of dread in her stomach. Her palms were damp, but Russ held her hand anyway, and she had lost a glove somewhere but didn't care.

A glittery tinsel garland on an evergreen tree beside the door shivered in the chill wind. Russ held the door for her, and the overheated air inside felt like a blast from a furnace on her cold cheeks. To the right of the door a long counter shone under the fluorescent light, and on the counter a two-foot-tall Christmas tree's lights winked and blinked. A clerk greeted her with a smile, but the smile faded when she announced that she was Leigh Cathcart, Wendy Craig's mother.

"Follow me," an aide said in a hushed tone, and Leigh hurried after her, holding tightly to Russ's hand.

They were led to an empty office decked with smiling pictures of Santa Claus but smelling faintly of mildew. Leigh stood uncertainly as the aide turned and went back out the door.

"I'll find the doctor," the aide called over her shoulder, and Russ looked at Leigh's pasty face and said, "I think you should sit down while we wait."

"I don't like this place," Leigh said.

"It's a typical small-town hospital," Russ said with a shrug.

"It smells bad," she said.

"Look at the ceiling. There's been a leak, but it's fixed now," Russ told her, and she looked up, saw the stain on the acoustical tiles and shuddered.

"In Spartanburg—" she began, but she stopped when they heard footsteps in the hall. They both stood up when a tall white-coated man entered. He was accompanied by a nurse, and his expression was grave as he held out his hand. "I'm Dr. Miller," he said. "Please sit down."

He looked so serious. "Wendy?" Leigh whispered as a wave of dizziness swept over her. The nurse quickly handed her a glass of water, but she set it aside untouched as she sank back onto the chair.

The doctor went behind the desk, sat down and studied her for a moment as if to gauge how much she could comprehend.

"Your daughter has a severe concussion and a nasty cut above the hairline," he said. "That's the bad news. The good news is that there's no skull fracture or intracranial bleeding, as far as we can tell. We've put her in the intensive-care unit, and she's still unconscious. We have listed her condition as serious."

"Serious?" Leigh said.

His expression softened. "I have a good feeling about your daughter, Mrs. Cathcart. Maybe it's because I have a daughter of my own, also recently married. I want Wendy to be okay. I'll take good care of her, I promise," he said.

"I want to see Wendy," Leigh said.

"I can arrange that," he replied. He picked up a telephone and spoke a few words into it. "You may go to the second floor; they're waiting for you in the ICU. Wendy isn't a pretty sight right now, I'm afraid. But we have every reason to be optimistic." His smile was tired but compassionate, and she took heart from it.

"My son-in-law, Andrew Craig, came in with Wendy. May I see him?" Leigh asked.

"We can wake him if you like, but we've given him something to help him sleep, and he dozed off about an hour ago," the nurse said.

"I'll see him later," Leigh said. "After I see Wendy."

"Mrs. Billings will take you to ICU, and if you have any questions, please feel free to ask. If you'll excuse me, I want to stop by the radiology department," Dr. Miller said. He stood and shook Leigh's hand.

After the doctor left, the nurse, Mrs. Billings, told Leigh that she had to check with her supervisor before leaving the floor, and Leigh nodded mutely. She stood and stared out the window while they waited for the nurse to return. Outside, a gray dawn was breaking. Leigh struggled not to cry; crying would do no good.

Russ's hand touched her shoulder. "If you'd like something to eat or drink while we wait, I'll get it for you," he said.

"I couldn't," she answered. She felt chilled through to her bones; her face felt stiff.

For a moment she managed to transcend her own misery to consider Russ's. His eyes were rimmed by bluish circles, and the lines on each side of his mouth looked deeper than they had before. He was being so kind.

She reached out toward him and he folded her in his arms. She nestled her head against his shoulder, drawing strength from the beat of his heart. They were standing like that when Mrs. Billings appeared in the doorway.

"This way," she said, and they rushed along the corridor to an elevator which led to the ICU. They followed the nurse's stiff white back until she stopped in front of a windowed room, and Leigh pressed her face to the glass and strained to see the person lying in the bed. She couldn't see much; there were too many monitors and machines in the way. Mrs. Billings, a calm-looking woman with an air of competence, held a cautionary finger over her lips as she swung the door open.

When she saw Wendy, Leigh's hand rose to stifle a cry. She wouldn't have recognized her own daughter if she hadn't known who she was. Wendy seemed overwhelmed by the tubes and monitors; her head was swathed in bandages, and her face was white and still.

Leigh fought back tears as she approached the bed. Wendy's hand lay on the blanket, and she stroked it gently.

"Wendy?" she whispered softly.

"She can't hear you," the nurse murmured.

Leigh kept stroking her daughter's hand anyway. Wendy's chest rose and fell rhythmically.

"Come on, Leigh," Russ said. "There's nothing you can do. You should try to get some rest. The nurse is going to make up a bed for you in a room down the hall. You are welcome to stay there as long as Wendy is in intensive-care."

"But—"

"We'll call you if anything happens," Mrs. Billings said firmly, nudging her toward the door. With one last heartfelt look at Wendy, Leigh allowed herself to be steered down the hall and lay down on the bed that the nurse indicated.

When the nurse had gone, her tread whisper-soft on the faded asphalt-tile floor, Leigh sat up.

"I've got to make some phone calls," she said.

Russ had stretched out on the shabby recliner in a corner of the room. He brought the recliner to a sitting position.

"At this hour?" he said.

"I don't care what time it is. I'm moving Wendy out of this hospital."

"Moving? Leigh, I don't think it's such a good idea. Dr. Miller seems more than competent, and he said that they can provide the care that Wendy needs here." He regarded her with a puzzled frown.

Ever since she first saw Wendy lying in that bed, tubes and monitors surrounding her, she'd known what she wanted to do. Get Wendy out of here, that was it; move her to the clean, modern hospital in Spartanburg where she knew the doctors and nurses, and where her own mother had once worked as a volunteer.

"I want Wendy close to home," Leigh said stubbornly.

"Leigh, sweetheart, it's not up to you. It's up to Andrew. He's her husband now." She paled noticeably, and too late he realized that he had challenged her authority in the matter of her daughter, and that it hadn't set well with her.

"She's still my daughter. I'll talk to Andrew as soon as he wakes up," Leigh said.

He crossed the room and pressed lightly on her shoulder. "Please try to get some rest. Perhaps you'll see it differently after you've had a nap." Moving Wendy seemed like the utmost folly to him. In his view, there was no reason. Dr. Miller seemed more than competent, and what's more, he was sympathetic and interested in Wendy. The prognosis was good; it stood to reason that moving Wendy all the way to Spartanburg might result in a setback. And the hospital was clean enough; it was just old.

Leigh twisted away from him and stood up. She looked exhausted and probably was.

"Would you like something to eat before you rest? Or something to drink?" he offered, not knowing where he would find food or drink but willing nevertheless to try.

"I can't rest, Russ. Thoughts of Wendy keep ricocheting around inside my head," she said, and tears pooled in her lower eyelids.

"Tell me about them," he said, pulling her close.

"Oh, things like the time she found a butterfly with a broken wing in the woods and brought it home. She fed it sugar water and managed to keep it alive for quite a while. It never could fly, of course, and then it died, but..." Her voice broke because she realized now why she had thought of that incident; Wendy, lying helpless in her hospital bed reminded her of the butterfly. She sobbed softly against Russ's chest.

"Leigh, she's going to be all right. I know it," Russ said with conviction.

Impatiently she pulled away. "I think I'll go see if Andrew is awake," she said.

"Not yet, Leigh. It's too early. Let him get as much rest as he can," Russ said.

Leigh crossed the room in five steps and had her hand on the door. "I can't wait," she said, but he was beside her in an instant, barring her way.

Leigh had the determined look of a woman who was used to being on her own and doing things her way. He had to make her see that, where Wendy was concerned, she must relinquish control to Andrew. And besides, Leigh was being unreasonable.

"Russ?" she said. "Please get out of my way."

She was growing angrier by the minute; he had seen this resolute expression on her face many times before. He hadn't let her win last time, the time he left for Canada, and look what had happened to them. He suddenly felt uncertain; maybe he should let her have her way now.

But it was constitutionally impossible for him to give in, when he knew he was right. It always had been and still was. And he knew he was right about this. His experiences with both his sick parents in their later years had given him a kind of sixth sense about hospitals and doctors, and he knew instinctively that Wendy was in good hands here.

"Don't do this, Leigh," he said quietly. "It wouldn't be best for Wendy."

He couldn't have anticipated the effect this would have on Leigh. Her face flushed angrily, and when she spoke it was with a stone-cold fury.

"Best for Wendy?" she said, her eyes hard. "How would *you* know what's best for Wendy?"

"Sweetheart, it's just common sense," he said, suddenly more exhausted than he'd realized.

"Common sense? Let me tell you about common sense. It's what I had to have plenty of, Russ Thornton, to raise her."

"Of course you did," he said in an attempt to calm her.

"And now you're telling me how to take care of her," Leigh said. "Well, I won't have it."

Russ felt deflated. Maybe she was right—he was interfering. He tried to think about what they'd need to do if Leigh insisted on moving Wendy to the hospital in Spartanburg. They'd need an air ambulance, and as a pilot he was in a position find out where they could get one; and of course there was the matter of a hospital room in Spartanburg, which Leigh could attend to, and—well, perhaps the other details would fall into place. If only he weren't so tired. He felt as though he hadn't slept in a week.

"I don't—" he said, and he was only going to say that he didn't want to interfere, but Leigh seemed to think that he was going to say something else that she wouldn't like.

"Didn't you hear me? Get out of my way! You weren't around to take care of your daughter during the first part of her life, and you don't have any business butting in now!"

Horrified, Leigh clamped both hands over her mouth before Russ realized what she had said. He stared at her, his emotions deadened by fatigue.

"What?" he said, thinking that he hadn't heard her correctly.

Leigh's eyes looked panicked. "I—I—" she gasped.

"*My* daughter? Wendy is *mine?*" he said. He felt as though he was slipping into a state of total paralysis.

All the color drained from Leigh's face, and her eyes were deep pools of dread.

"Ours," she said. "Wendy is *ours.*"

Chapter Thirteen

Russ slumped in the chair, his head in his hands. There was no doubt in his mind that Leigh was telling the truth; her anguish was genuine.

He lifted his head and looked at her. She stood above him, tears streaming down her face. He stood and turned to the window; patches of blue sky showed above the trees. It was finally morning.

"She doesn't know?" he asked.

"No," Leigh whispered.

"David knew?"

"Of course. I told him before we were married."

"It's the reason you married him, isn't it?"

"Yes," she said. He felt her standing close behind him, but he didn't turn. All he could think of was that he had a daughter, and that Leigh had deliberately withheld that information for all this time. He wondered if he'd ever be able to forgive her.

"What else haven't you told me?" he asked bitterly.

"Only that. I couldn't," Leigh said.

He wheeled around. His eyes felt bloodshot, and his mouth was dry. "But you could blithely invite me to the wedding," he pointed out on a rising note of anger.

"I—I wanted you there," she said.

"You wanted me present on that day but not on any of the other days in her life? So when did you intend to tell me that I had watched another man walk my daughter down the aisle?"

"I don't know," Leigh said miserably. She lifted her shoulders and let them fall. "I really had no plan. I suppose I wanted to see how things went between the two of us."

"Oh, so it was something like, 'If Russ and I get along and we fall in love, I'll casually inform him some night when the lights are low that Wendy is his daughter.' Is that it?"

Leigh shook her head. "I thought that—that if we ended up together—"

"'Together?' What kind of together are we talking about? Married?"

She pressed her lips together to keep them from quivering and shook her head. She couldn't look at him, she couldn't.

An ache seized Russ's throat. All the long and lonely years through which he had observed happy families together and yearned for a child of his own; all the occasions that he and Dominique had argued about whether or not she would become pregnant; all the times he had been saddened by the thought that he was past the age when he could reasonably expect to become a father—and he already had a daughter! A beautiful daughter any man would be proud to call his own.

As if over a great yawning chasm he heard her voice, a placating voice.

"It wasn't possible for me to tell you, Russ, can't you see that? Certainly not while David was alive and when I didn't know where to find you. And after that, even if I had wanted to tell you, would it have been in Wendy's best interests? She was still a teenager when David died, and then she was working hard so that she'd make good grades at Duke. How could I have told her something that was bound to tear her life apart, even if I wanted her to know? And I didn't want her to know, I'll admit that.''

Russ passed a hand over his eyes; his eyelids felt as though they were turned inside out.

"And now," Leigh said, "I wouldn't have chosen this time to reveal such a secret. It slipped out. Maybe it was the worst possible timing. But now you know. And I have nothing to hide anymore."

"You had everything I always wanted—a good marriage and family life, a child! You took that from me, dammit!"

"Russ—"

"Leave me alone. Go away. Please."

Leigh buried her face in her hands. She was going to lose Russ. Had already lost him, perhaps. And she could lose Wendy, too.

She heard a noise at the door, and, lowering her hands, turned around. It was Andrew.

"Leigh," he said, crossing the room in two steps and putting his arms around her. They clung to each other in their mutual sorrow until at last she held him at arm's length. His face had two really swollen bruises, one on the left cheek and the other on his chin, and there was a small cut over his left eyebrow. His left hand was bandaged.

"I'm okay," he assured her. "But Wendy—" and his eyes filled with tears.

"I know, I know," Leigh said, trying to comfort him. In the background Russ stared at them blankly.

Andrew pulled away and tried to get control of himself. Russ continued to look at her, a stranger now. Leigh knew she had to get out of there.

She picked up her coat from the bed, gathered her purse from the table beside it. She turned to face Russ, hoping he would keep his silence. She didn't want Andrew to get caught up in their own private hell; he had enough to worry about.

"Andrew and I will go to the coffee shop," she said to Russ. She couldn't stand the way he looked at her, his eyes so accusing. Russ nodded, his face as cold and as hard as granite. In that moment, she knew that he hated her.

What had she expected? Hadn't Katrina tried to warn her? All the deceit of the past twenty-two years pressed down upon her, crushing all hope for the relationship.

Blindly Leigh turned and took Andrew's arm, surprised that she was strong enough to walk out of the room and half expecting Russ to call her back. But he didn't. It was over.

In her state of mind at that moment, she grasped at anything that would help her go on. Wendy needed her. Andrew needed her. But Russ had never needed her, had never needed her at all.

Somehow she and Andrew found the hospital coffee shop and sat down at a booth. Somehow they ordered a breakfast of eggs and bacon that neither of them ate. As they sat watching the eggs cool and congeal on their plates, Andrew, who was almost too distraught to speak, told Leigh that the reason that he and Wendy had left the island was that the heater in the cottage where they were staying had stopped working altogether.

"At first we were going to go to my parents' house in Asheville, but when we called them to let them know, we found out that everyone had a cold, and they said that they didn't want us to get sick. That was when Wendy suggested that we drive back to The Briarcliff to surprise you and Russ. Wendy wanted to spend New Year's Eve with you in the worst way. So we set out, not realizing that it would be raining hard once we reached the middle of the state, and we skidded off the interstate when Wendy lost control of the car," Andrew explained, his voice breaking at the very last. He looked as though his entire world had fallen apart.

"She always drives too fast," Leigh said softly, remembering all the times she had cautioned Wendy to slow down.

"I didn't want Wendy to drive, but she insisted after we stopped for gas, and I wanted to let her have her way. I love her so much, you know," Andrew said, and he looked down at his full plate, fighting tears.

"I know you do," Leigh said consolingly.

"After the accident, before the emergency crew arrived, I found Wendy lying in the ditch and started to give her first aid. I sat beside her in the ambulance and held her hand, and when we arrived at the hospital I asked the receptionist who she thought was the best local doctor to deal with a head injury and made sure she called him. I tried to do everything I thought you would have done." His eyes seemed to plead for approval.

Leigh's eyes caught and held his. "You did everything you could. She's going to be all right, Andrew," she said, though she was far from believing that herself. Her son-in-law looked so desolate that she didn't have the heart to bring up the subject of moving Wendy to the Spartanburg hospital; she would save that for later.

When she looked up, Leigh saw Dr. Miller's face in the window between the coffee shop and the hospital lobby. He swung the door open and came inside, sliding into the booth beside Andrew.

"I was going to ask you to come into my office to discuss Wendy's condition, but we can talk here just as well," he said. Leigh thought his smile was encouraging.

"Have you seen her? How is she?" Andrew asked.

"I just came from her room, and I must report that she's doing very well indeed. Much better than I expected. In fact, she opened her eyes and was able to understand what I was saying to her. We've upgraded her condition to stable," he said. His round face radiated his own relief at his patient's turn for the better.

"May we see her?" Leigh asked.

"Of course. Come with me," he said.

They followed him upstairs, Leigh wondering where Russ was. Perhaps he had left. Perhaps this whole scene was more than he could handle. She wouldn't blame him if he had gone to the airport and flown back to The Briarcliff or even to Charlotte; he probably never wanted to see her again. That thought should have made her sad, and at another time she would have been devastated, but with Wendy lying injured in the intensive-care unit, all she could feel about Russ was a curious kind of emptiness, as though her revelation about Wendy had purged all emotion from her psyche.

They were silent as they walked through the wide, empty halls of the hospital; in one wing, breakfast was beginning to be served, and people were starting to stir in the rooms up and down the corridor. In the intensive-care unit, a nurse named Bernadette showed them into Wendy's room. Dr. Miller walked purposefully toward the bed and enclosed Wendy's small hand in his larger one.

"Wendy," he said softly. "Your husband and mother are here. Can you hear me?" Nearby machines and monitors blipped and beeped; an IV unit hung over the bed.

Wendy's eyes twitched, then fluttered open. Leigh held tight to Andrew's hand and walked closer to the bed until she was in Wendy's field of vision. She bent over her daughter, trying to keep the horror she felt at Wendy's condition from showing on her face.

"Hi, Wendy," she said, forcing herself to smile.

There was an interminable silence while Wendy struggled to focus her eyes. Andrew leaned forward and took Wendy's other hand.

Finally Wendy managed to whisper one word, "Andrew?"

"I'm here," he said.

"Mom," Wendy said.

Leigh longed to hold her child in her arms and kiss away the pain as she had done so many times when Wendy was young, but this hurt was beyond healing with a kiss and a few kind words. Her eyes filled with tears, but she didn't want Wendy to see her cry, so she blinked them back and struggled to keep smiling.

"We're both here, and we're going to see that you're taken care of," she said firmly.

Wendy's eyelids drifted shut, and Leigh stepped back. The nurse, Bernadette, was standing in the corner, and Leigh approached her.

"Is she in pain?" she asked.

"No, I'm sure she isn't. We gave her something for the pain when Dr. Miller came in less than an hour ago."

Dr. Miller beckoned Leigh to the bed.

"She's sleeping now, but she's comfortable. You can see her again when she wakes up," he said. Gently he stroked Wendy's hand; it was a kind, caring gesture. Perhaps Russ was right. Maybe Wendy shouldn't be moved.

Leigh leaned over and kissed Wendy's cheek; Andrew did the same. Quietly they tiptoed out of the room, and Dr. Miller ushered them into a nearby alcove where they could speak privately.

"Wendy knows you're here, and she realizes that you're pulling for her. That means a lot," Dr. Miller said.

"Is there anything we can do?" Andrew asked.

"Nothing. Let us take care of her. It's what we do best," the doctor told them. "Now, how about you? If

you need a place to stay, my office will arrange a room at
the local motel. It's not The Briarcliff, I'm afraid, but it's
only a block away and the people are friendly."

Leigh hadn't even considered where she would stay
throughout this ordeal; she was grateful for Dr. Miller's
help. She shot a questioning look at Andrew, but he
looked confused, and she realized that he was still in
shock and recovering from his injuries.

"We'd appreciate it," she said.

"How many rooms? Two?"

"Yes. Oh, but—" She had just thought of Russ. If he
were still here, he would need a place to sleep tonight, and
she was sure he wouldn't want to sleep with her. "You'd
better make that three," she said hurriedly.

"Three rooms at the Hawthorne Motel," the doctor
said, scribbling on a pad of paper. "My receptionist will
call the motel for you. All you'll need to do is walk in and
tell the desk clerk who you are. If you'd like, you may
spend today in the ICU visitors' lounge, which is across
the hall from Wendy's room. Help yourself to coffee and
doughnuts. And, please—don't worry about Wendy too
much. She's young and she's strong and she has a reason
to live—she wants to get on with her new marriage. I have
a feeling that this young lady is going to be all right."

Leigh gripped his hand gratefully. She had begun to
have positive feelings about this man and about the hospital staff. When they passed Wendy's room, she looked
through the window and saw the nurse, Bernadette,
standing beside Wendy's bed, speaking softly to her and
smoothing the covers. Wendy's eyes were closed, but that
didn't mean she couldn't hear. Leigh had lost all her desire to move Wendy to Spartanburg.

Andrew looked at her bleakly. "We could go check into
the motel if you'd like. You probably haven't slept
much," he said.

"I'm not sleepy," Leigh told him.

"Did you bring a suitcase?" Andrew asked.

"I left it in the doctor's office last night—I mean, this morning," she said.

"I could take it to the motel, check us both in and leave it there. Then if you would like to rest later, all the formalities will be taken care of," Andrew said.

She had the feeling that Andrew wanted to be doing something useful; he must feel as powerless in this situation as she did.

"Okay," she said. "That would be really helpful, Andrew. Are there any phone calls you want me to make while you're gone?"

Andrew shook his head. "I called my parents last night after I called you. They were frantic to jump in the car and drive over here, but I talked them out of it because of their colds. Mother said they'll come as soon as possible."

Leigh patted his arm. "I'll wait for you in the visitors' lounge," she said.

When Andrew was gone, she walked back to the window overlooking Wendy's room and watched with her hand pressed to her mouth as Bernadette changed an IV. Wendy looked so small underneath those covers. She waited for some sign that Wendy was awake, but she never opened her eyes. *At least she's alive,* Leigh told herself. There had been moments when she was not at all sure that Wendy would still be breathing by the time she arrived at the hospital.

Slowly she went to the lounge, opened the door and walked in. To her surprise, Russ was sitting on the couch in front of the window. He was drinking a cup of steaming hot coffee.

She searched for some kind of sign that he had softened in his feelings toward her, but his lips were set in a grim line and there was a steely look in his eyes. His face, unshaven since yesterday morning, looked ravaged.

"How is she?" he asked.

Leigh stood as if riveted to the spot. "She's improved," she said. Her heart raced; she wished Russ had left. She felt too uncomfortable with him staring at her from underneath his lowered eyebrows with intense dislike.

"Her condition?"

"Upgraded to stable," she said, moving to the chair opposite the couch and sitting down, then standing up again. She walked to the coffeepot and poured herself a cup, aware all the while of Russ's eyes upon her.

"If you're still determined to move her, you should know that I object strenuously. *If* it makes any difference to you," he said.

Her hand shook as she brought the cup to her lips. She remained standing with her back to him.

"I don't think it's necessary to move her now," she said. "The doctor and the staff seem capable and concerned."

"You've come to your senses," he said. "I should be thankful for that."

She slammed the coffee cup down, and coffee jumped out and drenched a pile of napkins. She hung on to the edge of the table, telling herself not to break down in front of him. If only he would leave her alone to deal with this!

He stood up and turned toward the window as though he couldn't bear to look at her. When she raised her head, she saw that his shoulders were shaking, and she felt a wave of despair wash over her. She had never seen Russ break down completely before.

She mopped ineffectually at the coffee, finally giving up when she realized that she couldn't accomplish the task with the few napkins at her disposal. She wanted to go to

Russ and put her arms around him, but not if he would shake her off, not if he was as angry as he had a right to be.

"Russ," she said, and he took a deep breath and turned to face her.

"Is she going to be all right?" he asked, and his face was convulsed with grief.

"The doctor says he thinks so," she replied.

"My daughter," he said. "She's my daughter."

Leigh could only shake her head yes.

"She looks like me," he said.

"I know. I was afraid at first when I saw you at the inn that you'd guess. She has your nose, your chin, your shoulders."

"She has your eyes," he said, and she looked away.

"Didn't anyone else ever guess?" he asked in a low tone.

"Katrina was the only one who knew," she said.

"What about David?"

"Yes, he knew the baby was yours."

"How he must have hated me," Russ said bitterly.

She crossed the room, stood in front of him. She touched his arm. "You mustn't think that. David liked you, and he loved Wendy from the very first. He was grateful to you, he said, because you gave us Wendy."

"That's difficult to believe," he said.

"It's true. He and Wendy had a very special relationship. She never had any idea that he wasn't her real father."

"And now? Will you tell her?"

Leigh's face crumpled. "Yes" was all she said. Her face was full of the anguish she felt, and Russ couldn't stay angry. He had never been able to stay angry with Leigh.

Without a word he folded her in his arms, listened to her heartbeat, felt her tears drench the front of his shirt.

He was still trying to make sense of it all; he felt over-whelmed.

After a moment he led her to the couch and they sat huddled together, holding hands. After all the years, after all the words, they had nothing to say to each other. They could only comfort each other in silence.

Later they went together to Wendy's room to look through the window for any sign that she was improving; afterward they walked aimlessly up and down the hall outside the ICU. Whenever anyone went into or out of Wendy's room, they both hurried to see what was happening, and later, after Andrew returned, Bernadette allowed all three of them in to see her.

"Hi, Mom," Wendy said, her voice stronger now. Her eyes searched for Andrew. "I'm sorry I wrecked the car," she said. She spoke slowly, as if it were a great effort.

"Don't worry about the car," Andrew told her, reaching for her hand. "Right now it's in better shape than you are."

A flicker of a smile, and then she looked at Russ. "Russ came with you," she said in surprise.

"He flew me here in his plane," Leigh said.

"We were..." Wendy stopped and licked her dry lips. "We were coming to The Briarcliff to go to the New Year's Eve party with you."

"I know," Leigh said. "Don't talk too much, dear. You need to rest."

"But...but I'm afraid I've ruined your vacation," Wendy managed to say.

"Don't be silly. There's no place I'd rather spend my New Year's Eve than right here in beautiful downtown Kettiston with you," Leigh told her, knowing that Wendy would see the humor in this.

Another smile, and Wendy's eyes closed.

"You'd better go," Bernadette said, and with lingering backward glances, the three of them tiptoed out.

"Leigh, you look dead on your feet. You should try to get some sleep," Russ said to her when they stood in the corridor. "Is there a motel in Kettiston where we can stay?"

"Dr. Miller arranged for us to stay at the Hawthorne Motel. It's down the road about a block, and Andrew already took my things."

"Here are the keys to your rooms," Andrew said to Leigh, pulling them out of his jacket pocket. "Why don't you try to rest? I'll stay here and call you if there's any change in Wendy's condition."

"I don't think I should go," Leigh said with a backward glance toward Wendy's room.

"You won't be able to help Wendy if you're exhausted," Russ told her, and Leigh saw the sense in that.

"All right," she said. She held her hand out for her key.

"I'll go with you," he said, and so they walked out of the hospital through the lobby with its big Christmas tree decorated with red velvet bows and out onto the narrow tree-bordered Kettiston street.

It was a warm day, and the sun was shining. Overhead, a large, bedraggled white plastic snowflake was attached to each lamppost, trying in vain to dress up the small, dreary town for the holidays. Across the street, someone had painted a Christmas scene on the big plate-glass window of the gas company with tempera paint, which had already begun to flake. The whole scene was depressing, and Leigh looked away.

They turned right toward the motel and walked silently, heavy with fatigue. Leigh was so tired she could barely place one foot in front of the other; her hair blew in her eyes on a gritty wind, and she brushed it away impatiently. Her mind was concerned with Wendy; had she made a mistake in deciding to leave her in this hospital? Should she investigate the doctor's reputation? Was Andrew capable of making any decisions that needed to be made, or would she have to do it? She hated being in such a situation so far away from home.

"I didn't think you'd leave Andrew there with Wendy," Russ said suddenly.

"He's an adult, and he's her husband," she said with a shrug.

She noticed a brief flicker behind his eyes when he looked at her. "A few days ago, I wasn't so sure you were ready to let go," he said.

"A few days ago, I probably wasn't. Now—"

"Now what?"

She scuffed at some fallen leaves. "Now I see that Andrew, even though he is hurt and in shock, is capable of taking care of her. He handled the emergency very well, finding the doctor, calling his parents, calling The Briarcliff. I couldn't have done any better."

"I'm surprised," he said. "Surprised that you're letting go."

"I'm not letting go," Leigh said as she began to understand. "I'm merely moving over to make room for Andrew in Wendy's life."

They had reached the motel, but she thought that Russ was looking at her in a new way as they walked through the parking lot.

The doors of the motel rooms opened directly onto the parking space for each room; it was an old motel. "You're in Room 103, I'm in 104," Russ said, looking at their key tags.

"Andrew arranged our rooms that way," she said. She wanted Russ to know that she hadn't put him next door to her on purpose.

Russ said nothing, but he waited at the door to her room while she went in and flipped on the switch to the wall heater. When she looked up and saw him standing there, framed by the light in the doorway, she didn't know what to say. He seemed to be waiting for something, but she only looked at him blankly.

"I'll see you later," he said finally. "Shall I stop by for you in three hours or so? We could go back to the hospital after we grab a bite to eat."

"You don't have to—"

His head shot up. "She is my daughter," he said. "Of course I do."

"What I mean is—"

"Don't give me a rough time, Leigh," he said wearily. "I'll be back to get you like I said."

She nodded in reluctant agreement, and after he closed the door she made sure it was locked, stumbled to the bed, threw back the bedspread and fell asleep in her clothes.

RUSS DID NOT FALL asleep right away. Instead he lay on his bed and stared at the ceiling, thinking about Leigh and his daughter.

His daughter. He should have guessed when he saw her; Wendy was the image of his paternal grandmother when she was a girl. She had the Thornton jawline, too prominent for classical beauty, but beautiful nonetheless. When he had looked at her, all he had seen was the eyes, Leigh's eyes.

If Leigh had only told him that she was pregnant back in 1969, he could have come home from Canada and married her. But she couldn't have told him. She didn't know where he was.

Why didn't Leigh contact his parents when she realized that she was going to have a baby? They could have found him for her. They always knew his address. Yet Leigh would have been too proud to do that. She wouldn't have wanted his parents to think she was chasing after Russ; she couldn't have told them she was pregnant because in those days nice girls didn't get pregnant before marriage. And anyway, Leigh had thought he didn't love her.

What a mess! So many problems, so many sorrows, and all because he and Leigh had been young and in love and too innocent to realize that the very private act of making love could have public repercussions. They'd never thought how an illicit pregnancy could affect other people's lives, and if they had they wouldn't have cared. The only thing that had seemed important to either of them in those days was to make love as often as possible, never mind the consequences. Leigh had relied on him for birth control, and something had gone wrong, and for that he felt immeasurably guilty and always would.

And Leigh—what about her? How had she managed to come through the experience as well as she had? A lot of the credit had to go to David, who had jumped in and solved the problem that he, Russ, had caused. From what Leigh had told him about Dave, the guy had been a prince.

He heaved a giant sigh and turned over on his stomach. He punched the pillow, trying to get comfortable, and he wished that Leigh was lying beside him. He'd been so hard on her, had said some things that he shouldn't have said. She'd suffered, they'd all suffered enough. Whatever was the outcome of all this, he didn't want any more suffering.

Before he did anything else, he'd better go to sleep. Things would look better when he woke up. Things had to look better, because it was hard to imagine their being any worse.

LEIGH'S WAKING UP was gradual, and before she was fully awake she wondered why Russ wasn't sleeping beside her. Then she remembered about Russ and about Wendy, and all she wanted to do was pull the covers up over her head and never come out. But that would never do.

Slowly she eased herself to a sitting position and rubbed the back of her neck. She was stiff and sore; her mouth felt dry. She went to the bathroom and filled a glass with water. Her face stared back at her from the mirror as she drank, her eyes red-rimmed and her cheeks gaunt. At her throat, Russ's locket, engraved with their initials, mocked her. Slowly she unhooked the clasp and, after staring at it for a moment, dropped it into the depths of her makeup case.

She showered quickly and put on lipstick, and she wondered if Russ had been serious about returning for her; his knock on the door convinced her that he had. When she opened the door, she found him looking rested. He had shaved and looked more like his old self.

"Shall we get something to eat?" he asked stiffly.

Leigh didn't think she should go with him. They clearly had nothing of importance to say to each other. But what else was she to do? She didn't want to walk around in a strange town by herself, when it would soon be dark. She silently put on her parka and joined Russ outside the room, pulling the door tightly shut behind her.

Neither of them talked as they walked to the restaurant two blocks away. The large plastic snowflakes on the lampposts had been lit, looking slightly better than they had in the daytime, and they lent a soft white glow to the night. Leigh had no idea where she and Russ were going from here. Nowhere, probably.

They found a table in a corner of the small restaurant that had been recommended to Russ by the desk clerk at the motel, and without enthusiasm they ordered the daily special, which was meat loaf and fried potatoes. Leigh was staring out the window at a plastic snowflake when Russ spoke.

"I thought at first that I could never forgive you," he said. She turned startled eyes upon him. She hadn't expected him to talk about what was weighing so heavily on their minds.

"I don't expect forgiveness," she said in a strangled tone.

"But I have forgiven you," he said, and she stared at him in shock.

"I've had time to think about it since you told me, and I understand why you did what you did," he went on as she focused disbelieving eyes on his face. "In those times, under those circumstances, there was nothing else you could have done. Nothing else that would have made any sense, that is. I want you to know that I understand."

Her eyes filled with tears, and she looked down at her lap, unable to risk looking at him. If she did, she was sure that she would fall apart before his very eyes.

He reached across the table and put his finger to her cheek with a touch as delicate as a feather.

"Please look at me when I talk to you," he said gently.

She lifted her brimming eyes to his and saw through the blur of tears that he was smiling. She couldn't believe it. She felt as though under the circumstances, his goodwill toward her was completely unwarranted.

His expression was one of infinite compassion. "I cared about you when we were twenty, and in those days the world seemed as young as we were. It was all an illusion, wasn't it? The world was old and careworn, only we didn't know it. The irony is that we become that way, too, as we grow older. We take all the burdens of the world upon our own shoulders, and sometimes we become weary and blasé about everything," he said, watching her intently.

"I—" she began, but he said, "No, let me finish," and she subsided.

"The point is that I've felt like a new person since I've been with you. Christmas seemed like Christmas again, and everything was fresh and new and yet it felt comfortable and right. We belong together, Leigh, now as never before. I've discovered that I love you more than ever, and I love our daughter. I need you, and I need her. I hope you need me, too," he said. His eyes were bright, too bright, and she saw that they were swimming with tears.

As the realization dawned that he was serious, that he was not only serious but was pouring out his heart to her, she was rocked by a rush of gratitude so strong that she felt as though she were drowning in it. Her heart expanded to take it all in, and she knew that this was more than gratitude, it was a love so perfect and so right that it could never die, that it had never gone away completely but had slept dormant in her soul until she had found Russ again.

"I do need you," she whispered. "So much. So *much*." Her hand rose and met his over the table, and he slowly lowered their clasped hands to the tabletop.

"Where do we go from here?" she whispered, still only half believing, and he said, dispelling all doubt, "Wherever it takes us, Leigh. Wherever you want to go."

Chapter Fourteen

Later that night, a jubilant Dr. Miller told them that Wendy would be moved out of the ICU the next morning.

"And then?" Leigh asked.

"We'll watch her closely. She's making wonderful progress, but we don't want her to overdo it," he said.

After the doctor left, Leigh and Russ simply stood and held each other in the hall, sick with relief and weak with the knowledge that it could have been much, much worse.

Andrew, his spirits bolstered by the positive report, volunteered to sleep that night in the room that had been made up for Leigh down the hall.

"You'll sleep much better at the motel, and there's no need for all three of us to be here," he told her. "I'll relay any information you need to know."

Leigh hugged him, this man who was so capable, and turned toward Russ, her spirits lifting.

"Will you stay or go?" she asked.

"I'll go with you," he said promptly, and when Andrew had started to walk away, he said, "Always."

They slept in each other's arms that night as they had at The Briarcliff. In the night Leigh woke often and when she did, she always opened her eyes, half fearful that Russ wouldn't be there. Each time she was immensely relieved to find him there, his face serene in the light penetrating the thin motel curtains. Once he stirred briefly and muttered, "What's wrong?" and she said, "I can't believe how lucky I am," and he pulled her closer and nestled her head in the hollow of his shoulder.

The next morning when they were walking back to the hospital, Russ said suddenly, "We're going to miss the New Year's Eve celebration at The Briarcliff," and he said it as though the thought hadn't occurred to him before.

"Do you think I care?" she said, swinging their hands between them. She thought guiltily of the black sequined dress that she had ordered but had never tried on. She would pay for it, of course, and wear it sometime, but not this New Year's Eve, which was tonight.

At the hospital they went directly to Wendy's new room and found Andrew sitting beside her bed holding her hand. Wendy's smile was weak and she looked groggy, but she had eaten oatmeal for breakfast and was feeling stronger. Her huge head bandage had been replaced by a smaller gauze pad.

"Dr. Miller says I might even be able to start the semester on time if I keep improving at this rate," she said.

"Oh, I don't know," Leigh began, but she checked herself in time, when she realized that this decision wasn't hers to make.

During the intermittent times that Wendy was sleeping, Leigh and Russ walked the hospital corridors until Leigh thought she would gag on the hospital smell, and then they walked outside until they couldn't stand to look at downtown Kettiston anymore. For dinner, Russ went to a nearby fast-food restaurant and brought back a pizza for Leigh and Andrew and fried chicken for himself, and they all ate in Wendy's room.

"A lovely New Year's Eve dinner," Wendy said apologetically.

"Any dinner is a celebration when you're with people you love," Russ said, and he meant it.

Later, when Wendy had closed her eyes for a nap, Leigh told Russ, "I should call Katrina. And Bett. And a lot of other people who will want to know about Wendy and Andrew's accident."

"I called Bett this morning," Andrew supplied. "I phoned some of Wendy's and my friends from the university, too. A couple of them will probably drive over to see Wendy tomorrow, if she's feeling up to it."

Leigh went to phone Katrina, thinking again that Andrew seemed to have things well in hand. It was good to be able to give him some of the responsibility; he was someone to lean on, and for that she was grateful. She thought, not for the first time, that Wendy had chosen a good husband.

She left Russ talking with Andrew and Wendy and went to the hospital lobby where she found a pay phone. She punched in Katrina's Spartanburg number from memory.

Katrina was stunned when Leigh told her about Wendy's accident and quickly volunteered to do anything she could do to help.

"You have your hands full with your mother and her broken foot," Leigh said.

"True, but my cousin Ginger is visiting us for a couple of days, and she could stay with my mother. Would it help if I came to Kettiston?"

"Andrew is taking care of things quite well, and I have Russ. Thanks, Katrina, but I don't think it's necessary."

"How is Russ, Leigh?"

Leigh jiggled the change-return pocket in the pay telephone; there was nothing in it. "He knows," she said.

"He knows about Wendy?" Katrina asked sharply.

"It slipped out. It was awful, Katrina, just like you, in all your wisdom, warned me it would be. After we came to the hospital and saw Wendy linked up to all those machines, I was upset and kind of crazy, thinking I wanted to move Wendy out of this hospital, and Russ was doing his best to talk me out of it, but I wouldn't listen. And I just started screaming at him, and suddenly I said it," she said.

"And then what?" Katrina sounded awestruck.

"I thought he hated me. Then later we went out to dinner and he told me everything was okay. He loves me, and he loves Wendy. Only she doesn't know yet that he's her father."

"You'll tell her, I suppose," Katrina said.

"Not now. Not yet. She's not ready to hear it. She's curious about Russ and our relationship, though, so I think there will soon be a time when we can tell her naturally and easily. She likes him, which will make it easier."

"What about everyone else? Bett and Carson, my mother, Andrew's family? Will you tell them, too?"

"You know, Katrina, I think I've carried this burden too long. I'm going to leave it up to Russ and Wendy to help me decide things like that."

Katrina expelled a sigh. "Maybe that's good. Yes, I'd say you're making progress."

Leigh managed a rueful laugh. "Finally," she said.

"Tell Wendy I love her, and I'll call her when she feels more like talking. And tell Russ—" Katrina stopped in midsentence.

"Tell him what?"

"Tell Russ that this year, he'd better drink a cup of kindness for auld lang syne," Katrina said.

Leigh had talked to Katrina much longer than she had intended, but she called Bett, too, mostly to assure her that Wendy was recovering. By the time Leigh went back to Wendy's room, it had been dark outside for a long time. Andrew was sitting beside Wendy's bed, and he and Wendy were holding hands, clearly enjoying a quiet moment. Leigh stayed for only a short time; she felt as though she was intruding on their privacy. They were, she reminded herself, technically on their honeymoon.

"Do you know where Russ went?" she asked Andrew as she was preparing to leave.

"He said to tell you not to worry, that he'd be back as soon as he could," Andrew said.

Leigh hesitated in the corridor looking for Russ, but he was nowhere to be seen. People were beginning to arrive on the floor with paper-wrapped packages shaped suspiciously like bottles of champagne, probably to cheer their friends and relatives who were confined to the hospital on this festive night. At the nurses' station down the hall, someone had set out several plates of hors d'oeuvres.

"Have one," offered the smiling aide who was sitting at the desk, and Leigh did.

"We try to make it as much like a party as possible for patients who are here during the holidays," said a nurse who arrived and sat down with a pile of charts. Behind her a tiny Christmas tree with bulbs too big for its branches glittered in the glare of the fluorescent light overhead and a red-and-green banner proclaimed HAPPY NEW YEAR. Voices rose in the patient's room nearest the nurses' station, and Leigh realized that the people in there were having a party. Several people were singing,

> Should auld acquaintance be forgot,
> And never brought to mind...

but someone had trouble singing on key, and the song fell apart as everyone laughed.

Leigh felt very much alone and out of it; she wouldn't feel comfortable going back to Wendy's room, and she was tired of waiting for Russ in the drafty hall. The hospital chapel was located around the corner from this station, and she supposed she could duck in there for a few minutes.

"If Russ Thornton comes back, will you please tell him I'm in the chapel?" she asked the aide, who would recognize Russ because he had given her the leftover fried chicken and pizza that they couldn't eat, and the aide looked up from her paperwork and said that she would.

The chapel was blessedly quiet and warm, and stained-glass windows glowed in the light of several candles that someone had lit on the altar. Leigh slipped inside, tiptoed down the aisle and sat down in the first pew, relaxing, thinking. She was glad she had found this peaceful spot. Tonight, New Year's Eve, it was deserted.

She bowed her head and said a short prayer for Wendy and Andrew, thankful that the accident had not been any worse. She lifted her head sharply when she heard the door behind her open.

It was Russ. He walked down the aisle and sat beside her, taking her warm hand in his cold one. He was wearing his coat, and she realized that he must have recently come in from outside.

"Where have you been? I was beginning to wonder if something had happened to you," she said.

"I had an errand to do," he said, and she thought she detected a shred of mystery about the way he said it. "You weren't worried, were you?"

"A little. I keep thinking you're going to disappear."

"Never again," he said comfortably, squeezing her hand. "Where you go, I go. And I can promise you I'll never go as far away as Canada again."

"I wish you hadn't gone that far before," she said.

"So do I. Have I ever mentioned how much I missed you after I left?" he said fondly, looking down at her with serious eyes.

"Missed me? No, I don't think you ever told me that," she said.

"Oh, I thought about you twenty-four hours a day. I even telephoned your parents' house in Spartanburg shortly after you went back to Duke for the fall semester to ask the telephone number of your new dorm at school, and I was plunged into a state of despair when your father wouldn't give it to me."

"He wouldn't *what?*" Leigh said, staring at him in disbelief.

"Your father said you didn't want to talk to me, and that you didn't want to have anything to do with antiwar protesters. Afterward I felt like crawling under a rock someplace and eating worms."

"He never told me you called," Leigh said slowly. "I had no idea. And it wasn't true that I wouldn't talk to you. My father probably just didn't want me to see you." She remembered that she and Katrina had moved to a different dorm that year, and the number of the lobby phone had been a new one and was not listed in the telephone directory. It had caused them no end of inconvenience, but she'd never known that it had also cost her the chance to talk to Russ.

"I'd called the old dorm, but no one seemed to know or care about the number of your new dorm, and after someone walked away and left the phone hanging, I gave up. I thought your parents could give me the new number, so I called them. After your father told me that you didn't want to talk to me, I figured there was no point in trying to reach you again. Later I heard that you were married. Anyway," he continued, "that was a long time ago."

"A long time," she agreed, but she was incensed that her father had told Russ she hadn't wanted to talk to him. She'd had no idea that her father would take it upon himself to censor her relationships. Of course she had wanted to talk to Russ! Those were the days when she'd been scared and worried about her pregnancy; she would have given anything to have spoken with Russ for only a few minutes. If she had, maybe things wouldn't have turned out the way they did. Everything would have been different. Or would it? And hadn't she been happy? Hadn't she loved David? Had things worked out for the best, after all?

The chapel door hadn't closed properly when Russ had entered, and through the open door came the soft strains of the group down the hall singing "Auld Lang Syne." They'd added a few good singers; someone was attempting the harmony.

"That song always makes me feel nostalgic," Russ said, pulling her into the shelter of his arms.

"They were trying to sing it before, and they had to stop. This time I think they're getting it right," she said.

"There's something *I'd* like to get right," he said. He moved away slightly, and his eyes sparkled at her in the candlelight.

She watched him pull a velvet box from his coat pocket; her eyes grew round as he opened it. Inside was a ring; a huge brilliant-cut diamond winked up at her.

"For me?" she whispered.

"If you'll say yes," he said.

"Yes," she said without hesitation. "Yes, yes, yes!"

"I've been waiting most of my life to hear you say it," he said, and he slipped the ring on the third finger of her left hand.

"I would have said yes the first time you proposed, you know. I'd have married you in an instant," she said.

"It's funny about that," Russ said. "I wonder where the letter was for all those years."

Leigh smiled. "All I can tell you is that the mail carrier was one of those temporary postal workers that they hire for the holidays. He was short and fat and had a long white beard and—"

"If you're going to tell me he wore a red suit with white fur trim, I'm not going to believe you," Russ said.

"No, I'm not going to tell you that, but it does make you wonder, doesn't it?"

They laughed together, and he pulled her close again.

"I love you, Leigh," he said. "And now I have a daughter to love, too. It's a wonderful present, you know."

She smiled up at him, at his curly eyelashes, at his square jaw, at his sharp nose; Wendy's features in Russ's face. She slid her arms around his neck.

"Where did you get the ring?" she asked.

"I made the town's only jeweler desert the New Year's Eve preparations at his house and open the jewelry store. He grumbled a bit, but not after I told him our story. I hope you like the ring," he said.

"It's beautiful," she said. The ring Russ had chosen for her was gold, and the diamond was flanked by four channel-set baguettes, two on each side. The diamonds flashed and gleamed in the light from the candles on the altar.

"I bought a wedding ring, too," he told her. "When will you marry me?"

"As soon as I can. As soon as we've told Wendy," Leigh said.

"Told Wendy—?"

"That you are her father. We'll find a way," she said, strong in her conviction.

"The two of us will always find a way," he assured her, and then he kissed her, and in that moment she knew that nothing, nothing and no one, could ever keep them apart again.

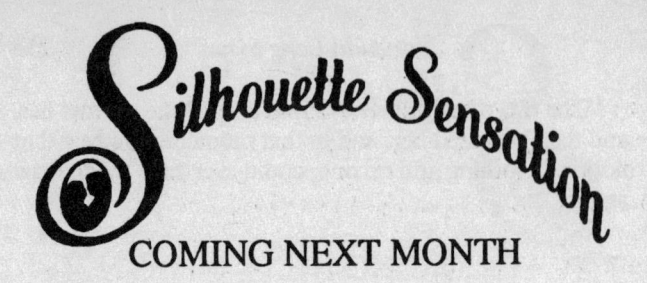

Silhouette Sensation

COMING NEXT MONTH

STEVIE'S CHASE
Justine Davis

The man who lived next door to Stevie Holt was a mystery. Tall and dark, he looked a little too menacing to be described as handsome. He didn't talk to anyone and clearly was not interested in making friends. But then, one day, Stevie gave him no choice. . .

It was hard to keep your distance from a bubbly, strawberry blonde who had broken into your apartment and was determined to nurse you. But Chase Sullivan didn't just look dangerous, he *was* dangerous—to anyone foolish enough to care about him. What was he running from?

OUT OF THE ASHES
Emilie Richards

The final story in Emilie Richards *TALES OF THE PACIFIC*

For Alexis Whitham, Australia's remote Kangaroo Island was the perfect place to begin a new life. Her young daughter would be safe from her ex-husband, safe in a new land with a new name.

But Jody brought a new man into Alexis's life—a man with a past just as tragic as her own. Matthew Haley had already loved and lost; he wasn't going to repeat himself!

Silhouette Sensation

COMING NEXT MONTH

THE ART OF DECEPTION
Nora Roberts

Adam Haines was visiting the Fairchild mansion under false pretences and he didn't like that. He liked to be straightforward and honest, but you didn't find a thief by declaring that you were an investigator. Moreover, you didn't get to sleep with the chief suspect's daughter if you told her you expected to have her father arrested!

The question was, was Kirby involved? If so, just how involved was she and could he compromise his ethics to save her?

CHARITY'S ANGEL
Dallas Schulze

Gabe London had been going to ask Charity Williams out but three, armed thieves prevented that. Suddenly, Gabe was a cop trying to control a hostage situation and prevent anyone being hurt.

But someone was hurt—Charity. And worse still, it was Gabe's bullet that injured her. The least he could do was offer her somewhere to recuperate. . .

Her lips were pink and soft and wet . . .

and, as he looked down at them, so inviting. He gazed into her eyes, those eyes that watched him, read him. He wondered if she saw everything.

"Well . . . good night," she whispered.

"Wait."

She didn't turn away, didn't back down, as he came as close as he could without touching her. He told himself to stop it now, that there was too much at stake, that if he let this happen again, there would be no more controlling his feelings.

"I want to kiss you," he said.

She felt his breath on her lips, and wet them again. "That's not a good idea."

"No," he said. "It isn't, is it?"

They looked at each other for what seemed a fragment of eternity. Then he lowered his face and his lips grazed hers, and before taking her completely, he whispered, "But I'm gonna do it anyway."

Dear Reader,

Season's Greetings!

The magic of Christmas has been captured in this special Silhouette collection. Read in *Second Chances* how the kidnapping of her young daughter forced Leah to seek out her embittered ex-lover. And how Bret in *Under the Mistletoe* was compelled to return home after receiving a long-lost mystery letter from his close friend, Dani. Our third seasonal novel, *For Auld Lang Syne*, celebrates a wedding at Christmas and we share in the warmth and hope which comes with the beginning of a New Year.

Join with us and celebrate Christmas – the season when wishes really *can* come true.

The Editors,
Silhouette Books,
Eton House,
18-24 Paradise Road,
Richmond,
Surrey.
TW9 1SR

TRACY HUGHES
Second Chances

SILHOUETTE BOOKS

*First published in Great Britain in 1992
by Silhouette Books, Eton House, 18-24 Paradise Road,
Richmond, Surrey TW9 1SR*

© Terri Herrington 1991

Silhouette Books and Colophon are
Trade Marks of Harlequin Enterprises B.V.

ISBN 0 373 58626 4

95-9211

Made and printed in Great Britain

Chapter One

Cassandra's life is worth two million dollars, to be delivered tonight. If you ever want to see her alive again, do not involve police and answer on first ring.

Leah Borgadeux wadded the damp, typewritten note in her trembling hand and bit her lip. She'd read it a thousand times since Casey had been snatched from her baby-sitter's yard over four hours ago, but each time she read it, her terror only heightened.

The noise of electronic equipment being set up in the corner of her small kitchen punctuated the cold reality of the nightmare that had her in its grip.

She stroked the threadbare baby blanket draped over her arm and hugged Casey's sticky old Bunny Fu-Fu to her chest. She closed her eyes and tried not to think about how lost the two-year-old would be tonight without these favorite items.

"Why don't they call?" she asked rhetorically, her voice hoarse from hours of near hysteria. "They said in the ransom note they would call."

"Pull yourself together," Lance Borgadeux said as he paced across the room, his large, intimidating frame dwarfing the tiny beach house. "They'll call."

She gave her father a cursory glance and remembered vividly why she had moved out from under his thumb before Casey was born, despite the fact that, ever since, he'd tried to paint Leah as insecure and irresponsible. The kidnapping was just one more piece of data in his "can't-take-care-of-herself" file.

"Of course they'll call," she echoed sarcastically. "They would never break their word to an almighty Borgadeux. Just because they snatched a two-year-old asthmatic baby from her sitter and left a two-million-dollar ransom note doesn't mean they'd break their word!"

"Calm down," her father replied. "They want the money. They'll call, damn it!" He turned back to one of the detectives. "Call a doctor. Get Leah a tranquilizer or something."

"I don't *need* a tranquilizer!" she shouted. "I need my baby! She's out there with God-knows-who—"

Her father caught her arms and shook her. "You're falling apart, Leah! You've got to stop this."

Leah pivoted out of his arms and shook her head. "No tranquilizers, Dad. Just make them find Casey."

"They will."

He came up behind her, turned her back around and pulled her into that rough, demanding hug that had been the benchmark of her security for most of her life. Long ago, she had stopped wondering if a mother's embrace would have been softer, more tender. Her mother had died in childbirth with Leah, leaving Leah with only the real-estate tycoon to parent her, and no basis for comparison. Until three years ago it had been enough.

But Leah hadn't known better then.

Slipping out of his arms, she walked to the open glass doors and out onto the deck that overlooked the Gulf, and tried to concentrate on the surf pounding against the shore. The ocean breeze whispered through her soft blond hair—hair that seemed so compatible with the sun and sea—but she couldn't feel the peace nor the healing that it usually offered.

"Maybe we can catch 'em before you 'ave to let go of the money." She looked over her shoulder to the three detectives her father had brought here with him. The one with the plaid tie and the Australian accent addressed her father instead of her. "We 'ave people working on it in the field right now."

Leah turned around and clutched the blanket and bunny tighter to her chest. "I don't care about the money," she said. "I don't want some idiot I don't even know jeopardizing my daughter's life. They said they'd kill her if they thought we'd gone to the police."

As if this was just another corporate game that wasn't going to ruffle him, Borgadeux put his arm around Leah's shoulder and escorted her back to the open doors. "No one's jeopardizing Cassandra's life, honey," he said in a quiet, condescending voice. "These are pros. I've used them over and over in my own business, and they're very discreet. The kidnappers will never know. But if you want to get Cassandra back, sweetheart, you'll have to cooperate with them.''

''Her name's Casey,'' Leah corrected, though she knew it hardly mattered now. ''I call her Casey, Daddy. Why won't you ever call her Casey?''

''Because it's a stupid name,'' he said. ''Cassandra is a beautiful name for a beautiful little girl.''

''You never give up,'' she said under her breath, a hopeless note of despair flattening her tone.

She moved away from him, stepped farther out onto the balcony and felt the cool wind blustering against her house. Yesterday it had been ninety-three degrees, not unusual for October in Florida. But today a cold front had moved in and the temperature had dropped to the seventies.

As always, with abrupt weather changes, Casey had awakened that morning congested and wheezing. Her theophylline, Ventolin and nebulizer treatments had stabilized her enough that Leah had felt safe keeping an appointment that afternoon. But once the medicine began to wear off around three, Casey was sure to have trouble breathing again. It was now five o'clock, and the thought of the little girl crying, coughing and wheezing was more than she could stand.

''She needs her medicine,'' she said aloud for the thousandth time that day. ''What if she gets really sick, and they panic and—''

''They won't. They'll call any minute now, we'll make the switch and you'll have Casey back.''

"Right." The hopeless word matched the look of doubt in her blue eyes as she gazed out over the Gulf. In the distance, the horizon was blurred with black clouds moving across the water. There was going to be a storm.

Already, it looked violent. Coastal storms always were. Lightning would perform its lethal show across the sky, the earth would shake, the sky would grumble. Electricity would flicker and, perhaps, go out altogether. And Casey would scream.

She brought the blanket to her eyes and tried to squeeze back the tears. It still smelled of the little toddler—baby powder, Tootsie Pops and Kool-Aid. She wished she'd followed the doctor's advice and broken Casey of that last bottle of the day months ago. At least that would be one less thing she'd expect. . . .

The thought of her baby's state of mind, now that she'd been in a stranger's hands for much of the day, made Leah's stomach knot and sink with nausea. Why didn't they call? Why couldn't they just tell her where to take the money and get it over with?

Ben, the detective who seemed in charge, stepped out onto the balcony and handed her a cordless phone. "They said t'answer on the first ring," he said, his soft accent momentarily distracting her from her terror. "Don't worry about us. Our equipment is all set t'start tracing the minute you answer. You'll want t' keep 'im on as long as you can. Tell 'im about the asthma and the medication she needs. Just keep 'im on."

She looked down at the phone, vaguely aware that her palm was sweating, making it difficult to hold. "Yes. All right."

He went to the railing of the deck, sat down and pulled a pencil out of his pocket. Flipping open his notepad, he made a notation, then glanced out over the water. "Storm's comin'. Hope it don't interfere with the telephone lines."

She swallowed and looked out toward the clouds again.

"Prob'ly won't," he added. "Listen, if you're up to it, I need t' ask a few more questions."

"Yes," she said. "Anything."

"Well we've already got people checking out everyone Casey sees from day to day, but I need ya t' rack your brain once more. Is there anyone you may 'ave left out? I know she's only two, but does she 'ave any friends she plays with on a regular basis? Any preschool teachers? Church nursery workers? Ballet instructors? Anyone who knows she's Lance Borgadeux's granddaughter and saw a quick buck to be made?"

Leah sat down on a patio chair and tried to steady her trembling hands. "I've already told you everyone I can think of. Since I left home and moved here, I haven't had a very high standard of living. Nothing to indicate my father's wealth. I don't think anyone here knows anything about the Borgadeux."

"Everybody knows about the Borgadcux," her father said, the pronouncement an aggravating combination of pride and long-suffering chagrin. "Everybody's suspect. Especially those who pretended not to know or care."

Frustrated, Ben jotted a few comments and shook his head. He seemed to hesitate on the next question, and he shot Borgadeux a tentative look. "Mr. Borgadeux, I know this next question won't meet with your approval—"

"Then don't ask it."

Leah snapped a look at her father. "What question?"

"I *'ave* t'ask," Ben said, still addressing her father. "If I didn't, I'd be overlooking a vital area that could 'elp us crack this—"

"What vital area?" She turned from her father to Ben, appalled. "This is *my* child we're talking about. *Mine.* If you have something to ask me, you ask it. And, Daddy, you have no right to stop him!"

"He wants to ask about the child's father, Leah!" her father bellowed. "I told him to leave him out of this—"

She swung back to the detective. "Her father didn't have anything to do with this, but damn it, *my* father had no right to stop you from asking."

She walked to the edge of the deck, trying to steady her breathing, and told herself that her father's manipulation was nothing new. He had successfully convinced her to walk out on Jeff over two and a half years ago, and she hadn't forgiven him for it yet. Now he thought he could manipulate the factors of the investigation just as he'd always manipulated the factors of her life.

The sky grew darker, and a few drops of rain began to fall. She made no move to go in. "Casey's father's name is Jeff Hampton. He lives in Tampa."

Ben scribbled the name on his pad. "Miss Borgadeux, I know this is painful for you, but we have t' know more about 'er father. In the case of two parents living apart, it's not unusual for a kidnapping t'occur.''

Leah twirled one of the bunny's ears around her finger and drew her brows together in a frown that bore more remorse than she'd ever known what to do with. "It would be unusual in this case," she said quietly. "He doesn't even know Casey exists. And I prefer to keep it that way."

Ben intercepted Borgadeux's I-told-you-so look and rose to face her. "Look, Miss Borgadeux, I understand your desire for discretion, for whatever reason, but suppose... just suppose... that the father discovered 'e 'as a child and decided to get revenge for your keeping it a secret. We 'ave to at least consider that possibility."

"Jeff isn't vindictive like that," she whispered. "He would never do anything like this."

"But 'e could 'ave found out. Dunedin isn't more than twenty minutes from Tampa. He could have seen you with Casey, or heard about her from a mutual friend. He could have—"

"He would have confronted me if he heard," she said with certainty. "He would have come to me."

"People change. They get bitter. Angry. Sometimes they don't react to things the way we think they will."

Leah wiped a stray tear off her face with the blanket, and tried to sort out the rhymes and reasons in her head. A drop of rain fell onto the ribbon edging the quilting, drawing her attention to a stain there. She wondered where it had come from. Had Casey dragged the blanket through the dirt at the park again?

"She said to leave him out of it," Borgadeux said, his powerful voice quieting the detective. "He doesn't have anything to do with this. He's gone this long without knowing about Cassandra. Just because she was kidnapped is no reason to drag him into it now."

The rain began to drizzle harder, but Leah still made no attempt to go inside. Neither Borgadeux nor Ben made a move to leave the deck, either.

"He'll find out now anyway, y'know," the detective pointed out. "When this is all over, regardless of the turnout, it'll be all over the media. Whether he was involved in it or not, he'll know then."

"He won't know Casey's his," Borgadeux said.

Leah snapped her gaze to her father, astounded. "Yes, he will. I wasn't sleeping around, Daddy. I was in love with him. I would have married him—" Her voice cracked midsentence, and she turned away.

The rain was falling harder now, and she could see the lightning moving closer. In moments they would hear its thunder and feel its wrath on her home. As much as she wanted to stand out here and let the cool rain wash away her mistakes and regrets, as much as she wanted to defy the sky and dare the lightning, she couldn't.

That would be as foolhardy, as devastating, as bringing Jeff in on this now.

She heard the door slide open, and her father tapped her arm. "We'll talk about it inside," he said.

"You and Ben go on in," she said. "I'll be right there."

"Don't wait too long, honey. The storm's getting ugly."

She nodded and watched the power of the lightning, still miles away on the water. It wouldn't take long to reach her. It never did.

It had been raining and thundering the day she'd left him, and now, as a fissure of lightning split the sky in the distance, she recalled when she'd told him it was over. His wet black hair had waved and slapped against his head, as if demonstrating the pain and anger she had seen in the obsidian depths of his eyes. And he'd had a right to be angry. Anyone would.

"You love me," he had pleaded, as though reminding her could wipe away the inevitable heartache she seemed so bent on inflicting. "I know you love me."

She had wanted to fall into his arms and scream yes, that she loved him. But her love was a weapon...a destroyer that brought ruin to those who had the misfortune of loving her back.

Images of her mother's face had danced like a phantom across her heart. The face had been an image she had only seen in photographs since Leah had never known her mother. Images of the dog she had loved, the dog who had gotten too rough in their play and had bitten her. Her father had gotten rid of it that very afternoon. Images of the nanny she had loved, the only woman who had molded her and cared for her and influenced her—too much, according to her father, who had fired her and refused to give references to account for the four years she had devoted to Leah.

Everyone who had ever loved her had met with misfortune...and regardless of how her father's hand had always helped it along, the threat remained real.

And then her father had handed down one of his famous ultimatums, at a time when Jeff was on the threshold of taking his contracting business from breaking even to breaking records. The contract on the Suncoast Dome in St. Petersburg had been all but his after years of hard work, but her father had the contacts and the means to destroy that dream, ruin his reputation and break the man.

Unless she refused to marry him and never saw him again.

Those were the things playing through her mind that day she had left him. So she had carried out the charade of fickle rich girl who didn't care about him anymore, and had aptly convinced him that it was over.

But neither of them had known then that she was pregnant.

Weeks later, when she learned that she was carrying his child, she had searched her soul and found that she didn't have the strength to keep this secret from him. Wouldn't a baby fill the void that a foiled business would cause? Together, couldn't they weather that storm? Wasn't this baby worth any fight?

But the questions had never been answered, for Jeff, so steeply entrenched in bitterness and hatred for her, had refused to take her repeated calls. When she'd tried to see him, he'd slammed the door in her face. Letters she'd sent had come back unopened.

Finally, she had accepted that the baby was hers alone, and she had moved away from her father's es-

tate, determined not to let him force any more ultimatums on her. She had hoped to never need him
again.

But she'd never counted on Casey being kidnapped.

Somehow, that changed things. She needed for Jeff
to know about Casey. She needed to be purged of that
sin for which she was certain she was being punished.

She went back inside, realizing only now that she
was soaked clear through to her skin. A shiver coursed
through her.

"I'll do whatever it takes to get Casey back," she
told Ben. "And if you think contacting her father will
help, then I'll go along with it."

"But, Leah! You're opening a Pandora's box.
You'll regret it!"

She didn't look at her father as Ben shoved the
notebook into his coat pocket. "Willy and I'll go
question 'im now, and Jack can stay in case we 'ear
from the kidnappers. We'll have t' take your Jaguar,
Mr. Borgadeux, since we didn't come in our own car.
If the 'ouse is being watched, they'll just think one of
you is leaving. They won't see us through the tinted
windows."

"Wait."

Ben turned back to her, and she saw relief draining
the tension from her father's face. He thought she was
going to back down, she mused.

New tears pushed to blur her vision as she stepped
toward the detective. "Could you . . . could you question him without telling him everything? I mean . . .
could you let me . . . ?"

"Let you what?" the confused detective asked. "Question 'im?"

"No," she said, her voice wobbling. "Let me tell him who Casey is. I want to be the one to tell him."

"Honey, don't do that to yourself," Lance said, coming to her side. "If they have to question him, let them do it and be done with it. It's none of his business."

"None of his business?" she asked her father, half laughing in disbelief. "He's her father. I don't think for a minute he could have taken her. But if he did find out, he'd have every right to want revenge. Besides . . ." Her voice trailed off, and she felt that defeated horror wash over her again. "I need to see him. I *need* to tell him. I've waited too long already."

"But he'll hurt you again. Just like the last time."

Leah looked fully at her father for the first time since he'd walked in here today with a briefcase full of money. And all the old anger came rushing back to remind her why she'd left home in the first place. "He didn't hurt me, Daddy. I hurt him, remember?"

And there was nothing Lance Borgadeux could say. For he remembered it well.

THE MEMORIES CAME RUSHING back to Jeff with confusing clarity the moment the gold Jaguar with plates bearing the name *Borgy 1* drove up to the trailer on the work site where he kept his office. From the scaffold on the fourth-floor level of what was to be the new home of the Sunshine Bank, he watched two men get out, look around, then start inside the trailer.

They were looking for him. He knew it instinctively, for he had never forgotten the way Borgy's "people" had tailed and harassed and bribed him before, when he'd been determined to marry Leah. But that was all history, and they had gotten what they wanted. He couldn't imagine what they wanted with him now.

Not anxious to find out, he stayed where he was. If they were to meet their deadline on this building, he couldn't lose one man-hour right now. Even if it was his own. They had all committed to working every daylight hour to complete the job, and from the looks of the sky, a storm would break soon, forcing them to quit for the day, anyway. Until it reached them, they had to move forward. That dedication to finishing the job was why he was so successful. He had the best crew in Tampa Bay, and he was a hands-on builder who saw his projects through to the very end. It might not look so good to a man who wanted only "the best" husband for his daughter...someone who spent his days philosophizing in an executive think tank, and drove a Jaguar with eighteen-carat gold trim...but it was what Jeff had chosen to do. It was good that he liked it, he mused cynically, because for the last two and a half years, it was all he'd had.

He glanced back toward the car and decided to let Jan handle them. He'd lost enough time on Borgadeux, he thought. The last thing he needed was to dredge up those old, buried memories again.

Bending down on one knee, he checked the bolts on the steel frame, and put the car and its passengers out of his mind. Jeff concentrated on wrapping his work up before the storm hit.

INSIDE THE TRAILER, Jeff's sister and secretary, Jan Hampton, gave her best shot at questioning the two detectives before they could question her brother.

"Just tell me one thing and I'll show you where he is," the woman said, running long fingers through her short-cropped raven hair and assessing the Australian carefully. "Tell me what two detectives would have to question him about. He hasn't done anything wrong."

"Maybe 'e has, maybe 'e ain't," Ben countered. "No way to tell till we talk to 'im."

"Where are you from?" Jan asked. "England?"

Ben snickered. "No, I ain't from bloody England. I 'ail from Australia. Now are you gonna show us where we can find 'im, or do we 'ave to—"

"Australia." Jan leaned back against her desk and crossed her arms. "How do I know I can trust some foreigner carrying a gun?"

"I ain't carryin' a gun, lady," Ben said.

"But he is," she said, undauntedly opening the coat of the man standing beside him. Willy slapped his hand over his pistol and straightened his jacket, indignant.

"I'll ask again. How can I trust a couple of pistol-packing foreigners looking for my brother?"

"Damn it, we'll find 'im ourselves," Ben said, starting back for the door.

"Good luck," she said. "There are eighty other men out there. And they get real quiet when strangers start asking questions."

Ben threw a look back over his shoulder to Willy. "Go back to the car, Willy, and radio for reinforcements. We're going to 'ave to use force, I guess."

Jan's eyebrows shot up. "Reinforcements? That won't be necessary." She pointed out the window. "He's up there, on the scaffold. Geez, you people. A girl tries to protect her brother from a couple of Dick Tracy clones, and you start threatening her."

The two detectives opened the door and started out, and Jan followed close on their heels. "Hey, you guys aren't gonna arrest him or anything without telling him what he did, are you? You can't do that, can you?"

Without answering, the detectives started toward the scaffold.

IT WAS JUST STARTING to drizzle when Jeff saw the two men coming toward him, and heaving a sigh and wondering what the hell was up, he made his way down and started toward them.

Jan trailed behind them, a look of distress on her face, but that was nothing unusual, he mused. Her feathers were always ruffled about something. The detectives wore a look of dead seriousness, and Jeff couldn't imagine why they'd be looking for him on old Borgy's behalf. Jeff had done what Borgadeux had wanted and let his daughter go over two and a half years ago. What else did the man want?

"You looking for me?" Jeff asked as he reached the men.

"They threatened me," Jan cut in. "One of them's carrying a gun."

Jeff gave them a slight frown, then glanced over his shoulder to see if any of his crew around him had heard. None seemed particularly interested in the conversation, for most were hurrying to reach stopping points before the sky opened up. "What's going on?" he asked in a quieter voice.

Again, Jan piped in before Ben could answer. "They're detectives, Jeff."

"Detectives?" He started to laugh, and shaking his head, pushed past them into the trailer. The men followed him.

"That's great," he said. "Detectives. Again. Isn't the jerk satisfied that I don't want anything of his? What kind of dirt is he looking for this time?"

Ben gave Willy a confused look, then took out his ID and flashed it. "Look, mate, I don't know what the 'ell you're talkin' about, but we're 'ere to question you about your whereabouts earlier today."

Jeff walked to the sink, set his hard hat on the rim, and began washing his hands. "That's easy. I've been here all day."

"Can you confirm that?" Ben asked.

"*I* can," Jan interjected. "He's been here since seven this morning and hasn't left all day."

"Anybody else around who can confirm it, mate?" Ben asked, ignoring her. "No offense, lady, but you ain't what I call a credible witness."

Jan started to object, but Jeff stopped her. "Help yourself," he said, drying his hands. "There's a whole team of guys out there who can vouch for me. I haven't left here all day."

"Guess 'e's clean, then," Ben said, glancing at his cohort with disappointment. "Willy, go on out and confirm 'is alibi."

The quieter detective started out of the trailer, and Ben looked at the scuffed floor and cleared his throat. "Uh, I'm sorry, mate, but I need you to come with me for an hour or so. Won't take long, but my orders are to bring you in for some . . . er . . . some questioning."

"About what? And what do you mean, check out my alibi? What do I need an alibi for?"

"I'll tell you when we get there. Come on now. It's easier if you come peaceful."

Jeff glanced at his sister. "Do you believe this guy?" He shook his head at the detective. "Tell old Borgy that he can't send his thugs out to pick me up at a whim. I'm not going."

"Then we'll have to take you by force. And all your crew 'll see their boss in 'andcuffs at gunpoint. Wouldn't look too good, eh?"

"You've gotta be kidding."

"No, joke, mate. I don't want to do it that way. I'd rather you just come with us for an hour or so, and we'll bring you right back 'ere."

Jeff set his hands on his hips and stared at the man, realizing he was dead serious. Finally, he unhooked his tool belt and handed it to Jan. "All right, I'll go and get this damn thing over with. It's Borgadeux's car they came in," he said. "Maybe I'll get the chance to bash the jackass's face in."

"Borgadeux?" Jan asked, still holding the tool belt. "I can't believe this. Does it have anything to do with Leah? Because if it does, Jeff, I hope I don't have to remind you that she dumped you. You spent a year scraping yourself up off the ground after she trampled all over you."

"Don't worry. I'm immune. She's like a disease you only have once. It can't get you twice."

The rain began to come harder, pounding on the aluminum roof of the trailer. Slinging down the towel, he started to the door.

"Jeff, please be careful."

Jeff's sarcastic smile held no joy as he looked back over his shoulder. "With Borgy or Leah?"

"Leah," his sister said. "You can handle that slimeball father of hers. But she's charmed your pants off before."

"I told you. I'm immune. I'm not the same person."

"But she is," Jan said.

"That's just the thing," he said. "I never really knew who that was."

Jeff started out into the rain, now pounding hard on the dirt, and Ben followed him. Already the structure had cleared and his crew were dispersing and heading for the cars and trucks lined behind the trailer. Some of the men who Willy had approached were now standing near the car, watching with curiosity.

"Alibi checks out," Willy said, dashing through the rain to the back door of the car. He opened the door and took Jeff's arm to urge him in.

"Get your hands off me!" Jeff told him. "Touch me again and I'll break your neck."

"Sorry." Willy raised his hands innocently and went around the car to the passenger side as Jeff got in.

"Look, nobody wants to hurt you," the detective in the front said as he started the car. "You've got a solid alibi, so you obviously had nothin' t' do with the kidnappin'. We just 'ave to take you in to—"

"Kidnapping?" He leaned forward in the seat and glared at Ben. "What kidnapping?"

"Never mind, mate."

By the way the man had shut up, Jeff wondered if it had been a slip. Kidnapping. He sat back, frowning out the black-tinted window, and tried not to dwell on that word.

Was it Leah? Had someone abducted her?

An irrational, maddening, self-betraying fear skidded up inside him as images of terrorists, of murderers, of rapists holding her at their mercy flashed like freeze-frames in his mind. Could they appreciate more than the dollar signs that hovered over her like a manmade halo? Would they hurt her?

He cleared his throat, swallowed. "Look, pal. I have a right to know." His voice sounded foreign, hollow. "When was she kidnapped? Where was she?"

Via the rearview mirror, he saw the condemning look pass from the driver to Willy.

"Did we say it was a 'she?'" the Aussie asked. "I don't remember sayin', do you, Willy?"

"Nope. Neither of us said."

"Give me a break." Jeff bracketed his hands over the seat in front of him and leaned forward again. "You questioned *me* about it. You picked me up in one of the Borgadeux chariots. You tell me someone's been kidnapped. Who the hell else could it be but Leah?"

"Try Cassandra, mate," the driver said. "Cassandra Borgadeux."

A flood of relief washed over Jeff as he sat back in his seat. Cassandra. Not Leah. He didn't know a Cassandra Borgadeux. Probably a cousin or aunt or something, he thought. But not Leah.

He stroked his lip with his rough, tanned index finger, and for the first time noted beads of sweat there, despite the air conditioning that filled the car. Damn it, why had he let the thought of Leah in danger shake him that way? She had chosen to lead the life of the pampered heiress, and had discarded him like trash.

He could never forget that.

They reached the Courtney Campbell Causeway that would take them from Tampa into Clearwater, and over the bay he saw darker clouds billowing in angry orchestration. Bolts of lightning cracked across the sky, and thunder shook the earth. There had been a storm the day she'd left him, he recalled. A storm much like this one, brilliant and magnificent in its force and power, but that brilliance could also be deadly and devastating.

His heart twisted at the bittersweet memory of the woman who had pierced his heart over two and a half years ago, and he wondered if he was about to see her. God, he hoped not. The last thing he needed in his life right now was Leah Borgadeux bringing him to his knees again.

So a Borgadeux had been kidnapped, and he was a suspect, he thought bitterly. Why not? He'd been guilty of the sin of falling in love with the Borgadeux heiress, and for that, he supposed, he deserved to pay some sort of penance. As if he hadn't already.

The storm grew more violent as they reached Clearwater, and he wondered how the Australian could see through the drenched glass. The windshield wipers worked furiously but the rain pounded too hard. The idea that he had gotten into Borgadeux's car with two of his thugs, and was sitting quietly while they drove him into the worst part of the storm, for some unknown reason and some unknown destination, enraged him.

"If you don't let me contact my lawyer the minute we get where we're going," he shouted over the noise of the storm, "I swear to God I'll slap you with the biggest lawsuit you've ever seen."

"Just sit tight," the detective called over his shoulder. "You're in no trouble. You won't need a lawyer."

"Then what the hell is all this about?" Jeff asked. "You know, I could charge *you* with kidnapping! That is, if we don't get washed away by the storm."

He saw the sweat beading on Ben's brow as he tried to negotiate the Friday-evening traffic that the storm had done nothing but convolute even further. "Look, mate, I'd appreciate it if ya could shut up until I get us to Dunedin. This ain't no picnic, and if anything 'appens to this car, Borgadeux'll 'ave my ass."

"What's in Dunedin?" Jeff pressed, refusing to let up. "The Borgadeux live in Tampa."

They came to a traffic jam on Highway 19, one of the main arteries through Pinellas County, and Ben began massaging his temples. "There's somebody who wants t'talk t'ya," he said. "That is, presuming we ever get through this bloody 'ell t'get there."

"Well, if it's anybody in the Borgadeux family, male or female, I'll pass."

"No, ya won't. I ain't goin' through this for nothin'."

Jeff sat back and tried to rack his brain for some clarity. It was Leah who had sent for him, he told himself, even though it seemed more her father's way to have him dragged in like this. But what on earth would either of them want with him now?

Something to do with this kidnapping, he told himself, and he had to admit to some degree of curiosity.

They turned west on Curlew Road as the storm continued to rage around them. It was a bad one, he thought, unlike the isolated electrical storms they usually had in Florida. They reached the bridge cutting across the Gulf to Dunedin Beach and Honeymoon Island, and he sat up straighter.

A crack of lightning split the sky directly over them, its thunder coming simultaneously, as Ben slowed the Jaguar and pulled into the driveway of a small beach house behind a cluster of condominiums.

Ben opened the garage with a remote control, slipped the car in beside a minivan, and looked back over the seat as the door closed behind them. "Look, just cooperate for a few minutes, okay? You'll understand it all soon enough."

Wary of the whole situation, Jeff got out of the car and looked around him. "Whose house is this?"

"You'll see," Ben said, and started up the stairs to the door.

Lance Borgadeux opened the door, and his eyes shot with hateful arrogance to Jeff, as if he'd have liked nothing better than to beat the hell out of him for having had the gall—someone as low as him—to love his daughter. The feeling was mutual.

"Well, if it isn't old Borgy himself," Jeff said, feeling a new power now that he no longer cared what the man thought of him. He had nothing left to lose. "Long time no see."

Borgadeux didn't answer. Instead, as if for once he wasn't in control of things, he crossed his arms and looked toward the living room as Jeff came into the kitchen.

"His alibi checked out," the detective was saying. "But we brought 'im anyway, like she said."

Jeff looked past Ben into the living room, waiting for whatever—whyever—they had brought him here to be revealed. Leah stood there, her face paler than he'd ever seen it, her eyes swollen as if she'd just spent a lot of time crying and her blond hair disheveled and sticking to her damp face. But damn it all, she was still just as beautiful as the day she'd left him. He steeled himself for whatever was to come, and honestly wondered if he was ready for it. Under his breath, he muttered a curse and turned back to the kitchen.

"Jeff." Her voice was raspy with emotion.

Slowly, he turned back around, disgust distorting his face.

"What do you want?" he asked through stiff lips.

"I . . . I have to talk to you," she said. She looked past him, to the other men standing around him.

"Would you all please leave us alone for a few minutes? We have to talk alone."

"What happened, Leah?" he asked, not waiting for them to clear the room. "Did you convince your father that I wasn't worthless? Did you tell him to track me down and drag me back for another shot?" The cruel comment seemed to drain her more than he'd expected, and he almost regretted saying it. Almost.

Her father pushed through the others, his face a study in controlled rage. "Leah, please. You don't have to do this."

"Alone, Daddy," Leah said again, though the determined word came on a flat monotone. "I'll call you when we're finished."

The door to the kitchen closed behind Jeff, and their eyes met and held for a painful stretch of eternity. She was still fragile, he thought. Still so breakable. And damn it, so was he.

He waited, but she made no move to speak, and finally his eyes fell to the blanket she had wadded under her arm, and the worn-out bunny she held against her chest. He met her eyes again, desperate and despairing, and forced himself to ask.

"What am I doing here, Leah?" The question came out impatiently, but some niggling panic began to rise up inside him as the second question came to his lips. "Who is Cassandra Borgadeux, and why the hell did they think I kidnapped her?"

Leah held herself still for a moment, and he thought she would never answer. Finally, she drew in a deep, quick sob. "She's my daughter," she whispered, almost too low to hear. "And you, Jeff . . . You're her father."

Chapter Two

For a moment, the words refused to sink in, and Jeff stood staring at her, his face blank and pale. Finally, slowly, the realization washed over him.

"What the hell are you talking about?" The question came out on a raspy whisper, and he took a step closer to her.

Tears crept into Leah's eyes. "I call her Casey. She's two years old, Jeff, and she looks like you, and she's the—"

Jeff held out a hand to stem the stream of information that seemed so incongruous, so unexpected, and reached out to a chair to steady himself. His face reddened, and his words shredded through tight lips. "Are you telling me...that you had a baby? *My* baby?"

Crumpling beneath the question, Leah brought the blanket to her face. "I'm so sorry, Jeff. I tried to tell you. You wouldn't take any of my calls."

"That was because you dumped me!" he shouted. "You didn't tell me you were pregnant!"

"I didn't know then," she shouted back. "Jeff, I found out after I left you. But by then you hated me...."

Her words seemed to blur into some unintelligible whirlwind of memories and pains that circled through Jeff's mind like a tornado ready to sweep him out of existence. He shook his head, remembering her expressionless face when she'd ended things with him, the countless calls he'd refused to take, the endless, sleepless nights. He looked up at her and saw that her tears were flowing harder. "So that let you off the hook? A few foiled attempts to contact me? For God's sake, Leah, you could have left a message! I would have answered if I'd known you were pregnant! Was that too easy for you?"

"I couldn't do it that way!" she screamed. "I tried to tell you in person, myself, but finally I convinced myself that it was better if you didn't know!"

"Better for who, Leah? The baby? Am I some horrible monster that has to be kept from my child?"

"No!"

"Was it better for you, then? Better for your almighty father? Would it have cramped your style to admit to your child that her father was a man with calluses on his hands?"

"No! I was confused and hurt and panicked! I didn't want to hurt anymore!"

"And it's always easier to fall back into your father's cushy prison, isn't it, Leah, and the big bad world just goes away?"

"No, Jeff! You've got it all wrong. It wasn't that way."

"Wasn't it?"

"No! I haven't lived with my father since I was pregnant. I live here, alone with Casey. I support myself and it's not always easy and cushy. And if you look around, you'll see that the only thing that's gone away is my *daughter! That's* the benefit of being a Borgadeux, Jeff. And I never asked for it!"

The rage and emotion and terror behind her words stunned him, and at once the reason for his being brought here hit him full force.

"Kidnapped." The word rolled from his lips on a note of horror, and he stepped toward her and grabbed her arms. "Your baby...*my* baby. She's been kidnapped?"

"Yes!" Leah's own terror distorted her face, and he felt her trembling beneath his touch as she clung tighter to the blanket and worn bunny. "She was snatched from the baby-sitter's this afternoon, and the kidnappers left this ransom note. That's why my father's here. I don't have that kind of money—"

Jeff let go of her, his rough release making her stumble back. He snatched up the note and read the fateful words that had been glued onto the page like something in a B movie. The words were filled with venom that could mean the end of his daughter. The daughter he'd never even seen.

His heart rate sped to an all-time high, and he sank onto a couch, dropped his face into his hands. A daughter. His daughter. Kidnapped.

A misty glaze filled his eyes when he ran his fingers down his face and looked up at Leah again. "How long has she been gone now?"

"About six hours," she whispered. "And she doesn't have her blanket...and she has asthma. She needs medication, Jeff. She must think I abandoned her.... She must be terrified...and this damn storm..."

He swallowed and tried to calm his whirling thoughts, quiet his tumultuous emotions. "What... what are they doing? Is anybody looking for her? Have they questioned anyone?"

"Of course," she whispered. "That's how you got into this, remember?"

He didn't answer, but reached out and took the bunny from her hands. He looked down at it, saw the worn fur and the dirty whiskers, and a newer, more profound sense of loss than he'd ever felt washed over him. "Why did you decide to tell me now?" he whispered without looking at her. "You could have just had me questioned without letting them tell me."

"You would have gotten curious. You would have found out." She swallowed, and a sobbing moan sounded in her throat. "Besides, I needed for you to know. I'm so scared...." Her words broke off on a sob, and he brought his eyes back up to hers. But he didn't comfort her.

"Look, I don't expect anything of you," she said when she could speak again. "Casey and I are doing fine on our own. Nothing really has to change because you know."

His expression grew harder, more strained, but still he only stared at her, clutching the bunny in his hands.

The door to the living room opened, and Lance Borgadeux stepped inside, not hiding the fact that he'd listened to every word of their conversation. "Now you know, Hampton. You're free to go now. My people will drive you back."

"The hell they will." Jeff met Borgadeux's eyes across the room, his as steady and unwavering as the tycoon's. "I'm staying here."

"Oh, no, you're not." Borgadeux started toward him, but Jeff came to his feet, undauntingly facing him. "You're not needed here anymore. We're in the middle of a crisis, and the last thing we need is you hanging around—"

"Daddy, stop it," Leah cut in.

"I'm staying if I have to break somebody's neck to do it!" Jeff bit out, his eyes reflecting his willingness to do just that.

"Is that a threat?" Borgadeux asked, amused. "Are you threatening me?"

"Take it anyway you want, pal. You had me dragged here against my will, remember? And now you spring this little revelation on me as an afterthought, and I'm supposed to run along back home like nothing ever happened?"

"If you want me to use force, Hampton, I have three capable detectives in there who can do it."

"Stop it!" Leah came between her father and the father of her child. "If Jeff wants to stay, he can stay. He has every right."

"To do what?" her father demanded. "Hang around here and get in the way?"

"I'm staying," Jeff said through his teeth again, his voice quivering with rage. "I've just been told that I have a daughter, and that she's been kidnapped. At the moment, I'd think you'd have more important things on your mind than me. If not, then maybe I should make a few calls and get my own detectives working on the case."

"That won't be necessary." Borgadeux took a step backward, breathed a heavy, long-suffering sigh and gave in. "All right, Hampton, you stay. But if you start to get in the way or upset my daughter any more than she already is, so help me God, I'll throw you out of here myself."

"And when you start getting in the way and upsetting your daughter, do I get to throw *you* out, Borgy?"

Again, Leah stepped between them. "Dad, just let it go, all right? We have to concentrate on Casey. She's the most important thing right now."

"Yeah." Her father started toward the door, where the detectives were waiting for him to call them to his aid, but he didn't remove his threatening eyes from Jeff. "I suppose what Leah needs right now is a nice little distraction, anyway. You're good for that, if nothing else."

The hateful comment hit its mark, silencing Jeff, and he turned his cold eyes back to Leah as her father left the room.

For a moment, they stared at each other, her eyes still wet with tears, her hands still shaking as she clutched the blanket.

"Just for the record," Jeff said in a steady, controlled monotone, "I'm not staying here to butt egos with your father, or to comfort you, or to distract you. I'm staying here because I have a little girl who I've never even met, who's in the hands of God-knows-what right now. And despite how you'd like for me to go along as if nothing has happened, I can't walk out of this now."

"I know that," she whispered. She went to the piano in the corner, to the framed picture of the little girl, and brought it back to him. Tears filled her eyes again. "I'd give anything if I could hand her to you, and introduce you and let you see how beautiful and wonderful she is. But all I have for now is a picture."

His lips trembled, and he wet them and took the picture. His brows came together as he stared at it, and she saw the fine mist forming in his eyes. Slowly, he dropped back to the couch and pinched the bridge of his nose. "I'll never forgive you for this, Leah," he whispered.

"I don't expect you to."

Not taking much comfort in her response, he let his eyes fall back to the picture in his hand, to the image of the little package of life with sunshine and rainbows in her eyes. He had already missed two years—the most crucial ones, according to psychologists—and now she was a little lady with a personality, a vocabulary, likes and dislikes. But he didn't know what any of them were.

Bonding…it was a word that had meant little to him a few hours ago. Now it meant the world…for he had missed doing so with his daughter.

But as he set down the picture and looked at the bunny again, the reality of what had brought him here hit home once more. Some stranger had taken his child.

Suddenly an urgency like he had never known washed over him. He looked up at Leah, and saw the terror swimming just beneath the surface of her eyes. And he shared it.

The phone rang, startling them both, and Leah punched the On button to the cordless phone and quickly brought it to her ear. In the kitchen, the recording equipment switched on and the three detectives began trying to trace the call by way of their cellular phones.

"Hello?" Her voice quivered.

"Leah? Have you found her yet? What's going on?"

Letting out a disappointed breath, Leah put her hand over the receiver. "It's just Anna, Casey's babysitter."

She watched Jeff wilt, then get up from the sofa and walk into the kitchen, where every word of the conversation was being taped, anyway. From the speaker on the recorder, he could hear the conversation.

"Leah? Are you there?"

Leah went back to the phone. "Yes, Anna, I'm here. And no, we haven't found her. We thought you might be the kidnapper."

She heard a sob on the other end of the connection, and instantly imagined Anna with wet, swollen eyes and her fingers forever plowing through her red curls. "I can't believe this," she cried. "I can't believe this could happen. Anna, I hadn't given her her afternoon dose of theophylline when they took her. What if—"

Leah's face contorted, and again, she brought the blanket to her face.

"Please," Anna said, "can't I come over and wait this out with you? You shouldn't be alone...."

"I'm not alone." Her eyes collided with Jeff's as he stood in the kitchen doorway; and she saw the coldness in them and shivered. "Besides, I want someone to be home at your house. Since that's where they got her...."

Her voice trailed off as the possibility that it had all been a mistake, that they had taken the wrong child, that they might not even know where to contact her, flitted through her mind.

"All right," Anna said with a shaky sigh. "Please, just keep me informed, huh? I can't stand this. I feel so responsible."

Leah closed her eyes and tried to stifle the memory of her reaction that afternoon when she'd first confronted Anna after being told about the kidnapping.

How could you be so irresponsible? How could you let a strange man put my baby in his car? It's all your fault!

Instead of defending herself, her baby-sitter and closest friend had pulled her into her arms, weeping as deeply and desperately as she had.

It had only taken a few minutes for Leah to come to her senses and apologize, for she knew that Anna would have laid down her life to protect the child.

"You're not responsible," Leah said now, meaning it. "It was going to happen anyway. They just used you."

"Leah, if there's anything you can think of for me to do, please..." Her voice cracked, but she went on. "I told that detective everything I know. But I panicked and didn't see the license plate.... Damn it, why didn't I see the license plate?"

Leah saw Jeff turn back toward her as he listened to the conversation playing in the kitchen, and the softness, the worry, the vulnerability in the eyes that could be at once hard and soft, cold and warm, touched her heart. Behind that hard, angry shell, she knew the old Jeff still resided. "Anna, I'll let you know as soon as I hear something." Her voice lacked its usual energy, and a soul-deep weariness kept the tone flat and lifeless.

"Yeah, I guess you have to keep the line open, huh?"

Leah didn't tell her that she had Call Waiting, and that any call would come through anyway. "Yeah, but I'll call you later."

She hung up the phone, stared down at it and looked up again to see Jeff at the doorway looking at her. He had been working that day, she realized in one of those random thoughts that the mind struggles toward in moments of crisis. His jeans—tight and faded over every curve and bend of his body—were dusty at the knees, and his blue work shirt, its sleeves rolled up at the elbow, bore various unidentifiable smudges. His hands—hands she remembered as strong and big and protective, so rough across her skin, though his touch was always nothing short of tender—looked dry and rough as he folded them under his arms. As if he sensed her thoughts, he drew his eyes away from her and back to the detectives in the room behind him.

"Why did you tape that call?" he asked. "Do you suspect the baby-sitter?"

"At this point, everyone's suspect, mate."

"She didn't have anything to do with it," Leah said, coming into the kitchen. "She's the best friend I have, and she's as upset as I am about what happened. She blames herself."

"She *should* blame herself," her father interjected. "The kid was abducted while she was taking care of her. I wouldn't be surprised if she set the whole thing up. Figured she'd take the opportunity to squeeze a little out of the Borgadeux while she had the chance."

"She didn't do that, Dad," Leah snapped. "I wouldn't have left Casey with someone like that. She's a good, caring person, and I trust her."

"Yeah, well, we know what kind of pathetic judge of character you are, don't we?" her father flung back.

"I've done just fine for two years!"

"And look how it wound up! You don't know where your daughter is and I'm the only one who can bail you out of this. Independence isn't all it's cracked up to be anymore, is it?"

Jeff looked from Leah to her father, trying to stay detached from either of the people who sent his emotions rocketing in different directions. He saw the toll her father's words had taken on her, when she already looked ready to collapse. For some unfathomable reason, that made him angry.

"Independence has nothing to do with this, Dad,"
she said through her teeth. "And if you don't mind,
I've had enough of your accusations and observations."

She left the room, ending the argument, and Jeff
watched, stunned at what he'd seen. In the past, she
had cowered from her father, but now...

Silence engulfed the kitchen in her wake, and finally, Jeff gave Borgadeux a look of disgust and went
into the living room.

The storm had calmed and the rain had slowed to a
drizzle, but still the surf pounded against the shore in
a frothy display of fierceness.

Jeff looked toward the hallway where Leah had
gone. Some indeterminate force drew him that way,
and he wrote it off to simply feeling alone and needing more information. Slowly, he walked into the
hallway and checked the master bedroom on the left.
The room was feminine and pink, and it smelled of her
unique scent—a scent that he doubted she had bought
in a store. It was a sent that floated around her like an
aura, lingering in rooms she passed through, trapping
itself in his clothes... and his memory.

She wasn't there, so he stepped to the door directly
across from it, and saw her sitting on a frilly little
Mickey Mouse bedspread draped over a twin bed that
had a wooden rail on the side. Her feet were crossed
Indian-style on the bed, and suddenly she looked very
young and lost. He stepped into the room and leaned
back against the Humpty Dumpty wallpaper, watching her.

"Why are you letting him stay here with you when he talks to you like that?" he asked.

She pulled her feet up and hugged her knees. Still, she clutched the blanket as if it, alone, could keep her bond to her daughter intact. He went to a white rocker in the corner, sat down and settled his elbows on his knees. A strange, warm feeling came over him, and he tried to picture the little girl he'd seen in the living room photographs lying asleep on that bed, sitting on the floor amid the Lego blocks in the corner, rocking in her mother's lap in that chair....

"She's so shy...and she gets spooked easily." Leah's voice cracked on a high-pitched note and her face twisted as she pushed out the words. "New situations...new people...always frighten her. She only feels safe with me and Anna. What must she be feeling right now? What must she be thinking?"

Jeff met her eyes.

She held up the blanket, shook it. "This blanket...she drags it around everywhere...holds it against her face and sucks her thumb. They could have at least taken it with her...so she'd have something familiar. Something that didn't scare her to death...."

She dropped her face into the wadded blanket, and the sobs that shook her shoulders frightened him. He got up, the chair creaking with the release of his weight, and he stepped toward her. "Listen, why don't you lie down? Try to get some rest. It could be a long night."

"Can't...I can't sleep when my baby's out there...."

"Then don't sleep," he said. "Just stay here where it's quiet for a while. Lie down and just rest." Gently, he set his hand on her shoulder and urged her down to the pillow.

When her head sank into the Mickey Mouse pillow sham, she looked up at him, her eyes raw and wet, her nose shiny and red, and for a moment he forgot his own pain, his bitterness toward this woman. He wanted to slide his arms around her, hold her against him and make all her problems his. Would it be that easy to forgive when he'd so carefully cultivated his hatred of her? Was he really that weak? Or were his emotions simply that strong—that disloyal to his own cutting memories?

He saw a soft comforter folded on a toy chest in the corner of the room, and taking it, shook it out and laid it over her.

"Thank you, Jeff," she whispered.

His throat constricted, and he found he couldn't answer. Instead, he nodded, and quietly backed out of the room. At the door, he stole one last look at her, wondering how a woman could look both tormented and beautiful at the same time, and how a man could feel both weak and strong. She had always made him feel that way—as though he were strong enough to protect her from any harm that came her way, yet powerless where his heart was concerned.

He saw a tear roll over her nose and drop on the hand cradled under her face. And feeling his power slipping away too quickly, he left her alone in his daughter's room.

BACK IN THE KITCHEN, Ben was talking on a cellular phone to one of his agents in the field. Listening, Jeff stepped back into the room where Lance Borgadeux leaned against the counter, reading the stock section of the newspaper. Willy, the other detective, studied a notepad on which he had jotted a conglomeration of scribbled notes.

"What's going on? Have they found anything?"

"Not yet. The baby-sitter seems clean."

Jeff pulled out a chair and sat down. Propping his elbows on his knees, he rubbed his face. "This is all so overwhelming." He looked at the men over his fingertips, and sat up straight. "I couldn't get enough from her. She's too upset. What exactly happened when the baby was kidnapped?"

Willy flipped back through his notepad. "Apparently, the child was playing in a sandbox in the front yard, when two men drove up in a car. One of them got out and asked the sitter for directions. As she was giving them, the man leaned over and picked up the child."

"Didn't the baby-sitter think that was strange?"

"According to our witness—a neighbor who was also out in her yard—she told him to put her down. At that point, the man took off for the car with the girl. Sounds like it was all planned. They knew who they wanted, where she'd be, how to best grab her—"

"God." Jeff got up again, raking his hand through his hair. "This is unbelievable." Ben hung up his phone, and Jeff turned to him. "The note. How did they leave the note?"

"It was stuffed into a pop bottle, and they threw it out the window as they took off."

Jeff stared down at the surveillance equipment set up on the table, sorting through the ugly facts and trying to make some sense of it. He thought of Jan, back at the work site, and his crew still scratching their heads and wondering why two detectives rode off with their boss. He pointed to one of the cellular phones. "Mind if I make a call? I need to tell my sister that I'm not being tortured."

Ben handed him the phone. "Sure, mate."

Dreading the call, Jeff dialed the number. The line was busy, and he surmised that his sister/secretary was on the phone telling everyone in town what had happened. Moaning, he clicked the button and dialed the other office number. It rang.

"Hello?"

"It's me, Jan."

"Jeff! Are you all right? Hold on."

He smiled when she put him on hold, presumably to hang up on her gossip-buddy, and thanked his stars that the call wasn't an emergency. In seconds, she was back.

"Jeff? Where are you?"

"I'm in Dunedin at Leah Borgadeux's house."

"Leah's?" He could hear the censure in her voice. "What does *she* want?"

"She had a little bomb to drop on me," he said. "I'll tell you all about it later. Just wanted to let you know that I'm going to be here for a while. Don't worry."

"Are they going to bring you back? Do you need me to pick you up?"

"No. I'll probably be here all night."

"Jeff, are you crazy? Do you have to be reminded how badly she hurt you?"

"No, Jan, I don't. It's not what you think." He sighed and rubbed his face. "Look, just close things down for me. I'll explain it all later."

He hung up the phone before his sister could protest further, and looked up to see that Borgadeux had folded his newspaper and had settled his steely eyes on Jeff.

"Where's Leah?" he asked.

"In Casey's room," Jeff said quietly. "She's lying down."

"Well, get her out of there. That's the last room she needs to be in right now."

"You care to explain why?"

"It's obvious to any moron," he said. "She needs to stay strong, not wallow in that room looking at all the things that remind her of Cassandra. It'll just feed her worry."

"I doubt seriously that she needs to be *reminded* of her daughter," Jeff threw back. "And I think it helps her to be around Casey's things."

"Who the hell cares what you think?" Borgadeux shouted. "Nobody asked you. As far as I'm concerned, you're an intruder right now in a very private family matter. So you can just sit there and keep your mouth shut—"

"Dad!"

The two men swung around and saw Leah standing in the doorway, a look of disgust and impatience coloring her pale features. "I'm getting real tired of hearing the two of you bicker. My nerves are already shot, and you two aren't helping—"

The phone shrilled, startling everyone in the room, and catching her breath, Leah grabbed it up.

"Hello?" Her voice came out raspy and unstable.

Jeff looked at Ben, who wore a pair of headphones through which he now monitored the phone call since Leah was in the same room, and from the look of him, Jeff could tell that it was the call they'd been waiting for. The call from the bastard who had kidnapped his child.

Chapter Three

"Do you have the money?"

Leah steadied herself and tried to control the overwhelming nausea taking hold of her. "Yes. Yes, I have the money. Where is my daughter? What have you done with her?"

Jeff stepped closer to Leah, putting his face next to the phone to hear the man who was speaking. He felt her arm trembling, and she swayed slightly, as though she might faint. With one hand, he touched her back to steady her.

"Shut up and listen if you ever want to see her again. I want you to deliver the two million to me at midnight tonight. And you'd better come alone, or you'll never see the kid alive again."

Before Leah could answer, Jeff snatched the phone from her hand. "Listen to me, you bastard," he said. "I'm Jeff Hampton, Casey's father, and if Leah's going anywhere tonight, I'm going with her. If you think she's going to walk into a trap—"

The phone cut off, and Jeff stood holding the receiver in his hand, listening to the dial tone hum in his ear.

"No!" Leah's scream shook the house. Her face turned a raging red, and she swung her fist against his arm. "How could you do that? Do you know what you've done? You've made them mad and let them know that I've brought someone into this! They could kill her for this!"

Jeff slammed down the receiver. "I was trying to help. I couldn't go with you without their permission, Leah, because they might see me. But if I told them—"

"Told them?" she repeated. "Jeff, we're not going anywhere now. I've waited *hours* for that phone call, and they never even got the chance to tell me where to deliver the money!" Her voice broke off on a sob, and shaking her head, she collapsed into a chair. "I can't believe you did that!"

Jeff turned around and confronted the men at the table. Ben was on the cellular phone, scrambling to get the call traced. The other two rewound the tape and listened through the headphones.

Only Borgadeux took the time to bore a lethal look through Jeff. "Why don't you get the hell out of here, Hampton, before you wind up getting the kid killed?"

"Why don't you get off my back!"

"Shut up, both of you!" The piercing order came from Leah, who then got to her feet and ran through the living room, out the glass doors and onto the balcony overlooking the Gulf.

Jeff stood paralyzed with remorse and defeat as he faced the man he despised so. Borgadeux only stared at him.

At last, Willy broke the silence. "We traced the call to a phone booth, and I put in a call to one of our men near that area. They just got there, and it's empty. We missed him."

"Damn." Ben stood up and paced across the room, trying to think. "Okay, don't anybody panic. The guy won't give up that easy. For two million, 'e'll call back. You can count on it."

"I didn't think the guy would hang up," Jeff said through his teeth. "I just couldn't believe you guys were going to even consider letting her deliver that money alone. And I figured if I was up-front about who I was . . ."

"We *weren't* goin' to let 'er go alone," Ben snapped. "We would 'ave tailed 'er the whole time to make sure she wasn't in danger."

"But that would be even more dangerous than what I just did," Jeff argued. "If they spotted you, it could jeopardize everything. Don't you see that if they knew I was coming, I could help protect her and my being there wouldn't jeopardize anything?"

"Your being here has *already* jeopardized everything," Borgadeux shouted.

Jeff turned back to the detectives, but they were already on the telephone, listening to the headphones, or typing things into a lap-top computer. He went to the door, looked out across the living room to the glass doors of the terrace and saw Leah, standing distraught on the wet deck.

He couldn't remember the last time he'd felt so low. Yes, he could, he amended. It was the last time he'd seen Leah Borgadeux, when he'd let her walk out of his life.

But this time it was by his own hand. He had screwed up big-time. He had acted on a gut instinct, but it had served him wrong.

Slowly, he started across the living room to the terrace. Sliding back the glass door, he stepped out to join Leah.

The air was thick with the smell of saltwater and rain, and the pounding of the shore provided little peace. Leah leaned against the wet rail, staring out over the angry Gulf. She made no move to look at him.

"Leah, I'm sorry I did that. I didn't mean—"

"If you knew her...if you cared about her...you wouldn't have risked that. You'd realize how much was at stake."

"I don't know her because you haven't let me."

"That's not the point." She flung around, facing him with raging tears and a mottled face. "The point is that this is not a game. This is my baby's life. You can't take things upon yourself like you just did." Her voice broke, and she brought the child's blanket up to muffle a sob. "Damn it, Jeff, if anything happens to her, I don't know what I'll do. She's all I have. She's everything...."

The phone rang again, like a torturous device that strangled the life from Leah's soul. Shooting past him, she ran to the extension in the kitchen. Sniffing to clear her voice, she whispered, "Hello."

Jeff followed her in, but this time he stood back, feeling like the intruder Borgadeux had accused him of being.

"Yes...yes, I understand but...please, can I speak to her? Just so I'll know she's all right? Please!"

The phone went dead, and holding it in her hand, she lowered it from her ear. "He hung up. I didn't get to tell them about the asthma!"

The detectives scrambled to trace the call, but this time the kidnapper hadn't been on the line long enough.

"What did he say?" It was Borgadeux who asked.

"He said that he would call me back at midnight to tell me where to deliver the money, and that if I do as they say, I'll get Casey back then." She threw Jeff a dull, heartless look. "And he said that Jeff could come with me, as long as he's unarmed. But if anyone else follows me or comes with me, they'll kill Casey."

Relief burst out of Jeff's lungs.

"Good goin', mate," Ben acknowledged, patting Jeff's back. "Guess you were right. We'll put a phone in the van, and you can call us the moment you 'ave Casey. We'll be close enough by to get there in time to apprehend them." Jeff didn't hear, for his gaze was locked with Leah's, assessing her for some sign that she didn't still blame him for interrupting the first call. "I'm glad Leah won't 'ave to go alone," Ben went on. "I didn't want to say anything, but I was a little worried they might think two Borgadeux would command higher ransom than one."

Borgadeux massaged his temples. "Oh my God. You don't think—"

"It won't happen." Jeff's words were issued with a note of finality that Leah couldn't deny. "I won't let anything happen to her."

Reluctantly, Leah looked him in the eye, noting the protective way he was prepared to come to her rescue. Something warm, secure, hatched inside her, but the fear still gnawed at her heart. "No more heroics? No more risks?"

"None. I swear it."

Relieved that he'd done what he'd done, but unable to reveal that relief so soon after her accusations, she nodded and wiped her face. "Okay. Then all we can do now is wait."

"You need to eat something," Borgadeux said. "It's going to be a long night. We all need to."

"I can't eat, Dad."

"You have to make yourself."

That taut, cliff-edge expression returned to her face. "If you're hungry, Dad, you know where the refrigerator is." Then drawing in a deep sigh, she left the room.

JEFF WATCHED HER GO, and feeling the sudden chill of abandonment, left the kitchen and walked to the sliding glass doors, where the rain was beginning to fall harder.

It had worked, he told himself. His instincts had served him right, and he would be there to protect Leah when she delivered the money.

So why did he still feel like he'd blown it?

The thought of how dangerous these kidnappers could be forced perspiration to break across his forehead, and reaching up to massage his temples, he turned around and looked toward her bedroom. He saw her come out and disappear into the bathroom. He heard the door lock, and the sound of the shower being turned on.

Without realizing what he was doing, he walked slowly toward the bathroom, stopped just outside it, and tried to imagine her inside, unzipping those tight pants she wore, sliding them down over her hips, stepping out of them with those long, silky legs. He could envision her blouse slipping over her flat stomach, the soft indention of her navel, the small breasts just big enough to fill his hands....

He wondered if she'd had a man since him, if any other had touched and loved her, if they had tasted the sweetness of her skin....

His throat went dry, and sliding his hands into his pockets and hauling in a deep breath, he went into Casey's room and recalled Leah lying there on Casey's bed, crying, sick with worry for her baby....

His baby...

Slowly, he stooped in the corner where the Lego blocks were scattered on the floor, and picked up one. He wondered if Leah played with her, if she taught her how to build towers and robots, if she praised her scribbled drawings, if she adorned her hair with big bows and dressed her in frilly dresses.

Sitting on the floor and leaning back against the wall, he let his eyes roam over the books in the red bookcase. Two photo albums caught his gaze, and

quickly he reached for them. Opening the first one, he
saw Casey's very first picture. She lay in Leah's arms,
all red and blotched and beautiful, and Leah was
smiling as tears rolled down her face.

Something painful twisted his heart, and he felt the
sting of his own tears.

And as he turned the pages and saw all the moments with Casey he had missed, one of those tears fell
to his stubbled cheek.

STEPPING INTO the warm spray of water, Leah closed
her eyes and let the heat wash over her, calming her
tense muscles and washing away the tears that had
created a salty film over her skin.

She would see Casey tonight. In just a few hours,
she would deliver the money where they said, and
Casey would be back in her arms. If nothing went
wrong.

But the truth was that all sorts of things could go
wrong. Her father could intervene and ruin everything, or the detectives could follow without her
knowledge and cause the whole thing to blow up. Or
Jeff could lose his temper and either frighten the kidnappers away or make them angry. Or the kidnappers
could just get cold feet, and decide to kill the whole
plan.

And Casey, too.

Even as she washed the old tears away, new ones
formed in her eyes and mingled with the water spray-
ing on her face.

She wondered if Jeff realized how badly he had
frightened her when he'd grabbed the phone. Al-

ready, nothing was in her control. Already, she was at the whim of the criminals who had Casey. When Jeff had done that, it was like he had deliberately and mercilessly severed the link between her and Casey.

He had only been trying to help, she told herself. Just like her father and the detectives were trying, and even though Jeff really *had* helped, it didn't settle her knotted stomach or calm the pounding in her head. It didn't make it any easier—right now—knowing that there were still hours to go before Casey would be safe.

There was no relaxing, she realized finally. Not while her baby was in a stranger's hands. Not until she had her safely back.

Stepping out of the shower, she dried her skin with a big towel, then slipped into her bedroom and dressed quietly in a big sweatshirt and jeans. Unable to join the others just yet, she went back to Casey's room.

Jeff was already there, huddled on the floor in a corner, looking at Casey's photo albums, studying pictures of the little girl who looked so much like him. His face held a poignant longing, a look that made Leah's heart melt into her toes, a look that revealed to her how good it was to share Casey with someone else who could love and appreciate her.

Slowly, she went to sit on the floor beside him. For a moment he didn't stir, and made no indication that he knew she was in the room with him. His eyes were glued to a recent picture of the child holding a Tootsie Pop, her face covered in sticky red candy. Instead of the smile she might have expected at such a comical portrait, she saw a fine mist glistening in his eyes.

"She loves Tootsie Pops," Leah said. "She always winds up getting it in her hair. Little pieces of it stick to her face, and her hands are covered with candy when she's finished. I usually have to bathe her right away."

He turned the page, and saw a picture of her at her first birthday party. Several other babies sat around the table in pointed hats, staring covetously at the birthday cake decorated with Minnie Mouse.

"Those are some of the kids from her Sunday-school class," she said. "And this one—" she pointed to a little boy of the same age as Casey "—he's Anna's son. They were born a week apart. That's how I met Anna. We were in the same Lamaze class. Her husband is in the Coast Guard and was gone a lot, so we helped each other. We got to be good friends."

He brought puzzled eyes to her, and Leah knew he was probably thinking how strange that was, since she had never had close friends before. She had been so sheltered . . . so protected . . . so smothered.

"When I went into labor, Anna went to the hospital with me and acted as my coach. She was the second person to ever hold Casey."

He frowned down at the pictures again. "I'm surprised your father didn't throw her out and insist on being there himself."

"I didn't call him until it was all over," she said. "I knew he'd just make me nervous and drive the hospital staff crazy. I kept it to myself until I was back home with Casey the next day. He wanted me to move back in with him, so I decided that the faster I got Casey settled at home, the easier it would be to convince him we were fine."

"And did you? Convince him, I mean?"

"No," she said with a smile. "He still harasses me about it. Every single day he has some new reason why I would be better off to move back."

Jeff turned the page, and saw a picture of Casey in what looked like an oxygen mask. "What's this?"

A haunted look returned to her eye, and she stiffened again. "Her nebulizer mask. She's asthmatic, and sometimes I have to give her breathing treatments to help her breathe." Tears filled her eyes again, and she covered her mouth with her hand. "She was wheezing this morning. After I medicated her, she was fine, but I shouldn't have taken her to Anna's. I had an appointment with a woman putting together a trousseau, but I should have canceled it and closed the shop and kept her home...but she was breathing fine by the time I took her. When she gets upset—"

"I was asthmatic when I was a child," Jeff whispered, cutting her off. He brought his fingers to his eyes and pressed hard.

"That explains where she got it," she said. "You outgrew it?"

"Yeah, I outgrew it," he said in a tight voice. "I also had nosebleeds at night, I'm allergic to poison oak and my family has a history of diabetes. Those are things that a parent needs to know about her child's genes, don't you think?"

Leah felt the sting, and accepted it. "I would have told you if something serious like that had come up. I had always planned to tell you someday."

The idea seemed ludicrous, and he gaped at her with disbelief. "When? When she was grown and had children of her own? When you accidentally ran into me on the street? Or just when she was ill and you needed a kidney or something?"

"I told you today," she said. "You know now."

"Yeah. Now I know." He looked back down at the child's picture, and shook his head. "Only I can't figure out what I ever did to make you hate me so much."

Leah caught his arms and made him look at her. "I *never* hated you, Jeff. Never."

"You couldn't keep something like this from me if you didn't hate me, Leah."

"I called you a hundred times. I left messages on your machine, with your secretary, with your friends. I went to your office and waited, but you wouldn't see me. I finally realized that *you* hated *me!*"

"Yes, I hated you," he shouted, flinging the album across the floor and getting to his feet. "I hated you because you walked out on me! I wasn't good enough for you or your family!"

Leah stood up and faced him across the room. "You've got it all wrong, Jeff. My family wasn't good enough for you. My father would have destroyed you. You were right on the verge of closing the Suncoast Dome deal. He said he could pull the rug right out from under you. He had important people in his back pocket, Jeff, and I knew he had the power and determination to bankrupt you."

"So you convinced yourself that you had made some supreme sacrifice for me? How magnanimous of you, Leah. How generous." His sarcasm died off, and he swung around. "It's a crock, and you know it. If you'd loved me, nothing your father said or did could have influenced you. And nothing you ever say will convince me that you kept my daughter from me for my own good."

"I thought my breaking up with you was for your own good. But then when I found out I was pregnant, I wanted you so much...." Her voice broke off into a sob, and she stepped toward him. "But it was you who put up a wall between us then."

"No, Leah, it was you! You're the one who robbed me of two years I will never get back! You're the one who robbed Casey of a father who could love her and protect her from those jackasses that have her right now. And it was all for a buck, wasn't it? So your father wouldn't cut you out of his will, or cut off your charge accounts. Was it worth it, Leah?"

Leah slapped away a tear rolling down her face, and without honoring him with an answer, turned away to pick up the photo album lying on the floor where Jeff had thrown it.

When her voice was calmer, more controlled, she gave him a searing look and pushed past him out the door. "You don't know what you're talking about," she whispered through quivering lips, and she left him standing alone in his daughter's room.

FOR THE NEXT SEVERAL hours, they avoided speaking to each other. The only thing to break the silence was the ring of the detectives' cellular phones in the kitchen, and her father's calls as he tried to conduct business as usual from her living room. Jeff found refuge on the wet deck, poring over the photo albums by the light of a single patio bulb around which a swarm of mosquitos bumped and buzzed, trying to fill the gaps of the past two years.

In the bedroom, Leah busied herself packing a duffel bag of things that Casey might need immediately when they found her. A change of clothes. Some diapers. Bunny Fu-Fu and her blanket. Her medication. The air compressor and nebulizer, in case they found her in respiratory distress. And two million dollars in cash.

It was nearing midnight when she took the bag and briefcase of money into the kitchen and gladly accepted the cup of coffee her father handed her.

"Sit down, sweetheart," Borgadeux told her. "I want to talk to you."

She picked up the cordless phone and held it near her face. "They're going to call soon, Dad. There's not much time."

"I know that," he said. "But I wanted to talk to you about what's going to happen after you get Casey back. I want you to come home with me. I have a room all decorated for her, and you can have your old room back. You'll have servants and nannies and guards, and you'll never have to worry about kidnappers or baby-sitters or struggling to make ends meet again."

Leah sat silent, expressionless, as her father rambled on, and when she glanced toward the door, she saw that Jeff had come in and was leaning against the kitchen door, listening.

"I don't struggle to make ends meet, Dad. Business is good, and I can provide for my daughter just fine. And I don't need servants."

Borgadeux's voice rose a decibel. "Are you going to deny that you need security? After all this? You would honestly go along as usual, knowing that little Casey is an open target? It's foolish, girl, to keep pretending like you're an ordinary person, when you're a Borgadeux. You can have the advantages of that. Don't be stubborn when your daughter's safety is involved."

Her temples began to throb harder, and she brought her fingers up to massage them. "Dad, I really can't think about all this right now. All I can concentrate on is this phone ringing and the kidnapper telling me where I can find my baby."

"I understand that," he said. "But I wanted to mention it to you, because you need to think about it. You need to have a battle plan when you bring Casey home . . . *if* you bring her home."

"If?" Her voice slipped on the word. "Dad, don't say that. I have to believe that everything's going to go fine tonight. Please—"

"We'll get her back," Jeff said, walking to her chair and setting his hand on her shoulder. "There's no if about it. I'm going to see my little girl tonight."

Thankful for his confidence and his secure touch, which she realized was more to rile her father than to comfort her, she watched her father shoot Jeff a dangerous look and rise from the table.

"As soon as I get her," she said, "I want a doctor to examine her to make sure they didn't hurt her. But I don't want to take her to the hospital. She'll need to be home." She looked up at her brooding father. "Dad, after we get Casey, would you call her pediatrician and see if he'll meet us back here?"

Borgadeux shrugged. "I'll call him right now."

"No. No one else can know until we get her back. *Then* you can call."

Before Borgy could respond, the phone rang, and Leah lunged for it.

"Hello?"

"Are you ready to turn the corner?" the voice asked.

"What corner?" she asked breathlessly.

"The corner in this nightmare. The one that determines whether you ever see your kid alive again."

Chapter Four

Leah swallowed back the sickness rising to her throat and tried to get the words out. "Yes, I'm ready. You can have the money . . . but please don't hurt her."

"Go to the phone booth at the corner of Belcher and Drew Street," the caller said. "Wait there for further instructions. And I'll tell you one more time, if you bring anybody other than the kid's father, she's dead. We know what he looks like. We've done our homework."

"All right." She clutched the phone tighter. "Please . . . is she all right? Is she wheezing or coughing? She's asthmatic, and she needs medication—"

"Belcher and Drew," he repeated, and hung up.

Leah's heart sprinted in her chest as she cut off the phone and turned to Jeff. "Are you ready?"

"Yes," he said, starting for the door.

Leah grabbed the duffel bag and briefcase that contained the money, and saw Borgadeux reach for his keys.

"Wait a minute," Leah said, swinging around. "What are you doing?"

"We're going to follow out of sight," Borgadeux said. "Ben put a tracer on your van so we would know where you're going to be. We'll be just a few blocks away. You can also take the cellular phone. Call us if you need us."

"No!" She stopped at the door, her heart pounding in terror. "Dad, this is dangerous. They might see you. If someone's watching the house and they see us all leave, they'll be suspicious."

"She's right," Ben said. "We'll have t'wait a few minutes before we go."

Borgadeux held back reluctantly. "I'm not going to sit around twiddling my thumbs."

"Yes, you are," Jeff said. "It's the only thing you can do."

"Dad, if you jeopardize this, so help me God, I'll never forgive you for it," Leah said. "If you're worried about getting your damn cash back, Casey's worth a hell of a lot more than two million dollars."

Borgadeux dropped into a chair as Leah and Jeff went to the garage and climbed into her van.

THE RIDE to the designated phone booth was quiet, for the prospect of what they were walking into, what Casey was already in the middle of, played havoc in their minds. It took twenty minutes to reach the booth, set conspicuously at what normally would have been a busy intersection. Now, at 12:30 a.m., the street was almost deserted.

Leah pulled into the gas station parking lot next to the booth and rolled down her window. She cut off her lights, leaving the van enveloped in the opaque darkness. The moon hid above a thick froth of clouds, blocking out all light, and it looked as if it could begin raining again at any moment.

"Should I get out?" she asked, breaking the silence.

"No. Just wait here until the phone rings. It could be a while. They would want to give us plenty of time to get here."

"Yeah." Her word came out on a whisper, and her eyes gravitated to the phone. "So what do we do in the meantime?"

"Wait, wait and wait some more."

"I'm getting good at that." She shoved her fingers through her hair, realized she was perspiring. Taking in a deep breath, she whispered, "This is worse than when I was nine and a half months pregnant without a sign of labor. I thought nothing could be worse than that."

"Casey was overdue?" he asked, drawing her attention from the phone.

"Yeah."

"I was late."

The soft words were almost inaudible, and Leah looked at him in the darkness. "What?"

"I was late. My mother carried me for almost ten months. Is that kind of thing genetic?"

"I don't know," she whispered.

He gazed out into the night, focusing on the haze around a street lamp a half block away, where moths and mosquitos swarmed. "Was it hard? Labor, I mean?"

She took in a deep breath. "Not too bad. It was over in about six hours and Anna was great. It was all worth it."

"What about afterward, when you came home? Wasn't anybody there to help you?"

"No," she said, her tone a little more defensive than she wanted. "But it was fine. I'm self-sufficient. I didn't need anybody."

"You didn't need anybody." He uttered the words on a dull, despairing note, and shook his head. "Leah, this may not be the time, but I have to know. Did it ever occur to you during all that to call me, that I could have been there for you? That I would have wanted to see my daughter born?"

That old familiar guilt surged through her. "Yes, it occurred to me, Jeff. A hundred times. And I always intended to. But I always lost my nerve."

"Lost your nerve? Are you kidding?"

A car drove by, its headlights illuminating the van, and Leah's gaze followed it out of sight. "Jeff, by then I had let so much time pass that I knew you'd be furious I hadn't told you earlier. I had planned to call you when I went into labor. I didn't have the courage, and afterward . . . well, it was all said and done, and it seemed too late to include you." Her gaze drifted to the phone again as sharp regrets scraped at her senses. "Jeff, I was selfish, I know, but you have to understand my state of mind."

"What was your state of mind, Leah? Tell me, because I'd really like to know."

She winced at his frigid tone. "I was out from under my father's thumb for the first time in my life. I was struggling to start a brand-new business. I was dealing with a pregnancy. I was angry at you—''

''Angry at me! For what?''

''I don't know.''

''You don't know? Leah, if you were angry at me, you owe it to yourself if not to me to at least figure out why. What in God's name did you have to be angry at me about?''

She cursed herself for ever admitting to that strange, unreasonable emotion, but it was too late. Now she had to find a way to explain it.

''It's stupid,'' she said. ''It's irrational.''

''So what else is new? I'm listening.''

''I was angry at you...'' She faded out and looked at the phone again, willing it to ring, to interrupt the honesty that seemed so bent on coming, but it didn't. ''...because you didn't fight for me. Because you let me walk out, and that was the end of it. I kept telling myself that if you really loved me, you'd have come after me.''

''So that's what it was? Some kind of insane test? To see how much I cared?''

''No, that isn't what it was at all. I told you it was irrational. None of what I was feeling made sense. When I realized I was carrying your baby, I suddenly realized that nothing my father did was worth breaking up the family we had created together. And I wanted you back.''

''But it blew up in your face, didn't it? I didn't want you anymore.''

''No, you didn't. And I didn't want you just for the baby's sake if you didn't want me.''

They both looked at each other across the van, both of them full of pain and heartache that would never easily be quelled. Another set of headlights passed, illuminating a sliver of tears in his eyes.

"I loved you," he said through stiff lips. "You knew that."

"And I loved you," she whispered. "As much as I knew how. But at the time, I didn't have a lot of experience with love. Just manipulation, and possession and emotional blackmail. It took Casey to teach me what real love is."

"But I didn't get that luxury," he whispered.

Silence filled the van again—surrounded it—wringing her heart and nerves tighter. She wished for the words that could heal the wounds, but she knew there were none. Above all, she wished the phone would ring, but it didn't. Finally, she brought her tense gaze back to Jeff. "Jeff, I swear, when this is all over, when I have my baby back with me again, I won't try to keep you out of her life. I want her to know her father. I've made terrible mistakes, and I can't change the past, but I can change now."

"Yeah, right," he said. "And what about when old Borgy threatens to huff and puff and blow my house down again? Are you going to throw me out again, for my own damn good? Or this time will I get a choice?"

"My father has no hold on me anymore," she said. "I told you . . . he wouldn't have been there today if I hadn't desperately needed his money. I didn't have anywhere else to turn."

"You could have turned to me."

"For two million dollars? You don't have that kind of—"

"I could have gotten it, Leah. But you wouldn't know that, would you, because you don't really know me anymore. I could have been there for my daughter. I could have come through for her."

"But I wouldn't have had the right to ask."

"No, you wouldn't have," he agreed. "But that wouldn't have mattered.

"After this," he went on, "your father's going to feel like you owe him. Like he has some kind of new hold on you."

"I can deal with that," she said. "But I can swear to you that nothing he ever does will keep you from seeing Casey . . . if you want to."

A moment of quiet followed, and they both watched the phone. It sat silent, mocking their anxiety. "Damn it, why won't they call?" she whispered.

She reached behind her seat and unzipped her duffel bag. "Oh, no. Did I remember to pack her blanket?"

"It's in there," he said quietly.

"What about the bunny? I was so distraught—"

"I checked," he said. "It's wrapped in the blanket. Just relax. It'll be over soon."

"When?" she shouted, surprising herself more than him. "When will it be over? Why don't they call?"

"I don't know," he whispered.

"Do you think we got the address wrong? Is it possible that we're at the wrong one?"

"No," Jeff said. "They're just making us sweat."

She brought her hands to her face, and felt her own fingers trembling. Her legs felt rubbery and shaky, and she feared that when the phone rang, she would collapse trying to get to it.

She opened the door and started to get out.

"What are you doing?"

"I'm going to stand beside the phone. I can't just sit here."

"No. It's not safe. I don't want you standing out there in the open."

"I have to do something! How long are we going to sit here?" She dropped her face in the circle of her arms over the steering wheel. "This is driving me crazy!"

It began to drizzle, the raindrops drumming against the roof of the van and beading on the windshield. "Raining again!" she cried. "And Casey's out in this wet night air, and they'll probably leave her alone somewhere in the rain and she'll be terrified and—"

Before she knew what was happening, Jeff's arms were around her, his big, comforting, calloused hands stroking her hair and her back as she wilted, sobbing, against him. "Shh. It's okay," he said. "It's all right."

For the first time in over two and a half years, in the secure embrace of Jeff Hampton's arms, Leah realized just how much she had lost. Instead of calming her misery, it only heightened it.

"We'll get her back," he whispered. "I promise. We're going to have her in just a short time, and we can take her home and rock her...."

The "we" uttered so naturally, so easily, calmed her spirit, for it had been a very long time since there had been anyone else to plan and hope and love with her. He could love Casey, she told herself. And Casey would love him.

Swallowing and breathing in a sob, she looked up at him. "Are you... are you sure? Will we get her... get her back?" The words hiccuped on the rise and fall of her sobs.

"I'm sure." He stroked the tears from her cheek, and she could feel his breath against her lips, see the reassurance in his eyes, feel the confidence in his heart. She saw him wet his lips, felt him narrowing the space between their faces....

His lips grazed hers, so lightly that she almost couldn't feel it, but even so, the slight touch sent emotion shooting through her. He pulled back, looking at her with pain and a little surprise, as if he couldn't decide whether to push her away or kiss her fully.

Reaching up, she framed his face, feeling the stubble against his fingertips, and his lips came back to hers.

Something—some long-held passion that had simmered for years—boiled to the surface as their kiss deepened and their hearts pounded out of control. His touch sent tiny shock waves through her, making her nerves tingle and her senses reel. He shifted slightly, pulling her closer against him, and his fingers slid through her hair, down her back....

And suddenly the phone rang, startling them as if they'd been caught breaking each other's heart again.

Catching her breath and forsaking his arms, Leah bolted out of the van and grabbed the telephone. Jeff was behind her in an instant, his face pressed close to hers, listening.

"Drop the briefcase with the money in the garbage bin beside the red bench at Osceola Park. It's behind the library."

"Will Casey be there? Will I see her then?"

"*If* you do as we say, and the money is all there, you can pick up the kid at the playground behind the First United Methodist Church on Drew Street. If we see any sign of your being followed, you'll find her dead."

"I'll do as you say," she blurted. "Please . . . don't hurt her."

The phone went dead, and she slammed it down and rushed back into the van.

"Let me drive," Jeff said.

"No," she argued. "I already know the way. I can get there faster."

Not arguing further, he jumped into the passenger seat and held on as they raced to the location where the money would be dropped.

The cellular phone in the van rang, and Jeff looked at her. "It's your father."

"Don't answer it," she said. "He'll want to know where we're going. I don't want him to know, or he might screw everything up."

She ran a red light, and Jeff touched her arm. "Take it easy or you'll attract the police. That's all we need."

"You're right." Her hands trembled as she clutched the steering wheel and forced herself to slow down. "Please, God, don't let them hurt her."

"It's going to be okay," Jeff said. "You have to believe that."

They reached the park, screeched to a halt, and leaving the van idling, ran together to drop the briefcase in the garbage can. Then, looking around for any sign of the kidnappers, they walked as quickly as they could back to the van, got in and started to drive away.

"Do you see anyone yet?" Leah asked Jeff as he strained to see out the back window. "No. Not yet."

"How will they get Casey there before we get there, if they haven't gotten the money yet? How could they do that?"

"You said two of them kidnapped her. They probably have some kind of communication with each other." Losing sight of the park, he turned back around in his seat. "He's probably grabbing the case at this very moment and calling his accomplice to leave Casey."

"Alone? In the rain? She's afraid of the dark, Jeff! She'll be terrified. You know they won't hang around. They'll just leave her—"

"We'll be there," he said. "That's all that matters. In just a few minutes, we'll be there."

Despite her efforts to go slowly, Leah ran another two red lights. The cellular phone began to ring again, but this time there was no discussion. They both ignored it. After a moment, it stopped ringing.

"Oh, God. I just thought of something."

"What?"

"Didn't Dad say that they had put a tracer on the van? They would know where we've been, where we've stopped. They'd realize that we dropped the money off at the park. What if they go there, and the kidnapper sees them, before we can reach Casey?"

Jeff sat stiffer in his seat, and found that this time he could offer no reassurances. "Let's go ahead and call them. Tell them not to do it."

"Yeah, okay. We don't have to tell them where we're going. Just tell them how important it is for them not to go where we've been."

Leah grabbed the phone and began punching out the number her father had written and taped to the back of it. He answered on the first ring.

"Dad, we dropped the money."

"At Osceola Park? We're almost there."

"No! Dad, please don't go there! Please! They're leaving Casey in another location, and it all depends on their not thinking anyone's following us! Please, if I mean anything to you, if Casey does, don't go there!"

"All right. We're turning off."

Leah wilted in relief.

"Where are you going now?"

"I can't tell you. Not until this is over."

"Leah, we can help you! We can be nearby, just in case—"

"No, Dad. I don't want you to do anything until I have Casey back."

She hung the phone up, and flung it to Jeff. "We're almost there. That's the church, right up there."

Jeff strained to see the playground behind it. There were no cars. No lights. No sign of life.

Leah skidded into the parking lot, threw the van into Park, and jumped out, leaving the van running as she bolted toward the fence surrounding the playground. "Casey!"

Jeff was behind her in the rain, searching the shadows for any sign of the child, when suddenly they heard a hoarse, raspy wail from across the yard.

"Casey!" Opening the gate, Leah burst across the yard to the little sandbox where her daughter sat, crying her heart out, what was left of her voice squeaking with soul-deep hysteria.

Leah grabbed the child and crushed her against her, instinctively rocking her body to stop her anguished cry.

Chapter Five

Jeff stood, awestricken, as Casey clung to Leah with a desperate embrace. He watched as Leah rose, holding her, and her little ringlets bounced against her shoulders.

Stepping close, he reached out a shaky hand to touch her hair. It was soft, baby-silky, but it wasn't enough. He wanted to see her face, wanted to touch her hand, wanted her to cling to him as she clung to Leah. Desperately, he wanted to ask if she was okay, but his voice would not function.

Leah seemed equally paralyzed, standing with the crying child, but finally she rasped, "Let's get out of here."

Nodding and trying desperately not to let his own tears shatter, he took them both back to the van. Quickly, he got into the driver's seat and pulled the van out of the parking lot.

In the passenger seat, the child still trembled and clung to Leah, still crying as if the ordeal had not yet ended. "Shh. It's okay, pumpkin. It's all right now. Mommy won't let them take you again."

Her voice wobbled as she spoke, and Jeff came to a red light and looked over at the mother and child. Casey was so small, so fragile, it was hard to believe she was two. He wondered if she was hurt physically. He swallowed the emotional obstruction in his throat. "Is she okay?" he asked. "Any bruises? Cuts?"

Leah's face broke with her sob, and she shook her head. "Nothing I can see. She's all right, except she's wheezing a little. Thank God, she's all right." She pried Casey away from her just long enough to see her face. "Honey, did those people hurt you? Were they mean to you?"

"I want my mommy," the two year old cried. "They said no."

"Mommy's here now, sweetheart. Nobody's going to take you again. I promise."

"I want blankie."

Ignoring the light that had turned green, Jeff kept the van at a halt and grabbed the duffel bag. Quickly, he handed Leah the blanket, watched Casey grab it covetously, watched her wad it next to her face, between herself and Leah, and bring her little thumb to her mouth. It seemed only then that she noticed him, and letting out a fresh round of sobs, she buried her face in Leah's chest.

"I'm sorry," Jeff whispered as the van still idled at the green light. "Did I scare you?"

"I want my mommy!"

Leah held her tight and cast him an apologetic look.

"Tell her I won't hurt her," he said in a soft, unthreatening voice. "I won't even touch her." The absurdity of that promise struck him in the heart, and he leaned closer. "She needs her mommy. Don't you, Casey? And Mommy's not going anywhere."

Her cries quietened a little, but she still kept her face buried.

"Why don't we pull over for a minute until we can calm her down?" Leah said.

Unable to make himself take his eyes off of her, he pulled the van into the Winn Dixie parking lot beside them, and left it idling.

He picked up the Bunny Fu-Fu that had fallen out of the blanket and slipped from his seat. "You want your bunny?" he asked.

Slowly, Casey stole a look at him. He handed it to her, and she took it by the ear with her thumb-sucking hand.

"Are you okay now?" he whispered, his voice a raspy wave of emotion.

Casey nodded and, laying her head against Leah's chest, closed her eyes.

"She's tired," he whispered, and he looked up in the darkness and met Leah's eyes. Tears blurred his vision, but he blinked them back.

"I'd let you hold her," she said, "but she's a little too frightened right now."

"It's okay. There's plenty of time for that," he whispered.

The little girl opened her eyes again—eyes that he guessed were as red and raw and swollen as her mother's—and assessed the man who had given her her bunny.

"Casey," Leah said softly, brushing her damp curls back from her face. "I want you to meet Jeff. He's our good friend. And he's going to keep us safe."

Casey stared at him for a moment, then looked up at her mother. "Mommy not leave me?"

"No. I'll not leave you. I'm staying right here. We're going home."

Accepting the answer, Casey coughed and looked again at Jeff, stuffed her thumb back into her mouth and closed her eyes.

Tears rolled down Leah's face again, but she tried to hold back the sob for fear of further frightening the baby. "She'll never be the same," she whispered. "She'll never trust anyone again." The child coughed again, a wet, phlegmy cough, and Leah dropped her head down and listened to her breathing.

Jeff brought his hand to Casey's hair, but thought better of it. He had promised not to touch her. "She'll trust me," he whispered. "I'll make her trust me."

He moved his hand, and looked at the thumb beginning to fall out of the baby's mouth. "I think she's asleep."

Leah smiled and kissed the top of Casey's head. "I really need to give her a breathing treatment and her medication. Let's take her home, Jeff. It's all over now."

The cellular phone rang, startling the little girl, but quickly she closed her eyes again. Jeff answered it.

"Yeah?"

"You got the girl, mate?" It was Ben who spoke, and Jeff glanced at the child again.

"We've got her," he said with a slight smile. "Did you catch them?"

"No such luck. We waited till your van left the scene, and then we 'eaded over there. There wasn't a clue. The police 'ave been contacted now, though, and they're combing the area. Was the kid all right?"

"Scared out of her wits and wheezing a little, but other than that we can't see any physical damage. We're taking her home now. Will the doctor be there?"

"We'll call right now. We're on our way home."

Jeff hung up the phone, and looked at Leah. Her hair was tangled and stuck to her wet cheek, and tears still rolled down her face as she held the sleeping child. "He says they didn't have any luck finding the kidnappers. The police have been called in now. Your father and the others are on their way to your house."

Leah nodded, but for a moment, she didn't speak. "What if they come back?" she whispered finally. "What if they think it was so easy that they try it again? I can't believe they're still out there...."

As he drove the rest of the way to her home, Jeff couldn't find an answer to calm her fears.

CONTROLLED CHAOS ABOUNDED around Leah's house as they pulled into her driveway. Three police cars and an ambulance waited on the street, their lights flashing and radios blaring. Neighbors had come out of the condos across the street wearing robes and slippers and had clustered in the street, watching.

"What the hell...?" Jeff threw a helpless look to Leah. "Your father doesn't waste any time, does he?"

Leah tightened her hold on the sleeping, wheezing child. "Jeff, I don't want them frightening her. I want her to have some peace—"

Someone knocked on the window, and he looked out into the blaring light of a television camera. "Damn. Can you open the garage? I can pull in—"

A police officer knocked on Leah's window, but ignoring him, Leah reached for the remote control garage door opener on the sun visor and brought the door up.

"They're following us in!" Leah said.

"Just answer their questions and we can get this over with," he said. "We want them to find the kidnappers."

He bent over her and opened her door and reached for the duffel bag as she slipped out, still holding Casey.

"How is she, Miss Borgadeux?"

"We have an ambulance waiting. . . ."

"Are you all right?"

"Did you find them?" Leah asked one of the officers. "Did you catch the kidnappers?"

"Not yet, ma'am. We need to ask you a few questions."

"Miss Borgadeux!"

She glanced aside at a familiar reporter who had stuck a microphone in her face. "Did you see the kidnappers?"

"No," she said, shielding Casey's eyes from the light. "Excuse me. I have to get her in—"

"Is she all right? Did they harm her?"

"She seems fine," she said. "But you're waking her up. Please—"

Jeff broke through the crowd as Casey lifted her head and began to cry.

"Get a close-up," the reporter instructed his cameraman. Jeff took Leah's shoulders and began guiding her to the door.

The child screamed louder as the crowd pressed in, and she blinked at the television lights and railed an octave higher. "Damn it, turn that thing off!" Jeff shouted.

"Miss Borgadeux how much ransom was involved?"

Jeff held a hand in front of the camera. "She's going in now, pal!" He found her house key on the key chain and opened the door. The reporter started to follow them in, but Jeff blocked the entrance. "Nobody's coming in here except for one cop and the doctor. No reporters, and that means you."

"And who are you?" the reporter asked, pointing the mike at Jeff.

He started to say he was Casey's father, but reality hit, and he realized that his family would hear it over the news before he had the chance to tell them himself. "A friend of the family," he said finally. "Now get the hell out of here."

Borgy's Jaguar pulled into the driveway, effectively luring the reporters away, and Jeff let the cop in and closed the door.

Leah took Casey into the living room and, sitting down, tried to comfort her. As Casey's cries weakened, Leah's own tears intensified. She closed her eyes and squeezed them tightly shut as she buried her face in the child's hair.

In the light of the living room Jeff got his first good look at the little girl who was his daughter. Mesmerized, he was helpless to do anything more than stare.

"Did you see the car, Mr. Hampton?" the officer who'd come in with them asked.

"No. We didn't see anything."

The radio on his hip blared static police calls, and Jeff had the sudden urge to rip it off the cop's belt and throw it as far as he could. "Was the voice familiar? Could you identify—"

The door burst open, and Borgadeux and his detectives spilled inside, bringing with them two more cops and the television crew.

"I told them to stay out," Jeff said. "Where the hell is that doctor?"

"Here," one of the last men to come in called. Jeff looked down at the man's black bag and parted the crowd for him.

"How's Casey?" the doctor asked, instantly making Jeff feel as if he knew her.

"She's upset," he said.

"Any wheezing?"

Jeff led him into the living room. "Yes. And this damned mob isn't helping matters any."

The doctor took a look at the frightened child, still crying in her mother's arms.

"Thanks for coming, Dr. Marks," Leah said over the cries. "See, Casey? It's just Dr. Marks."

The doctor saw the extent of Casey's despair and turned around to the crowd coming in behind him.

"All right, let's clear this room. She needs quiet, and I can't examine her properly with all this commotion."

"Everybody out!" Borgadeux's powerful voice boomed over the chaos. "We'll be out with a statement later. Come on. Everybody except the doctor and the police officers."

Jeff refrained from pointing out that over half the crowd still remained, but he left it up to the tycoon to get them out. Going back to Leah's side, he watched as the doctor slipped off Casey's clothes, talking gently as he worked, examining her for any sign of harm despite her weary whimpers.

Too nervous to sit still, he pushed past the cops waiting their turn and went into Casey's room to get the air compressor he had seen earlier, to set up the nebulizer for the child's breathing treatment. Bringing it back into the living room, he plugged it in. "Where do you keep the mask and nebulizer?" he asked softly.

"In the kitchen. Second cabinet on the right."

He went in and found the necessary pieces in a sterile bag, tore it open and grabbed the three medicine bottles and vial of saline, and brought them back to Leah.

She took them with her free hand. "Thank you, Jeff."

He stooped down next to them and watched the doctor listening to Casey's breathing. "I didn't know which medicines you needed, so I brought them all."

She pointed to the ones she needed, and instructed him on how to mix them. In seconds, she slipped the mask over Casey's pale face and turned on the machine. A fine therapeutic mist floated out of the airholes on the mask.

"Is she okay, Dr.?"

The doctor smiled, and Jeff decided at once that he liked him. Leah had made a good choice in pediatricians.

"She'll be just fine as soon as we get this wheezing under control," he said. "Everything else looks fine. They must have handled her with care. She's a very lucky little girl."

"Yeah, right."

He watched as Casey tried to shove her thumb through the air hole in the mask and put it in her mouth. Closing her eyes tightly, she relaxed against Leah and tried to sleep.

The cops sat down, their hip radios still blaring, and Borgy and his detectives came in.

"Did you see anyone at all at the park?" the cop began to ask. "Any parked cars? Anyone sitting on a bench, standing in the shadows?"

"Nobody," Jeff said. "It was dead quiet." He looked at Casey, falling asleep against Leah, still wearing the mask as if it was a familiar routine.

"Me and my men can give you all the details you need, mate," Ben told the cop. "We 'ave recordings in the kitchen as well as the note."

Two of the cops followed him out. The third one gave them a tentative look. "You know, it wouldn't hurt to talk to the reporters. Since the kidnappers haven't been apprehended, maybe someone who hears about it might have some information. Besides, they're going to report it whether you talk to them or not. You want them to get the facts straight."

"Dad can talk to them," Leah said, her voice flat. "He can tell them everything they want to know. I just . . . I just can't right now."

A flurry of activity followed in the kitchen, but Jeff stayed in the living room, his eyes never leaving the tiny child clinging in her sleep to her three favorite things—her bunny, her blankie and her mother—while she breathed the vaporized mist into her lungs. That he wasn't among those favorite things ate at him from the core of his being, and he felt his anger being crowded out by sheer despair.

An hour later, after he'd finished with the reporters outside, Lance Borgadeux ambled into the room, putting himself between Jeff and Leah. "Fumbling idiots let them get away," he said. "They're still out there. It was so easy for them. They'll try it again, you know."

Jeff saw the terror seeping back into Leah's weary eyes.

"I want you to come home with me . . . tonight," he said. "Right now. You and Casey will be safe there, Leah."

Jeff saw her drop her face into the child's soft curls, and he could see that she struggled with the decision.

"You can't stay here," Borgadeux said. "You'll be all alone . . . vulnerable. . . ."

"I'll stay with her."

Jeff's words sounded so foreign to him, that for a moment he wasn't aware that he had uttered them.

Borgy turned around, regarded him with a threatening look, and Leah looked up at him.

"I'll stay here," he repeated. "I won't leave her. She'll be safe."

Borgadeux came to his feet, his big form lacking the intimidation it once held for Jeff. "Who the hell do you think you are?"

"I think I'm the child's father," Jeff said, giving him a what-are-you-gonna-do-about-it look. "And if anybody's going to protect them, it's going to be me."

"And you think you can hold off dangerous criminals trying to get at my granddaughter?"

"Yeah, I think I can."

"And what if you're wrong, hotshot? What if you can't?"

"And what if *you* can't?" Jeff shot back.

"I live in a mansion," the tycoon said. "I have guards at the gates, guards at the doors, guards inside the house, security systems that alert the police at the drop of a paper clip, close-circuit televisions that pan the grounds. Just what do you have to offer her?"

"I care," Jeff said. "I care about what happens to that little girl, and by God, I'm not going to sit here and let you bully Leah into hiding her away from me now that I know about her. Not unless it's what she wants."

The qualifier seemed to please Borgadeux, and smiling, he turned back to his daughter. "Tell him, Leah. Tell him where you'd rather be."

Leah's voice was hoarse when she spoke. "I'll stay here, Daddy," she whispered. "If Jeff will stay with us, I'll stay here."

"Are you out of your mind? Do you know what kind of danger you're putting yourself and that child in?"

Confusion settled over Leah's eyes, and she turned them back to Jeff. Despair clouded over her expression, once again, as she kissed the top of Casey's head. "Maybe he's right, Jeff. We don't really know what we're dealing with."

"I can take care of you and Casey until the kidnappers are caught," he said without a doubt. "You owe this to me, Leah. You owe me the chance to do that."

"This isn't about owing," Leah whispered.

"No, Leah," he said. "It's about trusting. As far as I can see, nobody here really trusts anybody."

"I trust you," she whispered.

But I don't trust you, he thought. If she took the child to her father's and he locked them away there, Jeff's chances of seeing Casey again were next to nothing. And he didn't trust Leah to care about that one way or another.

"Then stay here," he told her. "Stay here with me."

The words, uttered so confidently, washed over her with warm security. Security that she hadn't known in such a long time. It was nice to have someone to take care of her, someone to worry about her, someone to take part of the burden off her shoulders.

Someone besides her father, who only added new ones when he took the old ones away.

The medicine ran out, and Leah removed Casey's mask and cut off the machine. "I'm staying here, Dad," she whispered, coming to her feet with the baby asleep in her arms. "I think it's best for Casey to sleep in her own bed tonight. If she wakes up in the middle of the night, I want her to know where she is. I don't want her to have to be afraid again." Not waiting for a reply, she headed toward her daughter's room.

Borgadeux swung around to the man who'd come between his daughter and him once before. "I'm warning you, Hampton, you'll regret the day you ever crossed me if you keep getting in my way."

"Funny," Jeff said. "I was just about to say the exact same thing."

"She doesn't want you," he said. "She made that clear two and a half years ago. She dumped you, then had your baby and didn't even tell you. Does that sound like a woman who wants you around?"

He couldn't deny that it didn't, but at this point, that wasn't the issue. "I don't care if she wants me around or not," Jeff said honestly. "The point is that I'm going to protect my daughter, I'm going to get to know her and I'm going to let her know that she has a father she can count on. And I don't give a rat's ass what you or your daughter think about it."

Borgadeux gave a frustrated, sarcastic, even threatening chuckle and shook his head. "You don't know what you're getting into, Hampton. This isn't wise."

"Your threats don't work on me anymore, Borgy. I'm immune."

"Nobody's immune," Borgadeux said, his eyes suddenly deadly serious. "I don't think you understand how far I'm willing to go for my daughter and grandchild's sake."

Jeff met his eyes with seething seriousness of his own. "And I don't think you understand how far I'm willing to go. This child casts a whole new light on the subject, Borgy. She's my flesh and blood . . . my family. And if you have any delusions that I'm going to disappear, think again. I can fight just as dirty as you can."

He saw Borgy's eyes dart to the bedroom door and turned to see Leah standing in the doorway. He wasn't sure how much she'd heard, but from the look on her face, he knew she'd heard enough.

"She's sleeping," Leah whispered.

Her hair was wild and tousled around her face, and she didn't wear a stitch of makeup. To look at her, one would never know that she was the pampered princess of the Borgadeux fortune. One would think she had character, and warmth and heart.

"Are the police gone?"

Borgadeux nodded. "They said they'd keep us informed. Ben and Willy and Jack left with the cops."

"And the reporters?"

Borgadeux shrugged. "I'll give them what they want in a minute."

Leah nodded silently. "I'm really tired, Daddy. I'd like to get some sleep."

Borgy looked back at Jeff, his eyes still threatening. "Leah, you have to—"

From the bedroom, Casey started to cry, and Leah turned and fled from the room.

"Give it up, Borgy," Jeff said.

Cursing under his breath, Borgy grabbed up his keys from the counter and slammed out of the house.

JEFF WAITED A MOMENT, staring at the closed door, listening to the quiet of the house, breathing the scent of Leah's turf. They were alone. Finally. And just in there, just beyond the hallway, was his little girl. Safe and sound.

She had stopped crying when Leah had gone to her, and quietly he stepped into the darkened hallway and to the door of Casey's room. Leah was sitting on the edge of the bed, holding her, and Casey's eyes were closed again.

"Is she all right?" he whispered, not wanting to disturb her.

Leah looked up at him, saw the apprehension in his eyes, the reluctance to step into the circle of love the little girl wore about her. She smiled and nodded. "She's fine. She just woke up and got scared."

He lingered at the doorway, as if he had no right to come farther into the room, now that the child was back.

"Thank you for staying," Leah whispered. "I really didn't want to go back with my father."

He didn't answer. Instead, his eyes fell from Leah's eyes to the child, whose head was relaxing back on Leah's arm.

"Is he gone?"

Jeff looked up at her. "Who?"

"My father. Is he gone yet?"

"Yeah," Jeff said.

"How'd you do it?" she asked softly. "Make him leave, I mean."

He shrugged. "Just let him know I couldn't be pushed around."

Realizing that the conversation wasn't about to be two-way, Leah hushed and looked down at the child in her arms. Casey's breathing had relaxed to a steady cadence, free of wheezing, and her thumb had fallen out of her mouth.

"You can sleep in my bed tonight," she whispered.

His eyes darted up to hers, and Leah blushed... something that surprised him, for in the last two and a half years, he had tried hard to forget those little vulnerabilities about her. Instead, he'd concentrated on her coldness, her selfishness, her unyieldingness on the day she had left him.

"I mean... I'm going to sleep in here with Casey. I don't want her to be alone."

"Fine."

She looked up from the child and settled her eyes on him again. It seemed that they were strangers, with nothing in common except the child. The child he didn't even know.

Quiet grew like a wall between them, defining the darkness of the voids in both their lives.

Finally, Jeff pushed away from the door's casing and started to walk away.

"Jeff?"

He stopped in the hallway, turned back.

"Would you like to hold her for a minute before I put her down?"

He froze, but despite his seeming paralysis, his heart accelerated. "Won't she...won't she wake up? Won't it scare her?"

"She's sleeping pretty soundly," she whispered. "I think it'll be all right. Besides, I'll be right here."

For a moment, he didn't make a move to come nearer. He only stood at the doorway, staring at the child, with eyes that held the slightest trace of terror.

Finally, he took a step toward her.

Leah stood up and met him across the room. For a moment they looked at each other, that trust that he had sworn to be so lacking in her radiating like candlelight in her eyes. She trusted him enough to hand over her child. Even if it was for only a moment.

Taking a deep breath and trapping it in his lungs, he opened his arms and allowed her to place the child in them.

She was light, he thought as a soft, poignant, yet sad smile came to his lips. And sweet. And warm.

Quietly, he backed to the rocking chair and lowered himself into it. Distributing her weight across his lap and pulling her closer, he looked down at her little face, which he hadn't had the chance to really see clearly since it had been hidden behind a thumb or crushed against her mother's breast ever since they'd found her.

Her face was shaped like his, he thought, long and narrow, and her little nose reminded him of his own baby pictures. But her mouth was Leah's—soft and full and pouting....

His heart burst at the sight and feel of the child in his arms, and slowly he bent down and pressed a kiss on her forehead.

Leah came closer, knelt beside him and smiled softly at the delicate gesture. She saw the tears mist over in his eyes. Saw the way his throat convulsed. Saw how his hands trembled.

Gently, she set a reassuring hand on his knee, letting him know that he was doing everything right.

The edges of his mouth trembled as he dropped his face down into Casey's curls, just like he had seen Leah do a hundred times since they'd been home. She smelled of baby shampoo and Leah, and suddenly, the sensation of loss welled so deeply inside him that he couldn't fight the feeling breaking out over his face.

Leah saw it, and the pain he struggled with found its own seat in her heart. "What is it, Jeff?" she whispered, desperate to help him with the burden of his pain, as he had helped her tonight. "What are you thinking?"

His lips tightened across his teeth as he brought his moist eyes to hers. "I was thinking," he whispered, "that I don't know how I'll ever forgive you for what you've done to me."

Chapter Six

In Leah's face, Jeff saw the pain his words had inflicted, but he told himself she deserved to hurt. He had every right to hate her.

And yet, there was Casey, lying asleep between them, curled snug and warm in his arms. The one bond that would unite them for the rest of their lives, despite all that had passed before.

"I can't blame you for that," she managed to say after a moment. "And for what it's worth, I never expected you to forgive me."

His eyes fell from Leah back to the little girl in his arms. He wondered how much she had weighed at birth, if she would have fit perfectly from the palm of his hand to the crook of his elbow, if he would have been able to burp her, feed her, diaper her. He wondered if Leah had breast-fed.

Idly, his eyes strayed to the woman kneeling in front of him, and slowly, pensively, dropped to her breasts, covered by cotton fabric. Tearing his eyes away, he began to rock as the child felt more comfortable in his arms.

Her curls spilled down his bare arm, and he wondered if she'd been born with a lot of hair, and if it had been curly at birth. He wondered if she'd slept all night at first, how old she'd been when she'd said her first word.

Again, his eyes drifted to Leah's small body, a body that had always made him feel so strong, so protective. And so miserable.

It was Leah's soft, sad voice that finally broke the quiet. "It's late," she whispered. "We should get some sleep."

Jeff nodded and looked down at the sleeping child, but he didn't want to let her go. If he could feel this way in one night, he thought, how intense must Leah's feelings for the child be after two years?

She stood up and pulled back the covers on Casey's bed. Slowly, Jeff came to his feet and laid the child on her side, repositioning the blanket against her face and the bunny near her hand, where she wouldn't have to look far to find them.

Leah watched as he remained bent over her, stroked the hair back from her face, pulled up the covers and pressed a soft, undisturbing kiss on her temple. He turned back to Leah, raked his hand through his hair and avoided her eyes. "Do you need anything from your room before I go to bed?"

She shook her head. "No, nothing."

He started for the door, but she reached out and caught his arm. "Jeff?"

Not looking back, he stopped.

"Thank you," she whispered. "I couldn't have gotten through this without you."

Jeff turned around and gave her a cold, heartless look. "You owe me, Leah. And I intend to collect."

"You will," she whispered. Leah waited until he was out of sight, until she heard her bedroom door close, before she pulled back Casey's covers and lay down beside the child. It didn't matter that she was still dressed. All that mattered was that Casey was back in her arms. And Jeff was here, too.

She dropped her head on the pillow, which Casey rarely used, and tried not to think about the shower that she heard running, or the fact that Jeff had opted to spend the night with her to protect her. It wasn't her safety he cared about, she told herself, but Casey's. And that was all right. That was enough.

The clock ticked on, until she heard the water cut off, heard the mattress of her bed squeak beneath his weight. She wondered if his hair was wet, what that day's growth of stubble felt like on his jaw, if her soap smelled differently on him than it did on her.

And then she told herself to stop wondering. It was no use. She had destroyed any possibility she'd ever had of resuming things with him.

But even knowing that, it felt wonderful to know he was there, in the next room, watching over her. Even if he could never love her again, she was glad to have him back in her life.

IT WAS HOURS LATER when Jeff gave up the idea of sleeping. How could he be expected to lie in Leah's house, in Leah's bed, between her sheets, on her pillow, and not think of her? The scent of her hair and her skin brought back a flood tide of memories that he lacked the energy to fight. Memories of their driving off to Sanibel Island on the spur of the moment, of their pitching a tent on the beach and making love with the autumn breeze sweeping across their skin.

Was that when they had conceived Casey? Or had it been the Christmas weekend they'd spent in his apartment, making tree ornaments out of popcorn, glue and glitter, painting the windows with artificial snow? Had it been before or after he'd given her the small diamond necklace he'd shopped for weeks for— the one that matched the ring he had planned to give her later?

The one she hadn't accepted.

Pulling out of bed, he went to the window, and looked out onto the Gulf lapping against the shore behind her house. The moonlight defined the white-caps ruffling the water, and he thought there was going to be another storm soon.

Restless, he walked around her bedroom, taking in the personal items that he didn't want to see, for he had no interest in knowing any more about her than the fact that she'd stepped on his heart and betrayed him in the deepest way.

He picked up her brush, saw flaxen hairs threaded through, and remembered the time he had brushed and braided her hair, that night on Sanibel Island. It felt like silken threads slipping through his fingers, without a tangle, without a kink. It was baby hair, he'd told her, and she had laughed.

He set the brush down and went to the picture of her and Casey framed and angled on the dresser. Casey was laughing, and Leah smiled with the most serene smile he'd seen on her. Had motherhood really changed her? Had it taken the restlessness from her spirit? The insecurity that her father had spent her whole life instilling?

Idly, he went from the dresser to her chest of drawers, and saw the little jewelry box lying on top. Knowing he shouldn't, he opened it. The diamond necklace he had given her was tucked in a satin pocket, and he pulled it out, held it in his palm. Did she wear it? Or did she keep it hidden away, like the ring he hadn't even looked at since he'd sworn to put her out of his heart.

You could sell it and get all that money back, Jan had told him more than once. *It must have cost a fortune.*

But Jan had never understood that, when he bought it for Leah, she had been *worth* a fortune to him. He just hadn't been worth that much to her. He kept it as a reminder not to make the same mistake again—not to trust that fickle, fatal emotion poets called love for want of any more accurate, more scathing word.

He heard a humming within the house and, instantly more alert, opened the door quietly and looked out. He realized the sound was coming from Casey's room.

Slowly, he made his way through the darkness to her door, and saw the source of the noise sitting on a towel in the corner of the room. It was the humidifier, blowing a fine mist of cool air throughout the room, making Casey's breathing come easier. He wondered how long ago Leah had filled it with water and turned it off.

He looked at the bed, saw Leah was sound asleep, her arms firmly around her child—his child—just as Casey's arms were firmly holding her blankie and bunny. Leah's hair was splayed across the pillow, and her mouth was slightly open, making her look innocent and pure rather than selfish and conniving.

He turned away.

He had watched her sleep many times before, and always, it had melted his heart. Like the child, she was beautiful.

But she was also dangerous.

She stirred slightly, and he saw her shiver. The covers had fallen off her in favor of the child, and he realized that the temperature had dropped. Looking around, he saw the afghan lying on the trunk in the corner of the room. He picked it up, feeling the soft knit of it, and laid it gently over her.

Quickly, he backed out of the room, desperate to put some distance between them. This wasn't going to be easy, he told himself, but he was doing it for his child, not for Leah. He wasn't going to let his feelings about her spoil his new relationship with his daughter. Nothing would keep him from knowing Casey, or from letting her know him.

More tired now than he had been before, he went back to Leah's room, climbed once again into her bed and laid his head on her pillow. Wrapped in the scent and softness of her possessions, he slept.

"I WANT GUMMI BEARS."

Casey's first words, at 7:00 a.m. the next morning, brought Leah instantly awake. The child was sitting up in bed. A tuft of curls fell over her face, and her eyes were still sleepy. She looked the way she did on any average morning. Healthy, happy, and here...right here where Leah could reach up and kiss her warm little cheek.

"Good morning, sweetheart."

"Gummi Bears, Mommy. Turn on the TV."

Leah's smile blossomed to a full flower, and she sat up and hugged Casey. "You got it, pumpkin. Come on. I'll race you to the TV."

Giggling, Casey hopped off the bed and, dragging her blanket behind her and still clutching her bunny's ear, she ran as fast as her plump little legs would carry her.

Leah reached the television seconds after Casey. "You won!" She raised Casey's fist in mock victory. "Even with a ten-pound diaper—" she said, patting the wet diaper dropping to the child's knees "—you still beat me."

Casey giggled and poked the power button on the television, where the Gummi Bears cartoon sprang to life. Then, ignoring the wet diaper, the child climbed up onto the couch, put her thumb in her mouth and began watching.

"You little rascal," Leah said, sitting down next to her and smoothing her hair. "You'd think it was any other morning." *Not the morning after you were kidnapped.*

Tears came to her eyes, and she smeared them away before her daughter could see them. "So are you hungry?"

Casey nodded. "I want a Tootsie Pop and five do-nuts," she said, holding up two fingers.

"No can do," Leah said with a smirk. "How about oatmeal, yogurt or cereal?"

"No can do," Casey said.

"All right then. How about eggs and bacon?"

"How 'bout cupcakes?"

"You mean *pan*cakes?"

"With syrup?"

Feeling as if she'd been outsmarted, Leah messed up the child's hair and planted a kiss on her neck, sending Casey into a delightful round of giggles. "All right, you little con artist. Pancakes with syrup. This morning you could probably talk Mommy into anything. But first, let's get you out of this diaper."

Casey's smile faded as her eyes focused on something in the door, and Leah turned around to see Jeff standing there, wearing only his jeans. His chest was bare, except for the sprinkles of hair curling across it, hair she had flirted with and splayed her hands through. His eyes were sleepy, and his hair was mussed.

She thought he had never looked better.

"Hi," she said with a smile.

"Hi." His greeting was soft, tentative and more directed at the child than her.

Casey's thumb headed for her mouth.

Leah smiled again. "She's in a good mood. Like nothing ever happened."

"That's a good sign. Isn't it?"

"I think so," she said. She turned back to Casey. "What do you think, squirt?"

"I think cupcakes," Casey said, looking up at Jeff with eyes the size of quarters, apprehensive eyes that seemed to fear his presence as though it meant she wasn't going to get those pancakes.

"Pancakes," Leah corrected.

"With syrup."

It was Jeff's turn to smile.

Leah picked Casey up, put her on her lap and pointed up to Jeff. "Casey, do you remember who this is?"

Casey was silent for a long moment as she studied the strange man who had come from her mother's bedroom, wearing only a pair of jeans. Her thumb gravitated to her mouth.

"He's Jeff," Leah prompted. "And he's..." She met Jeff's eyes, swallowed. "He's your daddy. Can you say 'daddy'?"

She saw the poignant expression on Jeff's face, but Casey shook her head.

Jeff stooped in front of her. "That's okay. She doesn't have to call me that yet. She can call me Jeff."

"Daddy's as easy to learn as Jeff," Leah said. "Isn't it, Casey?"

Casey took the thumb from her mouth, and cocked her head at Jeff. They held their breath, waited.

"You want cupcakes?" she asked.

Jeff grinned. "You feed her cupcakes for breakfast?"

Leah rolled her eyes. "*Pancakes*."

"With syrup," Casey added.

And as they all started for the kitchen, Leah wondered how long this feeling of pure, unadulterated happiness could last.

THE ANSWER CAME LATER that morning, when Casey sat at her little play table smashing clay pancakes, and Leah and Jeff finally found themselves alone in the kitchen.

"We have a lot to take care of today."

Leah turned around at the sink and saw Jeff rubbing his tired eyes and looking at her.

"Like what?" she asked.

"Like seeing to it that those kidnappers are caught. Plus, I would really like to introduce Casey to my sister and call my parents. They should be told about her." He breathed a dry laugh and brought his coffee to his mouth. "I can just hear it now. 'Hey, Mom, I just thought I'd give you a call and let you know that you have a two-year-old granddaughter. Why didn't I tell you? Well, because the mother forgot to tell me.'"

Leah dropped a pan in the sink and felt her face growing hot. "I didn't forget and you know it."

"No, you didn't forget," he said. "But that's infinitely easier to explain than the real reason."

She dried her hands roughly on a towel and turned back to him. "Look, Jeff, nobody would blame you if you just picked up and walked out of here right now. I can take care of myself and my daughter—"

"*Our* daughter," he corrected. "And you'd like that, wouldn't you? For me to just disappear again?"

"No," she said, emotion quivering on her voice. "As a matter of fact, I wouldn't. Believe it or not, I'm glad you're here."

"Yeah, right." He pushed back his chair and stood up. "Anyway, I won't leave you and Casey alone today... not while those kidnappers are still on the loose. You'll have to come with me."

Leah nodded. "I didn't plan on opening the shop today, anyway. All the publicity—"

"You mentioned that earlier," he said. "What is it you do?"

"I have a dress shop," she said. "It's called Leah's, and it's how I support Casey and me."

"Oh," he said. "I thought—"

"That I was living off of my father? I told you I wasn't. I opened the shop with a small business loan I got on my own. It hasn't been easy, either, but I've managed."

He looked at her pensively for a moment. "What do you know? You an entrepreneur...."

"And a good one," she said. "But since I'm not opening today, Casey and I can go with you to your work site. I'd like to see what you're working on."

Her interest surprised him, but he pretended to ignore it. "Before that, we'll drop by the office of a private investigator I know, get him started on the case—"

"But my father's people are working on it. And the police—"

"And they haven't found them yet," he cut in. "It can't hurt to have one more person on it."

"I guess not." Leah stepped toward him, a frown wrinkling her brow. She didn't have on a stitch of makeup, and her hair had yet to be brushed. He couldn't remember ever seeing her look so tousled . . . even after the night they'd spent on the beach, she had slipped away and put on a touch of makeup before he could see her the next morning.

But oddly enough, she had never appeared more beautiful to him. That thought made him angry.

"Jan will be at my work site, so I can take care of a few things while we're there."

Leah took a dishrag to the table and began to wipe away the breakfast spills. "Jan probably doesn't have real good feelings about me."

"Nope, she doesn't," he said in a you-made-your-bed-now-sleep-in-it tone. "And after this, she'll downright hate you. But hey, that's the breaks."

His nonchalant way of dealing with his pain made hers even more pronounced, and she shoved her hair back from her face. "Look, Jeff, I'm not fighting you on any of this. I'm grateful for your being here, whether I deserve it or not. I'm grateful for your attitude toward Casey, and I'm grateful for your protection and concern for her. But in order for both of us to tolerate this situation, you've got to stop sniping at me. Casey will sense it, and it won't do either of us any good."

Jeff looked through the doorway to Casey, who had begun making "beans" out of her clay. As she played, she hummed bits and pieces of "Itsy Bitsy Spider." The sight of her softened his lips.

"Do you think she remembers yesterday at all?"

"Of course." Leah sighed and went to stand beside him in the doorway. "I'm just hoping that her attitude today means that she wasn't traumatized too badly. Maybe they were nice to her."

"The police said she needs to see a psychologist for evaluation."

"Yeah," she whispered. "I'm not looking forward to it."

"I'll come with you," he said quietly.

She nodded, wondering how he could be sarcastic and angry one minute, then sweet and considerate the next. It frightened and confused her.

"So... do you want the bathroom first?"

She smiled. "If it's okay. Sorry there's only one."

He shrugged. "That's all right. I have a hot date for some clay pancakes with a cute little two-year-old I know." As he spoke, he went and sat down beside Casey, and she started to giggle.

For the moment, Casey was too distracted by the man molding teddy bears out of her clay to notice that her mother had left them alone. But the moment Leah turned the shower on, the child looked around for her mother.

"Where's Mommy?"

"She's taking a shower," Jeff said, handing her the molded teddy bear.

Casey stood up, knocking over her little chair. "I want my mommy."

"Take it easy," Jeff said quietly. "She's just in there."

Tears burst to Casey's eyes, and she ran to the bathroom door. "Mommy!"

"Wait. Mommy'll be right out."

The child's cries rose to high-pitched, terrified screams. "No! I want my mommy! I want my mommy now!"

Throwing herself against the door, Casey reached for the doorknob, turned it. The door opened, and a thick cloud of steam rolled out, its fragrant scent wafting over the house. "Mommy! Mommy!"

The water was cut off. "Mommy's here, honey. What's wrong? What is it? Jeff!"

Jeff stopped in the doorway, trying not to look toward the drawn curtain. "I'm here, Leah. She got spooked when she noticed you were gone."

The child's screams grew more panicked, and she tried to scale the bathtub to get in with Leah. Her foot slipped, sending Casey sprawling backward on the wet floor. A bloodcurdling scream tore from her throat.

Forgetting why he couldn't go in, Jeff burst into the bathroom and snatched her up.

Leah held the thin plastic curtain against her and looked out the side of it. "Is she all right?"

"No harm done," he said over the child's screams. "She didn't hit her head." He sat down on the lid of the toilet, struggling to calm her.

He looked up and saw the silhouette of Leah's bare body behind the curtain, the shampoo dripping from her hair, the water beading on her naked shoulder. His throat went dry and he stood up and started back for the door. "Come on, Casey. We'll wait for Mommy outside the door, okay?"

"No!" Squirming to get down, Casey screamed again, the sound breaking Leah's heart. "Mommy!"

Quickly, Leah turned the water back on. "Just let Mommy rinse out her hair, okay, baby?"

Jeff turned his back to the shower. "Leah, if I let her down, she's going to slip again. And I don't want to upset her by taking her back out."

"Then stay here."

He glanced over his shoulder. "What?"

"Just sit in here with her. She'll calm down if she realizes you aren't trying to take her. I'm hurrying."

Not knowing if her idea was such a good one, he readjusted the squirming, crying girl on his hip and sat again on the lid of the toilet. "Okay, Casey. We're going to sit right here and wait for Mommy, okay? You can see her right through that curtain. See?" As the child calmed, his own heartbeat accelerated. His voice, however, retained its soothing, honey tone. "Mommy's not going to leave you, and nobody's going to take you from her. Okay?"

Still hiccuping her sobs, the child rubbed at her eyes and laid her head back on his chest. "Be-cos I want my mommy," she whimpered.

"I know you do." His eyes strayed to the silhouette behind the curtain as Leah arched her back and rinsed out her hair. Her breasts were fuller than he remembered and her hips smaller. He wondered how it would feel to step into the shower with her and lather those soft, delicate curves, and feel her body against his just one more time.

She cut off the shower.

"Uh . . . could you hand me the towel?" Her voice sounded awkward, tense.

He lifted the towel off of its rod and handed it to her, keeping his head turned.

"I'm really sorry about this," she said from behind the curtain. Despite his efforts to keep his eyes diverted, his gaze gravitated to the naked shadow as she towel-dried her body. His mouth went dry as she moved the towel over her breasts, her arms, her flat stomach, her legs.... "Having a two-year-old can be pretty demanding."

Vaguely, he picked up the thread of her words. His voice sounded distant and distracted when he answered. "I can handle it," he said absently.

He watched her silhouette wrap the towel around her, watched her tuck a corner between her breasts. Slowly, self-consciously, she pulled the curtain back slightly. "I guess this insecurity answers our question about her remembering yesterday."

There was still a cluster of wet drops on her shoulder, and he fought the urge to smooth them away with his fingers. "Yeah."

She noted the clipped way he spoke and the way his throat convulsed as he looked at her. "You could probably set her down now. I can take it from here."

"Yeah." He felt silly, only uttering monosyllables, but he was afraid his voice would give him away if he tried to say more. He set Casey down and stood up.

"I'm sorry about all that. You should be able to take a shower without an audience."

Leah smiled. "You obviously have a lot to learn about parenthood. I haven't taken a shower alone in two years."

He turned back and gave her a soft smile, and of their own accord, his eyes fell to those bare, wet shoulders again, to the swell of her breasts, to the bare, thin legs and the wet feet with apricot-colored toenails.

As if she didn't notice his pensive scrutiny of her, she bent over to her daughter. "You okay now, Casey? You know Mommy's not going to leave you?"

Casey stuck her thumb in her mouth and nodded as Jeff closed the door behind him.

MOMENTS LATER, when Leah dressed and turned the bathroom over to him, he didn't even try to use the hot water. Cold, icy jets sprayed over him, but it did nothing to ease the physical ache produced by what he had seen earlier.

He tried to block out the memory of her body sliding over his so long ago. Tried to forget the honey-sweet taste of her mouth as she'd responded so completely to him.

When he came out, freshly shaven with the razor she'd left for him, he found them both sitting in the living room waiting for him. All remnants of Casey's tears were gone, and she was dressed in a frilly little sundress. Her hair, long ringlets to her shoulders, was pulled back from her face with a big white bow.

He smiled and stooped in front of Casey. "I think you might just look pretty enough to deserve a Tootsie Pop."

Casey's eyes lit up. "I want a red one."

"One red Tootsie Pop, coming up," he said. "We'll stop at the first store we come to."

Casey's smiled faded, and she gave Leah a troubled look. "Mommy come, too?"

Jeff glanced up at Leah. "Do I look like a man who would forget your mommy?"

The question, though meant innocently and flippantly, struck them both. Quickly, he rallied.

"Mommy's coming, too. You don't have to worry."

Demonstrating that she wasn't worried, Casey hopped down from the sofa beside her mother and headed for the bathroom. "Wanna see I'm big?"

He came to his feet. "Sure, I do."

"I can go potty."

Leah followed them back into the bathroom, noting that Jeff had dried the floor before he'd come out. "We've just embarked on the long road to potty training," she said as she tugged the little girl's training panties down.

She set Casey on the potty, and the child smiled up at them.

"You'd better get comfortable," Leah told Jeff. "This sometimes takes awhile."

Jeff stooped next to Casey. "I am just so profoundly amazed at how big you are," he said softly. "Up on the potty and everything."

"I'm big," she confirmed.

Promptly she slid off the toilet without having produced anything, and with her panties still at her ankles, reached over to flush. "See? All by myself."

Leah's smile matched his. "This is when we applaud."

The two began to cheer and clap as Casey struggled to get her panties back up. Continuing the jubilation,

Jeff swung her up off the floor, setting off a round of giggles. Slowly he lowered her to his face and set a kiss on her mouth.

Casey didn't object.

This must be what a family feels like, Leah thought as her laughter faded and fell into a soft smile. *Except that in a normal family, the father doesn't hate the mother.*

Quietly she started back out of the bathroom.

"Mommy!"

Leah turned around and saw the panicked look on Casey's face. "What, honey?"

"Don't leave me."

Exchanging looks with her, Jeff set her down and let the child scurry into her mother's arms.

"It's going to take some time," she said.

Jeff nodded. "I just happen to have a lot of that," he said. "Come on, let's go."

Chapter Seven

Together, they saw the psychologist, who evaluated Casey to the best of his ability and noted her fear of being separated from her mother again. Casey would have to learn how to trust, he told Leah. But that would take patience. It wouldn't happen overnight.

As they drove to the office of the private detective whom Jeff insisted on hiring to help in the search for the kidnappers, Leah thought of what the psychologist had said. Trust. It was something that Jeff was having trouble with, as well. And why should he trust her, after all? She had lied to him, hurt him, kept the most precious thing in his life from him....

She wondered what the good doctor might have to say about guilt, and self-forgiveness. She found it hard to believe that Jeff would ever be able to forgive her until the day she forgave herself. But that wasn't so easy.

Patience. She didn't know if she had enough, or if he did. Oh, it would be no problem to see Casey through her trauma. It would be no problem staying with her constantly until she was secure enough to be left again. It would be no problem letting Jeff into her child's life. What she wasn't sure of was whether or not she had the patience to wait for him to stop hating her.

They met with the private detective who bombarded them with new questions that she was happy to answer, praying all the while that he would be able to make headway where her father's people and the police had failed. The one time that she allowed him to question Casey, the child seemed to withdraw within herself and clung harder to Leah. Thankfully, Jeff had refused to let him ask Casey any more.

Casey conned Jeff out of a second Tootsie Pop sucker as they started to his work site to see Jan. Leah felt a new tension seeping into her bones. What must Jan think of her after what she'd done to Jeff? What would she think of her now, when she found out that her deceptions went much further than any of them had imagined.

If she'd had a choice, she would have stayed in the van. But Casey would never have gone in without her, so feeling like French royalty headed for the guillotine, she helped the child out of her car seat and started toward the trailer.

Jan was at the door before they had a chance to reach the trailer.

Instead of leaping on Jeff and chastising him for not telling her more, Jan crossed her arms and faced them squarely. "I saw the news this morning," she said, giving Jeff a guarded look and Leah a drop-dead one. Casey, she regarded with uncertainty.

"Hi, Jan," Leah whispered.

Ignoring her, Jan turned back to Jeff. "What's going on, Jeff?"

"Inside." He opened the door and motioned his sister in before him.

Reluctantly, Leah followed, carrying Casey, who still sucked on her Tootsie Pop and had a sticky pink ring around her mouth and coating her hands.

When they were inside the small trailer, Jan gave them all a sweeping look again. "Are you two back together or something?"

The question came with disapproval, sinking Leah's heart further. Jeff avoided her eyes.

"No," he said quickly. "Nothing like that. It's Casey." Reaching over to stroke her tendrils, he offered his sister a tentative smile. "Jan, Casey's my daughter."

Jan's face drained of all color, but from her expression, he knew she had already suspected after the news accounts on television. "Yours and . . . *hers?*"

"Yes." It was Leah who spoke this time.

"And you didn't tell me?"

"He didn't know," Leah said. "I kept it from him."

"You *what?*" As if the injustice had been directed solely at her, tears sprang to Jan's eyes. "You had my brother's child and didn't tell him?"

Jeff stepped between them. "Enough, Jan. We've been all through this, and now is not the time. For now, I wanted Casey to meet her aunt."

Slowly Leah set Casey down, and Jan's expression transformed into a sad, longing look as she bent over the child. "Aunt? I guess that does make me an aunt, huh?"

She stooped down, smiled at the candy on the child's face. "I see my brother's already spoiling you." Reaching for a tissue on her desk, she wiped the stickiness away then threw a look up at her brother. "Is she all right? I mean, after the kidnapping and all?"

Leah stooped next to Casey. "Yes. She's fine, except for being afraid to leave my side. They didn't hurt her. Not physically, anyway."

Jan gave Leah another cold look before turning her eyes back to Casey. "How old is she?"

"Two."

"Two." The word stuck in Jan's throat. "Two years you kept this from my brother?"

"Jan..." Jeff began, but Jan got to her feet.

"Jeff, can I see you outside for a minute, please?"

Jeff glanced awkwardly at Leah, then reluctantly at Casey. "Make yourselves at home," he said. "I'll only be a minute."

He followed Jan out of the trailer. When she reached the bottom of the steps she turned to face him, arms crossed. "Jeff, tell me that you aren't starting things back up with her. Instant family and all that."

"I told you I'm not. I'm just hanging around until the kidnappers are caught. Besides, I have a right to get to know my daughter."

"You're telling me! I hope you realize what kind of cruelty it takes for that woman to hide your child from you for the past two years. If she had ever known you, if she had ever loved you, she couldn't have done that. She would have known how much it would have meant to you."

"I'm well aware of that, Jan. And believe me, the last person in the world I want to get involved with is Leah Borgadeux. But she's the mother of my child. And right now, that's all that matters."

LEAH HEARD BITS and pieces of the conversation as it drifted through the open trailer window. She hadn't meant to listen, but there hadn't been a way to escape it.

The last person in the world I want to get involved with is Leah Borgadeux.

Jeff's words pierced at her heart, forcing a slow tear to trickle to her cheek. The funny thing was, she didn't blame him a bit.

How could a man who'd come from a loving home and a loving family ever understand the depths to which her father would have sunk to break them up? How could he ever understand that—at the time—she had believed she had no choices left?

But he couldn't, wouldn't ever understand that. It defied logic. The most she could hope for was that it wouldn't hinder his relationship with Casey. Or hers, later, when Casey grew up and learned what Leah had done.

Leaning over, she readjusted the bow in Casey's hair and pressed a kiss on her cheek. "Do you like your daddy?" she asked.

Casey nodded. "I like Tootsie Pops."

"That's all you're going to get for today, young lady." She wiped the tear off her face and lifted Casey into her lap.

The door opened, and Jeff came back in. Jan followed behind him. Offering Leah another cold look, she went around her desk. "Here are your messages," she said, handing a stack of notes to Jeff.

Jeff took them, flipped through. "I have to return a couple of these." He glanced at Leah. "Do you mind waiting a minute?"

"No, not at all." It was all so civil, she thought. The way they addressed each other over Casey's head, the way they pretended to get along.

He disappeared into his small office, and Jan went back to her desk and pretended to be absorbed in her work. But Leah wasn't fooled.

"Look, Jan..."

Jan held up a hand to stem Leah's words. "Don't. Whatever you're going to say, don't."

"I was just going to tell you that I don't blame you for disliking me. I'm not too pleased with myself right now."

Jan's sharp eyes met hers across the desk. "If you hurt him again, Leah, you're gonna pay for it. Somehow, you're gonna pay."

The words stung, and Leah thought of all the heartache she had suffered over the past two and a half years since she'd left him. It hadn't gone away, had only numbed into a manageable feeling that she'd grown used to. She thought of all the hard times she'd faced with Casey, times when she'd felt so lonely and so alone that she wondered how she would go on. She thought of all the men who had asked her out, men who by all rights should have held some attraction to her, but she'd turned them all away. And she thought of the constant, nagging memory of the man who possessed her heart, the man who now hated her. "I've already paid," she said.

The words seemed to make Jan angrier. "You've never paid for anything in your life."

Leah pulled Casey against her and gave Jan a look cool enough to match her own. "You don't know me," she said. "You don't know anything about me."

"I know enough."

The two women held each other's piercing gaze for a long moment, until a crash sounded behind Jan's desk. She swung around and saw a broken vase lying on the floor and a cat prowling away.

Casey gasped. "A catty! Mommy, look!"

The exclamation diverted their attention and brought the slightest hint of a smile to Jan's lips as she picked up the pieces of the vase. "He's a bad cat. He belongs to Jeff...I mean, your father...." She stooped to scoop up the cat and hold it out for Casey to pet. "What *does* she call him?"

"Nothing yet," Leah said softly. "But we're shooting for Daddy."

"Daddy." Jan repeated the word pensively as Casey reached out a tentative hand and touched the cat's soft fur. Her face resumed its tightness. "You know, I always looked forward to the day Jeff had a little one to wrap him around her finger, but I never expected it to happen like this."

"Neither did I," Leah whispered.

Jan tried to punch some life back into her smile as she looked at the child. "The cat's name is Sylvester, like in the cartoon. I think he likes you."

Casey giggled.

The cold edge to Jan's eyes died, and she touched Casey's curls. "She beautiful. She should be in commercials or something."

"Thank you." The words came softly, tentatively.

"She looks like him, doesn't she?"

Leah smiled. "I've always thought so."

They heard Jeff's footsteps across the trailer, and he came into the doorway and saw Casey petting the cat.

"Has Sylvester been sidling up to you?" he asked, bending over to Casey. "You have to be careful. He can get you into trouble sometimes."

As if in protest, the cat meowed.

Casey mewed back.

"Here," Jeff said, picking up Sylvester's ball off the floor, and handing it to Casey. "Throw this and he'll run after it."

Casey did as told, and the cat scurried after it, chasing the spongy ball as if it were a colorful little mouse. Casey slipped out of Leah's lap and followed the cat around the room.

"So…" Jeff said, looking from Leah to Jan. "What does Aunt Jan think of her niece?"

"I think that the minute you're out of here, I'm going to be on the phone looking for a talent agent. That kid belongs in the movies. We could put her picture on the front of a calendar and sell millions."

Smiling like a father, he stooped down and grabbed the ball. "Sorry, but I just found her. I'm not ready to share her yet."

Much to Sylvester's chagrin, he handed the ball to Casey, then messed up her curls. Jan looked at Leah again with an expression that warned she was watching her. Leah returned a look that said, *I know he's vulnerable right now. I won't take advantage of that.*

Jan went back to her desk and plopped into her chair. "The news said the kidnappers hadn't been caught. What are you going to do?"

The question was directed more to Jeff than to Leah, but Leah answered nonetheless.

"My father has a team of detectives on the case, the police are looking and today Jeff hired his own detective to look for them."

"Aren't you afraid?" she asked grudgingly.

"Yeah, a little." She glanced back at Jeff's strong shoulders as he bent over Casey, and thought how much more afraid she might be if she didn't have him.

"So when will you be back at work?" Jan asked her brother.

"I don't know. I'll let you know."

He leaned over, put his hands under Casey's arms to pick her up, and Leah held her breath, hoping that Casey would allow him to hold her. Her wish came true.

He pressed a kiss on her cheek and, smiling like a man who'd finally found his way home, headed for the door. "Come on, Mommy. We have to go now."

Casey looked back over his shoulder. "Come on, Mommy."

Leah smiled, but that smile quickly faded as she saw the look in Jan's eyes again. *Yes, it's a farce,* Leah's eyes seemed to say. *But it's for Casey. And it's worth it.*

THE MELANCHOLY of that afternoon turned to stark fear as the sun fell and the kidnappers still had not been caught. More reporters circled her house and hounded her phone line. Her father's calls came every hour. And the police and detectives were no closer to finding the two men who had taken her baby than they had been the day before.

It was only then, as she watched Jeff barbecue hamburgers on the grill on her deck, that she realized how afraid she was. Jeff hadn't made any mention of where he was going to sleep tonight. Surely she couldn't expect him to stay here. For all she knew, he had other commitments, other obligations, possibly other attachments. She hadn't even asked him if he was involved with someone. What if he was in love and wanted to be with her tonight, instead of baby-sitting Casey and Leah?

The phone rang again, and Jeff, who had been balancing Casey on one hip while he turned the burgers, looked up at her. "Don't answer it. In fact, go unplug the phone."

Leah shook her head. "I can't. It could be news about the kidnappers. I'll let the machine get it again."

They listened, and heard the voice of her father, telling her once again that he wanted her to bring Casey and stay at his house that night.

She sighed. "He may be right, you know. One or two nights wouldn't hurt, and we'd be safe."

Jeff flashed her a look and, closing the grill, set Casey down. Taking a step toward her, he assessed her with eyes that she feared could see right through her. And she wasn't ready for him to see all that was there.

"I'm staying with you tonight," he said. "I told you I'd stay until they were caught."

Leah handed him the plate she had brought out. He took it, but she didn't let it go. "I know what you said, Jeff, but why should I expect you to put your life on hold for us? If I went over there, you could go home...."

"But you don't want to go over there," he said. "At least, that's the message you've been giving me."

"No," she whispered. "I don't want to. But I'm getting nervous, Jeff. They haven't been caught yet. I thought they'd be in jail by now. They could come back."

"All right," Jeff said, accepting her fears as valid. "Tell me one thing. Why didn't you want to go to your father's before? Why were you so dead set against it? So much, in fact, that you opted to stay here with me?"

She couldn't tell him the real reason. At least not all of it, for she couldn't handle his scoffing at the feelings he would never believe. "Because I was afraid that if he got me home, it might be harder and harder to leave."

"It's comfortable there, no doubt about it. You'd have everything you need, everything you want...."

"That's not what I mean," she said. "You don't know him. If he got us there, he'd find more and more ways of keeping us there. It was hard to break free, Jeff, but I did it. I don't want to go back."

A knock sounded on the door, and Leah closed her eyes. "Another reporter. I can't take this anymore." Her hands trembled as she pushed them through the roots of her hair, and Jeff put the plate down and set his hands on her shoulders, gently urging her face up with his thumbs.

"You don't have to take it." She met his eyes, her heart beginning to burn at the touch that was so gentle that she wondered if he was even aware of it. "We'll go to my house. Chances are they'll leave us alone there, and if not, well, we won't be quite as bothered by all of it there. My house is a little bigger than this, and the land is fenced, so they can't come up and pound on the door anytime they want."

"Are...are you sure? I mean...I wouldn't be stepping on anyone's toes?"

The moment she asked, she felt silly, for it was blatantly obvious that she was fishing for information on his love life.

"You mean...like a woman?"

She felt her face reddening. "Is there one?"

He let her go and turned back to the grill. As he opened it, a white cloud of smoke billowed out. "Not at the moment."

She felt a smile breaking out over her heart, but she kept it from reaching her face. "Then...I guess it would be all right.

"But Casey..." She looked at the little girl who was chasing a lizard across the deck. "I wanted her to be able to sleep in her own bed."

"Then we'll stay here," he said, turning back to her. "It's your choice. But whatever you decide, I'm not leaving you."

The reassuring way he said that made her heart melt in gratitude...and much more. But along with those

feelings came regret greater than any she had ever
known. For the reassurances were meant for Casey,
not her.

"Good," she whispered. "I mean . . . I don't want
to go to my father's. It helps to know you're here."

Their eyes held for a moment, and finally, he turned
back to the grill. "It's ready," he said. "We can eat
now."

AN HOUR LATER, as they were clearing the dishes from
the table on the deck, a camera flashed. Instantly, they
both turned around and saw a reporter standing on the
sand below them. "Miss Borgadeux?" he called.
"May I have a few minutes of your time?"

Her face reddened, and she grabbed Casey and
pulled her back against her. "Go away or I'll have you
arrested for trespassing!"

Flashing one more picture before Jeff started toward him, the reporter trotted back around the house.

"*Damn* it," Leah said. "He could have been the
kidnapper. How do I know who's a reporter and
who's a criminal?"

Jeff took her arm and turned her around. "Hey,
take it easy. He's gone."

Tears burst into her eyes like a tropical wave held off
by a crumbling sea wall. "When can we leave?" she
asked.

He pushed her hair back and cupped her neck.
"Right now."

"Great," she said quietly as she grabbed Casey and
started inside. "Let's hurry before I lose my mind."

LEAH'S MIND was still intact by the time they got to Jeff's house, set on a three-acre lot surrounded by a chain-link fence in which two Irish setters romped. Outdoor floodlights illuminated the gravel driveway in the opaque darkness. As they pulled in, the dogs jumped up to the van windows, eagerly whining for their owner to acknowledge their itching ears and wet noses.

"When did you buy this?" Leah asked as they drew closer to the house hidden behind an enormous oak tree.

"About two years ago," he said.

That his purchase had happened just a few months after their breakup was obvious. "It's beautiful, Jeff. But it's just you. Why would you buy all this just for yourself?"

"Wanted some permanency," he said. "I got tired of waiting for something to happen." He parked the car and got out to greet the yelping dogs as Casey squirmed in her seat and squealed, "Puppies!"

"They're a little bigger than puppies," he said, reaching into the back seat and unbuckling Casey from her car seat.

Leah tried to focus on the dogs and Casey's reaction, but Jeff's words still hung on the air. "Something like what? What were you waiting to happen?"

He set the suitcase down and looked up at her as if she were an unwelcome intruder on a joyous moment. "I don't know. Look, the house isn't all that big. It only has three bedrooms."

"But you only need one."

"Not anymore, I don't."

He lifted Casey up to his shoulders, and the little girl, who had grown used to him throughout the day, squealed and wrapped her arms around his neck, giggling at the dogs still wagging their tails and nuzzling his legs. His attitude, concerned and caring just an hour before, grew guarded and distant from Leah as he unlocked the house and switched on the light inside.

The living room looked like a decorator's showcase. From the deep velvet sofa to the pecan coffee table and the wallpaper and trims that made the place at once lovely and unlivable, there were expensive and elaborate accessories generously placed throughout the house. None of them seemed to possess anything of Jeff's personality or preferences. It was as though he'd had nothing at all to do with arranging his home.

"Did a professional decorator do all this?" she asked, looking around.

"Most of it," he said.

She touched a lamp that she knew had cost hundreds of dollars. "Jeff, it's beautiful, but...when I knew you before, you weren't the extravagant type."

"Yeah, well, we all make mistakes," he said, taking Casey off his shoulders. "I guess I was trying to prove something."

"Prove what?"

"I don't know! That I wasn't just some slouch who wasn't good enough for the almighty Borgadeux."

"But who were you trying to prove it to?" she asked softly.

"Myself," he said. "That's all."

Casey ran across the room, exploring some of the expensive breakables he had sitting out. Jeff's eyes followed her with adoration rather than worry about his possessions.

"You never had to prove that to me, Jeff," she whispered. "I liked you the way you were."

"You *left* me the way I was."

As if he couldn't sit still under her scrutiny, he got up and set an expensive vase on the mantel, out of Casey's reach. But Leah wanted to continue the conversation. She couldn't leave it hanging.

"Jeff, I can see that you've been successful. But if you don't mind my pointing this out, that only proves my point. If we had stayed together, you wouldn't have had the means to buy any of this stuff. My father would have seen to it."

"But it wasn't the *stuff* I wanted in the first place, Leah," he said with an insufferable weariness that seemed to doubt she could ever understand.

"And it wasn't what I wanted, either," she whispered.

Casey found a tall bar stool, and whined to be put up on it. Jeff obliged.

"You can go check out the bedrooms if you want," he said, changing the subject. "I figure you can stay in the middle one, since it has access to the master bathroom. The one on the end can be Casey's."

She reached down to pick up the suitcase, and Jeff went on. "I plan to have it decorated for her as soon as I can. I want her to spend a lot of time here."

Leah turned back. "What do you mean, a lot of time?"

"I mean, I want to see my daughter on a regular basis, Leah. I want her on weekends, and a night or two during the week. I want her on holidays and, when she's in school, summers."

Leah's face paled. "Jeff, she's too young to be bounced around. She's not ready for this."

"You mean, *you're* not ready for it."

She swallowed. "All right. *I'm* not ready for it."

"Leah, you're the one who wrote this script. I suggest you start preparing yourself," he said. "I'll prepare Casey."

A lump of emotion lodged itself in Leah's throat as she started back to the bedrooms.

THAT NIGHT, AS SHE LAY next to Casey, with whom she had decided to share a bed since the child was nervous about the new room, she stroked her daughter's cheek.

"I love you, Mommy," Casey whispered.

Leah's heart melted. "I love you, too."

Casey looked around, her big eyes taking in the new surroundings enshrouded in darkness, except for the Mickey Mouse lamplight in the corner, which Leah had brought from home. "This Daddy's house."

Leah smiled. It was the first time Casey had called him that, and she regretted that he was across the hall, showering in the bathroom, and hadn't heard it.

Casey smiled. "I like Daddy."

"Yeah," Leah whispered. "Daddy's a pretty good guy, huh?"

"Daddy buy me Tootsie Pops."

Leah smiled. "Daddy spoils you rotten."

"I like Daddy," Casey said again.

"So do I," Leah whispered as her smile faded. "So do I." She stroked her daughter's hair back from her face and whispered for her to close her eyes. In moments, she thought, sleep would pull Casey under its spell. But as tired as Leah was, she knew that sleep wasn't ready for her yet.

She heard Jeff moving around his bedroom, and knew he was out of the shower. Would he go straight to bed or would he stay up awhile?

She shivered as she thought of his words earlier, when he'd told her he wanted Casey on weekends. The thought of handing her over to anyone, even Jeff, chilled her. Reaching down, she grabbed the blanket beneath Casey's feet and pulled it up to tuck around her daughter's shoulders.

Casey didn't stir, and she knew she had found sleep.

Getting up, she slipped on her robe, tied it at the waist and went back into the living room. Except for one small lamp, he had left it dark.

She went to the telephone and decided to call and listen to her messages, in hopes that there would be word on the kidnappers by now. She dialed the number and listened.

Most of the calls from the press had been hang-ups, thankfully, so the rest were primarily from her father. Sighing, she hung up the phone.

"Anything important?"

Jeff's question made her jump, and she turned around. He was leaning against the doorway, wearing only his jeans, which were noticeably unbuttoned at the waist. His hair was still wet and a shadowy stubble darkened his jaw.

"No, nothing. Just some more reporters and my father."

He lingered there a moment, taking in the sight of her white silken robe, and her hair falling straight and silky around her face. "You want some tea?" he asked, finally. "I have decaf."

The fact that he remembered how she loved to drink tea before bed moved her, and she nodded. "I'll get it, though."

She went into the kitchen and he came in behind her, handing her the cups and sugar. He was too close, and his scent was no longer that from *her* shower, *her* soap, but from his. A flood of memories washed over her, and she kept her eyes down, away from him.

"So Casey's asleep?"

"Mmm-hmm." She filled the kettle with water, turned on the burner. She felt her lips quivering at the corners, and she prayed she wouldn't cry. She could go numb for just awhile, she told herself. She could hold back the pain until later. Summoning all her strength, she finally had to look up at him.

He was leaning next to her against the counter, watching her with eyes that held traces of regrets of his own, and a wealth of memories.

Their eyes met, locked, held, and she asked herself where she could hope for this to lead. She was feeding her grief, adding to her remorse, by even entertaining the idea that he could still be attracted to her.

"She called you Daddy tonight," she whispered.

His face changed. "Really?"

"Yes. Just before she went to sleep. She told me she liked you."

His smile was undeniably sexy, and unaccountably vulnerable. "She said that? Really? What were her exact words?"

"I believe they were, 'I like Daddy.'"

He raked his hand through his hair and looked longingly back toward the bedroom where the child slept. "Damn. Why couldn't I have heard that?"

"You will," she said.

He was quiet for a long moment, and his eyes settled on her again. "Thank you," he said.

"For what?"

"For telling me. I know you weren't thrilled with what I said earlier. About taking Casey on weekends. You could have kept this to yourself."

The teakettle began to whistle, and Leah turned around and moved it from the burner. Again, she felt the ache of tears behind her eyes. "I knew you would want to know."

"I did. It helped."

She poured the tea, keeping her eyes averted, but she couldn't hold back the tears pushing into them. He saw them glistening in the soft light, and touched her chin to bring her face up to his. "What's the matter?" he asked. "What are these tears for?"

She swallowed back the emotion in her throat and took a deep breath. "Why do you want to take her from me?" she asked, her voice breaking. "Can't you see that she's all I've got?"

He took her shoulders and turned her to face him. "Leah, I'm not the bad guy. I'm not going to take her from you. I'm her father. I have a right to spend time with her, too, and it can't always be with you there. It's not fair to you or me."

"But it's not fair to either of us for you to take her alone. You've seen how she clings to me! She's never been away from me one night in her whole life. Even the night she was kidnapped, she still slept in her own bed, with me right there beside her. You may be her father, Jeff, but you're not the one she depends on!"

Her tears fell over her lashes, tumbled down her cheeks, but still he held her shoulders and stared down at her. "She'll come to depend on me over time. I've only had one day."

Leah covered her mouth to hide its trembling. "Jeff, she's my baby."

"She's my baby, too," he whispered.

"But you have others in your life," she said. "You have Jan, and your parents are great. You have two dogs out in the yard, and friends, and probably even a couple of girlfriends. Don't you understand that I don't have any of that? All I have is Casey!"

"If that's the case, it's because you won't let anyone else in your life, Leah. That's not my fault."

Leah's crying came harder now, and her shoulders shook beneath his hands. She dropped her face into her hand, and tried to hide the tears that had come so easily lately. "I know it's my fault, Jeff. But that doesn't make it easier."

He watched her cry, and something inside him stirred to life. Some protective instinct—the same one that had assaulted him yesterday when he'd thought Leah was the one who'd been kidnapped—emerged full force. He slid his hands down the silk of her robe and pulled her against him.

She curled into his bare chest, her cheek pressed against his heart, and she felt his hand combing through her hair. "Shh," he whispered. "I'm not going to take her away from you. We can love her together."

She looked up at him, still enclosed in his arms, and raised her hands to his bare shoulders. "Really, Jeff?" she asked on a sob. "Really?"

He wiped her cheek with the pad of his thumb, and cursed himself for allowing those tears to weaken his resolve. "Yeah."

What was he saying? some voice inside asked him. That he would let her have her way? That he would forego a relationship with his daughter just to keep from making Leah cry? Or that he would go on as they had the last day, hanging around in her life, being a third wheel in a family that wasn't really his?

It didn't matter, because for now, the only answers his heart could focus on, were the blueness of her eyes and the redness of lips wet with tears. She kept looking up at him, kept waiting for more promises, but he found he had none to offer her.

She wet her lips, and he saw the way her eyes fell to his mouth. She could feel his heart beating against her hand, he thought, could feel his reaction to her. It gave her power, and he didn't like it. But it was power nonetheless. And he wasn't strong enough to fight it.

Gently cupping her chin, he tilted her face up to his and descended slowly to her mouth. She tasted salty, like warm tears. Her mouth opened to him, as if it came naturally, and his tongue swirled gently against hers.

Her hands slid up his chest, around his neck, and he felt her raise up to her toes. His hands slid down her back, to the hips that fit his palms, and he pulled her against him.

He knew she could feel his arousal, and he could feel hers in the free, complete way she devoted herself to his kiss. He wondered what she wore beneath the robe, if it would slip easily off her shoulders, if she would balk if he scooped her up and carried her to his bed.

He felt her whimper within the kiss, felt her hand slide down his back, felt her pulling his hips closer against hers. She had always been a great lover...the best lover. She had always known what he liked, how he wanted to be touched.

His hand slid up to the neck of her robe, and he slipped one side off her shoulder. A spaghetti strap held her gown, and breaking the kiss, he nuzzled her neck, then slicked his tongue across her bare shoulder, pulling the strap down as he did.

His blood was hot as he felt her hands moving between them, to the open button at the waist of his jeans. Her hand splayed over his flat abdomen, slid lower, lower.

An urgency, a desperation, a hunger that lacked rationale or reason burned like a torch inside him, and he realized that he *had* lost all power. That she, once again, was completely in control of him.

The thought exhilarated, stimulated, excited him.

It also scared the hell out of him.

Pulling out every shred of control he still possessed, he stopped her hand.

Leah looked up at him, her eyes smoky with longing.

"We can't do this," he whispered. "We can't."

That disarming sadness returned to her eyes. "Why not?"

"Because," he said more firmly, "we can't go back. What's done is done."

She slipped her hand out of his, let it drop to her side, and stepping back, adjusted her robe. "You're right," she whispered.

He could see the embarrassment on her face, the humiliation, and he hated himself for putting it there. He had started it after all. *He* had kissed *her*.

And she had responded in a way that would keep him awake all night, keep his heart thudding whenever she came near, keep his hormones pumping for a long time to come. It made him furious.

"Sex was never our problem," he whispered.

She shook her head.

"It was always good," he went on, condemning himself further with every word. "That's why we can't. It would cloud too many things."

She tried to blink back the tears crowding her eyes, but he saw them. "Funny," she said. "I thought it might clear some things up."

"Like what?" he asked. "Like whether or not I'm still attracted to you? Well, you have your answer. I am. Physically, my body reacts just as strongly to you as yours reacts to me."

She didn't let the confession lift her hopes, for she heard the unspoken "but" hanging on the end. "And emotionally?"

"Emotionally, Leah, I'd like nothing better than to never see you again."

She stared up at him, her eyes as hurt as his and tried to breathe. But her lungs seemed to have collapsed.

"But since Casey's involved, I have no choice."

"*We* have no choice," Leah said, lifting her chin. "So I suggest that if you want us both to remember the way you feel, that we keep our distance, both emotionally and physically. That means no more long, wet, scathing kisses."

The subtle reminder that *he* had kissed *her* hit its mark. "Agreed," he said.

"Good." She turned around, starting back to the bedroom, and Jeff stopped her.

"Leah, there's one other thing."

She turned to face him and crossed her arms like a sentinel guarding a fragile treasure.

"This weekend I want to take Casey to meet my parents. Of course, you'll have to come along, too."

Leah's tough facade fell again, and for a moment he thought her tears would return. "Fine," she said. "I guess they deserve that."

"She's their granddaughter," he reminded her.

"I know that," she said. "We'll be ready whenever you say."

He watched her leave the room, then wilted back against the counter. His pulse was still pounding, and his hormones were still whirling. His body was still painfully aware of just how much he had wanted her.

And so was she.

It was a power he couldn't let her have over him again. It was too heady, too seductive.

And when it ended, the power could devastate him. He had let her do it to him once.

She would never have that chance again.

Chapter Eight

Instead of going in to work the next morning, Jeff decided to leave Leah and Casey in his home, where still no one had found them, and visit Borgadeux's detectives personally. The case was going nowhere, and even his own detective was drawing a blank. He wanted to make sure everything possible was being done to catch the kidnappers.

The office of Palm Investigations was smaller and more run-down than he would have expected for one of Borgadeux's teams, and from the temporary sign on the door, it looked as if they hadn't been around for very long.

He went in, saw a few desks scattered around the room, and only two people working telephones and computers, though none was active at the moment. The sight of inactivity gave him a sinking feeling, for it was apparent that the office wasn't all abuzz with worry over the kidnappers.

One of the women looked up when he came in. "Can I help you?"

He shrugged. "Yeah. I was looking for Ben or Willy. My name is Jeff Hampton."

Without getting up or picking up the phone, the woman let out a yell that shook the peeling walls. "Ben, someone's here for you!"

"Comin'!" came the reply from one of the offices.

In seconds, Ben was at the door to his office, and he peered out and seemed surprised to see Jeff. " 'Ow ya doin', mate? Didn't think I'd see you again."

Confused, Jeff shook his hand and followed him into the dirty office filled with boxes and new furniture. "Are you moving out of here or something?"

"No, movin' in." He knocked a stack of books off of a chair and gestured for Jeff to take it. "So what brings you 'ere?"

"What brings me here?" The question was ludicrous, and Jeff remained standing and gaped at the detective as he dropped into his seat behind his desk. "The kidnapping investigation, what else? I wanted to see what's being done to find my daughter's kidnappers."

"Well, nothin'."

Jeff wasn't sure he'd heard correctly. "Nothing?"

Ben frowned and leaned forward, setting his elbows on the desk.

"No. Mr. Borgadeux fired us right after the girl was found."

"He fired you! Why?"

"Got me. I thought it odd, too, but 'e paid us more money than we usually make on a case like that, then sent us on our way." He leaned up to his desk, set his hands on it. "I was a mite disappointed, too, if you don't mind my sayin' so. We'd kind of 'oped 'e'd give us more work. We sure coulda used it.''

Jeff lowered to the chair behind him, his amazed expression reflecting the profoundness of his rising anger. ''Do you mean to tell me that you've never worked for him before?''

''Never,'' the man said. ''Why 'e decided to 'ire us, I don't know. 'E retains one of our biggest competitors in the city. But who am I to argue, right? I thought maybe 'e was lookin' to replace 'em.''

Jeff stood up again, and prowled around Ben's office, trying to sort out what he'd just learned. ''His granddaughter had been kidnapped. Why would he hire someone he'd never worked with before, when he had an office full of crackerjack detectives already on his payroll?''

''Got me. And why'd he want to call off the 'unt just like that... Well, all I can figure is 'e decided to go back to 'is own PI's after all. Guess we won't get more business from 'im, but at least we made enough to 'elp pay for these offices. Nice, ain't they?''

Jeff looked absently around. ''Yeah. Nice.'' Still battling the questions raging in his mind, he started back to the door. ''Well, thank you for your time.''

''Right.'' Ben said, hopping up and holding out his hand. ''And just for the record, I apologize for the way we 'auled you outa your office the other day. You 'ave to understand, mate. In a kidnapping where the parents don't live together, one of the first suspects 'as to be the father. Borgadeux almost 'ad a 'eart attack when we started asking questions about you. 'E told us we might 'ave screwed up everythin'.''

"Screwed up everything? Why?"

"Guess 'e wanted you to stay in the dark about the kid. But it was Leah who told us to find you. No 'ard feelings, 'ey?"

"None," Jeff said. "Thanks for the information."

He went back to his car and started home, struggling to make sense of what he'd just learned. But there was none to be made of it. He only hoped that this niggling fear in his heart was unfounded.

"I WASN'T HIDING from you, Dad." Leah leaned over to hand Casey the apple she had cut up for her, and cradled the phone with her shoulder. She had returned his call after getting a dozen from him on her machine. The last few had been desperate, furious, and he'd threatened to put out a search on her if she didn't call him to let him know where she was. "I just had to get away from the phone calls and the reporters."

"How was I supposed to know you hadn't been kidnapped, too?" he bellowed. "How was I supposed to know that some sick maniac hadn't found a way into your house...."

"Dad, I'm fine. I'm at Jeff's. It's safe here, and no one knows we're here."

"Safe?" he scoffed. "Is he there with you?"

"No, not right now, but—"

"Does he have guards posted outside?"

"No, Dad, but—"

"Does he have a security system? Do you have a gun?"

She grabbed the phone and switched it to her other ear. "No. He has two dogs, though, and a fence around the property, and the phone doesn't ring off the hook and reporters aren't clustered outside waiting for a glimpse of Casey."

"Well, then you aren't safe, Leah. And this ridiculous stand you're taking in refusing to come home with me is only endangering your daughter's life."

Unable to argue with that, Leah took the cordless phone and crossed the room to sit next to Casey, as if her nearness could hold any harm at bay. Idly, she stroked the child's hair as she spoke. "Have they gotten any closer to finding the kidnappers, Dad?"

"They found a witness," he said. "Someone who saw a man with a little girl who looked like Casey. He was in a green car, and she seemed upset. Ben got a description of the man, and he's working on it."

"Really?" she asked, standing back up. "Can he do something with that?"

"It's a start," he said. "I'm paying them a lot of money to work around the clock on this, darling."

"The man. Was it the same one who took Casey from Anna's house?"

"Could be. The point is, they're making progress. We're going to crack this soon, Leah. But those men are still out there. They got two million dollars from us. They might try it again. The only way you can both be completely protected is if you're here with me."

Leah looked at Casey again and wondered if her father was right. Was she being stubborn? Was she risking Casey's life? She started to say something but heard Jeff's car coming up the gravel drive. "Dad, Jeff's home now. I'll call you later."

"Leah, you can't go on as if everything is business as usual! Give me his address, and I'll come over there and get you myself."

"No, Dad. I won't go with you. I said I'll call you later."

She hung up the phone just as Jeff came in. He was wearing a white dress shirt with the sleeves rolled up, and a pair of jeans. His eyes—as they swept down her freshly washed hair, to the tight tank top she wore, to the short white tennis shorts, to her bare legs and feet—were fatigued and troubled.

Casey smiled and started shyly toward him, instantly making him smile, as well. "Hi, there," he said, lifting her up and dropping a kiss on her cheek. He glanced across the room to Leah. "Who were you talking to?"

"My father," she said. "He threatened to put an APB on me if I didn't tell him where I was, so I called. But there's good news. He said that Ben had found a witness. Someone who saw Casey in the car with a man. He's working on some more leads, and—"

"Ben? He said that? That Ben found a witness?"

Leah faltered. "Well...yes. Why?"

He stared at her for a moment, trying to decide whether to tell her that for some reason he couldn't fathom, her father had lied to her. That no one was really working on the case. But he decided now wasn't the time. Not until he had a little more information.

"I guess...I'm just glad to hear they're making some progress."

The awkward, tense silence fell between them again, and Casey held an apple slice up to his lips. "I got apple. Want some?"

Jeff's grin was troubled as he took a bite. "Good," he said. "Thank you."

Trying to cross the bridge that loomed precariously between them, Leah got Casey's napkin and wiped her face. "Why are you back so soon? I thought you were going in to the office."

He shrugged. "I planned to, but I got kind of sidetracked. And I didn't feel good about leaving you two alone."

She let her gaze drop to the floor. "Well, you didn't have to come home. Casey's almost ready for a nap."

"You should take one, too," he said. "You look tired."

"So do you," she whispered.

"Maybe I will. But I have a few phone calls to make first."

The dismal feeling that she was intruding on his life washed over her, and she nodded. "All right. I'll lie down with Casey so you can be alone."

Jeff watched Leah leave the room with Casey, and for a moment after she was gone, he stared at the place where she had stood moments before. Something about the way she had believed her father tore at his gut, and he wondered what the man was up to.

Quickly, he picked up the phone and dialed the number of his own investigator. Almost immediately, the receptionist put him through.

"Yeah, Phil. This is Jeff Hampton."

"I was just working on your case, Jeff."

"Find out anything?"

"No. This case is incredibly clean. You got anything?"

"Maybe." He glanced in the direction of the bedrooms again, and lowered his voice. "I stopped by Borgadeux's detectives today. The ones who were there the night of the kidnapping. They told me he fired them from the case. And now I come home, and Leah tells me that her father told her that these same guys are making a lot of progress. What do you make of that?"

The detective was silent for a moment. "I don't know, but I'm gonna find out."

"Yeah, you do that."

When he had hung up, he sat down and stared back in the direction of the bedrooms. She was in there, lying with his daughter—her daughter. *Their* daughter.

The phone rang and absently, he picked it up.

"Hello?"

"Hampton, put my daughter on."

Jeff bristled at the overbearing tone. "She's sleeping, Borgy, but I'll tell her you called."

"Wake her up. This is important."

He thought of calling him on firing the detectives, but something told him not to. Not yet. The man would only rally with excuses, and cover his tracks before Jeff could get to the heart of it. Still, he couldn't squelch his sarcasm. "Is it about another lead on the case?"

Borgadeux hesitated. "I said I want to talk to my daughter."

"And I said she's asleep."

He could almost see the man's face turning crimson. "I'm warning you, Hampton. If you come between my little girl and me again—"

"Little girl? Are we talking about Leah? She's a grown woman, Borgy."

"She's like a little girl when it comes to making decisions," he said. "She doesn't know what she wants. She needs someone to take care of her."

"I'm doing just fine," Jeff said.

Another moment of silence followed.

"Hampton, before this thing is over, she's going to be begging me to come home, and you're going to be left with your heart splattered like the last time. She was raised too well to ever be committed to a nothing like you. Mark my word—"

Jeff slammed down the phone. "Bastard," he whispered through his teeth.

He got up and went into the hallway, looked through the open door and saw Leah lying on the bed with Casey cuddled up next to her. They were both still, and he wondered if she had fallen asleep as quickly as the child had.

The anger in his heart died by degrees, and he stepped closer, leaning against the doorway.

Lying there like that, so soft and vulnerable, she looked innocent. Not like the selfish heartbreaker Borgy had made her out to be. She looked fragile, and it made him want to protect her.

Crossing the room, he stepped closer to the bed and gazed down at her. What would she think, if he told her that her father had lied about the case? Would she think the best, or would she jump to the silly, ridiculous conclusion that his own imagination was jumping to?

But of course, none of that made sense. Her father couldn't be deliberately obstructing justice by calling off the dogs, could he? He would want to see the kidnappers caught as much as Jeff did. Wouldn't he? Even though their methods were different, their goals were the same.

Weren't they?

The doubts that nagged at him told him not to say anything to her until he had more facts. He had no doubt that Phil would have something for him soon.

Leah stirred, and her eyes fluttered open. She looked up at him with sleepy eyes and frowned.

"What?" she whispered.

Embarrassed that he had been caught watching her sleep, Jeff shrugged. "What do you mean, what?"

"Why were you standing there?" she asked softly.

He turned around, hiding the emotion on his face and started back to the door. "I... Your father just called. We sort of got into it again and... I thought I might have wakened you."

She sat up, self-consciously pushing back her hair. Checking Casey, she covered her with the afghan at the foot of the bed, then motioned for them to go out.

When they were in the living room, Leah turned around, "What did my father say to you?"

"The usual." He started into the kitchen, and she followed.

"I'm sorry. He never gives up."

Jeff opened the refrigerator, peered inside. "He wants you to call him back."

"Not now," she said with a laugh. "It'll just be another lecture designed to make me come running home."

She noticed that Jeff was staring at the contents, not seeing anything that was there. "What is it, Jeff? What's wrong?"

"I was just thinking. Wondering what kind of man your father is. What he's capable of."

He closed the refrigerator door and leaned against it, studying her with serious eyes.

Not certain what he was after, Leah shrugged. "He means well, Jeff. I'm sure of that. It's just that he's used to being in control. He can't stand the idea that I have a mind of my own."

"No," Jeff said, shaking his head. "I mean…what might he *do?* Before, when you talked about why you left me, you said he was going to ruin me. What kind of thing did he tell you he'd do?"

Leah sighed and left the kitchen, went back into the living room and sat down at the hearth, where the fire was crackling. Jeff followed her.

"Leah, answer me. I have to know."

"He said that he had contacts with your financiers. That they would pull the money out from under you. He also said there were rumors he would circulate about your business. Rumors that would ruin you professionally."

"Pretty tough words for someone who means well."

"Yeah, well…" She stopped, wet her lips, and went on. "You would have lost it all if we had stayed together."

"I'm a carpenter," he said. "I work with my hands. Nobody can ever take that away from me."

"You underestimate my father," she whispered.

He looked at her for a long moment, thought of how he had blamed her those two years, how he still blamed her, for screwing up his life. Did she really think she had *saved* it?

Memories of the kiss that night, the way her body had fit so familiarly against his, the way she had tasted, smelled… assaulted him with heart-rending force. That he could let her get to him that way infuriated him.

Hauling his thoughts back in, he stood up. "I have to go," he said.

"Go? Go where?"

Anywhere, he wanted to shout. *Anywhere but here where I have so little control.*

"To the office," he said. "I'll probably be back before Casey wakes up."

She watched him brood on his way to the table where he kept his keys, and giving her one last look over his shoulder, he left the house.

FOR OVER AN HOUR after he left, Leah sat alone in the growing dusk of his living room, arms hugging her knees, and tried to find the source of the gnawing pain in her soul. She was getting nowhere with him, because he would never forgive her for doing what she had to do. For being who she was.

She leaned her head back on the chair and tried to think of ways to make him stop hating her so. It was a feeling, an awareness, that she was not able to stand.

Because in her heart, she still loved him.

She closed her eyes and imagined a scenario in which she confessed to him, and he took her into his arms and told her that was what he wanted and needed to hear, and made slow, heartaching love with her until the sun came up.

But people didn't really live happily ever after, did they?

She got up, went into the kitchen and found a frozen roast in the freezer, some potatoes under the sink and various other things that had the makings for a good pot roast. Trying to get her mind off her heartache, she began to prepare him dinner.

When the roast was in the pressure cooker and there was nothing to do but wait, she went to the ironing board she had seen set up in his laundry room and turned on the iron. He ironed his clothes each morning before he dressed, she had noted, probably because he didn't have the time to iron them all at once, and he wasn't self-indulgent enough to send them out to be done.

She went into his bedroom, found all his wrinkled shirts and three pairs of jeans that had been left in the dryer until the wrinkles had set in and took them back into the laundry room.

Casey woke up an hour later, and as if sensing that it was safe to come home, Jeff came in soon after. Immediately he smelled the roast.

"What's that?"

She smiled. "Pot roast. I hope you weren't saving it for anything special."

He shrugged. "No. You cooked it?"

"Yes, I cooked it."

"I didn't know you could cook."

"There's a lot you don't know about me," she said.

She went back into the laundry room, where she had just finished ironing before Casey had gotten up, and brought out his clothes on hangers.

"What's that?" he asked again.

"Your clothes," she said. "I ironed them so you wouldn't have to."

He set Casey down, stared at her with confusion. "Why?"

"You seem to have a lot to do," she said. "It was something I could do to show my appreciation. Besides, I was bored."

"You could have watched television or taken a walk...."

"I wanted to iron your shirts," she said.

Before that baffled look had the power to sink her heart again, Leah went back into his bedroom to hang up the shirts.

THE SCENT OF ROAST wafted over the house, and suddenly Jeff was assaulted with the feeling of home . . . a feeling he hadn't ever felt in this house. There was dinner cooking on the stove, an adoring child at his feet, a woman in his bedroom, familiarly hanging his shirts back in his closet. The intimacy of what she had done, of going through his things and finding needs that she could fulfill struck him all at once. It made him want her more. But that desire made him desperately need to hang on to the anger he'd worn like a shield for so long.

They ate as if they were a real family, both telling Casey to sit up, to eat her carrots, to chew before swallowing. They passed the butter and the salt and talked about their daughter. It was nice. But it was also deceiving.

That night, as Jeff was putting Casey to bed, she looked up at him and framed his face with her little hands. "I like you."

His heart plunged then leapt, and he sat down and settled his soft, misty eyes on her. "I like you, too, Casey."

He pressed another kiss on her puckered mouth, gave her a tight hug, then backed away from the bed.

He caught the scent of Leah before he saw her, and he turned around. She was standing in the doorway in a long white robe, and her hair, just washed, was shiny and full around her shoulders. She was smiling, and he knew that she had heard the exchange between father and daughter. It didn't threaten her that her daughter could love someone else, he realized. It actually made her happy.

He diverted his eyes and slipped past her. Their arms brushed, and his heart jolted, but still he did not meet her eyes. "Good night," he whispered.

"Night," she said.

He left them alone in the room, and rather than staying up watching television as he usually did, he decided to take a shower. A cold, icy shower. A shower that could wash those irrational feelings away and make him forget how one look from Leah could make his heartbeat accelerate. A shower that cleaned his body but did nothing to cleanse his mind.

CASEY WAS ASLEEP in moments, but Leah found that sleep eluded her. It was around the corner, just out of her grasp. Just like Jeff.

She loved him. The admission seemed to make her feelings easier to deal with. She had established the problem, the source for her misery. Now all she had to do was act on it.

She had heard him take a shower, and the scent of his soap and steam still wafted across the air from the open bathroom. She wondered if he'd gone to bed. She wondered if he, too, were awake. She wondered if he was thinking of her.

Fleeting memories of an afghan tucked around her, of waking up to see him watching her, of the kiss that had seared both their souls and startled him into a retreat, assaulted her. He did want her. She knew that. But it was her job to make him *want* to want her.

And the first step would be telling him how she felt.

Slowly she drew out of bed, ignored her robe, wearing only the long silky negligee. Not knowing what she hoped to accomplish, if anything, she took a deep breath. Quietly she padded down the hall carpet and stopped at the open doorway to his bedroom.

He lay there motionless, staring at the ceiling, and for a moment, she didn't know if he saw her. Without a word, she started toward him.

He looked at her then, confused alarm flashing across his eyes as she drew nearer, and she saw his eyes dash down to her breasts, thinly covered by the white silk. His eyes moved back up to her face, anticipating what was to come. She saw desire there, lust and some emotion she couldn't name.

She also saw him tensing, as if he were the hunter's prey being stunned with a bright light.

She sat down on the edge of the bed, set her hand on his bare chest and stroked upward to his stubbled chin. Her eyes were serious, apprehensive, as she gazed down at him.

"Jeff, there's something I have to tell you."

She saw him swallow. "What?"

Her finger traced the curve of his ear, then slipped through the soft hair just above it. Slowly she bent down to kiss him.

His mouth opened in response, and their tongues grazed in a reluctant mating dance that neither seemed powerful enough to fend off. She felt his heart pounding beneath her hand, felt his breath seeping out in relief, felt his arms moving up her bare arms. One thumb moved across the silk at her nipple, inciting it to bud and peak in response.

He pulled her farther down, and more boldly now, his hand moved over her breast, palmed it, stroked it. His other hand moved down her partially bare back, to the hips covered with lacy panties.

Joy and ecstasy danced in her soul as she realized that he wasn't going to send her away... that he was going to love her as she needed to be loved... that he was going to allow her to love him as he needed to be loved.

Slowly he pulled her toward the center of the bed, laid her down and rolled onto his side. He slipped his knees between her thighs, and his hands began to move more urgently over her. His tongue played heart games in her mouth, and his ragged breath was swallowed up by her kiss.

His hands moved over her face, her shoulder. He slid her strap down, and the silky fabric slipped down over her breast.

His movements became more urgent, more rapid, as his desire grew. He broke the kiss, dipped his head down and grabbed her nipple in his mouth. She whimpered beneath his ministrations, and that very whimper seemed to heighten the urgency more.

He moved above her, and she could feel his tumescence beneath the briefs he wore. Then suddenly he peeled her panties off her and discarded them along with his own. She caught her breath as he filled her, and began to move harder, faster, with a contagious delirium that drew her to the brink of madness.

His body shuddered with the quick release, his heart pounding in dangerous rhythm, his skin perspiring and sliding against her.

Exhausted, he untangled himself from her and fell onto his back. She lay there beside him for a long moment, feeling the sudden rush of coldness—of incompletion. Lifting herself up on an elbow, she slid her hand across his abdomen and kissed the corner of his mouth.

His eyes came open, and she could see the smoky confusion coloring them. "Why did you do that?" he whispered. "I have to know why."

"Because," she whispered, her words a breath across his lips. "I love you. I've always loved you. I've never stopped loving you."

Roughly, he framed her face in his, stared at her with stricken eyes, as if he, too, had a confession to make. But after a second, she saw the shutters swinging shut over his eyes.

He pushed her away.

Tears burst into her eyes. "Jeff, I—"

"Don't," he said. "Don't say that to me again. I don't want to hear it."

"But it's true."

"It's not true," he argued. "It can't be true. Not after all this time. Not after all you've done."

Trying not to let the tears explode in front of him, she slipped out of bed, straightened her gown and found her panties lying on the floor. Grabbing them, she left the room without looking back.

Chapter Nine

The car radio droned out Tina Turner's cynicism as she wondered "What's Love Got to Do with It," and for the first time, Leah knew the meaning of the song. Love had nothing to do with it. Absolutely nothing. The lovemaking they had shared the night before was separate and apart from any connected emotion. Jeff had stroked her, cherished her, held her, quivered within her.... But it was only for a moment. And the moment passed.

They had gotten ready for the trip to see Jeff's parents without speaking to each other. Their avoidance of each other's eyes took a herculean effort, but Leah managed it. Anger, planted the night before, now grew and blossomed in her heart. But it was her problem to deal with, and she vowed to grit her teeth and endure the day for Casey's sake. If she found Jeff's distance disheartening now—and she did—she realized it was nothing compared to what she expected from his parents.

She had met his parents once before, when she and Jeff were in love and she'd believed nothing would ever separate them. But that was before her father had found out about him. Then, Al and Florence Hampton had embraced her as part of the family. Warmth and inclusion came easily for the couple who had spent twenty years operating the Hampton House, a country-music bar that was the hot spot of Brooksville's baby-boomer crowd. Everyone who came into their bar was family to them, but those who came into their home were treated even more warmly.

She wondered how that would change now.

Jeff had called yesterday and told them he was coming, that he was bringing a surprise and that they would like it. Jan, who'd claimed she didn't want to miss the looks on their faces, and added that Jeff might need a buffer to keep them calm, had gone on up the night before.

Leah didn't kid herself into denying that she was nervous. She was sick-nervous. The kind of nervous that clamped a vise over her chest and kept her from being able to breathe. The kind of nervous that made all the other negatives in life look even worse. The kind where tears seemed just behind her eyes, waiting for the worst possible moment to ambush her.

She thought about how stupid it had been to make love to Jeff last night. She thought how cruel it had been of him to accept it, then turn her away. She thought how miserable the day would be, considering that his parents would no doubt hate her for keeping Casey from him all this time.

The silence was so thick between them that she wanted to scream, or reach out and shake him, but it finally occurred to her that, if he did open up and start to talk, she really had nothing more to say. There came a time when words didn't matter, and actions mattered even less.

But still there was that little girl sucking her thumb in the back seat, the little girl who was getting attached to her daddy, the little girl who was now a part of both their lives. It was the hell Leah had to pay for keeping her secret.

AS HE DROVE, Jeff thought of the way Leah's skin had felt beneath his hand, the way she had tasted, the way they had fitted together like they had never been apart.

And he thought of her proclamation of love. The one he had ridiculed. The one that had sent her away in tears.

He was a bastard, he thought. He had hurt her deliberately, and he didn't even know why.

Quickly reeling those traitorous thoughts back in, he told himself that he did know why. It was because he still didn't trust her, and he hated himself for giving her power over him again. When she had loved him, then articulated that love, he had lost a little more of himself to her.

"I need to go potty," Casey said from the back seat.

Jeff glanced in the rearview mirror. "Potty?" He looked at Leah. "I thought she wore diapers. I thought that potty-training stuff was something she was just starting."

"Well, maybe she's more ready than I thought."

She looked in the back seat and smiled at the child. "We'll find you a potty, sweetie. Won't we, Daddy?"

Jeff glanced over his shoulder. "Sure will. Right up here's a McDonald's. If you go in the potty, I'll buy you an ice-cream cone. How about that?"

Casey smiled around her thumb and told him it was just fine.

Off guard, Jeff met Leah's eyes, and they shared a smile. It was one of those rare, unexpected moments of intimacy—spoken without a word—that the common love of Casey evoked. He knew there would be many more of those, and he supposed they'd be just as hard to distance himself from as their lovemaking last night.

TWO EMPTY POTTIES, a wet diaper and a melted ice-cream cone later, they pulled onto the street in Brooksville where Jeff had grown up. The house was set about a hundred yards from a big pond that contained a score of catfish that his father raised, and sat snugly in the shade of three giant oaks. Leah knew Casey would love it here.

Jeff parked the car on the gravel drive, and that vise over Leah's lungs tightened. She was here for Casey, she told herself again, and however his parents wanted to treat her, that was fine.

Jeff looked over at her. "You ready?"

She tried to hold back those threatening tears. "Not really."

"It'll be okay," he said. He twisted in his seat and looked at Casey. "How 'bout you, Casey? Are you ready to meet Grandma and Grandpa?"

Not taking her thumb out of her mouth, Casey nodded. Slipping out of her seat, Leah went back to

Casey and grabbed a wipe from her diaper bag. From her peripheral vision, she saw his parents and Jan come out of the house. Quickly she wiped the ice-cream cone off of Casey's face and hands, and removed her bib.

"Where we going?" Casey asked, looking past her to the people approaching the car.

The words got caught in Leah's throat as she unhooked Casey from her car seat and set her down on the floor of the vehicle.

"Mommy staying?"

This time Leah made herself answer. "Yes, darling. Mommy's staying with you."

Jeff opened the door, smiling like a proud father with a day-old infant. "Come here, short stuff," he said.

Casey took one look at the people approaching her and backed into Leah's arms.

"It's okay," Leah whispered, holding Casey and stepping out. "I'll hold her."

Coming closer, Florence Hampton looked at Leah, then at Casey, then at Jeff, the wrinkled lines in her forehead defining her puzzlement at Jeff's "surprise." "Hello," she said finally, and Leah didn't miss the coolness in her voice. "Jeff didn't tell us you were coming."

"I said I had a surprise, Mom," Jeff said, dropping a kiss on her cheek.

His mother tried to laugh but fell short. "I thought you'd gotten a new car or a haircut or something...."

"It's better, Mom," he said, setting a possessive hand on Casey's head. "Mom, Dad, this is Casey. She's your granddaughter."

"Our *what!*" The words of both parents came simultaneously, and Jan covered her mouth and began to laugh.

"I love it," she said. "I should have had the camera ready."

Her mother turned on her, as if she'd been somehow responsible for the shocking news. "Did you know about this and not tell us?"

"Just a couple of days, Mom," Jan said. "Jeff swore me to secrecy."

"Why?" Florence turned back to her son. "This child is at least . . . how old *is* she?"

"Two," Leah said quietly.

"For two years you've had a beautiful little daughter, Jeff, and you've kept it from us? *Why?*"

"I didn't know until a couple of days ago myself," he said.

Florence Hampton's face blanched and she turned her condemning glare back to Leah.

"It's a long story, Mom," Jeff said. "Come on. We'll go inside and I'll tell you everything."

His mother hesitated, and Leah saw the fine mist forming in her eyes as the woman looked at the child in Leah's arms. Her hand trembled as she brought it up to touch Casey's curls. "May I . . . hold her?" the woman asked.

For a second, Leah thought Casey would go to her, and she allowed herself to fantasize about sitting in the car all day—out of the chill of his family's hatred of her—while they got to know Casey inside.

But Casey recoiled from Florence and threw her arms around Leah's neck.

Her fantasy quickly vaporized, and kissing Casey's head and holding her securely, Leah started toward the house. "I'm not leaving you, sweetheart. I'm staying right here."

Casey's death grip embrace didn't loosen as they went into the house.

"SO WHAT ARE YOUR PLANS?" Al Hampton, Jeff's father, asked the question of both Jeff and Leah as Florence read Casey a book on the floor near Leah's feet.

"Plans?" Jeff asked. "We have no plans. I'm staying with Leah and Casey until the kidnappers are caught, and then there will be visitation—"

"No marriage?" Al cut in. "No resumed romantic affair?"

Jeff met Leah's eyes, and she knew he was thinking of last night. She looked away.

"Mr. Hampton," Leah said, "I didn't' tell Jeff about Casey so I could somehow trap him into a relationship. I was wrong to keep Casey from him—"

"Damn right you were wrong."

She faltered, took a deep breath and started again. "I realize that. And now I'm willing to make it up by letting him play a part in her life. That's all. I'm not out to rope a husband."

"It's complicated, trying to raise a child in two separate households. A child is not a possession to be passed around."

Leah's heart sank at the reality of his words, and her sad gaze drifted to Casey, who was warming up to her grandmother. It wouldn't take that long for her to trust Jeff and Jan and their parents as much as she trusted her. Before she knew it, she'd be *asking* to come see them. Still, the memory of Jeff's words the other night, when he'd promised not to take Casey from her—how much had been in reaction to her tears, and how much would he honor?

"We aren't going to do anything to hurt Casey," Jeff said. "Leah's a good mother. And I can be a good father."

"She needs good *parents*," his father said. "She needs a family. Not a fragmented facsimile of one!"

"This is the way it is, Dad," Jeff said on a sigh. "We only have this to work with."

Jan, also on the floor with her mother and Casey, piped in. "Come on, Dad. What do you want him to do? Marry her?"

The word was thrown out with such contempt that Leah's lips tightened, and she glanced toward the floor, wishing desperately for a means of escape.

"Hell, no, I don't want him *marrying* her," Al threw back. "I just want him to realize that this isn't going to be a picnic."

"I realize that, Dad. Leah and I will work it out somehow. Trust us."

Jeff's eyes met Leah's again, and she looked at him with a profound sadness that stirred his heart. His eyes, too, saddened. Getting up, he took Casey from the floor, kissed her cheek and held her close to him. "The bottom line, Dad, is that I have a little daughter. And nothing anyone says or does is going to change that. She's mine. And she's yours, too, if you want her."

Casey sneezed twice, and instantly the room exploded into a flurry of activity. Florence jumped up and grabbed a tissue from a nearby box. Al rose and began a baby-talk chant of "God bless you, God bless you." Jan's laughter overrode it all, as if the sneeze had been one for *America's Funniest Home Videos*.

And Leah stood back, feeling less a part of her daughter's life than she'd ever felt in her life.

AT MIDAFTERNOON, THEY SAT down to eat the traditional feast that Florence Hampton usually reserved for Sundays, but had broken the rules and cooked today, instead.

Casey could want for nothing, for Jan and Florence fussed over her with each bite she took. Jeff and his father sat at opposite ends of the table, talking over the noise as if they hadn't seen each other in years.

In the midst of all the hubbub, Leah was the outcast. The one whose eyes no one would meet. The one no one addressed. The one who could have fallen through a hole in the earth, and no one would have cared.

After a while, when Casey was occupied with chocolate pudding, Leah left the table quietly and went outside. Sitting down on the steps, she dropped her face into her hands and let the tears that she had held back all day fall at last.

The door opened behind her, and someone came out. She looked up and saw Jan.

"Tough day, huh?" Jeff's sister said without much sympathy.

Leah nodded.

"You know, we haven't meant to be rude to you, Leah. I can see that you feel as awkward as we do."

"You haven't been rude," Leah lied. "Everything's fine. I didn't expect to be welcomed here with open arms."

Jan sighed and sat down next to her. "Look, I know it's hard on you, but you have to understand. When you left Jeff... well, he hurt pretty bad. He didn't recover for about a year. He brooded and was irritable all the time. No one could talk to him. And he went on these wild spending binges, like he had to prove to the world that he would have been good enough for the Borgadeux. It was hard on the whole family to see him that way."

Leah smeared a tear across her face. "I know that. I don't blame them for hating me. And I don't blame him—"

The door opened, and Jeff stepped out, looked from Jan to Leah. His eyes lingered on Leah's tears, and quickly, he dashed accusing eyes to his sister. "Leave her alone, Jan. She hasn't done anything to you."

Jan came to her feet. "For your information, I didn't do anything to her, either. We were just talking."

"Leave her alone," he said again.

Leah looked up, surprised at his defense of her. "Jeff, she wasn't—"

"That's okay," Jan bit out. "I'm going in."

The door closed behind her, and Leah met his eyes, forgetting to hide her tears. He was no stranger to them these days. "You didn't have to do that, you know. I can take care of myself."

He lowered himself to the step beside her, and with both palms she wiped the remnants of tears from her face. "Where's Casey?"

"My mother took her to the back to see the kittens. Any minute now she'll be screaming for you."

Leah started to get up. "I'll go ahead and see about her."

"Wait." He caught her arm and pulled her back down. "Wait."

She looked at him, bracing herself for the pain that came so abundantly whenever he was near.

"I wanted to tell you that . . . I'm sorry for the way they're treating you. It's hard on them."

"That's exactly what Jan was saying," she told him. "But I don't have to be told. I can see how hard it is."

"But it doesn't make it easier for you, does it?"

She shook her head, and looked out over the trees across the road. "The last time I was here, they welcomed me like I was one of them. And I *felt* like I could be. Like this could be my family. I've never had that before, you know. Not really. That's something that I still don't think you understand."

"You had your father," he said, that cool edge returning to his voice.

"My father is a controller, Jeff," she said. "He tries to love, but he isn't good at it. It's unnatural for him, somehow. But for your family, it's so easy. They took Casey in like they had known her since birth, and I just can't help wishing—"

"That they could take you in, too?"

It seemed so ludicrous that she couldn't make herself say it. "I can't help wishing that things could have been different."

"So do I," he whispered.

They sat next to each other for a long moment, staring off into space, seeing the same dream. But the dream was only that, and they both knew the impossibility of it ever being fulfilled. Too much damage had been done. After a moment, Leah stood up. "I'm going to check on Casey."

He came to his feet and started to follow her around the house. "Leah, before you go, I have to ask you something. My parents wanted us to come to their bar tonight. They want to show Casey off. I thought we could stay for a couple of hours, then drive home late. Is that okay?"

She shrugged. "Sure, whatever you say."

Then not looking back at him, she left him standing there and went to find her daughter.

Leah surmised from the difference in his parents' moods that he had had a word with them. She was back inside, rocking Casey as she drifted into a nap, when Florence came in and gave her a cool smile.

"It must have been awful for you when she was kidnapped."

Leah nodded. "It was."

"Are you afraid? Of them coming back again, I mean?"

Leah looked at the woman who had such warm lines around her face. This coldness she displayed toward Leah was accomplished only with great effort, she told herself. It didn't come naturally to the woman. "Yes, I'm afraid. But I'm grateful to Jeff for helping us through this."

The woman compressed her lips and nodded. "You know, it was quite a surprise to hear about Casey."

"I know," she whispered. "I'm really sorry for that."

Florence nodded again. "I hope you'll keep your word and let Jeff see her after all this is over. I hope you'll let him bring her back here. A lot. Already we've gotten attached to her."

She closed her eyes and tightened her embrace on the sleeping child. "I promise," she whispered.

Florence left them alone in the shadows of the living room, and unable to put Casey down, for it had been a cold morning with only the child who cared about her, Leah continued to rock her throughout her nap.

JEFF STOPPED at the doorway and looked in. He saw Leah rocking the sleeping girl in her arms. Her own eyes were closed, and her head was leaned back.

It was the most beautiful sight he had ever seen. His child, and the woman he—

He stopped midthought and hauled his emotions back. The woman he once loved. The woman with whom he had conceived a child.

He wasn't sure how long he stood there, just staring at them, but his mother noticed it. When he finally turned around to go back into the kitchen, Florence was shaking her head.

"You're still in love with her, aren't you?"

"What? No, of course not. Not after what she did to me." He went to a pan of brownies and mashed some crumbs with his finger.

"Unfortunately, Jeff, your brain doesn't always dictate what's in your heart. I saw the way you looked at her."

"I was looking at Casey, Mom. I love Casey."

"And earlier today, when she left the table and you turned on us for being so cold to her, were you thinking of Casey then, too?"

He shoved away the brownies and looked at his mother. "Yes, as a matter of fact. Leah's my daughter's mother. We have to get along. You have to get used to the fact that she's a permanent fixture in Casey's life."

"Which makes her a permanent fixture in yours."

He set his hands on his hips and cocked his head impatiently. "What are you saying, Mom?"

"I'm saying, son, that sometimes convenience can make us believe what we want to believe. Knowing how complicated it is to raise a child separately, you might convince yourself that she's changed, that you're still in love with her, that you can be happy with her."

"Mom, you don't have to worry."

"I can't help worrying," she said. "I don't want to see you hurt again."

"Leah's not going to hurt me again," he said, feeling the heat rush to his cheeks. "She brought me to my knees once, but I'm stronger for it now. I'm not going to let it happen again."

BUT THAT NIGHT, at the Hampton House, where Jeff and Jan had spent most weekend nights throughout their lives, Jeff wondered if he could really stand behind those words.

Leah sat at the corner of the table with Casey tucked in her lap, swaying to the live music of the country band. A dim red light cast a glow over her head, painted the tops of her cheekbones, her nose, her lips....

He drew his eyes away and looked out over the dance floor, where lovers danced and laughed and flirted. His eyes gravitated back to Leah and Casey, and he saw the delight on his daughter's face at the excitement generated by the live music and dancing. Slowly standing, not knowing just whom he was approaching—Leah or Casey—he went around the table.

Casey smiled up at him, making his choice easy.

"Casey, will you dance with me?"

Casey cast her big eyes out over the dance floor and nodded.

He reached down, picked her up and held her against him with one arm extended as they went to the dance floor.

LEAH WATCHED JEFF dancing with her daughter, swinging the little girl around, dipping her and making her laugh louder than she'd ever heard. A soft smile played on her lips, and she decided that that sight was even more beautiful than the sight of Casey alone.

She saw him look back at her, saw him grinning with amusement at the way Casey was trying to throw herself into the dips and keeping her own kind of rhythm to the song the band was playing.

"He's good with her," Jan said, popping a peanut into her mouth.

Leah nodded.

"He's going to be a good father."

"He already is," Leah said.

The song ended, and Jeff started dancing Casey back to the table as friends applauded. Leah stood up to reach for her, but Jan came between them.

"Did you dance with Daddy?" Jan asked Casey. "Did you like that?"

Jeff surrendered the girl to his sister as the band launched into another tune, and his eyes met Leah's. She started to sit back down, but he stopped her. "You want to show Casey how it's really done?" he asked with a smile.

"Me?"

His grin disarmed her completely. "Yes, you. If I recall, you and I cut a pretty good rug together."

We did a lot of things well together, she thought. *But none of it meant anything.* Swallowing, she glanced back at Casey, saw that the child was preoccupied with Jan. "I don't know, Jeff."

Not taking her reluctance for an answer, he took her hand and pulled her to her feet.

The song the band decided to play at that moment was anything but a "cut the rug" song. Instead, it was a slow, weepy love song that forced couples to come together, to embrace, to sway against each other's bodies.

She hesitated. "We...we could wait for the next song."

He pulled her against him and took her hand. "There's nothing wrong with this one."

Their faces were so close that she could feel his breath on her lips. The way he held her brought back images of last night—images she desperately wanted to escape. "I just didn't think you'd want to...."

"Neither did I," he said. "But life's full of surprises."

She was silent for a moment, trying to decipher his words. Was he making some kind of revelation or just making conversation? For the life of her, she didn't know. They danced quietly for a long while as she tried to steady her runaway heartbeat and the fragile hope she knew better than to entertain. His face moved close to her ear, and she could feel the warmth of his breath. "You've been great today, Leah," he whispered. "I really appreciate it."

She dropped her forehead against his shoulder and refrained from telling him that she really had no choice. That it had been pure hell.

"And last night..."

Her head snapped up, and she met his eyes. He hadn't mentioned their lovemaking since it had happened. His eyes were smoky and direct as they looked into hers.

"Last night was wonderful...even better than I remembered."

She kept her eyes fixed on his, stricken, waiting for whatever was to come next.

"I'm sorry for what I said afterward. I can be a real SOB sometimes."

"You weren't being an SOB," she whispered. "You were being honest. You were saying what you feel. I can't blame you for that."

She saw the turmoil on his face as he looked down at her, and she wondered if it was her imagination that he had tightened his hold on her infinitesimally. Was he beginning to despise her a little less? Was he beginning to like her again?

She knew that love was too much to hope for, so she didn't even allow herself to. But maybe he didn't want to push her away anymore.

The song ended, but he didn't let her go as the dancers around them broke up and applauded. It was seconds later before he released her, and even then his eyes held hers with an intensity she wanted desperately to understand.

Finally he turned away from her and started back to the table, where Casey had just noticed that Leah was gone and was reaching for her.

Leah took her and, holding her close, glanced at Jeff over her head. He was watching her.

A tiny thrill ebbed inside her as she sat back down. Something was on his mind. Something to do with her alone—apart from Casey. Anticipation swirled in her head and her heart, and she couldn't wait to get back home with him.

Chapter Ten

The ride home was quiet, tense and rife with anticipation. The animosity had disappeared, and in its
place was a disturbing feeling of confusing desire. Jeff
feared saying anything, so he said nothing.

They reached his house, and while Leah put the
sleeping child to bed, he hung back in the living room,
deciding he needed to keep his distance until his feelings were more in his control. He couldn't feel desire
for her. Sleeping with her again would be cruel. It
would be dangerous.

It would be wonderful.

Trying to shake the thoughts from his mind, he went
to his phone and checked the messages on his machine. One was from his detective, and said to call him
tonight no matter how late he got home.

Quickly, Jeff dialed the number. The phone was
answered on the first ring.

"Phil? It's Jeff. What have you got?"

"You're not going to believe this," the detective
said. "Are you sitting down?"

Jeff switched the phone to his other ear and grabbed a pencil. "Let me have it."

"I did some checking on Borgadeux today. And I found out that the morning after the kidnapping, he deposited two million dollars back in the same bank account from which he had withdrawn it the day before. I don't know about you, but I smell something rotten."

Jeff frowned, unable to make sense of it. "You mean he took it out the day of the kidnapping, we gave it to the kidnappers and then the next morning he redeposited it?"

"Looks that way to me."

"Maybe he liquidated something to make up for it. Maybe he transferred some funds to cover it, or sold some stock...."

"I checked. The money seems to have come from nowhere, except out of that same account the day before."

"I don't get it." Jeff glanced toward the bedrooms, then lowered his voice. "What do you think is going on, Phil? Any ideas?"

"I don't know," Phil said. "Unless maybe the man was involved, which makes absolutely no sense. Why would he want to stage his granddaughter's kidnapping?"

"To manipulate his daughter, maybe?" Jeff asked, not realizing he had mumbled his thoughts aloud.

"Maybe. You'd know better than me. I've got a few more things to check tomorrow. Be available in case I find something, all right?"

"Yeah, sure."

Leah came into the room just as Jeff was hanging up. Her hair was disheveled from the day and the drive, and her eyes were sleepy and more aware than he wanted to admit. What little makeup she had worn today had all but worn off. Still, she looked beautiful. Too beautiful to walk away from.

"Any news?" she asked.

For a moment, he thought of telling her what he had learned, but it seemed premature. It could be a coincidence, he thought. And there was no use speculating about it until he knew more.

"None," he said. He leaned back against the couch and slid his hands into his pockets and looked at her standing before him.

"Well...it's late," she said. "I guess I'll go get some sleep."

"Yeah." He looked down at his feet, then stood upright, facing her. "Leah, I really appreciate your cooperation today. I know it wasn't easy."

She swallowed. "It could have been worse."

He looked down at her lips, pink and soft and wet, then moved his gaze back to those eyes, watching him, reading him. He wondered if she saw everything.

"Well . . . good night," she whispered.

"Wait."

His eyes dropped back to her lips, and his face moved closer. She didn't turn away, didn't back down, as he came as close as he could without touching her. He told himself to stop it now, that there was too much at stake, that if he let this happen again, there would be no more controlling his feelings.

"I want to kiss you," he said.

She felt his breath on her lips, and wet them again. "That's not a good idea," she whispered without moving away.

"No," he said. "It isn't, is it?"

They looked at each other for a fragment of eternity, hearts pounding so loudly and so hard that they weren't sure whose they heard.

He lowered his face, and she swallowed. His lips grazed hers, jolting her heart, and before taking her completely, he whispered, "But I'm gonna do it anyway."

When he took full possession of her lips, there was no turning back. It was as if they had signed in blood, sold their souls and now were sucked into the black spell that would own them forever.

The kiss grew deeper, and he pulled her against him, his hands moving over her in memory of last night's loving. She responded as he knew she would, as she always had, and that response filled a need deep within his soul, a need that it had always filled, a need that had always lain empty when she was not there.

He kissed her temple, her forehead, the bridge of her nose. Her trembling subsided as he kissed the corner of her mouth, then the center of her bottom lip, wet and smooth and downturned.

His mouth met hers, opening a floodgate of feeling, of latent passion, of burning desire that he didn't know he had endured for so long.

His kiss was like a drug that dulled her pain and replaced it with a burning of her own. She slid her arms up to his shoulders, laced her fingers through his hair.

Without realizing what he was doing, he slipped his arm beneath her legs, lifted her, and not breaking the kiss, carried her to his bed.

Jeff told himself that when he loved her this time, there would be no regrets, no recriminations. He would deal with the consequences of his feeling. He would live with it and whatever it meant.

They made love, discovering, once again, that the bond destiny had forged between them years before was still not broken.

AFTERWARD, AS SHE LAY soft and sleeping in his arms, he buried his face in her hair and tried to sort out all the misery in his life. He hadn't felt this whole, despite all the anger and confusion, since the day she had walked out on him.

But the pain wouldn't go away. It was like an old friend, a convenience, something he clutched to his heart like a shield. He couldn't forget what she had done to him by walking away and keeping Casey a secret.

But that anger wasn't as sharp as it was before, for now it came with a stream of reasons behind it. Reasons she had given him, reasons that only now possessed some validity. Borgy was a mean-spirited bastard. And if he was capable of lying and conniving to manipulate his daughter, maybe he would have tried to ruin Jeff's life.

He would have failed, Jeff thought, but how could Leah have known that? Deep in her heart, he knew that she knew that her father could be a heartless monster, that he could be capable of kidnapping.

Deep in her heart, perhaps, she had believed that Jeff would be ruined if she didn't do as her father told her.

Still, it was so hard to forgive her.

She stirred in his arms, and he held her tighter, not willing to let her go. Her hair smelled of lemons, and it felt like satin against his stubble. His heart felt heavy, not with the weight of her head, but with the weight of his emotion for her. He did love her, but that frightened the hell out of him.

"Oh, Leah," he whispered, knowing she didn't hear. "Make me believe in you again. Make it so I'm not afraid to love you again."

He looked down at her face, so soft and shadowed as she slept, and he knew that it was a wish that would die without reaching her heart. He doubted she could have made it come true, anyway.

THEY SLEPT TOGETHER, wrapped in each other's arms, until Casey woke them the next morning. As if nothing unusual lay in the fact that she'd found her parents sleeping together, the child climbed into bed between them and demanded the Gummi Bears cartoon.

They ate breakfast together, passing meaningful smiles and sensuous glances across the table, though neither of them spoke of what the night had meant. Neither chose to spoil the pure and unhampered feelings of the day with talk and speculation.

When the dishes were done and he had showered and dressed, Jeff called the office and learned that there was a problem on his work site. "I have to go to the site for a couple of hours," he said, "but I don't want to leave you. Do you and Casey want to come with me?''

"No," she said. "I have to make some phone calls. I want to make arrangements to have someone open my shop for me tomorrow. We'll be all right alone while you're gone."

He left them, Casey playing in his living room and Leah straightening the kitchen, and smiled all his way to work.

IT WASN'T LONG AFTER Jeff had left that Leah got Casey busy molding clay, and decided to check her machine for her messages.

Her father's voice, demanding and angry, came across the line three times. But the fourth call was from another voice... a voice she recognized... the voice that sent a shiver up her spine and made her heart plunge.

"Casey will never be safe," the voice said. "We could take her from her bed, or from your car, or from your patio. You could even find her washed up on that beach you live on. If I were you, I'd keep a little extra cash handy. You never know when you might need it again!"

"Oh, God!" She dropped the phone and jumped back, as if it had burned her.

"What, Mommy?"

She put her hand over her mouth and backed farther from the phone. "Oh, my God! Oh no!" Quickly reigning her thoughts in, she turned and grabbed Casey up off the floor. "Come here, baby. Let Mommy hold you."

Seeing her mother's state, Casey didn't argue.

Trembling, Leah ran back to the phone, snatched it up and began dialing the number of Jeff's work site that he'd left near the phone. It rang four, five, six, seven times before she realized that no one was in the office.

"Damn," she whispered, hanging it up.

It rang beneath her hand before she'd even let it go, and she brought it to her ear. "Hello?"

"Damn it, girl," her father shouted. "Where the hell were you last night? I've been trying to call—"

"Daddy!" She tried to steady her voice, but a sob escaped her. "They called back, Dad. They said—"

"Who called? The kidnappers?"

"Yes! Dad, Jeff's not here and I'm scared!"

"I'm coming over," he said. "I'll be there in fifteen minutes."

"No!" She swallowed and tried to stop her whirling thoughts. "I need to talk to Jeff first. I can't just pick up and go with you."

"Damn it, Leah, stop thinking of yourself and think of your daughter for a change! Her life is in danger! Do you want to take a chance with those lunatics?"

Casey put her arms around Leah's neck and hugged her, and Leah sobbed again. "You're right, I know. Oh, God, you're right."

"They can't get to either of you at my house," her father said. "It's the only right thing to do, Leah. I'll be right over."

"All right." The words, once out, seemed to fill her with relief to counter the fear in her heart. "All right, Dad. I'll be ready."

She hung up the phone and stared at it, wondering if she'd done the right thing. Her father had won, but if she didn't go with him, they could all lose. And it wasn't a gamble she was willing to make.

Setting Casey down, she took her hand. "Come on, pumpkin," she said, wiping her tears. "We have to go pack."

"Where we going?" Casey asked.

"To visit Grandpa for a while," she said.

"Daddy coming?"

Tears burst to Leah's eyes again, but fear propelled her onward. "No, honey. Not yet. But we'll see him later, okay?"

She tried to call Jeff again before she left, but there was still no answer in the trailer on his work site. Instead, she left him a brief note, telling him about the phone call, and letting him know how she could be reached. He would be furious, she knew, but there wasn't time to go into a lengthy explanation. There would be plenty of time for that later.

IT HAD TAKEN HOURS but Jeff solved the problem at the work site. He'd spent the entire time thinking of getting home and basking in Leah's smile and her sensuality again.

No, their problems hadn't miraculously evaporated. Some of the anger was still there, along with the pain and the knowledge of her deceit. He couldn't forgive that. He couldn't forget. But that desire riding higher in his soul seemed to be more pronounced. Despite himself, he wanted to hold her again. Wanted to taste the honey sweetness of her. Wanted to breathe in her scent.

And when Casey took her nap, he wanted to make love to Leah again, as he had done last night.

What he found, instead, was an empty house and a note that shattered his world. He stared at it for a moment, not believing it, when finally he started through the house, denying it with every step. The rooms were clean, empty, as if they had never been there.

"No!" he shouted, kicking the wall with his foot and leaving a scuffed imprint on the wallpaper. "No, damn you! You can't do this to me again!"

He ran to the phone, dialed Borgy's number, and listened as a servant answered the phone.

"Borgadeux residence."

"I want to speak to Leah!"

"I'm sorry," the maid said. "She isn't taking any calls."

"Damn it, tell her it's Jeff! Put her on the phone right now."

"I'm sorry—"

"No!" he shouted, gripping the phone as if it were the maid's neck. "Damn it, put Borgadeux on the line. Let me speak to him."

He waited a moment, then heard Leah's father's amused voice as he took the phone. "What's the matter, Hampton? You're not still a sore loser, are you?"

"Let me speak to Leah, Borgy!" he shouted. "If you don't, I'll make so much trouble for you you won't know what hit you!"

"Go to hell, Hampton." The phone went dead in Jeff's hand, and he yanked it out of the wall and flung it across the room. It landed with a ringing thud.

Grabbing his keys, he started to the door, deciding to pay a visit to the "Borgadeux residence." If the man wanted to play the game this way, then by God, Jeff would fight back. And he would use every resource available. He wasn't going to let Leah do this to him again.

THE ROOM her father had reserved for Casey was decorated with disturbing detail in Laura Ashley wallpaper with coordinating drapes, bedspread and accessories. Some of the most elaborate toys she had ever seen filled the room next to Casey's, never before touched by a child's hands but waiting for the day Casey would enter the room with delight and wonder.

Leah wanted to keep her from going in there now, but it was impossible. Her father had already dangled the temptation before the child, and Leah was powerless to stop him.

In fact, she was powerless to do much of anything now that she had succumbed to her father and come back into his house. Yes, she was safe. Nothing could break through her father's security.

But nothing could break out, either.

"You two settling in all right?"

She turned around and saw her father standing in the doorway, smiling with peculiar pride at Casey on the floor playing with a dollhouse that was too mature for her. "How could we not?" she asked. "It's been a long time since I've had everything done for me."

"You deserve it," he said. He walked into the playroom and patted Casey's head. "Dinner's at seven. I've been looking so forward to this. The family, all together."

He turned back to Leah, and smiled with a sincerity she had seen very rarely in him. "I've been so lonely without you, Leah. This house gets very cold when its empty."

"I know, Dad," she whispered.

"I want you to make yourself at home," he said. "As if you never left. The servants are all at your disposal. You can do whatever you like."

"Except leave," she said.

He frowned and stepped toward her. "Leah, it's just until the kidnappers are caught. They can't touch you here. You can wipe them out of your mind, forget they ever existed. You can go on with your life and—"

"My life?" she asked, her voice a dull monotone. "What life? I have a business to run, Dad. I can't do that locked away in here. And I have a home. And Jeff—"

"You did just fine without him before all this. You don't need him now."

"But he's Casey's father, Dad. I promised him he could see her. When he calls, I'm going to tell him he can come here whenever he wants. He can see Casey here, and if you try to stop him, I'll have to leave."

"No, I wouldn't do that," Borgadeux said. "Your business can wait and Jeff can wait. What's important is your safety. That's the only thing."

She looked at the phone that had sat so silent all afternoon. The maid had always answered the unit downstairs, then rung whatever room Leah was in if the call was for her. Jeff hadn't called, and she couldn't understand it.

"Are you sure Jeff hasn't called?" she asked. "Are you sure Tessa just didn't forget or something?"

"Sorry, sweetheart. No word."

She sighed. "Then I guess I should try him again. I just don't know where he could be."

"Who knows what the carpenter son of a bartender does with his time?" he asked. "He'll call when he gets around to it."

OUT AT THE FRONT GATE, Jeff's car pulled up to the little security house where two guards stood watch.

A benign-looking guard with a German accent came to his window. "May I help you?"

Jeff got out of the car and faced the guard squarely. "I'm Jeff Hampton, and my daughter is in there. I want to see her now, or I'm—"

The other guard joined the one facing Jeff, and he could see them both bracing themselves for a fight. "I'm sorry, Mr. Hampton, but we have strict orders not to let anyone through those gates."

"Wait a minute! I have the right to see my daughter! Tell Leah I'm here. I want to talk to her."

"She isn't taking calls," the guard said. "Now if you'll just get back in your car—"

"Damn it, she can't do this! She can't run this time! There's a child involved!"

The guards grabbed Jeff by each arm, and he tried to shake them off. Strength honed by hard outdoor labor enabled him to make it difficult for them, but they had him almost in his car when he heard footsteps on the other side of the locked gates. He shook free of the guards and went to the gates, facing Lance Borgadeux with venomous rage.

"You get Leah out here right now, Borgy!"

The guards grabbed Jeff again, and Borgadeux laughed. "That's right. Put him back in his car. If he won't leave, call the police."

Jeff struggled. "I'm warning you. If you try to keep my daughter from me, so help me God, I'll get a lawyer! I'll make you walk through hell with me, Borgy!"

"Notice that I'm growing weak in the knees," Borgadeux said. "My hands are trembling. I might even faint. Now, gentlemen. He's worn out his welcome."

Before Jeff could shout further threats, the guards took him to his car, and one of them drove him, himself, out of the drive.

Leah never even knew he had come.

CASEY WAS SLEEPING later that afternoon, when Leah went downstairs to confront the maid who answered the phone. She didn't like the woman, for she rarely looked her in the eye when she spoke to her, and it gave Leah the uneasy feeling that she wasn't someone she could trust.

"Miss Beel, are you sure that I haven't had any calls today?"

"None, miss."

"But have you answered the phone every time it's rung? I mean, maybe the cook got it or—"

"I always answer the phone, miss, except for your father's private line. No one's phoned for you."

"I see."

Sighing, she went to the phone in her father's study, closed the doors and once again dialed Jeff's number. Again, his machine answered, and again, she left a message. "Jeff, why haven't you called? I need to speak to you. Please, call me at my father's as soon as you get—"

The machine beeped as the phone was snatched up, and Jeff yelled, "Damn it, Leah! Why did you do it?"

"Jeff? Why did I do what?"

"Why did you run away again?" He was out of breath, as though he'd just run into the house.

"I didn't run away. Haven't you gotten any of my messages? Didn't you get my note?"

"I got your note and left," he said. "I haven't been home to get any godforsaken messages. I've been too busy brawling with those guards at your front gate!"

"Here? You were here?"

"Hell, yes, I was there. They wouldn't let me in."

"What?" She turned around, but the maid had left the room. "It must have been a mistake. You should have called first so I could make sure they let you in."

"Damn it, Leah, I've called a dozen times today. That maid of your father's keeps telling me you aren't taking calls! Short of helicoptering in and landing on your roof, there wasn't any way to reach you."

"I can't believe this." She felt her face mottling with patches of heat. "Miss Beel told me no one had called, and I've been calling you all day. Jeff, I told my father when I came here that it was only with the condition that you could come whenever you wanted. I'm not trying to keep Casey from you, but if you read the note you know that the kidnappers called again. I felt like an open target, Jeff, and I couldn't reach you—"

"Leah, your father is conning you. And you're letting him do it."

"Jeff, I had no choice. This is not a question of pride anymore. It's a question of survival. I can't risk Casey's life just to make a point!"

"Leah, she's my daughter, too."

"I know that, Jeff. And I'm not taking her from you. And what had started happening between us...I don't want to destroy that. I just want to be safe until those men are caught."

"Leah, there aren't any *men,* damn it! It's a hoax. It's all a stupid, cruel hoax!"

"What?"

His breathing was still heavy, but he lowered his voice to a calmer pitch. "Leah, listen to me. I didn't want to tell you this before I had more facts, because I don't know what it means. But you have to know before you let your father manipulate you any further."

"Manipulate me? He's trying to *protect* me!"

"Listen to me!" he said, silencing her. "I lied to you about there not being any news. There is some news. A lot of it."

"What? Tell me."

He plowed his hand through his hair and turned around, trying to decide where to start. "A couple of days ago, I went to see Ben and Willy. You remember? The detectives your father hired.''

''And?''

''And they told me that your father fired them from the case the night Casey was found.''

''He what?'' She shook her head. ''Well, there must be some explanation.''

''Is there?'' he asked. ''Didn't he tell you just yesterday that Ben was working on some leads?''

She sat down on a Chippendale chair next to the telephone table, suddenly dizzy from the confusion. ''Yes. And even today he mentioned them. Why would he lie, Jeff?''

''I found out that he had never worked with them before, that he had just hired them that day for this. He retains a very good, very reputable detective agency, but he went to these fly-by-night guys to find his granddaughter. Does that make sense to you?''

''No!'' she said, her voice shaking. ''He said he'd worked with them a lot.''

''And when I checked with the other agency he often uses, they hadn't been called in on the case at all.''

She sprang to her feet and began pacing. ''Why? Why would he call off the search?''

''Maybe he didn't want anyone to dig deep enough.''

Her head was beginning to throb. ''That doesn't make sense, Jeff.''

''Right. It doesn't make sense. And neither does the other thing I found out. Your father made a two-million-dollar deposit back into his bank account the day after the kidnapping. And there's no record of any stock or property being liquidated, or any transfer of funds from any other accounts.''

For a moment she froze, trying desperately to put the pieces together. ''What are you saying?''

''I don't know,'' he whispered. ''You tell me what your father is capable of.''

''Not that,'' she said. ''Not having my baby kidnapped for some bizarre manipulative reason. He wouldn't do that, Jeff.''

''I know it's hard to believe, Leah. I know—''

''He wouldn't, Jeff! He's my father! He has a lot of problems, a lot of shortcomings, and he'd do a lot of things. But not that!''

''Okay, take it easy.'' He was quiet for a moment, listening to the breathing pattern of her crying.

''He wouldn't,'' she said again. ''He wouldn't. Jeff, you don't believe that, do you? You don't think—''

''I don't think anything,'' he whispered. ''I don't know anything.''

She sucked in a deep, cleansing breath and wiped at her tears. ''Well, I do. There are kidnappers, Jeff. They did take my baby. And they'll take her again. My father is the only one who can protect me right now, and if you can't handle that, then I'm truly sorry.''

''Leah, I'm not making this up. It's all true.''

''I have to go check on Casey,'' she said. ''I'll call you later.'' And before Jeff could say any more, she had hung up the phone.

Chapter Eleven

Leah stared at the telephone for a moment before she backed away from it. Her lips trembled, and she hugged her arms around herself and started for the door.

Jeff was wrong. There was some explanation for the things he'd said. Her father would never do anything that malicious, that underhanded, simply to manipulate her.

Wiping her tears with a trembling hand, she went back upstairs and into Casey's room. Lance Borgadeux was standing over the bed, smiling down at the napping child.

He loves her, she thought. *He would never do anything to hurt her.*

"She's beautiful," he whispered.

Unable to speak, she tried to smile.

"Just like you when you were a baby," he went on in a gentle voice that belied the ugliness Jeff had accused him of. "You didn't suck your thumb, but you had a pacifier. They told me not to let you have it, that it would ruin your teeth, but I couldn't help it. I let you have it."

She leaned back against the wall and gazed at her father, loving him despite his tyranny—as she had always loved him.

"Remember that day, when you were almost three, and the dentist handed you the wastebasket and told you to throw the pacifier away? You tossed it right in and never asked for it again."

"I was afraid of him," she said. "I've always responded to fear."

"Well," he said. "It was just a pacifier."

And my baby.

She reeled her thoughts back in and told herself again that none of what Jeff had said was true. Her father was strong, decisive, authoritative... even threatening.

But not malicious.

She cleared her throat and gestured toward the door.

"Dad, I need to talk to you," she whispered.

Still smiling, he nodded and came out into the corridor, where a handwoven Aubusson rug ran the length of the floor. Her mother had designed it herself and had laid it the month before Leah was born. She hadn't lived to see her daughter walk on it.

"What is it, sweetheart?"

Leah looked up at him, dread darkening the color of her eyes. "I just talked to Jeff. He said he's been trying to call, but that Miss Beel wouldn't put the call through to me. He also said he was turned away at the gate. That you knew he was here and didn't tell me."

"Oh, honey." He sighed and stroked her hair, and gestured for her to sit down on a gold-gilded bench beside the wall. "You were so upset when you came here this morning," he said. "I wanted you to have time to get your bearings before he started badgering you to risk your child's life and go back to him."

Tears sprang to her eyes, and she swallowed. "I'm only staying until the kidnappers are found, Dad. You do realize that, don't you?"

"Of course," he said. "I didn't expect anything else."

She looked down at her hands that were suddenly very cold and folded them to conceal the trembling. "Has . . . has Ben come up with anything else?"

Her father sat down next to her and patted her clasped hands. "A few little morsels of clues here and there, but nothing substantial."

She felt a lump forming in her throat, a lump that made it difficult for her to speak. She knew he was lying, but she couldn't face what that meant. "But he is still looking?"

"Of course," her father said. "Night and day."

Her heart plunged farther. So he was lying about the detectives. That didn't mean he had staged the kidnapping.

"About Jeff . . ." she said, and her voice sounded thin and shredded. "I told Jeff he could come here anytime, Dad. I told him—"

"Leah, wake up," he cut in gently. "That two-bit construction worker is after only one thing. Your money."

Leah moved her gaze back to her father. "I don't have any money, Daddy. You cancelled my trust fund when I moved away from home."

"Well, I plan to reinstate it. Besides, if he isn't after your money, he's after Casey's. He's manipulating you to get control of her trust fund."

"Then cancel it, too. Give the money to charity. Casey doesn't need your money. I can provide for her. As soon as the kidnappers are found I'm going back home—"

"And what if they aren't found?" her father asked, his voice rising by degrees. "What if the detectives and cops can't come up with anything? What if weeks, months go by, and they're still not caught? They could get her again, Leah. This time, they might kill her! Meanwhile, you have to be settled *somewhere.* It's not good for a child to move back and forth—"

"Dad, listen to me—"

"They'll terrorize you for years, kidnapping that child and blackmailing you. They could take her from her bed, or your car, or from your patio—"

As he spoke, she rose to her feet, staring down at him with eyes that, for the first time in a long time, saw him as clearly as Jeff did. "How do you know what they said?"

Her words cut into his monologue, slicing to the heart of his deception.

"What? What who said?"

"What the kidnapper said on the machine? How did you know?"

"You told me."

"I didn't tell you that. And it's kind of strange that you would know it, because those were their exact words."

"Well, that doesn't surprise me." He turned around, but she could see the distress on his face, the same distress that he harbored when he was cornered in a less-than-straight business deal on any given day. "All it takes is a little common sense, a little thought, to figure out what they're capable of."

"I guess they're capable of just about anything," she whispered.

It was at that moment that she realized the things Jeff had said were true—that her father had used her baby, manipulated her, lied, stolen and cheated. It was at that moment that she realized the extent of the prison he had created for her.

Borgadeux hugged her and pressed a kiss on her cheek. "You don't have to be afraid, darling. I'll always be here."

"You're right, Dad," she whispered flatly. "We can always count on you."

THAT EVENING when her father was busy on the telephone in his study and the staff had all retired to their own quarters, Leah sat in the bathroom, watching Casey frolic in her bubble bath. A froth of white smattered across her nose, and she giggled and lay down, stretching out and pretending to swim.

"I'm Little Muh-maid," she told Leah.

Leah smiled. "Wash your face, Little Mermaid."

Casey scooped a handful of bubbles and rubbed them across her face, as if that would do the trick. Instead, it made her look like a poor imitation of Santa Claus. Leah tried to smile again, but her mouth quivered and tears filled her eyes.

What am I going to do?

The question had gnawed at Leah's mind since her conversation with Jeff, reminding her incessantly that her father had lied, that Jeff had been right.... But what did it mean?

She had run the gamut from wanting to confront her father with the dirty truth to wanting to run as far and as fast as she could. Confrontation seemed a waste of time. Borgadeux was a smooth operator. He could talk his way out of anything, and turn the tables around as if she'd been the one who'd committed a crime. If he would have her baby kidnapped, there was no telling what other horrors he could exact in the name of love. As long as she was near him, she was at his mercy. And merely going back to her own little house and her own little life were not enough. She had to get farther away. So far that she would never have to fear his threats again.

The decision jelled in her mind even as she pulled Casey from the tub and dried her off. They would go tonight. And by the time her father realized they were gone, it would be too late to get her back.

But as her resolve hardened, her heart ached, for she knew that leaving her life behind meant leaving Jeff, too. He could never understand her need to run, and their relationship was far too precarious, too embryonic, for her to expect him to go with her.

Smearing her tears across her face, Leah dressed Casey and quickly packed the few things they had brought here with them. Then, when she was sure that no one was around to stop them, she grabbed the child and left from the back door.

"Where are we going, Mommy?"

"Home," Leah whispered. "Be quiet now. We don't want anyone to hear us."

She spirited the child to the huge garage, where her father kept his limousine and two Jaguars. The key, as always, was in the ignition, for the garage was locked each night. She put Casey in one of the Jaguars, hooked her seat belt, then punched the digital code on the remote control garage opener. The lock disengaged, and the door quietly came up.

The car windows were tinted black and as she pulled to the front gates, the guards assumed she was her father. Without hesitation they opened the gates, and she pulled out onto the street.

A breath of profound relief escaped her as she drove farther from her father's estate. She glanced over at Casey, saw her sucking her thumb and staring up at her with wide eyes. "It's okay, sweetheart. Everything's going to be fine now."

THE DARKNESS HAD INVADED Jeff's house like an army of demons, surrounding and attacking while he sat alone on his recliner, staring at the nothingness Leah had left behind. Between two fingers, he held the neck of a half-empty, lukewarm bottle of beer—the strongest thing he'd been able to find in his house to quell the aching in his soul.

Like the percussive beat of a cavalry's hooves, he heard a knock at the door, then his sister calling, "Jeff? Are you in there?"

He sat still, paralyzed, for he didn't want to confront Jan right now. I-told-you-so's were particularly hard for him to swallow. Especially when his own heart screamed them louder than ever.

He heard her try the knob and vaguely remembered that he'd forgotten to lock it. It came open, and Jan stepped inside. "Jeff?"

"When people don't answer the door it usually means they don't want company."

Jan flicked on a lamp and gaped at her brother, sitting in the shadows. "Jeff, are you all right? You sounded so bad on the phone—"

"I didn't feel like talking. Still don't."

Jan closed the door and crossed the floor. She sat down facing him, not hiding the poignant concern on her features. "Jeff, what's wrong? Is it about Leah?"

"Let it go."

"Jeff, what did she do?"

A slow, heartless, whispered laugh escaped him. "She got me again, Jan. She moved back in with her father. Only this time, I guess I deserved it. I knew better than to let her back under my skin."

"Damn her!" Jan came to her feet and paced across the room, then turned back to him. "I knew she'd do it. I told you—"

"Save it."

She let the thought die and came to her brother, bent over him. Her eyes glistened as she looked into his. "I'm sorry, Jeff. I'm so sorry. But what about Casey?"

"Who knows?" He pulled the recliner's lever and dropped his feet. "She says she isn't cutting me off, but Borgy won't let me near them."

Jan sat on the chair's arm and hugged her brother, but he didn't respond. "You're in love with her again, aren't you?"

Slipping out of her embrace, Jeff stood up and ambled across the floor, rubbing the back of his neck. "Yeah," he whispered. "I guess I am. And that makes me the biggest kind of fool." He turned back to Jan, his eyes reddening. "I thought she had changed, that she had separated from her father. That she wouldn't do this again. But then that bastard told her lies, and she believed every word."

"It's Casey," Jan whispered. "She's scared out of her mind for Casey."

"But it's all a lie, Jan. He set her up. It was a hoax, and I tried to tell her—"

"A hoax?" She frowned and stood up. "Jeff, are you sure?"

"As sure as I can be," he said, his voice rising as the anger took hold of him. "The man will do anything, *anything* to get her under his wing. He's dangerous, Jan. He's ruthless. And now Leah and *my* daughter are his puppets, and I'm locked out."

"Leah doesn't strike me as the kind of woman who could be anyone's puppet, Jeff. Maybe you just need to give her some time."

"Time to do what?" he asked. "Time to make Casey forget she ever *had* a father? Time to let Borgy fill Leah's head with more lies and raise Casey to be just as afraid to move as Leah is?''

The phone rang, and Jeff threw back another mouthful of beer and ignored it.

"Do you want me to get it?" Jan asked.

He shook his head. "I don't want to talk to anybody."

"Maybe it's her, Jeff."

"I especially don't want to talk to her. Damn her, she's ruining me, Jan. She's ripping me up again—"

The phone kept ringing, and his voice trailed off as he looked at it with dull eyes. His face turned red, and finally, he threw down the bottle of beer, watching it shatter on the floor as he snatched up the phone. "Yeah?" he yelled.

"Jeff!" It was Leah's voice, rushed and breathless.

"Leah?"

"Meet me at my house," she blurted. "I'm on my way there now. And hurry."

"Leah, what's wrong? How did you talk your father—"

"You were right about him, Jeff." Her voice wobbled, and he could hear that she was crying. "He lied. He must have set up the whole thing. We'll talk when I see you."

Adrenaline filled his veins, and his heart swelled with relief. Suddenly the anger was gone, and in its place was a different emotion that set him back on track and opened the dark places in his soul again. "I'll be right there," he said.

The phone went dead, and Jeff hung it up and swung around to Jan, who had bent over to clean up the mess. "I've got to go," he said, life returning to his eyes. "She needs me."

Jan didn't utter a recriminating word as she watched her brother bolt out of his house to rescue the woman he had cursed just moments ago.

JEFF WAS WAITING in her driveway when Leah pulled up to her house and quickly she threw the car into Park and pulled Casey out. "Hurry," she told him when he reached the Jaguar. "I've got to go in and get some things. He'll realize I'm gone soon and come after me."

Baffled, Jeff took Casey and the suitcase and followed her in. "Leah, what are you doing?"

She ran to the bedroom and grabbed two more suitcases, opened them and began emptying the contents of her drawers into them. "Leah! Where are you going?"

"Away from here," she said. "Anywhere!"

"Wait a minute!" He sat Casey down and went toward her. "Leah, talk to me. Stop just for a minute and look at me!" When she kept throwing things into her bags, he took her arms and turned her from the suitcases. Suddenly she wilted like a flower snapped at the stem, and he felt the sobs shaking her body.

"He did it!" she cried, muffling her horror with her hand. "You were right, Jeff. He staged it all. My own father. How could he have done that to me? To my baby?"

Jeff gathered her up and held her close, as though his own warmth could dispel the chill in her soul. Beside the door, Casey watched her mother weep. Her thumb went to her mouth.

"It's the betrayal that hurts so much, Jeff. That someone I love could deceive me so deliberately. Could betray me in the worst kind of way...."

"Leah, what are you about to do?" he asked. "What are the suitcases for?"

Leah reined in her shattered emotions and looked up at him with the deepest dread she'd ever faced. "Oh, Jeff," she whispered sadly. She wiped her face with a trembling hand and shoved her hair back as she slipped out of his arms.

"I could prosecute him, but how could we really prove what he did? A bank account, his detectives fired. Those aren't enough. Or we could expose him publicly, but the press would turn it into some sort of greedy tabloid feud, and Casey's life would be marked forever. I don't want her to grow up with that."

Jeff stood motionless, watching her pace the length of the room as she spoke. Casey, looking distraught, herself, went to Leah and held up her arms to be picked up. Leah bent over and lifted her.

"The only way to beat him, Jeff, is to make sure he never sees Casey again," she said, pressing her face against Casey's and closing her eyes. "I'm willing to do whatever that takes. I won't let him do this again."

"Then you aren't going back there at all?"

"No!" she cried. "I want to get away from him. So far that he can never find us."

She turned around to Jeff, the sadness in her eyes so profound that Jeff wondered if anything could ever wipe it away completely. "Jeff, I don't want to take her away from you," she whispered, "and I don't want to leave you, either."

"I don't want you to." He swallowed the intense lump of emotion in his throat and fixed his gaze on the desperation in her eyes.

"I know I have no right to ask this of you, Jeff, but if you wanted to come with us . . ."

For a moment, he didn't answer, and a barrage of fears assaulted her. She'd had no right to ask. No right to assume that his feelings for her had been reborn. Just because they were lovers again, didn't mean that he loved her. "I'm sorry," she whispered. "I didn't mean to presume anything about you . . . about us. . . . What's happened between us . . ."

"Presume."

Her words died out, and she stared at him for a moment. "What?"

"Go ahead and presume," he said. "You'd be right."

She caught her breath on a sob and covered her mouth with her hand. "About what?"

"About the way I feel about you."

"And . . . and how is that?" she whispered. "Don't make me presume."

He went to her and Casey, and slid his arms around her. His expression was more serious than she'd ever seen it. "The other night, when we made love, I realized a lot of things, Leah."

Her tears clouded her eyes again. "What things?"

"The way I still feel about you . . . even apart from Casey."

She swallowed and clung to every word . . . even the ones he hadn't yet uttered.

"And then . . . when you went back to him, Leah, I didn't think I could take it. Losing Casey again . . . losing you . . ."

"I don't want to leave you," she said, realizing he wasn't going to say the words but accepting what he had said instead. "But I have to go. Please understand."

"Where, Leah? Where are you going? Are you going to just leave your business? Your home?"

"Yes," she said. "And I don't *know* where I'm going. Just . . . anywhere. I can get a job in a town where no one knows what the Borgadeux name means. But I understand if you can't do that with me, Jeff. You'd have to leave everything, too, and if you can't, I really do understand." She sobbed and turned her face away, anticipating his answer.

Jeff rubbed his face, wondering at the irony of her leaving him once before to save his business, and now asking him to leave that same business for her. The greatest irony of all, however, was that it didn't require a second thought.

"Let's get packed," he said simply.

Leah muffled a cry of joy, and he crushed her against him again, holding her with all the grief and despair he had felt for the past two and a half years. No matter what it meant, he wasn't going to let her father take her away from him again. This time, Borgy would be the one to grieve.

LESS THAN A HALF HOUR later, Leah strapped Casey into her car seat in Jeff's car and made one last trip through the house for anything they might have forgotten.

Jeff was waiting beside the passenger car door when she came out of the house. His eyes were sober, yet serene, as he framed her face and stroked her cheekbone with his thumb. "You realize what this means, don't you? We won't come back here. We're saying goodbye to everything."

"I realize it," she whispered. "But are you sure you do?"

"I know what I'm doing," he said.

He kissed her then, long and hard, without the inhibitions he had possessed the first two times they had made love this week. This time, a full heart of emotion, of commitment not yet expressed, of hope too new to look fully upon, played in their kiss.

"Let's go, Daddy," Casey called out.

Jeff broke the kiss and leaned into the back seat, looking at the child who had never called him Daddy before. "What, Casey?" he asked, his voice shredded. "What did you say?"

"Let's go, Daddy. I ready."

He stood, paralyzed, for a moment, savoring the sound of the word he had longed to hear and trying desperately to stop his mouth from trembling and his eyes from welling.

When he looked back at Leah, he saw the tears glistening on her cheeks, and he smiled. "She called me Daddy."

"I know," she whispered. "And the look on your face means more to me than anything I could think of."

He drew in a deep, shaky breath and pressed a kiss on Casey's puckered little mouth. "I love you, Casey."

"I love you, Daddy. Let's go!"

Laughing, Jeff slipped into the driver's seat and closed his door. "Okay, Casey. We're going."

In less than an hour, Casey was sound asleep and quiet had settled over the car. Jeff looked over at Leah.

"Where are we going? Any ideas?"

"I don't care," she said. "Anywhere."

He smiled, but a hint of a shadow darkened his eyes. "I can't believe you're willing to do this."

"I can't believe you are."

"Why wouldn't I?"

She dabbed at the tears in her eyes. "Because of the way you've felt about me for the past two years."

He frowned and stared at the road for a long moment. Streetlights illuminated his face briefly, then cast it in darkness again. "Well, like I told you, maybe that's changing."

Leah leaned across the seat, following her impulse to hug him. He slipped his arm around her, possessively, and she knew that he was healing from the hurts she—and her father—had inflicted upon him. She couldn't expect sudden pronouncements of love, or any emotions articulated. She would take whatever he gave her, whenever he was ready.

Awkward with the newfound tenderness between them, Jeff broke the silence. "We'll drive for a few hours and stop in Fort Walton Beach,'' he said. ''We can get a hotel room, spend the rest of the night there and decide where to go from there.''

She nodded. ''Dad's probably discovered we're gone by now. He's probably going nuts.''

''He won't find us,'' he said. ''We'll be able to relax in Fort Walton. And then we can think.''

IT WAS AFTER MIDNIGHT when they checked into a hotel in Fort Walton Beach, and it was only after Jeff let them into the room that Leah realized he had gotten only one.

He carried the sleeping child in first, laid her in the middle of one of the double beds, and gently covered her with her blanket. He took her Bunny Fu-Fu from Leah and tucked it under her arm.

''You and I can sleep in that one,'' he whispered.

Her eyes collided with his, then quickly skittered away. ''All right. If you'll get the suitcases, I'll stay here with Casey.''

He nodded and went back out to the parking lot. Leah locked the door behind him. Turning back to the beds, she watched Casey sleep. She looked so peaceful, so unhampered by turmoil and deceit, so satisfied.

And that was how Leah felt. It was funny, she thought, but her father's deceit had actually liberated her completely. It had caused her to put her past behind her. To go on with her life. To see Jeff as someone she could have a life with.

He came back to the room and she let him in, and together they unpacked the things they would need for the night, though Jeff had brought nothing with him. "When we get wherever we're going," he said quietly, "I'll call Jan and get her to send me some of my things."

"What will you do in the meantime?" she asked.

"Buy some things. I have my credit card. Tomorrow I'll buy a couple pairs of jeans and whatever else I need."

Leah sat down on the bed and pulled her feet beneath her. Her head dropped, and she traced a pattern on the bedspread with her finger. "I feel so guilty for doing this to you," she whispered. "I never wanted to cost you everything. That's what I tried so hard to avoid."

"Hey," he said, coming to sit across from her on the bed. "I get my daughter out of all this. That's a hell of a lot more than anything I left."

She looked up into his eyes—wishing, hoping that he would say that she was worth leaving it all for, too—and saw that the sadness and distrust she had read in his eyes so many times was lifting, but still there were a few shadows. He was still afraid to love her.

But she didn't need words or endearments from him. When he leaned over to kiss her, soft and sweet and unhurried, touching her face as if he couldn't fathom the softness of it, she realized she had everything she could ever hope for right here. Her baby safe and sound, and the man she loved sharing her bed.

As they made love, delightful images tiptoed through her mind. Images of white picket fences, and wisteria-covered arbors in the yard, and growing her own food, and making her own clothes, and being happy. Images of deep, long talks in the night with Jeff, of loving him with her body and soul, of hearing him say that he loved her.

He couldn't say it tonight, but he showed it, more than the first time when he had turned her away afterward, and even more than the second time when she had felt his barriers slipping. Tonight he loved with his whole being, with the part of him that was vulnerable to pain and heartache, the part of him that was still wounded from her own blade. He loved her without control, without inhibition, without despair. And she loved him in the same way.

They fell asleep in each other's arms, clinging lest one of them slipped away during the night. But the peace that blanketed them and protected them took away the fear, the paranoia, the distrust. They had each other, and they had Casey. And that was all either of them would ever need.

IT WAS 3:00 A. M. when they woke to a loud, urgent banging on their door, and clutching the blankets to them, they sprang up. Jeff grabbed his jeans and slipped them on. "What the hell?"

The pounding came again, louder, more frightening, and Casey sat up and began to cry. Leah tied the belt around her robe and grabbed Casey as Jeff started for the door.

"Open up!" someone shouted from outside.

"Who is it?" Jeff called.

"Police. Open the door."

Throwing a confused look back at Leah over his shoulder, Jeff opened the door. "Haven't you guys ever heard of plain old knocking? There's a baby in here—"

Three uniformed officers burst inside, and Casey screamed. Leah clutched the crying child to her and backed up against the wall.

"Jeff Hampton?" one of them asked.

"Yes."

"You're under arrest," the cop said.

"Arrest? For what?"

"For kidnapping. You have the right to remain silent...."

"Kidnapping? Who did I kidnap?"

"Miss Borgadeux and her daughter," the officer said, snapping cuffs on Jeff's wrists. "You have the right to an attorney...."

"No!" Leah rushed forward, trying to stop them from cuffing his hands. "It's not true. We came with him on our own. For heaven's sake, isn't anybody going to ask *me?*"

"You can make a statement at headquarters, Miss Borgadeux. Meanwhile, our orders are to take him in. He's a suspect in several other crimes, and we have to question him."

"Other crimes?" Jeff shouted. "What did Borgy tell you? That I'm a thief? A criminal? Is that what he told you?"

"That you'd kidnapped this child once before."

"*What?* He's the one—"

Two of the cops grabbed Jeff's arms and began escorting him out of the room. "If you cannot afford an attorney—"

"Stop, damn it!" Leah shouted. "You don't understand. He didn't kidnap us! Look at me! Why would I be defending him if I were being held against my will? Look at me!"

The two cops dragged Jeff out to the car, and the other one stopped in the doorway. "You can ride in the other squad car, Miss Borgadeux. We'll need you to make a statement."

"You bet I'll make a statement!" she cried. She ran to the door and watched as they manhandled Jeff into the back seat, and Casey began to scream louder.

"Daddy!"

"Jeff, don't worry!" Leah shouted across the parking lot. People began to open their doors, and a few dared to come out onto the landing and strained to see what was going on. "I'm coming, too. They won't get away with this."

"It's your father," he said before they closed the car door. "You know this is your father's doing."

"They can't hold you," she cried. "Any more than he can hold me!"

But she wasn't sure he heard, for as she shouted that out, the squad car he was in pulled away to take him to jail.

JEFF SAT in a questioning room under a glaring hot light as four officers who had nothing better to do surrounded him, staring at him as if he'd just committed a string of murders. They had brought him stale coffee, probably aged for the occasion, and the room was thick with smoke and bad breath.

"We can't let you go, pal, until you tell us what we need to know," the cop with the biggest mouth told him.

"You mean until I tell you what you want to hear, *pal*," Jeff returned. "I've already told you everything I know. I did not today, nor have I ever, kidnapped anyone. Lance Borgadeux, on the other hand, set up Casey's kidnapping, held his daughter against her will and set up this whole charade."

"He said you stole his car."

"His car? I haven't *touched* his car. Leah drove his car so she wouldn't get stopped at the gate of his estate. Otherwise, they would have hauled her back in." He leaned forward, beseeching the officers to pull some little thread of common sense from what was going on. "Think about it. Would she have to sneak off like that if she could come and go freely? And would she decide to run in the middle of the night?"

"So you didn't break into his home and abduct Miss Borgadeux and her daughter?"

"*My* daughter, and no, I did not. Leah called me to meet her, and I did."

"At which time you forced her into your car and headed north?"

Jeff rubbed his weary face and began to laugh mirthlessly. "Do you guys not speak English or what? She was going to leave alone. She was going to go so far he'd never find her. I decided to go with her. Why don't you just ask her?"

One of the cops who'd come into the room late—presumably because he was questioning Leah—stood up and nodded toward the others. "Story checks out. She backs it up a hundred percent. We can't really book him under the circumstances."

"If you want to book someone, book Borgadeux," Jeff said. "The man needs to be taken off the streets. He's dangerous."

The big-mouthed cop stood up. "We're letting you go, but we'll be watching you, Hampton. I'm not totally convinced you're without blame in all this."

Jeff scraped his chair back and got up. "I don't care what you're totally convinced of. Now, if you'll excuse me, I want to go see if my fiancée and my daughter are all right."

"Fiancée?"

Jeff locked eyes with the man who'd caused him the most trouble in this ordeal. "Yes, fiancée. Tell Borgadeux that, *pal*. Tell him I'm going to marry his daughter. This time he isn't going to stop me."

MORNING HAD DAWNED before Leah and Jeff stepped out of the precinct, carrying the sleeping child, and rode back to their room in a cab, since they both refused to accept a ride in the squad car.

When they had been returned to their hotel room, exhausted and so angry that neither of them was able to sleep, they began to pack.

Leah looked at Jeff and came up behind him. She touched his back and laid her face against it. "Jeff, I'm so sorry he did this. I'm so sorry that it keeps falling on you."

"He's got to be stopped," he whispered. "We can't go on like this."

She felt him pulling away from her, changing his mind about wanting to go through all this with her, about all the sacrifices he was making. And she didn't blame him.

Taking a deep breath, he turned around and took her arms, making her look up at him. "Leah, we have to talk," he said quietly.

Tears came to her eyes, but she tried to blink them back. Gently she took his hands, brought them to her mouth. "You're having second thoughts," she whispered. "I understand, Jeff. Really I do."

He nodded. "I'm having second thoughts, all right, but not about us. Not about you."

"What then?"

"I had a lot of time to think when they had me in there," he said. "And I decided that there's no way I can let him control us this way. We're letting him send us running blindly. We're letting him take everything we have. We're letting him manipulate us again."

"But what else can we do? He could take Casey, make up lies about you, set you up again, ruin both of us."

"No. Not if we let him know that we're more than ready to expose him and prosecute him. Not if we stand up to him."

"You want to go back." It was a statement, steeped in disappointment and apprehension. It was a statement steeped in fear

"Yes. I want to confront him, Leah. I have to do this. It's right."

Leah looked over to the bed where Casey slept as they packed. She wondered if all the turmoil was doing harm to her little spirit, or if she really took things in stride, as she appeared to. "But if he would have Casey kidnapped, and you arrested—"

"Now we know what we're dealing with, Leah. We'll make sure that he never sees Casey again. *I'll* make sure."

Her tears fell over her lashes, trickled down her cheeks. "I'm scared, Jeff."

"I'm scared, too," he whispered. "But I'm scared of what will happen if we don't stop him. I'm scared of what will become of us if we let him manipulate us." It was his turn to take her hands and folding them in his, he pressed them to his chest. "Leah, the year after you left me was the worst kind of agony. I learned to be numb after that, and it's taken me a long time to trust anyone again. But I feel myself trusting you again."

She slid her arms around his waist, laid her head against his chest as he continued. He cupped his hand over her head, began to stroke her hair. "Maybe it took seeing how low your father would sink to make me believe what you must have been going through when you left me before. Maybe I'm just starting to see that you really had no choices."

A sigh of relief escaped her lungs. "Oh, Jeff, I couldn't let you lose everything you had worked for because of me."

He tilted her face up, looked hard and deep into her eyes. When he spoke, his voice was cracked. "Nothing he could have taken from me would have hurt as bad as losing you, Leah. Nothing.''

She sucked in a sob and tried to stop the quivering of her lips. He lowered his face and kissed away one of her tears. "I love you, Leah. I still love you. I guess somewhere, under all the anger, I always have.''

She tightened her embrace, and he held her with the strength and determination of the only person who had the power to save her.

Slowly he pulled back so that he could look into her eyes. "We have to go back," he said. "I can't walk away and let that man win. I can't walk away after he destroyed our relationship, had my baby kidnapped, had me arrested.... Please understand, Leah. I have to confront him, once and for all. It's the only way you and I will ever have a happy future together.''

The word "future" fell upon her heart like warm sunlight on a snow-covered lawn. "All right, Jeff. We'll go back.''

"We'll go today," he said. "I'll take you to my parents'. We'll spend the night there, and tomorrow you and Casey can wait there while I confront your father. While I tell him how it's going to be.''

"Your parents won't like it," she whispered. "Having me around. They'll hate it.''

"It'll be okay. Sooner or later, things will be clearer to them.''

THE MOMENT THEY PULLED onto the gravel drive at his parents' house that night, Florence and Al Hampton rushed out to the car.

"Where have you been?" his mother cried, bursting into tears.

"They said you had kidnapped Casey and Leah. And that awful man, that Lance Borgadeux, has been harassing us with his phone calls and his thugs—"

"I'm sorry, Mom. I didn't mean to worry you." Jeff hugged his mother, then his father, and turned back to the car to help Leah and Casey out. "It's just that we left suddenly."

"What the hell is going on?" his father demanded.

Leah clutched Casey tighter to her and faced his parents. "Mr. and Mrs. Hampton, if there were rumors, my father started them."

"They weren't just rumors. They were news reports, in the newspaper, no less! Jeff, you should have never gotten tied up with that family. It's poison!"

"Stop it."

Jeff stepped closer to Leah, took Casey from her and set his free arm protectively around her. "Leah's as much a victim as I am. Borgadeux set up the kidnapping himself so he could manipulate Leah. As soon as we figured it out, we decided to put ourselves as far from him as we could."

"But he still had Jeff arrested in Fort Walton Beach," Leah added. "He'll go to any lengths."

His parents looked stricken. "He had his own grandchild kidnapped?" His mother turned her teary eyes on her son. "And you were in jail? Are you all right? Oh, my God, *he's* the one who should be locked up!"

"He won't get away with it," Jeff assured his parents. "We need for you to let us stay here tonight. Tomorrow, I'm going back to Tampa to confront him, and Dad, I need for you to protect Leah and Casey. I'm counting on you."

"But what about you? Who's going to protect you from him?"

"I can take care of myself," he said. "I have ammunition now. I have enough on him to prosecute, but he won't want that."

"You will prosecute, won't you?"

Leah gave him a dreadful look.

"We don't know yet," Jeff said. "We don't want Casey marked forever. What we really want is just to be left alone. Just for him to get out of our lives. If I have anything to say about it, that man will never see either his daughter or his granddaughter again."

Both parents gave Leah an assessing look—a look that said they still didn't trust her, they still didn't like her and they still could not accept her into their family. But it was a tentative look, one that offered the slightest hope that they might be wrong.

They went into the house and got Casey settled into bed. Since he didn't want to upset his mother further by sharing a bed with Leah, she was sleeping with Casey that night.

"Don't worry about me tomorrow, okay?" he whispered, holding her tightly against him before he left her for the night.

"I won't," she whispered. "I just wish your parents didn't hate having me here so much."

"They'll come around," he said. "In time, they'll love you, too. Remember, we have all the time in the world."

"Do we?" she asked. "Because to me, it seems like we just have a few more hours."

"He's not going to ruin us again," he whispered. "I promise you, this will all be over tomorrow."

Chapter Twelve

Leah and Casey were the first ones up the next morning, for Jeff's parents slept late since they always stayed so late at the bar. Casey, who didn't care where she was, popped up at the crack of dawn with a man's appetite.

Setting Casey up on the counter, Leah began quietly moving around the Hamptons' kitchen, trying to find Casey something to eat without waking anyone.

"There's cereal in the pantry." Leah turned and saw Florence in the kitchen doorway, looking at her with that drawn, reluctant expression. "Here, I'll get it."

"Thanks. I hope we didn't wake you. Casey never sleeps late."

"I'll never mind waking up to my granddaughter's voice," Florence said, softening as she picked Casey up. "Where's Jeff?"

"Still sleeping, I guess. I made coffee if you want some."

For a few minutes, they worked quietly, only speaking to Casey as they prepared her breakfast, passing each other with "excuse me's" and "sorry's."

Finally, Casey was eating and there was nothing left to do. Leah gave Florence a tentative look. "Will you sit down with us? Have some coffee?"

Looking trapped, Florence poured herself a cup and sat down, fixing her eyes on Casey.

"Look, Mrs. Hampton, I know how you feel about me, and I can't blame you. But I really appreciate you letting us stay here."

"Casey," she corrected. "I'm letting Casey stay. You're just here because you happen to be her mother."

The sting hit its mark, and Leah swallowed and tried to start again. "I realize that."

She took a deep breath and looked down at her coffee, as if some answers would materialize on the obsidian surface. "You know, when I left Jeff before, it wasn't because I wanted to. It was because of the kind of man my father is. The kind of man who could ruin Jeff if I didn't do what he wanted. You must see that now, after all he's done."

"All I see, Leah, is that you've brought nothing but heartache and despair and turmoil into my son's life." The words were spoken calmly, gently, but the bite of them was devastating. She sipped her coffee, pushed Casey's hair back from her face and looked at Leah again. "Leah, I know that it may not have been your fault. But the fact is, you hurt him deeply before, and now, finding out that you've deliberately kept his daughter from him... I just don't know if I can ever forgive you for that."

"I don't know if he'll ever forgive me, either," she whispered. "I don't even know if I can forgive myself. All I know, Mrs. Hampton, is that I still love him with all my heart, and if there were even a remote possibility that he would give me another chance, I would make it up to him. And to you. You'd see."

"But second chances are hard to come by, Leah. And to be perfectly honest, I don't think he *should* give you one."

Through the tears clouding her eyes, Leah noticed a movement in the doorway, and she looked up to see Jeff standing there, his face a mask of controlled anger.

Blinking back her tears, she whispered, "Good morning."

"Is it?" he asked, his eyes settling on his mother.

Florence slid her chair back. "I'll get you some coffee."

He came farther into the room as his mother went for the coffee and sat down next to Leah. Their eyes met for a moment, and she knew he saw her tears. Feeling awkward, clumsy, silly, she scooted her chair back. "Can you watch Casey, Jeff? I'll be right back."

He nodded, and quickly she left the room.

His eyes followed her until she was gone, and he felt his heart sink for the pain she was feeling. He wanted to stop it, to heal it, as she had started the healing within him.

His mother brought his coffee cup to the table and sat down across from him. "I was just telling Leah that—"

"I heard what you told her, Mom," he said. "And now I have something to tell you."

He saw her stiffen, saw her take a deep breath and hold it, bracing herself.

"I don't think it's up to you to decide whether or not I give Leah a second chance. It's between her and me. And as for you accepting her, that's up to you. I'm not accepted by her father, and that's just fine with me. We can live without your acceptance, too, if we have to."

"What are you talking about?" his mother demanded. "Are you going to get back together with her?"

He looked down at his hands, studied them, then clasped them on the table. "I'm in love with her, Mom. She's the only woman I've ever felt this way about. Yes, she's dragged me through hell, but she went there, too. She had more of it than I did."

Casey looked up at them, her eyes widening at the sharper tones in their voices, and Florence waited for a moment before answering. Trying to smile a shaky smile, she poured Casey some more cereal.

Softening her tone, she said, "I want you to be happy, Jeff. That's all. Is that such a bad thing for a mother to want for her son?"

"Leah makes me happy, Mom. Since she walked out on me, I've been miserable. Now she's back, and I feel like my life has started over again. She gave me Casey, and I want to give her the family she never had. I want you to love her, too."

"That'll take time," she said, taking his hand. "But if that's the way you feel, son, I'll do my best."

WHEN CASEY HAD EATEN her fill, Florence took her outside to see the litter of kittens, and Jeff went to Leah's bedroom. "Leah?" he called quietly through the door.

"Come in."

He opened the door, stepped tentatively inside. She had been crying harder, and her nose and lips were red with the strain of it. But she had wiped her eyes dry so that she could hold up that brave front—that front she had been born to wear.

"Are you all right?"

"Sure, fine," she said, turning away from him and busying herself folding Casey's clothes. "Where's Casey?"

"She went out to see the kittens with Mom. She's warming up to her."

"Yeah," she said. "She doesn't scream when I'm not around anymore. Kind of amazing, with all that's been going on. I guess kids are more resilient than we give them credit for."

He stepped closer and reached out to still her hands. She looked at him, and he saw the tears forming again. "I talked to my mother," he whispered.

"About what?" Her lips quivered with the effort of not crying.

"About you. About us."

"Us?" Her voice was shaky, unsteady.

"Yes. I told her, Leah, that I'm in love with you."

Those tears she struggled so hard to hold back splashed onto her cheeks, and her eyebrows lifted in disbelief. "You did?"

"Yes, I did," he whispered, framing her face and wiping a tear with his thumb.

She sucked in a breath and covered her mouth with her hand. "And what did she say?"

He smiled. "She promised to go easier on you."

He pulled her against him, buried his face in her hair and felt his own eyes stinging with emotion as she wept into his shirt. "I'm sorry she hurt you."

"She was just being honest," she said. "She had every right."

He lifted her face to his, met her lips and pulled her into a kiss so deep she would have gladly drowned in it. But he was there to breathe life back into her, passing his strength through the gentleness of his touch, carrying the burden of love and loneliness she had carried alone for so long.

When the kiss ended on a sigh, he threaded his fingers through her hair and pressed his mouth against her temple. "I've got to go," he said, reminding her of the dread that had kept her awake all night. "It's time to confront your father."

"I want to come with you," she said. "I want to be there."

"No."

"Jeff, please. It's my battle. . . ."

"It's *our* battle. Besides, Casey would fall apart if she didn't know you were nearby. And it could get ugly. There's no reason for you to be in the middle of it."

"But I *am* in the middle of it."

"Please," he said. "Let me do this. It's very important to me."

Seeing that his mind couldn't be changed, she nodded quietly. "All right, I'll stay. Just be careful, Jeff. I don't think he would hurt you physically, but I didn't think he'd kidnap Casey, either. Please be careful."

"I promise," he said, slipping out of her arms. "I'll be back in a little while, and then we'll have some plans to make."

Leah choked back a new surge of tears as he left her there.

FROM THE WAY Borgy's staff buzzed around him, one would have thought Jeff was a fugitive from the law who had finally come to turn himself in. Borgy's secretary dropped a stack of papers she was holding as she reached for the telephone to buzz her boss. A cluster of security men, or "thugs" as his mother had called them, immediately appeared in the room outside Borgy's office. And the man himself appeared in less than thirty seconds after Jeff announced who he was.

"Where's my daughter?" Borgy shouted, his voice shaking the very walls of his office. "What have you done with her?"

"In the office, Borgy," Jeff said, breaking loose from the security guard's grip. "This is just between you and me. No bodyguards, no detectives, no cops. Just you and me in the office. You wouldn't like it if they heard what I have to say."

"I have no secrets from my staff," Borgy said, but his imperial tone had slipped a note.

"Oh no?" Jeff asked. "Then I guess they'll all go to jail with you, Borgy. I mean, if they knew what you were doing—"

"Jail?" His secretary came to her feet, staring at Borgadeux.

Jeff saw his face redden.

"I don't know what you're talking about."

"I'd be happy to elaborate," Jeff obliged. "Since everyone knows and all...."

Borgadeux flung open the door to his office and gestured for Jeff to go in.

"Great idea," Jeff said, slipping his hands into his pockets and ambling into the elaborate nerve center of Borgadeux Enterprises.

He walked to the middle of the carpet, turned and watched Borgy follow him in and close the double doors behind him. His face was still crimson when he turned around.

"I warn you," Borgadeux said. "You're in a hell of a lot more danger with me alone than you would be in front of witnesses."

"Oh, I don't doubt that you're dangerous, Borgy," Jeff said, holding his cold stare. "But I'm the one who was in jail yesterday. At the moment, I'm more dangerous than you are."

A vein at Borgadeux's temple pulsed as he crossed the room toward Jeff. "Where's my daughter?"

"She's not in Fort Walton Beach waiting to bail me out, if that's what you hoped," he said. "And she's not talking to the DA about the fact that her own father had his granddaughter kidnapped."

The surprise on Borgy's face was worth every moment of anger and rage Jeff had experienced. "What did you say?"

Jeff grinned. "We know, Borgy. I have my own detectives, and really, it doesn't take a genius to figure out what you've done and why."

"Are you accusing me of—"

"Yes. I'm accusing you of hiring strangers to kidnap my daughter so that you could manipulate yours. I'm accusing you of harassing and terrorizing and threatening Leah so that you could get her back under your control."

"You must be crazy! Why would I do something like that? I would never—"

"You did it, and we can prove it." The words were so calm, so unemotional, that Borgy only stared at him. Jeff picked up a framed photo of Leah and Casey, looked at it and set it back down. "Now, as I see it, Borgy, we have a few options. My preference is the one where I expose you for what you are and turn you over to the DA, and stand back and watch while they cuff you and haul you off to jail like they did to me. But that's only second to the one where I take you on myself and tear you limb from limb until I have satisfaction that you've gotten what you deserve…which is to live in the same kind of hell you've put Leah through."

Borgadeux's shoulders stiffened, and his hard expression held firm, not cracking. "The DA is a friend of mine. He would never believe you."

"Oh, he'd believe me," Jeff assured him. "And you couldn't keep it quiet, Borgy, not with it all over the news. Hell, it just might ruin you."

He paced across the room, stopped at a pair of bronze baby shoes displayed on a marble shelf, saw the inscription of Leah's name and birth date. Borgadeux waited, solid and expressionless, holding his breath. "But Leah and I have opted for something else entirely," Jeff said finally.

"What?"

"Well, Leah wanted to move to another town where you'd never find her again. Someplace where she didn't have to look over her shoulder for fear her father's thugs would snatch her daughter to manipulate her. Someplace where they could live in peace. I was glad to take her to that place. That's where we were headed when you had me arrested like a drug lord in the middle of the night. And that kind of got me thinking."

"Get to the point, Hampton. I'm not a patient man."

"And neither am I," Jeff said, squaring off with the man across from him. "Which is why I decided that I can't let you get away with this. You aren't going to run Leah away from her home and her business, you aren't going to force us to uproot our daughter, and by God, you aren't going to ruin me the way you threatened Leah you would. You're not going to do a damned thing, because if you do, I'll smear your name so bad that you'll be happy to wind up in jail."

The vein in Borgy's temple twitched, but his expression did not change.

"The fact is that I'm still in love with Leah," Jeff said. "And I'm going to marry her. I'm going to move her and Casey into my house, and we're going to be happy there. And if you ever come within a hundred feet of my wife or my child, I'll splatter your ass all over the newspapers and television screens for as far as they know your name, and then I'll take my family so far away that it'll be like they never existed. Have you got that?"

For the first time, the man's hard facade began to crack. "Hampton, whatever I did, it was in the best interest of my daughter. She knows that—"

Venomous rage bled into Jeff's eyes as he came within inches of the man. "I know that you are capable of horrible things, Borgy. I'm going to document every bit of my proof and keep it locked up where I can pull it out any time I need it. You just never know when the mood might strike me to do you in. You just never know."

WHEN THE TELEPHONE RANG at the Hamptons', Leah fought the urge to spring for it. It wasn't her house, she reminded herself as Florence answered in the kitchen. If Jeff wanted to speak to her, he'd have to go through his mother first.

But it wasn't Jeff, she gathered the moment Florence stepped into the dining room where she and Casey sat putting together Lego pieces.

"It's your father," Florence said. "Do you want me to tell him you're not here?"

An alarm went off in her heart, and she tried to think, tried to put together broken images of what might have happened to make him call here. Had Jeff reached him yet? Had something happened to him? Had her father hurt him?

She raked a hand through her hair and came slowly to her feet. "Did...did he say if Jeff's been there yet?"

"No," Florence said. "He's very rude and obnoxious, and he just demanded to talk to you. I can hang up on him if you want—"

"No." She swallowed and reached for the phone. "It might be about Jeff. I'll take it."

Florence sat down next to Casey as Leah put the phone to her ear, and Leah could see from the disapproval on her face that she expected Leah to defect to her father's side of this fight again. "Hello?"

"Leah, he's filling your head full of lies, sweetheart. He's brainwashing you. You've got to get out of there—"

"Shut up!" The harsh words startled both Florence and Casey but not as much as they startled Borgadeux. "Just shut up!" she shouted again. "You're the one who tried to brainwash me!"

"Leah, I'm your father! I love you!"

"You don't know what love is!" she shouted back. "Love is not fear, and it's not intimidation. It's not lying and stealing and hurting!"

"I never hurt you, Leah. I would never have hurt you or the baby!"

"You let your lowlifes take my baby!" she screamed. "You watched me die a little at a time! And it was all so you could have your almighty power!"

"Leah, this is crazy. We've got to meet somewhere, darling. We've got to talk."

"Not without a team of reporters with television cameras, a battalion of cops and the DA," Leah said. "Still want to talk, Dad?"

Borgy's voice faltered, and she could hear that he wept. Oddly, she felt no sympathy for the man. "He told me I could never see you again," Borgy said. "Don't you understand that I can't accept that? You're all I have, Leah."

"Then you have nothing," she said. "Jeff meant every word he said about turning you in if you ever come near us again. I'm getting a gun, Dad, and I'm going to learn how to use it. And I'll do whatever I have to to protect myself and my daughter. Even from you."

Without waiting for her father's response, she slammed down the phone. Florence stood up, and the look on her face revealed that she was letting down the barriers. She opened her arms for Leah, and wilting like a delicate flower too long in the heat, Leah fell into her embrace and cried until her tears ran out.

LEAH WAS WAITING OUTSIDE on the front porch with Florence and Casey when Jeff drove up, and Florence took her hand. "No obvious cuts or bruises," she said. "Guess he's all right."

Leah gave her a smile that was full of gratitude, a smile that thanked her for opening her arms to her, for seeing her true colors at last, for accepting that she was someone who deserved a chance. "I'll go see."

She ran down the steps to the car as Jeff was getting out. "Are you okay? He didn't hurt you?"

Jeff laughed. "Of course not. He was so scared, he wouldn't have touched me."

"I know," she said. "He called here."

"He *what?*" Jeff's smile crashed, and his face resumed the murderous expression with which he had confronted Borgadeux. As if to fulfill that rage, he started to get back in the car. "I *warned* him to leave you alone. I'll kill him."

"Wait!" Leah cried, pulling him back out. "I handled it, Jeff. I told him I was getting a gun."

Jeff turned back to her. His breathing was heavier as he waited for a reason not to go after the man again. "What did he say to that?"

"What *could* he say? I think he knew it was the end when you told him, but he had to hear it from me."

Florence came up beside them, holding Casey on her hip. "You would have been proud of her, Jeff, the way she told him off. She really let him have it, and there's nothing I like better than a good fighter."

Jeff seemed to relax, and he set his arm across Leah's shoulders, as if to feel for himself that Borgy hadn't done her more harm. Then, as if he only now recognized the significance of what his mother had said, he passed a questioning look from Leah to his mother. "Did I miss something?"

Waving him off, Florence turned him around and gave him a quick once-over. "Are you sure he left you in one piece? Didn't even try to cripple you?"

"That's not his style," Jeff said, still frowning. "It's too obvious. He likes doing things the underhanded way. But I think he's the one who's been crippled. He's losing Leah and Casey for good."

"His loss is our gain," Florence said. She started back up to the house.

Jeff stood still, a slow smile dawning across his face. "Did she say what I thought she said?"

Leah smiled. "Your mother and I are going to get along just fine," she said. "Come on. Let's get our stuff and go home."

LATE THAT NIGHT, when they were back in Jeff's home and Casey slept soundly in her room, Leah lay on the couch, cocooned in his arms.

"There's one thing I told your father that I haven't told you, yet," he whispered, gazing into her eyes and fingering her hair.

She looked up at him and touched his face, wondering at the texture of the stubble across his chin, the angle of his jaw, the shape of his chin. "What?"

"I told him..." He swallowed, and moved his mouth to her fingertips, caught one in his mouth. His eyes met hers as he laced his fingers through hers, bathed each tip and traced the pad of her thumb across his lip. "I told him I was going to marry you."

Their eyes locked softly, foreign beacons meeting across a night sky—his apprehensive, hers stunned. "You did?"

"Yes," he whispered. "Maybe I should have asked you first, but—"

"No." She got up on her knees and looked down at the face she loved. Her eyes were misty, soft, vulnerable as they beheld him. "It's...it's all right. If you meant it."

"I meant it." Releasing her, he reached into his pocket and pulled out the small velvet box he had put there the moment he'd come home. He had waited until Casey was asleep, until they could be alone, and over and over he had slipped his hand in his pocket and felt it against his fingers, a reassurance that the light wouldn't die the moment his happiness blossomed fully. "I didn't mean to tell him first. What I really wanted to do..."

Leah's eyes fell to the box, the box he had offered her once before. She had never been able to take it, for her father had already drawn the lines. Now, knowing what was inside that box that she had never dreamed he'd kept, her eyes filled with tears. "Jeff?"

His hands shook as he lifted the lid, and Leah saw the diamond ring she had wanted so badly to wear the first time. It had dazzled her then, as it did now, and she knew it had been way more than he could afford when he'd bought it. "You kept it," she whispered.

"Yeah," he said. "If I had taken it back, they would have sold it to someone else. I couldn't stand the thought of anyone else ever wearing it but you." He took it out of the box and reached for her hand.

"Leah," he whispered, "I love you more than you could ever imagine. I don't ever want to face the thought of losing you again. I want to live with you for the rest of my life." His own eyes filled with half-moons of tears as he breathed out the words. "Will you be my wife?"

Her tears rolled down her cheeks as she pressed her forehead against his. "I love you, Jeff Hampton," she said. "And I've never wanted anything more in my life than to be your wife."

He slipped the ring on her finger, brought the finger to his lips. Closing his eyes, he kissed her knuckle, then moved her hand against his cheek. "I wanted to marry you the first day I met you...." His eyes opened and he framed her face and caught her lips. "I wanted to marry you the day you left me...." He slid his hands down her neck and pulled her against him. "And I want to marry you now. I want to love you forever and make you the happiest woman on earth."

"You've already made me the happiest woman on earth," she said. "Now just make me your wife."

Their loving was slow, selfless, sensitive, as each moved to prove how deep their love was. And as they came together in a union more perfect than either had experienced before, they knew that nothing would ever come between them again. They were solid, they were whole.

They were one.

Epilogue

"Hurry, Mommy! Daddy'll be home soon."

Leah smiled at Casey and took the three strands of Christmas tree lights from her. It was going to be a surprise for Jeff. Casey had seen the "invisible Christmas tree" at the mall, made of lights coming from a center point and angling out to the ground. She had been fascinated that it looked like nothing but wires and bulbs when the lights were off, but when the strings were plugged in, it became a glorious display that lit up the building. She had convinced Leah to make one in the center of their front yard.

To the child, it was a miracle, making something magnificent out of a mess of tangled wires. To Leah, it was more than a miracle. It was a symbol of the beautiful union she and Jeff had created in marriage.

The door to the house opened, and Jan stuck her head out. "Hey, Leah! Mom's on the phone and wants to know if you want lace or ribbon to edge that baby blanket she's making."

Leah got to her feet and, smiling, set her hand over her swollen stomach where her and Jeff's baby continuously made his presence known. "Tell her, ribbon. Yellow or white." She felt the baby kick as if in protest, then shook her head. "Never mind. Tell her I'll call her back."

Jan waved and retreated back inside, where she had engaged in hanging the decorations she and Leah had found at a craft fair that morning. They had saved the tree-trimming for Jeff to help with, but the rest would be a surprise.

Leah turned back to the "invisible tree" and saw that Casey was tangled up in the two remaining strings. "Casey! What are you doing?"

"I can do it myself," she said. "I'm big."

"Not that big." She stooped down and began trying to untangle her.

"Plug me in, Mommy! Let's see if I look like a tree!"

"We have enough trees around here, thank you." She stood up and stretched out the strand and stapled it to the plywood on the ground. "There. Almost finished."

"Who's that, Mommy?"

Leah stood up, dusting off her knees and saw a black limousine coming through the gates that she had forgotten to close after she and Jan got home. A skein of fear shot through her. "Come here, Casey."

She picked up the three-year-old and, holding her close, stood motionless as the limo approached.

"Is that Daddy?"

"No, honey."

The car came to a halt, and Leah felt the blood drain from her face as her father got out of the car.

She hadn't seen him in a year, and the age and weathering of his face surprised her. She hadn't expected these months to do so much damage.

"Leah." The word, broken and soft, made her back away.

"I don't want you here," she said. "I told you—"

"Please, Leah." He burst into tears and held up his hands. "I've given you a year. I haven't contacted you once. But you're my daughter, and it's Christmas."

Afraid that his emotional state was upsetting Casey, she set her down. "Run in, Casey. Aunt Jan needs your help."

Casey didn't move.

Borgadeux bent over and started to pick her up.

"Put her down!" The words came too harshly and Casey started to cry. Reaching out, she took her away from him. "Don't you ever touch my daughter again."

"Leah, I wouldn't hurt her! She's my grandchild!"

"You had her kidnapped! You let people who commit crimes for money take my baby for an entire day. How dare you say that you wouldn't hurt her?"

"I've paid!" His tears came harder, and his big, slumped shoulders shook. "I've learned. All I ever wanted was to keep you close to me. I didn't know any other way to do that. Instead, I drove you away."

He broke down, and Leah only stared at him, unable to lift a hand to comfort him.

THE LIMO WAS THE FIRST thing Jeff saw as he came up the drive, and he felt his heart rate shift into high gear. He saw Borgadeux standing with Leah, and Casey between them.

Throwing the car into Park, he got out and bolted toward the man, ready to beat him to a pulp, ready to call out all the legal dogs he could find, ready to make good on his threat.

"I warned you, Borgy—"

The man turned around, and the tears and wrinkles and age on the man's face stopped Jeff. "I'm going," he said, like a defeated, broken old man. "But I had to come. I had to try."

Jeff stepped close to Leah, set a possessive arm around her, and touched Casey's shoulder as if the mere touch could protect her from the debilitating love of this man who was her grandfather.

"I don't blame you for hating me," Borgadeux told him. "I'm responsible for more pain than any man should have to suffer. But if it's any consolation, I've suffered, too."

"It is," Jeff said.

Slowly Borgadeux turned back to the car, opened the back door and looked around the yard at the newly hung Christmas decorations, the swing set on the side of the house, the sandbox. He looked at Casey, plump and healthy and full of life. And then he looked at his daughter, standing silently beside her husband, her belly full with the new life they had created together.

"I've been a fool," he whispered. "Maybe some-day you'll find it in your heart to give me another chance."

Jeff held Leah as she watched her father get back into his limo and ride out of sight.

IN THE WEE HOURS of morning when the night wind sang its doleful song against the corners of the house and the full moon lit the window, Jeff woke to an empty bed and found Leah sitting on the windowsill, staring out into the darkness.

"You okay?" he asked, sitting up.

She smiled. "The baby was doing gymnastics and woke me," she said. "He'll be the world's first infant gold medalist."

Jeff scooted onto the sill behind her and reached around her, feeing her stomach with both hands. "Feels quiet in there to me. Are you sure something else isn't bothering you?"

"Like what?"

"Like your father?" He rested his chin on her shoulder and nuzzled his face against hers.

"I don't know," she whispered. "It's all so confus-ing. I thought I hated him, and then today when I saw him, he looked so old and so alone—"

"And you felt sorry for him."

"I don't know what I felt," she said, leaning back against him.

They were quiet for a while, staring out into the night, listening to the wind and relaxing in the warmth of their love. Finally Leah spoke again.

"If I hadn't had a second chance," she whispered, "I wouldn't be here with you. Maybe everyone—no matter how cruel or hateful—maybe everyone deserves a second chance."

For a long time Jeff was still, his face pressed against hers and his hands cupping her stomach. After a while, a slow sigh escaped him, and he dropped his hands, releasing her.

She sat up straight and turned around as he stood up. "Jeff?"

Quietly he walked across the room, got the telephone and brought it back to her. "Ten to one he couldn't sleep tonight, either."

Leah took the phone and stared at it, unable to believe what he suggested. "You want me to call him?"

He touched her face and tipped it up to his. "If you need to. If he's left an empty hole inside you, Leah, then I think it needs to be filled."

She looked at the phone again, an uncertain frown tugging at her brows. "I don't know, Jeff. The things he's done.... We've had such a good life this past year. I don't want him to spoil it."

"Leah, look at me." She looked up at him again, saw the face that had at last taken away her insecurities, the face that meant everything to her. "We've built something too strong for him to knock down again. He can't hurt us now. Go ahead and call him if you need to."

Leah pulled him into her arms and kissed him with the gratitude and love he had cultivated in her so carefully over the last year, for he had taught her the true value of second chances. And as he turned her around in his arms and pulled her back against him, holding her, she smiled...and began to dial her father's number.

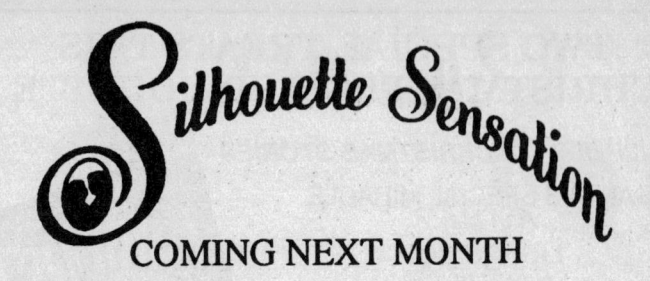

Silhouette Sensation

COMING NEXT MONTH

STEVIE'S CHASE
Justine Davis

The man who lived next door to Stevie Holt was a mystery. Tall and dark, he looked a little too menacing to be described as handsome. He didn't talk to anyone and clearly was not interested in making friends. But then, one day, Stevie gave him no choice. . .

It was hard to keep your distance from a bubbly, strawberry blonde who had broken into your apartment and was determined to nurse you. But Chase Sullivan didn't just look dangerous, he *was* dangerous—to anyone foolish enough to care about him. What was he running from?

OUT OF THE ASHES
Emilie Richards

The final story in Emilie Richards *TALES OF THE PACIFIC*

For Alexis Whitham, Australia's remote Kangaroo Island was the perfect place to begin a new life. Her young daughter would be safe from her ex-husband, safe in a new land with a new name.

But Jody brought a new man into Alexis's life—a man with a past just as tragic as her own. Matthew Haley had already loved and lost; he wasn't going to repeat himself!

Silhouette Sensation

COMING NEXT MONTH

THE ART OF DECEPTION
Nora Roberts

Adam Haines was visiting the Fairchild mansion under false pretences and he didn't like that. He liked to be straightforward and honest, but you didn't find a thief by declaring that you were an investigator. Moreover, you didn't get to sleep with the chief suspect's daughter if you told her you expected to have her father arrested!

The question was, was Kirby involved? If so, just how involved was she and could he compromise his ethics to save her?

CHARITY'S ANGEL
Dallas Schulze

Gabe London had been going to ask Charity Williams out but three, armed thieves prevented that. Suddenly, Gabe was a cop trying to control a hostage situation and prevent anyone being hurt.

But someone was hurt—Charity. And worse still, it was Gabe's bullet that injured her. The least he could do was offer her somewhere to recuperate. . .

TAKE 4 NEW SILHOUETTE SENSATIONS FREE!

Silhouette Sensation is a thrilling series for the woman of today. They are a specially selected range of narrative fiction with a mix of suspense, glamour and drama. Featuring modern realistic stories, they are daring and sensual.

NOW YOU CAN ENJOY 4 SILHOUETTE SENSATIONS, A CUDDLY TEDDY AND A MYSTERY GIFT FREE

♥ ♥ ♥ ♥ ♥ ♥ ♥ ♥ ♥ ♥ ♥ ♥ ♥ ♥ ♥ ♥ ♥ ♥ ♥

Now you can enjoy 4 Silhouette Sensations, a cuddly teddy and a mystery gift absolutely FREE and without obligation. Then if you choose, you can look forward to receiving your new Sensations delivered to your door each month at just £1.75 each (post & packing free) plus a FREE newsletter packed with author news, competitions offering great prizes, special offers and lots more. Send no money now. Simply fill in the coupon below at once and post it to:-
Silhouette Reader Service, FREEPOST, PO Box 236, Croydon, Surrey CR9 9EL.

----------- NO STAMP REQUIRED -----------→

Please send me, free and without obligation, four specially selected Silhouette Sensations, together with my FREE cuddly teddy and mystery gift - and reserve a Reader Service Subscription for me. If I decide to subscribe I shall receive 4 new Silhouette Sensation titles every month for £7.00 post and packing free. If I decide not to subscribe, I shall write to you within 10 days. The free books and gifts are mine to keep in any case. I understand that I may cancel or suspend my subscription at any time simply by writing to you. I am over 18 years of age.

EP22SS

Mrs/Miss/Ms/Mr _____

Address_____

_____

_____ Postcode _____
(Please don't forget to include your postcode)

Signature _____

"Do you know the mistletoe legend?"

Bret strained to reach the cluster of mistletoe and detach it from the snowy branch. Suddenly, the cluster came free and tumbled through the tree limbs, raining berries and leaves and snowflakes amidst Dani's shouts of delight.

She stretched her hands upward to catch the cluster, laughing.

Bret sprang to the ground beside her. He said softly, "Do you mean the one about kissing?"

Suddenly, their eyes met. The moment between them was poised and expectant, and either one of them, with a word, a breath, a shifted gaze, could have broken it. But no power on earth could have persuaded Dani to move away from Bret then.

She whispered in a husky voice, "Absolutely."

Their lips touched, as they had done many times before. But right from the first instant, they both knew that this time was different. . . .

Dear Reader,

Season's Greetings!

The magic of Christmas has been captured in this
special Silhouette collection. Read in *Second Chances*
how the kidnapping of her young daughter forced Leah
to seek out her embittered ex-lover. And how Bret in
Under the Mistletoe was compelled to return home after
receiving a long-lost mystery letter from his close
friend, Dani. Our third seasonal novel, *For Auld Lang
Syne*, celebrates a wedding at Christmas and we share in
the warmth and hope which comes with the beginning
of a New Year.

Join with us and celebrate Christmas – the season when
wishes really *can* come true.

The Editors,
Silhouette Books,
Eton House,
18-24 Paradise Road,
Richmond,
Surrey.
TW9 1SR

REBECCA FLANDERS
Under the Mistletoe

SILHOUETTE BOOKS

*First published in Great Britain in 1992
by Silhouette Books, Eton House, 18-24 Paradise Road,
Richmond, Surrey TW9 1SR*

© Donna Ball, Inc 1991

Silhouette Books and Colophon are
Trade Marks of Harlequin Enterprises B.V.

ISBN 0 373 58627 2

95-9211

Made and printed in Great Britain

Chapter One

The sound of the mail truck's horn interrupted Bret's fifth lap across the pool. By the time he pulled himself out of the water and dried his face with the towel that was draped across the webbed chair at the pool's edge, the door chimes had already echoed once. Like most California homes—even those as luxurious as his—there wasn't much of a walk from the street to the front door.

He could see the mail carrier's uniform through the glass inset of the front door as he crossed through the kitchen and foyer, leaving wet footprints across the quarry-tile floor. He could also see the registered letter that was the reason his morning swim had been interrupted—a packet of documents from his father's attorney in Clayville that Bret had specifically directed should be sent to his office but that Johnson Webb, with typical small-town stubbornness, had apparently mailed to his home instead.

Towel-drying his hair with one hand, Bret opened the door. "Morning," he said, accepting the pen the carrier offered.

"Just sign right there by the *X,* if you will."

Bret glanced at the man as he did so. "You're new on this route, aren't you?"

Bret had a natural eye for detail, but it didn't take an experienced detective to realize that this middle-aged, rosy-cheeked man bore no resemblance to the slim, young woman who usually delivered his mail. He was short and round, with a neatly trimmed white beard and a fringe of snowy hair peeking out from his cap from ear to ear and a deep, warm voice that reverberated with more than the usual Southern California friendliness. He looked like a man who enjoyed his job and he made Bret want to smile even through his annoyance at having to interrupt his morning routine to sign for the package.

The letter carrier's blue eyes twinkled as though with some private joke as he replied, "Just filling in during the holidays."

Bret grimaced a little as he glanced across the street at the houses of his neighbors, many of whom had already started decorating their doors with tacky foil wreaths and paper Santas. "Yeah, I guess it is that time again, isn't it? Seems to start earlier and earlier every year."

"Never too early for me," the mailman replied cheerfully, and handed him the package, plus several other envelopes. "Here's the rest of your mail. Have a good day now."

Bret had never heard of a mailman who actually looked forward to Christmas, and he grinned a little as he turned away from the door, glancing through the mail. He tossed the package on the foyer table next to his briefcase so he wouldn't forget to take it to the office, but the rest of the mail wasn't worth saving. Fliers, mail-order catalogs, sweepstakes entries, credit-card offers... How had his name gotten on all those mailing lists, anyway?

Then he stopped. There was one envelope that was completely blank—no return address, no postmark, not even an address. "Hey!" he called, going back to the door. But the mail truck was already gone.

He frowned as he closed the door and started toward the kitchen, examining the envelope. It was probably more junk, he thought and he started to throw it away with the rest of the trash. Then common curiosity got the better of him. He tore open the envelope and was startled to see a hand-written message that began "Dear Bret." He skipped down to the signature and his heartbeat actually jumped as he read "Dani."

For a moment, he could do nothing but stare at the page. Then quickly, he snatched up the envelope again, examining it both front and back. Dani! But how... and why...?

"Weird," he muttered. He hooked his ankle around a chair and pulled it out from the kitchen table. He had to sit down to read this.

Dear Bret,
   I'm never going to mail this, and no one but you would understand why I have to write it down. Tonight, you're getting married...

His heart thudded again. Married? He glanced at the top of the letter, but there was no date. Of course, there wouldn't be, she had never intended to mail it. Married . . .

Ten years ago, Bret Underwood had married Laura Wheeling, a bright, beautiful liberal-arts major with enough ambition for two women and enough charm for five. He had thought she was exactly what he needed, he had thought he was the luckiest man alive. He had thought, young and starry-eyed as he had been, that he loved her.

His eyes went back to the letter, seeing the words but not reading them. Ten years ago, Dani Griffin had sat down to write this letter because that was what they did when they had a secret too big to keep and too important to tell . . . they wrote it down. Once it was out of their systems, they tore the message up or hid it away and the urge to tell was gone. Except Dani hadn't torn up this letter. What was the secret she had kept from him on his wedding day that was too important to tell?

He made his eyes focus again. His throat felt dry but he did not reach for the cup of coffee that was cooling at his elbow.

Tonight, you're getting married, and I've tried to be happy for you, I really have, but I think you know I don't approve. What you don't know is why, and that's the secret. There's someone who loves you, Bret, more than Laura ever could, and I think if you knew, it might make a difference. And that's exactly why I can't tell you . . . because you love Laura, not her, and it might make a difference. I've never kept a secret from you before, and I hope you understand why I had to keep this one. But even if you don't, remember that I'll always be

Your best friend,
Dani

He read the letter again, then once more, slowly. Then he just sat at the table and gazed out the open French door that led to the pool.

"Dani, Dani," he murmured, dropping his eyes to the letter once more. "You always did know how to get a fellow's day off to a helluva start, didn't you?"

He lifted his cup, but the coffee was cold. He poured the contents into the sink and refilled the cup, leaning against the open door as he read the letter again. Ten years ago...

Ten years ago, he had been ready to shake the dust of Clayville, Indiana, off his feet and conquer the world. He had a job lined up that paid more than his father had ever made in his life, he had Los Angeles, with all its glamour and tinsel, and a wife who had dedicated herself to helping him get to the top. He wouldn't have been able to imagine, nor would he have believed it had he been told, that everyone wasn't as happy for him as he was for himself.

Of course, he knew Dani hadn't completely approved of Laura, but that was only natural. Laura was a stranger, and no girl, in Dani's eyes, would ever be good enough for him just as no man would ever be good enough for Dani as far as Bret was concerned. But she had never given him any indication that she objected this strongly to his marriage...or if she had, he had ignored her.

A wry smile touched his lips as he lifted the coffee cup. If she had given him this letter ten years ago, it might have saved him a lot of pain...or it might not have made any difference. At any rate, it was too late to start crying over spilled milk now.

If you knew, it might make a difference. He read the line again, frowning. *There's someone who loves you, Bret....*

Who? Who was it who had loved him all those years ago, and who, if he had known about it, might have saved him from making the biggest mistake of his life? Who could it possibly have been?

His mind drifted back into the past, over the girls he had known...hometown girls with sparkling eyes and curly ponytails, sophisticated college girls, voluptuous starlets... A wistful smile crossed his lips then faded with puzzlement. Which one of them could have changed his life? And how could Dani have known about it when he didn't?

Unless...it was Dani herself.

Embarrassed color stung his neck, and the thought was dismissed almost before it was born. Not Dani. To even consider the possibility made him feel conceited and foolish.

He had a collage of pictures inside his head, pictures of Dani and pictures of himself that when strung together, formed a diary of his life. Dani at five, her fists balled and her eyes glittering as she flung herself into a free-for-all to defend him from some real or imagined insult. Himself at nine, doing the same for her. A mountain of peanut-butter sandwiches shared from Flintstone's lunch boxes in between. Dani in her first grown-up party dress, trying to keep him from trampling all over her new pumps as she taught him to dance. And himself, threatening to tear some poor freshman limb from limb because he had gotten fresh with Dani at the Valentine Ball.

It would be ridiculous to say Bret had never thought of Dani sexually. Every teenage boy thought about every teenage girl sexually. He and Dani used to practice kissing so they'd be sure to do it right with their "real" dates, and there had been times when Bret thought he might like to do more than practice. But they'd been kids then, and Dani had certainly never thought of him that way.

Since they were three years old, Dani Griffin had been his sparring partner, his confidante, his tutor, his counselor; sometimes his worst enemy, but always his best friend. When they'd gone away to separate colleges, her twice-weekly letters were the only things that had kept his head on straight. When his marriage broke up, his long-distance phone bill averaged four hundred dollars a month; God only knew what hers had been. When he had gone home for his mother's funeral five years ago, he and Dani had sat up all night and talked, and he hadn't been ashamed to cry on her shoulder. He had never been as close to anyone in the world as he was to Dani Griffin.

And that night, the night before his wedding, she had kissed him. It was a congratulatory kiss, a good-luck kiss, an I'm-going-to-miss-you-and-hope-you'll-be-happy kiss. But for a moment—for one fleeting, dangerous and wildly promising moment—Bret could have sworn that kiss hovered on the edge of something more. And then it was over and Dani was laughing, and he was sure he imagined it. The next day, he got married and Dani waved goodbye to him from the steps of the church.

She had known all along. But she'd never said a word. And what difference did it make now? What difference would it have made then?

Abruptly, he picked up the phone and started to dial Dani's number. He had barely punched out the area code, however, before he hung up again. Just what was he supposed to say to her? "Say, about this letter you wrote me ten years ago and never intended to mail..." And how had it gotten here, anyway? He went back to the table and looked at the envelope. The whole thing was entirely too disturbing for this hour of the morning, and the only thing that was clear was that he couldn't confront her with it via long distance. In fact, the smart thing to do would be to forget about it—just as Dani apparently had for ten years.

But he couldn't forget about it. He put the letter into his briefcase and took it to work with him, and all the way downtown, he kept wondering. Who was she? Who was the girl who had loved him? And what was he supposed to do about it now?

IN BRET'S OPINION, THERE was no place in the world as depressing as Los Angeles at Christmastime. It was bad enough that the temperature was already eighty-three degrees and the smog layer so thick you could cut it with a knife, but why did all the stores have to use that garish, glittery garland in colors like neon pink and lime green? One window display featured Santa in Hawaiian-print swim trunks and a surf board. Another suggested that Santa's helpers were all models with platinum hair and gold-sequined bikinis. And there was nothing quite as gaudy as a tinfoil Christmas tree flashing with oversize gold bulbs.

Almost every Christmas in Clayville had been a white one, and even without the snow, they had always been cold enough to justify Santa's fur-trimmed suit and cherry red cheeks. After his first year at Berkeley, Bret had sworn he would never spend another frost-bitten winter as long as he lived. Funny how much he missed the cold now. And how he couldn't get the picture of Dani, with her nose chapped and red, and snowflakes in her hair, out of his mind.

By the time he arrived at the fifth-floor offices of Underwood Security Agency he thought he had figured out how the letter had gotten to him, at any rate. Obviously, it must be connected with the envelope from Webb and Webb, Attorneys at Law. Maybe it had accidentally gotten mixed up with the other papers inside and had fallen out.... Maybe Dani had intended to send him a letter or some kind of important paper via the lawyers and had mistakenly sent this letter instead.... Maybe she *had* sent it to him ten years ago and it had only now resurfaced among his father's papers.... None of those solutions was completely acceptable of course, and each of them left a great deal more unanswered than not, but at least they were a start.

Generally, he felt a surge of perfectly justifiable pride every time he saw the gold-stenciled letters on the door that read, Underwood Security Agency. To own one's own business in a town as competitive as Los Angeles was no small accomplishment; to make the kind of success of it that Bret had was little short of a miracle. He liked to remind himself of how well he had done—even though his present success still fell short of his original dreams, and even though he had done it all without the help of the perfect wife. But today, he didn't even glance at the lettering on the door. He was too distracted.

It should have come as no surprise to him that his secretary had already set up an ugly snow-flocked Christmas tree in the corner of the reception room and was now in the process of tacking miles of red garland across her desk, the walls and every other available surface.

"What's the rule around here, Miss Cranston?" he greeted her on the way to his office.

Linda Cranston was twenty-seven years old, blond, slim and California sexy. For that reason, Bret always addressed her as "Miss Cranston" and made sure every man on his staff did as well. She climbed down from the stepladder and quoted, "'No Christmas decorations before December 15.'"

"And what's the date today?"

"November 13."

"You're fired."

"Scrooge."

"Ho-ho-ho."

She followed him into his office with a handful of pink message slips. "You've got a dentist's appointment at noon, and Carol Weatherly wanted to know if you were free for lunch. I told her no, but I set up a tentative date for tomorrow...."

Bret glanced through the messages as he flipped on the monitor that connected him to the com center. Joel Phillips, night-shift supervisor, came onscreen, the row of consoles and operators who ensured the security of hundreds of exclusive, highly overpriced homes in the greater L.A. area forming a busy backdrop behind him.

"Morning, Joel," Bret said. "Anything?" He scrawled "no" across two party invitations, "yes" across a request to speak at a club luncheon, and "$500" across the bottom of a message from a charitable organization.

Joel grinned. "We had an intruder alarm at 4:15 from the Carringtons'. Turned out it was her boyfriend trying to get out the window when they thought they heard her husband come back early from a business trip. Boyfriend is fine. Husband is still in New York."

Bret returned the message slips to Linda. "Get Harold Syms on the phone for me, will you?" He turned back to Joel. "Anything else?"

"The usual. Gabe Riley's cat set off his motion detector again. We've told him to keep that cat locked up, but he insists the fault is in the system. I sent a man over there this morning. And Margaret Holloway swears she saw a man lurking outside her window last night. I told her there was no way anybody could get that close to her house without alerting every cop in L.A., but the poor old gal hasn't got anything else to do but worry, I guess. She wants more security.''

Bret nodded. ''Where would we be without the paranoia of the rich and famous, hmm? Go home, Joel, get some sleep.'' He grinned. ''And don't forget to set your security alarm. Mrs. Holloway's Peeping Tom might decide to try your house next.''

''Then he's in for a thrill,'' drawled Joel, and he switched off.

Linda came back in. ''Mr. Syms is out of the office, but Julia Lymon is on line one. They're taking a three-week cruise and want private patrols while they're gone. She wants you—'' Linda waggled an eyebrow at him meaningfully ''—to make the arrangements personally.''

Bret stifled a groan. Julia Lymon was a middle-aged, oversexed, Chanel-drenched dragon with too much money and too little self-restraint. He never left a meeting with her without feeling as though he were fleeing for his life—or his virtue, at the very least.

''Did you ever wake up one morning and discover you hate your job?'' he murmured.

Linda feigned innocence. ''Who me? Working for the sweetest guy in the world? Surely you jest.''

He winced. ''I guess I haven't exactly been a pussy-cat around here lately, have I?''

''More like a pit bull,'' Linda told him frankly. ''And it's going to be like this till after the holidays. Why don't you take a vacation?''

Bret glanced at the blinking light on the phone. ''No vacation. The crime rate always goes up during the holidays, you know that, and this year promises to be a beaut. Our client list will double.''

She made a face. ''What a cynic!''

''That's what pays the rent, babe. I don't make the statistics, I just—''

''Take advantage of them,'' she finished for him.

He looked at her steadily for a moment. ''Just to show you what a sweetheart an old cynic can be, if you'll tell Julia Lymon I'm not in, you're not fired.''

''If I tell her you're in the hospital, can *I* take a vacation?''

''In your dreams. Oh, and Miss Cranston—'' he opened his brief case and pulled out the envelope from Johnson Web. ''—send this over to Craig Notions with a letter. 'Enclosed are the documents relating to the Clayville property, which we discussed putting on the market last Thursday, et cetera, et cetera. You know what I mean.''

She accepted the envelope. ''I still don't understand why you're having an L.A. real-estate firm handle property in Indiana.''

He shrugged. ''There aren't a lot of wheeler-dealers in Clayville. There're over two hundred acres there, and I'll have a better chance of selling them if I get somebody who knows what he's doing.''

''I don't know,'' she commented on her way out. ''I'd think about it if I were you. A nice quiet farm in Indiana sounds to me like exactly what you need right now.''

Insurrectionist that she was, Miss Cranston had hardly closed the door before she began to pipe Christmas music through the intercom. The song was

"Carol of the Bells," and it always reminded Bret of Dani.

Bret started to close his briefcase, but his eyes caught the plain white envelope on top. Slowly, he took it out but didn't read it again. He had every word memorized.

"Not fair, Dani," he muttered. He leaned back in his chair, balancing the envelope between two fingers and frowned at the opposite wall. He had enough on his hands this time of year trying to protect other people's peace of mind without a mystery like this unraveling his own. He didn't have time for dreary reminiscences of ten years ago; he didn't have room in his life to be sitting here, wondering how a small-town boy from Clayville, Indiana, had ended up in a suite of fifth-floor offices gleefully studying the rising crime rate and calling women "babe."

Maybe his secretary was right. He was a Scrooge and a cynic and it always got worse this time of year. But what could he expect after seven years in a business like this?

At first, building up a business, taking the chances, fighting off the competitors and scraping to make ends meet—it had all been exciting. Every day was a challenge, and he couldn't wait to get up in the mornings. But over the past few years, he had settled into a routine that was wearing on his nerves more and more each day, and the thought of the upcoming holiday season filled him with weariness and dread.

What he needed was to talk to Dani. Not about the letter—though how he could avoid mentioning it, he didn't know—but just to talk to her. There had never been a time in his life so bleak, so lonely or so desperate that talking to Dani hadn't made it right. From playground brawls to adolescent heartbreaks to those shocked, empty months after his divorce, somehow, the sound of her voice had always had the ability to put things in perspective, to reassure him, to make him laugh at himself again. He'd just give her a call, and if the matter of the letter came up...

His hand was on the telephone again, and then he stopped. Because he really didn't want to talk to Dani. He wanted to *see* her.

It was crazy. He didn't have time to go flying off to Indiana, especially not now. It would be cold in Indiana. He couldn't just desert his business on a moment's notice, leave his employees stranded, turn his back on the potential boom in new clients the holidays would bring, and all for the sake of something as stupid as a letter he was never supposed to read.

There's someone who loves you, Bret...

But he hadn't had a vacation in eight years, and it wasn't just the letter. There was the matter of the property he was trying to sell. Hadn't he been telling himself for years that what he really needed to do was make a trip out there and look at the place for himself? Now that he had decided to put it in the hands of a real-estate agent, *somebody* should look it over in person. Why put it off?

His hand was still on the receiver when the interoffice line buzzed. "Beechwood Promotions wants to know if you can handle the security for Neon Ecstasy on the fifteenth," Linda said.

"Who?"

"You know, the rock group. You're really out of it today. He needs six bodyguards for eighteen hours, and don't forget, you've promised to handle the Century Center party that night. And I've got Harold Syms on line three."

For the second time that morning, Bret stifled a groan. Guarding rock stars constituted hazardous duty for most of his staff; he practically had to force the men to draw lots in order to assign them. Without fail, he'd be called on site himself to deal with some trumped up problem or the other, and the Century Center people always expected him to show up and make a tour, just to reassure them everything was under control. Not to mention Harold Syms, who handled a dozen of Hollywood's most valuable—and temperamental—personalities; who knew which one of his "properties" Bret would be called upon to baby-sit this time? That was the trouble with building one's reputation on personalized service: everyone expected you to do the job personally.

Bret ran his fingers through his hair as the upcoming weeks began to look bleaker and bleaker. He looked at the letter lying on his desk. He tapped his fingers on the telephone receiver. Then he made a decision.

"Tell Beechwood we're booked," he said abruptly. "Confirm with Century. The guys can handle that without me. Tell Syms— Never mind, I'll tell him myself. And better cancel all my appointments for the next couple of weeks."

The silence on the other end of the line was stunned. "Are you okay?"

"No." Bret took the white envelope in his hand and then smiled. "I'm not okay. I need a vacation."

Chapter Two

"And that's the legend of the Christmas cactus," Dani finished, leaning one hip against the corner of her desk as she picked up the withered potted plant. "Every year, it blooms to remind us of what we're celebrating, and when it does, you know that Christmas has really come."

Four rows of semiattentive third-graders regarded the plant she held in her hand. Then Jimmy Skinner commented skeptically, "It looks dead to me."

"It's supposed to," she explained patiently. "All year long, it hibernates, and then at Christmastime, it suddenly comes to life again, and it's covered with flowers."

"How does it know when it's Christmas?" Melanie Kane wanted to know.

Dani smiled at her. "That's the miracle."

"What color are the flowers?"

"White, like Christmas snow."

Dani set the plant on her desk. Bret had sent the cactus to her five Christmases ago, and every year since, she had brought it up from the basement on December 1 and enthralled her class with the suspense of waiting for it to bloom. And every year, by the time the children left for the Christmas holidays, it had been covered with snowy white blossoms. The cactus had become one of the best parts of the season.

Jimmy said, "I think the bugs got to it. It's deader'n a doornail."

Dani tossed him a look of mild exasperation. There was always one in every class. "You just wait, Jimmy."

The bell rang, signaling a mad scramble for books and belongings. "All right," Dani called over the uproar. "Remember tomorrow starts the auditions for the school play, and start thinking about what you want to make for your parents for Christmas. Don't leave before you copy your homework off the blackboard!"

A few of the more conscientious students stopped to copy their homework; most of them rushed for the coat locker. Days were short this time of year and too precious to be wasted inside a schoolroom. Dani was in perfect sympathy, which was why, from the beginning of December to the end of the year, very little of academic value was built into her curriculum.

"Bye, Miss Griffin!"

"I want to make a birdhouse!"

"That's stupid—I want to make a bow and arrow!"

And Jimmy paused by Dani's desk, gave the cactus one last disgusted look and repeated, "Deader'n a doornail."

"Bye, Miss Griffin!"

"Goodbye, Karen. Be sure to have your mother look at that scrape on your knee. And, Tim, that hat goes on your head, not in your pocket!"

Tim pulled the stocking cap over his head as he ran out the door, only to rip if off and stuff it back into his pocket as soon as he thought he was out of sight.

Dani turned to her desk with a smile and a shake of her head, gathering up her papers to a chorus of "Bye, Miss Griffin" and "See you tomorrow!" In three minutes flat, the room was clear.

Though she was technically on duty until three-thirty, Dani had better things to do than spend the afternoon at school, too. At this time of year, she had approximately two hundred better things to do, and none of them involved filling out forms or picking up trash. She decided to come in early tomorrow to straighten the room, and the forms could wait until the beginning of the new year. She had just begun to give the blackboard a quick once-over with the eraser when a voice came from behind her.

"If I'd had a teacher who looked as good as you do, I might never have gotten out of third grade."

Dani turned. She dropped the eraser.

He stood leaning one shoulder against the door frame, sandy hair tousled by the wind, tweed overcoat open over a white cable-knit sweater and sleek gray slacks. He was wearing amber-tinted wire-framed glasses, and the faint bristle of blond beard on his jaw gave him a rakish, devil-may-care look. Broad shoulders, slim hips, perfect tan...

"Bret!" she cried, and flung herself at him.

She launched herself into his arms, throwing her arms around his neck and leaping up, winding her legs around his. He caught her, laughing, and stumbled backward against the desk. "Bret, you're here! What are you—"

"Get off me, you wicked woman, before I have to call the police!"

She sprang down lightly, and he held her at arm's length for a moment, flooded with a grin of pure pleasure, then he said, "Come here, funny face." And he pulled her to him again, hugging her hard.

They laughed again and hugged each other, then she broke away, striking out at him playfully. "Bret, you snake, sneaking up on me like that! And look at you, standing there as fresh as new money! What is this?" She lifted his tinted glasses and let them fall onto the bridge of his nose. "A new Hollywood trend or are you going blind in your old age?"

"A little of both," he admitted when she paused for breath.

She stood back with her hands on her hips. "Why didn't you tell me? When did you get in? What are you doing here?"

He looked at her, and he couldn't seem to stop grinning. She never changed. How was it that she never changed?

She was wearing a challis-print skirt, tan cowboy boots and a canary yellow blouse with big shoulders and a wing collar accented by a purple tapestry vest. The rich colors reflected the jewel tones of her eyes, which were sometimes violet and sometimes gray. Right now, her eyes were dancing with excitement. Her brown hair was wound into a flat braid and tied with a perky yellow bow at the back, just like the bows he used to take such delight in untying when he sat behind her in third grade. There was that same spattering of freckles across the nose she had always hated because it was too short, and her face was glowing with color just as it always did when she was happy. It was not a gorgeous face, or even a striking one—a little too round, with a broad forehead and cheeks that were quick to dimple—but her smile was as big as Indiana and could light up a room, or Bret's heart, in no more than an instant.

"What are you doing here?" she asked. Then her expression changed, quickening with concern as she took his face in one hand and examined it intently. "You look awful. Have you been driving all night? Is something wrong? What's wrong? Why did you come? Tell me what's wrong."

The letter lay like a guilty stain in his shirt pocket, and suddenly he knew he couldn't tell her why he had come. It was clear she knew nothing about his having the letter, and why embarrass her—or himself—by mentioning it now? She *would* think he was crazy if he told her he had driven eight hundred miles because of a letter she'd forgotten writing and had never meant for him to read. Besides, that wasn't really why he had come...not entirely.

"What?" he retorted, pulling his face away from her grip. "A guy can't come home for the holidays without getting the third degree?"

Her face lit up again. "Are you really? Are you going to stay?"

"For a while, at least. I've got some business to take care of, and I don't know—"

"That's great! I can't believe it, Christmas together just like old times! Bret, what a wonderful idea, but you could have *told* somebody, you know!" As she spoke, she had wound her arm through his and was leading him toward the door. "Mom is going to have a fit, she'll be so excited, but you'd better shave before you see her or she'll think you've gone and joined some weird religious group out in California— though as far as she's concerned, the whole state of California is a weird religious group—"

"Whoa, hold on!" He stopped her, laughing. "Come up for air, will you?"

"Can't help it, I'm too excited." She tugged on his arm impatiently. "This is perfect. If you don't take all day about it, you can wash up and change, and we can still get downtown in time to help string the lights. And tonight is the first bonfire down at the lake—"

"Change into what? You're looking at the only clothes I have suitable for this North Pole you call home, and I had to stop at Sears in Omaha to buy the coat. I haven't even checked into the motel yet. And I hope this little burg has come up with something better than the Route Fifty Inn in the past five years because—"

"We'll go shopping later," she decreed cheerfully. "First you've got to drive me home. And for heaven's sake, will you *tell* me what possessed the city slicker to take a down-home holiday all of a sudden? What's been going on, anyway? What happened to that decorator you were seeing—did you ever get rid of her?

Last I heard, she had roped you into taking her to that banquet...."

Laughing, Bret scooped up Dani's coat and draped it over her shoulders as they walked outside. On the way, he told her how he had dumped the decorator—politely, of course—on the night of the banquet. Dani told him he was a jerk, and he agreed he probably was. He ended up driving her home even though it meant he would have to take her back to school the next morning to pick up her car. Because they were laughing and talking so much, it didn't occur to him to do anything else, and because Dani was, as always, as uncontrollable as wildfire and just as contagious.

DANI DID NOT LIVE WITH her parents, but her living arrangements were the next best thing, and for an unmarried woman in a town as small as Clayville, the only acceptable compromise between independence and propriety. Her parents still lived in the century-old farmhouse where she had grown up. They had never worked the land on any large scale and over the years, the property had been reduced from hundreds of acres to twelve. Dani's home was a converted barn at the end of the long driveway that led to the main farmhouse. Her father had restored and redesigned the structure into what Dani's friends called a dream cottage. For Dani, the best thing about it was the hundred or so yards of hedge-lined drive that separated her house from her parents' home.

Of course, Bret could not just drop her off in front of her house, so he proceeded up the drive to the farmhouse. Harold Griffin's hand was evident in the

well-kept, restored and improved main house, too, and
it had always been a matter of some pride to Dani that
theirs was the most attractive house on the road.
Dani's father owned the local lumberyard, but Dani
often thought that, had he not inherited the business
from his father, he might have gone on to be one of the
great architects of the time—or at the very least, a
highly successful contractor. But Harold contented
himself with "fixing up" their place or other peo-
ples', and when neighbors came into the store asking
him for advice on how to add a porch or modernize a
bathroom, he would likely as not go out and do the
job himself—for free.

Dani pulled Bret up the three steps and across the
wide porch at a semirun, calling, "Mom, company!"
before she even got the door open. Bret paused in the
slate-tiled front hall to take off his coat and let the
sights and scents of home rush over him, pushing him
back through three decades of memories.

The house smelled of something sweet and spicy
baking in the kitchen, with the undertone of that dark
furniture polish his own mother had always used on
the family heirlooms. The starched lace curtains at the
front windows hadn't changed in twenty years, and
neither had the overstuffed chair in the living room or
the braided rugs on the hardwood floor. Bret remembered when Dani's father had caught the big bass that
was now stuffed and mounted over the fireplace and
when Bret, at age sixteen, had helped the older man
install the flying staircase that had been rescued from
an old church tower. He had learned more than he ever
wanted to know about building that summer.

"Bret Underwood, as I live and breathe!"

Anne Griffin stood at the threshold that led to the kitchen, and Bret went toward her with his arms open. "Miss Annie," he said. "It's good to see you!"

"What on earth—" But she interrupted her own exclamation to hug him, and Bret thought Thomas Wolfe must have been crazy in saying you can't go home again. Nothing had ever felt more like home to Bret.

Anne Griffin was a short, sporty-looking woman with straight brown hair cut in a pageboy. She had grown a little plump over the years, but that only gave her a more motherly look. She was wearing a gray sweatsuit and her husband's oversize white socks, and though there was presently a smear of flour on her oven-flushed cheeks, Bret knew she had just as soon be out chopping wood or replacing broken shingles as baking a cake.

She held his shoulders and looked at him, beaming. "Well, I couldn't be more surprised if the Archangel Gabriel just walked into my front room! Dani, why didn't you say something? And here the house is a mess—"

"Oh, Mom, get real!" Dani made a face. "Your house wouldn't be a mess after an earthquake, flood and fire. Besides, Bret's family."

Annie touched his cheek, looking worried. "Are you growing a beard? You haven't joined some cult, have you?"

Dani's eyes twinkled, and Bret replied soberly, "No ma'am. I've been driving all night."

"You know better than that! Pull over every two hours, that's what your daddy always said, and you should listen to him. I'll tell you something else, you're too thin—all California folks are, aren't they? It's from eating all that seaweed and tofu and whatnot, but we'll fix that! Now, you just give me a minute to get your room in order—"

"No, wait, I didn't come to impose. I planned on staying at a motel—"

Anne gave him a look filled with patient disgust. "Don't talk nonsense. Do you want to end up with some kind of disease? You're staying here. Go on out to the kitchen and make yourself something to eat. I'll just put fresh sheets on the bed and straighten up the bureau. Dani, check that pie in the oven for me, will you?"

Bret watched Anne disappear up the stairs, shaking his head helplessly. "Your mother..."

"You didn't really think you were going to get to stay in a motel, did you?" Dani said over her shoulder on the way to the kitchen. "Folks would think we'd turned you out—we'd never live it down."

"Yeah, I guess you're right," Bret admitted ruefully. "And your mom's cooking beats diner food anyday. Do you think I protested enough?"

"Hardly enough to be polite."

The kitchen was big and airy; the floors and one wall were covered with age-darkened brick Harold Griffin had scavenged from a riverfront warehouse, and there was a big brick fireplace that, in Bret's youth, had been boarded over to conserve heat. Now it was open and a couple of logs crackled with merry flames, adding the scent of seasoned oak to those of cinnamon and cloves that filled the room.

Bret got a glass from a cabinet and poured himself some milk, just as he had done when he was twelve. "Funny, I never can remember where the glasses are in my own house."

"That's because you keep going through decorators so fast." Dani opened the oven door and slid out the rack with a mittened hand. A perfectly crusted pie sat bubbling on it, but apparently, it was not quite brown enough because Dani closed the door again and tossed the oven mitt onto the stovetop.

Bret hoisted himself to the kitchen counter and helped himself to the contents of the cookie jar. "This place never changes," he said, looking around contentedly.

"Sure it does." Dani scooped up a couple of cookies and sat down at the breakfast table, swinging her feet onto the opposite chair. "We've got cable now."

She took a bite out of the cookie and regarded him with alert, bright-eyed interest. "So," she demanded. "What's going on?"

Dani knew Bret too well to imagine that he had left his business and driven all this way just to spend the holidays in his old hometown. But she also knew him well enough to have seen this coming for some time now. Over the past few months, she had been able to read the restlessness and dissatisfaction in his phone conversations and notes. He was working harder and enjoying it less, but that was only part of the problem. The rest of the problem he would tell her in his own time... or when he figured out what it was himself.

But that time was apparently not now. He bit into the cookie and answered, "I've decided to put the old place on the market. Thought I'd come down and look it over, see what needs to be done, that sort of thing."

Dani waved a dismissive hand. "You've been talking about selling the place for years. You're never going to do it."

"Oh, yes, I am. What do I need to keep paying taxes on it for? The rent I get barely pays the upkeep. So I listed it last week."

She lifted an eyebrow. "No kidding? Well, good luck finding a buyer. Nobody around here has that kind of money."

Bret glanced down at the half-eaten cookie. "I wasn't thinking about anybody around here. Actually, I listed it with an L.A. broker. He thinks he might be able to stir up some corporate interest."

Dani stared at him. He sounded serious. "What do you mean, 'corporate interest'?"

"You know, shopping malls, office complexes, resort hotels..."

She gave a little bark of laughter. "You nut, you had me worried there for a minute!"

"What, you don't think I can do it?"

"Yeah, right, the minute you strike oil on the south forty." She smiled at him, eyes twinkling. "You know what I think? I think you just missed me, and all this business about selling the farm is an excuse."

"Well, in that case, I'd better call the Saudis and tell them to cancel their inspection tour." And his face softened. "Yeah, I missed you, skunk. I want to know what's going on with you."

There was a gentle intensity to his question that touched Dani's heart. It didn't matter why Bret had come or what excuse he had used; he was here. He had always known when she needed to talk to him; he had always managed to somehow be there for her just as he was now. She had never needed her best friend more than she did at this moment, and the funny thing was that she hadn't even realized it until he was there.

But as good as it was to have him here, to know that he was ready to listen as soon as she was ready to talk, Dani was also, strangely, a little uncomfortable. She didn't know where to begin.

Fortunately—or perhaps not so fortunately—her mother did it for her. "Dani," she called down the stairs. "I forgot to tell you—Todd called. He has to work late and won't be able to take you to the bonfire tonight. He wants you to call him back."

"Todd?" Bret frowned sharply. "Who's he?"

"Okay, Mom," Dani called back. "Thanks!" And to Bret she said, "I told you about Todd. He's the new editorial manager at the newspaper."

Bret was still frowning skeptically. "I don't think so. I would've remembered somebody named *Todd.*" He made the name sound like something nice people didn't repeat in mixed company.

She scowled irritably as she got up and took his empty glass, rinsing it under the faucet. "I did, too. You just never listen. And what's wrong with his name? It's a perfectly nice name."

"For an eighteen-year-old beach boy, or maybe the cover model on *Musclebound*."

"Good Lord, where do you come up with these things? You don't even know him!"

Bret was watching her closely—too closely—and it made her cheeks sting, to her further annoyance. She twisted the tap off with a snap and dried her hands.

"So, what's the deal?" His voice was too mild. "How'd you meet this dude? Are you sleeping with him?"

"I never sleep with anybody who lives within a twenty-mile radius of this town, you know that," she replied airily, but her cheeks were only getting hotter.

"You are!" he declared softly. "You're hot and heavy with a guy named Todd! Well, this is going to take some looking into."

"You're impossible!" She tossed the towel at him.

The teasing faded from his eyes and was replaced by a look she couldn't quite read as he took another cookie from the jar, then popped it into his mouth with a gesture too studied to be casual. "So," he said after a moment, "are you going to tell me about him?"

Dani hesitated and then realized that as much as she had wanted to talk to Bret about this only a few moments ago, she really did not want to think about Todd now. And at the same time, she realized something that should have disturbed her, but didn't: she was glad Todd canceled their date for tonight because that meant she would get to go to the bonfire with Bret.

She said, "Later," and gave him a gentle push off the counter. "Right now, you'd better get moving—we've got Christmas lights to string!"

Bret silently accepted her wish to change the subject as, being Bret, he would. But he gave a groan of protest as he sprang to the floor. "Have mercy, girl, I've been driving sixteen hours straight. What I need is a shower and a long nap."

"What you need," she corrected, pushing him toward the door, "is to get in the spirit. Only twenty-four days left till Christmas, and Santa needs every helping hand he can get."

"Ah, Dani, don't start with me. You know I hate all that holiday stuff."

She stopped and stared at him. "You do not! You love it."

"I hate it," he insisted. "I hate stringing lights and chopping trees and standing in the freezing rain singing 'Deck the Halls' and God, do I hate shopping. So please, just do me a favor and leave me out of all the holiday falderol, okay?"

She continued to stare at him as though he were an alien species, then abruptly dismissed it. "You're lying. You love it, and you know you do."

"Hate it. Always have and always will."

"You love it. Now come on, we're going to miss all the fun."

Bret tried to remember a time when he had ever considered standing atop a cherry picker in the icy wind and stringing Christmas lights from lampposts fun, but he couldn't. Still, it was easier to pretend resignation than to argue with Dani, so he let her push him out the door.

And the single consolation was that, no matter how cold it was and no matter how tired he was, he was spending the afternoon with Dani. She had a way of making nothing else matter, and he was glad he had come home.

Chapter Three

Clayville, Indiana, was one of those postcard-perfect towns that dotted the Midwest. "Downtown" consisted of three intersecting streets six blocks long with a steepled church at the intersection square. There were benches outside the bank where old men really played checkers, and a small park shaded by an enormous spreading elm tree and accented by a granite watering trough that these days was more frequently used by birds than horses.

The population—excluding those in the outlying rural area—was just over six hundred, and every one of those six hundred people knew not only their neighbors' names, but their neighbors' secrets. It was the kind of place that had been built on barn-raisings and quilting bees, and the sense of community had flowed effortlessly into the twentieth century.

In Clayville, one did not have the option of being uninvolved. When the one-room police station and jail was struck by lightning and burned to the ground, Harold Griffin donated the lumber and everyone pitched in to rebuild. When the school budget was too small to afford computers, local merchants and businessmen ran contests and drives until enough money was raised for four new computers for the upper grades. And when the first of December rolled around, every able-bodied man and woman with an hour to spare donated that time to dragging out the boxes of town Christmas decorations, uncoiling wires and rolls of garland, hanging lights and draping greenery across the streets.

And in Clayville, nobody ever forgot who you were. Bret was greeted as though he had only been away on a short vacation, and before he knew it, Dani's father had slapped a pair of work gloves into his hands and assigned him—of course—to the bucket of the cherry picker.

"Some welcome-home party!" Bret called down to Dani, who was sorting through a pickup truck full of evergreen boughs and wreaths.

She grinned up at him, her cheeks chapped and her hair tossed by the wind. "You ain't seen nothing yet!"

When they were younger, Bret and Dani used to watch this same ritual every year, resentful of the childish tasks they were assigned, like tying bows on wreaths and replacing light bulbs, impatient for the time they would be grown-up enough to do the important jobs. Now other children tied the bows and other grown-ups admonished them to be careful not to break that box of ornaments. Watching it all from his bird's-eye view, Bret felt a weird and uncomfortable sense of déjà vu.

He still hated it. The cold stung his ears and crept inside his thin Italian-leather loafers to freeze his toes. He couldn't imagine anything more stupid than risking life and limb and electrical shock to hang strings of red and green lights across a main thoroughfare. But when twilight came and the switch was turned on to a clamor of cheers and applause, even Bret had to admit it was all kind of pretty...in a tacky, small-town way.

"I can't believe I let you talk me into this," he said, rubbing the small of his back. "Every muscle in my body aches, and I've got blisters on my hands, and I can't feel my toes. Can we go home now?"

"Only sissies get blisters," Dani retorted, slipping her arm around his waist. "That's what you get for living the soft life. And, of course, we're not going home. Now's our reward for working so hard—the bonfire."

"Which you've, no doubt, volunteered to build," he returned wryly, and she laughed.

"Now, Bret, isn't this fun? Aren't you having a good time?"

"On a scale of one to ten," he answered, "with dental surgery being a one—this ranks maybe two and a half."

"What's ten?"

"Sex."

They walked back to his car with their arms around each other's waists. Bret walked close to Dani for warmth, and because he liked the way she smelled in the crisp, early-night air—like cinnamon and vanilla.

"So, what would you be doing if you were at home?" she asked.

He chuckled. "It wouldn't be a ten, I'll tell you that."

"What?" She slanted a dancing glance at him. "I'm disappointed. I always pictured you wallowing in that wild every-night's-a-party, Southern California lifestyle. You know, wearing a purple silk kimono and sipping Dubonnet and filling the hot tub with bubble bath...."

"Only on alternate weekends."

"So what *would* you be doing?"

"As a matter of fact, I'd probably still be in the office." And it surprised Bret to realize that he hadn't thought about the office once all day. That was gratifying, he supposed, though it was scant compensation for stiff muscles and frostbite.

"And then?"

He opened the car door for her. "Then I'd probably pick up some Chinese food on the way home, watch the late news and go to bed."

"Wow. Even I do better than that."

Bret couldn't help wondering, then, just how she did. And he wondered about Todd.

As he slid behind the wheel, it occurred to Bret how little they really did know about each other these days. There had been a time when every detail of her life, big and small, had been a part of his. They had never had to ask what the other was thinking because they always knew. And they never had to write down secrets because, between the two of them, there simply were no secrets.

But something was lost in the translation over long distance. He told her about his loves and losses, his triumphs and defeats, just as he always had. She told him about her hopes and dreads, just as she always had. They exchanged funny stories and sad news, they gossiped and they philosophized, and yet…something was missing, and he hadn't even realized it until now.

He reached across the seat and squeezed her hand. "I've missed you, sweetheart," he said simply.

She looked surprised for just a moment, then she smiled and wrapped her gloved fingers around his. He held her hand all the way to the lake.

The annual bonfire was the first official event of the Christmas season. Women had been baking and simmering their prize-winning specialties all day, and as soon as it was dark, families would pack up their covered dishes, drive through town to "ooh" and "ahh" over the Christmas lights, then rendezvous at the lake. A select committee had been working on the bonfire since just before sunset, and by dark, a respectable blaze was shooting sparks into the air. Beneath the covered pavilion, casseroles were kept warm over Sterno pots, and baked goods of every description were spread out on picnic tables. Barbecue pits were fired up for roasting hot dogs and German sausages, and there was always plenty of caramel popcorn and candied apples. Neighbors filled their plates and gossiped back and forth. Children, delighted by the spectacle of the bonfire and the opportunity to play outside after dark, ran wild while their parents constantly shouted at them to stay away from the lake and not get too close to the fire.

More marriage proposals and other, slightly less-acceptable, romantic encounters had taken place at the annual bonfire than at any other time of the year. There was something intoxicating about a cold, star-studded night with a centerpiece of leaping flames bathing faces and figures in soft yellow light; something intimate and even a little pagan about the lush scent of evergreens and tangy wood smoke. Voices were always a little louder, laughter more uninhibited, and the sense of secrecy and adventure inherent in sneaking away from the crowd for a stolen kiss or a few moments of shared body warmth always made the experience doubly exciting.

"Boy, does this bring back memories," Bret murmured as he got out of the car.

"Carla McBride," Dani teased him.

He gave her a withering look. "I never came out here with Carla McBride."

"Then you were the only boy in town who didn't."

"Whatever happened to her, anyway?"

"She married a shoe salesman from Indianapolis, had five children and got as fat as a cow."

"See? I knew there was a good reason I never came out here with her."

"Dani! Hi!" Mary Witt waved to her, a parka-clad two-year-old in tow as she made her way across the snow-spotted ground toward them. "Is that— Good heavens, it can't be! Bret Underwood?"

It wasn't long after that that other people spotted Bret. Those who hadn't had the chance to do so welcomed him home and barraged him with questions, someone thrust a cup of hot chocolate into his hand, and someone else insisted he come have a bite of her mincemeat pie and tell her if it wasn't just like the recipe his own mother had made famous county wide.

Dani sneaked away to help Mary carry her two casseroles to the pavilion.

"Imagine that," Mary said, hoisting her son on her hip and tucking the casserole under her arm. "What do you suppose he's doing back here?"

"Here, let me take that. I can carry both of them." Dani took the casserole from Mary and stacked it on top of the one she already had.

"Isn't he some kind of important businessman in California? Banking or something?"

"Security agency. You know, locks and burglar alarms and body guards?"

"Oh." Mary seemed momentarily confused. "Well, anyway, I hear he's as rich as God."

Dani shook her head in pure amazement at how tangled small-town gossip could get—even though she was sure she herself, at one time or another, had probably been a party to it. "Richer than you and me, maybe, but he's no Howard Hughes. Not that I know of, anyway."

"I guess there must be a lot of call for that kind of thing in Los Angeles," Mary mused. "All those movie stars and such."

"Bret always was smart," Dani agreed, and was aware of a touch of motherly pride in her voice.

Mary glanced at her shrewdly. "So where's Todd tonight?"

Dani felt a small prickle of guilt that she had forgotten to return his call. "Working late. You know how it is."

"Does he know about, umm, Bret?"

Dani stopped and lifted the casseroles out of harm's way as a group of squealing children raced past, but she did not miss the insinuating tone in Mary's voice. She chose to ignore it. "Bret just got in this afternoon. I haven't had a chance to introduce them."

"Now *that* should be interesting," Mary murmured.

Dani couldn't ignore that. "What do you mean?"

They had reached the pavilion, where lines were already forming for food and compliments were being shouted back and forth as people warmed their hands around cups of cider and called out requests for Miss Annabelle's rice pudding or Laura Crow's three-bean casserole. Bret was, of course, in one of those lines, surrounded by high school friends and beaming matrons. Mary lowered her voice conspiratorially as she glanced at him.

"Come on, Dani, you and Bret have been an item as long as I can remember. What's Todd going to think when he finds out the competition is in town?"

"Mary Witt, for heaven's sake!" Dani set the casseroles on the table and dodged the groping fist of Mary's son as he grabbed for her braid. "Hi, Mrs. Carpenter. Everything looks great, doesn't it?"

She lowered her voice as she said to Mary, "We were not an item! Bret's always been like a brother to me."

"If you say so," Mary replied innocently, but her eyes were twinkling with a secret mirth as she turned to uncover her casserole. "Still, I think Bret's even better-looking now than he was in high school, don't you? If Todd's got any sense at all, he's going to be jealous."

Dani liked to think that the color that fanned her cheeks was due to nothing more than irritation with Mary's teasing, for she had always blushed too easily. But the truth was, she was remembering a time when she hadn't thought of Bret as a brother at all, and whether the blush was caused by embarrassment or regret, she couldn't be sure.

She stole a quick glance at him through the crowd. He was talking to one of the girls they had grown up with, and even though the woman in question was happily married and pregnant, Dani could see how she responded to his smile and his joking banter. In fact, most of the people surrounding Bret were female, many of them single, but Dani told herself that wasn't too surprising. After all, it wasn't every day that the women of Clayville were treated to the sight of a man with professionally styled hair and Italian shoes. The home-town-boy-made-good was bound to generate a little excitement. But it wasn't as though he was a football star or a politician or anything, and it began to occur to Dani that those women were seeing something in Bret she wasn't...or perhaps something she had always known but thought no one else did.

Of course, Bret was good-looking. She had begun to understand that about the time they were juniors in high school when, all of a sudden, Bret's ears didn't seem too big for his head anymore and his arms and legs weren't too long for his body and the face that had once seemed thin and angular became masculine and arresting. The transformation had taken Dani by surprise, but it was more than the metamorphosis of an awkward adolescent into a striking young man. The

confidence and charm Bret had always had evolved
into style, a distinctive way of moving and talking and
laughing that complemented his handsome profile and
strong masculine form and set him head and shoulders above his peers. Somehow, Dani had always
thought no one appreciated that but her.

Looking back, she realized she had had a dreadful
crush on Bret those last couple of years of high school.
But it was so difficult to allow changes in a relationship that had remained virtually impenetrable for all
their lives. She hadn't even recognized the emotion for
what it was at the time. She made excuses to be with
him, she dressed for him, she wore her hair for him,
she even cancelled dates with other boys to spend an
evening doing nothing but watching television with
Bret . . . and why not? He was the most popular boy in
school, and all the other girls were jealous when she
went out with him. Plus, he was her best friend.

It was only toward the end of that last wonderful,
frantic, desperately intense summer between high
school and college that she began to realize that Bret
had become more to her than a friend. By the end of
the summer, they would be going their separate ways,
they would be apart for the first time in their lives, and
Dani could not imagine surviving without him. Convinced he was the only man she could ever love, she
had spent the summer torn between ecstasy and despair, her misery further compounded by the fact that
Bret was completely unaware of how her feelings for
him had changed. She would never know what might
have happened had she somehow gotten up the courage to tell him, but it didn't matter. Toward the end of

the summer, they had a fight—she couldn't even remember what it was about now—and she had been only too happy to flounce off to Indiana State on her own, while Bret went on to Berkeley.

Their relationship was too strong, of course, to be destroyed by one fight, and over the course of their college years, they once again settled into the comfortable, dependable roles of best friends and confidants. When Dani thought about the grand passion she had nursed for him that last summer, it was with the embarrassment of a newly formed adult for the childish things of the past. Bret was her lifelong friend and closer than a brother, but he had his life and she had hers, and all those silly romantic fantasies were long since forgotten.

She had really believed that, until she saw him again the summer after they graduated—Bret with a degree in business administration and she with one in education. There he was, tall and tan with sun-streaked hair and twinkling hazel eyes, as familiar as childhood but as fresh as tomorrow, and she had fallen helplessly, hopelessly in love with him all over again. And even though she fought it, though she tried to deny it and devoted every ounce of her energy to convincing herself it wasn't so and to preventing him from finding out, this was no girlish crush. This was love, quiet and genuine and desperately real. But he was in love with another woman.

Dani never told him, and at the end of the summer, he married someone else and broke Dani's heart for the last time.

It was all so long ago, a mere thread in the rich tapestry of history they had woven between them, and looking at him now, Dani felt a little uncomfortable with the memories. She was thirty-three years old and liked to think she knew something of life; loves had come and gone and so had heartbreak, disappointment and failure—for both of them. They were different people from those they had been twenty years ago, or even ten. Childish infatuations and secret devotions belonged to the past, and she was very happy to keep them there. Still, she couldn't help wondering what would have happened if, at any juncture, her relationship with Bret had taken a different course.

Her mother called to her, and the real world burst the bubble of speculation and memories. For the next hour and a half, as she dished out food and drink, all Dani saw of Bret was a glimpse through the crowd.

The traditional climax of the evening was the ritual tossing of the final logs on the fire, and when everyone agreed that the blaze was roaring as brightly as it could possibly get, they would all gather round to sing Christmas carols. That was, for Dani, one of the most moving and uplifting moments of the entire season, and this year, it would be doubly so because Bret was here. She couldn't remember how long it had been since the two of them had stood side by side with the fire stinging their cheeks while the clear, sweet voices of the entire community were lifted on the winter's air. But she knew her best memories were of nights like this, cold hands warming each other's, collars turned up against the wind, their voices straining to outdo each other with "Deck the Halls" or "The First Noel."

She went in search of Bret while the men were heaving the last of the big logs on the fire to the enthusiastic cheers of the onlooking crowd. She found him talking to Lenore Skinner who, with her husband George and son Jimmy, had tenanted Bret's farm for the past four years.

"Of course, we're not going to terminate the lease," Bret was saying, "and you'll have plenty of notice before I sell. But people will be coming out to look at the place from time to time, and I thought you should know what my plans were."

Lenore Skinner smiled weakly. She was a thin, work-worn woman in a shabby cotton coat that last year had belonged to someone else. Not even her attempt at a polite smile made her look more attractive or less tired. "You really should talk to my husband about this, Mr. Underwood."

Bret glanced around. "Well, I was hoping I'd get to see him tonight."

Lenore smoothed her hands on her coat nervously. "No. He couldn't come. I think he's coming down with a bug."

"Maybe I could drive out in a couple of days. But meanwhile, I don't want you to worry. You've been fine tenants over the years, and I'll do everything possible to make the transition easy for you."

Lenore shook her head, no longer smiling. "It doesn't matter, Mr. Underwood." Her voice sounded weary. "It's probably for the best, anyhow. George and me...well, I don't reckon we'd be staying on long after the first of the year, anyhow.''

She walked away, and Bret looked after her, puzzled. Dani came up to him. ''They've been having a hard time,'' she explained quietly. ''George Skinner doesn't know anything but farming, and you know that land has never been good for much more than weeds. With the drought the last couple of years, they haven't been able to even grow that. He's tried to hold down other jobs, but the plant over in Centerville started laying off last year and, well...'' She finished the sentence with a shrug.

Bret frowned. ''I'm sorry to hear that. I know they've been late with the rent a lot, but it never bothered me, and I just figured they came up short sometimes, like people do. I didn't know it was that serious.''

''The rent comes mostly from the tips Lenore makes at Harry's Café out on Route 20. She had two jobs for a while—one at the café and another at the dime store in town. Then Ruby Likes decided she couldn't afford full-time help at the store, so they're back to living off just tips.''

''Well, I guess selling the farm is going to be good for them, too,'' Bret said. ''It'll give them a chance to get out of this place and start over.''

Something about the way he said that disturbed Dani—so easily, so matter-of-factly, almost callously. Did he really think people like the Skinners could just pull up roots and start over? Did he really think being forced out of one's home could be good for *anyone*?

But a quick glance at his face assured her that Bret did not mean to be callous or self-serving, and wasn't even aware of how his response had sounded. Everything had always been easy for Bret, the solution to any problem simple and straightforward, and he just didn't understand that it wasn't always so for other people. He had been living in Los Angeles so long, he had forgotten what it was like in the real world. He would remember soon enough.

Meanwhile, the whole issue of the Skinners was academic because he would never be able to sell that farm.

Dani said, "The worst part is, their money problems are only the tip of the iceberg. Their son, Jimmy, is in my class, and I gather there's real trouble at home. George Skinner wasn't sick tonight—he just doesn't go out anymore. Not to church, not to town, especially not anywhere with his wife. He just sits at home, with a bottle most likely, and watches that old black-and-white television day in and day out."

Bret gave a small shake of his head. "Welcome to Norman Rockwell's America, huh?"

The shadow of depression crept toward them, threatening to ruin a perfect evening, and Dani pushed it back determinedly. Not on Bret's first night home. Not at her favorite gathering of the year, and not when they had so much to celebrate. She wound her arm through his and said cheerfully, "Come on, they're about to start the Christmas carols."

Bret groaned. "Dani, I'm freezing. Couldn't we just—"

"It's warm by the fire." She tugged on his arm.

"But Christmas carols! Anything but Christmas carols! It's not even the middle of December and I'm already up to my eyeballs in Christmas carols. Can't we just skip it?"

She dropped his arm, staring at him. "We certainly cannot! What's wrong with you anyway? How'd you turn into such a boring old man?"

"Scrooge," he corrected. "My secretary calls me a Scrooge, and it's a reputation I've worked hard to earn." But he could tell by the expression on Dani's face that she was not amused, so he compromised. "Couldn't we just sit in the car and listen? I'm not kidding. If I stand out in this cold any longer, I'm going to turn into a popsicle. Buy you some caramel popcorn," he coaxed with a grin.

He could tell she was disappointed, but she relented. They went to the car with a bag of caramel popcorn between them, and he ran the engine for a few minutes to warm the interior.

Dani decided after a while that a break in the tradition wasn't entirely bad. The windows were steamed up, turning the inside of the automobile into a cozy, private niche through which muted sounds of carolers were still perfectly audible. It was nice being alone with Bret, away from the crowd, munching on caramel popcorn and not feeling compelled to talk. Thinking, perhaps, a little too much about the past, but they were good memories.

She glanced across the bucket seat at him. "The first time you ever kissed me was here, do you remember?"

"Hmm." His voice sounded lazy and content. "Do you know, if cars had had bucket seats back then, I probably wouldn't have kissed a girl till I was twenty."

She chuckled in agreement. "You were the first, you know."

"The first what?"

"Boy to kiss me."

"Yeah. You were the first girl I kissed, too."

She was surprised. "Really? I never knew that."

"That good, was I?" he returned smugly.

"As far as I was concerned, you were." She popped a kernel of caramel popcorn into her mouth. "Too bad you couldn't have been the first for other things, too."

His eyebrow shot up in a pretense of shock. "Why, Dani Griffin, I can't imagine what you mean."

She shifted a little uncomfortably in her seat. "Well, anybody would've been better than that big jerk of a quarterback I thought I was so in love with in college."

"Pretty bad, huh?"

"The first time?" She shuddered. "Awful. God, nineteen-year-old girls can be stupid."

A silence fell, and in its wake, an awkwardness developed that was as unexpected as it was inexplicable. They had always talked as freely about sex as they had about everything else; never had embarrassment or constraint gotten in the way. Why should this time be different?

Maybe it was the close intimacy of the car making Bret's long, lean body seem to fill even more space than it usually did. Maybe it was the opaque windows and the singers just outside, heard but not seen, and the fresh, poignant memories of adolescent experimentation. Maybe it was in the way she said it: *Too bad you couldn't have been the first . . .*

And maybe it was because she had accidentally, involuntarily, almost told him more than she ever wanted him to know.

It was Bret who broke the awkwardness, as he could always be counted on to do, by delving into the popcorn bag and commenting, "I hope it got better over the years."

Dani relaxed. "Oh, sure. Doesn't everything? All it takes is finding the right guy."

Bret asked, "Like Todd?"

Dani looked at him. His voice was deliberately casual, but his expression was just as deliberate and trying very hard not to appear so. He was half-turned from her, pretending to be very interested in what he could not see through the front windshield, munching on popcorn, affecting a total lack of concern. But the hazy firelight reflected on his jaw and outlined a certain tightness there, played in his eyes and illuminated a tense expectation he could not entirely conceal.

Dani said impatiently, "For heaven's sake, Bret, you've been dying to ask me about Todd since this afternoon. Why don't you just come right out and say so?"

He turned to her, his eyes sober and concealing nothing. "I thought I had."

And so he had. Dani had evaded him then, and she hadn't known why. Now she did, but it was too late.

There was no way she could avoid telling her best
friend the most important secret of her life.

But suddenly, it was the last thing in the world she
wanted to do.

The carolers began singing "Good King Wences-
las." Dani wished with all her being she were out there
with them, instead of trapped in this car having this
conversation with Bret. But she took a breath, and
without looking at him, she said, "I've been seeing
him for about eight months. He's—he's great Bret,
really smart and fun to be with, and he has this fantastic sense of commitment...you know, to the world,
the environment and society as a whole. He's the
newspaper editor—I told you that didn't I?—and you
wouldn't believe the changes he's made. It's like a real
newspaper now instead of that twice-monthly rag we
used to have. He's on the town council, too, but he's
not really a politician—not that he wouldn't make a
great one, he just doesn't play those games. But he's
involved in everything. I mean, he's only been here
two years, but already people know that if there's a
job to be done, they can count on Todd Renshaw to do
it."

She paused for breath, still not looking at him, and
Bret said guardedly, "He sounds like a terrific guy."

"He is," she agreed quickly. "You'd really like
him."

Bret waited.

She reached for more popcorn, changed her mind
and folded her hands in her lap. "He's asked me to

marry him,'' she said. She pulled at the fingers of her gloves, straightened them again and forced herself to look at Bret. ''And I think I'm going to say yes.''

Chapter Four

Bret drove Dani home and rather absently refused her invitation to come inside for cocoa. As he went up the warmly lit steps of the main house, he realized he had arrived before the elder Griffins and that he didn't have a key—but the front door was unlocked, as he should have known it would be. With a rueful shake of his head, he went inside, for what should have been a sign of trust and welcome only served to remind Bret how little he belonged here.

It would be rude to go to bed before his hosts arrived home, but suddenly, every bone in Bret's body ached with fatigue. He scrawled a note on the back of a sheet torn from his address book—"Exhausted. Made myself at home. Thanks again! Bret"—and propped it up on the mantel. He made his way upstairs to the room that had always been his, and wondered how much of his exhaustion was physical and how much was sheer emotional shock.

He couldn't remember exactly what he had said to Dani following her startling announcement—something snappy and clever about old-maid schoolteachers, most likely, followed by a witty assault of teasing, which was exactly what she would expect from him. Pretty soon, she lost that uncomfortable, anxious look and started to respond in kind. When he left her, she was laughing. Bret was reeling.

The room had not changed much since he was a boy and had stayed over for early-morning hunting trips with Dani's dad or had stayed late after a party when the roads were too icy to drive home. The bed was an old oak four-poster, the bureau, a slightly mismatched turn-of-the-century piece, the curtains forest green and the braided rug faded with washing. It was always a little chilly up here, even with the furnace Harold Griffin had put in in 1972, and the bed was piled high with hand-made quilts. It had always been a comfortable room to Bret, a familiar room.

In deference to the quilts, Bret kicked off his shoes before lying back on the bed. He folded his arms beneath his head and stared up at the ceiling. Dani, getting married. Well, what had he expected? That she would wait for him forever?

Wait for him... He frowned at the unexpected slip and couldn't imagine where it had come from. It wasn't as though he wanted to marry her or had ever even thought about it. But neither had he planned on her marrying somebody else, and the possibility was so alien, so new and surprising, that it was going to take him longer than one evening to adjust to it. No, he didn't want to marry her. But he didn't want to lose his best friend, either.

This must have been exactly the way Dani felt when he told her he was getting married ten years ago.

And the irony was, of course, that it was a ten-year-old letter that had brought him back here now, only to find the same scene being played out again—in reverse.

Slowly, he withdrew the letter from his pocket and looked at it for a long time without opening it. Well, this answered one question, anyway. Dani certainly hadn't meant for him to read this—not then, not now—and there was no way in the world he could ask her about it now. It would sound entirely too much like sour grapes. The past was the past, and whatever secrets it held would just have to remain secret for another ten years or more.

After a time, he got up and put the letter in the bottom of the top bureau drawer, covering it up with socks and underwear from his suitcase. Much later, climbing between the crisp-smelling cotton sheets and weighed down by quilts, he managed a smile. Dani, getting married. He resolved to make it top priority to find out all he could about this man who thought he was good enough to be her husband. Bret felt it was a good thing he had come home when he had.

But sleep was a long time coming, and he was beginning to wonder whether it had been a good idea to come home at all.

"GOOD HEAVENS," exclaimed Pauline Westmeyer, examining the scrawl on the back of the boys' bathroom door with an expression of distaste. "Where do kids learn words like this, anyway?"

"What do you expect to find on a bathroom door?" Dani replied. "A love poem? I'll call the janitor."

The two women proceeded down the hall, dodging an occasional overenthusiastic student, who, upon seeing them, immediately pretended to remember the rule about running in the halls—only to forget it again the moment he passed them. Pauline cast Dani a side-long glance. "Speaking of obscenities," she said, "who was that gorgeous fellow you were cuddled up with last night? The one who, I might add, bore no resemblance whatsoever to a certain Todd Renshaw?"

Dani muffled an exclamation of exasperation. Pauline had been teaching at Clayville Elementary almost as long as Dani had, and she could be reasonably counted as one of Dani's best friends. But she had not grown up in Clayville and could, therefore, have no idea of who Bret Underwood was or of the history between Dani and him. Dani wasn't sure whether, in this case, that was a good thing or bad.

"Good heavens," she said, scowling, "the way people talk in this town..." Then, moderating her voice with hard-won patience, she explained, "In the first place, I wasn't cuddling up to anybody. In the second place, he's an old friend. He's staying with my folks for the holidays."

"Is that right...?"

There was an expectant tone to Pauline's murmur, but Dani remained stubbornly silent. She was growing a little irritated with the speculation and innuendo that seemed to be as necessary to her neighbors' survival as the air they breathed. Odd, because usually she found such harmless gossip merely amusing. She reflected wryly that being the target of gossip gave one a whole new perspective on the word *harmless*.

When it became apparent Dani did not intend to elaborate, Pauline prompted, "Well, old friend or not, he's definitely a hunk—to use the vernacular. What does Todd think about this latest development?"

"Nothing yet. I haven't introduced them."

"Are you going to?"

"I guess I'd better," Dani retorted, pushing open the door of her classroom, "before Todd reads about my passionate affair with an out-of-town stranger in his own newspaper!"

Pauline chuckled as she crossed the hall to her own classroom. "Sounds good to me. Nothing like a little scandal to liven up the holidays."

If Dani had been closer, she would have had a pithy reply for that, too. It was perhaps fortunate that Pauline was already out of hearing range.

Dani dumped her books onto her desk and looked skeptically at the withered cactus that sat on the corner of her desk, showing little improvement since yesterday. Not, of course, that she could expect much in a mere sixteen hours, but it did seem that the cactus looked worse this year than it ever had. Maybe she should stop by the library this afternoon and find a book on cacti.

She took a pitcher from the arts-and-crafts cabinet and filled it with water from the girls' bathroom— where, she noticed, there were no unsightly scrawls on the door—and by the time she returned, she was able to put the conversation with Pauline in perspective. She had done enough teasing in her time to be able to take it in good measure from someone else, and there was absolutely no reason why she should be so sensitive on the subject of Bret Underwood. One thing was certain though: she was going to have to get the two men together, and the sooner the better. Maybe tonight, for dinner.

Bret had been sleeping that morning when Dani left for school and her mother absolutely refused to let her wake him. Since her car was still in the school parking lot, Dani had had to accept a ride into town with her father, and she tried to push away the disappointment she felt. It was just that she had counted on having a few moments alone that morning with Bret, and she couldn't shake the feeling that too much had been left unresolved last night.

Certainly, he had not done or said anything to make her feel that way. All in all, the announcement of her almost, not-quiet-certain, possible engagement had gone very well, and Bret had reacted no differently than she had expected; probably not much differently than she herself had reacted when he made the same announcement to her ten years ago. Good humor, goodwill, light banter—those were their trademarks, and Bret had not disappointed her.

Still, she was left *feeling* disappointed and a little uneasy and not quite right about the whole thing in her own mind. Part of it, she supposed, was guilt for not having told Bret before—coupled, of course, with the guilt of enjoying herself with Bret while Todd was working overtime at the paper, and not to even mention the fact that she had not, as of this moment, returned Todd's phone call. But another part was some indefinable feeling that she had let Bret down in some way or he had let her down. She wanted to talk more. She wanted to know what he thought. She wanted his advice.

Which, of course, was ridiculous. What advice could Bret give about a man he didn't even know? What could he possibly say that would be of any value concerning the man she had all but decided she wanted to spend the rest of her life with?

Maybe all she really wanted from Bret was his approval, and looking back over the evening, she realized that for all his easy humor and nonsensical pleasantries, approval was one thing Bret had explicitly not given.

And that, Dani scolded herself as her classroom began to fill, was utterly ridiculous. She was a grown woman and had been delegated the right to make her own decisions for quite some time now. She didn't need Bret Underwood's permission—or approval—to make this, certainly one of the most personal decisions of her life.

But she knew she would never be comfortable until she at least had his opinion.

PAULINE MIGHT HAVE welcomed a scandal to liven up her holidays, but for Dani, the holidays were more than lively enough. The first three hours of the classroom day were spent in diligent application to study, but Dani tried hard to disguise the lessons with so much holiday cheer that the students did not suspect they were actually learning. In social studies, they began a study of Christmas around the world; she passed out math work sheets that consisted chiefly of arranging an even number of Christmas ornaments on the seven branches of a tree, and in English, she assigned a Christmas story to be turned in Friday. After lunch, she passed out permission slips for the annual Christmas-tree-cutting field trip, accepted suggestions for the craft projects the children would make for their parents and—by clever manipulations that only another teacher could appreciate—persuaded the class into unanimous agreement on clove-studded oranges for the mothers and spool tie racks for the dads. During recess, she finally got a chance to call Todd.

"Well," he greeted her, "if it isn't my favorite person. And just in time for my coffee break."

"You know what I don't like about you?" she challenged him.

"Wait a minute, let me get my list."

"I haven't returned your phone call for almost twenty-four hours, and you're not even mad."

"Do you know what I don't like about you? I break a date with you at the last minute, and you're not even mad."

"Who says I'm not?"

"If you were mad, you wouldn't have returned my phone call for at least forty-eight hours."

Dani grinned as she leaned back in the creaky swivel chair and adjusted the blinds so that she could watch the playground. She was sitting in what was euphemistically called the "teachers' lounge"—in reality little more than an extension of the janitor's closet with a desk, a chair and a window—but it afforded a good view of both the front entrance and the playground. There were three teachers on duty outside, and everything appeared to be as much under control as it could be at recess, so she turned her attention back to the telephone.

"As a matter of fact," she informed Todd blithely, "I would have been more than forty-eight hours' worth of mad, but lucky for you, I was able to get another date at the last minute."

"So I hear."

Dani smothered a groan. "News spreads faster in this town than head colds. Who needs a newspaper?"

"Hey, watch that kind of talk. So who is this combination Greek god and Wall Street genius I'm supposed to be losing you to?"

"Not Wall Street," she corrected. "Lemon Street, California. Why can't anybody understand the difference between *securities* and *security?* It's just Bret— you remember, I told you about him. My old friend from—"

"Sure, I remember. When did he get in?"

"Just yesterday afternoon. It was a real surprise. He didn't let anybody know he was coming. I want you to meet him."

"Sounds great. How about this afternoon? I can knock off early and pick you up after school."

"Can't this afternoon. I start auditions for the school play. Anyway, I was thinking more along the lines of dinner. Seems to me I owe you one somewhere along the line."

"A free meal? Even better. Who's cooking, you or your mom?"

"Don't push your luck, wise guy. My place, seven-thirty."

"I'll be there. What can I bring—besides the main course?"

"I'm warning you—"

"Okay, okay." His voice was smothered with laughter. "I'll bring the wine and a mouthful of compliments on your cooking. Love you."

"Me, too."

Dani hung up the phone, smiling. She didn't know why she had dreaded the call so much; talking with Todd always made her feel good, just as being with him did. Everything about him made her feel good: his smile, his easy humor, his quick grasp of problems and his straightforward approach to them. She really *liked* him, and there weren't very many people anyone could say that about. And why shouldn't she like him? Todd was a great guy; anyone could tell that. Furthermore, anyone could see that she and Todd were perfect for each other. Certainly, Dani had never known anyone with whom she got along better... except, of course, Bret.

And with all of that in mind, there was no reason at all why she should be so ambivalent about marrying Todd Renshaw.

Dani had not exactly had a stellar social life since she'd finished college and settled down for good in Clayville. Part of it was due, of course, to the limits of living in a small town where she knew everybody and everyone knew her and there wasn't much mystery left to lend excitement to romance. Part of it was undoubtedly because of Dani's own high standards. Over the years, she had had casual dates and one or two long-term love affairs, but she had never considered any of them serious.

But from the time she and Todd had started dating, they had been linked in the minds of every onlooker as a couple and for the first time, Dani hadn't minded. Maybe it was because she was getting too old to fight it, maybe it was because everything about her relationship with Todd had seemed to follow the course of least resistance. She had been expecting his marriage proposal since August; by the time he finally made it just before Thanksgiving, she had been more than prepared to say yes. And no one had been more surprised than she was when the words that came out of her mouth were, "I need to think about it, Todd."

Todd took it in good grace, though, of course, he wouldn't have done anything else. He understood that they had both been single for a long time, and there was a lot to think about—finances, living arrangements, careers, children. There were adjustments to be made, and he was willing to give Dani time to get used to the newness of the idea. Deep inside, Dani was sure, he had no doubts as to what her answer would eventually be. Just as she, until yesterday, had had no doubt herself.

Why should Bret's unexpected appearance make any difference?

She didn't know the answer to that, and just thinking about it was threatening to give her a headache. But she knew now she wouldn't be able to make a decision until she talked to Bret.

IF DANI HAD KNOWN HOW much Bret had been counting on those few moments alone with her that morning while he drove her to school, she would have awakened him no matter what her mother said. As it was, with the time-zone change and Bret's restless night, it was after nine o'clock before he awoke, and he was sharply disappointed to find that he had missed her.

There were two reasons he had wanted to get up early. The first was that he still felt he had handled things badly the night before and he wanted a chance to make up for it. The second was that he knew unless he got out of the house early, there would be no way to avoid the years of catching up Dani's parents would insist upon.

Dani's parents were almost as close to him as his own, and he had always enjoyed their company. The two families had been neighbors all their lives and close personal friends, as well. When Bret's father passed away when Bret was nine, Harold Griffin had stepped into the surrogate role as easily as an uncle might have, making the loss much easier for Bret to bear. Holidays had been celebrated around the Griffin table; summer vacations, Labor Day picnics and Sunday dinners had always been joint affairs. Bret had spent as much time at Dani's house as he had at his own, for they were family.

But families entailed certain responsibilities as well as pleasures. Bret didn't mind pitching in to help Anne with the dishes—and he certainly hadn't minded the first hot breakfast he'd had since he'd given up power brunches two years ago. He endured her questions about the state of his health, business and personal life with the same amused tolerance he would have given his own mother, but he didn't object when Harold rescued him just before lunch with the suggestion they take a walk around the place. He enjoyed slipping back into a simpler time with fish stories and tall tales, and there was a basic, uncomplicated pleasure in the sound of their footsteps crunching over icy, stubbly ground, as he listened to the older man's expert comments on everything from the state of the nation to the state of last year's crop. He didn't even mind—not much, anyway—the half a cart of wood he split after lunch; the exercise was good for him. But with one thing and then another, with so much to talk about and so many memories being evoked, he never got around to bringing up the subject of Todd Renshaw, and that was really the only thing on his mind.

It was after three when he finally got away, and he could only hope Dani was still at school. He followed the sound of a slightly out-of-tune piano to the combination cafeteria/auditorium, and that was where he found her.

She was sitting at one of the child-sized gray Formica tables in a child-sized red molded plastic chair, a sheaf of papers spread out before her and a pencil stuck behind her ear. Her attention was on the stage where a dozen or so children were belting out a fair rendition of "Jolly Old St. Nicholas." He stood there for a moment, overwhelmed by that slightly queasy feeling of déjà vu every adult experiences when confronted by a schoolroom situation—as though he should look over his shoulder for the principal before he threw that next spitball—and he wondered why in the world Dani would want to teach in the same school in which she herself had grown up. When viewed like that, she had spent her entire life surrounded by the same four walls. How did she stand it? Convicted criminals served shorter sentences than that.

He moved toward her, glancing dubiously at the undersized chairs before selecting one and sitting down beside her. He wrinkled his nose a little and said under his breath, "Spinach and yeast rolls. The place even smells the same."

Dani's face lit up as she turned to him. "Oh, Bret, good! I was hoping you'd stop by. We're auditioning for the Christmas play. See that little boy with the red hair? I think he'd be perfect for the part of the Mischievous Angel, don't you?"

"Type casting," he replied. And then he grinned. "Remember when old Mrs. Hawkins put on the metronome and made us all skip around the stage to pick the best dancers for her musical production of *The Three Billy Goats*?"

Dani nodded. "Her idea was if you didn't have enough coordination to skip you couldn't be much of a dancer. Good theory. You were the first one out."

"I was the *only* one out," he corrected. "Possibly the only fourth grader in the history of the world who was too clumsy to skip. It was humiliating."

"It was a little cruel, come to think of it."

"I still carry the scars. And you—star of every school play since kindergarten and so graceful you wouldn't trip if somebody tied your shoelaces together—immediately pretended to lose the rhythm so she'd kick you out, too."

"She made me mad."

"You just didn't want me to feel bad."

Dani grinned at him. "We sure had fun, didn't we, drawing scenery backstage while all the other kids were getting yelled at for two hours every afternoon by Mrs. Hawkins just so they could be in her stupid play?"

Bret could still smell the dust of the pastel chalk that had clung to his clothes and hair and dyed his hands blue, but it wasn't that memory that made him smile. It was Dani. "We always had fun," he agreed.

The music stopped, and Dani turned back to the stage. "That was great," she called. "Now, all the girls line up on the right side of the stage—no, Sarah, the right—and all the boys on the left, and get ready to read your lines. Laurie, we'll start with you. Talk real loud now. Pretend your mom's in the back row and you want her to hear you."

"My mom always sits on the front row," Laurie replied smugly.

"Go ahead, Laurie."

Laurie shouted, "Don't cry, little pony! I'm the Christmas Angel and I've come to make all your dreams come true!"

Bret groaned. "This is depressing. Like one of those nightmares when you're back in school again and you discover you've forgotten your algebra book *and* your pants."

Dani arched her eyebrows at him. "I never have nightmares like that. Must be one of those type-A personality things." Then lifting her voice. "That's fine, Laurie. Boys, settle down. Robert, read your line.''

For the next half hour, Bret listened to a dozen or more students alternately shout, mumble and stammer their lines. He entertained himself by waggling his fingers at the pianist—a young sandy-haired woman who kept staring at him and then was continually embarrassed to be caught staring—and by wondering, once again, why Dani had ended up here.

She was good with the children, there was no denying that. She had the patience, the humor and the natural energy it took to work with youngsters, and no doubt she was an excellent teacher. But she also had a great deal more, and in all their childhood plans and dreams, teaching had never even been mentioned as one of Dani's ambitions. Of course, there weren't many options open in a town the size of Clayville for a college-educated woman. He would never understand why she had stayed so long and settled for so little.

When the last little girl reassured the pony and resumed her place among her giggling schoolmates, Dani called out, ''Okay, kids, that was great. I'll be handing out your parts tomorrow morning, and tomorrow afternoon, we'll get together here and start practicing. Does everyone have a ride home?''

To judge by the clamor and excited rush for the door, everyone did. The pianist gathered up her sheet music and came over to them. ''Hi,'' she said, directing herself to Bret. ''I'm Pauline Westmeyer. You must be Dani's friend—''

"Bret Underwood," he supplied, grinning as he got to his feet.

She blushed again. "Sorry for staring. It's just not often that we see an unfamiliar face around here. Are you staying long?"

"I don't know yet."

"He'll be staying," Dani assured her colleague. "I've got enough for him to do to keep him here till Christmas."

"Well, great." Pauline smiled. "I'll be seeing you around, then."

She made a circle of her thumb and forefinger behind her back when she thought Bret couldn't see as she left, and Bret laughed softly.

"Watch it, Hot Stuff," Dani said as she gathered up her papers. "She's divorced and on the prowl, and you're prime pickings."

"I'll consider myself fairly warned." He picked up Dani's attaché case as they started for the exit.

"So, who do you like for the Christmas Angel?"

"The little blond girl," he replied promptly, "in the plaid jumper."

"Type casting," she scoffed. "I'm going to give it to Lisa Carp. She's never played anything more important than a tree, and the part would be good for her confidence."

"Mrs. Hawkins would turn over in her grave. Don't you know the first requirement for being a teacher is to torture the little monsters for everything they're worth?"

Bret pushed open the heavy fire door and they walked into the bright, crisp afternoon.

"How about coming for dinner tonight?"

He glanced at her skeptically. "I don't know. Your mom is making apple dumplings."

"So tell her to send over a few."

"And pork chops."

"I'm making eggplant casserole. Take it or leave it."

"Some choice."

She didn't break stride or alter her tone as she said, "Todd's coming, too."

Bret lifted one eyebrow. "And you want me to chaperone?"

She stopped then and gave him a look he knew too well to ignore. "I want you to be polite, charming and supportive. I mean it, Bret. Best behavior."

"I guess that means I can't eat with my feet on the table."

"Bret..."

"Okay, okay. Sounds like an offer I can't refuse." And then he hesitated, squinting a little in the bright winter sunlight. "Listen, Dani," he added, trying not to sound as uncomfortable as he felt, "I guess I was a little insensitive last night. All that joking around when I should've known you wanted me to just shut up and listen. It's just that you caught me off guard, you know? I'm looking forward to meeting your Todd, and I'll be nice to him, even if I hate him. I promise."

The smile that spread across her face was as much in gratitude for what Bret had not said as for what he had. "You won't hate him," she assured him, slipping her arm through his. "And if you do, you don't have to be nice to him. Fair enough?"

He ruffled her hair as he walked her to her car. "You've got a deal."

And he hoped Dani wouldn't be too disappointed when it turned out that he did hate Todd Renshaw, because that was exactly what he was fully prepared to do.

Chapter Five

Bret pushed aside the lingerie that was scattered over Dani's bed and stretched out across it on his stomach. "You know," he said, "this is really nice."

He was looking out over the living area from the loft that was Dani's bedroom. When he had last seen the place, it had barely been completed: she had slept on a hammock in the loft, and the only furniture was her grandmother's maple dining room set. The dining set was still there, but it had been joined by a collection of braided scatter rugs, an oversize plush sofa, and several colorful, mismatched chairs and a spinet piano. She had painted the walls a deep Colonial blue with off-white trim and wainscotting. Brass trunks and wrought iron plant stands served as occasional tables, and the built-in shelves her father had designed were crowded with books and collectibles. It was casual, eclectic and fresh; as colorful and energetic as Dani herself, and just as warm. Looking at it, Bret felt the faintest stirrings of envy. She had built a home; all he had was a house.

"All right, what about this?" She came out from behind a country-chintz screen wearing a long, burgundy skirt of some kind of floating, clinging material and a cream-colored sweater with a wide, lace collar.

He turned over to look at her, scrunching a pillow behind his head. "Looks fine." He was careful to keep his voice noncommittal because, of course, she looked more than fine. He was amazed at how fine she looked when she got dressed up, and he was a little puzzled about why he had never noticed it before.

"What about my hair?" She pirouetted toward the mirror, pushing her hair up off her shoulders into a pouf on top. "Up or down?"

He made a face. "Ah, Dani, don't make me do this. Don't you have a girlfriend you can call? What do I know about hair?" She gave him a warning look in the mirror and he relented. "Down. Wear it down. I don't know what the big deal is anyway. You've already hooked the guy, what do you have to impress him for?"

She bent over at the waist, brushing her hair forward. It rippled like exotic silk in the lamplight. "I'm not trying to impress anybody. You're the one who made me change the first dress—"

"It was too tight. I could see your panty line."

"And you're the one who made me snag my only pair of blue stockings—"

"Which wouldn't have happened if you'd worn jeans like I told you to."

She straightened up, caught the whirl of her hair in one hand before it could fall to her shoulders again, and twisted it into a loose knot atop her head. "Why do I get the feeling you'd be just as happy if I served dinner in a chenille bathrobe and bunny slippers? Speaking of dinner, will you run downstairs and put the rolls in?''

"You already did. Jeez, Dani, you'd think you were serving an eight-course dinner for a head of state. What are you so rattled about?''

"I am not rattled," she retorted. "This is the way I always get before a dinner party. I can never remember how to time the vegetables or whether I salted the soup or— Oh!''

"What?''

"My earring's caught! Oh, damn, I hate these earrings, I never wear them—''

"Come here. Stop jerking your head, you're going to hurt yourself." He sat up and caught her waist, pulling her back to sit on the bed between his legs. The earring, a dangling contraption of silver wire that greatly resembled a medieval torture device, was snagged in the lace collar of her sweater, and her ineffectual strugglings had only ensnared it further.

"Relax," Bret said, working to loosen the delicate lace. Her cinnamon scent drifted up to him, warm and feminine. "I was a brain surgeon in a former life.''

"You're going to tear my sweater.''

"I'm more concerned about tearing your ear. Stop wiggling.''

"What are you doing with my stocking around your neck?''

Bret glanced disinterestedly at his shoulder, where a dark blue stocking was draped like a scarf. "That's where you threw it, I guess. Oh-oh.''

"What?'' She sat stiffly, not daring to move.

"The earring's free. My watch is caught."

"Oh, Bret, for heaven's sake!"

"Be still—"

They both froze at the sound of a knock on the door. A second later, the door opened and a man who could only be Todd walked in.

The loft bedroom was perfectly visible from below, and though Bret felt a brief twinge of sympathy for Dani, it did not override the mischievous—and, he had to admit, unworthy—sense of satisfaction he felt for the view Todd must have had. There were the two of them, sitting on the rumpled bed amidst a pile of lingerie in what could very well be mistaken for an embrace; his arms were around Dani and their faces were almost touching as she turned to look at him. Anyone could be forgiven for misinterpreting.

But Todd, seeing them, merely grinned. "Am I early?" he asked.

He set the bottle of wine on the bar and started up the stairs.

"Hurry!" Dani ground out.

For her sake, Bret did and got the watch disentangled just as Todd reached the loft.

Dani leapt to her feet. "Hi, Todd. I want you to meet Bret Underwood. Bret, this is Todd Renshaw."

Bret got to his feet, making a deprecating gesture toward the bed. "I guess you're wondering what's going on."

"With Dani," Todd replied easily, "I've learned not to ask." He extended his hand. "Good to meet you, Bret."

Bret accepted his handshake, but couldn't prevent a puzzled glance at Dani as she plucked her stocking from around his neck. No one, he thought, had the right to be that confident.

Then Dani gasped out, "The rolls!" and pushed past them. "Come downstairs," she called over her shoulder. "Make yourselves at home. Somebody pour the wine."

Todd grinned at Bret. "Great little hostess."

Bret got the glasses while Todd opened the wine. Dani kept herself busier than she probably needed to be in the kitchen in order, Bret suspected, to give the two men time alone together. That was not necessarily a good idea.

Bret guessed Todd was probably close to Dani's age, around Bret's own height and—he had to reluctantly admit—looked to be in pretty good shape for a newspaper man. He wore tortoiseshell glasses, a tweed jacket and a sweater vest over an Oxford shirt. He had probably, Bret reflected, been a nerd in high school, the kind of guy Dani wouldn't have looked at twice. But then, none of them was in high school anymore.

"So, Bret," Todd said, handing him a glass of wine, "tell me about yourself."

"I think that's supposed to be my line."

"I anticipated as much," Todd replied, and reached into his coat pocket for a folded sheet of paper, "and thought I'd save us both some time."

Bret glanced at the paper Todd handed him and had to fight back a grin. It was a typed résumé, complete with salary, family history, career goals and golf handicap. "I see Dani's dad has already given you the third degree."

"After the second date," Todd admitted.

They walked back toward the living area. "Did you pass?"

"The jury's still out."

Bret chuckled. "The Griffins aren't known for making hasty decisions."

"That's okay. I'm a patient man."

Bret did not imagine the underlying meaning behind those words—it was not a warning, merely a statement of fact. He turned to add another log to the fire he had built earlier, and when Todd took the big, comfortably worn chair by the fireplace, it was with the natural ease of a man who had sat there many times before. Bret sat on the hearth.

There wasn't much room, and Bret accidentally upset one of Dani's collection of bells when he straightened out his legs. There must have been a hundred of them, arranged along the mantel, grouped on the hearth and on the two small shelves flanking it—sleigh bells, doorbells, hand bells, glass bells, silver, gold and copper bells. Bret wondered how she ever found time to keep them all dusted.

He righted the small clapper bell he had overturned, murmuring, "'Bells, bells, bells, bells...'"

"'The tintinnabulation of the bells,'" Todd finished, and Bret looked at him sharply.

"Bret started me collecting them," Dani said, coming into the room with a plate of hors d'oeuvres. She diplomatically chose to sit on a cushion on the floor between the two men and first offered the plate to Todd.

"Don't put that on me," Bret objected. "That's one vice you developed all on your own."

"You were into bells?" inquired Todd.

"He was into cows." Dani thrust the hors d'oeuvres platter into Bret's hand and stood up, lifting a rust-scarred cowbell from its place on the mantel. "Bret gave me this when I was five. It was the first present a boy ever gave me."

"You were easily impressed," Bret admitted. "Why do you keep that filthy thing? It ruins your whole decor."

She made a face at him, and Todd reached for the bell. "Who did the artwork on the side?" he asked. He turned the bell to face them, clearly showing the crooked letters carved into the tin: BU + DG.

"Dani did," Bret said.

"Bret did," Dani answered at the same time. Then they looked at each other and laughed.

"Who knows?" Bret shrugged. "That was over twenty years ago. God, I never thought I'd be old enough to say that."

"Did any of us?" Dani took the cowbell and replaced it carefully on the mantel, then resumed her place on the floor, smiling at him.

Bret resisted the impulse to slip his arm around her shoulders in a friendly hug and contented himself with smiling back at her. It was a good moment, and even Todd's presence couldn't spoil it.

Bret was amazed, as a matter of fact, at how little Todd's presence did to spoil any part of the evening.

He kept waiting for the other man to do something or say something to irritate him, but Todd never did. Either Todd Renshaw was incredibly well rehearsed, or he was really pleasant company. The fact that Bret couldn't find anything wrong with Todd was, in truth, the only thing that annoyed him.

They talked about the changes that had occurred in Clayville since Bret's last visit, and Todd was able to put personal stories into a social and economic context in a way that formed a fascinating picture. Bret asked about real-estate prices and discovered Todd knew more off the top of his head than Bret's expensive L.A. firm had uncovered in a month of research. Eventually, the talk turned to Bret's business and Bret learned Todd knew a great deal more about the psychology of crime than he did. In fact, Todd knew more about almost everything than he did, and it was easy to see why Dani liked him. Bret should have resented that, but he was too interested in the other man's conversation to pause for reflection.

He watched Dani and Todd carefully, trying to read between the lines into the nature of their relationship, but that, too, proved futile. There were no lingering touches, no secret glances. That could indicate a couple so secure in their relationship, they had grown past the need for open displays of affection. It could mean they were simply being polite for Bret's sake. Or it could mean...nothing.

Bret only knew if he had a girl who looked as good as Dani did that night, he would have been hard put to keep his hands off her. Maybe Todd was used to it, but Bret's eyes were continually drawn back to Dani in amazed appreciation at the way the soft sweater outlined her figure and the way the skirt alternately floated and clung when she moved; the way her eyes sparkled when she laughed and the way soft tendrils from her upswept hair escaped to frame her face. When had she gotten so grown-up, so feminine? Did Todd have any idea how lucky he was?

The only awkward moment came at the end of the evening, when neither man could decide who was supposed to leave first. Though it would have been against his better judgment, Bret would have accepted a signal from Dani if she had wanted to end the evening alone with Todd. He knew her well enough to realize that the point of the meeting would not be served until she and he had a chance to talk about it, so he made no move to go. And when Todd finally glanced at his watch with a rueful expression and made some comment about the time, Bret knew he had read Dani correctly. She walked Todd to the door, and though Bret should have been ashamed of himself, he made sure that he could see them at all times. Todd, observing this, kissed Dani on the cheek and waved good-night to Bret.

Bret had to admit that any man who could take that kind of treatment in such good humor deserved a Good Sport of the Year award at the very least.

"So." Dani leaned against the door, her cheeks flushed and her eyes bright with expectation. "What do you think?"

Bret lounged back on the sofa and swung his feet onto the brass trunk in front of it. "I think he's charming. Another hour, and we'd probably be picking out a china pattern together."

"Be serious."

"I am serious. He's a great guy."

Bret patted the place beside him on the sofa, but Dani was too keyed up to sit. She began gathering up coffee cups and cocktail napkins.

"I knew you'd like him. Do you think he's good-looking?"

"Not my type."

"Well, I do. I like that swarthy, intellectual look."

"He's not swarthy. And his nose is too big."

Dani glanced at Bret critically. "Well, maybe he's not as good-looking as you—"

"Am I?" Bret pretended to preen.

"But I think he's got interesting looks. Character."

"And I don't?"

She took the coffee cups to the sink. "You're too blond, too tan, too perfect."

"Don't forget built."

She returned, wiping her hands on a dish towel, and looked at him assessingly. "You're too...Hollywood. You need a flaw."

"I've got plenty of them. You just can't see them because you adore me so much." He reached for her hand and pulled her down beside him. "What is this, anyway, a beauty contest? Your Todd's a nice guy, and looks aren't everything. What's really on your mind?"

She tossed the dish towel aside and sighed as she leaned her head back against his shoulder. "You know that."

"Yeah, I do. But I want to hear you say it."

"Oh, Bret. Marriage..." She twisted her head around to look at him, uncertainty in her eyes. "What's it like?"

He chuckled. "I'm the last person you should ask about that."

"But at least you did it," she insisted. "Why?"

"Oh, honey, I don't know." Absently, his hand caressed her shoulder. "Looking back, I really don't know."

And then something struck him. *If you knew, it might make a difference.* Maybe that was the key. If he had known, back then, about this other person who loved him, it *would* have made a difference, and it shouldn't have. Not if the marriage was right, not if the love was real....

That was something he had never realized before, and it disturbed him. There was something there he needed to think about, but he was aware that Dani's expression had become puzzled, so he added thoughtfully, "I'll tell you one thing. If I had it to do over again, I wouldn't marry in the heat of passion. I mean, there should be that, but it takes more, I think. A lot more."

"Like what?"

"I've got a better question for you. Why didn't you ever do it before?"

"Get married?" She shrugged and settled back against his shoulder again, curling her legs beside her on the sofa. "I don't know, lots of reasons. It took me so long to get a place of my own—well, almost a place of my own—and I guess I had to fight so hard to show my independence, it became sort of a habit. And I never found anybody I liked well enough to settle down with—or anyone who could put up with me for more than a few months. The time just never seemed right.''

''And now?''

She hesitated, but only for a minute. ''I'm thirty-three years old,'' she said. ''I'm tired of living alone. I want to care about someone and know someone cares about me. I want to build a future with somebody, maybe have children, and that kind of thing can't wait forever. I don't want to grow old alone.''

Bret ruffled her hair. ''Hell of a reason, kid.''

''And I love Todd,'' she added. ''I really do. He's easy to talk to. We get along great. Everybody says we make a perfect couple.''

''It's looking better and better.''

She sighed again. ''I know how that sounds. I couldn't talk like this to anyone but you. I mean, everyone expects you to just go into raptures about the man you're going to marry, but you have to be practical. You have to think about these things. Like you said, there should be more than passion.''

''But a little passion never hurt.''

''I never said I wasn't passionate,'' she objected. ''I just don't let it go to my head.''

''And nothing scares Dani Griffin more than change.''

''Right,'' she admitted.

A silence fell and Bret wished he knew what to say. He wished he knew what Dani *wanted* him to say. The whole situation would have been a great deal easier if only he had been able to find something wrong with

Todd, and he hadn't realized until that moment how much he had counted on disliking the man.

He gave her shoulders a reassuring squeeze and lowered his chin to rest atop her hair. She smelled wonderful. The sweater was as silky as kitten fur against his fingers, and the shape of her arm beneath it was soft and feminine. He had never noticed before how well they fit together, her head coming just beneath his chin, her hip resting naturally against the curve of his. How good it felt to sit with her like this, holding her.

"You know," he said after a moment, "I didn't expect any of this when I came home. It seems like all my life, you're the one thing that never changed. The one thing I could always count on."

"Maybe that's not a good thing."

Without his realizing it, his arm had drifted down, encircling her, his hand resting lightly on her rib cage. He could feel the delicate pulse of her heart just beneath her left breast. An awareness went through him that started as a tingling in his fingers and spread to a warmth that tightened his muscles. The reaction shouldn't have surprised him: she was a beautiful woman, soft and feminine, and she was lying in his arms. But she was Dani.

His voice was a little thick as he replied, "I don't think I'm the one you should be asking about this."

She turned to look at him. Her eyes were a silvery, candlelit shade, and so close that, had she been anyone else, he would have closed them with a kiss. And there was something in those eyes... something that caught him off guard and made his heart beat a little faster, almost as though she knew what he was thinking. And she didn't mind.

She said softly, "You're the only one I can ask, Bret."

He could feel the faint stirring of her breath on his cheek and the silken brush of her hair tickling his throat. Her scent tantalized him, making him wonder if traces of it lingered on her skin and what it would be like to taste. They were fleeting thoughts, ephemeral feelings that would hardly bear close examination, not even with that open, almost expectant look in Dani's eyes all but urging him to do so.

His throat felt a little dry as he swallowed, and he straightened up, forcing a smile. "Tell you what, then," he said. "Better let me think about it awhile."

He kissed her on the forehead and stood up. "Meanwhile, don't do anything rash."

"Who, me?"

She walked with him to the door, her arm looped around his waist. "Thanks for coming, Bret."

"Have you ever known me to refuse a free meal?"

"No, I mean..." She stopped and looked up at him, resting her hand lightly on his chest. "Thanks for coming home when you did. You always know, don't you?"

"*We* always know," he corrected gently.

She smiled. "And thanks for being nice tonight. Even if you didn't want to."

"I did outdo myself, didn't I?"

"You're amazing when you apply yourself."

He opened the door and they stood for a moment in the cold draft of night air. "I knew you'd like Todd," she told him. She leaned forward and brushed his lips lightly with a kiss. "He's a lot like you. Good night, Bret."

The scent of cinnamon and vanilla lingered on Bret's skin through the crisp walk home and followed him into his dreams.

Chapter Six

"What kind of perfume does Dani wear?" Bret asked Anne the next morning.

Her eyes twinkled as she glanced over her shoulder at him. "Christmas shopping, are you?"

She bent to take a pan of muffins out of the oven—blueberry, from the smell of them—and Bret was glad she missed the look of discomfiture that came over his face. He didn't know where the question had come from, except that it had been on his mind all night, and now that the words were out, they almost seemed too personal.

Besides, he hadn't given the first thought to what to give Dani for Christmas.

"Do you know," Anne said, a little frown playing with her brow as she straightened up with the muffin tin, "I don't believe Dani ever wears perfume. Aunt Ida sends her a bottle of toilet water every year, and every year it ends up in the box for the poor. But I'll try to find out if there's any particular fragrance she likes, if you want."

"No, I guess not." Bret made his voice casual as he took a bowl from the counter and helped himself to the oatmeal that was simmering in the big kettle on the stove. "Perfume's not the right kind of gift for Dani, anyway. I was just trying to think of something girlie."

Anne laughed. "You have been away a long time! Her father and I are trying to decide between a pair of snowshoes and a new bobsled. 'Girlie' has never been her style."

"Maybe she'd like a new puppy," Bret teased.

"Don't you dare!" Anne set the basket of muffins on the table and gave him a sidelong glance. "Of course, this year, she might be easier to buy for. China and silver should be high on the list. How did dinner go last night?"

Bret brought the coffeepot to the table. "Not too bad. She didn't burn anything."

"You know that's not what I mean."

Bret sat down with his bowl of oatmeal, choosing his words carefully. "Her new fella is a nice guy."

Anne sat next to him, buttering a muffin. "We think so, too."

"Miss Annie," Bret said abruptly, "could I ask you something?"

"Of course, dear."

"Do you remember when I got married?"

Her eyes twinkled again as she bit into the muffin, reminding Bret very much of her daughter. "Why, yes, now that you mention it, I do vaguely recall something of the sort. Why do you ask?"

Bret kept his eyes on the cup of coffee he was pouring. "I just wondered if you remembered how Dani felt about the whole thing at the time."

Anne's attention seemed to quicken, and Bret wondered if he had revealed too much—and then he wondered why he thought he had anything to hide from Anne Griffin in the first place.

"I'm not sure I know what you mean," she said.

He pushed the coffee cup across the table to her and poured another for himself. "I mean..." And he looked at Anne. "Dani never liked Laura, did she?"

Anne seemed to hesitate, and then she smiled, almost apologetically. "Bret, you know how it is with you two. You're the only brother Dani's ever had, and all her life, she's worshiped the ground you walk on. If she didn't like your wife, it was only because she didn't get to pick her out herself."

"She never told me," Bret said slowly. He was thinking of the letter that was hidden upstairs in his underwear drawer. After last night, he had promised himself he'd forget about it. Now, he supposed he should've thrown it away, because it was obvious he would never be able to forget about it.

Anne smiled at him over the rim of her cup. "Would it have mattered?"

Bret hesitated and then reached for the milk pitcher, pouring a little over his oatmeal. "Yeah," he admitted. "I think it would. If I had known...I might have thought twice."

"And now you resent Dani for not saving you from a painful divorce."

Bret looked at Anne in surprise. Resent Dani? A protest formed on his lips but died unspoken. Because now that Anne had said it, he realized that it *was* resentment he had been feeling, ever since he read that letter. Deeply buried and carefully disguised, but, yes, resentment. Anger, as much as he tried to deny it, because of all the times in their lives, why did she have to pick that one to keep the truth from him? *It could have made a difference, damn it.* And though he was ashamed of himself, he couldn't help it. Dani had cheated him of the most important thing she had to give—her honesty. How could he not resent that?

He tried to smile as he glanced down at the cooling oatmeal. "After all these years, I guess I'm still looking for someone to blame. Stupid, isn't it?"

Anne said sympathetically, "I know it was hard on you, Bret."

"They say it's harder on the woman, but I don't see how that can be."

And again he hesitated, looking for the right words, shaking his head a little when they wouldn't come. "Don't misunderstand me, it wasn't that I was still in love with her when we broke up. It's just that, growing up like I did, with my folks and you, I expected marriage to last forever. There just wasn't any question in my mind that was the way it was supposed to be. It was hard to adjust to—I don't know, losing an illusion. Facing up to the fact that I had invested so much of myself—so much of my expectations—in what turned out to be a temporary arrangement. Do you understand what I mean?"

"Of course, I do. But it's not always an illusion, Bret, and it's not supposed to be temporary. I'd be very disappointed in you if you turned out to be a cynic."

"Not a cynic," he told her, lifting his spoon again. "Just cautious. And a little scared. I think Dani wants me to tell her whether or not to marry Todd," he confessed suddenly.

"Ah." She nodded, sipping her coffee. "And now the shoe's on the other foot."

"I guess it is."

"You're afraid she'll do what you tell her."

"Or she won't."

"No, she probably will. Or she'll at least think about it."

A rueful smile touched Bret's lips as he heard his own words repeated back to him. "And I don't want that responsibility."

She smiled at him.

"All right," he admitted, turning back to the oatmeal again. "I guess I understand where she was coming from all those years ago. But it doesn't make it any easier." In fact, it made it harder. He knew the end of his own story, but who could tell the end of Dani's? He didn't want her to hate him in ten years for what he hadn't said, any more than for what he had.

"Just out of curiosity," Anne said casually, "what would you tell her?"

And that was the hard part. He liked Todd. Dani liked Todd. The two of them seemed perfect for each other. If he were any kind of friend, he would tell her not to be a fool, to grab the guy before he got away and have a great life. So why was he holding back? Why was there any doubt in his mind at all? Marriage was more than a change in life-style, it was a lifetime commitment, and he still believed that despite his own failure. Marriage was a sacrament, a huge, soul-altering progression. Was it the shadow of his own mistake that stood in the way? Or was it that he was afraid Dani would take his advice?

The back door opened with a gust of cold air and Harold came in, his cheeks ruddy from the outdoor temperatures, his eyes twinkling like a good-natured Santa. "I've got the tractor hooked up," he announced, rubbing his hands. "Is everybody ready?"

"What are you doing, going out in that cold without your breakfast?" Anne scolded. She got to her feet to help her husband off with his jacket. "I told you, we've got plenty of time before they get here."

Bret was grateful for the reprieve from disturbing thoughts. "Before who gets here?" he asked. "Where are you going?"

"We," corrected Anne, hanging her husband's jacket on a hook by the door. "It's a family affair, always has been, always will be, though heaven knows how it ever got started."

"Don't be a Scrooge, young lady," Harold said, pinching his wife's cheek. "You know you love it."

"As if I didn't have enough to do around here," Anne pretended to complain, but her smile gave her away.

"Annual Christmas-tree expedition," Harold explained to Bret as he filled his coffee cup. "I'm sure Dani mentioned it to you. She reminded me only this morning to get out an extra jacket for you."

"No, she didn't mention it. She never tells me anything." But it didn't sound too bad, tromping through the woods in search of a tree. It might even be fun. Of course, it would be a lot more fun if Dani were along. "I'm surprised she didn't want to come," he added, sipping his coffee. "It's not like Dani, leaving something as important as a Christmas tree in somebody else's hands."

"Oh, she'll be here," Anne assured him.

"But it's a school day," Bret pointed out.

Harold's eyes twinkled as he sat down and buttered a muffin. "Exactly."

THE BRIGHT YELLOW SCHOOL bus that pulled up in front of the Griffin house forty-five minutes later disgorged twenty chattering, laughing, hyperkinetic eight-year-olds. Dani stood on the bus steps, calling out instructions and admonitions while Anne and Harold greeted the children and tried to arrange them in some semblance of order. Bret stood a little to the side, looking confused and somewhat overwhelmed.

"All right," Dani called, clapping her hands for attention. "All right, you know the rules. Has everyone got his partner?"

There was a great deal of scrambling around, squealing and coattail pulling, followed by a chorus of "I do!" and "Here she is!" and "Miss Griffin, tell Tammy to stop holding my hand!"

Dani waited until they had quieted down. "Remember, stay ten feet behind the tractor. And what happens to anyone who runs or leaves the group?"

The consensus was that the offender would have to go back to the house or wait in the bus or something equally unpleasant.

"Jason, give Mr. Griffin the trees."

A proud little boy walked over to the wagon that was attached to the tractor and presented Harold with a flat of seedling pines. Harold made an appropriate fuss over them before settling them securely against the bed of the wagon. He then climbed onboard the tractor, started the ignition and raised his hand. "Wagons, ho!" he shouted.

The children loved that, and fell into place a safe distance behind the wagon as the tractor chugged down the path that led toward the woods at the back of the house.

Anne took up her place on the left flank of the group, and Dani fell behind, waving to Bret to join her. "Surprise," she said, her eyes sparkling as he came up to her. "Sorry I forgot to mention this last night, but I knew you wouldn't want to miss it."

"You didn't forget. You just knew if you warned me, I'd be sure to sleep late."

She gave him a playful punch in the ribs. "And I'd be sure to wake you up."

Bret looked wonderful today in one of her father's plaid flannel jackets, jeans and borrowed work boots. His hair was tousled and seemed to pick up sun highlights even through the dull, overcast sky, and his skin was roughened and weather chapped. Already, he had begun to lose that polished California boy look, and was beginning to resemble the Bret she had once known.

"So, now that I've been recruited," he said, "what am I supposed to do?"

"Just keep your eyes open—for trees and kids."

"I don't know. Twenty kids and four adults— there's something wrong with those odds."

She laughed. "Coward."

"Where are we going, anyway?"

"Where we always go. That pine meadow at the back of your place."

He repeated blankly, "My place?"

"You don't mind, do you?" she teased him. "Should we be paying you a finder's fee?"

He shook his head, looking a little distracted. "No, it's just that it sounded funny when you said that...my place. I'm not used to thinking of it like that."

"How do you think of it?" she asked curiously.

He hesitated, then shrugged. "The property, mostly. Or sometimes my folks' place. Not mine."

It struck Dani suddenly that there was something sad about that, almost lonely. Bret had deliberately distanced himself from what was rightfully his, he had practically made himself a self-proclaimed orphan, and she would never understand why. She wondered if even he did.

She wanted to slip her arm around him in a gesture of comfort, but wasn't sure how that would look to the children. There was no chance to pursue the subject further because just then Tommy Anderson hit Kathy Sewell and it was clear this expedition was not going to leave much time for socializing.

Dani was amazed and amused at how, after an initial awkwardness and pretended reluctance, Bret stepped in to help with the children as naturally as though he had spent half his life surrounded by noisy eight-year-olds. Dani had observed that it took most people, particularly unmarried men, some time to adjust to being around children, to try to find an attitude toward them with which they were comfortable. Bret didn't have that problem; he simply treated them as he would any other perfectly capable, reasoning human beings. Within twenty minutes, half the girls had a crush on him and the boys were hanging on his every word.

"Do you know something?" Dani commented when she caught up with him again. "I think you'd make a good daddy."

"No, I wouldn't."

"Why not?"

His eyes twinkled as he replied, deadpan, "Because I don't like kids."

"Oh, right." She smothered a grin. "Doesn't exactly fit in with your Hollywood image, does it?"

"Right." Then he lifted his face, grimacing a little as a flake of snow drifted down. "And neither does thrashing through the woods in the middle of a snowstorm."

Dani laughed and slipped her arm through his. "*I* think it's romantic," she declared. "I hope it snows and snows!"

Bret smiled down at her, and there was a tenderness in his eyes, a simple, unabashed pleasure at her touch, that made her feel warm all over. And then she was embarrassed because *romantic* was not what she had meant to say at all, but when he looked at her like that, she almost wished that he was someone different, or that she was, and that romance was what they both had on their minds . . . she didn't know what she wished.

It was a confusing, tangled train of thought that made her look away from him uncomfortably, and she was glad that she did not have the opportunity to pursue it further. Just then, the children noticed the snow and an excited clamor grew up. Dani dropped Bret's arm and moved forward, leading the children in a rollicking rendition of "Frosty the Snowman."

The snow was not heavy, nor was there enough accumulation to do more than dust the tops of the tall grasses and frost the branches of the pines. A gentle mist of white, however, was all that was needed to add authenticity to the search for the perfect tree, and Dani didn't care what Bret said: it *was* romantic. The entire day was. This time with the children in the woods was always her favorite field trip of the year, and having Bret here made it twice as special—almost magical. Having Bret here made *her* feel like a child again with the entire world laid open at her feet, full of possibilities and bursting with promise. Having Bret here made everything seem right again, and she had not felt that sense of rightness since . . . since the last time he had been here. She realized with a sudden pang how much he had taken out of her life when he went away. And how unfair it was that he couldn't stay.

Harold was an absolute wizard when it came to children, and managed—by some method Dani never could figure out—to get them all to agree enthusiastically on the perfect tree, which also happened to be one he had marked weeks ago for that very purpose. He took saw in hand and everyone cheered and applauded as the small tree fell, then Bret helped him load it into the wagon.

"Well, that's that," Bret declared, rubbing the pine sap off his hands. "One less unsightly pine cluttering up the forest. Let's get out of here before all these little darlings catch cold."

Dani laughed. "What a wimp! It must be all that California wine in your blood. We're not even half-finished yet. We've got two more trees to cut—one for my folks, and one for me."

Bret groaned and shivered elaborately. "I should've known. Nothing's ever easy with you in charge."

Two more trees fell to the blade of the hand saw, both were loaded safely onto the wagon, and then as Anne spread out a picnic of hot chocolate and sandwiches on the tail board of the wagon, the tree-planting ceremony began.

Each year, a boy and a girl were chosen to do the honors, and this year Jimmy Skinner and Amy Carney had been elected. Amy carried the little box of saplings proudly, but Jimmy complained, "How come we have to plant trees, anyway? There's nothing but trees everywhere you look. My daddy says you can't grow rocks out here for the trees."

Bret, who had taken the shovel from Harold to dig the six small holes, paused and grinned. But Dani explained patiently, "We always give back what we take from the land, Jimmy. You know that."

"But we only took three trees," Jimmy pointed out. "How come we have to plant six?"

"The other three trees are our Christmas gift to Mother Nature."

"I don't know what you're complaining about," Bret said. "You don't have to dig the holes. Come over here and give me a hand."

Jimmy pretended to be put out, but Dani could tell he was secretly pleased at being given a man's job. And Bret stepped back to let him do it, despite the fact that the holes were already deep enough for planting.

"I don't know why we have to put 'em way over here, anyway," said Jimmy, grunting a little as he dug the tip of the shovel into the frozen soil. "We should've put 'em near the creek, where the digging's easier."

Bret raised his eyebrows, but replied, "There are too many big oaks near the creek. They'd choke out the seedlings."

"Don't matter." Jimmy turned over another spade tip full of earth. "They're gonna freeze, anyhow."

Bret moved over to Dani and murmured, "Smart kid. I'd say he's got the makings of a farmer."

She shrugged and stuffed her hands into the pockets of her parka. "Seedlings are cheap, and replanting is a good habit for the kids to get into. Besides, some of them do make it through the winter—which is why we always plant more than we need. You'd be surprised."

Bret nodded toward the boy. "Who is he?"

"That's Jimmy Skinner," Dani replied. "I guess he did pick up a few things about farming from his father—like how hard this land is to work. Your dad always did say if there was a profit to be made in rocks and pines, he'd be rich."

Bret nodded absently, and Dani noticed that a shadow had fallen over his face.

"What?" she inquired, looking at him closely.

"Nothing." He glanced back at her. "You just reminded me of two unpleasant things I have to do. Call my office and go talk to Skinner. Will you come with me?"

"Do you mean now?"

"No, but maybe this weekend."

"Sure. I can understand why you wouldn't be looking forward to kicking your tenant out...." He scowled at her and she ignored him. "But why is calling your office so unpleasant?"

He looked surprised as he considered the question. "Maybe because I'm having so much fun freezing my butt off out here with you, I can hardly bear the thought of all that dreary sunshine I left behind?"

"Or maybe," she suggested, unable to keep from pushing just a little, "you're just beginning to realize what you really left behind here a long time ago."

Bret looked at her for a moment, and though his expression was unreadable, it made her heart beat just a little faster and for no reason whatsoever. And then he turned back to Jimmy.

"All right, friend," he called, "that looks deep enough." He went over to Amy, who stood ready with the box of seedlings. "Young lady, will you do the honors?"

DANI DISTRIBUTED peanut-butter-and-jelly sandwiches, paper cups of hot chocolate and homemade cookies, and Anne spread blankets and cushions beneath the shelter of the trees for the children to sit on. When everyone was settled down, they begged Dani for The Story, as they always did. Somehow, through the magic grapevine of childhood, rumors of The Story were passed down from generation to generation, so that every class was just as eager to hear it as the one before.

Dani brushed a light film of snow off a rock and sat down, cuddling a cup of chocolate with her gloved hands. Her eyes twinkled as she pretended to protest, "Oh, it's a dull story. You don't want to hear it."

"I want to hear about the bear!"

"I want to hear about the Indians!"

"But it's history," Dani insisted with a dismissing wave of her hand. "You don't want to hear about history when we're not in school."

"Tell us about the bear!"

Bret sat beside her on the rock, grinning. "Yeah, tell us about the bear."

Dani smiled and scooted over to make room for him, deliberately prolonging the suspense by drinking from her cup. Then she said, "Well, all right. But you have to be very quiet and still, and no throwing food."

"We will!"

"We won't!"

Twenty pairs of eyes turned expectantly on her as she began. "A long, long time ago, a man and a woman called Hannah and Zaccariah came all the way from Pennsylvania in a covered wagon."

"Like that wagon?" interrupted Billy Sims, pointing to the wagon that held the Christmas trees.

The other children shushed him, but Dani nodded. "A lot like that, except they put a roof on it with wire and canvas to keep the rain and wind out. Those kinds of wagons were called prairie schooners because, when a whole bunch of them moved through the tall grass on the prairie, they looked just like boats on the ocean, and *schooner* is another name for a boat. Now Hannah and Zac—we'll call him that for short—they came out here all by themselves, because that was in the time before many people knew about the good farm land out here, and they wanted to be the first to get here and start growing wheat and corn. And so they were. This whole state—" she made a wide sweeping gesture with her arm "—was big and empty, so empty, you can hardly imagine it, and hardly anybody lived here except prairie dogs and a few buffalo and bears... and Indians."

The snow made a tinkling sound as it struck the tops of the trees, but beneath their branches the children were dry and protected from the wind. Harold and Anne leaned back against the wagon with their arms around each other's waists, watching the scene benevolently. Bret sat close to Dani, munching a handful of cookies and sipping chocolate, keeping her warm. The children listened expectantly.

"Well," Dani went on, "they got here just about this time of year. It was cold, and snowing a lot harder than it is now. And it so happened that Hannah, Zac's wife, was going to have a baby—"

"And there was no room for her in the inn," piped up Tiffany Wales, and Dani smiled at her.

"There weren't even any inns," she said. "So you know what they had to do? They had to make a tent from the canvas that came off their wagon to live in until Zac could cut down enough trees to build a house. And they built their tent right over there—" she raised her arm and all eyes followed "—underneath that big oak tree.

"But first," she went on, "they had to find something to eat. They had used up most of their food coming out here, and Hannah didn't have anything left in her barrels except a handful of coffee, a scoop of flour, and a few beans. So all day, Zac would go off hunting while Hannah stayed here by the tent, chopping down branches to prop up against the tent to keep the wind out. How would you like to camp out here in the woods in the middle of the winter?"

Several boys volunteered enthusiastically that they'd like it just fine, but Dani assured them, "It was cold. And they were hungry. Do you know why?"

"Because old Zac wasn't much of a shot," murmured Bret, and Dani shot him a warning look.

"Because they used up all their beans," said one little girl.

"Because the animals were hiding," suggested another.

"That's right," Dani said. "It's winter, and you don't see many animals running around, do you? The smart ones are up in their nests, staying warm. So poor Zac and Hannah used up the last of their provisions, and they thought they were going to starve. Zac kept going out every day, looking for game, but he was getting weaker and weaker. Pretty soon, he wouldn't be able to hunt at all.

"And then one morning..." Dani paused for dramatic emphasis, her eyes sweeping the assembly. "Hannah got up and pushed back the flap of the tent and looked out. And there, right at her doorstep, was a haunch of venison, all ready to be cooked. And leading away from the meat were footprints in the snow."

"Indian footprints!"

"Bear footprints!"

Dani smothered a smile and went on. "That venison saved their lives. With something to eat, Zac got stronger and was able to hunt again. But they kept wondering—who had brought it to them? They were all alone here. Who had left the footprints in the snow?"

"A ghost," someone whispered.

"A spaceship man," suggested someone else.

"One day," Dani went on, "Zac managed to shoot a couple of squirrels. And you know what he did? He took one of them and tied it to a low branch of the oak tree. And the next morning, it was gone, with nothing left but footprints in the snow."

There were murmurs of awe among the children. Dani loved it.

"And so it went all winter," she continued. "Whenever Zac and Hannah thought they were surely going to starve, there would be a squirrel or a rabbit or a pile of winter berries left on their doorstep. And whenever Zac had a little luck at hunting, he would leave half of whatever he caught tied to the old oak tree for their mysterious visitor. And that way, they survived the winter.

"Then the snow began to thaw, and it was almost time for Hannah's baby to come. One day while Zac was out cutting trees, Hannah went down to the creek for water..."

"Long walk," commented Jimmy Skinner skeptically.

"Yes, it was," agreed Dani. "But people didn't have electric water pumps back then, and the only way to get water was to draw it from the creek with a bucket."

"Should've pitched their tent closer," Jimmy said.

The other children looked irritated, anxious to get on with the story, but Dani explained patiently, "If they had done that, the creek might have flooded when the snow melted and washed them both away."

Jimmy looked satisfied, and Dani continued with the story. "While Hannah was bent over, dipping the bucket in the water, she heard a rustling noise behind her. She looked up and—"

"A bear!"

"An Indian!"

"It was the biggest, meanest, *hungriest* looking bear you ever saw. This bear had been hibernating all winter, you know, and Hannah must have looked like she would make a pretty good breakfast, because he reared up on his hind legs—and when he did, he was almost twice as big as Hannah—and he let out a roar that shook the treetops, and he started charging toward her."

Her audience was spellbound, and Dani played it for all it was worth. "Poor Hannah. She screamed as loud as she could. She threw the water bucket at the bear, but it just bounced right off him, he didn't even seem to feel it. He just kept on coming. She tried to scramble up the bank and run away, but she fell down, and when she looked up, there was that bear still coming toward her. He was almost on her, with his big, yellow teeth gleaming, and his black claws stretched out...and all of a sudden, the bear stopped and fell down dead.

"Now, Zac had heard his wife scream, and about that time, he came bursting through the bushes with his shotgun in his hand, and he saw Hannah lying there on the ground where she had fallen. He ran over toward her and just about reached her when he heard a noise and he spun around. He was face-to-face with—" Dani paused for effect. "An Indian! And, oh, was this Indian a fearsome sight! His hair was all shaved off except for one long strip down the middle, and he had designs painted all over his face and feathers dangling in his ears and animal skins around his neck. He just stood there, frowning at Zac and looking as fierce and mean as the devil himself. Zac thought for sure both he and Hannah were goners, and he was so scared that when he lifted his gun and tried to aim, he couldn't even pull the trigger because his hands were shaking so badly."

Her audience was rapt, and Dani lowered her voice, leaning toward them a little as they leaned toward her. "Zac got the Indian in his sights. He put his finger on the trigger. He started to squeeze it. And then.... And then he noticed the bow in the Indian's hand, and the bear lying dead with an arrow through its heart. And he knew he'd almost made the biggest mistake of his life. He had almost shot the man who had kept them alive through the winter. The man who had left the footprints in the snow.

"The Indian's name was Walks-Among-Trees. Funny name, isn't it? But it sounded a lot prettier in Indian language. Walks-Among-Trees went home with Hannah and Zac, and that night, Hannah's baby was born. They named him Walker, after their new friend, who had saved their lives. And do you know who that baby Walker was? It was Mr. Underwood's great-great-great grandfather."

There was a chorus of "Wow!" and "That's great!" and "Is that true, Mr. Underwood? Is it really true?"

Bret looked somewhat embarrassed to find himself the unwitting star of the story, but he replied, "If your teacher says it's true, you'd better believe it. Every word."

And he murmured in Dani's ear, "I don't think there were any bears in this part of the country back then."

She widened her eyes at him. "Are you calling your own grandmother a liar?"

He grinned. "You are amazing. Absolutely amazing."

Dani gave him a flirtatious toss of her head and replied, "And it's about time you realized it, too." She jumped lightly to the ground and brushed off the back of her coat. "All right, children, finish up your lunches. You know what to do with your trash, don't you?''

Anne was already passing among them with a plastic bag, but most of the children had been so entranced by the story, they had not even begun their lunches yet. Dani didn't rush them. She was no more anxious to get back to the schoolroom than they were. She walked out of the shelter of the trees, tilting her face up to catch the sprinkles of snow, and thought about Hannah and Zaccariah Underwood, who had come here so long ago and endured so much hardship for the sake of this land. On days like this, they were so close, she could almost touch them.

Bret stood beside her. ''If they had the whole state to choose from,'' he commented, following her thoughts, ''looks like they could have picked a better piece of land than this one.''

Dani shot him a dry look. ''They did, as you know perfectly well. This whole county and more was Underwood land at one time or another.''

''Figures they'd end up with the only uncultivatable plot this side of the Rockies. But, then, what can you expect from a family that started out with a couple of greenhorns who didn't even have enough sense to bring provisions with them to last through the winter?''

''Honestly, Bret, you're impossible. Don't you have any pride in your heritage at all?''

''Nope,'' he replied cheerfully.

She caught the glint in his eye and knew that he was teasing her, but the fact mollified her only slightly.

''You're a disgrace to your name,'' she grumbled.

"I do my best."

Dani's eyes moved to the old oak tree, and she tried not to be too irritated with Bret about his cavalier attitude toward a past that, to her, was more magical than Christmas. As close as they were, there were some things about him she would never understand, and knowing that disturbed her.

But suddenly, she caught his hand. "Bret, look!"

He followed her upraised arm in some confusion. "What?"

"Mom, Dad," Dani called over her shoulder, "watch the kids for a minute, will you? We'll be right back." She tugged at Bret's hand.

"What?" he demanded. "Where are we going?"

"Mistletoe!" she exclaimed, and she broke into a run, pulling Bret across the snow-dusted field beside her.

Chapter Seven

The mistletoe was nestled in the fork of a thick branch midway up the oak tree. Dani stopped beneath it, panting a little as she pointed upward. "Right up there, do you see? Climb up and get it for me, will you Bret?"

He turned an incredulous gaze on her. "Oh, yeah, right. Just shimmy a hundred feet up a tree in the middle of a snow storm."

"It's not a hundred feet!" Then she said impatiently, "Oh, all right, I'll do it." She reached for a low branch of the tree. "Just give me a boost."

He stared at her for a moment, then announced, "You're crazy." He took her shoulders and moved her firmly aside, grabbing hold of the branch himself. "I'll probably break my neck." He swung himself up.

"Be careful," Dani said, and he spared her a dark look as he reached for a handhold on the next branch.

Dani stepped back, clasping her hands behind her back, tilting her head back to follow his progress. "Do you know the legend of the mistletoe?" she said conversationally.

The branches creaked and rustled with the remnants of a few dead leaves as he made his way upward. "Yeah, it has to do with somebody getting murdered, doesn't it?"

"It does not."

"Sure it does. The man who shot Achilles in the heel used a mistletoe arrow, and the stuff has been killing innocent men who climb up slippery trees ever since."

She choked back a giggle. "That's the most unromantic thing I've ever heard."

"You want romantic? I'll tell you what romantic is. Romantic is Carmel Beach at sunset. Romantic is sitting by a fire with a glass of wine. Romantic is not—"

A branch snapped suddenly and Dani's breath caught in her throat, her hand going up automatically as though to shield him from a fall. But Bret continued easily, "I repeat, romantic is *not* freezing to death in the top of a tree trying to snag mistletoe for some...silly...woman."

The last few words were punctuated with grunts of exertion as Bret strained to reach the cluster of mistletoe and detach it from the branch. Suddenly, the cluster came free and tumbled through the tree limbs, raining berries and leaves and fragile, broken stems amidst Dani's shouts of delight.

She stretched her hands upward to catch the cluster, laughing. "My hero!" she called.

Bret grinned down at her, his feet braced on a sturdy limb and his hand balanced on a branch above him. Dani thought if ever there had been a picture-perfect portrait of a hero, it would be him. His hair frosted with snow, his eyes twinkling like sunshine, his broad shoulders and well-fitting jeans...he looked like a woodland god, poised up there in the tree, master of all he surveyed. The sight of him made Dani's heart catch for a minute, like a schoolgirl struck by the glimpse of a fantasy come to life.

He began to descend the branches, and in a moment, he sprang to the ground beside her. His face was slightly flushed with exertion, and his eyes danced with sparks of light.

"Well done!" she said, applauding him. "I'm glad to see you haven't forgotten everything I taught you."

"I'd make old Walks-Among-Trees proud, wouldn't I?" he agreed. "You've got that junk all in your hair."

"*That's* the mistletoe legend I was referring to," she replied pertly. She reached up her hand to pull the stems and leaves out of her hair, but Bret moved to do the same thing at the same time, and their fingers became entangled.

He said softly, "Do you mean the one about kissing?"

Their eyes met. Their fingers twined together lightly and did not move. The moment between them was poised and expectant, and either one of them, with a word, a breath, a shifted gaze, could have broken it. But no power on earth could have persuaded Dani to move away from Bret then.

She whispered, "Absolutely."

Their lips touched, as they had done many times before, but both of them knew from the first instant that this time was different. The memory of Bret's eyes just before he lowered his face to hers swirled in Dani's head—the surprise, the quick darkening of intensity, the same spark of irresistible excitement and curiosity that quickened in Dani's own veins. Her heartbeat took on a breathless, leaping rhythm even before his lips touched hers and when they did, it was with a rush of heat and weakness she had not expected.

His kiss went through her like something liquid and shimmering, stroking nerve endings into a sudden shock of awareness, flooding her with warmth, taking away her breath. Not the kiss of a friend, not a brief affectionate embrace, but a natural melding of man and woman, a chain reaction of swift-flowing sparks, of bodies coming together in perfect chemistry and muted wonder. Dani realized dizzily that she had waited all her life for this kiss.

There was surprise, yes, for both of them, but it was more like something that caught them off guard than something that was completely unexpected, for they both must have known deep in their hearts and secret memories that it would be like this. Every sensory receptor in Dani's body seemed to suddenly energize and flare to life. She could hear the soft whisper of the snow and feel its feathery touch as it drifted down on her hair. She could smell the crisp scent of pine and the subtle, woodsy aroma of mistletoe and Bret's warm, quietly masculine fragrance—like sunshine and tanned skin. She could feel the silky texture of her own hair against her cheek and each individual tendon and bone of Bret's hand, clasped around hers. The slightly coarse texture of his chin, the cottony softness of his jacket, the cold air around them and the pocket of heat they created between them, and Bret, who invaded every part of her with his touch, his kiss.

She could feel his restraint, even as she struggled with her own. Their entwined fingers, which were resting against the curve of Dani's neck, tightened briefly and then slowly, deliberately released. And even as they separated, the kiss seemed to linger, breaths mingling and heat flowing as they gradually, a fraction of an inch at a time, moved apart.

Dani's heart was pounding so forcefully that she thought he must surely be able to hear it, or see it, shaking her rib cage. She could feel the color staining her cheeks and see it in his, and for the longest time, all she could do was stare at him. She saw in his eyes the same kind of slow, pleasured astonishment that she felt, as though he couldn't believe what had just happened or understand why, as though he didn't know what to say or feel or whether he should apologize or she should. . . .

And she wouldn't. Her head was spinning, and her emotions were like a tangled skein of yarn that grew more tightly knotted the harder she tried to sort them out. She only knew that she could not think about it now. She could not risk this moment.

She turned away, brushing the last of the mistletoe out of her hair. "We'd better be getting back," she said brightly. "They'll send out a search party."

He didn't answer.

She glanced at him quickly and made no effort to disguise the pleading in her eyes. *Not now, Bret. Don't talk about it now. . . .*

But aloud she said, with that same false, almost frenetic cheer, "Tree-trimming party tonight. First course at Mom's, dessert at my house. No begging off. It's a tradition."

He hesitated, and then he forced a smile. "Right. Wouldn't miss it."

He dropped a hand atop her shoulder in an exaggerated gesture of companionability, and together, they walked back to the others.

THE AFTERNOON PASSED IN A blur of schoolroom colors, of construction-paper chains and the smell of wheat paste, popcorn strings and the sound of childish excitement. Dani felt a semblance of that excitement inside, and it had nothing to do with the pine tree in the corner that was gradually transformed with paper birds and homemade ornaments into a Christmas spectacle. She felt feverish, a little breathless, distracted and delighted. She also felt disturbed and confused and very guilty.

She wasn't guilty for having kissed Bret, nor was she sorry. She wasn't even guilty for having enjoyed it. And that, in truth, was exactly what she did feel guilty about. Because in that one delirious moment when the whole world seemed to open beneath her feet, past and present flowing together to form nothing but an endless vista of possibilities, she had not thought of anyone or anything at all except Bret. And that was very wrong. And very confusing.

After school, she held a rehearsal for the play, but it wasn't easy to keep her mind on what she was doing. Finally, she asked Paula to take over and she went to call Todd. The sound of his voice should have been reassuring, but it wasn't.

"Christmas party tonight," she announced brightly. "Want to come?"

"What? Nobody told me. Or did I forget?"

"Well, it's not really a party," she admitted. "Just tree trimming and eggnog with the folks. But I'd really like you to come, Todd. We've never done that together."

There was a pause. "Ah, honey, you know I'd like to, but it's kind of short notice. I was planning to work late."

Dani tried to feel disappointment. She really did. "No problem, I understand. Just thought it was worth a try. We'll miss you."

"Not as much as I'll miss you."

She forced a smile, even though he couldn't see.

"Say, how did I do last night?"

She blinked. "What?"

"With your friend. Did I pass?"

She swallowed hard and pushed the smile back into her voice. "With flying colors."

"Ha! The master at work!"

"Listen," she said quickly, "I've got a stage full of kids waiting for me, and you need to get back to work. Call me this weekend, okay?"

"Sure thing. Bye, sweetheart."

She went back to the cafeteria, feeling no calmer than when she had left, yet with a strange pricking emptiness inside she couldn't quite explain.

She loved Todd. She knew she did. Why should anything be different just because Bret had kissed her?

No... because they had kissed each other, willingly, thoroughly and as adults. Because they had wanted to. And they had enjoyed it. More than enjoyed it...

She cut rehearsal short and promised herself she would make it up next week. Pauline gathered up her sheet music and came over to Dani as she was stuffing her papers harum-scarum back into her briefcase.

"You feeling okay?"

Dani wouldn't look at her. "Why? Don't I look okay?"

"You look like a woman with something on her mind." Pauline sat down at the small table, hands folded patiently. "So, what is it?"

Dani hesitated, then sighed. She sat down, too. "Pauline," she said carefully, "with men, even when they're married—happily married—they can still be attracted to other women, can't they?"

"Oh-oh." Pauline's eyes rounded. "Todd's got a roving eye already?"

Dani shook her head impatiently. "No, what I'm trying to say is—do you think it's possible, even if you're really in love with somebody, to be—well, attracted to someone else?"

"Of course, it is," Pauline responded immediately. "That's what God made fantasies for."

Dani tried to keep the anxiety out of her voice. "And it's okay. I mean, it's perfectly normal."

Her friend shrugged. "Sure it is. I don't care if I was married to a guy with the sex appeal of a rock star and the sensitivity of a talk-show host, if some twenty-three-year-old Adonis walks by in a French bikini, I'm going to look."

"And lust?"

. She grinned. "And lust."

Dani took a breath. That was all it was, and it was completely understandable. Bret was an incredibly attractive man; what woman wouldn't, if given half a chance, succumb to his charms? Could she be blamed for her curiosity, hormones or whatever impulse had prompted her to step into his embrace? There was nothing to be ashamed of. It had all been perfectly harmless.

Pauline reached out and patted Dani's hand. "Listen, you want some advice? You're not married yet. You're not even engaged. Let Todd get it out of his system. As long as he's just *attracted* to other women, neither one of you has anything to be worried about. But if it's more than that...well, he—and you—deserve the chance to find out. You know what I mean?"

Dani nodded slowly. *If it's more than that...*

Pauline grinned and got to her feet. "This from a woman who's been divorced twice. You sure know where to go for advice, friend. Let me know if I can do anything else to help."

"Thanks, Pauline," Dani murmured absently. "I'll see you tomorrow."

Pauline laughed and waved on her way out the door. "I hope not! Tomorrow's Saturday."

Dani was thoughtful but a great deal more composed as she made her way home. She had never been given to self-deception, and she was not going to try to convince herself now that what had happened between her and Bret was an accident, an aberration, something to be forgotten and ignored. The truth was, she had wanted his kiss, she had not turned away from it, and it had been wonderful. And the further truth was that it was only natural that she would want to know whether or not anything remained of the old school crushes she had had on him. She had her answer now, and it shouldn't surprise her. Bret was very sexy; he always had been and always would be. There was nothing wrong about the surface attraction she felt for him . . . as long as that was all it was. And that *was* all it was.

She was almost sure of it.

BRET REMEMBERED VERY well the traditional tree-trimming buffet at the Griffin household. Cold cuts, sliced pumpernickel, homemade bread-and-butter pickles—anything that could be eaten with the fingers between trips to the ornament boxes, because Anne had learned early on that it was impossible to keep the children seated at the table for the length of a meal when there was a tree waiting in the living room and boxes full of Christmas magic to be unearthed. There were no children anymore, but the excitement was just as high as it had been twenty years ago, and the warmth of memories was contagious.

Bret stayed busy in the kitchen with his own soon-to-be-famous eggnog recipe while Dani helped her mother tack evergreen boughs and bright red bows over the doorways and along the banister, and Harold grumbled and mumbled over the strings of lights. Bret assured himself that he wasn't avoiding Dani. There was nothing to feel awkward about. He wasn't ashamed of what had happened beneath the oak tree, and he wasn't going to apologize for it.

The last thing he intended to do was apologize for it.

He carried the big bowl of eggnog into the living room and announced, "All right, friends and neighbors, prepare yourselves for the taste sensation of a lifetime. From your own living room to the shelves of finer food stores everywhere, this may be your last chance."

"After a buildup like that, how can we refuse?" declared Anne.

Harold abandoned a tangled string of lights and agreed, "Sounds like just what the doctor ordered to get me through the night."

Dani picked her way carefully around the strings of lights and boxes of ornaments spread out over the floor. "Don't believe a word of it. He used a mix."

Bret pretended insult. "If you were a man, I'd call you out for that."

Dani made a face at him.

The same old Dani... and not. Just looking at her filled him with delight, as it always did. She was wearing faded jeans that hugged her thighs and her rounded bottom in an intimate, hard-to-ignore way, and a red sweatshirt with a Santa face painted in white on the front. Her hair swung in a glossy pony tail that fell just below her ears, and her eyes twinkled with the familiar playful mischief. But were her eyes a little brighter when she looked at him now, her cheeks a little more flushed? Bret knew it probably wasn't right, but he found himself hoping so.

He ceremoniously dipped the thick creamy mixture into cups, receiving the elder Griffins' enthusiastic compliments and Dani's noncommittal, "Not bad...for a California boy." They filled paper plates with selections from the buffet, and Bret sat on the floor beside a cardboard box marked "Xmas," pulling out ornaments between bites of ham and cheese.

"I think we should have gotten a bigger tree," he commented.

Dani sat cross-legged on the floor before him, balancing her plate on one knee. "Some of them are for my tree," she told him. "Mom's going through this designer phase—she only uses pink and red on her tree."

"And it's always perfectly beautiful," Anne said proudly.

"Yeah, for a department-store window," Dani shot back. "I prefer a more eclectic look."

Bret chuckled. "You would."

They smiled at each other, caught in one of those moments of perfect understanding that only a lifetime of shared memories can produce, an intimacy of knowledge that encompasses good and bad, faults and weaknesses, and accepts without question. That was what they had, Bret and Dani, and it had survived far more challenging episodes than a kiss in the snow. They smiled at each other, and suddenly, everything was all right.

Bret pulled out a ceramic bell ornament, a little chipped in places, its paint fading. "Your tree," he decided.

"Right." Dani dug into the box and came up with a pink velvet bow carefully wrapped in tissue. "Mom's tree."

They began to sort the ornaments into two separate piles, and Dani said, "You look ten years younger."

He looked at her in surprise. "What?"

"Than when you first got here," she explained. "Well, maybe not ten years, but two, at least."

Her mother laughed, but agreed, "She's right, Bret. I think the country air is good for you."

He shrugged. "I don't know about that. But I do know I've had more fun today than I have in a long time." He was surprised to hear himself say that, even more surprised to realize it was true. All these hokey Christmas traditions, the kids with all their noise and unpredictability, the snow falling in the woods and the smell of fresh-cut pine . . . and that wondrous, joyous moment of discovery and disbelief when he had taken Dani in his arms. It was all part of the magic, not one element separable from the others. It was a package of memories, and he knew he would be able to taste the texture of this day for years to come.

He was aware of Dani looking at him thoughtfully, but she did not look as surprised by his admission as he was. And, of course, she wouldn't be. He always had said Dani knew him better than he knew himself.

Then Anne said, "What do you usually do for Christmas, Bret?"

He chuckled and shook his head. "I'm embarrassed to say."

The solemn look vanished from Dani's face as she teased, "It's something lewd. I knew it would be."

"Dani!" Anne reprimanded.

Bret grinned at her. "I go sailing," he confessed. "I know it sounds pagan, but that's what I do—when I can take the time off from work, that is. This friend of mine has a boat, and hardly anybody else is on the water on Christmas day, so..."

"All by yourself?" inquired Anne, looking distressed.

"Usually."

"All alone in a boat on Christmas day...that's the saddest thing I ever heard."

"Oh, leave the boy alone, Mother Hen," Harold told her. "A man likes to get off by himself once in a while. Many's a Christmas afternoon I've spent out in a deer stand—"

"But you always had your family, and the tree in the morning, and Christmas dinner together..." Anne broke off, shaking her head. "I'm sorry Bret, I am an interfering old mother hen. But it *is* sad, I don't care what anybody says. And if I had known that's how you spent Christmas, I would've made sure you came home a long time before now."

Dani grinned at Bret. "That's right, Oliver Twist, play it for all it's worth. Poor abandoned boy, all alone on some playboy's yacht, nothing but champagne and smoked salmon for his Christmas dinner, nothing but the false glitter of the distant lights of Catalina to guide him...."

Bret threw a handful of tinsel at her. "I'm starting to remember why I prefer spending Christmas by myself."

The tinsel caught like stardust in her hair, and Dani pulled it out, throwing it back at him strand by strand until Anne broke up the fight with some exasperated comment about children.

It was Christmas like a dozen other Christmases before it, with Harold admonishing Bret to "Check this bulb—no, the other one" and Anne scolding Dani for tossing the tinsel on by handfuls instead of draping it one strand at a time, and Dani finally giving up and going to the piano, keeping them all entertained with Christmas carols while the work went on much faster without her. Then there was the magical moment when the room lights were turned out and the Christmas tree was lit, and when they stood bathed in the blinking pink-and-silver glow of the tree, Dani's hand slipped quite naturally into Bret's and she leaned her head against his shoulder. A magical moment.

They boxed up the leftover ornaments and lights and trooped across the snow-frosted lawn to Dani's house, where they began it all again. They ate homemade ginger cookies—one of Dani's specialties—and drank cinnamon-spiced coffee and hot chocolate. Dani thoroughly enjoyed herself as she gave specific orders as to how *her* tree was to be decorated, which was as gaily haphazard as possible.

It was after eleven when the elder Griffins, pleading exhaustion, left Bret and Dani to put the finishing touches on the tree—the last few ornaments to be hung, the last few handfuls of tinsel to be tossed. Bret sat on the floor with a fire crackling in the grate behind him and the smell of pine filling the room, as he threaded a hanger into a gray felt mouse. The little ornament must have been twenty years old, its whiskers were crushed and one ear was missing, but Dani insisted absolutely nothing was to be left in the box.

"What does your mother want for Christmas?" Bret asked. "I want to get her something really nice."

"A pressure cooker." Dani took aim at a high branch and tossed a handful of tinsel as though it were a softball. "She wants a new pressure cooker. They have them on sale at the hardware store."

Bret made a face. "That's no kind of present for a woman."

"What's wrong with it?"

"I'm not getting her a pressure cooker."

"That's what she wants."

"I'm not getting her a pressure cooker."

Dani shrugged. "There's always that diamond bracelet she's had her eye on in the Tiffany catalog."

"I'm serious."

"So am I. A pressure cooker is about the best you're going to do around here. Todd's taking Mom and me to Centerville for shopping next weekend. Do you want to come?"

Bret placed the mouse on a low branch and reached for the last ornament. It was a miniature silver bell that made a tinny tinkling sound in his hand. There must have been three dozen such bells on Dani's tree.

"Why Centerville?" he inquired. "It's not much bigger than Clayville."

"Oh, that's right, you haven't been there since they redid it. It's the cutest little tourist trap now—all the storefronts are done in turn-of-the-century, and the streets are cobblestone. It's a great place to find all kinds of unusual gifts." She stepped back to observe the tree. "Todd keeps trying to talk to the town council about doing something like that here. It's really been great for Centerville's economy. The only trouble is, we don't have anything to make a tourist attraction out of."

Bret felt himself tensing every time she mentioned Todd's name, but she seemed perfectly unselfconscious about it. And that was sensible. The kiss they had shared that afternoon was an accident, a harmless exchange of affection that had drifted, for a moment, beyond the borders of friendship, and he would have felt terrible if Dani allowed herself to feel guilty about it. There was no reason at all he should feel hurt that she appeared to have forgotten it, but he did not want to talk about Todd any longer.

He stood up to place the bell on the end of a middle branch. It made a pleasant jingling sound and winked with sparks of firelight as it bounced on the branch. "You and your bells," he said. "I don't guess I ever think of Christmas that I don't think of bells."

"Okay, the lights," she said excitedly. She ran to the switch and turned off the other lights. "Plug them in."

For a moment, the room was illuminated only by the glow of the fire and the glitter of tinsel, and then Bret made the connection between outlet and plug. The tree sprang to life in a twinkling, blinking network of red, blue, yellow and orange.

Dani stood beside him. "Now *that's* a tree," she declared in satisfaction.

He chuckled. "I suppose it would be unnecessary to point out that having two trees—one for you and one for your folks—is a little silly. You can only have Christmas in one place.''

''Just another symbol of my independence,'' she said. ''Besides, I like it—I like decorating it and looking at it. And, tell the truth, my tree *is* prettier than Mom's, isn't it?''

Dani's tree was gaudy and overdone, so heavily decorated in places that the branches sagged. There was no color scheme or theme, just a gay collection of random memories and treasured tradition without order or plan, spontaneous, colorful and energetic, just as Christmas was supposed to be. Just as Dani was.

Bret grinned at her. ''It's you,'' he admitted.

''There's some coffee left. Do you want some?'' She started toward the kitchen.

''No, I've still got some cocoa left.'' He sank to the hearth and picked up his half-empty cup. ''I wouldn't mind another one of those cookies, though.''

''You're going to get fat.''

''No chance, the way I've been working.'' He propped a cushion behind his shoulders and leaned back against the warm stones of the hearth, drowsy and content. ''I never thought I'd say this, but that's what I miss about farm life. Getting outdoors, doing something with my hands and my own two legs.... Not that cutting down trees is a particularly noble calling, but that was fun today. And tonight, I'm going to go to bed tired, which is something I haven't done in a long time. Working out in the gym just isn't the same.''

Dani placed the platter of cookies on the hearth and sat in front of him on the floor, drawing up her knees, sipping her coffee. "Is that why you've been unhappy?" she asked. "Is it your work?"

He hesitated and she thought he wouldn't answer. Then he glanced down at the cocoa in his cup and replied, "I guess. That and midlife crisis."

"You're too young to have midlife crisis."

He sipped the cocoa. "It's not just work. Nothing is turning out like I planned."

"You have everything you wanted," Dani reminded him. "You wanted to be successful, in charge, make lots of money...."

He looked at her thoughtfully. "Is that what I wanted?"

"That's what you told me."

"Then I guess you're right. I must be happy."

"Why did you come back here, Bret?" she asked gently.

He could have told her then. The firelight, the twinkling, dancing glow of the Christmas tree, and Dani sitting so close, looking at him so tenderly...it was the perfect time. But the taste of her lips was still too fresh, the firelight was too soothing, and she was too lovely.

He said, "I'm not sure." He put the cup on the hearth. "But I know I'd better be getting to bed now, before I fall asleep on your floor. We'd have a hell of a time explaining *that* to your parents."

He started to rise, and Dani had every intention of walking him to the door and telling him good-night. But instead, her hand came out to rest upon his knee, staying his movement, and once it was done, she wasn't sorry. It seemed that everything that had happened today, everything, perhaps, that had happened from the moment she looked up from her schoolroom to see him standing there, had been leading to this moment—this quiet warmth, this understanding, this intimacy. She could not let him go. She could not pretend that they had not been on the verge of discovering something new this afternoon. She couldn't pretend it had never happened. If she ignored it, it would haunt her the rest of her life. If she denied it, she would never know for sure what it was she was hiding... and she simply had to know. Because wondering would cloud her future for as long as she lived.

Bret looked down at her hand, resting lightly on his thigh, and she could feel his muscles tense involuntarily. Her heart was beating hard and fast. She said softly, "Bret, did you ever wonder... what it might have been like between us?"

He looked at her and she saw surprise there, followed by uncertainty and a jumble of possible answers flickering through his mind, some flippant, some not. He swallowed. He said uncomfortably, "Come on, Dani, it's late."

His refusal to answer, instead of frustrating her, only made her heart beat faster with a secret, unexpected excitement. He made no move to rise, and she held his gaze, insisting on an answer.

And eventually, he gave her one because they could not lie to each other. He glanced away briefly, then back at her again. His voice was a little husky as he answered, "Of course, I have. I spent most of puberty wondering."

"Lately, I mean." She felt breathless. "When we were adults."

His eyes were steady, troubled, yet lit with a dozen conflicting little flames. Dani was lost in his gaze, seeing things there she had never expected to see before, uncertain and exhilarated and a little scared.

"I've thought about it," he said lowly. His words were rushed, almost clipped, but the tenor of them went through Dani with a little thrill, like wind moving through the aspens. "You're a sexy woman, Dani, I've always thought so. Of course I'm attracted to you, any man would be. And your Todd is a lucky man. And I don't think we should talk about this anymore."

He thought the mention of Todd's name would break the spell, but it didn't. He started to get up, but Dani's eyes held him, glowing and intense in the firelight, her fingers like a brand on his thigh. He couldn't move.

She said softly, unblinkingly, "Bret... kiss me."

His heart lurched in his chest. He said, with difficulty, "Dani, listen. This afternoon—"

"I know." Her words came out in a rush, backed with breathlessness, and he could see the color in her cheeks that was more than the glow of the fire. "I know, it shouldn't have happened, and maybe it was a mistake, and maybe it was just the snow and the romance of it all, but I've got to know for sure, don't you see? I can't spend the rest of my life wondering if I imagined it, I've got to—"

He had every intention of getting up and walking away; he even moved to do so, but suddenly, before she had even finished speaking, his mouth was on hers. And this time, there was no restraint; there couldn't have been even if he had wanted it.

Dani knew the minute he touched her that the kiss they had shared that afternoon was not an accident, a mistake or a trick of imagination...and she must have known all along that the only mistake was in coming to him again, risking the fire again. But she was as helpless as any moth that had ever danced around the flame as the brightness flared inside her, as Bret's mouth covered hers.

There was no gentleness this time, no hesitance or uncertainty. Bret slid down on the floor beside her, and his hands were hard on her back as he pulled her close. Her lips parted with a helpless breath and she tasted his tongue; she felt the hot, dark flush of passion and the secret invasion, the power and the wonder of physical intimacy. She was trembling inside, hot and dizzy and breathless with the suddenness of sensory shock. And only then did she realize how many times she had dreamed it might be like this with Bret.

Her hands moved along his arms and to his shoulders, then dropped weakly to rest against his chest. She could feel the strain of his muscles and the beating of his heart. She could feel the heat and the dampness of his skin against hers, the tingling and hardening of her nipples in response to him. And no, it did not feel like a betrayal. It felt as right and as natural as anything she had ever done in her life. And it was for that reason that it was so frightening.

Bret broke away almost roughly. His hands tightened for a moment on her arms and then released them abruptly. Dani could hear his unsteady breathing through the roaring in her head, and she felt weak and ill with the sudden absence of him. It was a moment before she could make herself open her eyes and look at him.

His face was flushed and sheened with perspiration, his eyes dark and quick with passion he could not hide. Dani knew that look. She had just never expected to see it on Bret's face. And she knew the look was reflected on her own. The thrill of need, the shock of wonder, the question...

The question that had only one answer.

Bret looked away from her. He said in an almost steady voice, "I trust the experiment was a success."

Dani caught her breath on a sudden stab of hurt and brought her fingers to her mouth. Her lips felt swollen, still damp with his moisture. She could still taste him inside her, still feel the gentle abrasion of his skin on her cheek. All she wanted to do was to lean her head against his chest, to feel the comfort of his arms around her. She was in tumult inside; she needed him. But he was the last person to whom she could turn now.

She whispered, "It—it wasn't an experiment."

He turned on her harshly. "What was it, then? A comparison test?"

She saw the flash of remorse on his face even as the words were spoken, even as she pressed her lips together against the shock, the pain. And then, he stood abruptly.

"I'd better go," he mumbled, not looking at her.

Dani's limbs were still trembling as she stood up, her chest still aching. But her heart was pounding now with alarm, with emptiness, with fear. "Bret—don't be mad."

"I'm not mad."

He went to the coatrack and fumbled for his coat. Dani followed him quickly, touching his arm. His muscles jerked as though she had burned him, and his jaw tightened. And then his shoulders forcibly relaxed. He retrieved his coat, but he wouldn't look at her.

"I'm not mad," he repeated more evenly. "I'm embarrassed, okay? And sorry, because I don't want you to think—"

"I won't," she insisted quickly, ready to promise him anything, ready to plead for anything, as long as he didn't despise her for this, as long as he didn't leave her with the residue of his anger filling up the ache in her chest.

He looked at her then. There was strain in the tight lines of his face and sorrow in his eyes and confusion and an awful kind of defeat. "Look," he said with difficulty. "It was a mistake coming back here. I've got things going on in my life that you don't understand—that even I don't understand. It's not fair to make you the victim of them. I think...I think it's probably best if I just went home. Back to Los Angeles."

The slamming of her heart was like an explosion in her chest. For a moment, she couldn't get her breath. "No!" she gasped.

And then she had to turn away because she didn't want him to see the desperation in her eyes or the struggle it took to compose herself. She pushed her fingers through the hair at her temples, drawing a deep breath, trying to marshal her wildly crashing thoughts and emotions. Finally, she managed to say tightly, "Don't do this to me—to us. Don't make me think I've driven you away and make us remember this like a—like a wall that will be between us for the rest of our lives."

She took another breath and made herself turn to face him. Her cheeks were scorched. She felt miserable and hurting inside. "Bret, I'm the one who's sorry. It was my fault, and it was stupid, and ... don't let it come between us. Stay and enjoy Christmas and— Can't we forget it ever happened?"

Even as she spoke, she knew the impossibility of the suggestion, and his sober gaze reflected it. "No," he replied. "I don't think so."

Because neither of them wanted to. Because forgetting was the last thing Dani wanted to do, even though it made no sense, even though there was no point to remembering, even though it complicated her life unbearably.... She couldn't forget.

Her fists closed at her sides to still the trembling and she said, "Then—we can deal with it. We're both adults. These things happen."

The fleeting corner of a smile caught his lips, then vanished. And his eyes darkened again with the weight of anxiety. "Dani," he said quietly, "you've got your life together now. I'd never forgive myself if I thought I did anything to mess it up."

She shook her head adamantly. "You won't. You didn't. I promise."

The anxiety didn't fade. "I don't want anything to change between us, Dani."

She took an unsteady breath. "It won't, unless we let it."

She watched him, her breath stilled in her throat and expectation straining every muscle, hoping the words would be enough. Then at last, he nodded and slipped on his jacket. He even managed a smile, though it didn't quite reach his eyes. "I don't really want to go back to Los Angeles," he said. "Not before your mom's Christmas turkey, anyway."

Dani returned his smile, weak with relief. "Good night, Bret."

Any other time, he would have kissed her goodnight or she would have reached for him. But this time, he merely opened the door, said, "Lock up behind me," and then didn't look at her again as he left.

Dani closed the door and leaned against it, staring blankly at the shifting, dancing glow of the Christmas-tree lights. Their last words seemed to echo hollowly around the room, empty reassurances, frail comforts. She couldn't forget, not if she lived to be a hundred would she forget the way it felt to be in Bret's arms; she would dream about it, she would muse about it, she would grow hot thinking about it at unexpected moments of the day, and she would yearn over it for a long, long time. Everything was changed. She knew that.

And she suspected Bret knew it, too.

Chapter Eight

Bret walked over to the Skinner place—his old house—by himself the next morning. He followed the path through the woods they had taken the day before with the children, even though there was a shorter route across the fields that he and Dani used to take on their bicycles. But to go that way meant going past her house, and he didn't want to take the chance of running into her.

He couldn't believe that he was up before she was for once, and in fact, thought that was unlikely. She had probably been awake for hours, just as he had been, waiting for daylight and wondering how she was going to avoid seeing him today.

He still got flashes of hot and cold when he thought about the night before, of how close he had come to making love to her there, on the floor beneath the Christmas tree. Of how much he had wanted to. Hundreds of available women, thousands in the world, and he had to pick Dani on whom to vent his sexual urges. Dani, the most important woman in the world to him. Dani, who was in love with another man. Dani, for whom he could do nothing but ruin her life.

He still didn't understand how it had happened, how he had let it happen. Of course, Dani was uncertain and confused; who wouldn't be at a time like this? He had felt the same way right before he got married, which was why he had imagined so much more into that kiss Dani had given him all those years ago than there had been. He *had* imagined it, hadn't he? Or was it possible that even then...

But he refused to think about it any more, to let things get any further out of hand than they were already. He wasn't twenty years old anymore. Dani and he had too much history between them, precious history, to risk destroying everything for one moment of self-indulgent passion. His first instinct had been right; he should just go home and get out of her way, let her get on with her life.

But he couldn't do that. Dani was right, if he ran away now, it would only enhance the whole episode, it would make her feel guilty and make him feel worse, and they would never get past it. Their relationship had survived over twenty turbulent years of change and growth; they had too much at stake to let one indiscretion destroy it now. Somehow, they would work through this.

But he could still taste her warmth, and even the memory of her softness beneath his hands brought a tingle of excitement to his skin. He just didn't know how he was going to face her again.

The morning was cold and damp, fogged with ice crystals and miserably gray. Patches of snow had frozen in places and crunched beneath his feet, chilling him even through Harold's heavy boots. Faraway, a distant machine hummed—a chain saw or a tractor—but otherwise, the woods were still and bleak. The walk would have been a great deal cheerier if Dani had been along; she had a way of finding beauty in even the ugliest landscape.

The tangled woods gave way to scrubby pine growth and then stubbly field as Bret emerged behind the house that had once been his home. It had been years since he had seen the place, and he didn't know what he had expected, but the flood of memories caught him off guard.

It was a simple frame house, two stories, not much different from the Griffins' or from any other place along the highway. It was set well back from the road and had once, very early in Bret's memory, been surrounded by a cornfield. Now it was surrounded by nothing but barren, frozen stubble and weeds. There was a screen porch on the back where Bret used to play on rainy days and where his mother used to serve lemonade in the summer. A trailing rose climbed the side of the house, and when Bret was eight, inspired by some boys' adventure story he had read, he tried to climb from his bedroom window down the trellis to the ground. He had torn gashes in his hands, legs and clothes on the thorns, and still ended up falling halfway down and breaking a rib.

The screen on the porch was rusted and torn now, and the rose was nothing but a dried, unsightly skeleton clinging to the side of the house. As he came around the side, he noticed a light was on in the kitchen, and he remembered the smell of ham frying on cold mornings and buckwheat pancakes sizzling on the griddle. The kitchen had always been a warm, yellow place, sparkling bright, smelling good. Despite himself, he felt a wave of homesickness, even though he had not thought of this house as home in years. He supposed you never got over certain feelings for the house you grew up in . . . nor could you ever quite resign yourself to seeing it change.

The closer he moved, the more dramatic those changes became. In his youth, the house had been painted bright yellow with green shutters. At some time over the years, the color had been changed to a battleship gray, but even that was beginning to peel and flake badly. He noticed an effort had been made to repair a sagging gutter, but one of the front shutters had been removed or had fallen off and was leaning against the side of the house. Several of the storm windows were cracked and had been covered with plastic. The roof had been patched with mismatched tiles. The paving stones that led from the garage were cracked and overgrown with dead weeds, and the garage itself was badly in need of a new coat of paint. When he started up the front steps, a chunk of badly set concrete fell out from the underpinning. How had the place gotten so run-down? He had always had an understanding with Skinner, giving him a break in the rent in exchange for maintenance on the house, and the last time he had asked about it, Harold had told him Skinner was doing a fine job. Why hadn't Harold told him about this? Bret tried not to be angry, but this was his *home*.

He pushed the bell, but it obviously didn't work. He knocked loudly. He heard movement inside and after a moment, the door opened cautiously.

The man on the other side of the door was wearing a rumpled sweatshirt and a three-day growth of beard. His hair was greasy and his eyes suspicious.

Bret said, "Mr. Skinner? I'm Bret Underwood. I hope I'm not bothering you too early."

Bret extended his hand and after a moment, the other man opened the door long enough to take it in a brief, disinterested clasp. "Yeah, my wife said you might drop by. Come to throw us out, I reckon."

"No," Bret said quickly. "I just wanted to talk to you for a minute."

"You might as well," Skinner said, meeting his eyes defiantly. "I don't have this month's rent and don't intend on getting it."

"I didn't come all the way from California to collect rent," Bret said patiently. "I just wanted to talk to you about my plans for the property."

"Ain't no business of mine." But after a moment, Skinner's shoulders slumped in resignation and he pushed the door open wider. "Guess I can't keep you out. It's your house."

Bret stepped inside, and the annoyance he felt at the state of disrepair became mitigated with dismay. His mother's "front room" as she liked to call it, which had once been so cheerily filled with overstuffed couches and polished wood tables, scatter rugs faded by the sun and crisp cotton draperies, was now all but bare. There was a spindly-legged couch with a hole in one arm and a couple of molded plastic chairs of the kind Bret always associated with dentists' offices. The coffee table, a cheap mail-order piece, was scarred and watermarked. A twisted coat hanger served as an antenna for the small black-and-white television, and Jimmy Skinner was stretched out on the bare floor in front of it, watching Saturday-morning cartoons.

"Wife's at work," Skinner said ungraciously. "Ain't no coffee. Jimmy, shut that racket off. Get outside and play."

Jimmy looked at Bret with a semblance of his father's suspicious defensiveness, and Bret smiled at him. "Hi, bud. How're you doing?"

Jimmy mumbled something in reply, then turned the television off and left the room.

"Blasted kid," Skinner muttered, "always underfoot." He sank to the sofa. "That's the trouble with kids today, they don't have enough to do. 'Course, that's the trouble with a lot of us."

Bret sat down uncertainly on one of the plastic chairs. Skinner had not offered to take his coat, and Bret was glad because it wasn't warm in the room. He could feel a draft from the front windows, where plastic substituted for a pane, and the flame on the gas heater was turned down to a feeble glow, probably to conserve money. But despite its poverty, the room was scrupulously clean, which only made it sadder somehow. That was the evidence of someone whose pride was all that was left.

Abruptly, Bret was convinced, beyond any doubt there might have been, that selling this place was the best thing he could do. He shouldn't have held on to it this long. There was nothing of his childhood left except the ghosts of memories, and the two hundred acres certainly weren't doing the Skinners any good. It would be best for everyone, just as he had always thought.

George Skinner said, "Look, I know what you come for, so no point in us sitting here staring at each other. We'll be out by the first of the year. The wife, she's about had it with me. Can't say's I blame her." He lifted the bottle again, his eyes bleak and bloodshot. "Said she'll stay till after Christmas, for the boy's sake, but after that..." He shrugged. "Reckon she'll be moving back with her folks, out in Minnesota. And me, I don't need a house if I don't have a family."

Then he looked at Bret, his expression abruptly anxious and his tone somewhere between a plea and a demand. "Just till after Christmas. That's all I ask. Let us stay that long."

Bret did not want to hear this. He did not want to be here. He could not recall ever having been so miserable, uncomfortable or completely at a loss in all his life. But he managed to meet the other man's eyes directly, and he said, "I'm sorry for your trouble. I know the land didn't turn out to pay like you hoped—"

Skinner waved a dismissing hand. "Weren't your fault. You never charged us a penny's rent for the land we worked, and I appreciate it, I really do. Trouble is, good land costs money, and I don't know nothing but farming." He took another drink. "Anyways, it don't concern you. You've been more than fair."

"There's no hurry about leaving," Bret said. "I just wanted to let you know I'd be putting the place on the market. When it sells, I'll give you plenty of notice before you have to vacate. Maybe..." He hesitated. "Maybe it will be good for you to move on. Find some place you can make a decent living."

The minute he spoke, Bret knew how false the words sounded and he was ashamed of them. But Skinner just mumbled, "Yeah. Maybe."

Bret got up, and Skinner walked him to the door. On the porch, Bret looked around, struck again by how sad and neglected the old house looked in the dull morning light. He said quietly, "I would've paid for the repairs."

The other man avoided his eyes. "I couldn't afford the raise in rent. We had a deal. I do the repairs, you keep the rent low. I did the best I could."

Bret felt small and miserable. He said, "I wouldn't have raised the rent."

He drew up his collar against the cold and started back home, thinking about the false glitter and tacky glamour of Los Angeles. He had never thought he would miss it, but it seemed to him a very welcoming place to be right then. Nothing very real, nothing very demanding, nothing, really, very important at all. It wasn't such a bad way to live.

On impulse, he decided to take the shortcut across the fields. But the old path had gone the way of the children who once had ridden it, and twenty feet into the field, he found himself hip deep in a tangle of briars and scrub brush. For a moment, he just stood there, letting the cold seep into his skin and bleakness chill his soul. "What a mess," he said. And he turned and fought his way back out.

BRET FOUND HAROLD WARMING up his pickup, preparing to go into work. He took one look at Bret's glum expression and said, "Yeah, I figured that's where you'd gone. I'm sorry about the shape the place is in, son. I would've talked to you about it sooner, but when you said you were going to sell…" He shrugged.

For a moment, it seemed as though there was no more to say. Then Bret spoke abruptly, "Do me a favor, will you? Check the place out and see what it needs. I didn't get a chance to look around inside much. Whatever it takes, just make out a bill. And listen, don't do the work yourself, okay? Hire Skinner to help you, whatever the going rate is. Tell him…tell him you're subcontracting and the real-estate company is paying for the work."

Harold grinned. "That's the spirit. I'll take care of it today." He started toward the truck, then looked back. "Of course, you realize we won't be able to paint until spring—"

"Aluminum siding, then."

Harold frowned. "That's an awful lot of expense for a place you're not planning to keep."

Bret knew that. The whole idea was foolish and impulsive and not the move of a good businessman at all. But he rationalized his request, saying, "If I want to sell the place, it's got to look good. So just fix it up. Whatever it takes."

The grin returned. "That'll be good news to an awful lot of men who need the work at Christmas. Not to mention what it'll do for my store. You get a discount, of course."

Bret knew that arguing with Harold would do no good, so he returned the grin, feeling a little better. "Of course."

Harold climbed inside the truck, shifting into reverse before he closed the door. "Wouldn't be surprised if we had it done in a week," he called. "You won't recognize the place!"

Bret stepped out of the way, his hands stuffed into his pockets against the cold, and replied, "That's not the point. I *want* to recognize the place."

Harold nodded his understanding, smiling, and waved as he backed out of the drive.

Bret found Anne in the kitchen, cleaning up the breakfast dishes. Never had a kitchen looked so good to him. Never had home felt so warm.

"You didn't have any breakfast," she announced as he hung his coat on the rack by the door. "Sit down, I'll fix you something."

"No, thanks, I'm not hungry." And because he knew he wouldn't get away with that, he added, "My stomach's a little upset." He forced a smile. "Too many cookies last night."

That Anne understood. "Well, have some juice, anyway. You can't go around all morning without anything at all."

Obediently, Bret took a bottle of apple juice from the refrigerator.

"By the way, your office called."

Bret stifled a groan. "I should've checked in before now. I knew something would go wrong."

"Nobody said anything was wrong. The young lady sounded very sweet and cheerful, and she said it wasn't urgent."

Bret poured the juice and returned the bottle to the refrigerator. "I'd better call her back."

"And, Bret, if you don't mind, could you take some things down to the church for me this afternoon? Just some candelabra and some poinsettias. I would've asked Harold, but they'd blow away in the back of that truck, and he won't take the car to work."

Bret smiled at her, happy to feel useful after the futility that had settled over him with the events of the morning. "Glad to. Just let me make that call."

"No hurry."

He took the glass of juice to the living room and settled back in a wing chair, using his credit card to make the call.

Linda Cranston answered on the first ring.

"What's wrong?" he demanded.

"What? No 'hi, babe?' And I thought a vacation would improve your manners."

Bret replied, "Hi, babe. What's wrong?"

"That's better. And nothing's wrong, for your information. As a matter of fact, the place never ran smoother. It's amazing what the mice can do when the cat's away—"

"Miss Cranston." His voice took on a warning note.

"Yes, Mr. Scrooge. Right away, sir."

That made him smile. It *was* good to hear her voice, to be connected for a moment to the bright, busy world in which he belonged, where everything was routine, nothing was complex and he always knew the answers. He couldn't remember, for a moment, why he had ever left.

"All I wanted to tell you," Linda went on, "was that you had a call from Craig Notions yesterday. Something about your property, I imagine. He wants you to get in touch with him."

Bret lifted an eyebrow. "Well, that's timing for you," he murmured.

"What?"

"Nothing. Listen, about the Christmas bonuses—"

"You made out the checks the first of November, remember? It's all taken care of."

He did remember, now that she mentioned it. "Right. But the schedule for Christmas day—"

"That's taken care of, too. I know this might come as a shock to you, but the world actually does go on spinning without you turning the crank. Everything is just fine. Are you having a good time?"

Bret hesitated, not certain whether to be reassured or depressed by how little he seemed to be needed. "Yeah, sure," he answered, but he wasn't even certain whether that was true anymore. "But, listen, I was thinking—"

"If the rest of that sentence has anything to do with your coming back early," she said sternly, interrupting him, "don't say it. If you show your face here before New Year's Day, I'll quit, I swear I will. You need this vacation—almost as much as the rest of us need a vacation from you."

Bret smiled through a half-smothered sigh. "Why does it seem to be my fate to be surrounded by bossy, overbearing women?" he grumbled.

"Because you love it," she returned pertly. "Merry Christmas. And don't call me—I'll call you."

Bret's smile turned reflective as he hung up the phone. Yes, there were things he missed about California, but now, he was beginning to realize that work wasn't one of them. And Linda had unwittingly put her finger on the exact source of the dissatisfaction that had been troubling him for months: he wasn't needed there. The challenge was gone, the routine flowed uninterrupted with or without him. As George Skinner had said, everybody needs something to do.

He dialed Craig Notions's real-estate office a little absently, wondering what it was, then, that he wanted to do... and if he had ever really known.

"Do I have news for you!" Craig said boisterously when he got on the line. "You are dealing with the shrewdest, fastest broker this side of the Mississippi, and if you had a shred of decency, you'd double my commission."

"Not until I hear what you've done."

"I, my dear fellow, have all but closed the deal on your Clayville property, sight unseen. Is that a stroke of genius or what?"

Bret was stunned. "It's a stroke of something. What are you talking about?"

"The Japanese, Bret, the Japanese!" He was practically chortling. "How would you like to be the beneficiary of the excess cash flow of one of the largest electronics manufacturers in the world? We're talking millions here. Millions!"

"This is starting to sound like a scam," Bret said cautiously.

"Well," Craig conceded, "I don't expect to get millions for the property, or even close. But we will get a hell of a lot more than it's worth, and that's the name of the game, isn't it?"

"Will you cut the bull and get to the point?" That, Bret realized impatiently, was the one thing he had gotten used to in Clayville that was utterly lacking in L.A.—straight talk.

"All right, here's the deal. Inushu Electronics is looking to open a new plant in the Midwest. All they need is a highway, a couple of hundred acres and a fairly central location from which to draw their labor force. And guess what I just happened to have for sale? We've done the demographics. We've shown them the maps and the plat. They're interested. They're more than interested. They're sending a rep down next week to draw up a report."

Bret felt a little overwhelmed. And the only thing he could think of for the moment was that, if the Japanese were going to build a plant on the property, there was hardly any need to fix up the house. The first thing they'd do would be to bulldoze it.

Still, he was cautious. "Then it's hardly a done deal, is it? I mean, they've got to be looking at other pieces of real estate."

Craig sounded exasperated. "But this is the one they're going to buy. Jeez, don't overdo the gratitude, will you? You're embarrassing me."

"Sorry, Craig. It sounds great, it really does. It's just that..." But he wasn't sure what it was.

"Yeah, I know, you always were a conservative son-of-a-gun. So let's just say this is an early Christmas present. I'll get back with you as soon as we're ready to come out and look at the property. I'll tell you this, though. Be as skeptical as you want, but these guys are no fools. If they want to beat the new tax laws, they're going to have to move before the end of the year, so don't be surprised if you have a big, fat check in your stocking Christmas morning.''

For a long moment after he had disconnected, Bret sat there, trying to let it sink in. Of course, nothing was certain, but this was a good thing. If it worked out, it could be a very good thing for everyone concerned, and after the rotten morning he'd had, wasn't it about time something started looking up? This was what he wanted. Why in the world should he feel even the least bit uneasy about it?

There was no reason, he decided firmly. No reason in the world. It was the best thing that could possibly happen; he couldn't have asked for more. And, as though to prove it to himself, he jumped up and started toward the kitchen. "Hey, Miss Annie!" he called. "Guess what?"

THE CHURCH WAS REDOLENT with the smell of evergreen and beeswax, rich with the glow of polished pews and the muted light that poured through the stained glass windows. It was a soothing place to be, comforting and calming—or it should have been. It would have been on any other day of Dani's life, but today, she was so bogged down in guilt and uncertainty that church was the last place she wanted to be.

She was the first of the decorating committee to arrive—except for Todd, who had come early to go over the score for the cantata they would be rehearsing that afternoon. She hadn't really planned on meeting Todd, and what he thought was a happy coincidence was, in fact, an unpleasant shock for Dani. She had wanted to be here alone, to compose herself before the others arrived, and she had wanted to get away from the house early, before she ran into Bret.... Spending the morning with Todd had not been in her plans.

But it was probably the best thing that could have happened. She was tense and distracted, and, of course, he noticed, but he never made an issue of it, never forced her hand, never let her mood affect his. He made her feel ashamed of herself in more ways than one, but more importantly, he made her remember just what a special man he was and how lucky she was to have found him at this stage of her life. When at last she mumbled some apology about too little sleep and P.M.S., he just grinned and held the ladder for her as she climbed up to tack a wreath over the door.

He was working at the piano now, the bright glow of the music lamp casting an aura around his profile, and she thought, *A saint, that's what he is. He's a saint, and I'm a fool for ever doubting for a minute that he's the man I want to marry....*

And that's what it was with Bret, she was sure. She was starting to feel overwhelmed by the choices that faced her, and she wanted to check out all her options. It wasn't as though she was the first woman in the world to feel such doubts. She had nothing to be ashamed of. She hadn't really made a commitment to Todd yet; she hadn't really betrayed him. They were both adults, and did she think for one minute that Todd hadn't slept with other women before he met her? Not, of course, that she had done anything of the sort with Bret . . . but that was the trouble. She had wanted to. And no amount of rationalizing or reexamining could convince her otherwise. She had wanted to make love with Bret last night, very badly, and it was he who had pulled away, not she.

She had no intention of telling Todd about it, but she had an awful feeling that if she did, he would understand. It was Bret she was worried about. She had thrown herself at him. She had behaved like a wanton, sex-starved teenager. What must he think of her now? She was supposed to be in love with another man, yet she had gone into Bret's arms without a moment's thought or hesitation or even a twinge of guilt.

She felt plenty of guilt now. She felt guilty for Todd's sake, because if he had been with another woman after all they had shared, she would never have forgiven him. She had no right to expect better from him on her behalf—but she did. She felt guilty for her own sake because it wasn't like her to behave like that, and she didn't understand what had come over her. But most important, she felt guilty for Bret's sake. She had almost driven him away. What was he thinking now? How could she ever face him again?

She had an opportunity to find out sooner than she expected or even wanted. She was tacking garlands of fresh evergreen along the choir loft when she heard the vestibule door open. She turned, expecting to see the rest of the decorating committee. Instead, Bret stood there, holding a potted poinsettia beneath each arm and balancing a candelabrum in either hand.

He looked as surprised to see her as Dani was to see him, and for a moment, she was helpless beneath the flood of inevitable memories. Her cheeks went hot, and her skin prickled, just as though she could feel his hands caressing it now. Her eyes were drawn to his mouth, and her stomach tightened as she remembered the swift, hot invasion of his tongue, the taste of him, the feel of him.... And he was remembering, too. She could see it in his eyes.

They both felt Todd's gaze and they broke eye contact quickly, speaking at once. Bret said, "Hi, Dani."

Dani said, "What are you doing here?"

Their voices sounded forced, a little too casual, a little too loud.

Todd got up from the piano. Dani might have noticed something strange in the glance he gave her, but his attitude was easy and relaxed as he approached Bret. "Here, let me give you a hand."

"Thanks." Bret handed over a potted plant and a candelabrum. "There're more in the car. Dani's mom sent me over with them."

"The Garden Club supplies the poinsettias for the church every year," Dani explained, wiping her hands on her skirt and hoping the gesture didn't seem too nervous. "They always end up dumping them at Mom's house."

Todd placed the poinsettia on the altar table, and Bret followed him, looking around curiously. "So, what's going on?"

"The Christmas cantata is tomorrow night." Todd took the other candelabrum from him and set it on the altar. "We're trying to get the church decorated before final rehearsal this afternoon. The other ladies should be here any minute."

"Cantata, huh?" Bret's smile seemed almost natural. "And I guess Dani's directing it."

"Actually," Dani said, coming down the steps to them, "Todd's the choir director."

Bret looked at the other man in surprise. "No kidding?"

"Just amateur," Todd admitted. "It's a volunteer job. But this year's cantata looks pretty good, if I do say so myself. You'll be here, won't you?"

"Wouldn't miss it." Bret glanced at Dani, then away before she could meet his eyes. "Well, you two do have a lot in common. Music, I mean. Dani's always been the biggest star this town ever produced. Singing, dancing, you name it."

Todd caressed the back of Dani's neck in brief affection. "She's still a star," he said.

Dani said hurriedly, "Do you want us to help you bring in the rest of the plants?"

"No, you go ahead with what you're doing. I'll get them."

But Todd followed him out, and they brought in the remainder of the poinsettias in one trip. Dani began to arrange the plants in clusters around the altar and the pulpit, and she tried to convince herself the silence wasn't too awkward. But it must have been because Bret broke it with a sudden, almost too boisterous, "Well, I had some interesting news today."

"What's that?" Dani spoke without turning.

"I think I've got an offer on my property."

Todd exclaimed, "Is that right? Well, I never would have thought you'd sell it this quickly. Who is it, someone from out of town?"

Bret chuckled. "Way out of town. The Japanese, actually. They're considering it as a possible site for a new electronics plant. Inushu—maybe you've heard of them."

Dani turned around slowly, staring at him. "You're kidding."

He shook his head. "I don't think so. It's not settled yet, of course, but my broker sounds pretty excited. They're sending someone down next week to do an on-site survey."

Dani said incredulously, "You're going to sell your property to the *Japanese?*"

"If the price is right, which I'm sure it will be."

"You'd actually *do* that?"

Bret frowned a little in confusion. "Why not? They're not communists or drug dealers or even racketeers—what's the big deal? Why are you looking at me that way?"

For a moment, Dani could only stare at him, then she stalked past him, grabbed her coat and went outside.

In only a few seconds, Bret was beside her. "What's the matter with you?" he demanded. "What did you run out here for?"

She turned on him. "Because it's a sin to fight in church! Bret, are you crazy? You're really going to sell your daddy's house to some foreign concern who's going to build an industrial *plant?*"

He still looked confused, but there was annoyance in his eyes, too. "Why not? It's not like they're going to manufacture insecticides or poisonous chemicals, but even if they were, it wouldn't have anything to do with me. Besides—"

"I don't believe you!" she cried, gesturing wildly. "I don't believe you can actually stand here and tell me you don't care about toxic waste—"

"There *isn't* any toxic waste!"

"How do you know that? How can you say that? How can you do that to your own land, the place we grew up, where your family has lived for generations! Where Zac and Hannah—"

"Spare me Zac and Hannah!" His voice rose in tone to match hers, and shoppers on the sidewalk across the street turned to stare. "For God's sake, Dani, I told you when I came here this is what I intended to do—"

"I didn't think you'd do it! You grew up here, Bret, you know—"

The door to the church opened and Todd came out. "Private conversation?" he inquired mildly.

"Tell him, Todd!" Dani demanded. "Tell him he can't do this!"

And Bret turned on him, as well. "Can you believe this woman? She's acting like I'm a war criminal or something! Do you know how many jobs a thing like this could bring to the county? New roads, new housing, not to mention outside revenue—the whole economic standard would go up two hundred percent. How can anybody possibly object to that?''

Todd said cautiously, ''A thing like this could be really big news, and it certainly bears some looking into. But I've got to tell you, I'm pretty much like Dani—a traditionalist at heart. That's why I moved here. I'd hate to see things change.''

Dani looked smug. ''That's why *everyone* lives here,'' she told Bret. ''Because we like the small town and the quiet life-style. If we wanted superhighways and high-rises, we'd move to the city. I can't believe you want to put an industrial plant in my backyard!''

''It's not your backyard,'' he told her, ''it's mine. Besides, the deal isn't settled yet. It's not even a firm possibility. I thought you'd be happy for me, that's all.''

''Well, I'm not!''

Bret might have responded, or Dani might have said more, but just then, a group of ladies from the decorating committee rounded the corner, calling and waving to her. Bret glanced at them and then at Dani, his jaw tight and his eyes angry. Then he said shortly, ''I'll see you later.'' He spun on his heel and walked away.

Dani started to call him back, but let the words die unspoken. She didn't want to apologize. She wasn't sorry. She wasn't wrong. She was hurt and betrayed and angry, and why shouldn't she be?

And she was also scared. Because this wasn't the Bret she knew. Because she was afraid of losing him. And because the fight really hadn't been about the Japanese. She was shocked and angry, but that was not why she had yelled at him. She had fought with him because fighting was easier than facing up to what she had really felt when he walked into the church a few moments ago.

She greeted the members of the decorating committee automatically, and Todd draped his arm around her shoulders as they walked back inside the church. But she couldn't get over the disturbance her harsh words with Bret had left. The Christmas spirit was fading fast.

THAT AFTERNOON, ANNE WENT to rehearsal with Dani, and supper was a pot-luck affair concocted between the two men. Afterward, Harold turned on a movie on cable and invited Bret to join him, but Bret pleaded fatigue and went to his room early.

He lay on his bed with his arms folded behind his head, staring at the ceiling, angry and unhappy and trying to figure out what he had done wrong. Except that it really wasn't such a puzzle. It was all very easy to understand. Dani just couldn't accept change. She expected everything to stay the same year after year, decade after decade, handing down memories like those worn-out Christmas ornaments. But Bret was a man who thrived on change, who made changes happen, and this wasn't his home anymore.

If she couldn't accept the changes that went on in the world around her, how could she possibly be expected to accept a change in their relationship? How, for that matter, could Bret?

There was a timid knock on his door, and he turned his head toward it just as Dani pushed it open. She was carrying a small basket wrapped in red cellophane. "Peace offering," she said, indicating the basket. "Can I come in?"

He propped the pillows a little higher under his head, but didn't get up. "Only if you're carrying cookies."

"How did you guess?"

She came inside, leaving the door open a little. He could hear the drone of the television set from downstairs. She set the basket on the night table, and Bret moved his legs over, making room for her to sit beside him on the bed. It was a natural thing to do, just like old times, but when she sat beside him, he could feel his pulses speed and the scent of her perfume drifted over him like a warm caress.

"Look," she said, glancing down at her folded hands, "I feel really dumb. Mom told me how you're fixing up your house."

He said nothing.

She looked at him cautiously. "You could have called it all off after you found out about the Japanese, but you didn't. Seems like a waste. The Japanese won't have any use for the house."

He lifted one shoulder uncomfortably. "The deal might not go through. I'll need to have the place spruced up if I put it on the open market."

"Or maybe," she suggested, "you wanted to give some men around here some work and Mr. Skinner some extra money and his family a decent place to live."

She was wearing a long, bulky-knit sweater and a print skirt, hardly a sexy outfit by anybody's standards. Her hair was pulled back at her nape with a bright red bow, and she wore no makeup. She was just Dani, familiar, honest, comfortable... and beautiful.

"So I waste a little money," he said. "If I make the deal, I won't even miss it. If I don't... it can't hurt to spread a little Christmas cheer around. I'm getting tired of being called Scrooge."

"I never said you were a Scrooge."

"So now that you think I'm a sentimental tower of Jell-O, you like me again, is that it?"

She grinned. "Right."

He tilted his head to the side, examining her gravely. "Then we'd better get one thing straight. About that fight this afternoon—I was right and you were wrong."

She rolled her eyes in exasperation. "Are you going to start it all over again?"

"I just don't want any misunderstandings."

She sighed a little, looking at him with a mixture of sadness and apology. "Bret, I know that what you do with your land is your business. And I know that you really don't see anything wrong with your plans. It's just—it shocked me, that's all, to find out you felt so differently about things than I do. You're my best friend, and I guess I always assumed we thought alike on everything, and Bret, the world is changing so fast and things are so messed up that sometimes, it seems like our memories are the only things we can really count on. I just always thought that you treasured those memories as much as I do. And that's why I yelled at you."

Bret reached down and took her fingers lightly in his. "We've always thought about things a lot differently than either one of us wanted to admit." He kept his eyes on their hands, fascinated by the differences in size and texture and color. Her small, slim fingers, flower-petal white, entwined with his large brown ones, her neat, pale pink nails trimmed into delicate ovals...softness and hardness, male and female.

He raised his eyes to her face. "But you were right about one thing. You didn't mean to be, but you made me see something today, something very important. I do treasure those memories, Dani, but that's all they are—just memories, and I can't live on them. That's what makes us different—what makes me different from everybody around here, I guess. And that's why I don't belong here."

Her eyes were quick with protest. "Bret, that's not—"

But he shook his head, silencing her. "It's not that I don't want to," he went on, trying to make her understand. "There's so much about this place I love, and these last few days have been more...well, more *real* to me than anything I've done in the past five years. But I've changed too much, Dani, and I just don't fit in anymore."

"You could change back," she said gently, "if you wanted to."

He shook his head against the pillow. "I tried to change to fit into Los Angeles and I couldn't. Not really. I did a pretty good imitation, I guess, but..." He turned her hand over in his, playing with it absently, stroking the palm, curling the fingers. "You asked me yesterday about work, and I think I've figured it out. When I left here, it was to do something great, to make my mark, to conquer my own part of the world...and what I've got is just a business. A successful business, a money-making business most of the time—but it's not great, it's not earth shattering...it's not the dream. And I feel, after all these years, like I've wasted my life and I don't belong there, either."

Dani closed her fingers around his, aching for him. There had never been a time in her life that Bret's pain was not her own, that his emptiness did not make her feel alone, and she fought against her own helplessness, she strained to make it better for him. Why couldn't he see that *this* was where he belonged? Here, at home, with her?

It came to her so naturally, so totally without surprise, that it was a moment before Dani fully realized the significance of what she felt. And then, on the very heels of that revelation came another, more startling thought. *I'm not sure I love Todd anymore... or that I ever really did.*

She felt disoriented for a moment, shaken to the core, afraid to examine too closely what was slowly being revealed to her. Hesitantly, she unwound her fingers from Bret's and found herself suddenly unable to look at him. But she had to say the rest. There had been too many secrets between them already.

"Bret," she said, and she made herself meet his eyes. Her cheeks felt uncomfortably warm. "There was another reason I yelled at you this afternoon. I think you know what it was."

He didn't drop his gaze. She loved him for that.

"It was—it was awkward seeing you again after last night," she managed with difficulty. "And I guess—well, you know how I am when I'm uncomfortable. I'm not used to it, I guess, and I get irritable. More angry with myself than with anybody else."

"I know," he said softly. "I felt the same way."

The gratitude in her eyes turned to anxiety as she said in a rush, "Bret, I don't want you to think badly of me. That I—well, that I'm a tramp or—"

His hand seized hers. "I don't think that. I don't want to hear you say that."

"Or," she said, making herself finish with difficulty, "that I was using you. Because—"

His fingers tightened. "Don't," he said huskily. "I know."

She saw the quiet urgency of conviction in his eyes, and it seemed in that moment that he did know, that he knew too much and understood too well, and that the sum of it was something she did not want to hear right now or even to think about.

She dropped her eyes and made herself withdraw her hand again. The next words seemed very difficult to say, and her voice was hoarse with anxiety. "So, is everything all right between us, then?"

He smiled. "Everything's always all right with us, Dani."

After a moment, she returned his smile and stood up.

She was almost to the door when he said, "Dani."

Her heart skipped a beat, and she turned. His face was sober and for a moment, she was certain she saw something forming in his eyes—a question, a statement.... And then it was gone.

He merely smiled again, and said, "Thanks for the cookies."

It was a moment before she could catch her breath, and then she wasn't sure whether it was relief she felt, or enormous, overwhelming disappointment. She nodded, but her throat was too tight to speak. She opened the door and left him alone.

Chapter Nine

"Dani, this is ridiculous," Bret said, pulling up the suspenders of the red felt pants. "I feel like an idiot."

"You look adorable," Dani assured him, handing him the heavily padded red jacket. But even she had trouble repressing a grin. "Tall, skinny Santas are in vogue, everyone knows that. It's the fitness craze."

The schoolroom was empty except for the two of them, but the sounds of revelry from the last-day-of-school Christmas party in the cafeteria drifted down the hall to them. Bret, who had thought Dani's last-minute invitation to join her for the school holiday party would involve nothing more strenuous than drinking green Kool-Aid and eating sugar cookies, eyed the fuzzy white beard and wig skeptically. "Who usually gets to do the honors?"

"Sometimes Dad, sometimes Principal Hollyfield." She tried to hook the beard over his ears but he squirmed away.

"And?"

"And Mr. Hollyfield has the flu, and Dad's working on your house."

Bret, too, had spent a great deal of his time working on the house over the past week, replacing shingles, reinforcing banisters, building steps. It was good, solid, muscle-straining work, and there was an indefinable sense of satisfaction at the end of the day to step back and be able to see the tangible results of what he had done, along with a certain sense of pride to realize that he had not forgotten, in all these years of desk work, the skills that Harold Griffin had taught him in his youth. It was good, too, to see George Skinner out there working and feeling good about his work, for although he wasn't the most skilled carpenter on the job, he was inexhaustible and had a perfectionist's pride that wouldn't let him walk away from any job until it was done right. Bret kept thinking how unfair it was that a man like that couldn't find work, and he found himself wishing there was something more he could do.

When—or if—the electronics plant was built, hundreds of jobs would be created and a lot of problems would be solved for a lot of people, but Bret didn't kid himself that any help would be forthcoming from that quarter for men like Skinner. It could be years before any hiring was done at all, and the best George was qualified for was janitor or night watchman—the latter position fast becoming obsolete, thanks to firms like Underwood Security.

Speculation had been rampant about the electronics plant over the past week. Bret had met Bill Lars, Inushu's forward representative—who was not Japanese at all, but thoroughly west-side Chicago—briefly, just long enough to be cordial, for the project was far too early in development to call for any serious input from Bret at all. But from other sources—Todd, mostly—he had learned Lars had met with town councilmen, county officials and representatives from the utility companies. Apparently, Inushu was very serious, indeed, about making a move, and everyone in town had an opinion on the proposed project. There were times when Bret was reluctant to walk down the street for fear of being assaulted by yet another well-meaning citizen with strong advice—pro or con—on what he should do with his daddy's land. But Dani had not said another word.

Bret got the beard on, and the wig, and topped the costume off with the droopy fur-trimmed hat. He said morosely, "How do I look?"

Dani stepped back, covering her mouth with a curled hand, her eyes twinkling madly. "Like a pregnant track star."

"That does it." Bret grabbed for the hat.

"No, Bret, stop it." She moved forward quickly, laughing, and reached up to straighten his hat. "All you need to do is fix your beard and keep your hat on straight...."

She was leaning against him, reaching up to rearrange the costume hat and beard, her eyes bright with laughter and her face flushed. It was one of those moments that caught them both off guard. The touch, the nearness, the warm sweet fragrance of her perfume... And then she said, perhaps a bit too brightly, "There. Perfect."

She stepped away quickly, bumping the corner of her desk. The movement tipped over a dried out plant, that Bret hastily righted. "What happened to your flower?" he asked.

"It's not a flower," she said, "it's a Christmas cactus. Don't you remember? You sent it to me five years ago."

He examined the plant in his hands uncertainly. "Well, I hope it was in better shape then. Honey, I don't know how to tell you this, but this thing is dead."

"It is not." She took the plant from him firmly and replaced it on her desk. "You sound like Jimmy Skinner. It's supposed to look that way, but it always blooms before Christmas."

"I don't think so." He cast the plant another skeptical look. "Not this year. You'd better throw it out."

"I will not! Do you think I'd throw away something you gave me? It'll bloom. You wait and see. Christmas is just a little slow in coming this year, that's all."

Bret could not repress a grin of familiar, unmitigated affection. "You never change. Hope springs eternal, huh?"

"Right," she replied with a decisive nod. "Now, let's get this show on the road." She picked up the lumpy red sack that matched the costume. "All you have to do is a few ho-ho-ho's and hand out the presents. The kids drew names and put their presents under the tree. The ones in the bag are just little things from the teachers. So every child should get two presents."

"Well, some of them might get three." Bret reached under the desk and pulled out a big box filled with wrapped gifts, and began to transfer them to the Santa sack. "When you mentioned the party," he explained, looking a little abashed, "I thought it wouldn't hurt to get the kids in your class a little something—since I knew them and everything."

She tightened her lips in mock reprimand, her eyes sparkling. "What would Scrooge say?"

He looked up at her. "What did your dad say when you told him he wouldn't be playing Santa this year?"

Dani simply smiled. "He agreed with me—it was about time you got into the Christmas spirit. Are you there yet?"

Bret stood up, hoisted the sack over his shoulder, and replied deadpan, "Ho-ho-ho."

THE SCENE IN THE cafeteria was utter mayhem: the noise level almost at the pain threshold; children, wrapping paper, cookies and punch everywhere. Dani stayed close to Bret, partly to help keep the gift-dispersement going in an orderly fashion, mostly because she was afraid if she didn't stay within grabbing distance, he would run away.

But he surprised her. He made a comical, sometimes satirical Santa Claus, but he threw himself into the part wholeheartedly, booming out his voice to be heard over the clatter, taking little girls on his knee, throwing in a generous sprinkling of ho-ho-hos for effect. Though he did his best to disguise it, there were times when Dani thought he might actually be having fun.

When Jimmy Skinner's name was called, Bret went through his usual routine. "And what do you want for Christmas young man?" he demanded boisterously.

The boy looked at him in disgust. "You're not Santa."

Bret played along. "Now, what makes you say that?"

Jimmy lifted his hand to pull at the beard, but Bret blocked his move with his arm. "Touch the beard and die, kid," he said.

"Santa!" Dani hissed, but she could see a grin tugging at Jimmy's lips.

"There ain't no Santa Claus," Jimmy declared, rocking back on his heels. "And even if there was, you ain't him. Give me my present."

Bret lifted the gaily wrapped package of Christmas candy out of Jimmy's reach. "What do you want for Christmas?" he repeated.

A shadow crossed Jimmy's face that was painful to see on one so young. He mumbled, "Nothing you can give me."

Dani started to intervene, but Bret insisted gently, "Give it a try." Dani held back, watching Jimmy's face.

Jimmy looked at Bret defiantly. "I know who you are. You're fixing up our house. You feel sorry for us, I guess. That's what Daddy says. But it don't make no difference. Nobody's gonna be living there after Christmas. They think I don't know, but I do." He stuck out his hand, his jaw set belligerently, and Dani was alarmed to see the glitter of tears in the boy's eyes.

Bret placed the candy in his hand, and Jimmy turned away.

"Hey, kid." Bret's voice was gruff.

Jimmy turned around and Bret reached into his sack, digging out another present. "Merry Christmas," he said.

Dani placed her hand on Bret's shoulder, and they both watched as Jimmy took his presents across the room, squatted down on the floor and tore the wrapping paper off the biggest one. It was a model airplane. There was wonder in his eyes as he looked back at Bret.

Dani forced a smile, her fingers automatically massaging the tight muscles at the back of Bret's neck. "That was nice," she said softly. "Probably the best present he'll get all Christmas."

Bret shook his head slowly. "I think we both know what that boy wants for Christmas. And he's right, I can't give it to him."

Dani heard the bleakness in Bret's voice, she saw the sorrow and frustration on his face, and she knew what he was feeling because she felt it, too. And she also knew something else, suddenly, simply and without any fanfare at all: that she loved him, more than she had ever loved anyone in her life.

And it really was no surprise; she did not know why she had been fighting it for so long. Hadn't she known, after all, since she was three years old?

She squeezed his shoulder briefly, filled with a quiet and overwhelming joy that needed no words, no further expression. Soon, she knew, the joy would fade and the doubts would surface, the problems would assail her, the complexities and impossibilities would leave her wracked and torn and filled with loss. But for now, she had this happiness inside her, this secret truth, and she wanted to savor it.

"Back to work, Santa," she said, handing Bret another wrapped package. She felt so full of wonder that she was sure he could see it shining softly in her eyes. "Only twenty-five names to go."

TELL HIM, THE LITTLE voice inside Dani kept whispering. *Tell him.*

A light snow was falling through the darkness as they walked across the school parking lot. Bret carried a box filled with the small gifts Dani's students had given her that afternoon—dusting powder, brooches shaped like little birds or Christmas wreaths, hand lotion, little plaques emblazoned "Teacher," pocket handkerchiefs, and the usual assortment of odds and ends—and Dani carried the dried-up Christmas cactus.

"No wonder you like Christmas so much," Bret commented. "You make out like a bandit."

She chuckled. "It makes up for the salary." She glanced at him, wondering if anyone had ever looked so handsome, so strong, so wonderfully familiar and so completely hers. Snow dusted the shoulders of his coat and glistened in his hair under the streetlights. His face was easy and relaxed in profile, tilted upward a little to catch the flakes of snow. Dani found it suddenly impossible to remember a time when he had not been beside her, or to imagine a time when he would not be again.

"I must say," she commented, "you've been an awfully good sport today."

Neither of them had gone home after the school party. It had taken an hour after the last child had gone home for the teachers and staff to clean up the cafeteria, and then it was time to start setting up scenery for the Christmas pageant that night. The children had started arriving for dress rehearsal just as Dani, Bret and several of the teachers returned from having a quick sandwich at the diner across the street, and the past two hours had been an insane whirl of lambs and little ponies, Christmas angels, shepherds and wise men. The children had been stricken with everything from hyperactivity to amnesia. The parents had broken into several spontaneous standing ovations. And Dani, if she had had any sense at all, would have been exhausted. But she wasn't. She was euphoric.

Bret balanced the box on the snow-frosted trunk of Dani's car as she searched for her keys. "At the risk of ruining my image," he admitted, "it was kind of fun. Like walking through a time portal and losing twenty years." And then he smiled at her a little ruefully. "It's like that every time I'm with you. I think you do it on purpose."

"I do," she replied, turning the key in the lock. "My Christmas gift to you—your childhood."

She straightened up, and found that he was still smiling at her. Her heart started beating faster as the little voice insisted again, *Tell him. Tell him now, in the snow with the Christmas lights twinkling in the back-*

ground, while he's close enough to touch and wanting you to touch.... Tell him. Just tell him.

How many times had she heard that voice over the years, and how many times had she refused to listen to it? There had always been some reason for keeping silent: embarrassment, uncertainty, fear of change... fear that Bret would not love her back, fear of making a mistake. Once, she had even—almost—written it down when she thought she couldn't stand the secret feelings that were bursting inside her anymore, but Bret had never seen the letter. When she looked back over the years, it seemed she had made a career out of falling in and out of love with Bret. And it was only now that she realized she had never fallen out of love with him at all.

So why couldn't she tell him now? Tell him that the sister he thought he had was not a sister at all, that the friendship he thought he could count on from her had never been friendship at all, but the love of a woman who only wanted him to love her back...like so many women who had gone before her in Bret's life. Why? There were a thousand old reasons, and almost as many new ones. Because a love affair, once ended, was gone forever. Because she couldn't have stood it if the warmth in Bret's eyes should turn to awkwardness and embarrassment, or even disappointment. Because she had always known it had to come from him because she was frightened and unsure, and she had already risked losing him once when she had kissed him.

Because she already had a man who loved her, who wanted to marry her, who would make a perfect home for her. Because her future was settled and secure and because Bret had always accused her of being a sucker for fantasy, especially at Christmastime. Because she had never done anything impulsive in her life and because, quite simply, she was afraid.

So with her heart beating far too fast and the words she couldn't say choking up her throat, she looked at Bret, and she said instead, simply, "Bret, why don't you stay?"

He looked surprised and then puzzled. "Do you mean . . . here?" He glanced around. "In Clayville? Forever?"

She could only nod.

She cursed the darkness that disguised his expression from her, the eyes that she could read so well. Because when he returned his gaze to her, all she could make out clearly was the puzzlement, as he replied, "Why would you want me to?"

"There you are!"

A voice behind them made them both turn and the moment for answers and all that hung in the balance with it was gone. Todd lifted his hand to them as he made his way across the crunchy snow.

"Great show, madame producer," he said, dropping his arm around Dani's shoulders. "As usual, I might add."

Dani forced a light laugh as Bret opened the trunk and put the box inside. "Thank you, kind sir. I assume I can look forward to a stellar review in tomorrow's paper?"

"The presses are rolling as we speak." Todd looked at Bret. "We're on our way for a cup of coffee," he said. "Will you join us?"

Bret took the cactus from Dani and locked it in the trunk with the box. "Thanks," he replied with an easy grin, "but this sounds like one of those two's-company situations. Guess I'll go on home and stretch out in front of the fire. I think I heard something about popcorn later."

Dani started to protest, but when Todd said nothing, she hardly could. So she just smiled. "Good night, then. And thanks for all your help."

"Be careful coming home. The roads look slick."

Dani walked across the parking lot with Todd, leaning into the shelter of his arm for balance in the slippery spots, and she could feel Bret watching them. As they moved into the shadow of the building, Todd turned her toward him and kissed her gently, and all Dani could think about was whether or not Bret was still watching.

She knew then why she couldn't tell him. And it broke her heart.

Chapter Ten

Over the next week, Bret was plunged into such a frenzy of Christmas gaiety that he couldn't help but suspect a conspiracy. He was recruited to help collect canned goods for the poor, make Christmas wreaths for the hospital and distribute fruit baskets at the nursing home. People he hadn't seen in twenty years and whose names he barely remembered invited him to Christmas parties and skating parties and hay rides. And behind every face, every invitation, every gaily decorated door and tinkling silver bell, there seemed to be the unspoken questions *See, isn't this what you want? Isn't this what you miss? Isn't this worth preserving? Bret, don't you want to come home?*

He accepted the invitations, he decorated the wreaths, he wrapped big packing crates in foil paper as collection centers, because he was as helpless as anyone else under the Christmas spell and because he knew, deep in his heart, that this might be his last chance. He had been briefly privileged to visit a way of life that had been arrested in time, to return to the streets of his childhood, and it was something to be treasured. But it wouldn't come again. Even as he looked, that small-town innocence was dying out and he might well be the instrument of its final destruction.

He ignored, as much as he could, the business with Inushu. People asked him questions, and he could honestly say he didn't know. He didn't want to know the whens, wheres or hows of the deal, or even how great was the possibility that there would be a deal at all. He was having enough trouble answering his own essential question: Why?

A week ago, the answer had been obvious. Business was business, and if there was one thing he was good at, it was that. But a week ago, Dani hadn't looked up at him through the drifting snow with eyes that were big with unspoken yearning and demanded simply, "Bret, why don't you stay?"

Why don't you stay? His head had reeled with the implications of that question for an hour or more. And it wasn't just the words, but what lay behind them. She had wanted to say more, he was sure of it. He could feel the thoughts crackling through the cold night air like a half-finished sentence, an unresolved chord. *Why don't you stay and...*

And what? Be an usher at her wedding? Play poker with Todd on Thursday nights and watch her children grow up calling him Uncle Bret? Could he do that? *Could* he?

That was why he was so thoroughly determined to enjoy this Christmas. He knew he would never come home again.

He kept himself so busy during that week that he rarely saw Dani, and never alone. He wouldn't have gone shopping in Centerville with them on Saturday except that Miss Annie begged him to come, for the last thing he wanted to do was be a third wheel with Dani and Todd. But it turned out to be a far more pleasant morning than he had anticipated.

Bret remembered Centerville as a dusty, dying town not much different from Clayville, but it had been transformed into a winter wonderland that could have rivaled any eastern tourist trap. The downtown area had been refinished to resemble a quaint turn-of-the-century village that was European in flavor, with gas street lamps, horse-drawn carriages and hand-painted signs. Pricey boutiques lined every street, Victorian Christmas decorations abounded and all the sales personnel wore nineteenth-century costumes. It was charming, business was booming and Bret was amazed. Todd explained how Centerville's success with the tourist industry had attracted bigger business, the new hotel was at ninety percent capacity and a mall and luxury condominiums were already under development. The contrast between Centerville's prosperity and Clayville's seemed unfair.

After the initial tour of the town, they split up into what Bret dryly referred to as "shopping teams." Bret had always hated shopping, and he still did, but Anne was so cheerful and full of fun, it was hard to be in a sour mood. With Anne Griffin as his guide, he bought a new power saw for Harold, which was the only thing he had indicated he would like to have. Then, Bret took Anne to the jewelry store, hoping she'd give some hint as to what she would like. She didn't, but he spent a long time looking at bracelets and charms until he found just what he wanted for Dani—a small, silver bell.

Anne took Bret with her to pick up the coat she had put on layaway for Dani. "I know it's awfully expensive," she confessed, her face glowing as the clerk brought out the russet-colored wool with its soft, white, fur collar. "And this hasn't been our best year at the store, but Dani will never buy a nice coat for herself, and won't it be beautiful on her?"

Anne's own coat had seen many a better day, and impulsively, Bret put his arm around her, hugging her. "You know something, Miss Annie?" he said. "I love you."

And he wondered why it should be so hard to say those same words to her daughter.

Anne looked up at him, laughing. "Why, we love you too, Bret. Now, tell me, what do you want for Christmas?"

All he could think of was Jimmy Skinner's words. *Nothing you can buy me. Nothing anyone can buy me.* But he forced a smile and said, "Surprise me."

At eleven o'clock, they met up with Todd and Dani outside the china shop. "Okay," Dani declared, "now it's boys against the girls." Shifting half her packages into Bret's arms and the other half into Todd's, Dani was just as bright-eyed and as energetic as she had been when she started out two hours earlier. "We'll meet you for lunch at one, in the café across the street. Mom, I want to show you what I found in the window of Odds and Ends...."

Todd and Bret, each loaded down with the women's purchases, watched Dani and Anne hurry off, then looked at each other. Without another word, they crossed the street and took a booth in the café.

"And we call them the weaker sex," Todd commented, groaning a little as he stretched out his legs.

Bret rested his arm along the back of the booth, agreeing, "I think I've had enough Christmas to last me three or four years."

It was quiet inside the restaurant, too early for regular diners, and they had taken a booth by the window so that they could watch for the arrival of the women. Christmas music played softly in the background, and Bret smiled when he recognized "Carol of the Bells."

"That song always reminds me of Dani," he said.

"That's Dani's favorite song," Todd said at the same time.

The moment between them was a little awkward, and then the waitress came to take their order. They both asked for coffee, black.

"This place is pretty impressive," Bret said when the coffee arrived. "Dani said you had something similar in mind for Clayville."

Todd shrugged. "Not the motif, but the idea. Tourist attractions work best in clusters. With Centerville already attracting a lot of traffic, particularly this time of year, there ought to be some way we could capitalize on it. But we haven't even been able to come up with an idea we can all agree on yet, much less starting to put it into practice."

"Put Dani on the town council," Bret suggested lightly, "she'd turn it into a Christmas village."

"Actually, that's not such a bad idea, and we've talked about it. I don't guess I'd be accused of overstating it if I point out there's a lot of money in Christmas. The trouble is, there's no one on the council—in the whole town, really—who has the kind of experience or expertise it would take to put a plan like that into action. Or any kind of plan."

Bret nodded, sipping his coffee. "Well, the first thing you'd have to do is look into alternative financing. Take this place, for example—it all didn't just spring up full grown and polished overnight. Somebody had to pay to refurbish all these buildings, redo the streets, conceal the wiring.... There are government programs, of course, and you could offer the business owners incentives, but what I think I'd do is try a lease-back plan—have the city buy whole blocks of downtown property and lease the commercial spaces back to the business operators. That way, you'd have a built-in quality-control system. Of course, that would just be the tip of the iceberg," he went on, warming to the idea. "You'd have to set up a standards-and-practices committee and a financial overseer, but you'd be amazed at how much funding is available for landmark buildings, and there are definite tax advantages. Of course, what you'd really need is a program administrator to carry something like that through."

Todd was smiling at him so complacently that Bret knew he had been trapped. He dropped his gaze to his cup. "Of course," he said in a much more subdued tone, "none of that is really my field."

"No," agreed Todd. "But it's too bad we don't have a few men like you on the council, who aren't afraid of change and know how to get things done. Then again—" Todd lifted his cup "—it'll all be academic if your sale goes through."

Bret very wisely said nothing.

"Do you know," Todd said after a moment, "I like you. Pretty amazing when you consider how hard I worked at disliking you before I ever met you."

Bret tried not to show his surprise, but Todd just smiled. "Sometimes, I wish you would stay. Like I said, the town needs you. You have a lot of friends in Clayville. All things being equal, I'd probably be one of them eventually. But there's just one problem, isn't there? Dani."

Bret held his silence, but his hand involuntarily tightened on the coffee cup. Todd's gaze wandered casually around the room.

"I knew you'd be trouble," he went on. "I've got to tell you, I got sick of hearing your name this past year, and when I heard you were in town, it was kind of a relief. I figured it would be over, whatever mystique Dani had built up around you, or at the very least, I'd discover your fatal flaw and expose you for the lowlife you had to be...but, of course, that couldn't happen. And you know why, don't you? Dani picked in us carbon copies of each other. We can't dislike each other, and Dani can't choose between us."

Bret thought he could find it very easy in that moment to dislike Todd...except that he knew the man was speaking the truth. He knew it, and he hated the easy, nonchalant way in which Todd declared it. But

Bret couldn't deny it. The only thing he was sure of, suddenly and fiercely, was that he did not want Dani to marry Todd. And it didn't matter that he couldn't think of a good reason why.

Todd brought his gaze back to Bret, and his tone was quiet and sober. "So here's the deal," he said. "I'm thirty-five years old, and I've spent a lifetime preparing to be the kind of husband Dani needs. I know I would be good for her. She's already good for me, better than I can tell you. I've loved her from the first minute I met her, but I guess you know how easy that is. All I want is her happiness, and I've never been able to say that about any other person I've ever known. So what I want to know now is this—do you love her enough to let her go?"

And there it was. Clear, simple and out in the open. What Bret had been avoiding trying to say to himself since he had come back; the reason, ultimately that he had come back: if he lost Dani now, it would be forever. If he let her go, there would be no second chance. She would marry another man, and that man would be good for her, he would make her happy, he would give her everything she needed. How could Bret keep her from doing what was best for her, the only possible choice she could make? If he loved her, why would he even want to?

But how could he let her go?

He met Todd's eyes, and he responded softly, "Do you?"

For a long moment, the two men looked at each other; stalemate. Then Todd glanced at his watch.

"Well," he said, "I still have a few things to pick up. Will you watch the packages?"

Bret picked up his coffee cup. "Yeah. No problem."

Todd stood up and looked down at Bret for a moment. "So," he said. His voice had a note of finality in it, but no hostility. It was simply a matter of lines being drawn. "I guess there's nothing more to say except...may the best man win."

The bell over the door clanged as Todd left, and Bret sank back against the booth, staring into his coffee. "Yeah," he murmured. "That's what I'm afraid of."

"LOOK, MOM." DANI flipped excitedly through the pages of a book. "*The History and Settlement of Calvin County.* It's got Zac and Hannah's story in it."

Her mother looked appreciatively over Dani's shoulder at the chapter headings. "I'm going to get this for Bret," she decided. "He's always half accused me of making that story up."

Her mother smiled. "Bret has never been as sentimental as you are."

The excitement faded from Dani's face, and her eyes grew thoughtful, even a little sad, as she agreed, "No. I guess not." But she took the book to the counter and asked to have it gift wrapped.

"He's a hard man to buy for," her mother went on as they waited. "I thought about a nice sweater—the poor boy doesn't seem to own anything but jeans and T-shirts—but then, I suppose that wouldn't do him much good in California, would it?"

Inexplicably, Dani felt her throat tighten. "Maybe he won't go back to California," she said.

"Of course, he will." Anne sounded surprised. "Is there any reason he shouldn't?"

Unexpectedly and totally unpreventably, Dani's eyes flashed with tears. She didn't know why, and if she had had even a moment's notice, she certainly would have been able to prevent them. But with her mother's plain, matter-of-fact words, it was as though all the strain, the secrecy, the yearning of the past week combined into one searing stab of hopelessness; her throat burned and her eyes filmed and the truth was like a leaden weight settling in her stomach.

She turned away quickly, but not before Anne's eyes softened with sympathy and concern and gentle understanding that tore at Dani's conscience like shredded glass. She paid for her purchase blindly and left the bookstore.

Her mother gestured to a bench just outside the store, and Dani followed her there without protest. They sat in silence for a time while Dani struggled to regain control of herself. The laughing shoppers, the gay decorations, the tinkle of bells from sidewalk Santas all faded into a blur, and Anne covered Dani's gloved hand with her own. "Honey, what are you going to do?" she asked tenderly.

Dani swallowed hard, hardly trusting herself for speech, unable to look at her mother. "Oh, Mom, I feel so bad. Todd is so wonderful, and I can't hurt him. I thought we had a future together, I really did, and you know I've had a crush on Bret since I was—

was a kid—'' Here her voice broke, and her mother
patted her hand.

"Does Bret know?"

Dani shook her head mutely, tightening her jaw
against the tears that surged and receded and surged
again.

Anne was silent for a time, and then she said,
"You're right. Todd is a wonderful man. He's all your
father and I ever could have wanted for you, and the
two of you make a beautiful couple. I know that he
adores you. But it's more than a crush you feel for
Bret, isn't it?"

Dani looked at her mother, miserable and helpless.
"Yes," she whispered. "And it's been going on so
long that I—I hardly realized when he stopped being
my friend and started being the only man I've ever
loved.... But he doesn't feel the same way about me,
and even if he did, he would never tell me because..."

Anne nodded. "Because of Todd."

"And other things." Dani looked down at the sidewalk, blotting her eyes with the back of her coat
sleeve.

"Bret's an honorable man," Anne said. "And sensible."

Dani looked up at her, pleading. "Mom, do you
think it's wrong the way I feel? What should I do?"

Her mother smiled, tiredly it seemed, and slipped
her arm around Dani's shoulders, drawing her close in
a gentle embrace. "No, darling," she said. "I don't
think it's wrong. I think it's...inevitable. As for what
you should do, I wish I could tell you. I really do."

She leaned away and took Dani's chin in her hand, looking into her eyes as though she could impart courage with her smile. "You'll make the right choice, Dani," she said. "But you have to make it alone."

"It's scary," Dani whispered.

Anne sighed as she drew Dani's head onto her shoulder again. "I know, baby," she said softly, "I know."

But that was of no help at all.

BRET HELPED THE WOMEN carry their packages inside, then made himself scarce as they went upstairs to giggle and whisper over their purchases. He himself had come away with a down-filled parka for Miss Annie in addition to the power saw he'd bought for her husband, and, on an impulse, he'd purchased a whimsical coffee mug with a cartoon-character cat exclaiming "Bah, Humbug!" for his secretary. That one he had already had the store ship; he hoped to persuade Dani to wrap the others...except, of course, for the bracelet he'd gotten her. That one he wanted to wrap himself.

He was in the kitchen, making a pot of coffee, when the phone rang. "I'll get it!" he called upstairs.

Miss Annie's voice floated down to him. "Thanks, Bret."

He was surprised when the voice on the other end asked for him. "Speaking."

"One moment, please. Mr. Notions is calling."

The secretary transferred the call and in record time, Craig's voice boomed over the line. "Well, young man, you must have been a very, very good boy this year."

Then tension that went through every fiber of Bret's body was as sharp as a headache. "Don't play games, Craig."

"All right, short and sweet. Inushu is ready to make an offer."

Bret's voice was flat. "How much?"

"Well, I don't want to jinx it, but let's just say I threw out a figure roughly the equivalent of twice the appraised value and they didn't blink an eye."

Bret sank back against the wall. His throat was dry, and his fingers were tight on the receiver. He tried very hard to make his mind blank.

"Now, the project developer wants to go over the site personally, so what do you say to next Wednesday? We'll be coming in by private plane, so let's say ten o'clock at the property."

Bret cleared his throat. "Umm, I don't known. There's someone living in the house...."

"What house? Nobody cares about houses. It's just a formality. The guy wants to see what he's getting. Nobody has to even know we're there. Ten o'clock Wednesday, and be ready to sign on the dotted line."

"Right. Sure, Craig, sounds fine." Bret gathered his scattered thoughts long enough to inquire, "So that's it, then? It's really a go?"

"All that's missing is the signatures. And don't bother to thank me. All part of the job."

Bret managed a dry smile. "And the commission."

"Well, there's always that. Wednesday, then. I'll call if there's a change."

"Thanks, Craig."

For a long time after he'd replaced the receiver, Bret stood there, leaning against the wall, trying to take it all in. He had done it. He had come here to sell the property and, as though it were a special-order miracle, he had sold it. Not only had he sold it, but in a way that would change the face of this town forever, and it was a good thing. The *best* thing.

The view through the window was of another leaden day, and he could hear the rhythmic sound of an ax as Harold split kindling for the fireplace. *Wood splitter,* Bret thought absently. *That's what I should've gotten him.* But somehow, he didn't think that was a gift that would be greatly appreciated. Harold was a man who liked to do things the old-fashioned way. A wood splitter would be as out of place around here as ... as an electronics plant.

Bret did not know how long Dani had been standing at the door before he sensed her presence, but from the expression on her face, he knew it had been long enough to overhear at least part of the telephone conversation. He forced a smile and gestured toward the telephone.

"My real-estate agent," he explained. "Maybe you gathered."

Her voice was cautious. "You have an offer?"

"A whopper." He went over to the coffeepot, straining for enthusiasm he didn't feel. "Sounds like they want to finalize the deal as early as Wednesday, can you believe that?" He took a mug off the rack. "Coffee?"

Dani crossed the room, moving as if the floor were strewn with booby traps. "So they're serious, then. This could really happen."

"It *has* happened." He abandoned the effort at bright spirits and let his voice fall flat as he filled his cup. Then he turned to her, bracing himself. "I guess a lot of people around here are going to be pretty upset with me." *Including you,* he thought. *Mostly you.*

But she kept her emotions very tightly disguised, even though her voice was beginning to show the strain. "Just because they made an offer doesn't mean you have to accept."

His laugh was short and devoid of mirth. "You haven't heard the offer yet."

"So what did they do?" she shot back, and the careful dance around emotions they had been doing was completely abandoned. "Threaten to break your knees? Put a dead horse's head in your bed? Come on, Bret, you're not that greedy! You've lived without their money for years, the world's not going to come to an end if you don't take it now!"

"It's not greed!" Tension knotted in his muscles again, and though he tried to keep his voice calm, he did not succeed very well. "It's good business, but it's more than that. Damn it, Dani, let's not start this again. This is progress. It's good for the town—it may be the only chance this town has. Why do you keep trying to make me out to be the bad guy?"

"You're not doing this for the town!" she cried. "You're not even doing it for you—because you need the money or because it's good business or anything else! You're doing it because you can't stand to see anything stay static, because you want to put as much distance between you and the past as you can, and if you have to destroy the past to do it, then that's okay, too, isn't it?''

"That's not true," he said hoarsely.

But she shook her head violently, her ponytail lashing across her face with a gesture that was swift and abrupt, as though she were trying to shake off the aura of him or rid herself of a bad taste. "You couldn't wait to get out of here when you were a kid, you couldn't get far enough away—"

"For God's sake, Dani, that was college!"

"You never came back. You didn't even think about it—"

"I came back!"

"You never *cared* about things the way I do!" she cried. "I always thought you did, but I was wrong. All these years, I've been wrong about you."

"I cared," he said fiercely. His hand was wound so tightly around the coffee cup that his fingers hurt. "I've always cared." And suddenly, he realized he was not talking about the land or his hometown or any of the things from his past...or perhaps he was. Perhaps, all of those things and Dani were inextricably mixed. He only knew that when he looked at her, the hurt and the disappointment in her eyes went through him like the slow-cutting edge of a dull knife and an emptiness filled him that was bigger than any defeat he had ever known.

He said quietly, tiredly, "We were always different, Dani. I guess the only thing we ever had in common was each other."

Her eyes were big and far too bright. He saw her raise her hand to her throat as though it hurt her. He turned away, looking out the window, focusing his gaze on the trampled, churned up snow, the stark silhouette of an ice-glazed tree at the turn of the drive. The silence pulsed between them, heavy and desolate.

After a moment, he murmured, "Footprints in the snow."

"What?" Her voice was hoarse, confused.

He did not turn around. If he saw tears in her eyes now, even tears of anger, he would not be able to stand it. "Zac and Hannah. I always wondered why they didn't just follow those footprints in the snow."

"Maybe..." She drew in a soft, unsteady breath. "Maybe they were afraid."

"Maybe."

She said softly, "Are you afraid, Bret?"

He could feel her eyes on him, as gentle as a questing caress, as hesitant as a whisper. His muscles tensed against it, he made himself stand still. Afraid? Oh, yes. Afraid of making another mistake, afraid of hurting Dani, afraid of being wrong...maybe just afraid of being happy.

He glanced down, surprised to find the coffee cup still in his hand. Though he didn't want it, he took a sip. And he kept his gaze fixed on the view through the window. "When I was a kid," he said, "it was all so simple. There was so much to do, so much to explore. I didn't find what I expected to, and maybe now, it doesn't seem as important as it once did, but somebody once said the only thing worse than wanting and not having is not knowing what you want."

Her voice was tight and strained behind him, but strangely low, with a husky, seductive quality that reverberated in his blood. "You know what you want, Bret. You're just afraid to ask for it."

He drew in his breath but couldn't release it. His chest was tight, and his blood was racing. He felt disoriented; he wasn't sure what they were talking about anymore. Because he did know what he wanted and he would never, ever ask for it.

Dani moved forward. She reached out her hand to touch his arm, but let it drop. Bret looked at her and saw a jaw that was tightly set, eyes that were wide and unafraid, a face that was filled with all the stubborn, unflinching honesty he had ever loved, and it was with all the will at his command that he refused to reach for her. She said steadily, "You have choices, Bret. You always have choices."

It was as though a line had been drawn through time, separating one moment from the next, what was from what might be, and whatever he said now would change his future—both their futures—forever. There was no shying away from that line; time moved on.

"Yes," he agreed huskily. "I have choices." And then, deliberately, he turned back to the window. "But none of them appeals to me."

He took a sip of the coffee, trying to make the gesture casual, and then he said the words. "I guess I'll be going back to L.A. after I meet with those people Wednesday. I know I said I'd stay for Christmas, but it's really a bad time to be away from the office. All I really came here for was to check out the property, you know." The words tasted like poison on his tongue and he could feel them sting her flesh as though it were his own. "Of course," he added, lifting the cup again, "I'll come back for your wedding."

"My wedding?" The words were repeated blankly, like a recording.

He turned, making himself smile, making it look genuine. "You did mean to invite me, didn't you?"

Her face was as blank as her voice, as though all the life had been drained out of it. Only her eyes remained animated, busily searching, probing his. He withstood the assault manfully. "Of course. Of course, I'll invite you. But I never— I didn't say—"

He deliberately deepened the smile. "Come on, Dani, you've tortured the guy long enough. You know you're going to marry him. Give the poor fellow a break. Say yes."

Still the searching, almost a plea, maybe even a hint of desperation. Bret made himself put the coffee cup on the counter before his tight fingers crushed it.

"Is that what you want me to do?" she said, so softly he almost had to strain to hear.

He shrugged. "What I want doesn't have anything to do with it. But if you want my advice, you're a fool to let this one get away. I know how it feels to be over thirty and alone, Dani, and guys like Todd don't come along every day. Not in this hick burg, anyway."

"No," she whispered. She never took her eyes off him. "They don't."

Her gaze was like a laser, burning away the layers of his defense. Any moment now, she would break through the final thin barrier and discover "lies" written in black letters all over his soul. He couldn't look at her anymore. He couldn't stay here anymore. He couldn't lie to her anymore.

He turned for the door as casually as possible. "I think I'll go give your dad a hand."

"Bret."

He almost made it. He had one hand on his coat, the other on the door. He looked back.

Her face still looked stunned, her eyes ravaged, but her voice was almost normal. "I came down to see if you had anything you wanted me to wrap for you."

It actually hurt to smile, but he managed it. "Thanks. I'll bring them up to your place later."

She nodded, and he left as quickly as he could.

HE HAD DONE THE RIGHT thing. Bret breathed deeply of the sharp, icy air and repeated the assurance to himself in time with the crunch of his footsteps on the snow. He had done the only possible thing.

Do you love her enough to let her go?

He had let her go because he had no choice. Because one of them deserved to be happy and because it had to be Dani. That was all.

The ax was stuck in the chopping block, but Harold Griffin had apparently abandoned the chore. Bret picked up the tool, centered a log and began to swing with a vengeance. He brought the ax up and down, back and forth, taking satisfaction in the thud of each swing, the flying of chips. Sweat filmed his face and chilled him beneath his coat. His hands stung, and more than once, he came very close to losing a foot, but he didn't stop.

Then a mild voice spoke up behind him. "You fixing on killing something, son, or you figure you just need the exercise?"

Bret staggered back, panting, and let the ax drop as he turned to face Harold. He pushed his hair back, waiting for his breath to return, and he could have tossed off some off-hand explanation for his sudden burst of energy. But he was too defeated, too worn out and bruised inside to dissemble. Not again.

He bent and began to gather up the splintered wood. "I got an offer on my property."

The other man's voice was mild. "Good for you."

"It is good," Bret said tightly. "It's good for everybody. Your property values will go sky high."

"Yeah, I reckon they would, if I had a mind to sell. Which I don't."

"People will be moving in from all over. You won't be able to keep up with the business at your store. And if Todd Renshaw thinks he's got a newspaper now, just wait until he has something to really write about. Circulation will double, just like the population. And with the revenues the county will be bringing in, there'll be plenty to put into the school—they might even build a new one. The teachers can get the supplies they need and—"

"Yep," agreed Harold. "Sounds like it's going to be good for everybody. And two young people couldn't ask for a better wedding gift than the future you've got plotted out for them."

Bret tensed, then straightened up. He couldn't keep the belligerence out of his voice or his pose. "But you don't want an electronics plant in your backyard."

Harold just smiled, adjusting his cap a little more snugly on his head. "I've seen a lot of changes, Bret. I guess I can handle this one."

"I know people are going to accuse me of selling out. There's going to be an uproar, there always is in small towns like this. Shortsightedness, that's the problem. Nobody can accept progress."

"Seems to me you're a lot more upset by this than anybody I know."

Bret dumped an armload of kindling into the wood box and turned for more.

"Nobody's forcing you to sell, you know," Harold went on. "I've often wondered about it, Bret. Why don't you just come on back home here and settle down?"

"I can't."

"Why not?"

"Because I'm in love with Dani." He hadn't meant to say that; he couldn't believe it when he heard the words leave his mouth. He let the kindling slip from his fingers, and he looked up at Harold, stunned.

But the other man just smiled. "Well," he said mildly, "it's about damn time."

Bret stood up slowly, expecting to feel embarrassed, shocked, apologetic. What he felt was an enormous sense of relief. He had said it, if not to her, then to someone. It was out and he didn't have to hide it anymore. No more lies.

Harold shoved his hands into the pockets of his coat and rocked back slightly on his heels. "We've been expecting this for some time now, you know. About twenty years, I'd say. But let me see if I've got this straight. You're in love with my daughter, so you figure the best thing you can do is the one thing that will make her mad—sell the old homestead. Then I guess you'll go on back to California without her." He nodded. "Makes sense."

Bret drew an arm across his face tiredly. "There's nothing else I can do. Dani's life is here. Mine's on the coast. She's got everything going for her now. I can't just come in and tear it all apart."

"What does Dani have to say about all this?"

"Nothing. I haven't told her."

"I can't say that's the smartest thing I've ever known you to do."

Bret shook his head tersely. "She's in love with Todd."

"Maybe. Maybe not. But she's got a right to know and to make up her own mind."

Just as Bret had had a right to know ten years ago.

He returned Harold's gaze bleakly. "Even if I wanted to stay here, even if Dani wanted me, I couldn't make a living here. There's not a lot of call for burglar alarms and security patrols around here, and I don't know anything else."

"You could always learn."

But Bret shook his head. "I lost one marriage," he said simply. "I can't take a chance with Dani. Besides, it's too late." He looked back toward the house. "I just told Dani I wanted her to marry Todd."

"Maybe she won't listen to you."

Bret managed a smile, though it was weary and sad. "She always listens to me," he said. "That's the trouble."

FROM HIS WINDOW BRET could see Dani's house. There was a light on in the loft, and when he strained, he thought he could see a shadow pass before it, but it turned out to be only a branch moving in the wind.

She's got a right to know....

And she did. She had a right to know the one thing he could never tell her, but if he had to lie to her one more time, the stain would be on his conscience forever. She had a right to know, and he had a right to tell her.

He went over to the small writing desk beside the closet and opened a drawer. Among the odds and ends, he found an old ruled notepad and several ballpoint pens. Bret tore a sheet off the pad and picked up a pen.

Dear Dani,

I know it doesn't make any difference now, but I love you. I love you as a man loves a woman, and I want you like a man wants a woman, and I think I have for years. I wish it could have been different for us, but I only want you to be happy. Please believe that.

Your best friend,

Bret

He looked at the paper for a long time, aching inside, wishing, wondering.... And then he folded the paper, tore it neatly in half, folded it again and tore it again. He opened his hand and watched the pieces drift into the trash can.

Chapter Eleven

Dani had not spent an evening alone with Todd since Bret had come home. She hadn't planned it that way—she was sure she hadn't—but the holidays were always hectic. Tonight, they had been to a party and it was only natural that he should come inside when he took her home. It made Dani a little nervous, for reasons she didn't want to think about.

She hadn't wanted to go to the party, but once there, she had deliberately—somewhat fiercely—set out to have a good time. It was almost as though she was desperately trying to prove she could have a good time without Bret, which was ridiculous because she had had plenty of good times before he had arrived. Hundreds of good times.

"I was surprised Bret wasn't there tonight," Todd commented, helping her off with her coat.

"He doesn't know everyone in town," she replied a bit sharply. And then, forcing a more casual tone, she added, "Besides, I guess it's getting a little awkward for him, explaining about the land deal. He thinks the whole town is going to get up in arms over it." And then, refusing to let the conversation focus on Bret, she said brightly, "Look, there are still a few embers in the fireplace. Think you can get a fire stirred up?"

"At your service." Todd hung his coat on the rack beside hers. "How about something to drink?"

"Wine or coffee? Or I think I've got some eggnog left." Bret's eggnog.

"Wine, I think."

She hurried to the kitchen, and once there, she braced her hands on the counter, taking a deep breath, trying to steady her nerves. But it wasn't just nerves. She felt raw inside, battered, exposed and shaken, and she had felt that way ever since the encounter with Bret the afternoon before. She went through the day, she laughed and she talked and she moved and she kept busy, but she was still in something of a state of shock.

Over and over, she told herself how lucky she was. She had done everything but throw herself at Bret's feet—more than once she had literally thrown herself into his arms. She had given him every possible chance to reciprocate her feelings...but he hadn't. He must have known; there had been a moment yesterday when she was sure he knew, when she felt with every fiber of her being that he was on the verge of telling her the same thing—but he hadn't. He had let the moment slip by, and he had done it so easily, so gracefully, that not even a dent was left in their friendship to show how close she had come to stepping over the line. She should be grateful. She *was* grateful. She had almost made the biggest mistake of her life, and Bret had saved her.

Except that she did not feel as though she'd been saved. She felt lost and numb, and she couldn't explain it.

Bret was right. Men like Todd didn't come along every day and she was lucky, so lucky to have found him. She wanted to get married, to have children and grandchildren and the same man by her side day and night... and Bret did not want her. She had almost thrown it all away for a man who didn't want her, and in so doing, she would have lost twice: Todd, the man who should be her husband, and Bret, her best friend. She was very, very lucky.

She poured the wine and came back into the living room. Todd was sitting on the floor before the fireplace, coaxing a blaze from the logs. He had plugged in the Christmas-tree lights, and the twinkling lights added their play to the glow of the fire that planed his face. Dani felt a rush of tenderness looking at him, and reminded herself again how lucky she was. Suddenly, she wanted to be held, needed to be taken into strong, loving arms and kissed and stroked.

But not by him.

She pushed the treacherous thought out of the way and crossed the room, dropping onto the hearth rug beside him. He took the glass of wine from her, smiling. "Did I tell you how pretty you look tonight?"

"Several times." The party had not been formal and she was wearing winter white wool pants and a bright red overblouse with a floppy bow. She did not feel particularly ravishing, but it was nice to hear Todd say that she was. Nice to know that to some man, somewhere, she would always be beautiful.

Todd said, "So Bret's leaving after he makes the deal Wednesday."

Dani took a sip of her wine. "That's right."

"I've been looking into the Inushu plans. I'm starting to come up with some pretty interesting information."

"I don't want to talk about that," Dani said abruptly.

He looked surprised. "You might want to know what I've found out."

She shook her head. "I don't want to talk about electronics or Japanese or Bret, not tonight. I'm not interested and I don't care, not about any of it."

He smiled. "Well, I've got to say I don't believe you don't care. But it is nice, I'll admit, not to talk about Bret for once."

He lifted his hand, encircling her neck, his expression tender and adoring in the firelight. Dani thought he was going to kiss her. She wanted to kiss him. She was sure she did.

And then he let his hand trail down her arm. He said, "I brought a little something for you to put under your tree." He put down the wineglass and reached into his pocket. "But I think I'd rather have you open it now."

"Oh, Todd, it's too early for presents," she said starting to protest, and then she stopped as he drew out a small, square box wrapped in gold paper.

Dani's heart pounded and her fingers shook a little as she took it from him. She knew what was inside. She knew it by the shape of the box, by the look on his face, by the simple perfection of it all. A Christmas engagement, a New Year's announcement, a spring wedding... Perfect. Just perfect.

Visions of bridal showers, shopping trips, flower girls and white lace were skating through her head as she tore off the gold wrapping and lifted the lid. The small solitaire gleamed like a droplet of ice against the blue velvet, catching the glow of the fire and the spark of the tree lights. All engagement rings should be seen by firelight, she thought. It was perfect.

The ring glowed like a promise there on the velvet, and Todd's hand was warm and loving on her arm. She reached to draw it out and slip it onto her finger. But she couldn't.

The tears burned her eyes, trembling on her lashes. "I'm sorry," she whispered, and closed the lid.

The fire popped, and outside, an icy branch creaked in the wind. The silence between them was long and full and aching. Then Todd smiled a little and said, "Overplayed my hand, huh?"

She swallowed hard and shook her head. He wouldn't take the box from her, so she placed it on the hearth. Then he said one word.

"Bret."

Not a question, but a statement of fact.

Dani stood, hugging her arms, pressing her lips tightly together to stop the tremors, but still, her voice was broken. "Oh, Todd, I've been so unfair to you." She tried to draw a breath, but it sounded more like a sob. "I didn't mean to be, I swear I didn't. I always knew I wasn't sure, but I never knew why until... Still, I wanted to marry you, I wanted to believe we could be happy together, that—that he would go away and everything would be the way it used to be, but it can't be. I know that now. And I can't marry you when I'm in love with another man.''

After a long moment, Todd said, ''Well, thank you for that, at least.''

He stood up slowly, standing very close, but Dani couldn't turn to look at him. She stood with her head lowered, gripping her arms and choking back tears, and after a moment, Todd laid his hand lightly on her shoulder in a comforting, reassuring gesture. ''I had to know, Dani,'' he said. ''I couldn't go on like this. I just had to know.''

She watched as he bent to pick up the jewel box and turned toward the door. Then he stopped. A strangely sad half smile curved his lips as he said, ''You know something? If you would've had me, I think I would have married you anyway.''

Dani squeezed her eyes tightly shut and listened to the sound of his retreating footsteps, to the soft closing of the door. Then she couldn't fight it any longer. She began to sob, and once she started, she couldn't stop. She cried far, far into the night.

BLUE SKIES WERE spilling in through her window when Dani awoke late the next morning. Her eyes were swollen, and her chest felt stuffy, as though she were coming down with a bad cold, but she knew it was only the residue of tears. She had fallen asleep atop the bedspread, exhausted from crying, fully clothed, with only an afghan to keep off the night's chill. She had cried for Todd and for Bret and for herself; she had cried in anger and hopelessness and self-pity and frustration and in sheer, raw pain. Dani rarely cried; in fact, she could not remember a time in her life when she had wept so helplessly and for so long. Surely she had plumbed the depths of human misery.

People said such a catharsis was therapeutic and that things always looked better in the morning. Nothing could have been farther from the truth. The bright winter sunlight mocked the bleakness inside her soul when she opened her eyes, and all she wanted to do was pull the afghan over her head and lie there, numb with despair, until spring.

She should have been relieved it was over. No more lies, no more deception. She had made her choice... and she had lost everything.

She moved her eyes around the room, trying to take comfort in the familiarity of her surroundings. The Christmas cards that Bret had helped her string along the loft railing, the garland that Bret had wound around the bannister, the mistletoe... the Christmas cactus, as withered as her dreams, on her bedside table. But she hadn't lost everything. She still had her home, her family, the friends she loved, the town in which she had grown up.... But even that was changing, slipping away from her, outgrowing her. Soon, there would be nothing left.

She made herself get off the bed, shivering a little as her stockinged feet struck the bare floor. She might feel as though the world had ended, but in truth, life went on and she had plenty to do today. One night of mourning was enough to give to a man who didn't love her and to an engagement that had never been. She refused to wallow in self-pity. She couldn't afford to.

She started for the shower, but on her way, she paused and picked up the cactus. She looked at it for a minute, then dropped it into the trash can. Bret was right. She did have a tendency to hold on to things long past their time...things like hope—and even love. And the plant was as dead as it was ever going to get.

The hot shower restored her body, taking the puffiness out of her eyes and the soreness out of her muscles, but the physical well-being was abrasive, even painful, in contrast to the ache she felt inside. She would have to tell her mother. She'd have to tell a lot of people who would be expecting to see Todd and her together during the holidays, make a lot of excuses, face up to a lot of disappointment...and Bret. Bret would have to know. But she couldn't face him. Someone else would have to tell him, because she couldn't. He would be leaving in a few days anyway, and once he was gone...

Once he was gone, he wouldn't come back. She knew that as clearly as she had ever known anything in her life.

Someone was knocking on her door when she came out of the shower, wrapped in a terry cloth robe and drying her hair with a towel. Her heart started pounding as she gripped the banister. Her parents never knocked. Bret. Or Todd...

She went down the stairs quickly, uncertain whether to feel dread or anticipation, and not fully able to feel either, thinking only, *Not this morning, not now. I can't deal with either of them now....*

But when she opened the door, it was neither of them. A stranger in a postal uniform stood there,

smiling at her. "Morning, miss. Package for you." He
offered her a medium-size box, with the rest of the
mail stacked on top of it.

She stared at him. "You're not the usual mailman.
Where's Mr. Redman? He's not sick, is he?"

"Not that I know of." The stranger's blue eyes
twinkled with good humor beneath the visor of his
cap, and his cheeks were as red as cherries in the cold.
A shock of white hair encircled his head beneath the
cap in the back, and he looked like a thoroughly
pleasant, very cheerful fellow. Dani was just surprised that she didn't recognize him; she knew everyone in town. "I'm just helping out for the holidays."

"Oh." She took the package from him. "I'm sorry
you had to come to the door. I've been meaning to get
a bigger mailbox."

"No trouble." He tipped his hat to her. "Have a
Merry Christmas, now."

"Thank you. You, too."

The package was from Aunt Flora in New Jersey,
and even though the box inside was wrapped with an
expensive department-store wrapping and promi-
nently displayed a Do Not Open Until Christmas
sticker, under other circumstances, Dani wouldn't
have been able to resist peeling open a corner and
taking a peek. Today, she wasn't interested. She put
the package under the tree and flipped through the
other envelopes in a desultory fashion. Christmas
cards, bills . . . she didn't feel like opening those, either. She tossed the lot on the end table, and then
something caught her eye.

It was a plain white envelope, not Christmas-card size, and it didn't have a return address. It didn't, in fact, have any address at all. It was completely blank, front and back, and as Dani examined it curiously, she started toward the door, wondering if the new post-man had made a mistake. But she could already hear his Jeep moving down the road, and there was only one way to find out. She opened the envelope and pulled out a single sheet of lined note paper.

Dear Dani,
    I know it doesn't make any difference now...

THE WORDS FROM THE OLD song, "California Dreaming" were going through Bret's head as he crossed the drive toward Dani's house. At another time, the irony of the song would have brought a wry smile to his lips, but today, it simply haunted him, chilling him to his soul. He wasn't dreaming about California. If he dreamed about any place from now on, it would be here, where she was.

One hand was shoved deep into his coat pocket for warmth, in the other, he carried a snow shovel slung over his shoulder. The temperature was supposed to go above freezing today, and Harold had wanted to make sure Dani's porch and drive were cleared of snow before it turned to slush and then refroze into danger-ous ice. Bret had volunteered for the job because men Harold's age shouldn't be wielding a snow shovel, and because he knew he couldn't go forever avoiding Dani.

She had gone to a party with Todd last night. He had watched them drive away with a bitterness in his throat and an ache in his heart, then he had turned away from the window and set about being the most cheerful, entertaining and helpful houseguest Harold and Anne Griffin had ever had. It would be hell getting through the next three days, trying to act normal with Dani, trying to give the people he loved memories they could treasure of his last visit home, trying, above all else, not to let any of them know that every minute he stayed here was killing him inside.... And yet, three days was not nearly long enough.

It wasn't long enough to make things right between them. It wasn't long enough to see her laugh again, to hear her joke with him as she used to, to walk with her in the snow, talking about nothing at all, just feeling good being together. It wasn't long enough to see her eyes light up like a child's when she opened her presents on Christmas morning or to go caroling with her or to dance with her in the light of the Christmas tree... because everything was changed now. And he didn't have that magical power of Dani's to turn back time, to erase the years and bring back innocence. He couldn't undo what he had done or take away the memory of the hurt and disappointment in Dani's eyes his words had caused.

He had almost reached her porch and was debating whether to go up and knock or to simply get on with his work when, suddenly, the door flew open and Dani burst out. She was wearing a bath robe, her eyes were blazing as she plunged down the steps toward him.

He dropped the shovel. "Dani, what's wrong!"

"You dirty, rotten, lying *snake!*"

She drew back her arm to strike him, and it was only instinct that caused him to catch her arm, fending off the blow. She struggled, slipping on the snow-packed ground, and the robe parted to give him a glimpse of her naked chest and one slim thigh. "You lied to me!" she shouted at him. Her color was high and her face wild with fury. "All this time you—"

"Are you crazy?" He grabbed her and shook her because he didn't know what else to do. "Running out here in your bathrobe and bare feet—your hair is wet!"

"Let go of me!" She wrenched away violently, her eyes and her face like fire. "How dare you! How *could* you? Do you know what you put me through? Do you have any idea?"

He was becoming angry now himself. "What are you talking about?"

"This!" She raised a closed fist at him and he saw that it concealed some kind of crumpled paper. "Is that it, then? Were you just going to sneak away and forget about me? Was that the plan, never telling me, letting me wonder? You lying, cheating, lowdown son of a—"

"Get in the house, for heaven's sake!" He shoved her toward the door. "You can't stand around half-naked in the snow screaming at me for no good reason—especially not if you're going to use that kind of language!"

"I can scream at you wherever I want!"

"Get inside!"

He grabbed her arm and half pushed her up the steps, slamming the door behind him with a little more

force than necessary when they were inside. "Now
what in God's name is this all about?"

"This!"

She shoved the paper at him again, and this time he
snatched it from her, scowling as he unfolded it. "Get
something on your feet," he commanded her shortly.
"You're going to catch cold."

But then the words on the paper leapt up at him. His
words. His paper. His handwriting. He could feel the
blood drain from his face, but he couldn't tear his eyes
away from the writing. "Where did you get this?" he
demanded hoarsely.

"What does it matter where I got it? Did you leave
it in my mailbox? Were you just going to walk away
and leave that for goodbye? Or were you going to mail
it from California? Damn you, Bret, why couldn't you
just *tell* me?"

He looked up at her, numbed beyond all feeling. "I
tore it up. It was a secret, like we used to—"

"A secret!" Her voice had gone from righteous
outrage to despair. "For the love of heaven, don't you
know what I've been going through these past weeks?
Why would you want to keep it a *secret?*"

"I tore it up..." he repeated dully. "I threw it
away..." But there were no tears in the letter, no tape,
not even any creases, except the ones Dani had made
with her angry fist.

"Oh, Bret, I've been in love with you most of my
life! When we were teenagers, when you went away to
college, even when you came back—to tell me you
were getting married..." Her voice broke, and was a
note lower in pitch as she continued. "Oh, God, I did

everything but *beg* you to love me back! And these last weeks—you *knew* what was happening between us, you knew how I felt, and yet you—"

"You shouldn't have this," he said, looking at the paper. "There is no way you could have this."

"Bret, are you listening to me?" she cried. "Have you heard one word I've said? I love you!"

And then he did hear her, or he thought he did. The words drifted to him as though through a heavy fog, and he looked up at her, feeling numb, disbelieving, a little drugged. "What?" he said hoarsely. "What did you say?"

She stood less than three feet away from him, her cheeks stained with color and her eyes defiant, her chin lifted coolly. "I said," she repeated deliberately, "that I'm in love with you. I said you're a fool for not realizing it before and doing something about it. I said I'm the best thing that could ever happen to you, and if you don't realize that by now, then you deserve to lose me!"

"Dani." It was hardly a breath, and when he reached out his arms, she was in them. He didn't know how it happened, he didn't know how any of it had happened. He could feel her shaking, and he held her tighter. The paper slipped from his fingers as he brought his hands up to caress her damp hair, and her fragrance, warm and lovely, drifted up to him, cinnamon and vanilla. Her shampoo. It had been her shampoo all along.

He could feel her breasts pressing into his chest, and her arms were tight and straining as they encircled his back. He felt a surge of strength and hot desire, a wash of weakness and disbelief, and he thought, *This is it. This is why I came home, this is all I ever wanted.* None of it made sense. He couldn't understand the miracle that had brought her to him, nor could he fully believe it was real, but it was, for the moment, enough that she was here, holding him, loving him. He parted his lips against her hair to better drink in her scent, her warmth, the dizzying, intoxicating *sureness* of her, and in a moment, he would turn his mouth to hers and then it would be too late for making sense, too late for second thoughts. So he released an unsteady breath and made his arms loosen a fraction. He looked down at her.

"Dani," he said hoarsely, "this is not a good idea."

And though it cost him more strength than he thought he possessed, he let his hands move down her arms, and he stepped back. "Just because I—I never should have written it down, and you never should have read it. I didn't want to mix up your life, I didn't want to cause trouble. Todd..."

She shook her head firmly, pressing her lips tightly together for a moment. "I gave Todd his ring back last night, before—before I even read your letter. I thought I had lost both of you, that's why I was so mad at you.... If I had known you felt the same way I did, I wouldn't have been so confused. I could have done the right thing a lot sooner. Oh, Bret, we've wasted so much time!"

"Years," he agreed softly. And he stood only inches away from her, drinking her in, aching for her, adrift in wonder and disbelief, yet paralyzed with uncertainty. Some things were too good to be true. Some things were never meant to be. He couldn't afford to make another mistake, not with Dani.

He made himself look away from her, half turning. He tried to take a breath, and found it more difficult than he anticipated. "Dani, this is...wow." He ran his fingers through his hair. "This isn't easy. We should talk."

"All right," she said quietly. She stood very still, watching him, and her gaze held him as tightly as her embrace had done. "I'll go first." She took a breath. "You always accused me of being afraid of change, but it's you, isn't it? You're the one who's afraid."

He started to shake his head in denial, but then heard himself saying, "Yes." He looked at her helplessly, wanting her and knowing he shouldn't, needing her and feeling the moment poised between his fingers, ready to grasp... seeing his whole life in her face, all that had ever had any meaning to him reflected in her eyes—and he was afraid, desperately afraid, of losing it.

"Things have already changed between us, Bret," she said softly. "They changed the first time you kissed me, and you know that, don't you? There's no going back. Why don't you kiss me now?"

"Dani, there's so much..." But he couldn't, at that moment, think of any of it. All the things that needed to be said, all the reasons this was wrong, all the cautions to be careful...they all seemed insignificant, faraway, and they diffused into meaningless puffs of smoke the moment he tried to grasp them. He wanted to be sensible, he wanted to do what was right for Dani, he wanted her to be able to count on him the way he had always counted on her.... But the only thing that seemed to matter was Dani, only a finger's length away, wanting him as much as he wanted her.

"Let it be easy," she whispered, and there was a hesitance in her eyes, almost a plea. "Things have always been so easy and right between us. I've wanted you for so long, and I hurt for you so much. Don't make it hurt now."

And it was easy. Her fingers touched his in a light gesture of reassurance, and his hand closed around hers. He turned her into his arms, meaning to comfort her, to hold her, to give them both a chance to think. But instead, his mouth was on hers, drinking in her startled breath of surprise, tasting her, drawing her in and letting himself drown in her, and it was easy and so right. She made him dizzy; she took away his power of thought. Her warmth baked through his skin, quickening his blood. He felt the frantic beating of her heart, almost lost in the thunder of his own, and the curve of her breast, just beneath his cupped hand, the length of her waist. He felt the straining of her small, tight muscles against his and the caress of her hand on the back of his neck, and the heat that filled his loins was heavy and painful, but that was right, too, inevitable and good.

Her hands were beneath his open jacket when the kiss ended, pulling it down, and that was the first time Bret realized he was still wearing his coat. He lowered his arms and let the jacket fall to the floor, and then he returned to her, caressing her face, the damp strands of her hair, the curve of her collarbone where it was exposed by the robe, and the shape of her shoulder. Her face was radiant, her lips swollen from his kisses, her breath as unsteady as his own. His eyes moved over hers, anxiously searching, then inevitably downward across her throat, the V of naked chest, the shape of her breasts.

He smiled, and said huskily, "You're not wearing anything under that robe, are you?"

She shook her head, and there might have been a flash of shyness in her eyes, or embarrassment. But it was gone in an instant and she held his gaze. "Are we going to make love, Bret?"

His heart lurched and pounded. Make love...with Dani. After all these years of thinking about it and pretending not to, of wanting and making himself not want... He traced the shape of her lips with an unsteady finger. "I don't see how we can help it."

She closed her eyes and swallowed. "Me, either," she whispered.

She lifted her hand to his, which was resting against the side of her face, and closed her fingers around it. She opened her eyes and made no attempt to hide what was written there: shyness, uncertainty, even a little fear, but most of all, wanting. She said, "Let's go upstairs."

Dani had climbed those stairs with Bret dozens of times before, but never had the walk seemed so long, so self-conscious, so fraught with tension. She wondered if they would have changed their minds before they arrived. She wondered if they were making a mistake. She wondered if she really wanted to do this, or if he did, and if, once they crossed this line, there would ever be a chance to go back to what they had been before…and she knew the answer to that was no, and she was afraid.

The bright morning sun streamed with unforgiving cheer over the bed, still made but rumpled with the imprint of Dani's restless night. Automatically, she moved to straighten the covers, but Bret caught her hand, smiling. After a moment, she returned the smile, recognizing her own silliness. He caressed her hair affectionately, a calming, soothing gesture.

"Feels funny, doesn't it?" she said.

He nodded. "I'm nervous."

Dani brought her hand uncertainly to her damp, tangled hair. "I look awful."

"You look like Dani."

She relaxed a little, entwining her fingers with his. "We never did have to pretend with each other, did we?"

His expression was sober. "Except about our feelings."

Tugging at his fingers, she crossed to the bed, and they sat down together. She was overwhelmed by the newness of it all, by expectation and excitement and uncertainty. Her stomach felt quivery and her muscles tight, and she knew Bret could feel her tension because he didn't rush her. She knew he wouldn't. He just sat there, holding her hand, watching her.

She tried to smile as she looked at him. "What have you got to be nervous about?"

A smile creased one corner of his mouth. "What all men have to be nervous about at a time like this, I guess. And more." His eyes sobered. "That you'll be disappointed. That we won't be good together. That we both expect too much and we're risking everything to find out. That we can never go back to what we were."

"I can't be disappointed," she said softly. "I've waited so long, wondered so long...."

A spark of surprise touched his eyes. "You've wondered about me?"

A soft laugh bubbled through her lips. "Don't tell me you didn't think girls had thoughts like that."

"Well, sure," he admitted. She could feel the tension leaving him in a low, easy ebb, just as it did her. "I knew you thought that way about other guys, but not about me. I never had a hint."

"How would you have felt if you'd known?"

He grinned. "I'm not sure I should answer that."

"Tell me," she insisted, bouncing on the bed a little as she rearranged her position, tucking one leg beneath her.

His grin became rueful. "Well, let's just say it wouldn't have done a whole lot for a teenage boy's self-control."

She was surprised. "Do you mean you used to think about me, too? About having sex with me?"

He nodded. "Remember all those times we used to practice making out in the backseat of my car? It's a good thing for both of us I had such strong character—and that I was so afraid of your father."

She laughed. "God, Bret, we were crazy. Both of us."

The smile in his eyes grew thoughtful. "Funny, I never thought about it before. I guess you taught me everything I know about the opposite sex, without even meaning to."

"You taught me, too," she agreed softly. "A lot of things."

He looked at her soberly. "It wasn't just as a kid, either. Over the years... I've thought about making love to you a lot. It always made me feel kind of strange."

"Like now," she agreed.

He dropped his gaze, and his fingers traced the undercurve of her knee where it was exposed by the parting of her robe. Her skin prickled with the touch; her heart beat a little faster.

"I know everything about you," he said softly, "except this. I don't know what you like, how to make it good for you, how to even begin. I feel like I'm with a stranger...or like this is the first time I've ever made love."

Dani's throat tightened a little. "I don't know how to please you, either."

He looked up at her and smiled, his hand resting on her knee. "We could always talk dirty to each other for a little while."

"We could," she agreed slowly, and there was a touch of wonder in her voice. "We really could. And it wouldn't embarrass us, would it?"

The deepening of understanding in his eyes reflected her own, and with the simple dawning of truth, the last residue of awkwardness between them slipped away. "No," he said simply. "We're too close to be embarrassed about anything."

"But I'm still shy," she admitted.

"Why?"

"Because you've never seen me naked before."

His eyes twinkled. "Wrong. We took baths together until we were six, remember?"

"I've changed a little since then."

"You're forgetting the hole the boys drilled in the wall of the girls' locker room in high school."

"You didn't!" She struck out at him playfully, and he caught her arms, laughing, overbalancing her until she fell backward on the bed and he was poised above her, one leg thrown lightly over both of hers, his face only inches from hers.

Her breath caught, and then was released in a shallow flutter, fanning across his face. His eyes were a mixture of darks and lights, intense and penetrating, yet welcoming, wonderfully familiar. He said softly, "How do you feel now?"

"Kind of...hot and quivery inside," she replied breathlessly. "Nervous, but not afraid. Happy." So happy.

He dropped a slow, gentle kiss on her forehead. "I think I know where to start now."

He stood up and began to remove his clothes.

Dani turned onto her side, pillowing her cheek with her hand, and watched as he pulled off his boots and socks, then drew his sweatshirt over his head in a single, fluid motion and discarded it on the floor. His hands dropped to the snap of his jeans, then hesitated. He came over to the bed and sat beside her.

"Change your mind?" Dani teased, but her voice was a little husky because, although she was sure she had seen his naked chest before as an adult, possibly even been this close to it, his nearness made her pulses skip and her throat go dry.

The crinkles at the corners of his eyes deepened, and he wound a strand of her hair around his index finger, releasing it into a damp corkscrew. "You never heard of the allure of the wrapped package?"

"I kind of like what's unwrapped," she said. But he was right. The excitement of having him sit beside her shirtless was more enticing than had he taken her in a naked embrace, because what was happening between them deserved to be savored moment by moment, because there was the promise of more and because so much time had been lost to them now that nothing could be rushed; every second was precious.

She had always known Bret was an attractive man, but she had never known it in such a personal way before. His chest was lean and tanned, lightly sprinkled with golden hair. The pectoral muscles were firm, centered by flat, brown nipples that were slightly puckered in the room temperature. She could kiss his chest if she wanted to. She could touch him. And she did want to.

She lifted her hand, trailing her fingers down the sharp divide of his collarbone, spreading her palm over the expanse of one pectoral muscle, then sliding it down over his ribs and his waist, until her fingers met the impediment of his jeans. His pleasure at her touch was reflected in his eyes, and he smiled, tucking his fingers under her chin. "Something else I don't know about you," he said.

"What?"

"Whether you like to do the unwrapping yourself."

A flush went through her, excited and weakening, and her heart beat harder with surprise for the intimacy of the suggestion—the one thing she had never imagined herself doing, undressing Bret. Her fingers moved along the circle of his waistband, and she whispered, "Yes. I think I do."

"So do I." He leaned forward and tugged at the sash of her robe.

He parted the material, and she caught her breath as his eyes moved over her, filled with slow, gentle lights of pleasure. And following his eyes were his hands, pushing the sleeves of the robe off her arms, caressing her arms, cupping her heavy breasts in his hands, moving down over her stomach and outlining the shape of her hips, upward again along the length of her thighs. She was suspended in the wonder of his touch, tingling with new sparks of surprise in every caress; she could hardly breathe.

And then he lifted his eyes to hers again, smiling. "Not fair, Dani," he murmured huskily. "I thought you were going to do some unwrapping."

Her throat felt swollen, her heart beating hard as she moved her fingers to the snap of his jeans. The zipper was stubborn, and she could feel his heat and hardness against her fingers. She tugged the zipper downward and he stood up, allowing her to pull his jeans and his briefs over his hips. He stepped out of the garments and came back to her, resting his weight on one knee on the bed beside her. She looked upon the part of him that she had never known before, strong in his arousal, and she wanted to touch him. She felt the catch of his breath as she reached out her hand, brushing his inner thigh with her fingertips, encircling the strong, hard length of him with her hand.

He smothered a groan and stretched out beside her, drawing her into his arms. Their mouths met in a single surge of hunger and need, a wash of heat, a perfect blending. With an eager, almost desperate greed, Dani's hands moved over him, delighting in his broad angles and lean lines, the intimate parts of him, the strong and the soft. Bret, just as he had always been; hers, just as he had always been.

He drew her onto her side, encircling her with one leg, his hand sweeping down her back and cupping her buttocks, pressing her close. "Dani," he murmured against her neck, "look how well we fit together."

"Yes," she whispered, dizzy with wonder, and then she lost her breath as he lowered his head, placing a deep kiss upon her breast, drawing her nipple into his mouth, encircling it with his tongue. His hand slipped between her thighs, and her heart shattered in her chest as his fingertips caressed the sensitive inner flesh of her legs, then moved upward, his palm pressing firmly against the swollen, aching center of her. The sensation was so intense that a cry caught in her throat, and her fingernails dug into his shoulder.

"I know," he whispered, his lips brushing across her face. "I know..." He shifted above her; her legs opened to receive him, and in the space of one long, suspended heartbeat, he filled her.

He caught her face between his hands, and she opened her eyes to a delirium of joy: the beauty of his face poised above her, flushed and damp, his eyes a blaze of lights and darks, of tenderness and wonder; the fullness that was him inside her, a part of her, complete. Never had she known such completeness, because it was Bret, and it was so right.

She moved her hands over his back, she threaded her fingers into his hair. He kissed her face, his tongue lightly tasting her lips, and he began to move inside her, gentle-stroking caresses that caused her to gasp out loud with pleasure, with wonder, with the power of the sensations he built within her. She rose to meet him, and their rhythms became more urgent, a spiral of need and wanting that went beyond physical union. And as the power of fulfillment burst upon them, they touched in that moment the parts of each other they had never known before, each a part of the other; they knew and they held and they treasured what had been missing for all their lives. It was right. It was perfect.

Sunshine danced over their perspiration-slickened bodies, warmer than summertime as it was magnified through the high window. They lay on their backs close together, Dani's ankle curved over one of his. Bret's arm rested across her stomach. Sunbeams broke in slow, colorful explosions behind Dani's closed eyes in rhythm with the gradually slowing thunder of her heart. She could hear Bret's breathing; she could feel the glow of his body heat spreading over her and through her, still a part of her. She opened her eyes, experiencing a renewed thrill at seeing him naked beside her, at discovering his eyes adoring her even before she looked at him.

She threaded her fingers through his, turning her face on the pillow so that it was only inches away from his. "So what do you think?" she said softly. "Are we good together?"

He released a long, low breath and moved his arm to encircle her waist, drawing her close. "Ah, Dani, I could spend the rest of my life making love to you."

And they would, Dani thought. A little shiver of wonder went through her as she tightened her arms around him. They had the rest of their lives to do just that.

She lay back against the pillow, smiling with simple, silly joy. "Are you surprised?" she questioned. "Everything we do together is good."

"Yeah," he admitted slowly. His own smile was drowsy and love dazed. "I am surprised. It seems too good to be true, somehow. More than I deserve."

"Oh, Bret." She caressed his face, loving him so intensely that she had to close her eyes for a moment, lest the emotion spill over into tears. "I think…I know what you mean."

They lay together in silence for a while, locked in wonder and the simple, quiet pleasure of being together. Dani stretched out her hand, caressing his thigh. She loved the feel of that strong length of musculature, the light furring of hair, the heated crevice where his leg joined his pelvis, the stirring of his arousal against her fingertips. She felt his slow, indrawn breath, and then, reluctantly, he reached down and caught her hand.

"Honey, don't," he said huskily. "We can't stay here all day."

Her eyes sparkled as she playfully struggled to free her fingers. "Why not?"

"Because," he replied, determinedly tightening his hold and bringing her fingers to his lips. "It's the middle of the morning and I've got to get out of here. I'm supposed to be shoveling your walk, and you're supposed to be doing one of your busy Christmas elf things. And if we stay here much longer, your parents are going to start to wonder."

"Still afraid of my father?" she teased.

"You better believe it." Bret started to sit up, but she trapped him with one leg thrown across his abdomen. Delight sparked in his eyes even as he caught her shoulders, gently but firmly turning her back to her own pillow, holding her with a light pressure of his hands. "You are a witch," he said. "Something else I didn't know about you."

The playfulness in his eyes faded into gentle reluctance as he added, "But I've got to get serious with you for a minute, okay?"

Dani's hand, which had been playing with his hair, came to rest against the side of his face. She met his eyes a little uncertainly, but not afraid. She nodded.

"Dani," he said, "this isn't going to be easy for a lot of reasons. And one of them is your parents. I wouldn't hurt them or have them think badly of me for anything in the world. They still think you're— Well, you're with Todd. And until you can get things straightened out, we're going to have to be discreet."

Dani nodded, understanding. "So you're going to go shovel the walk, and I'm going to get dressed and go help Mom bake fruitcakes, is that it?"

She could see in his eyes that he found the idea just as bizarre, just as impossible as she did. But he said, "I think it's best."

She sat up, and Bret watched as she reached for the telephone, punching out a few digits. In a moment, she spoke into the receiver. "Hello, Mom? I broke up with Todd last night and now I'm sleeping with Bret. Is that okay?"

She moved the mouthpiece away a little and told Bret, "She says it's okay."

It was all she could do to keep from shouting with laughter at the look of stunned horror on his face, and the amusement in her eyes must have given her away. For just then, he noticed her finger remained on the disconnect button. He snatched the receiver from her, pushing her down on the bed, covering her with his body. "You *are* a witch!" he declared, his eyes dancing with laughter. "And I love you more than I ever loved anyone in my life."

"Oh, Bret." She cupped his face, adoring it, adoring him. "Why did it take you so long to tell me? Why did you have to keep it a secret?"

His eyes sobered a little. "Maybe," he answered, "for the same reason you kept it a secret ten years ago."

She looked confused. "What?"

"You wrote it down," he reminded her. "The night before I got married. That's why I came home, Dani. I finally got your letter."

"My letter?" Bewilderment and uncertainty tangled within her. "But... but I threw it away. I'm sure I did...."

"Just like I threw mine away."

"All those years ago..." She shook her head against the pillow, suffused with confusion and disbelief. "But that's not possible. Bret, you must be mistaken. There's no way..."

He smiled, slipping one hand beneath her, stroking her hip. "Do you know what I think we've got here?" he said.

The bewilderment left her, and she hardly heard the words, concentrated as she was on the caressing strokes of his hand, moving now around and upward, urging her thighs apart, teasing and caressing.

"What?" she whispered.

"A miracle," he answered.

And as she felt him move against her, sliding slowly inside, she wrapped her arms around him, and she thought with wonderment, *Yes. A miracle...*

Chapter Twelve

When Bret awoke the next morning, a hazy early sunlight was filtering through the loft window and Dani
was sleeping in his arms. He hadn't really spent the
entire previous day and night in her bed, though it felt
like it. The time when he had been away from her was
so blurred and indistinct in memory that it seemed not
to have existed at all, and in a way, he supposed it
hadn't. Nothing was real to him except the time he had
spent with her.

Sometime after lunch, he had gotten around to
shoveling the walk, and Dani had come outside and
thrown snowballs at him. When Harold pulled up in
his truck and asked Bret if he wanted to ride into town
with him, Bret thought it would be politic to accept.
When the two men returned, Dani was in the kitchen
with her mother, the house smelled of cinnamon and
nutmeg, and Dani asked Bret casually if he would like
to come over and help her make spaghetti for dinner.
He went.

She had told her mother about Todd, but Bret had
not gotten around to asking what else she had said.
Not that it mattered, now. His hosts would have had

to have been blind not to realize he hadn't come home last night, and not to guess where he had been.

He hadn't intended to spend the night. He must have started to leave four or five times, only to be stopped by one last kiss, one more embrace or some tart remark from Dani that would make him laugh or remind him of a story or set off a shared reminiscence. For they had not spent all of their time making love. In fact, some of the best hours had been spent simply holding each other, talking quietly or not talking at all, feeling good and warm and secure, making up for all the time that had gone before.

On Dani's bedside table sat the withered cactus. She had plucked it out of a trash can yesterday and had refused to tell him why. It had made him smile then, and it made him smile now, as he looked at it. Only today the smile was a little sad.

It was amazing. Yesterday, in the heady euphoria of physical love, of runaway emotions, of simple, obsessive joy, the problems that confronted them had seemed to simply disappear. He couldn't think beyond the moment, time did not exist beyond the next embrace, and it simply had not occurred to him that there was any life outside the sparkle of Dani's smile, the warmth of her arms. And maybe that was why he had spent the night, despite his better judgment. Because he knew, on some deep inner level, how precious the moments were and that daylight would inevitably come.

She was so beautiful, cuddled up in the curve of his arm, her hair tousled and her cheeks flushed with sleep. It was so easy to imagine a thousand mornings like this, a hundred thousand....

He grasped her shoulder and shook her gently. "Hey," he said softly. "Wake up."

She was smiling even before she opened her eyes. He smiled back, adoring her.

"We are in big trouble, kid," he said. "It's morning."

"I know." She stretched up her arms, encircling his neck, looking up at him with drowsy, love-sated eyes. "It was wonderful sleeping with you, Bret. Not just making love, but sleeping together."

"I know." He drew her close, bringing his face to her hair, inhaling deeply. She smelled incredible. "Like we've been doing it for years. Like it always should have been."

She bent her head back, looking at him with a slightly studious expression.

"Can I ask you something?"

"What?"

"Do you always sleep in the nude?"

His eyes picked up a spark of delight that came from nothing more than looking at her. "Not always. Sometimes I wear my shorts."

"Don't you get cold?"

He kissed her lightly on the nose. "Not in California."

And there it was, the moment they had both in their secret ways been dreading, the subject they had been trying to avoid. He saw the shadow touch her eyes even as it chilled his soul, and she started to speak.

He sat up abruptly. "Wait," he said, perhaps a bit too cheerfully. "I almost forgot. I have a Christmas present for you. I was going to give it to you yesterday, before I—" *Before he left town.* He didn't have to say the words; they rang implicitly in the air.

He reached over the side of the bed and brought up his pants, digging in the pocket for a gift-wrapped box. Dani smiled a little hesitantly as she took it. "The last time I got an early Christmas present, it made me cry. For about eight hours."

He ruffled her hair gently. "This one won't make you cry, I promise. At least, not for eight hours."

She looked up at him, suddenly stricken by a superstitious fear. "Do I have to open it now? Can't it wait for Christmas?"

He seemed to understand and smiled in quick reassurance. "Sure it can. Put it under the tree, and if you can keep your hands off it till Christmas morning, it's yours."

He swung his legs over the side of the bed and began to pull on his pants. "If you'll tell me where you keep the makings, I'll go down and do the coffee."

Dani tried to keep the anxiety out of her voice as she said, "It's just that giving it to me now makes me think that... well, that you might not be here for Christmas."

She saw the long muscles of his back tense, and his silence stabbed at her heart, taking her breath away. "Bret?"

He turned around. "I'll be here for Christmas," he assured her quickly, but the words were not enough. There was a mixture of reluctance and dread in his eyes as he searched hers, and the tension did not leave his shoulders.

"I'll probably have to go home for a little while," he went on carefully, "to take care of the final paperwork on the sale. And I need to check in with the office. But I'll be back."

She spoke hesitantly, not wanting to, knowing she shouldn't. "To stay?"

He looked away and didn't answer.

Dani reached for her robe and pushed her arms into the sleeves, feeling suddenly numb and cold. Bret stood up and pulled on his sweatshirt. Dani swung the covers aside and bent to put on her slippers, trying to pretend as though everything was normal, as though the weight of the whole world wasn't suddenly pressing her down... but she couldn't.

Her voice was small and a little shaky as she said, "Oh, Bret, what's going to happen to us?"

He drew in a breath and turned. His expression was cautious, not quite hopeful, and his eyes were busy searching her face, anticipating her every thought and reflecting it back to her. "I've been thinking. When the electronics plant opens, I can make a bid for the security contract. That doesn't mean I'll get it, but even if I don't, if there's one thing I do know, it's electronics. I can get a job."

The relief that went through Dani came in waves, uncertain and hopeful. He didn't want to leave her. They could work it out. There was a chance....

But he wasn't finished. "Honey, we've got to be realistic. A thousand things could go wrong. At best, it'll be a year or two before the plant is even open, and in the meantime, I have a business to run. I can't afford to keep two households. You'll have to come back with me for a while."

Of course. It was a simple solution, the only possible solution. She couldn't let him go, not after all the wasted years; he couldn't stay here, not without a job. But... "California?" she managed, in a tight, uncertain voice. "You want me to go with you to California?"

A flash of impatience crossed his eyes. "It's not Jupiter, for God's sake. They've got schools there, hundreds of them. You can get a job anywhere. And it'll only be for a little while—"

"Or maybe not," she said softly.

For reality, as clear and certain as it had ever been, spread itself before her. This was not a daydream, and even miracles like the one she had found with Bret were not always perfect. He was talking about an entirely new way of life, leaving behind the only home she had ever known, her family, her friends, the children she loved and the people she had grown up with. Herself. She would be leaving behind *herself*.

And once there, anything could happen. Bret had a business, roots, an entirely separate life on the West Coast, and it would be hard to give it up. And even if they did come home in a few years... there would be no home to come back to. Everything would be different.

She felt ill inside, disoriented and unsure. It shouldn't be this way. Things between them had always been so easy; why couldn't this be, too? But she couldn't help it. She was afraid.

Dani turned away, hugging her elbows, but not before she saw an expression of the most exquisite sadness come over Bret's face. "Now I remember," he said quietly.

"What?" Her voice sounded tinny and dull.

"The fight we had just before I went away to college. I wanted you to come with me, remember? With all your talent, you could have made it in Hollywood, you could have at least given it a try...."

She shook her head fiercely. "That's not what I wanted to do. I never wanted—"

"To take a chance," he finished for her flatly. "You let your whole life pass you by because you were afraid to find out what was on the other side of the mountain."

"That's not true!" she cried, turning to him. "You never understood that! I knew what I wanted, Bret, and it wasn't in California. *You're* the one who didn't know, who had to keep searching—"

"All those years," he said bitterly. "All those years wasted because you wouldn't come with me. I loved you then, Dani, just as much as I love you now, I just didn't know how to say the words. And now it's happening all over again."

"It doesn't have to!" she insisted desperately. "Don't you see Bret, the life I have here is good. It could be good for you, too, you know it could, and for our children! You don't have to walk away from it all. You don't have to destroy it. Why can't you just be happy? Why can't you let *us* be happy?"

But the look on his face was one of utter defeat and deepest regret, and he did not have to put his feelings into words. He sat on the bed and began to pull on his boots. "It was never a matter of life-styles," he said tiredly. "Or even values. I guess I was just hoping that this time, maybe you'd trust me enough to take a chance on me."

He stood up, his expression bleak and weary. "I'm sorry, Dani. I don't have any other solution."

He went down the stairs and out the door.

Dani pressed her lips together tightly, gripping her elbows to stop the trembling, refusing to give into despair, refusing to accept this as the end. They had come so far; they had found so much. It wasn't fair. How could he give up now?

How could she?

There had to be an answer. There just *had* to be.

Her eyes fell on the small wrapped package on the bed, and she picked it up. She knew she shouldn't open it. She knew it would make her cry.

She pushed aside the wrapping paper and opened the box. Slowly, she drew out the charm bracelet with its single silver bell and held it up to the light from the window. On the side of the bell, much like another bell from long ago, was an engraving: BU + DG.

She had been right. It made her cry.

BRET LET HIMSELF INTO the house through the enclosed back porch, stripping off his muddy boots and adding them to the stack by the door, angrily discarding his coat. He started toward the kitchen, from which the bright warmth of a light was already glowing, but he couldn't make himself go in. His lips tightened as he braced his hands against the door frame, and he wanted to beat his head against the wall, driving out the anger, the pain, the confusion. Instead, he brought his forehead slowly to rest against the cool wood, breathing deeply, trying to think clearly.

He had known this was going to happen; he had expected it. He had expected it so much he had *made* it happen, and he felt like a fool. All these years of loving Dani without even knowing it, of needing her, depending on her... was he going to throw it all away now because of one stupid argument about where they were going to *live?*

It was more than that, of course. He had asked her to share his life, and she had cut him to the core with her hesitance, that look of shock and reluctance in her eyes. She loved him, but he wasn't worth changing for. But he had hurt her, as well, by refusing to share her life, by insisting, in fact, on taking away everything she had built her life around. They had both opened wounds from the past that should have long since healed, but neither one was able to let go.

He kept telling himself that it was impossible to stay here with her, as much as he wanted to, and in a practical way, it was. But now he was forced to admit that the only reason he had left in the first place was fear: fear of losing himself in this place, of settling for small dreams and simple victories, of never taking the chance on finding out what he could be. But he had found out. He had followed the dream, he had climbed the mountain, and now he had come home. And he was too stupid to realize that he was still fighting a battle that had been won a long time ago.

He straightened up slowly, a weight dropping from his shoulders, the cobwebs melting away from his mind. He *had* been stupid. Both of them had. Each of them had been deliberately, although not entirely consciously, reenacting the past, and the past didn't matter anymore. They had found what they wanted. Now they simply had to decide whether they were strong enough to accept it.

He opened the kitchen door and went inside.

The room was bathed in good, clean, kitchen light and smelled of perking coffee and cinnamon rolls. Miss Annie, in a bright, flowered robe, turned from the stove and smiled at him, just as though it were the most natural thing in the world that he should come sneaking in the back door at six o'clock in the morning after an all-night tryst with her daughter.

"Good morning, Bret. Coffee's almost ready."

The warmth of home washed over him, a familiar, loving face, redolent with memories and continuity and all that was solid, dependable and good about life. Was he really going to sweep all this aside? How could he ask Dani to turn her back on them? How could he ask it of himself?

He stood there for a moment, feeling dazed and a little overwhelmed, but strengthened inside with a growing certainty. Then he murmured, "Umm, excuse me, Miss Annie. I've got to make a phone call."

He found his address book and searched through the pages for Craig Notion's home number. He paused for only a minute with his hand on the receiver, wondering if it could possibly be he, Bret Underwood, who was about to blow the deal of a lifetime, wondering if he could possibly be considering snatching away a whole town's future for the sake of one woman's happiness... and then he punched out the numbers.

Craig's voice, heavy with sleep, answered on the third ring.

"Are you crazy?" he demanded groggily when Bret identified himself. "Do you have any idea what time it is here?"

"I wanted to get you before you left for the office."

"Well, you sure as hell did that."

"Listen, Craig. I want you to do something for me." He took a breath. "Cancel the Inushu deal. I've decided not to sell."

There was a pause, and Bret braced himself for the storm of accusations, protests and invectives. But when Craig's voice came back, it was laced with sarcasm and sounded slightly bored. "Yeah, well, smart boy. For this you wake me up before sunrise?"

Bret frowned at the receiver, uncertain he had heard correctly. "You're not mad?"

"I might be one of the fastest wheeler-dealers in Southern California, my boy, but even I don't get my clients in bed with companies that are getting ready to go bankrupt."

"What?"

"What's the matter, you don't read the financial pages anymore? Or don't you get newspapers out in the sticks? It was all over the *Wall Street Journal* yesterday—and just in damn time, too. Looks like they were trying to keep their real financial picture secret until they could fatten up their assets a little, hoping for a takeover. Yours wasn't the only deal they were trying to rush through before the end of the year.''

Bret sat back in his chair, the strength suddenly leaving his muscles. "Do you mean—if I had made the sale, there never would have been any electronics plant?'' No new jobs, new housing, roads, county revenues....

"Hardly. The whole company would probably have fallen victim to some corporate raider, been parceled off...you know how these things go. You might've gotten your money, and you might not have, but it would've been years, and maybe ten cents on the dollar. As for the property, who knows? Not that it would've mattered by that time.''

"No,'' Bret murmured, stunned. "Not that it would've mattered.''

"I'm surprised you don't know more about this than I do. Seems I remember a sidebar that said the whole investigation was stirred up by a newspaperman down your way. Can you beat that? The best financial journalists in the whole country scooped by some hick reporter who didn't want an electronics plant built in his backyard.''

"Todd." But it was hardly more than a whisper, and Craig didn't hear.

"Well, I'm sorry it worked out this way." Craig's voice was heavy. "Good thing I didn't spend that commission. Merry Christmas, as they say.''

"Yeah." Bret's lips began to twitch with the beginnings of a slow, disbelieving grin. "Merry Christmas.''

The grin spread along with the wonder, and by the time he hung up the phone, Bret was laughing, softly, all to himself alone in the room.

DANI SPLASHED WATER ON her face, shook back her hair and squared her shoulders determinedly. "Dani Griffin," she told the woman in the mirror, "you are an idiot."

She took the stairs two at a time, pulling on her coat as she left the house, and plodded through the snow across the drive.

"Mom," she demanded breathlessly as she burst into the kitchen, "where's Bret?"

Her mother complacently set another place at the table. "He went for a walk. He didn't say where."

"That's okay." Dani turned quickly for the door. "I think I know."

"Dani." Her mother looked up, the faintest trace of concern shadowing her brow. "Wait a minute. There's something you should know."

DANI TOOK THE FAMILIAR path through the woods, pushing aside ice-stiffened branches, following the footprints in the snow. The footprints ended at the edge of the woods, and there Bret stood, his hands shoved into his pockets, gazing out over the pine-studded fields toward the house beyond. Dani hesitated for a moment, infused with wonder and adoration for the figure he made, standing alone in the snow. Then she made her way over to him.

He must have heard her footsteps, but he did not turn. They stood together in silence for a while, sharing the view. Then Dani said, "Remember in second grade when Len Bueler and his buddies tried to ambush you after school?"

A small smile of reminiscence touched Bret's lips. "You came out swinging with your lunchbox. Len had to have stitches."

"And in eighth grade, when we both auditioned for first chair in the school orchestra?"

"You played badly so that I would get it."

"And then you played so badly, neither one of us got it."

His smile deepened.

Dani touched his arm, making him look at her. "If I stood by you all those times," she said softly, "what makes you think I won't stand by you in this?"

Bret's expression softened in wordless love and gratitude, and he slipped one arm around her waist, drawing her close. Dani leaned her head against his shoulder, filled with the strength of his nearness, the wonder of loving him. For a time, she couldn't speak.

Then she said quietly, "Mom told me about the land deal."

Bret's voice was heavy. "You and Todd were right all along."

"You called off the sale before you even knew about the bankruptcy."

"Still, it was a close call. If it hadn't been for Todd . . ."

"Another Christmas miracle," she said, coaxing a smile from Bret.

But his eyes were a little sad. "We've about used up our share, haven't we?" He shook his head a little.

"The funny thing is, I kept telling myself I was doing it for you, for the town—even for Todd—despite what you all wanted. I thought progress was the only way. But now I see there are some things worth preserving. The world moves so fast, we're very, very lucky if we can hold on to the good things. Only now...I just don't know how."

Dani squeezed his arm bracingly. "So we go to California. I'm about due for a change. All this snow and slush is starting to get on my nerves."

He turned to her, smoothing back her hair with a gloved hand. Tenderness and wonder gentled his eyes. "You'd do that?"

"You'd do the same for me," she told him simply. "As a matter of fact, you just did."

He drew her into a slow, loving embrace. "Ah, Dani," he murmured into her hair. "You'd hate it in California. I hate it there. I just wish—"

"Ssh..." She lifted her hand to touch his face. "We don't have to decide right now. There's plenty of time to make plans. After Christmas. It can wait till after Christmas."

Their lips met in a long, deep kiss that spread its glow like radiant embers, full of promise, strong in its certainty. Yes, they had had their share of miracles. They didn't need any more.

When the kiss was over, they stood together, Dani's head against Bret's shoulder, their arms around each other's waists. They had no need for words, but simply stood in warmth and silence, watching the sun rise.

The scrubby, barren fields no longer looked ugly to Bret. The rising sun glinted off the snow-frosted pine trees, making them dance with a hundred Christmas lights. In fact, everything around him, as far as he could see, was dressed up like a Christmas-tree lot, a winter fantasy land. And slowly, tenuously, an incredible idea began to stir within him.

He could feel a slight reciprocal tension in Dani's body, and her voice was small with cautious excitement. "Do you remember," she ventured, "your dad used to say if there was a profit in rocks and pine trees . . ."

"Not only pines," he heard himself murmuring, "but spruce and fir . . ."

She lifted her eyes to him, and they reflected the shock and the wonder that was in his own. It was so simple. So absurdly simple.

"I don't know anything about tree farming," he said, but his hands gripped her arms as excitement began to buzz through his head—plans to be made, possibilities to be explored.

"George Skinner does!" she declared.

"If he would stay on and manage it for me—"

"And not just trees, but greenhouses! A nursery—"

"It doesn't have to stop here. The other farmers in the county have hundreds of acres going fallow—"

"A co-op!" she cried. "Evergreens will grow anywhere! We could ship all over the country!"

They were in each other's arms, laughing, hugging, holding on tight. He seized her shoulders, trying to think carefully, trying to be practical, but unable to keep the excitement from blazing in his eyes. "I could sell the business," he said, "and maybe make enough to get us through the lean years. But, honey, it's a hell of a chance—"

"And about time we took one," she replied.

She went into his arms again, and he buried his face in her hair, breathing deeply, cherishing the moment. "Sometimes," he murmured, "I guess we have to make our own miracles."

And Dani smiled, holding him. "Most of the time," she said.

ON THE NIGHT TABLE in Dani's loft, a single cactus blossom slowly unfurled beneath the husk of a long dormancy, and Christmas had arrived.

COMING NEXT MONTH

STEVIE'S CHASE
Justine Davis

The man who lived next door to Stevie Holt was a mystery. Tall and dark, he looked a little too menacing to be described as handsome. He didn't talk to anyone and clearly was not interested in making friends. But then, one day, Stevie gave him no choice. . .

It was hard to keep your distance from a bubbly, strawberry blonde who had broken into your apartment and was determined to nurse you. But Chase Sullivan didn't just look dangerous, he *was* dangerous—to anyone foolish enough to care about him. What was he running from?

OUT OF THE ASHES
Emilie Richards

The final story in Emilie Richards *TALES OF THE PACIFIC*

For Alexis Whitham, Australia's remote Kangaroo Island was the perfect place to begin a new life. Her young daughter would be safe from her ex-husband, safe in a new land with a new name.

But Jody brought a new man into Alexis's life—a man with a past just as tragic as her own. Matthew Haley had already loved and lost; he wasn't going to repeat himself!

Silhouette Sensation

COMING NEXT MONTH

THE ART OF DECEPTION
Nora Roberts

Adam Haines was visiting the Fairchild mansion under false pretences and he didn't like that. He liked to be straightforward and honest, but you didn't find a thief by declaring that you were an investigator. Moreover, you didn't get to sleep with the chief suspect's daughter if you told her you expected to have her father arrested!

The question was, was Kirby involved? If so, just how involved was she and could he compromise his ethics to save her?

CHARITY'S ANGEL
Dallas Schulze

Gabe London had been going to ask Charity Williams out but three, armed thieves prevented that. Suddenly, Gabe was a cop trying to control a hostage situation and prevent anyone being hurt.

But someone was hurt—Charity. And worse still, it was Gabe's bullet that injured her. The least he could do was offer her somewhere to recuperate. . .

TAKE 4 NEW SILHOUETTE SENSATIONS FREE!

Silhouette Sensation is a thrilling Silhouette series for the woman of today. Each tale is a full 256 pages long - a beautiful blend of sensitivity and sensuality. When you've enjoyed your FREE Sensations there's an extra treat in store!

You could go on to enjoy four more exciting new Sensations, delivered to your door each month - at just £1.75 each (we pay postage and packing). Plus a FREE newsletter and lots more!

No strings attached - you can stop receiving books at any time.

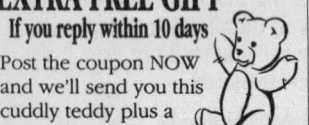

EXTRA FREE GIFT
If you reply within 10 days

Post the coupon NOW and we'll send you this cuddly teddy plus a surprise mystery gift!